F mily history (he is half Nor... ... fi ion of Bernard Cornwell ins... ... S in the Viking world, his bestselling 'Raven' and 'The Rise o igurd' trilogies have been acclaimed by his peers, reviewers a l readers alike. In *The Bleeding Land* and *Brothers' Fury*, tells the story of a family torn apart by the English Civil r. He also co-wrote Wilbur Smith's No.1 bestseller, *Golden L n*. Giles plunged into the rich waters of the Arthurian legend for his most recent novel, the *Sunday Times* bestselling *L ncelot*. It's a myth to which he returns in *Camelot* – a thrilling re magining of the story of Lancelot's son, Galahad.

Giles Kristian lives in Leicestershire.

To find out more, visit www.gileskristian.com; you can o follow him on Twitter @GilesKristian and Facebook/ lesKristian.

Acclaim for Giles Kristian's
CAMELOT

'A powerful, dark vision of Arthur's Britain, where magic has its limits and the worst monsters are human'
ANTONIA SENIOR, *THE TIMES*

'This is SUCH a good book . . . a vital, glorious story: rich, rewarding, and utterly revealing of our times'
MANDA SCOTT, author of the *Boudica* novels

'*Camelot* gave me one-hell of a punch . . . some of the best writing in historical fiction today . . . a phenomenal read'
***GRIMDARK* magazine**

'What a wonderful book. Beautifully evocative and bone-crunchingly bloody, filled with characters I loved and hated, all conveyed in beautifully lyrical prose and edged with the sense of hope and tragedy that is essential for any retelling of the Arthurian tale'
JOHN GWYNNE, author of the *Of Blood and Bone* series

'In some ways, even better than the first book . . . it is, in short, a triumph. Highly recommended, especially to fans of Bernard Cornwell's seminal Warlord Chronicles'
ANGUS DONALD, author of *The Last Berserker*

'Kristian's writing weaves a spell on the reader as surely as Merlin at the height of his powers . . . *Camelot* is a wonderful book'
MATTHEW HARFFY, author of the *Bernicia Chronicles*

'Kristian once again works his sorcery, and weaves a superb blend of high fantasy and historical fiction . . . herein lies the beauty of *Camelot*, it is a book where the past hauntingly mirrors the present . . . with sweeping battles, and prose that makes a reader want to savour every single word, this is an Arthurian retelling that I hold with high regard'
FANTASY HIVE

'An immense achievement . . . together these two novels represent something altogether more monumental. Nothing short of a new milestone in British myth-making. It deserves to be an instant classic'
THEODORE BRUN, author of the
Wanderer Chronicles

'A great book for anyone looking for a different take on the Arthurian legends or, indeed, an interpretation of Britain and its peoples and gods and struggles during the coming of the Saxons and their seizing control of the land from its kings'
ANNA STEPHENS, author of
***The Godblind* trilogy**

'*Camelot* sees the storytelling brilliance of Giles Kristian reach for and attain new heights . . . this duology for me is now the go-to Arthurian tale, surpassing Bernard Cornwell's . . . a classic'
PARMENION BOOKS

'Everything in this book is brilliant. That is partly due to my love for anything Arthurian, but it is also due to the intricate and powerful story Giles Kristian has magically created'
BOOKNEST

CAMELOT

GILES KRISTIAN

CORGI BOOKS

TRANSWORLD PUBLISHERS

Penguin Random House, One Embassy Gardens,
8 Viaduct Gardens, London SW11 7BW
www.penguin.co.uk

Transworld is part of the Penguin Random House group of companies
whose addresses can be found at global.penguinrandomhouse.com

First published in Great Britain in 2020 by Bantam Press
an imprint of Transworld Publishers
Corgi edition published 2021

A CIP catalogue record for this book
is available from the British Library.

ISBN
9780552174015

Typeset in 11/13.5 pt Adobe Caslon Pro by Jouve (UK), Milton Keynes
Printed and bound in Great Britain by Clays Ltd, Elcograf S.p.A.

The authorized representative in the EEA is Penguin Random House Ireland,
Morrison Chambers, 32 Nassau Street, Dublin D02 YH68.

Penguin Random House is committed to a sustainable
future for our business, our readers and our planet. This book
is made from Forest Stewardship Council® certified paper.

Camelot *is for Freyja and Aksel.*
You will find your own paths through bramble and briar,
And I will love you every step of the way.

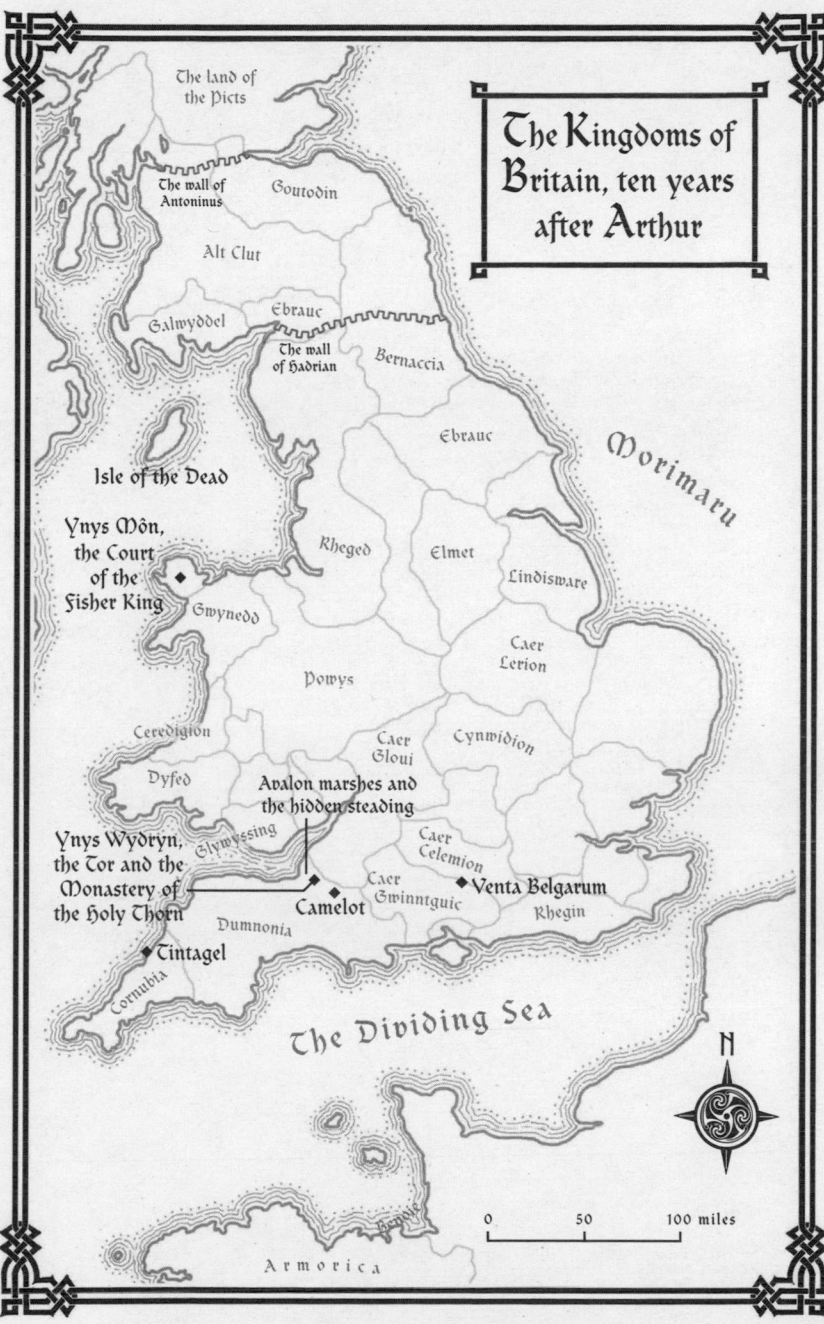

The Kingdoms of Britain, ten years after Arthur

The land of the Picts

The wall of Antoninus

Goutodin

Alt Clut

Galwyddel

Ebrauc

The wall of Hadrian

Bernaccia

Ebrauc

Isle of the Dead

Ynys Môn, the Court of the Fisher King

Gwynedd

Rheged

Elmet

Lindisware

Caer Lerion

Powys

Ceredigion

Dyfed

Caer Gloui

Cynwidion

Avalon marshes and the hidden steading

Glywyssing

Ynys Wydryn, the Tor and the Monastery of the Holy Thorn

Caer Celemion

Caer Swinntguic

Venta Belgarum

Camelot

Rhegin

Dumnonia

Tintagel

Cornubia

Morimaru

The Dividing Sea

N

Armorica

0   50   100 miles

For the fire of vengeance, justly kindled by former crimes, spread from sea to sea, fed by the hands of our foes in the east, and did not cease, until, destroying the neighbouring towns and lands, it reached the other side of the island, and dipped its red and savage tongue in the western ocean.

Gildas, excerpt from 'Concerning the
Ruin of Britain' (*De Excidio Britanniae*)

The Saxons are strong again. They are rapacious and without mercy. Their war bands stalk the land from Bernaccia in the north-east of these isles to Rhegin in the south, and they have come west even as far as Caer Gwinntguic, so that I fear they will never now be driven off, but will subjugate and oppress our people, and still their savage appetites will not be sated. I find myself yearning for the old days. When there was hope still. And though he himself lived in shadow, beyond the light of God, I cannot help but wish that we still had Arthur. I have even dreamt of him, riding out of Camelot at the head of his glorious horse warriors. How the ground trembled beneath their hooves! But Arthur is gone. The kings will not rally. They will not fight. Armed only with our prayers, and drawing courage from the Holy Thorn, we are left to watch the encroaching darkness.

Excerpt from a letter from Prior Drustanus
of the Monastery of the Holy Thorn in Britannia,
to his Holiness Pope Laurentius of the
Apostolic Palace in Rome

Prologue

*H*E IS GONE. MY LOVE. *I feel it as a severing, a ripping away. Sudden and brutal and I am falling through the darkness, down and down like a stone cast into the ocean. Fading towards the black depths, cold and unbreathing. Memories and faces falling away from me like the last autumn leaves from the oak.*

Disintegrating into my own wake as I descend. I am coming. Then light. A silver slash in the darkness. No! I am coming! Flying now. Whipping this way and that, my soul an ember in the storm's maelstrom. He is gone and I reach out after him. Questing into the whirling dark. Grasping in vain as light flares. Wait! Flaring light. Too bright, so that I cringe away, seared with pain, gasping and tasting blood. Breathing iron and foulness. And somewhere in the thunderous clamour I hear myself shrieking. I feel my great muscles bunching, my heart thumping, the blood hot and urgent in my veins. Wait for me!

But he is gone. Up! I scream, silently. Get up! And the stallion, his stallion, flails and struggles in the mud. Rolls and screams in hatred and defiance. Rolls again, forelegs stretching, hooves plunging into the churned filth and the gore of men. His heart thumps. A thunder clap and his hind legs thrust us upward and now his voice and my voice are one and we shriek. Standing now, blood flowing back into muscle, my will raising the stallion as though the gods themselves had cast a lunge line over him and hauled him up onto his feet. But not just my will. His own pride, too. The stubbornness that they both shared. But he is gone, and I wheel round and round, tossing my great head, throwing men back. I scatter them. Those fiends who took him from me. Now galloping, hooves drumming the earth, parting the struggling, bellowing mass and running as though along a causeway with the iron sea on either side, closing in. Keep going, brave Tormaigh. Run! I feel the stallion's life spilling away, as sand from a fist which I clench but know I cannot hold.

Yet I must. We are one, the stallion and I, and the world is madness. All hate and fear and death. The end of things. Run, Tormaigh. Run, my good boy. We burst from the swarming flesh and we stumble but do not fall, and now canter up the rise, coursing the channel through the tall grass, the channel of the stallion's own making, when his master, his friend, drove him down towards the heinous strife.

Up now. The roar of it all receding, rolling away like a wave back down the shingle. Up. Panting. Each breath stolen. Up. Staining the grass with hot blood and sweat lather as we sweep along this pathway which leads back to the boy.

I

Voices for the Lost

THE INFANT LIVED FOR as long as it took the tallow candle beside his crib to burn down to the iron socket. When his blue-veined abdomen sucked against his tiny ribs for the last time, his life departed with no more fuss than the smoke from that sooty hempen wick curling up to the rafters. Earlier, when it was still hoped that prayer might bear the child through the mortal danger, as the basket had borne little Moses among the bulrushes, I heard Father Judoc moan to Father Brice that it was a waste to use a candle when a rushlight would serve.

'You know as well as I that the child has been called to heaven to sit at our Lord's right hand,' Father Brice replied. 'Let his poor mother keep vigil over her babe without fear that the flame might extinguish and she not know if the child will be in this world or the next when it is relit.'

The baby had come too soon and there had been no time to send for the nuns across the water, nor to send Father Yvain to take a cutting from the Holy Thorn to place in the woman's hand as she laboured. The brothers had done what they could, but it was not enough, and Judoc had sent me to fetch Father Phelan and some of the others so that they might sing the child's soul to heaven now that his leaving was inevitable.

By the time they had gathered in the infirmary and decided

which hymn would best fit such a sombre occasion, it was too late. That scrap of a boy had left his mother alone in the world once more and gone to sing with the angels on high, or so Father Brice said, though the babe had barely squawked or made any sound at all since he had struggled into the world.

Neither did his mother shriek or wail. Not at first. From the stool beside the little bed, she turned tired eyes up to Father Brice, the stamp of the crib's rail livid as a birthmark across her pale cheek. I saw such sadness in that face, a pure desolation, and felt ashamed to be there, helpless, as Father Brice nodded that the moment had come.

The old monk rubbed an ashen cheek as if suddenly aware of the new white bristles rasping beneath his fingers, and I saw in that moment how tired he was. Weary not from this vigil alone but from hundreds like it. From a lifetime of shepherding souls to the borders of hereafter. From simply enduring, too, year upon year, as our little island of Ynys Wydryn endured, though the world beyond failed as everything must. Because our tor, a hill rising from the murk of marsh and lawlessness, offered rare sanctuary from a land in turmoil.

Just as the marsh tides flood and recede, eroding our muddy shore little by little, day after day, so had the years and the lives and the deaths scoured Father Brice, body and soul. And now I feared that the angels' wings which beat in that room, unseen by mortal eyes, might draw the tired old monk to heaven in their wake.

The mother – I did not know her name then – closed her eyes, perhaps to bid her babe farewell, and when she opened them again twin tears spilled onto her face. She stood, strength summoned from where I do not know, and stared at that silent little body. It possessed a stillness more profound than even the deepest sleep can induce. So much promise in those stick-thin legs. So perfect those knotty little hands, which would never clutch at his mother's breast nor tug her dark hair nor grip her finger. I whispered a prayer that I might grow in God's grace and one day glean some small understanding of His plan.

Then, with a gentleness beyond any mother's for her living child, the woman picked up the little body and held it against herself. I thought that she was taking the last fading echoes of her little boy's heart into her own.

Father Brice and Father Judoc looked at each other, their hands signing the Holy Thorn in practised harmony, the prayers on their dry lips as soft and quiet as the greasy tallow smoke wisping upward to the thatch.

Then the screaming. The tormented howl of an animal in pain. I had wanted to leave that place even before Father Judoc last trimmed the candle wick, but I knew I must stay.

'Your novitiate draws to an end, Galahad, and you will be a brother of the order,' Father Brice had said, soon after they noticed that all was not as it should be with the little one. 'It is not enough merely to contemplate the mystery of salvation, to read and meditate on the sacred scriptures. You must experience at first hand the miracle of life . . . and the enigma of death.' With that he had placed a hand on my shoulder, for he knew well enough that I had intimate knowledge of death, that the eyes into which he peered had borne witness to unspeakable violence. Years ago, now.

'I should be out gathering thyme and parsley for Father Meurig and I must check the eel traps,' I had protested. I wanted to be anywhere other than there in that room with that sorrow.

Father Brice's eyes had hardened. 'You will stay, Galahad, and pray.' Then he had glanced over to where the woman sat by the crib, her linens fouled from the labour and staining the air with iron. 'Let us hope that the child rallies. That the Lord will let him abide with his mother. At least a while.'

But the Lord in His wisdom had taken the child in spite of our prayers, and the monks, neither knowing how to comfort his mother nor having the courage to try, gave themselves to mournful song instead.

'My child. My child is lost,' the woman wailed. 'See?' Her eyes bored into mine and for a terrifying moment I thought she would hand the little body to me. 'He is too small,' she told me. 'How will he find his way to Annwn?'

I could not answer that but made the sign of the Thorn at her mention of the otherworld, the abode of the pagan dead, and, to my shame, looked away, shuffling closer to Father Phelan and the others, taking up the solemn chant in praise of God.

The men's voices were reed-thin at first but grew in strength, their breath blending in veils of fog in the chill dawn as they poured a balm of song into that small room which should instead have filled with a baby's cry and a mother's cooing.

I was in full spate when Father Brice pulled me aside. 'Fetch Brother Yvain,' he said. 'I need him to go across the water.'

I nodded and turned to leave, grateful to be given a task, but Father Judoc grabbed my sleeve and hauled me back. 'A moment, Galahad.' He held up a finger and lifted his chin at Father Brice. 'What do you intend, Brother?' he asked. He stood a head taller than Brice and revelled in it, not that I'd ever seen Father Brice intimidated.

'There is a man in the village who is sick,' Brice said. 'Eudaf the cobbler. His son came to me two days ago, begging me to send someone to sing the Litany for his father.' He lifted an eyebrow and turned an upward palm towards the grieving mother. 'I did not find the opportunity.' He frowned. 'Now I fear that I have failed the child, the mother and the cobbler.'

'God willing, the man has recovered.' Father Judoc placed his hands together, the straight fingers threaded to represent the Holy Thorn.

Father Brice tilted his head towards another possibility. 'But if he has died, and is not yet buried, it may be that this Eudaf can help the poor child,' he said. 'Help this young woman, too.'

'It is sacrilege,' Father Judoc blurted out, glaring at Father Brice.

'It is a kindness,' Father Brice countered with a thoughtful nod. I saw that his tonsure was in need of a blade, for there was new white growth, as fine as cankerwort down, sprouting on the front of his liver-spotted scalp. 'A simple kindness, nothing more,' he said, glancing at the woman.

The look on my face must have told them both that I did not know what they were talking about, and it was Father Judoc who took it upon himself to enlighten me, presumably hoping to win an ally against Father Brice.

'Brother Brice would have the dead child placed in the earth with this villager so that the man's soul may escort the little one to heaven.' Father Judoc curled his lip in distaste. 'It is a pagan ritual. I have seen it done.'

'Her grandmother served King Deroch back in Uther's day,' Father Brice said. 'Her father fought in Lord Arthur's shield-wall. I would assuage her pain if I can.' *For we did not save her child*, was what he left unsaid.

Judoc shook his head. 'It is not Christian.'

'Not Christ-like to seek to comfort those in pain?' Father Brice asked us both. 'And is it not wise,' he went on, inclining his head to give this next point more weight than the first, 'to keep the peace with those who may yet turn back our enemies? Their gods were powerful here, once.'

'The Saxons cannot be turned back,' Father Judoc said. 'They will not relent until they have slaughtered every last Briton or else driven us into the Western Sea. Britain is lost, Brother. You are a fool if you cannot see that. And helping non-believers will only anger the Lord further. It will only hasten the end.'

Father Brice gave him a sad smile. 'If we are already lost, Brother, then what harm can this small kindness do?' With that he turned his face, guiding our eyes back to the dismal scene of the young mother holding the dead infant to her bosom. Her mewling was pitiful to hear, all the more for being muffled by the little thatch of fair hair against her lips. It glistened with her tears, that hair, as though she offered the child a second baptism, just a candle's length after we had watched Father Brice wash the child with water from the White Spring. The mother had not seemed to know what Father Brice was doing. Or if she knew, she did not care.

'Do it if you must, Brother, but it will not be on my conscience,' Father Judoc said, making the sign of the Thorn again.

'Of course not,' Father Brice said, one eyebrow arching. Then he turned to me and lifted his white-stubbled chin and I went to find Father Yvain.

'The poor wretch has left us already, then.' Father Yvain nodded at Father Dristan to keep working the lathe, which the younger man did, pulling backwards and forwards on the leather strap that was wrapped around the piece, turning the wood one way and then the other. Over and over.

Yvain did not look up, his iron hook tool casting chips and curls of creamy wood onto the floor rushes. 'Boy or girl?'

The smell of that place changed as often as the weather, depending on which wood he was working and whether it was seasoned or freshly cut and still wet. Today, I caught the sweet smell of cherry mixed with the cat-urine tang of elm.

'A boy,' I said.

He made a gruff sound in his throat, whether at that revelation or because of how the green wood was turning, I could not say. 'Knew something wasn't right when I heard no squawking,' he said. 'Not since the girl stopped labouring.'

Sweating in spite of the chill day, Father Dristan pulled the leather strap with the fluid consistency of long practice, and Father Yvain pressed the little hook into the wood, gouging some decoration into it. Creating by taking away. 'Poor little soul,' the older man said, blowing away from the sharp iron a sliver of wood, bright as a curl of fair hair. He sighed. 'May the Lord be merciful.'

'Amen,' Father Dristan breathed.

Father Yvain seemed to fill the low-beamed workshop, seemed as much a part of that place as did the bowls stacked to dry on shelves, and the old, scarred work benches and the piles of ash-shafted hook tools and spooning knives forged by Yvain himself, each for a specific task. He could be found there most of the day, even at those times when the rest of us were gathered at prayer. Not that the others begrudged Father Yvain's absence from Sext and None, or from Vespers, where we almost never saw him. Aside from his wood-turning, Yvain shouldered certain responsibilities, undertook tasks which none of the others would. There was an unwritten covenant among the brothers that in return he be allowed to spend more time at his lathe than at prayer, which was why I now stood in the workshop, fighting the temptation to lift my foot and search for the splinter which was tormenting me.

'So?' Father Yvain said.

Broad-shouldered and black-bearded was Yvain. His hands were thick-fingered and gnarled as an old yew tree, and yet so many times I had marvelled at the graceful shapes which he teased from apple and ash, beech and blackthorn. Gaming pieces, bodkins and spoons, lidded boxes for salves and herbs, stool legs, shepherd's crooks and walking sticks for the older monks. All came from his lathe and his rough hands.

'Everything I make, I make as if the High King of Britain himself will hold it in his own hands,' Yvain had told me once, when as a child I had watched some spinning piece being kissed into shape by bright iron. Not that there had been a High King of Britain these past thirty years or more.

'Father Brice sent me to fetch you,' I said now. A sudden sting in my right foot, in the soft flesh of the arch.

That grunt again in the back of his throat. 'Tell him no.'

I looked from Yvain to Dristan, who gave the slightest shrug of his narrow shoulders, his eyes fixed on me as he worked the strap back and forth.

'Father?' I wondered how Yvain could refuse before he had even heard what Brice wanted of him.

'He wants me to go somewhere,' he said. 'To the village or to the nuns. Somewhere.' He lifted his chin and Dristan stopped pulling the strap, so that the workpiece went suddenly still. Yvain blew on it, examining it closely as Dristan caught his breath. 'Whatever it is, tell him no. I'm not going out there.' Again, he lifted his beard, all flecked with wood chips, and with nimble hands Father Dristan unwound the strap so that Yvain could remove the workpiece from the lathe. 'I'll not leave this island again, Galahad. Not in this body.' He turned the piece in his big hands, seeming less than satisfied. 'I've work to do. Tell Brother Brice that.'

'It's for the child,' I said, 'and . . . for his mother. Father Brice would put the infant in the grave with the body of a grown man.' Father Dristan was frowning at me. 'A man on the crannog was dying—'

'And Brother Brice wants me to go over there and bring his corpse back to Ynys Wydryn,' Father Yvain interrupted me, turning the workpiece over in his big hands. 'To go out there and risk my neck to bring a dead man back for a dead child.'

Father Dristan's eyes widened at that, but he knew better than to question Father Brice's wishes in front of Yvain, even if those wishes seemed at odds with our faith.

'I'll not go,' Yvain said. 'Not this time.'

I nodded and could not help but wonder at the things, the terrible things, that Father Yvain must have seen out there in the marsh and even beyond. Things of which the brothers whispered, wide-eyed, in the dormitory. Tales which grew yet sharper fangs and claws in night's ensuing silence, preying on us each in the lonely dark.

'Well, Galahad,' he said, and held up the fruit of his labour, turning it this way and that in the pale shaft of daylight which quested through the smoke-hole along with spitting gusts of rain.

'It is beautiful, Father,' I said.

Yvain frowned. 'It might be. When I bring out the grain and if it doesn't crack.'

It was a goblet made of spalted beech. A simple thing. But I knew that Father Yvain would work the beeswax into the wood until those strange, dark patterns told stories as rich as those of any bard.

'Off with you then, lad. And remember what I told you: I'll not go.'

'Yes, Father.'

'And get that splinter out of your foot.' He took a knife and sliced a burr from the underside of the goblet's base. 'A little thing like that will kill you if it can.'

He didn't miss much, Yvain. I nodded and pulled my cowl over my head, wondering how the rough wool would feel against my bare scalp come the new moon, when my novitiate would end and I would take the tonsure and become a brother.

Then I stepped out into the damp day and for a moment stood looking up at the sky. Above me, several rooks bickered and cried, tumbling like black ashes against the vast emptiness. Dusk was gathering, the day retreating, and I could feel the light leaching out of the sky. The brothers' voices, rising and falling with the breeze, seemed as much a prayer against the coming night as a liturgy for the poor child who had not lived but a day.

Father Brice glowered all through Compline, though his ire was wasted as Father Yvain was not there to see it. Of the others, only Father Padern had supported Brice's idea of seeking a recently deceased adult to share the infant's grave. Not that the old cellarer volunteered to risk the marsh and venture to the folk on the crannog when I relayed Yvain's refusal.

'I will go myself,' Father Brice had declared, pressing his mottled hands together, each gripping the other. But if he had believed that at all, his resolution faded like the fog of those words on the cold air. Father Padern arched a brow at me. Neither of us thought Father Brice was seriously considering leaving the monastery. But for Padern and Prior Drustanus, who had lain on his sickbed since the first ospreys had been seen in the marshes, gathering their strength before flying south for the winter, Brice was the oldest of the brothers. And while his mind was talon-sharp, his body was more suited to prayer than to sculling through the bogs in midwinter. Besides, there was evil out there among the reed-beds and fens. Evil lurking in the carrs and twisting with the willows' roots. Malevolence moving in the mires.

We had all heard the tales the folk of the island villages told of the thrys, a race of human-like creatures who dwell in the darkest reaches, sometimes underwater, waiting to murder unsuspecting travellers. Every few years, word spread of folk who had gone into the marshes never to be seen again.

And there were the mists which rose from the black water as though pyres, as many as there are stars in the night sky, burned in the underworld, their smoke passing through the veil into our own world. There was also the dreaded marsh fever, which could be caught from these unholy fogs and which would have you vomiting and yellow-skinned, your bones rattling in your flesh until you died.

Of us all, only Father Yvain dared the marsh, carrying messages from Prior Drustanus to Prioress Klarine at the convent, or to fetch Ermid the smith from the lake village when we needed something forging which was beyond the wood-turner's own talents.

'I've faced worse than some stinking fen-dweller,' he had told me once when I had asked why he was unafraid to take the coracle out onto the dark water, not knowing what was out there beyond the safe haven of our island. Father Yvain had been a warrior once, had even fought as a spearman for Lord Arthur, though he would rarely talk of those days now. If Yvain was not willing to leave our little sanctuary and go out there, then no one was. Father Brice would have to resign himself to laying the child in its grave alone and hope that our Lord's angels would find their way through the mists of Avalon to guide the infant's soul to heaven.

And so the old monk glowered through the night prayers, and Father Yvain turned his wood in the workshop, and the poor exhausted woman sobbed because she feared her baby would for ever wander the shadowy realm between our world and the next.

For myself, I wondered if the Lord God even knew we were

here, we ten clinging to that island in the marshes where the old gods of Britain had once abided before the Saxon gods came to the Dark Isles. I could speak the prayers by rote, leaving my mind free to roam, and though I felt some guilt at pondering such a thing at such a time, I decided it was better to seek the answers to these questions now, in my novitiate, than later. That way, by the time I took my vows and Father Brice himself gave me the tonsure, my mind would have been put at ease that I might devote myself fully to God.

And yet even such thorny contemplations withered in the damp cold of this night, so the Lauds of the Dead found me shivering and yawning in the reedlight-flickered dark at the rear of the church, thinking of my bed and of sweet sleep, when I should have been thinking only of my devotions.

For the little church was draughty in winter, when the apple trees beyond the pasture were black skeletons and bitter gusts blew from the west across the marsh and rolled up the tor like a wave. The reed thatch leaked, and we waited for drier days to replace it, in the meantime huddling beneath it, warmed only by our own breath as we sang and by the illusion of heat provided by the fragile flames of tallow lamps. And even though Father Yvain joined us for Lauds, his habit strewn with wood shavings, there were not enough voices to drown the sobs of the grief-stricken woman which seeped through the wattle wall and pierced the rhythmic rise and fall of our song.

Someone somewhere hissed, but in the gloom I could not see who. Then Father Dristan's elbow in my ribs drew my attention to Father Judoc, who was glaring at me from where he stood, to our right beneath the driest of the old thatch. He beckoned me with his eyes and so I wriggled through the brothers, still singing as I went, until I stood before Judoc and bent to put my ear near his mouth.

'The girl, Galahad; it will not do. She is distracting the brothers from their prayers.' I knew Father Brice had given her permission to spend the night in the infirmary with the little corpse, that our prayers might pass through the walls to give her solace. But from the sound of her sobbing, it seemed our devotions were giving her no comfort at all. 'Take her some wine,' Father Judoc hissed, 'and only a little water.'

'Yes, Father.' I turned to leave.

He grabbed my arm. 'Only a little water, Galahad,' he repeated. 'She will find some peace in sleep.' He grimaced. 'And we shall be spared a woman's wailing.'

I nodded and went to fetch a jug of apple wine, wondering if I would still be at the brothers' beck and call once I became fully one of them. When I rapped the cup's base on the infirmary door, I realized that my palms were slick with sweat and my stomach was rolling over itself like a pot of eels. I thought of what I had heard Father Folant say, that the dead baby was Britain itself. But then, Folant was ever the voice of doom, filling our ears with his dark prophecies about the future.

There was no answer from within. The sobbing quietened, though, and I heard a rhythmic gasping as of someone trying to catch their breath. I lifted the jug to my nose and inhaled the aroma of fermented apples and honey, a smell of summer days conjured brightly in the mind as if by some charm. I pushed the door open and went in.

An oil lamp burned with fitful, sooty splutters which seemed to mimic the woman's own breathing. By its light I saw that the bundle was back in its simple crib of pale birch, which Father Yvain had made on the day the woman's husband had brought her to the tor. No one knew where her husband was now. Against the brothers' advice, he had gone to fetch a healer who was known to live on a spit of land in the Meare Pool, but he had not returned and perhaps never would.

'I am sorry,' I told the woman, who sat by the crib as she had when her child still clung to life. She looked at me with such sadness as I had not seen for a long time. Her eyes were swollen and red. Her face glistened with snot and tears, and if I had felt trepidatious before entering that dim room, I felt contemptible now, standing there with an offer of apple wine, as if that would make things better. And yet she tried to smile.

'Thank you, Galahad.'

I was shocked and must have shown it.

She frowned. 'That is your name?'

'Yes,' I said, pouring the wine into the cup. I had added only half a beaker of water to the drink.

'They talk of you,' she said.

I moved closer and offered her the cup. She took it and drank, emptying it before I had the chance to place the jug on the table beside her. I refilled the cup and put the jug down. My name was known in Avalon. I knew that, and I hated it.

'What is your name?' I asked her.

'Enid,' she answered.

I nodded at the wine in her hands. 'It is strong, Enid,' I warned her. 'I'll add more water. If you like.'

She shook her head and drank again, then looked into the crib. 'My child is lost.'

'No. He will find his way to heaven,' I tried to reassure her. 'We all prayed for him. The one true God will welcome his soul.'

She scowled at me. 'There are no gods here, Galahad,' she rasped. 'Not yours, not mine. My poor little boy is lost. We are all lost.'

I did not know what to do. What could I say? The brothers'

devotions carried through the wall and I wished that I were with them and not here with this woman whose pain was like a living thing, a beast with grasping hands and talons which seemed to claw into my own flesh in search of my heart.

I picked up the jug and filled Enid's cup again, but she would not take it this time. She gripped the crib's rail, her knuckles white by the guttering flamelight, new tears making her eyes pools of misery.

'He is lost. My baby is lost and all alone.'

'I'm sorry,' I said. 'I am so sorry.' And with that, to my shame, I turned and hurried from the room.

I rejoined the brothers and lifted my voice to heaven with them, singing a little louder than before, even more afraid of hearing Enid's sobs through the wall now that I knew her name and she knew mine.

But later, in my bed, when the only sounds were the mice scrabbling among the floor reeds and the snoring of men and, beyond our thin walls, the occasional screech of an owl or bark of a dog carrying across the dark water, I lay thinking of that woman and her dead child. I heard her words over and over in my head, as monotonous as the Litany and as forlorn as the marsh around our refuge. *There are no gods here . . . not yours, not mine.*

Cold words. Terrible words which pulled and plucked at me and would not let me sleep. And so, being as careful as I could not to make any sound or movement which might haul the others from their slumber, I rose and crept through the darkness towards the sliver of deathly pale light which showed beneath the door.

The sea's breath was in my face, thin as hate. It stung my cheeks, made cold wells of my eyes and chafed my hands raw on the oar's shaft as I pushed the coracle on through the reeds. *Go no further,* those brittle reeds seemed to whisper whenever the Hafren's breeze quested through them, stirring the mist like the breath of some creature slinking low now that night gave way to dawn. *You should not be out here,* it hissed. *The marsh is no place for one such as you.* And neither was it, I knew, as I sculled the oar through the cold water – slowly, that my presence might go unnoticed by man. By creature. And by spirit.

Around me, the first curlews stabbed the muddy fringes with their long, downward-curving beaks, their plaintive and lonely calls weaving a sad sound. *Cour-leee. Cour-leee. Cour-leee.* Behind me, the tor loomed in the fog, humped and vast. A dragon's back as old as the world. A dark mass in a dawn which, like the infant soon to be laid in the grave, seemed too weak to survive. For it was an unformed, insubstantial day. The kind when the veils between the worlds are thin as smoke and folk stay indoors by their hearths, busying themselves with work which can be grasped and held and felt by the flesh.

So why was I out in the reed-beds now? Woven willow rods and bullock hide all that was between me and the water and whatever lay beyond its obsidian blackness. What had I been thinking, skulking past the brothers out into the pre-dawn gloom, down to the jetty where the little coracle rocked gently among the reeds? Perhaps it was not too late to go back. To tie the boat to the piling and scurry up to the dormitory before anyone knew what I had done. For, once I lost sight of the tor in the marsh mist, I might never find my way back.

You are not him. Turn back now.

My flesh shivered. Last evening's food and ale had curdled in my stomach and my bowels were sour water, so that I felt that the marsh was *in* me as much as around me. It pressed on me, heavy with threat, and I could not help but wonder at the fates of those folk who ventured here never to be seen again. Were they taken by the thrys, those creatures who dwell among the sedges and feed on human flesh? Did some madness come upon them, inhaled with this drifting fog? Some dark desire which compelled those doomed souls to give themselves to the marsh, the way those who believe in the old gods offer gifts of iron or silver to the water? Or perhaps the wading curlews around me had been men once, now turned by some enchantment into birds and bound to the marsh for ever.

Why would you want to be him? Turn back.

Some movement drew my eye and I started, almost tumbling off the coracle's narrow thwart, the craft tipping dangerously, and I held the oar above my head, using it to balance as the rocking subsided. Just a marsh harrier out hunting, sweeping over the reed-beds, swooping in a flash of silver throat and nape, her brown back the same colour as the seed heads. Then she dropped into the reeds and was gone, and I wondered what prey she had seized with her killing talons. What little body she had punctured with those deadly claws.

'Lord, give me courage,' I whispered, afraid to speak aloud in such a place, even to God.

There are no gods here . . . not yours, not mine. Enid's words rippled through the dark mire of my fear. Something plopped into the water off to my left and I glimpsed the sleek brown shape of an otter before it vanished, leaving a wake of bubbles behind it. I caught my breath, inhaling the sweet, musky scent of death and decay. I licked dry lips, tasting the salt of the Hafren and the bitter draught of my own despair, and I sculled the oar through the water, the blade describing a serpent twisting over itself, forever seeking to grip its own tail. On and on. Deeper, ever deeper into this insubstantial world, this girdle between land and water, keeping the weak dawn light on my right cheek. Towards the lake village. Now and then catching sight of the ancient causeway which the first people had built that they might more easily travel between the island settlements, though no man would trust that trackway now. No living man, anyway.

I saw something and cried out, raising the oar before me as though it were a weapon, or a staff imbued with the Lord's own power against evil. Something was on that causeway. Or above it. Some fen-dweller looming in the mist, watching me with hungry eyes. Or a spirit? The ghost of someone who never crossed to the afterlife. Perhaps even one of the unknown men who had laboured on the trackway so long ago, a thousand years or more before the Romans came.

I made the sign of the Thorn but otherwise just sat there, the coracle rocking beneath me, my fear gripping me so entirely I could not move. Whatever the thing was, it was turning slowly, and I was drifting towards it, as though it commanded the currents of the dark water and summoned me to it. A breeze stirred, sickly and weak, as if lost to wander the marsh these hundred years, and now clawed at the mist, shredding it to reveal a face. Not some ungodly creature or spirit, but a face of flesh. Old, rotting flesh. Sunken cheeks and black hollows where once there were eyes which beheld God's creation, before death fogged them and, after that, crows and gulls savaged them with greedy indifference to all that they had witnessed.

The corpse was suspended from a crude gibbet; an ancient pile robbed from the track and driven into the reed-bed. I whispered a prayer for the dead man's soul, for all the good it would do him now, and thrust my oar into the water again, wondering who had strung him up like that, robbing the poor man of his life and surely damning their own soul in the foul deed.

I had made only a dozen strokes when the next victim

revealed herself through the thinning mist. A woman with long red hair, her nakedness a shocking and shameful sight to behold. I tried to look away from that poor wretch, but my eyes kept finding their way back, until I had passed and could not gaze upon her without turning round, which I would not do. And these were not the only ones. Seven more corpses I saw, twisting slowly on creaking ropes, and one of them a child, a boy no more than nine years old, and I asked the Lord on High how any man could put a noose around a child's neck and watch his life snuffed out like a candle flame.

'The world beyond this island is a terrible, cruel place, Galahad,' Father Brice had told me the previous summer, when Father Yvain had returned from one of his trips with news of all he had seen and heard. 'Be grateful that you will never have to leave our sanctuary.'

'Should we not try to help others resist all that is evil?' I had asked, in my naivety. And the old monk had given a sad smile and touched my head, perhaps recalling a time long ago before he had completed his own novitiate and shaved his hair.

'All we can do now is protect the Holy Thorn and ensure that our order survives,' he said. 'I fear Britain is lost, Galahad, her people scattered like chaff on the wind. But we few shall remain here, so long as we have breath. And we shall protect the Thorn.'

One of the dead boy's eyes had been spared beak and claw. It glared at me through the sullen vapours and I felt the bitter accusation. The envy. The rage at a life cut short. I shivered, trying to ignore the burning ache of needing to empty my bladder. And I followed the channel, my eyes drawn skyward by the urgent mewing of gulls, a flock of hundreds flying into the west, turning like a shoal of fish, their white bodies flashing in a shaft of dawn light.

Soon after, I saw living children, doubtless long after they had seen me. Five of them, two boys and three girls, none taller than the bulrush and bur-reed around them. All filthy, wild-eyed and hungry-looking. They were the offspring of fisher folk or salt farmers, I guessed. Creatures of marsh, fen and bog, who watched me in silence, not afraid but wary, and I signed the Thorn at them, but they gave no indication of comprehending the blessing.

I caught the sweet smell of peat smoke on that thin breeze now. Could see it hanging in the wintry dawn, a darker grey smudge against the wan sky. Aiming for it, I came among thicker reeds and, leaning over, saw the silty bed of the shallows. I knew I must be close. I spied another channel and took it, sculling between low ridges of land thick with blackthorn, and eventually I came to the lake village, sweating now despite the chill and comforted to smell hearth smoke. I whispered thanks to God that I would soon be on dry land among men and women, safe from the unknowable dangers of the marsh.

I tied the coracle to a jetty thronged with similar craft and sleek, long dug-outs, and greeted a heron which stood looking out across the water. Beside that unmoving bird were piled half a dozen willow baskets ready to be set out in the marsh to trap perch and roach, trout and eel, and my stomach rumbled at the thought, for I had not broken my fast.

'A brother of the Thorn,' someone called. I looked up to see the broad shoulders and bearded face of a man above the willow fence which circled the cluster of roundhouses, keeping wind out and livestock in. 'What brings you here?' he called.

'Eudaf the cobbler,' I replied, slipping and sliding on the mud towards him.

The man frowned. 'We sent his boy to you two days since,' he said. 'Your songs will do Eudaf no good now. He died in the night.'

'I am sorry for the loss,' I said, lifting the hem of my habit out of the filth before signing the Thorn in respect for the cobbler's passing. And yet my spirits lifted upon wings of hope, that an infant's soul might yet be guided to heaven and into the Lord's keeping.

2

A Wolf in the Reeds

I HAD BEEN AFRAID BEFORE. Now I was faint with terror as I made my way back across the dark water, the mist wreathing around me like the ghosts of serpents. Cold sweat soaked me, and my heart was clenched tight as a fist in my chest. My breathing was shallow and ragged, and I felt that there was a scream in my throat ready to break free at any moment.

Where did Father Yvain find the courage to venture into the marsh whenever the brothers needed him to? I would never again set out across the water after this, I thought, glancing over my shoulder at the corpse of Eudaf the cobbler lying behind the thwart. His kin had wrapped him head to foot in two threadbare woollen cloaks, and I was relieved that at least I did not have to see his face, nor would he witness my fear. The man had lain in his dwelling on a bed of skins and stiffened there so that now he did not fit in the coracle but stuck out of it, his legs wedged beneath the bench upon which I sat with the oar, tracing knots in the water.

Just me and a dead man alone out there in the marsh. Or so I thought.

I heard them before I saw them. Heard their guttural voices speaking the Saxon tongue. I pulled the oar from the water and held it still, my heart thumping against my breastbone in time with the drips falling from the oar blade. The coracle slowed and stopped, as I twisted on the thwart, peering through the tall reeds around me for any movement. Sound carried unnaturally far in the marsh, so that I could not know if the men I had heard were within spitting distance or an arrow's flight away. Yet I did not hear the dip of oars and so thought they must be walking along the spine of gorse-crested land ahead, which I could just make out through the reeds.

Laughter now, and more voices, one growling, low and ominous as thunder. Another with a weariness to it. This man trying to make peace between the others, perhaps. But all of them louder than before. Closer. And if they came to the brow of that ridge, they must surely see me below them, and if they had spears or bows, I would make an easy target before I could put any distance between us. Yet, even knowing that, I was too afraid to move. I sat there, gripping the little craft's sides as we bobbed on the still water. And the Saxons drew nearer with every shallow breath.

Hide. Quickly.

I wanted to. My mind demanded that I do something, but my limbs refused to move. I couldn't breathe.

Hide. Now!

I leant forward and slowly, softly, sank the oar blade back into the water and propelled the craft towards the bank. If I could hide in the lee of that ridge, the Saxons might pass by, never knowing I was there. But they were almost upon me, their gruff voices grating in the heavy marsh air.

Faster!

I sculled as quickly as I dared, given the sound of the oar sweeping its knots through the water, and barrelled into the thick vegetation of the bank, the craft tipping forward so that I had to thrust the oar down into the mud to stop myself falling overboard. Behind me, the corpse rolled and tipped on the edge, but I threw myself across the thwart, grabbing fistfuls of cloak before Eudaf the cobbler was given to the lake.

A shout from the other side of the ridge. They had heard me. They were coming.

I scrambled back over the bench and took up the oar, but looked up to see the Saxons coming down the bank, tearing through thistles and blackthorn. Shields and spears and fierce, bearded faces. Heathen voices yelling ungodly words.

I spun the coracle and worked the oar through the water, then heard a splash and the coracle bucked beneath me and I was being pulled backwards, my efforts with the oar useless. Another savage buck and I fell against the willow ribs. Hands on me then, snarled in my habit and in my hair, and I was on my back being hauled through the cold water, reeds breaking off in my hands as I grasped at them. Onto the muddy bank. The reek of warriors. The blur of fair beards and hair and teeth as they dragged me through thorn and briar, up onto the ridge, barking like ravens.

I screamed in terror and shock and called God's wrath upon them, though they showed no fear nor understanding. Then one of them hammered his fist against my face and my lip popped like a pea pod, spilling blood into my mouth and down my chin. I yelled still, spitting blood as they threw me down and stepped back to see what they had caught.

There were three of them, two grizzled-looking, scarred warriors and one younger man, perhaps my own age, with the little square-headed hammer amulet of their god Thunor hanging at his throat. These warriors from across the Morimaru were the men who had taken Britain from us and I knew they would kill me now. My only chance was to wriggle free and run, but in the heartbeat that I moved, the biggest of the three warriors knew my intention and stepped forward, turning his spear to slam the butt into my shoulder, knocking me back down. Pain replaced fear and I lay on the wet earth looking up at the sky, the *click* of reed buntings all around me, and I saw a marsh harrier high up, its pale underside blending with the wan day, and even in that moment, as I waited for death, I wondered if it was the same bird which I had seen earlier.

The leader of these Saxons growled something at me. An order or a curse. For a moment I looked into his eyes and all I saw there was cruelty. My life measured in no more than a dozen sour breaths. And so I closed my own eyes and commended myself unto God.

'Lord of Heaven, receive me,' I said. And in that breath, I saw my mother's face, the memory flooding me with sadness, and when I opened my eyes the spear blade was blurred by tears.

The spear fell. The Saxon's mouth hung open, his eyes bulging in their sockets as he gurgled and choked on a froth of bloody bubbles. Then he toppled to the ground beside me, and I am certain I looked as shocked as he that the Lord of Heaven had made good my threats and struck him down.

The other two Saxons crouched and raised their shields, turning away from me, which was when I saw the arrow embedded in their dead companion's side. The elder of the two warriors roared a challenge at the reeds, fear keeping him hunched behind his limewood shield, anger filling his beard with spittle as he yelled.

No one replied. The only answer the Saxon received was an arrow which streaked from the reed-bed and took him in the shin, making him screech in pain, though he kept his shield up and his head down. It was too much for the other Saxon, who turned and ran, though he did not outrun the next arrow. It thumped into the back of his neck and burst from his windpipe in a spray of gore.

That young man was dead before his thin beard touched the grass, and I got back on my feet and moved away from the remaining warrior, who paid me no heed now. This last Saxon had more sense than to turn his back on his unseen enemy. Not that he could have run far with that arrow in his leg. Blood stained his trews and trickled in rivulets across his shoe as he yelled challenges at the hidden bowman who was the cause of his unexpected misery. He spun the spear in his hand and thrust it into the ground, then drew his sword, whose iron gleamed in the dull day. He roared to his god, Woden, and keeping his shield high, limped down the slope towards the reeds, repeating his chant of 'Woden! Woden! Woden!'

The next arrow thunked into his shield. The one after that took him in his right eye. He staggered three more paces and dropped, gone from this life to the next, and I made the sign of the Thorn at the devastation wrought by that warrior upon whom I had yet to lay eyes.

There was a rustling and movement of the reeds and I held my breath as the archer came out, using the bow to force a way through the tall stalks. Then I muttered an oath which would have seen me punished with cleaning the byre for a month back at the monastery. The archer, this killer who had slaughtered three Saxon wolves, was a young woman.

'You owe me two arrows, monk,' the woman said, having collected all but one of her shafts and examined them to see which could be used again and which would first need repairing. She was on her knees now beside one of the Saxons, bent over him, her face hidden by unruly auburn tresses, and I realized that she was spitting onto the dead man's hand, trying to loosen the ring on his middle finger.

'Though you're not a real monk, are you?' She looked up at

me, her grimace becoming a grin as she twisted the ring over the knuckle and pulled it off. 'You'd be shorn.' She put the ring into the drawstring purse beside the arrow-bag tied to her belt. 'From ear to ear. But you're not. Why do your kind do that?' she asked. 'And why are there no women on Ynys Wydryn?'

I couldn't find the words to reply. I was as shocked as a fish in a net pulled aboard a boat. I stood there slathered in mud, a hand pressed to my bleeding lip, watching this young woman who had undoubtedly saved my life. My stomach heaved. Were it not empty, I would have puked into the grass.

She took the dead Saxon's long knife and thrust it into her belt, then moved back to the man whose throat she had ripped open with one of her deadly arrows.

'That arrow was surely guided by God,' I said, hearing a shiver in my words, the same trembling that gripped my hands and the muscles in my legs, as the young woman went down on one knee and set about trying to pull the arrow from the ruined flesh.

She put her head on one side, frowning at me. 'Your god?' she asked. 'The Christ god?'

I nodded. I could not have spoken sensibly of the mysteries of the Holy Trinity then even if I'd wanted to. I saw one copper eyebrow lift behind the errant strands of damp hair which fell across her face and could hear the gristle tearing as she twisted the shaft this way and that. Could see the young man's head jerking horribly.

My stomach lurched and I retched, but nothing came up. With one final effort the arrow came free, but only the shaft. The iron head clung on somewhere in the mess of the wound.

'Then your god owes me an arrow, monk.' She wiped her bloody hands on the dead man's tunic and stood.

I made the sign of the Thorn in case she had meant any

impiety, my tongue questing into the raw, stinging split in my bottom lip. I saw that she held the little hammer amulet which had hung at the Saxon's neck. A dedication to his god Thunor. Somewhere a raven croaked, and I looked up, expecting to see more Saxons coming over the rise.

'We should go,' she said.

I looked back at her. I was staring. My tongue felt too big for my mouth. She had killed three men. She had taken rings and buckles, the brooches from their cloaks and their knives, and now she pulled the scabbard from the one who had owned a sword.

'Bring me the sword, monk.' She nodded towards a clump of wind-stirred grass in which I could just see the dull gleam of the long blade.

I looked down at the man, at the blood-pooled hole of his eye, hearing in my mind a faint echo of his last words. *Woden! Woden! Woden!*

'The chief of their gods has one eye,' the young woman said. I wondered how she knew such things, but I did not ask, and I bent, for a moment afraid to touch the dead man's sword. But this strange young woman was watching me and so I wrapped my hand around the sweat-stained leather of the hilt and lifted the sword into the day.

'They make good blades. Better than ours,' she said, looping the bow over her shoulder.

I tilted the sword this way and that, trying to catch the weak daylight in the blade, in which a watery pattern had been trapped during its forging. Or perhaps it looked more like smoke than water. I had heard Father Yvain speak in awe of *the breath in the blade*, almost as though a warrior's sword were a living thing, hungry for blood.

'Here.' I handed the sword over, relieved to be rid of it, but gazed at my own hand as if it remembered something which I did not.

She stepped back and slashed that iron and steel blade through the fetid air. Testing its balance, though for the thrill of it too, I thought. Then she thrust it into the leather scabbard. 'We should go,' she said again, lifting her chin.

I looked behind me to where the coracle sat among the reeds. The shroud-wrapped corpse of Eudaf the cobbler still lay there. Assuming his spirit had not yet flown from his body, I wondered if Eudaf had any understanding of what had just taken place on this mist-wreathed embankment in the marsh. Had the cobbler's spirit heard the souls of those Saxons shrieking in terror and perhaps even disbelief, at their lives being unexpectedly cut short that winter day?

'*We* should go?' I asked. She was close. I could smell the wood smoke in her clothes. I could smell her sweat too, which was unlike that of the brothers. Sharper but not unpleasant.

She pointed the sheathed sword northward towards a swirl of rooks that were flying back to their roosts. 'These Saxons were scouts.' She pulled a fur hood onto her head. Our breath was fogging in the air. It would be getting dark soon. 'There are raiding parties everywhere. I've seen them.' She turned her head and spat in disgust. 'They are like rats crawling over a corpse.'

I put two fingers to my mouth, feeling the swollen lips which throbbed with pain, though at least the bleeding had slowed. 'I don't need you to protect me,' I said, wanting to know the colour of her eyes. Impossible now with that hood.

'You cannot protect yourself,' she replied, walking over to where one of the dead men's spears lay. She burrowed a foot beneath the shaft and lifted the spear into the air, catching it with ease.

'God will protect me,' I said, watching her.

'You know what those men were going to do to you?' she asked.

I did not answer that and felt my cheeks flush with heat and shame despite the cold.

She looked past me to the coracle and shrugged. 'I knew Eudaf. He made some shoes for my mother.'

I looked down at her own boots, which were sturdy and well made, and somehow I knew that they were not Eudaf's work but rather that she had taken them from a young Saxon whom she had killed with that bow of hers.

'He was a good man,' she said. This young woman who was out here in the marsh, a bow on her back, two long knives in her belt, a spear in one hand and a Saxon sword in the other. 'Why are you taking him to Ynys Wydryn?' I did not answer. She shrugged. 'It doesn't matter. I'll see that he gets there.'

'I don't need your help,' I said. Just moments ago, I had been lying in the mud, helpless and terrified. I knew what the Saxons would have done to me, just as this woman knew it, and the shame of it swamped me.

'You know the ways?' she asked, pointing the spear at the water, which was flat and dark and still, though the reeds bristled gently in a thin breeze. 'You are not very skilled in that boat.' It was almost raining now, a fine mizzle hanging in the air.

'You've been watching me?' I asked, appalled to think that she had followed me through the marsh without my knowing.

'I wanted to see if you'd fall in,' she grinned.

I looked at the coracle hedged in by the reeds, then at the eastern skyline where huge flocks of starlings moved like smoke. Really, I was trying to summon a reply the way a warrior might counter a spear thrust. But it would be dark soon. And I did not know the marsh well. And even those who did sometimes vanished, never to be seen again.

'God will protect me,' I said again, thinking of the corpses I had seen hanging above the old causeway, watching me though their eyes were long gone. The memory put a bad taste in my mouth, a sourness mixing with the coppery tang of blood.

'Good, because my bow will not shoot when the string is wet,' she said, walking past me down the bank to where Eudaf and the little boat waited.

'What is your name?' I asked.

'Iselle,' she answered, giving it to the breeze as much as to me, as if names were unimportant.

'I'm Galahad,' I called after her. Not that she had asked. A moment's hesitation, and then I followed her down to the water.

Rain came. Vengeful and cold, shafting into the water and hissing amongst the reeds. It lashed us in our little boat and soaked through Eudaf's shroud so that his face appeared through the worn wool, the mouth open but the eyes closed. I tried not to look back at him, keeping my eyes on the channels ahead, looking for signs of the ancient causeway, searching the bank for a willow or alder whose shape I recognized, or the lightning-struck oak I had seen earlier. Anything that would suggest we were going the right way.

I kept warm from paddling, but for my hands which were raw and growing numb, and my feet chilled by the water sloshing in the bilge. I wondered how Iselle fared, crouching behind me, thinking she must be terribly cold though she did not say it. The only time she spoke was to tell me to take this passage or that, and even then she had to raise her voice to be heard over the seething rain and the wind, too, which had been gathering when we set off, jostling the lapwings and stonechats against the darkening grey sky. Now that wind buffeted the little coracle, seeking through the weave of my habit. It keened from the west, sweeping across the marsh to bend the tall grasses and send furrows racing across the water.

Sometimes the wind was with us, leaning into the stretched hide which covered the boat, pushing us on. Other times it drove us into the reeds and muddy shallows so that I had to scull fiercely with the paddle, my muscles burning, and Iselle had to work with the Saxon spear, thrusting it into the sludge to push us back into the channel. Eudaf the cobbler was not much help, but in the end we three threaded our way through the web of saltwater channels unmolested by spirits and fendwellers, perhaps made as invisible as spirits ourselves by the veiling rain and winter gloom. And we came, wind- and rain-flayed, to Ynys Wydryn as the light was draining from the world.

I swept my loops through the water, looking up at the tor, which loomed in the dusk like a whale breaching the grey sea. It was Iselle who saw the figure up there on the crown of the hill, a dark speck against the sky. One of the brothers, I knew even before my eyes found him, thinking how miserable it must be, keeping watch up there in that foul gloaming. Looking for me.

'You went without their permission, didn't you?' she called. I could not tell if her words were of admonishment, or even respect. Or mockery, that I might need the consent of others to leave the island.

The wind howled. Frenzied now, as if it had snarled itself on the island of Ynys Wydryn and could not tear free. I battled the fretted water and took us in to the jetty, where Father Yvain was waiting, the rain spilling down his face as it would course over a crag of rock.

'Damned fool!' he bellowed into the wind, grabbing hold of the coracle and pulling it alongside the mooring. Behind him came two torches, the flames hissing and bucking, and in the light they cast I saw the faces of Father Padern and Father Dristan. 'God-damned fool!' Yvain said, as Iselle and I wrestled Eudaf's corpse across the rocking craft to the monk's waiting hands.

You're not him, Galahad, Yvain's eyes said. *You're just a frightened fool who should have known better.*

Yvain threw the body over his shoulder and I lifted the coracle out of the water, fighting to keep hold of it in the wind.

'What's got into you, Galahad?' Father Padern demanded, his firebrand hissing. 'In the name of the Thorn, what have you done?'

'Father Brice is going to flay you alive,' Father Dristan told me, helping me steady the coracle and carry it to a sheltered spot, where we turned it over beside its twin, weighing it down with stones. 'And who is that woman?' Rain pattered on the hide which he clutched at his neck, drops beading on the waxed surface and spilling off in rivulets. 'What's she doing with you?'

'I'm alive because of her,' I said, clenching and unclenching my hands, trying to work some feeling back into them as I watched Father Yvain hefting the corpse along the track towards the cluster of buildings huddled together beneath the tor, out of the prevailing winds.

Father Dristan stopped me, grabbing hold of my arm. 'You don't need to prove yourself to us, Galahad,' he said, rain spitting from his lips. He followed my gaze to Father Yvain. 'He has been looking for you since you missed dawn prayers. Even took the other boat out when he realized you'd gone into the marsh.'

I looked up at the tor and wondered which of the monks was on his way down now, soaked to the marrow and wind-blasted, having been up there looking down onto the reed-beds.

'Come along, Galahad!' Father Padern swept his arm to usher me towards the monastery, his troubled expression lit now and then by the failing torch. 'Let us get inside before we are all carried off into the night.'

I looked at Iselle, who was standing on the jetty still, the elm bow over her shoulder and the spear and sword in her hands. A striking figure against the rain which lanced the water behind her. Some of her hair had escaped the hood and now whipped about in the wind. She gripped those weapons as though she might use them again at any moment, and for a little while we held each other's eyes.

Then I turned and went to meet my fate.

'She cannot stay,' Father Brice said again. Father Dristan had built up the hearth fire and those of us who had been out in the night now stood around it, holding hands or the hems of our habits near to the flames as we dripped onto the rushes. The stink of wet wool cloyed the air and men coughed and spluttered with the smoke, because the applewood which Dristan had brought in was not properly seasoned.

'You can't send her into this storm, Father,' I said.

'You forget your place, Galahad,' Father Judoc warned, pouring himself a cup of wine. 'You are a novice, nothing more. Remember that, unless you wish your punishment to be more severe.'

Iselle had yet to speak, though the brothers had allowed her into the warming-house and given her a space near the hearth. She stood there now, gazing into the flames which flapped in the draw of the smoke-hole.

'Brothers.' Father Yvain was rubbing his huge hands and spreading them near the fire. 'Galahad must be punished, no one says otherwise.' He glared at me from the shadow of his furrowed brow. 'He'll be punished for being a bloody fool and going into the marsh—'

'And for leaving the island without the Prior's permission,' Father Judoc cut in, getting a grunt from Yvain and some murmurs of agreement from the others.

'But the lad is right about the girl,' Father Yvain went on. 'We cannot send her out.'

Iselle swept the sodden hood from her head and twisted it in her hands so that water dripped onto the hearth stones. By the fire's light, and because the blinding terror had ebbed from me now, I saw her properly for the first time.

'A woman cannot stay the night under our roof,' Father Padern said. The way he looked at Iselle, you would have thought she was a thrys, one of the fen creatures said to feed on human flesh.

'There is a woman in the infirmary now, Brother,' Dristan reminded him, and though his voice was timid there could be no denying it.

'She has no boat,' I told them. 'Would you have her swim back to the village?'

'I don't live in the village,' Iselle said, but received only stares in reply.

'I've warned you, Galahad,' Father Brice said, holding an ink-stained finger up to silence me. 'Do not make it worse.'

'There are ways,' Iselle said. 'Old paths through the marsh.'

'Not where a God-fearing soul can walk,' Father Padern creaked, tugging at his white beard. A log rolled out of the flames and lay hissing.

'We know of this young woman.' Father Judoc frowned at

37

Iselle, who showed no sign of hearing any of us now, so absorbed was she with the fire. Her eye was caught by a spider scuttling across the rough bark of the errant log, seeking escape. 'She is a wild creature.'

'She is a brave young woman who saved Galahad's life,' Father Yvain said, using the iron poker to push the log back into the fire's red heart, his words stirring more murmurs and low talk.

'You saw her kill three Saxons?' Father Brice asked me, even though I had already told him the story. 'Saw it with your own eyes, Galahad?'

'I swear it by the Thorn, Father,' I said.

The monks looked at one another in the way of men who did not need words to share thoughts. On the one hand they struggled to accept that Iselle had killed three Saxon warriors. On the other, they could not believe that I would lie about it.

'And you had no part in the killing?' Father Brice asked.

Father Judoc scoffed at that. 'Galahad is not his father,' he said, glaring at me. 'I cannot even imagine what delusions compelled you to go into the marsh. Are you sick?' He turned to Father Dristan. 'Has anyone felt his brow?'

'I'm not sick, Father,' I said. 'And I did not kill anyone.'

He was right about who I was, though. I had been a helpless, frightened fool, and had it not been for Iselle I'd be dead.

'That is a Saxon sword, I can tell you that much,' Yvain said, at which every eye turned towards Iselle, who looked up from the fire, raking her gaze across each of the monks in turn, as if challenging them to question how she had come by the blade. Her fierce eyes seized on Father Judoc, who seemed to shudder in his skin before letting his own gaze slide away.

'You've rare courage, girl,' Father Yvain told Iselle. 'Plenty of seasoned warriors would not have taken on three Saxons with nothing but a hunting bow.'

'Someone has to kill them,' Iselle said, with no less flint in her eyes for Yvain than for Judoc. 'My arrows work better than your prayers.'

Father Brice and some of the others made the sign of the Thorn at that blasphemy, though none found the words to argue with her.

'While you hide here on this island, the Saxons slaughter and rape and burn.'

I stood there gaping like a fish in the bilge. That this young woman dared to speak to the brothers in such a way. At the steel in her voice and the fire in her eyes.

'While you hide here, fear spreads among our people like flames in dry straw,' she rasped, throwing an arm out behind her.

But Father Judoc would hear no more. 'Enough!' he snapped, glancing at Father Folant as though he feared the man would embark on one of his rants about the death of Britain and the end of our order. But Father Folant, who stood back in a dark corner, was lost in his own thoughts.

Iselle bit her lip, as though fighting to keep further words unsaid. Then she looked back into the flames.

'Well, Galahad,' Father Brice said, 'if there is any good to have come out of your reckless disobedience, it is that we may bury the babe with the cobbler. I pray the mother will find solace in knowing her poor child will find his way to heaven with Eudaf's help.'

'Or to Annwn,' Father Judoc said through his teeth.

Father Brice dipped his tonsured head. 'Which of us can claim to truly see beyond the veil, Brother?' he asked, at which Judoc was not the only one to thread his fingers in the sign of the Thorn. 'We will bury the child and the man tomorrow and, afterwards, Galahad will accept his punishment. I do not think we need trouble Prior Drustanus with this matter. It would only hurt him to know that Galahad had broken our rules and put himself in danger.' He looked up at me and I held his eye. 'Thirty strikes of the Thorn upon his flesh. One for each shoot which sprouted from Joseph of Arimathea's staff when he thrust it into the earth.'

Father Yvain made a gruff sound in the back of his throat at this, and even Father Brice frowned. 'You *do* accept this punishment, Galahad?' he asked. Perhaps he feared I might not, as was my right, seeing as I had not yet taken the tonsure. None of them could stop me leaving Ynys Wydryn altogether. But where would I go? The brothers had taken me in, and I would not abandon them. But thirty strikes! I doubted even Father Judoc would have pronounced a harsher penalty.

'I accept, Father,' I said, to Brice's relief. I chanced a look at Iselle and, from the expression on her face, she thought me a fool or a coward or both.

'What about the girl?' Father Judoc asked.

'No good can come of her being here. You mark me, Brothers,' Father Folant said, the first words he had spoken since Dristan had built up the fire.

'She saved Galahad's life,' Father Yvain said, and there was weight in his words. Apart from Yvain himself, they had all been Brothers of the Thorn when I was brought to Ynys Wydryn. They had all heard the stories about me. They had listened as Prior Drustanus proclaimed that I was given to the order by God.

'And she helped bring the cobbler here,' Father Brice added, 'for which we are grateful.' Saying the words seemed almost to cause him pain, yet he persisted. 'I say she may stay with us until the storm yields. With us, not *among* us,' he clarified. 'She will sleep in the byre. It will be warm enough in there, I think.'

My eyes met Iselle's and she gave a slight nod as if to say that she was content to sleep in the byre with the cows. Perhaps she would even prefer it, and who could blame her after how we had treated her?

'We are all tired,' Father Brice said, 'and some of us are soaked to the skin. Let us rest before prayers and be thankful that our brother Galahad has returned safely.'

'And give thanks that three Saxons who were breathing this morning are feeding the fox this night.' Father Yvain nodded at Iselle in a gesture as solemn as it was respectful.

'Have Brother Meurig make you some hot food, Galahad,' Father Brice ordered. 'You must be hungry and will need your strength tomorrow.' He saw me look at Iselle. 'She will be fed, Galahad,' Brice assured me, then nodded at Dristan, who half scowled, picked up a horn lantern and asked Iselle in a quiet voice to follow him to the byre.

I stood by the fire a little longer, letting it warm my wet clothes, then I went to find Father Meurig, who made me a bone broth thickened with parsnips and sweet chestnuts that soured with his chiding.

'What got into you, Galahad? Going into the marsh alone! And without the Prior's consent. Are you unwell? Did some malevolent spirit compel you?'

'Perhaps,' I teased, though I still shuddered to think of it.

'Well, what did you see out there? Tell me or I shall not feed you.' On and on he went, drawing the day from me like a man wringing foul water from a cloak's hem. 'The Saxons. Tell me about them. What did those devils look like?'

I slurped the hot broth down and made my escape, but even at prayers I felt the brothers' questions weighing in their stares. They watched me from beneath heavy brows and from the corners of their eyes as they sang their praises to Christ and the Thorn. I felt their suspicions as a presence in the flame-played dark, as the storm tore at the thatch above our heads. I felt their mistrust, as sharp as the wind which sought through cracks in the old walls where the hazel and ash wattle showed.

For I had been out there in the marsh, beyond the sanctuary of Ynys Wydryn. I had seen with my own eyes things which only existed amongst us as whispers and rumour. The children of the reeds, as thin as the bulrushes, their swollen eyes watching me as I passed. The gallows creaking with the weight of the hanged. And, of course, our enemies the Saxons, who had been alive and fierce-eyed one moment and dead the next, their souls released to the afterlife by Iselle's arrows. I had seen all these things and perhaps they had left a mark on me which changed my appearance in the brothers' eyes. Like a scar which I had not had the day before, but which now compelled them to stare.

I was the youngest of us, and in one day I had seen more than most of them had seen in years. It perturbed them. It perturbed me, too, and though I sang the praises by rote, I was still out there in the marsh, shaking with fear. Stomach-sick. Appalled. Perhaps the brothers saw that, too. But worst of all in their eyes, I had brought Iselle.

The next day, we buried the child and the man, bound up in the same winding sheet. It was a wet, miserable affair, but at least Dristan and I had little trouble digging a grave because the earth was sodden and soft. We stood around the excavation, cowled against the day, hands clenched within our sleeves as we lifted our voices above the wind's keening and sang the two souls to heaven. The old apple trees behind us creaked and moaned. The grasses and ferns hissed, and the rain roared into the earth and roof thatch, flung one way and then another like handfuls of gravel thrown by a god. But the infant's mother, Enid, wept silently as Father Yvain and Father Dristan, on muddy knees, lowered the corpses into the puddle already rising in the grave.

I had not spoken with Enid since my return. Did she know it was I who had fetched the cobbler's body to Ynys Wydryn and nearly died in the attempt? Or that I would be whipped for it? Why would she care? What mattered to her was that her son was no longer alone. He would find his way to the afterlife, guided there by Eudaf the cobbler, as a man leads his own child by the hand through tall grass or darkening woods.

I did see her share a knowing look with Iselle, who had come to pay her respects but who kept her distance, sheltering beneath the canopy of the ancient yew, watching from its shadow. It was possible that the women knew each other, but more likely, I thought, was that they shared some innate feminine compassion, an appreciation for the loss which we men could never wholly comprehend.

Yet we sang, and the wind howled. And as Father Yvain worked with the spade and wet earth thumped onto the winding sheet, I watched a flock of rock doves being buffeted and tossed about inside the wind's fury. If they did not turn into the wind soon, they would be flung out across the marsh and lost to it. But if those birds cried in fear, I did not hear it for the storm and our singing. Instead, I watched them tumbling eastward towards that grey water churned to a muddy brown, and I thought of three Saxons lying dead out in the marsh.

Father Brice did not linger over the rites. Even as Father Yvain was piling the spoil back onto the grave and slapping it down with his spade, the brothers scuttled away, shivering and dripping, to the warming-house. Yet Father Brice himself stood a while longer, his face turned up to the scudding grey cloud and his eyes closed against the rain.

It seemed to me that he was listening. To what or whom, I could not say.

'Come, Galahad,' Father Judoc called, his face hidden in the shadow of his cowl as he waited beneath the eaves of the warming-house. 'It's time.'

I looked back at Iselle, who still stood amongst the gnarled, reaching boughs of that yew, beneath which Joseph of Arimathea had once regaled the folk of Avalon with stories of Christ and the sunbaked lands far to the east. And even through the rain and the smoke which swirled down from the warming-house in billowing grey palls, I could see the challenge in Iselle's eyes. She thought me weak for submitting to the coming punishment. She did not know me and yet she wanted me to defy my brothers and refuse their discipline. I could see it in her face.

'Galahad!' Judoc called again. I tore my eyes from Iselle and left her standing beneath that ancient tree. And as I walked towards the bite of the lash, I prayed that I would find the courage to endure it.

3

Warriors from the Storm

I BIT DOWN ON A short length of rope to keep from crying out as Father Judoc struck me. I had wailed when the Saxons caught me in the marsh. I had shrieked and begged God to help me. Now, knowing that Iselle was out there, I vowed I would not whine if I could help it. Yet with each strike I gave a strangled yelp, and after the third time Father Brice told the brothers to sing.

'Let us not trouble the Prior,' he said, gesturing to the wall beyond which Drustanus lay dying in his own small cell. 'The Psalm of the Cup, Brothers,' he added with a nod, and they took it up at once, their voices smothering my stifled cries even as they winced with each blow of the crooked wand.

Father Dristan, I noticed, would not watch, but held his gaze on the floor rushes, though his voice flowed like clean water over smooth pebbles. For he had been the one sent to the Thorn to cut off the spiny switch and it seemed he felt in some part responsible for my suffering now, as each lash bit into my back and Father Judoc hissed the count, and red berries flew from the Thorn like drops of blood.

There were no berries left on that switch by the time Judoc finished, and when it was over, Father Brice rinsed the raw abrasions with soured wine. I gasped with the stinging agony of it and Father Brice smeared honey into the wounds and bound them in clean linen, muttering that I must never again leave the monastery without the brothers' consent or put myself in danger.

When he had tied off the dressing, he stood back to inspect his work, then raised a hand towards the door beyond which the wind howled. 'Now you have seen what is out there, let us hope you are eager to take your vows and stay among us here on Ynys Wydryn. To serve the Thorn with a steadfast heart.' He put a hand on my shoulder. 'Perhaps the Lord was at work in this.'

I watched the flames dancing in the hearth as I considered his words. 'If that is so, Father, might God have sent Iselle to protect me and bring me safely back?'

His brows lifted and he scratched a bristled cheek made ruddy by the wind. 'It is possible,' he said.

I frowned. 'And in return, rather than showing her kindness and hospitality, we make her stay in the byre with the cows while we warm ourselves by the fire?'

Father Brice gave that some thought but did not get the chance to answer, because Judoc growled that I was talking nonsense. 'She is a creature of the marsh, Galahad. As wild as the hawk and the wolf.' He clenched a fist, from which a finger extended to point at the roof. 'The Lord does not work through such creatures,' he said.

'God may not, Brother,' Father Folant rasped from his stool on the far side of the hearth, not taking his eyes off the flames, 'but the Devil does. The girl is *his* servant. Galahad brought her here and the end will follow.' He spat into the fire, the flames hissing in reply. 'I've seen it.'

Father Padern and Father Meurig made the sign of the Thorn. Judoc looked up at the soot-stained thatch as if he feared that at any moment the wind would rip it off and cast it away. 'This storm blew up when the girl came ashore,' Father Folant said. 'None can deny it.'

Father Meurig nodded. 'The Devil has sent her to tempt us.' His gaze slid from one man to another.

'It is worse than that, Brother,' Father Folant said. 'You'll see.' His flame-gilded face lifted, and his eyes fastened on me. 'You'll all see.' He tapped a finger against the side of his head. 'And when you do, you won't think that Brother Ridras was so cracked in the head after all.'

Mention of Brother Ridras deepened the creases in the monks' brows. Father Padern and Father Judoc whispered blessings upon his soul and Father Dristan visibly shuddered. For Ridras had been tormented by visions of the ruin of Britain, just as Father Folant now was. He had claimed to dream of the fires of Hell sweeping across the land to consume the children and the old. He believed that the suffering and the degradations which had stalked these isles since the disappearance of Arthur were just the beginning, and that even the marshes of Avalon and our island of Ynys Wydryn would be swallowed by encroaching darkness.

We had watched Father Ridras sink ever deeper into the mire of his own dark thoughts until, one day last summer, Father Dristan had found him in the orchard hanging from the branch of an apple tree. A shameful and cowardly act, Father Judoc had said, so that whenever Ridras's name was spoken, the brothers made the Thorn and squirmed as though plagued by lice.

'Well,' Father Yvain exclaimed above the pop and crack of the hearth wood, 'so long as we're still breathing and have a roof over our heads, I've got work to do.' He drained his cup and thumped it onto the table. 'It'll keep me warm enough and I won't have to sit here listening to this,' he said, and on his way to the door he stopped and placed a gentle hand on my shoulder.

'You do anything like that again, Galahad, and I'll flay you for a wine skin,' he said, then he leant down and put his mouth close enough to my ear that I could smell the drink on his breath. 'I'll take her some spiced wine and a fur,' he whispered, 'and you won't be a damn fool. Understand?'

I nodded, and when he opened the door rain gusted in and wind buffeted the hearth flames, making the coals seethe and glow.

'More wood for the fire, Brother Dristan,' Father Brice said. 'It will be a long night.' Dristan dipped his freshly tonsured head and went to fetch his damp cloak from the peg. I watched the flames and drank wine to ease the pain of my ravaged back. And the next day, warriors came out of the storm.

They came from the marsh like wraiths. Grey and grim and looming. Ghosts from another time summoned by the wailing wind and brought to Ynys Wydryn.

Father Meurig saw them first. At dawn he had gone down to check the eel traps and was up to his knees in the storm-driven water when some sense made him look out into the channel where, through sweeping veils of rain, a shape formed. The prow of a boat, he realized, a huge figure standing at the fore, guiding the small craft as if escorting souls to the hereafter.

Meurig had not stayed to learn more. 'Devils!' he had gasped, dripping water onto the rushes, bent double from running up the hill to warn us. 'Devils from the marsh are coming.'

'Saxons, more likely.' Father Brice looked back to the door. Most of us had slept in the warming-house, it being the sturdiest building and best able to withstand the wind's wrath.

My stomach clenched with fear. I wondered if the ghosts of the Saxons whom Iselle had killed had somehow followed us back to the monastery.

'Fetch spears, Brother,' Father Judoc told Dristan, then he turned, glaring at those of us who had been huddled near the hearth, drinking warm apple wine. We were standing now, though, frozen with dread, and my back seared from the lash, my muscles tight as knots.

'No matter what happens, they must not learn the whereabouts of the Thorn,' Father Brice warned us. His eyes were wild but knowing, as if he had been waiting for this day. 'We will die and be with Christ and Joseph before we tell the heathens where it is.'

'Yes, Brother,' we said in a ragged chorus.

Then the door was flung open and Dristan stumbled in, clutching a sheaf of spears.

'They are almost here!' he said, eyes bulging like boiled duck eggs as Judoc, Meurig, Father Folant and I each grabbed a spear.

'For the Thorn,' Father Brice said, pulling his small eating knife from his belt and leading us out into the swirling madness of the day.

Father Yvain was already out there. Having come from his workshop, he stood in the clearing with his back to us, a long-hafted axe in his hands. We hurried to him, instinctively arraying ourselves either side of him because he was the broadest and biggest of us and had once been a warrior. Then I looked across to the byre and through the wind-flayed shrouds of rain I saw Iselle standing in the doorway to keep her bow string dry, a half-dozen arrows planted in the earth by her feet.

Yvain saw her too and grunted with grim respect. 'Do as I say, Brothers,' he barked, flexing and tightening his fingers on the axe haft.

'God preserve us.' Old Father Padern threaded his fingers in the sign of the Thorn and held that gesture up with trembling arms, aiming it at the wraiths emerging from the tree line onto the slope of the hill.

'Four,' I heard Yvain say under his breath and knew he was weighing our chances of living to see the storm blow itself out. 'Stay behind me, lad,' he growled. 'You're in no condition to fight.'

'I can throw a spear,' I said, and had proved it, if only when hunting waterfowl in Ynys Wydryn's reed-fringed ditches or, now and then, bringing down a deer or boar in the high woods of Pennard Hill. Though I must have made for a pathetic sight now, standing there naked to the waist but for the linens wound around my torso, my lank hair running with rain, my flesh quivering with fear and cold.

The figures were halfway across the pasture now and I watched Iselle pluck an arrow from the ground and fit it on the string. She caught my eye and gave a slight shake of her head, the meaning of which I could not fathom, though it turned my gaze back to the striding, grey forms. Not ghosts but warriors. Broad-shouldered and shield-bearing, clad in furs and bronze. Spears in their hands, swords slung on baldrics across their shoulders or bouncing against their thighs as they trudged towards us. Faces grim-set beneath iron helmets whose long red plumes fell like streams of blood.

'Their shields, Galahad.' Father Yvain's eyes narrowed against the rain. 'Can't make it out.'

I stepped up to Yvain's shoulder, raising a hand to shelter my eyes from the downpour and willing them to identify what was on the leading man's shield.

'A black beast,' Father Dristan offered. 'A hunting dog, I think.'

'A bear,' I said. 'A black bear on a white field.' I could see it clearly now despite the rain. The shields of all four men were covered with bleached white leather and painted with a black bear standing on all fours upon the iron boss.

'Ha!' Father Yvain exclaimed. 'Not Saxons! Closer to ghosts than Saxons.'

'The bear? Truly?' Father Brice said. 'Can it be?'

Father Yvain looked at Iselle, but she had already lowered her bow, though she kept the arrow kissing the string. 'You might end up wishing they *were* Saxons, lad,' he said to me in a low voice. I was about to ask why but he strode forward to meet those men with their bear-shields and their helmets and their swords. Those lords of war.

'Yvain, you old ox!' the leader of the bear-shields called, holding his shield and spear wide apart as he came, teeth showing amid a silver beard. 'How long has it been, old friend?'

'A lifetime. More,' Father Yvain replied, swinging the axe and sheathing its head in the earth before embracing the other man, the two of them like bears themselves. The other three warriors' smiles could not fully dispel the bleak set of their jaws, though, or soften their hard eyes. Eyes which slipped from Father Yvain to me.

'I'll get some wine warmed,' Father Meurig said, and to my bemusement he and Father Padern walked off through the rain past Iselle, who was coming towards me, the unstrung bow stave in one hand. She frowned at my bandages and I knew she could not understand why I had let the monks beat me.

'You know them?' I asked her, realizing that she had known before any of us that these strangers were not Saxons.

'They are Lord Arthur's men,' she replied in a quiet voice, awe lighting her moss-green eyes.

'Arthur,' I whispered, the name feeling strange on my lips. Feeling almost like a blasphemy. 'Lord Arthur.'

Father Brice turned and flapped a hand at me and said

something, but his words were lost in the gushing rain and I was a leaf on the storm, swirling into the past. Lost in some half-remembered dream. *Arthur.*

A hand slapped against my upper arm. 'I said, fetch our guests some dry blankets, Galahad,' Brice hissed. 'Go now. Off with you.'

'Wait,' the man with the silver beard said, walking towards me. He was thick-set and broad-shouldered, his face scarred, his nose bent, and his jaw clenched. It was a terrifying face, but for the eyes. The eyes were smiling. 'Galahad,' he said, exhaling as he spoke my name. As though he had been waiting to say it a long, long time. Then he glanced down at the bandages which were sopping wet now and would need to be changed. 'What in the name of Taranis happened to you?'

Father Brice began to mumble an explanation, but the warrior raised a hand to silence him. 'Later,' he said. He was just staring at me through the rain which dripped from the rim of his dented, plumed helmet. 'It is good to see you again, Galahad,' he said. Then the smile in his eyes spread to his lips. 'You've grown, lad.'

Some part of my memory knew those eyes. Knew that battle-scarred face, albeit the years must have left tide marks of their own since I had known it.

'Who are you, lord?' I asked, keenly aware that the others were looking on. Those of the brothers who had not already retreated from the day and from these men.

'I am Gawain,' he said.

'Gawain, son of King Lot of Lyonesse and slaughterer of Saxons,' Father Yvain said, as the rain swirled around him. 'And these three tough old bastards,' he added, pulling his axe from the earth and pointing its muddy head at the other warriors, 'are Gediens ap Senelas, Hanguis ap Brodan, and Endalan ap Plaarin.'

The three men nodded at me in greeting. At *me*! Like Gawain, they were scarred and hard-looking and none of them young.

'I knew your father.' Gawain extended to me a hand which was crisscrossed with the cicatrices of old wounds.

The saliva soured in my mouth. I looked at Yvain, who dipped his head in a gesture which assured me that all was well, and so I took Gawain's offered hand, and it seemed his grip would crush the bones in mine. *My father?* I felt a dragging weight in my stomach. Felt a strange sense of dread writhe like a serpent in my soul.

'It is so very good to see you, Galahad,' the warrior said.

For a long moment we just stood there, our eyes fixed on each other, as if we were both trying to take the past and the present and join them together, the way you knot two lengths of a severed rope.

'Come, Lord Gawain of Lyonesse,' Father Brice said, shepherding the other three rain-drenched warriors towards the monastery. 'Now that we know we are not going to be murdered by Saxons, let us not catch our deaths lingering in this foul day.'

'I'm just glad we did not have to fight you, Father,' Endalan said, giving the smile of a hungry, tired man who knows he will soon be dry and filling his belly.

Yvain halted and nodded at Iselle. 'She's the one you should have been worried about. A killer with that bow of hers, as three Saxons would attest, if they were not dead.'

We all stopped and Iselle planted the end of the bow stave on the ground and lifted her chin, glaring towards the warriors, challenging them to be scornful. But though they eyed her with curiosity, I saw no disbelief in their weathered faces.

'Her name is Iselle,' I said, at which Iselle hissed something foul, annoyed at me for presuming to give up that which was hers to offer or not.

'Well, Iselle,' Gawain inclined his head at her, a rivulet of water pouring from his helmet, 'I hope these monks are as wealthy in wine and beer as they are said to be.'

'The girl may not join us.' Father Judoc swept an arm towards the building. 'She is quite comfortable in the byre.'

Gawain frowned at me and then at Iselle. 'She kills three Saxons and you make her live in the barn with the cattle?' He glanced at Father Yvain, who shrugged uncomfortably.

'She's a wildling, lord,' Father Brice said.

'We cannot have women among us,' Father Judoc added.

'Yours is a strange god.' Gediens shook his head.

'She gets wine and a place by the fire.' Gawain's eyes were all flint, at which Judoc and Brice looked at each other, neither willing to argue with the warrior.

'Well, come along.' Father Brice rounded us up again. And so we took shelter from the storm which flayed Ynys Wydryn, keening like a hundred lost and maddened souls. And before the wind-scattered starlings and rooks found their roosts that night and darkness fell over the marshes, I learnt that a far worse storm was coming.

Gawain and his men sat on stools by the fire, wolfing down their food and drink as their furs and cloaks and coats of bronze scales hung to dry. The air was cloyed with the stink of wet wool and sweat and the strong, animal scent of these warriors whose skin was begrimed with filth. They were ravenous. We watched them eat, none of the brothers daring to interrupt, knowing that only when they had taken the edge off their hunger would they tell us why they had come. And in that time, I looked at their swords in their stained leather scabbards. At Gawain's armour, the long leather jerkin covered with thousands of small overlapping bronze plates which resembled the skin of a fish. At the helmet with its iron rivets and hinged cheek pieces and the plume as long as a horse's tail and as red as blood. Even from across the room, the weight of all that iron and bronze and steel seemed to press down on me.

'You must leave this place and you must do it without delay,' Gawain said, not looking up from his bowl. He fished out a scrap of meat and blew on it as it steamed between his finger and thumb. Then he thrust the scrap into his mouth and closed his eyes for a moment as if seeking to commit the taste and pleasure of the food to memory.

Father Brice and Father Judoc, standing across from Gawain on the other side of the hearth, looked at each other. 'We cannot leave Ynys Wydryn,' Father Brice said.

'Why would we?' Judoc asked. 'We are safe here. Hidden.'

'*We* found you,' Gawain said, chewing, juices running into his beard.

'The Saxons do not know we are here,' Brice said. 'The ones who attacked Galahad—'

'If they *were* Saxons,' Judoc interrupted.

'—They must have wandered in search of plunder, straying far from King Cerdic's army,' Brice went on, 'which I believe is some miles east of Camelot and—'

'The Saxons are already here,' Gawain cut him off, looking up now, holding Brice's gaze. There were murmurs and rumbles around the fire then.

'We had to slip past them to get across the White Lake,' Gediens said, thumbing at the east wall. He was the youngest of the four men, though he could not have been less than forty years old. 'And not just a few scouts and foragers but war bands. Spearmen by the score. Saw their fires on Pennard Hill. Too many to count.' He turned his attention back to his bowl, spooning mutton and broth between his remaining teeth.

Gawain lifted his cup and drank deeply, then dragged a hand across his mouth and moustaches. 'There is no time to argue amongst yourselves or seek advice from your god, or whatever else it is you do here,' he told us. 'The Saxons are all around. Clustered like flies on a corpse. They will see the tor and they *will* come.' He glanced around at the modest walls and thatch, our only refuge from the wild storm. From the world, too. 'And when they find this place, they will burn it and they will kill you.'

The brothers looked to each other and I saw the fear in their faces, in the widening of their eyes and the flare of their nostrils. I felt the same fear, seeing in my mind again the dead I had seen out in the marsh. I felt the creeping dread stirred up by this warrior's words, and we looked at him, expecting more, but he said nothing, instead taking a moment to fill his cup again. Letting the blade of his foretelling sink deep into our guts.

It was Father Yvain who broke the silence. 'What of Camelot?' he asked. 'The Lady Morgana's spearmen have always kept Cerdic's raiders at bay. The Saxons rarely leave Caer Gwinntguic.'

'Lady Morgana does not have the strength to face Cerdic in open battle,' Gawain said. 'Just like the other lords and kings of Britain, Morgana hides behind her walls and watches the fires redden the night skies. Cerdic pushes west and the land bleeds.'

'Any that do not swear allegiance to him are butchered,' Hanguis said through a sour grimace. He was a brutal-looking man. Almost completely bald, he boasted a livid scar of white flesh across his forehead where someone had nearly opened his skull.

'And Constantine?' Father Yvain asked. Because of his occasional forays to the island villages around Ynys Wydryn, he knew more than any of the brothers about the happenings in the kingdoms of Britain.

'He still fights in the east, striking from the forests of Caer Lerion,' Gawain replied, and I wondered how well he and Yvain had known one another back when they had both fought for Lord Arthur. 'Two hundred men. A few more perhaps.' He shook his head. 'But he will not last long alone. He cannot.'

I had heard of Lord Constantine, son of Ambrosius and nephew of Uther Pendragon. A warlord of Britain and self-proclaimed king. Though he must be an old man by now.

'Perhaps Camelot will hold out,' Gawain conceded. 'I dug those defences with my own hands.' He raised an eyebrow at me and shook his head as one does at a memory which seems too strange to be real. 'Long time ago now,' he said. 'But Camelot can be held with three hundred spears. Lady Morgana will hold. Everything else will fall.'

The brothers fell into discussing the threat we faced, arguing about whether or not the Saxon war bands would find a way through the marsh to Ynys Wydryn. I felt Father Brice's eyes on me but, as I looked up, his gaze fastened back onto Gawain. 'Why have you come here, Lord Gawain?' he asked. 'If simply to warn us, we are grateful and will look to protect the Holy Thorn.'

A guttural sound escaped Gawain's throat. 'I care nothing for your tree, monk.' He looked up and his eyes were on mine. 'I've come for him. As you knew I would.'

I felt the blood run cold in my arms then. My stomach rolled like the storm-tossed water around Ynys Wydryn, and all eyes were on me as the hearth flames leapt and the rain seethed in the thatch above our heads.

'I would have come sooner, lad,' Gawain told me. 'Many times, I meant to come.' There was regret in his voice and in his eyes. Eyes which clung to me as if we had shared a past, though I barely knew him. 'Other matters have kept us away. Other pledges.' He lifted his cup and drank.

Father Yvain stiffened. 'Have you found him?' he asked, his big beard jutting towards Gawain.

Gawain glanced at Hanguis.

'Found who, Father?' I asked.

'The druid,' Father Judoc spat. 'They speak of the druid Merlin.' The other monks made the sign of the Thorn. Yvain, I noticed, did not.

'These last ten years we have searched,' Gawain said, the words given to the fire. 'Those of us that were left. We took an oath and we have held to that oath. We have sought Merlin in every corner of the Dark Isles. Many who set out have never returned. Men have given their last good years to it.' He shook his head, seeing the faces of old friends in his mind, perhaps.

'But you have found him?' Yvain said. He had walked round the hearth and was now looming over Gawain, who still sat on his stool, the cup of apple wine in his hand. He did not answer, though his eyes seemed to catch light in the flame glow.

'We will not talk of the druid here,' Father Brice said, his jaw clenching, eyes narrowed in determination. 'Nor will we hear of you coming to take young Galahad from us. You know he is of the order.'

Gawain looked up into the monk's cold glare. 'He is not shorn,' he said. Then he turned back to me. 'Have you taken the oath of the Thorn?' he asked.

Father Brice shot me a warning look.

'No, lord,' I told Gawain.

'The moon is waxing, Lord Gawain,' Father Brice cut in before I could speak again. The monk lifted a hand and scythed its edge through the tendril of black smoke curling up from the rushlight's flame. 'When it is full, I will give Galahad the tonsure myself. He has been with us these last ten years—'

'I know how long he's been here, monk,' Gawain growled.

Father Brice gave a curt nod. 'And you know that he has dedicated his life to Christ and the saint who lowered our Lord's body down from the cross. Galahad will be a brother of the order.'

'Galahad will come with us,' Gawain said.

Father Judoc took a step towards Gawain, his finger pointing at the warrior. 'You do not command us here,' he said.

'Prior Drustanus has always known I would come for the lad,' Gawain growled. 'Fetch him. He'll tell you.'

'The Prior is dying,' Judoc said, at which we of the Thorn made the sign.

Gawain gave a tired shrug. 'Galahad is coming with me.' He looked up at me. 'You remember?' he asked. 'You remember I told you I'd come for you one day?'

My thoughts swirled in my skull as Father Brice and Father Judoc complained and protested, and the others murmured amongst themselves. And I searched the silver-bearded warrior's face, my eyes following the old scar which ran up through his eyebrow to meet his hairline.

'I remember you, lord,' I said. Every tongue went still. 'I was a boy.'

Gawain nodded. 'What do you remember?' he asked.

I looked at the faces around me and saw concern and curiosity. Disquiet and even anger. But Yvain gave a slight nod which said, *go on*.

'It was the day of the great battle,' I said, casting my mind back through the years to that day. I looked at Gawain and it was all suddenly there within reach, the memory bright and as sharp as a blade which I feared to touch.

'And?' Gawain urged.

I looked into the hearth flames rather than into the warrior's eyes. I could not breathe deeply enough. The air of that place was foul, and my throat clenched like a fist and my breath was caught in my throat, fitful as a hare caught in a snare trap.

I did not want to remember.

'Go on, Galahad,' Gawain said again, the muscle beneath his bearded right cheek twitching.

I cleared my throat. 'You found me. Found us,' I corrected. 'After.'

The image of the raven-haired woman filled the eye of my mind. Guinevere, the woman whom my father had loved. Even when my mother was alive, he had loved this other. I had thought this cruel truth only came to me years later, in those times when I failed to stop my mind fetching up memories like sea-wrack spewed upon a shingle beach. Now, I realized that I had always known it, even before that day when she had come to our door in the forest, as though she were a spirit made flesh and sent by some god to damn my father and me. The way she and my father had looked at each other. The pain in their eyes. The longing. The hopelessness. I had not the words for any of it back then, yet I *had* seen it. Even with my child's eyes I had seen it.

'I found you, Galahad,' Gawain confirmed with a nod, and I could see that that terrible day could have been just yesterday for him. 'All was lost. We had fought the Saxons and the traitors for as long as we could. As hard as we could. In the end, both sides broke.' His teeth pulled at his lip. 'It was sheer bloody madness. That's what it was.'

Gediens grimaced, Hanguis shook his head and Endalan touched the iron hilt of the sword at his hip to ward off ill luck, the memory of that day still fresh in their minds. A seeping wound.

Gawain's eyes found me again. 'When I got clear of that mess, I found you and Guinevere. I can't say what had happened to her.' His brows lifted, as if retreating from all his eyes had seen. 'I suppose she couldn't accept it. Losing them both. And just as they'd become brothers of the sword again. After everything.' He shook his head. 'Her mind was gone, you see.' He fluttered his fingers in the smoky air. 'Just . . . gone.'

'I remember,' I said. I looked at my hands. Moved my thumb and fingertips across each other, almost feeling Tormaigh's coarse mane on my skin. Brave, proud Tormaigh, my father's war stallion. I closed my eyes and I could hear his hoofbeats on the ground and the din of battle receding like the sound of the ocean at my back. I had clung on to him and he had carried me to a copse of birch. There we found Guinevere lying amongst pink willowherb and cream-coloured meadowsweet.

'I thought she was dead,' I said, 'but could see no wounds. Then I thought her asleep but could not wake her.'

'Trapped somewhere between life and death, they said.' Father Yvain's words broke upon me like a wave. The memory twisted my insides. Dizzied me. I opened my eyes and looked at Gawain. A glisten of tear on his cheek held a tiny rushlight flame.

'We lost brothers that day.' Hanguis drained his cup. 'But we shall see them soon enough.'

'I found you on a deer path in the woods,' Gawain told me. 'Somehow, you had got Guinevere up onto that horse. *I* found you, lad. And I brought you here.' He looked around, as if judging his own memory of the place against the reality. 'The brothers took you in and I am grateful to them.' He nodded at Father Brice and Father Judoc. 'Carried Guinevere to a woman in Caer Gloui. A healer.' He shook his head. 'But the woman could not help her. Could not even name the affliction. So, I brought Guinevere to the nuns across the water.'

'Enough,' Father Judoc said. 'We will not talk of that woman here. She lived beyond the shadow of God.'

'If not for her betrayal, Arthur would have thrown the Saxons back into the sea,' Iselle said, and those brothers of the Thorn who had not wanted Iselle under their roof nodded solemnly.

'Perhaps,' Gawain said, watching the flames leap and dance. He nodded. 'Perhaps.'

The hearth wood cracked and spat into the silence.

'You may of course spend the night with us, Lord Gawain,' Father Brice said after a while. 'But if this storm passes and it is safe to leave in the morning, you and your men will do so.'

Gawain nodded. 'We'll leave,' he said, 'but we'll be taking Galahad with us.'

I felt suddenly cold. My breath caught in my chest and I looked at Father Brice.

'Father?' I needed his reassurance. Needed him to oppose this scarred warrior by means of his venerable age and wisdom and by the strength of his faith.

'It's all right, Galahad.' Father Brice lifted a hand towards me. 'Lord Gawain does not command here.'

'Even so,' Gawain said, feeding a stick to the fire, 'I'm taking the lad, when I go.'

I took a breath, emboldened by Brice's temerity, though the chill yet lingered in the pit of my stomach. 'I am not leaving Ynys Wydryn, Lord Gawain,' I said. 'My place is here.' I gestured at the three warriors huddled by the fire at Gawain's shoulders. 'You have your brothers, and I have mine.' Father Brice and the others nodded and murmured their approval of my words.

'Your place?' Gawain searched the flames with his eyes and shook his head. 'Wherever your place is, it's not here, Galahad. A man can't hide from the future, no more than he can hide from the past.'

'Even if he wishes it were otherwise,' Hanguis muttered under his breath as the fuel crackled and the flames capered, and Father Brice and Father Judoc shared a knowing look.

'Until you came here, I had not thought of the past,' I lied. 'Only the future. My future here, as a brother of the Holy Thorn.' I hardened my eyes on him. 'When you leave tomorrow, I will visit the Thorn and pray for you, Lord Gawain. When I finish my prayers, I will not think of you again. I will not think of that day again.'

Gawain searched my face. I did not know what he was seeking in it, but I saw in his eyes that whatever it was could not be found.

'You look tired, Brother,' Father Judoc told me. I could not recall him having used the term before. 'Like this storm, Lord Gawain has stirred up things that should be left alone.' He gestured to the door beyond which a walkway of planks led across the mud to the dormitory. 'Go and rest, Brother. And do not let your thoughts stray.'

I did not move, but looked at Iselle, who was watching the warriors with an awe which verged on reverence, the way the brothers looked at the Thorn on its lonely hill. In truth, I did not want to leave them all to talk without me. And yet neither did I want to remain in the company of Gawain and his men. Did not want to breathe the iron smell of their armour and the sheep-stink of the grease on their blades, for it was the scent of ghosts.

'Do as Brother Judoc says, Galahad.' Father Brice smiled at me. 'I will be along shortly to change your dressings.'

'Yes, Father,' I said, turning, and did not look at Gawain again before the door shut behind me.

I slept only a little that night. The wounds from the Thorn felt like fire, so that I could not lie comfortably but curled around my bolster, clinging to it as a shipwrecked man clings to a timber. And in a way I *was* drowning. Perhaps it was the rising waters of the marsh, or the rain which still thrashed down upon the thatch and pelted against the dormitory walls. But I think not. I think it was the coming of Gawain and the past he brought with him which had me fearing that I was suffocating. That I was sinking back into the dark mire from which I had been free these last years.

Perhaps I could have slept if I'd drunk more apple wine, but I was afraid of the dreams that might haunt me if I gave myself to sleep's capricious rule. And so I lay awake in the dark dormitory, trying and failing to think of anything but that day ten years past, when everything I knew was ripped from my hands. When everything I was and everything I had hoped to be vanished like smoke on the breeze and became no more than a memory.

When I was sure that the brothers were deeply asleep, when Father Yvain and Father Meurig were snoring like a pair of hogs, and Father Folant had ceased his impenetrable somnolent mumbling, I eased out from beneath my blankets and knelt in the rushes at the end of my bed. The only light came from a lamp horn beside Father Judoc's bed, which he watched to know when to wake us for the night prayers. But its jaundiced glow did not reach far and so my hands followed my eyes to the humped dark shape of the oak chest which held all my worldly belongings. For a moment I did nothing but let my palms rest upon the smooth wood. Remembering.

The creak of the hinges was no louder than the squeaks of mice in the thatch. No one woke and for a moment I breathed in the smell of my old home and the past. I felt my way down into the chest, rummaging beneath my spare habit of worn wool, and the poor cup which I had made under Yvain's tutorship in my second year on Ynys Wydryn. The cup had cracked in the drying, but I kept it anyway. Delving deeper, I felt the straps of Tormaigh's bridle; the headpiece, cheek piece and throatlatch, and could smell the old cracked leather just by feeling it. I thought I caught Tormaigh's scent too, lingering still in the few strands of his mane which even now remained caught between the crown strap and cheek piece. I felt the cool hardness of the bit, which I remembered Gawain taking from the dead stallion's mouth and from which I had cleaned the animal's blood-flecked spittle. I had brought Tormaigh's bridle with me to Ynys Wydryn because I had loved him, and he had never betrayed me, and for the first months I had polished the leather and iron, thinking it did the stallion honour. After that first year I had never again taken it out into the light of day.

I felt the soft leather purse, inside which were a handful of haws from the Holy Thorn. Prior Drustanus himself had pulled them from the thorny briar and given them to me during my first winter on Ynys Wydryn. I worked at the drawstring, then sought inside the purse, feeling for the haws, which were shrivelled and hard between my fingers and thumb. But I let them be and drew the string tight again, for I had come to wade deeper than that. And then I found it in the dark. The leather still smooth. Still hard.

A sheath to protect the inside of a boy's forearm against the stinging lash of the bow string. I took the bracer out, amazed at how small it was. In my memory it had been worthy of a grown warrior. I held it to my nose and smelled the beeswax which had been carefully worked into the leather, and in the dark I could just make out the simple pattern, incised with meticulous care on the outward-facing side. A sun. Its rays streaking out all around. A blazing sun. The same, only smaller, as that which adorned Tormaigh's breastplate of boiled leather.

Just holding that bracer, I felt an echo of the thrill that had shivered through me the first time I put my left arm into it and felt the leather against my skin. Kneeling in the floor rushes still, I closed my eyes, immersing myself deeper in the past. I saw my father sitting by the hearth, leaning into the firelight to see better as he worked. Piercing the leather with his knife. Threading the thong ties. Rubbing the beeswax in until he could see the flames reflected in the leather. His eyes were narrowed, his expression unsure, as if he feared his work was too poor, even though I had never seen anything finer.

In the end he had been proud of the bracer. Wearing it, I had been the king of the forest.

Father.

4

Into the Earth

I FOUND GAWAIN AND HIS men in the warming-room, working at bowls of hot wheatmeal, milk and honey with spoons I had turned myself. There was an empty bowl on the floor beside Iselle's Saxon sword and two damaged arrows, and my stomach lurched. I was not sure why, but then, to my surprise, I realized I did not like knowing that Iselle had spent the night by the hearth with these men.

As for the warriors themselves, they seemed bright-eyed and determined, renewed from a comfortable, dry night's sleep. They had combed the knots from their hair and beards, scrubbed the dirt from their armour and polished their helmets so that they gleamed in the dawn light flooding into the room, the door being open to let the clean air scour the damp stench from the place.

The wind had died sometime in the night. The rain, too, had slowed to a haze of drizzle which hung in the air like dew.

'I hope you slept well, Galahad,' Gawain said, pointing a spoon at me.

I had not slept before night prayers and, after, had lain awake until the first light seeped through the window slits, praying to Joseph of the Thorn to guide me.

'I did not, lord,' I said, wondering where Iselle was now.

Gawain half smiled. 'You're young enough that it doesn't show in your face.' He arched the eyebrow through which that savage scar ran. 'I was like that once. There was not enough wine and not enough women. I could drink the night away and still be in the saddle hunting deer or boar come the dawn.'

His men chuckled at that, as Father Meurig came in and gave Gediens a small, bulging sack. 'Cheese, bread, a fowl, some smoked mutton and plenty of hazel cobs which are still good. And three flasks of our most . . . warming apple wine,' he said.

The warriors thanked Meurig, even if it was clear that the food was a parting gift, telling them that they must leave that very morning.

'You will need to fetch another flask,' Gawain told Meurig, who followed the warrior's line of sight to where I stood.

'Galahad?' Father Meurig looked down at the knapsack in my hand, then up to my face.

'I've told you, monk,' Gawain said before I could answer, 'Galahad is leaving with me.'

Meurig stood a moment, blinking and pulling on his ear, not knowing what to say or do. Then, without a word, he hurried off, leaving me alone with the four men.

'It will be hard.' Gawain nodded at the doorway beyond which a sullen day brooded under a heavy sky, angry still, but exhausted from raging.

'I have not said I am coming with you,' I said.

He ignored that. 'There is no coming back. This place is finished. Your days of hiding from the world, hiding from yourself, well, they're over.'

'I have not decided yet,' I said, thinking that was true despite the knapsack in my hand. Despite having that dawn stuffed it with a waxed deer skin, my old habit, some bread and cheese and smoked meat stolen from the pantry and six apples and a cup which did not leak. At some point in the night I had decided I would go with Gawain, though now, in the day's pale light, the thought of it was absurd. Furthermore, Gawain's expectation of it was riling. Still, I clung to the knapsack.

'Can't deny who you are,' Gawain said. 'Who your father was.'

Gediens and Endalan shared a sideways look and made to rise from their stools. Gawain growled at them to stay where they were.

The creature stirred in me then. It seemed to shake itself. I felt it in my guts and in my chest and shivering into my limbs. 'Do not talk of my father,' I snapped. 'I hate him.'

Gawain winced, as if those words had stung him.

'I understand, Galahad,' he said. 'Your father and I . . .' He stopped, searching for the words. 'Well, we were not always friends. And worse than that, too.'

I saw the shadow of a snarl on Hanguis's lips, though whatever harm my father had done him, he kept it to himself.

'Even so,' Gawain went on, 'your father was the greatest warrior I have ever known. He was better than me. Better than Arthur,' he said in a softer voice, his eyes losing their sharpness. In that moment, Gawain's soul seemed to fly from the room. He was somewhere else and twenty years away. And wherever he was, my father was with him. 'I have never seen such skill,' he murmured. 'Could neither be taught nor learnt. Not a talent like that. It was god-given.'

I made the sign of the Thorn.

'Not your god of bramble and briar, lad,' Gediens sneered. 'Taranis, Master of War. That's who loved your father.'

I felt foolish. Why was I standing there clutching a knapsack of food and talking to these men who were as different from me as the gyrfalcon from the jackdaw?

Gawain shook himself free of his memories and returned to us from across the years, his gaze burrowing into my soul. 'You are Lancelot's son.'

My limbs felt heavy and numb, but not from a lack of sleep. 'I am not a warrior,' I replied.

'I just told you, Galahad. Your father was not made but rather born. Where he fought, the enemy withered and our own spearmen became champions. Having Lancelot with us was like having Arthur's bear banner flapping above our heads. Or the Pendragon's banner in the time before. It bled the Saxons' courage and fed our own.'

'He is nothing to me,' I said.

'His blood runs in your veins,' Gawain said.

Why had I taken the child's leather bracer from my chest and put it in the knapsack? I should have carried it down to the jetty and cast it into the marsh. Perhaps my memories would have sunk with it.

'What's happening here?' Father Brice said, appearing in the doorway with Father Meurig at his shoulder.

'We are leaving.' Gawain stood. The other warriors did the same, collecting their coats of scale armour, their cloaks, helmets and weapons which were scattered around the warming-room.

Father Brice looked at me. At the knapsack in my hand. 'Galahad?'

I did not know what to say or how to say it.

'Tell him, lad,' Gawain said.

'I have to go with them, Father,' I said.

'Go where?' Brice asked.

I looked at Gawain and felt like a fool again, for I had not asked him where we would go or even why. All I knew was I had to go with him.

'I've told you, monk.' Gawain was shrugging himself into the long coat of gleaming bronze scales. 'The Saxons are closing in. They will find this place, if not in a matter of days then surely in the spring. Come with us. Or die here.'

'Our place is here. On this holy island into whose earth Joseph of Arimathea thrust his staff, which took root and grew into the sacred Thorn.' Brice signed the Thorn, as we all would when we spoke its name. 'We do not fear death.' He grabbed at the cloth of his habit with a gnarled hand. 'We have no need of armour. No need of shield and sword. Besides which, Prior Drustanus lies on his deathbed. Would you have us abandon him?'

'I'll not let Galahad die for a tree,' Gawain said. 'Or for a man who is already halfway dead.'

'I'm going with them, Father,' I said again.

Father Brice came up to me and took my hand, turning his back on Gawain and the others. Father Judoc and some of the brothers had now gathered outside. I could hear them talking in low voices.

'Do not feel any obligation to go with this man,' Brice told me, 'no matter the past. His path is not your path.' The skin of his hands felt as rough as linden bark against my own. 'You are not your father.'

'Perhaps God wants me to go,' I suggested weakly. I had no reason to believe this was true, but then nor had I ever heard the Lord of Heaven's voice in my mind telling me that I was destined to be a servant of the Thorn.

To my surprise, Father Brice nodded. 'That may be true, Galahad,' he said. 'It does seem fateful, perhaps, that after all these years Gawain has returned here just days before you take the tonsure and swear yourself to the brotherhood.'

He pursed his lips and considered all this for a long moment as, behind him, the warriors prepared to leave. 'Give me a day, Galahad,' he said. 'Let me speak with the brothers and seek guidance from the saint.' He turned to Gawain. 'You may stay another night. Eat and rest. Will you give us that?'

Gawain looked at his companions. Gediens shrugged and Endalan nodded. Hanguis inclined his tall spear towards me. 'Give him another day to be sure of himself,' he told Gawain. 'Won't do us any harm getting more warmth into our bones. More food in our bellies.'

Gawain scratched his beard. 'One day, monk,' he said, 'because you took the lad in and have been a friend to him these past years.' He took up his own spear from where it leant against the wall and strode out, parting the gaggle of monks who clustered beyond the door.

'Well, Galahad,' Father Brice looked up at me with a tired smile, 'it seems I may enjoy your company a little while longer. There's something we must do. Come with me.'

'Where to, Father?' I asked. But he had already turned and walked out of the warming-room into the bruised day, and so I followed him.

Father Brice took me to the Thorn. It stood upon a wind-scoured hillside to the west of the tor, black, lonely and ancient. Patient and persistent, a shelter for sheep and, in a way, for a people. Keeping watch over us as it had done for five hundred years.

Even from a distance I could see the rags flickering amongst the branches. Hundreds of scraps of wool or linen tied by pilgrims over the years, each one fluttering in the breeze, as though whispering the prayer that was on the lips of whoever tied it there.

Approaching the tree, we disturbed a flock of rooks. The birds flapped up from the Thorn's knotted and fissured branches, cawing and rasping indignantly in a scatter of dark, reflective green-and-blue plumage, as though the timeworn tree itself were disintegrating into the wind. I counted nine birds taking to the sky, vanishing into the grey, and I could not help but mark that to be the same number of souls who lived below the tor, bar one.

Father Brice paid his respects to the Thorn, thanking the saint for having chosen Avalon and Ynys Wydryn as the place to start his church. Then he drew his small knife and took a cutting from the tree, the effort leaving him red-faced and puffing.

'To think, Galahad,' he mopped sweat from his brow, 'that Joseph's hand, that gripped the staff from which the Thorn grew, had also touched the body of Christ when he took him down from the cross and laid him in the tomb.'

He held the cutting towards me, expecting me to grasp it, which I did, careful to avoid those long, sharp thorns. 'Thus, do you hold Christ's body now,' he said, then dipped his head, the skin of which was raw from being freshly shaved, 'in a way.'

I nodded and withdrew my hand, and he tucked the cutting into his belt, a gift for the Prior, I supposed, and I imagined old Drustanus holding it at the end of his life as he passed from this world to the next.

I knew what Father Brice was trying to do. And in truth I did hold the Thorn in awe. For its own sake, having grown from a staff as a sign of God's will, but also because it represented a new beginning for the peoples of Britain. The old gods had fled these isles or turned their backs on the Britons. That was what folk whispered by their hearths. But here was a god who would welcome all into his fold. So the brothers of the Thorn believed. So we hoped.

After that, Father Brice gathered a handful of red haws

from amongst the thorniest reaches where the birds had not scavenged and placed them in the scrip on his belt. When it was done, he looked into the east, sucking his finger where a barb had stabbed him. The sky there was almost black. Heavy with swollen cloud and menacing. But I did not think the threat of rain was what had turned Father Brice's expression as ominous as the day.

'We had best be getting back,' he said, and so we hurried down the saint's hill and across the reed-beds back towards the shelter of the great tor.

Now, I was helping Father Judoc and Father Dristan repair the sheepfold, where an eight-foot length of the wall had collapsed in the storm winds. Moving gingerly because the lacerations on my back stung like burns.

Father Meurig had driven the small flock into the byre, where they seemed happy enough, so there was no pressing need to be out in the rain piling the stones back into place. But our working on the wall was Father Judoc's way of showing Lord Gawain that the brothers had no intention of leaving the monastery, nor would they quake in terror at the warrior's talk of Saxons. And so, wincing whenever the others weren't looking, I hefted stones and set them one upon another, hoping that Saint Joseph or Christ or God in His heaven would send me a sign which would portend that it was my fate to stay on Ynys Wydryn. For I could not say what had led me to fill my knapsack and stand before Gawain as though I would leave the monastery and go into the savage lands with him. I could only ascribe it to a moment of confusion which had since passed.

Having found me on that crimson day long ago, Gawain had then abandoned me, just as my father had done. The brothers took me in when I had nothing and no one, and so I would take the tonsure and join them, and Gawain would vanish like marsh mist back into the past where he belonged.

That thought had me wondering where Iselle had gone. Were it not for the Saxon sword which leant against a stool in the warming-house, I would have believed she had left us. But that fine sword was hers. She had won it and I could not think that she would just leave it behind.

'I trust you have come to your senses, Brother,' Father Judoc said, pointing at a particular stone which he wanted me to heft up to him. 'And that Brother Brice has reminded you of your place here among us.' I gave him the stone and he turned it one way, then the other, until it nestled amongst those around it. 'Of your . . . importance,' he added with a satisfied nod. Then he took a moment to appraise our work. 'The Prior would tell you himself, were he not busy preparing his soul for heaven.'

'God receive him,' Father Dristan muttered.

I said nothing. I knew what Father Judoc referred to by my *importance*. It was said that when I came to the monastery, the Thorn had blossomed that autumn. Previously, so the brothers said, the holy tree had flowered once in a year, in spring. But ever since my coming, it had flowered most winters also, which Prior Drustanus had proclaimed was a great miracle, though it had meant little to me as a ten-year-old boy. There had been scarce talk of the miracle since, but Father Judoc raised it now as a way of urging me to consider my place among them. As though my being one of them was somehow preordained.

Father Judoc eyed the tumble of stones still lying in the mud, then pointed at the one he wanted. 'We all have our place, Galahad,' he said, making his point by taking rather too long to position the next stone.

'But how can we be sure where that place is, Father?' I asked.

That was when Father Folant shouted in alarm, dropping

the firewood which he'd been carrying to the warming-house and pointing to the apple orchard at the foot of the slope. Iselle was running among the trees, her bow in one hand and a brace of ducks strung by the neck in the other.

'Fetch the others,' Judoc barked at Dristan, who ran off towards the buildings.

'What's happening?' Gawain roared, striding through the rain, throwing his cloak around his shoulders. His men came in his wake and together we watched Iselle hare up the hill towards us, her tresses thrown back from her pale face, whipping like flame.

Somewhere, one of the monks was sounding the hand bell, its hollow, metallic beat as fast as a terrified heart.

'Shields,' Gawain called, and Hanguis and Endalan turned and hurried back to the warming-room as Iselle reached us, dropping the bow and her kill and bending to suck in breath as she turned her flushed face up to meet Gawain's eyes.

'They're here,' she said.

'Here? On the island?' Father Judoc asked, caught between disbelief and fear. The brothers had gathered behind us, their wide eyes scouring the tree line, hands busy signing the Thorn, lips moving in prayer. Phelan still beating the bell, his face red with the effort.

'How many?' Gawain asked, in no doubt that *here* meant *here*.

'A dozen,' Iselle said. 'Spearmen. No lords or men with iron coats that I saw. But they saw your boat.' She picked up her bow and the ducks and straightened. 'They're coming.'

Gawain nodded, watching the trees below. 'We're leaving.'

'How?' Gediens asked.

Gawain grimaced at the thought of having to fight his way through the Saxons to get to their boat.

'There is another way,' Father Brice said. He stood at my shoulder and I saw that he held my knapsack, which I had left on my bed in the dormitory. 'There is a way through the caves beneath the tor,' he said.

'If it is not flooded.' Father Padern was eyeing the grey sky from beneath whiskery white brows.

Gawain turned to Father Brice. 'You'll come with us?' he asked.

The monk shook his head. 'Our place is here.' He looked at Father Judoc, who nodded and turned his face to the iron-grey, rain-veiled west. Towards the Thorn.

'But we will show you the way,' Judoc told Gawain.

'Galahad.' Father Brice handed me my knapsack. 'Go with Lord Gawain.'

I took a step back, pulling my hands away as if from fire. 'No, Father.' I tried to match the cold sharpness in his eyes with flint of my own. For in that moment I knew that I should stay with the brothers. That to do anything else was to forsake them, which only a feckless coward would do. It was clear now. The most luminous truth on the bleakest of days. 'I will stay, Father,' I said.

Gawain thrust his big spear into the earth, turned and grabbed a fistful of my habit. 'You will not,' he said. 'If I have to knock you onto your arse, sling you over my shoulder and carry you off, you're leaving this place with me.'

I threw up an arm, knocking the warrior's hand away, and glared at him, hating him then. Who was he to decide? This man whom I did not know. Whom I had not seen for ten years.

His eyes were fire now. 'I did not leave you here that day so that you could die like a lamb on some Saxon's blade.'

'Go with them, my son.' Father Brice offered me my knapsack again.

'Here they come!' Gediens called.

The Saxon spearmen had cleared the apple trees now and arrayed themselves in a line at the foot of the slope, shields raised as they eyed us, appraising our strength.

'You'll find no silver here!' Father Padern yelled down at them, his thin voice sluiced away by the wind and rain. 'Be gone, heathens! There is nothing for you here!'

I doubted the Saxons would understand what he was saying, though his words seemed to give them pause. Perhaps they thought the Brothers of the Thorn were druids. Perhaps they feared old Padern was cursing them with spells.

'Go, Galahad,' Father Brice said, then nodded at someone over my shoulder. I turned to see Father Yvain, a spear in his hand, a bear skin around his shoulders and an old, dented iron helmet on his head.

'I'll show you the way,' Father Yvain told Gawain.

'They're coming,' Father Judoc said. The Saxons were advancing up the rise, chanting some war song in low voices. 'Go, now.'

Iselle came from the warming-house, her bow in her hand, the bag of arrows and the brace of ducks tied to her belt, and the Saxon sword strapped onto her back.

'You would leave the brothers to be slaughtered, Lord Gawain, son of King Lot of Lyonesse?' I asked, speaking his bloodline to shame him.

'They choose to stay,' Gawain said. 'We have other fights.' He gestured with his spear at the humble buildings of the monastery. 'We have more to lose than this.'

Father Brice reached up and put the knapsack over my shoulder. Then he took my hands in his own. 'You are our future, Galahad,' he said. 'So long as you live, there is hope.' Tears came to my eyes then, hot and angry and tasting of the past.

I could hear the Saxons' words now. They were invoking their gods: Woden, Thunor and Tiw. I caught their animal stink on the wind. I heard the *whip* of Iselle's bow and the *thunk* of the arrow embedding in a shield.

'There are more coming from the trees,' Endalan warned.

Hanguis shook his head and spat a curse.

'Go, Galahad,' Father Judoc said.

'Go or stay, it matters not,' Father Folant added, and with that he set off walking down the hill towards the Saxons, who were just a spear-throw away now. None of the monks tried to stop their brother, and as Father Brice and Father Yvain entreated me to go, their voices lost in a swirling, dizzying daze which overcame me like a fog, I saw a Saxon plunge his spear into Father Folant's belly. Saw the bearded, snarling Saxon stamping his foot down onto the monk, trying to haul the blade from the flesh and the snag of Folant's woollen gown.

I saw Father Padern walk forward, towards the spearmen, his fingers intertwined in the sign of the Thorn. Father Meurig and Father Phelan followed, their own hands clasped in the same gesture of defiance and invocation, as though the sign itself might turn aside blades and hatred and heathen ignorance.

'We shall join the saint,' Father Padern yelled, his voice stronger than I had ever heard it. 'Come, Brothers! Come now!' That voice cut through the fog and pierced me. 'Be not afraid,' he commanded. I saw the spear blade, a silver leaf flashing in the grey. Saw the bright blood fly, stark and shocking. Too bright for an old man's blood.

A Saxon came on ahead of his spear-brothers. Eager to prove himself. Hanguis strode out to meet him, taking the man's spear thrust on his shield and turning it aside, then launching himself forward and driving his sword into the man's guts. He twisted the blade and hauled it out, then raised his shield and walked backwards with even, unhurried steps.

Iselle ran back past the unfinished sheep pen towards the buildings, and I thought she was fleeing but then she stopped by the wood pile, turned and watched, holding her bow low across herself, an arrow nocked on the string.

Something struck me and I stumbled and almost fell. It was Father Brice. 'In the name of the Thorn, go!' he screamed at me, a fury in his face which I did not recognize in him. 'Go or be damned!'

I watched Father Phelan's severed head tumble to the ground and his legs give way.

Another shove, from Gawain this time, and the next thing I knew I was staggering towards the byre.

'Remember us, Galahad!' Father Brice called after me. 'Remember us!'

'Move, lad,' Gawain growled, pushing the shaft of his spear against my back, so that the raw lesions beneath my habit bit into my flesh all over again. I saw Iselle take the arrow from the bow string and plunge it into the bag, then she turned and was running, and I was running too, gasping and sick in my stomach and needing to vomit.

I did not look back. I heard appalling shrieks of pain and strangled gurgles. I heard men bellow, 'Woden. Woden. Woden.'

But I did not look back.

We followed the narrow track up the south-west side of the tor, along the whale-backed ridge. Rising into the grey. Swathing ourselves in a shroud of unnatural dusk.

'They chose their end,' Gawain muttered through laboured breaths, convincing himself rather than me, it seemed. This famed warrior, this lord of war who had fought beside Lord Arthur and who had just turned his back on his enemy, leaving peaceful men to be slaughtered.

Up into the cold rain. Seven souls dissolving from the world, the clink and clatter of the warriors' war gear and our ragged breathing all faint, faraway sounds to me. I stumbled off the path into the wet grass, fell to my knees and vomited. The liquid steamed and stank, and I retched in stomach-clenching agony, my throat burning.

'We left them to die.' I spat bitter strings of saliva. Dragged a sleeve across my mouth. 'We left them to be hacked apart,' I said, louder this time. Full of hatred and shame. Full of fear.

'And we'll be next, lad. Is that what you want?' Gawain called from the path. 'Answer me! You want to stay here and watch your own guts spill onto the grass?'

In my peripheral vision I saw Father Yvain silence Gawain with a raised hand and the next thing I knew, the monk was behind me and his hand was on my shoulder.

'Up you get, Galahad.' His voice was low and hoarse. The rasp of a hook tool on an ash bowl. 'Our brothers knew what they were doing. They fought in their own way. They defied those Saxon dogs with their last breaths. No man can do more when it's his time.' His strong fingers burrowed into my flesh. 'But now is not *our* time, lad. We have to go. We must get away from here while we can.'

I spat the foul taste away and stood, my legs unsteady, my stomach squeezing into itself like an empty purse being drawn by the string. I turned back and my eyes found Iselle, but she looked away into the gloom.

She detests me, I thought. *Or worse, pities me.*

'We could have fought them,' I said, but I knew my words were hollow. Thin as the tawny smoke hanging above the hill fort of Camelot to the south-east. Who was I trying to fool?

Still, Gawain nodded, his eyes dark and unreadable beneath

his helmet's rim. 'We'll get our chance, lad,' he said. 'Today we live. Tomorrow we fight.'

I kept up the pretence, tightening my jaw and nodding curtly, as if grudgingly accepting some painful compromise.

'Come, Galahad.' Yvain beckoned me. 'To stay here is to die.'

I believed myself a coward for leaving, but I did not want to die on that hillside in the rain, and the next thing I knew I was reeling along the ridge again, Father Yvain leading us as before, his bear fur giving him the look of some shambling beast fleeing a hunting party. And soon after, when we had gone thirty or so paces past the great egg-stone beside the trail, he stopped and pointed his spear into the grey.

'Here. This is it, I think.'

'Here? I see nothing,' Hanguis said.

All I saw was the tufted grass and, here and there, piles of days-old sheep droppings glistening in the rain. But Yvain was already stalking across the slope and so we followed him, as unseen crows cawed, and I looked up to see a blur of lapwings belting over the tor, their shrill *peewit* notes sounding like a warning that we must hurry.

'Aye, this is it,' Yvain muttered under his breath, standing beside a single small boulder which was mostly hidden by the grass. The rest of us stood on the slope behind him, but for Iselle, who was a little way off, looking back along the track for sign of the Saxons.

'This some Christ magic?' Gawain asked, eyeing Yvain with suspicion. Hanguis and Endalan touched the iron of their shield bosses. Gediens spat into the wet grass. They seemed nervous, these once-famed warriors, their heads turning this way and that, as if they expected some strange fog to sweep down from the tor and carry them off. I made the sign of the Thorn.

Then Yvain thrust his spear into the earth.

The big man pulled the blade free then rammed it home again and this time the earth seemed to give way, the spear burying itself up to Yvain's leading hand, halfway along the shaft.

'What, in the name of Taranis?' Endalan said, scratching his bearded cheek with the leather-bound rim of his shield.

'Are you going to help, or just stand there like trees?' Father Yvain asked, for he had hauled the spear free again and thrust it back into the same place, twisting and levering to enlarge the hole he had created.

Gawain laid his shield down, so that rain bounced off the bear painted on it, then thrust his own spear into the earth near Yvain's hole. A moment later, they were all digging, breaking into the wet soil, stabbing at the tor as men might attack the vulnerable belly of a great dragon. And it became clear that the turf in that place was just a foot deep, like a thin skin over an old wound, and beneath it was a larger hole. With the opening revealed, the men discarded their spears and we fell to our knees, using our hands to pull the soil away, frenzied as dogs digging for bones.

Iselle had gone back along the trail until I could no longer see her, but now she ran across the slope to us and I knew what she was going to say before I heard the words.

'They're coming,' she said.

Still, the words stabbed into my heart. If the Saxons were on the track, following us up the tor, then it surely meant that their slaughter of the brothers was complete. Father Judoc and Father Brice were dead. The monks of the Thorn martyred in the mud. I imagined their killers stalking into the infirmary, wary of offending our god, perhaps, yet lusting after silver. In my mind I heard them calling to their hateful gods as they speared the Prior in his bed; good, gentle Drustanus hastened to heaven by heathen blades. I imagined his killers running rampant in search of riches which they would never find, our only treasure being the lonely Thorn on its wind-scoured hill.

We dug. Clawing at the soil, which was warm in my cold hands, with desperate haste now that we knew that the Saxons had not settled on the monastery as a wolf falls to devouring its prey, but were on our heels, thirsting for more blood.

'Nearly there.' Yvain was blowing hard with the effort, his big, clever hands plunging deeper, tearing the void wider still, and I saw that this opening in the earth was framed with stones. Whether these stones had been placed by human hands or were a natural part of the hill, I did not know, nor did I have the breath to ask as we revealed its extent and sat back on our heels, panting and exchanging questioning looks.

But it was too late. The Saxons were on the track near the egg-stone. Six of them. Young men by the looks, spear- and shield-armed. Talking in gruff voices amongst themselves as they watched us through the rain, as though trying to understand what we were doing.

'They think we're burying silver,' Gediens said.

Iselle stood on my right, her bow raised towards our enemies, an arrow on the string.

'Go,' Hanguis told Gawain, as we stood, the warriors wiping their muddy hands on the grass before gathering up their shields and spears.

Endalan nodded. 'We'll hold them.'

Gawain looked at the Saxons, his eyes aflame in the wet day, and I knew then that he hungered to fight them. To reap their lives as he had cut down so many of their brothers and fathers over the years. But he knew that he could not.

'Buy us a little time,' he told Hanguis and Endalan. 'Then follow.'

The two warriors nodded grimly, and Gawain gripped hands with each in turn, as did Gediens, the four warriors sharing a look which held within it years and brotherhood and an understanding which needed no further words. Then Hanguis and Endalan lifted their spears, hefted their shields and strode towards the Saxons, who levelled their own spears and came on, perhaps wary of the men in their fine war gear, yet eager to kill and strip them of it.

Father Yvain crouched low, poking his spear into the darkness of the hole. 'I'll go first in case the devils are waiting for us at the end,' he said. 'Then the girl, then you, Galahad.'

I nodded, and Father Yvain burrowed into the tor. I turned back to see Hanguis and Endalan clash with the Saxons, their scale armour and grey helmets glinting dully in the dying day. They cut and moved, thrust and leapt back, and I saw a Saxon go down. Saw another reel back in a spray of crimson, and heard Hanguis or Endalan, I could not say which, roaring the name *Arthur* as he killed.

'In you go, lad,' Gawain said. I crouched, seeing Iselle disappear into that strange and ancient darkness. A flash of pale skin and dark copper hair and she was gone. I put my head inside and smelled the loamy, wet earth, then crawled right in on my hands and knees. It was warm in there, out of the wind and rain, and the world I had left was suddenly distant and muted. I could not hear the fighting but somehow I knew that Hanguis and Endalan would still be on their feet, dealing death. Men such as they, long in war, lords of battle, would exact a terrible price from lesser warriors such as those Saxon spearmen who boasted neither iron helmets nor mail tunics.

Whereas I scrambled like a mole. Or like a hound in a badger set, eager to root out its prey, not stopping to consider the width of the tunnel or where it led, but pushing on as fast as I could, panting on the thin, stale air, the front of my habit wicking up the water which flowed along the winding passage. I did picture what would happen if the tunnel narrowed. If my shoulders became wedged between the slick rock sides and I could not turn round and go back the way I had come. If I was entombed within the tor and condemned to a handful of terrifying, mind-breaking days, slurping the water beneath me, only to die of hunger. And yet I took some measure of comfort in supposing that if Father Yvain could fit, anyone could.

When it seemed that I had been crawling for an eternity, I stopped, panting into the sleeve of my habit to let my ears work. For a heart-wrenching moment I heard nothing. Just the thump of my own heart in my chest, the gush of blood in my ears and beyond that, a heavy, crushing quiet. The eternal silence of the grave.

Then I heard a grunt and a curse, and I exhaled deeply in relief, for I knew that Gawain was behind me, perhaps five spear-lengths back. This was far worse for him, I knew, in his war gear, and because he was not a young man, and this knowledge shamed me into going on.

Down and down through the pitch dark. Following the coursing water which had been a trickle before but was gushing now, its sibilance a whisper in the blackness of night. Like the soft murmurings of spirits.

'How much further?' Gawain behind me said, his voice strange and dead and yet so close-sounding that it might have come from my own mouth.

'We must be near the foot of the tor by now,' I gasped, though for all I could tell in that twisting dark, we might have only crawled a couple of hundred feet. Soon after that, however, I noticed that my shoulders were scuffing the sides less often. Little by little, my cramping neck was stretching out and my head was not so bowed. The tunnel was growing wider. By the time it levelled out, I was able to get to my feet and progress in a crouch, my habit soaked and heavy, my knees stinging where the skin had been torn away, and soon after that I entered a cavern and could stand to my full height below the low rock ceiling. Still, it was oppressively dark, so that I could only see my hand in front of my face as a shadow amongst shadow.

'Galahad?'

I turned towards Father Yvain's voice.

'Over here,' he said.

'Father.' I clambered over the smooth stones, dropping down with a splash into a pool which I had not seen because it was as black as the rest of the cave. Above the constant chime of flowing water, I heard Iselle hiss and I knew why. This spring, which rose beneath the tor, was a sacred place to those who still venerated the old gods of Britain. It was a place where people now and then came to be healed. To drink the waters and commune with Morrigán, Queen of Demons, goddess of war; Cernunnos, the horned one; and Arawn, lord of the underworld.

And now I, a would-be Brother of the Holy Thorn, who had been raised in the light of Christ and Saint Joseph, and to whom the gods of Britain were but dark, forbidding shadows, was wading through their sacred pool in my filthy habit of undyed wool. It must have pained Iselle to witness. Still, the cold water felt wonderful on my grazed and bleeding knees and I stopped to cup my hands and drink, the water tasting sweet and clean.

Father Brice had shown me this spring before, when I was a boy new to Ynys Wydryn. By the guttering flame of a torch, he had explained the awe in which many folk held it, and I had been awestruck myself, thinking that gods resided somewhere beyond the glassy surface upon which the flame danced. In time, the monks had sluiced those gods from me. But Father Brice had never told me of the tunnels.

Father Brice. A clenching knot squeezed my heart and I drank from the pool again and lifted the water to my face, trying to wash away the pictures from the eye of my mind.

'Here,' Father Yvain said. 'The way out.' There was a splash as Gawain's shield dropped into the water, followed by the man himself. I was amazed he had managed to bring his shield through the tunnels. Also his iron, silver-chased helmet with its plume, which seemed to glow a little, the only visible thing in that place. But then, I suspected the man's war finery meant more to him than most of the people he knew. It was easier to imagine Gawain drawing his blades and carving his way through the tunnels of the tor than abandoning his accoutrements.

Gediens followed close behind, stumbling and falling headlong into the water. Cursing and spitting as he stood and gathered up his shield and spear.

It *was* lighter in this cavern than in the tunnels, I realized, or else my eyes had grown accustomed to the dark, for as I followed Father Yvain's voice, I made out the pale oval of Iselle's face and the cream colour of her yew bow. I felt a wave of relief wash over me at the sight of her.

'The others?' Father Yvain asked.

Gawain looked at Gediens, whose teeth flashed in the dark. 'I saw them put four down before I followed you,' Gediens said. 'Maybe they're behind us.'

Gawain shook his head. 'We can't wait.' He turned back to Father Yvain. 'Get us out of here.'

And so Father Yvain did.

We emerged into dusk like ghosts returned from Arawn's realm, startling an owl, which rose from an oak's crooked bough and vanished on silent wings. Gawain and Gediens led, shields raised before them in case there were Saxons waiting for us. But there were none and so we made our way through the gloaming, threading between the trees down to the marsh. More than once, I turned and looked up at the tor and its fringe of woods, beyond which our monastery had nestled for so many years, safe and hidden. A sanctuary untouched by the fires which raged across the land. Untouched until this foul day, which had brought blood and Saxon slaughter to our door.

'Where now?' Father Yvain asked Gawain.

The rest of us gathered around, drawing close to each other.

'There is something we need to do,' Gawain said. 'It is the reason we came to Avalon.' He looked at me. 'Other than to bring you out of that place.'

'Well? What is this thing?' Father Yvain asked, his thick brows drawing in, his expression ominous. Like me, he had lost his brothers, those men with whom he had passed these ten years, and whatever friendship he may have once claimed with Gawain seemed brittle in the aftermath of that.

'You'll see soon enough,' Gawain replied, looking out across the night- and mist-swaddled reed-beds. The rains of the last days had raised the waters, drowning the ditches, distorting the channels and tree lines by which we navigated. It was a shadowy, sunken world and treacherous. 'If we can find it.'

Gediens pointed his spear towards a stand of hazel and ash on a hump above the reed-beds. 'The boat is that way,' he said. 'If the Saxon swines haven't taken it.'

Gawain nodded, but before he could lead the way, Father Yvain took hold of his shoulder. 'I need to know if what you seek is worth the risk,' the monk said. 'I have my own charge, as you well know.'

I did not know what Yvain meant by that, but Gawain

glanced at the hand on his shoulder and turned hard eyes on the monk.

'Careful, Yvain,' he warned. 'We have not been spear-brothers for many years. Not since you came here to hide from the world. To worry fish and fowl and give your helmet to the mice to nest in.'

Beneath his beard, Father Yvain's face hardened. He took his hand from Gawain's shoulder and pointed a finger at him. 'You know why I came here,' he said, his voice the low rumble of distant thunder. 'Or are you calling me a coward?'

Gawain straightened, his lips forming round an answer which he never got to speak, because Gediens saw the torches. The warrior hissed, pointing towards the copse on the low hill, and we crouched down in the mist which rose from the marsh, wreathing around the willows. There were flames among the trees. There were flames everywhere. Dozens of them, bobbing and floating in the near-dark.

'Behind us, too,' Iselle said. We looked and saw flames flicker and burst into life, each born of another, then dispersing to dance like fireflies as the Saxons spread out, searching for us.

'Looks like Cerdic's whole army,' Gawain said, his face and helmet materializing as a cold light permeated the gloom. I looked up to see the cloud slowly ripping apart and the moonlight bleeding through to silver the world. Gediens put three fingers to his iron helmet to ward against ill luck, for in that celestial occurrence he saw the hand of some god. Some god who Gediens believed sought our destruction.

'Do we still try for your boat?' I asked.

Gawain's teeth gnawed at his bottom lip as he wrestled with the prospect of fighting our way to the boat beyond the copse, for surely now we could not pass the Saxons unseen. Then he shook his head. 'We go to ground,' he said, his decision made. 'But not here. We need to find somewhere to hide.'

Gediens held his shield and spear wide. 'Where?' he asked, looking from me to Father Yvain. I looked back towards the tor. The Saxons were all over the higher ground, so we could not go that way. The west was more like sea than marsh, unrecognizable even in the moon glow. No Saxons that we could see in that direction, but we would need Gawain's boat and for now that was beyond our reach. North or south, then, into the marsh. Into that brackish, insubstantial world which could swallow us alive as easily as a man eating a berry from a bramble.

'I know a place,' Iselle put in. We all looked at her, but she was looking north, the moonlight on her cheek and in the iron hilt of the Saxon sword on her back. She shrugged at Father Yvain. 'I told you I did not live in the lake village.'

'You want us to go into the marsh?' Father Yvain asked. 'How?'

She turned to him. 'We'll use the old ways.'

I thought of the sections of causeway of which I had caught glimpses when I took the coracle across the marsh to fetch the cobbler's corpse.

'It will be under water,' I said.

'I can find it,' Iselle assured us. Gawain was all frown. Even Father Yvain seemed unsure, pulling at his lip as he looked off in the direction Iselle had indicated.

'Maybe we should try for the boat,' Gediens said. 'I'd rather fight than drown.'

'I can find it,' Iselle said again.

Looking at her, her coppery auburn hair swept back now, tied behind her head so that her eyes were revealed in all their hawkish intensity, I believed her.

5

Ghosts from the Past

THE WATER WAS UP to our waists and terribly cold, and I would not have been surprised if the Saxons could hear my teeth rattling in my skull. And yet, now and then, we still managed to surprise some or other bird, a raptor or tufted duck which would clatter up from the reeds and set our hearts hammering as we edged along that ancient causeway. It was slow going because we could not see where we were treading, but had to follow the person in front and hope that our feet found the track below. At least the others had spears, and in Iselle's case her unstrung bow, which they used to feel their way ahead of every step, poking the causeway beneath the water. I had nothing and could only hold my arms out either side for balance. But I was glad not to be burdened by scale armour, sword or helmet. Should Gawain or Gediens misstep and fall, they would sink in a half-breath, down and down into the black depths, never to be seen again.

Iselle led the way, stopping now and then to explore with the bow stave or to wait for the rest of us to catch up before following the causeway in a new direction. How she had known where to find the old track was beyond my understanding. Father Judoc would have seen devilry in it. I think Gediens saw the gods of Britain in it. I did not know what to think, other than that this was the second time Iselle had saved my life.

Not that we were safe yet.

Sound carries far across the reed-beds in winter and so we did not speak as we inched along, shivering and numb, going deeper into the marsh. Ever further from the tor and from everything I knew. I wondered about the people who used to travel this track. Had they ever fled from their enemies along this very causeway on a night such as this? Had they feared the spirits and the demons of the marsh as I feared them now?

But I saw no thrys rising from the reeds to devour us. I gritted my teeth against the breath-stealing cold and followed Father Yvain, who followed Iselle. And every step along that sunken timber walkway took us further from the searching torches until they were but pinpricks of flame against the backdrop of the tor, which was seen not as a long, whaleback ridge now, but as a high hill whose summit was washed in moonlight.

And after the time it would take one of Father Padern's rush-lights to burn down to the nip, Iselle led us off the old track, out of the frigid water and onto ground that felt almost firm underfoot. Shivering, our breath still smoking around our faces, we followed a narrow ridge of land which rose proud of the flood marsh and upon which several stunted willows stood creaking in the breeze, then cut westward into a wood of skeletal beech, birch and alder. It was warmer among the trees, the air pungent with the sweet scent of wet decay and tanged with wood smoke which made my heart ache. To be warm by the hearth now, with Father Meurig grumbling that his barley bannocks needed more salt, yet watching us eat them with proud eyes. I could almost hear Father Brice and Father Judoc arguing about whether or not Joseph brought to these isles vessels containing the blood and sweat of Christ. Bickering about whether the saint had planted his staff in the ground knowing that it would take root and grow, or whether he had simply leant on it, seeking rest, and had been surprised to see roots worm into the earth and buds burst forth soon after.

Threading these woods, we came to more water, which looked impassable without the causeway. But Iselle led us down a bank to where a skin boat sat among the rushes, tied to a stake which had been driven in deep. She took us across two at a time, sculling with great adeptness though the boat was heavily laden, and upon reaching the other side tied the craft to another mooring post with such fluid, familiar ease that I was sure she must be taking us to her home.

'She's a resourceful young woman,' Gediens said, scuffing his boots against the grass to get the mud off them. Iselle had told us to follow the thistle bank until we came to a windbreak of stunted birch trees, then she had gone ahead, vanishing into the night. 'Proud and fierce as a hawk.'

'And too young for an old dog like you, Gediens,' Father Yvain said, giving me his spear to carry as he took the bear skin from his shoulders, shaking the water from it as we walked.

'True enough,' Gediens admitted, a note of regret in his voice. 'Wild and beautiful.' He shook his head. 'Safer to fight Saxons, I think.' He lifted his chin towards Yvain. 'But you must have missed a woman's company, monk,' he said, the last word spoken as though it tasted bad in his mouth. 'Someone to warm your bed furs.'

If Father Yvain took offence, he did not show it. 'I was not chained to the place,' he said, and glanced at me to see what I made of that tacit confession. Even in the dark he no doubt saw the surprise in my face. 'It's like spear work. You never forget.' He winked at me.

We had walked a few paces more when some creature cried in the night. Gawain stopped, lifting his spear in a gesture which told us to be still and listen.

'A screech owl,' Gediens said.

Even so, I was peering into the darkness around us, my eyes trying to sort the dark shapes, some still, some moving, into blackthorn and birch, reed-bed and hillock, darting hare or black-crowned night heron sweeping over us with a shout of *wok* as it passed. I felt each thump of my heart. Even though I was cold, I felt sweat prickling as it seeped out of the skin on my back, the salt in it stinging the wounds made by the Thorn.

'Smoke,' Gawain said.

'Iselle's kin's hearth,' I suggested. 'We must be nearing it.'

Gawain's scowl told another tale. 'Heads up and stay close,' he said, lifting his shield and spear and breaking into a loping run along the bank. We three followed on his heels, looking this way and that and failing to avoid clumps of thistles which snagged my habit or clawed the skin on my shins.

'What is it, Father?' I asked as we ran.

'The smoke,' Yvain said, puffing hard, unused to running. The smell was stronger now. More acrid. And suddenly I understood, even as Father Yvain said the words. 'That's no hearth fire.'

The place had not burned well. The rain had seen to that. But some of the thatch on the inside had taken a flame and burned, the heat seeping through to partly dry the roof outside, which now smouldered and steamed, pouring a thick stream of yellow-grey smoke into the night sky. Some of the more sheltered east wall was burning, weak flame eating into the wattle and old straw and dung, spewing a bitter-smelling, sickly-coloured breath. That was what Gawain had smelled. What

Iselle had smelled before him, which was why she had run ahead.

We found her in the shadows, kneeling in the scorched rushes, holding the hand of a woman, the two of them indistinct shapes in the hanging haze of that dark place. But I could see that the woman was dead. No one alive could be so still, and, as I ventured deeper into that room, by the flickering light of a patch of burning thatch and the glow of dying embers in the hearth I saw the wound which had killed her. Which had ended her suffering, by the looks of it. A gory smile in the white of her throat. Mocking our frail grasp on this life. Iselle's long Saxon knife lay in the rushes beside her, its blade slick. I shuddered.

'I'll see if they are still close,' Gediens said, stepping back out and disappearing into the night, though I doubted he would be able to see much out there. Father Yvain fetched a rain bucket and doused the flames as best he could, raising hisses of steam which sounded like the malice of demons in the dark.

Iselle's head was bowed, her hair loose now so that it fell across the dead woman's face, a tress kissing that dark gash.

'Your mother?' Gawain asked, his voice soft and low.

Iselle did not answer. Did not even look up. Gawain nodded at me, wanting me to go closer. To offer some comfort to Iselle, though I did not know how to do that. Still, I took a step forward and Iselle's head lifted, her eyes meeting mine.

'Her name was Alana,' she said. I had expected to see tears but there were none. Instead her eyes were sharp, burnished arrow heads in the dying flamelight. 'She raised me.' Her jaw clenched on her next words, then she shook her head at some memory. 'I told her the Saxons were close. I told her to go to Camelot. To seek the Lady Morgana's protection. She would not listen.'

'Camelot is where we should all go,' Father Yvain said. 'The Saxons are thick as fleas on an old hound.'

Gawain took off his helmet and ran a hand through his silver hair, glad to be rid of the weight of the armour. 'We're going west,' he said. 'As soon as we've done what we came here to do.'

'You would think you'd be safe, living out here like this.' Father Yvain gestured at the simple dwelling. There were only two beds, suggesting that Iselle and Alana had lived alone. 'Never thought the Saxons would trouble the fen folk.' He lifted the pail and flung the last of the water at a roof timber and a flame which crackled amongst a bunch of dried herbs. White smoke plumed, sweet and woody, and the place was plunged into a deeper dark. 'Seems to me King Cerdic means to deal with us as a man runs a flame along his tunic and breeks to be rid of lice,' he said.

'I told you,' Gawain said to the monk, lowering his voice out of respect for Iselle, 'told all of you. There is no one standing against Cerdic now. The kings of Britain look to their own walls and no further. Only Constantine bleeds the Saxons and he cannot fight much longer.' With the last of the flames doused, Gawain bent, turned a stool back onto its legs and sat down beside the hearth, exhaling with a weariness that betrayed all his war finery.

I went to Iselle and squatted beside her, trying not to look down at the woman whom she cradled still. Knowing that Iselle had loved her, but not having known Alana myself, it felt wrong to look at the dead woman's face, to see her for the first time without her soul.

'Let me help you,' I said. I did not know how, but I had to do something. 'Please, Iselle.'

She looked at me as though all she had heard was the wind in the bulrushes.

'I'll check the pen,' Father Yvain said, 'in case they left any of your animals alive.' And with that, he went into the night.

Gawain was building up the fire, blowing softly onto the embers. Lost in his own thoughts.

'What will you do, Galahad? Pray for her?' Iselle asked, her voice edged with scorn. So, she *had* heard me.

'I could. If you would like me to,' I replied. But I knew she had no use for my prayers. Her gods were the old gods of Britain: Cernunnos and Arawn, the horse goddess Rhiannon and Taranis lord of war, and a dozen more besides; compared to those, our god must have seemed weak. 'I can help you to bury her,' I offered.

'I don't need help,' Isélle said.

'What will you do?' I asked her. 'You can't stay here.'

'Why not?' she challenged me, but she must have known it was a foolish question.

'We'll stay here a day or two.' Gawain was looking into the new flames which capered amongst the sticks and split wood, his scarred face cast in their molten copper glow. 'If Iselle doesn't mind. When the Saxons have moved on and the water has receded, we'll leave. We'll go west.' His lips warped. 'They will have taken our boat. So, we go west on foot.'

'After you have found what you're looking for out there?' I asked.

Gawain nodded. 'After that,' he said.

'And you know where to find it?' I said.

'I will when the water recedes.' He looked over to us then, his face grim and gaunt in the wash of firelight. 'Will you help me, girl?' he asked. 'You know the marsh better than any of us.' But Iselle did not reply. She was staring at Alana's face. And now, at last, there were tears in her eyes.

*

Two days later, we burned the roundhouse properly. It was Iselle's idea. She laid Alana's corpse on a thick pile of rushes beside the hearth and we set several fires amongst the thatch and furniture, using dry reeds and wood from the animal pen. It had not rained since the night we came there, so the flame took hungrily to the wood, running along timbers like a living thing and leaping to the reeds, which belched yellow smoke before bursting alight. We left the place burning like a great pyre.

Gediens had been against setting the dwelling aflame. He feared that the smoke would bring Saxons the way hounds will prowl downwind of roasting meat. But Gawain pointed to three other distant and faint plumes of smoke against the blue sky, reminding us that the Saxons were busy killing and burning elsewhere and would take little notice of another smudge of smoke hanging above the marsh.

'Let the girl burn it,' he had said as we left Iselle alone to say her last words to the woman who had nursed her, raised her and loved her as though she were her own. 'She can't live in the ashes. And I need her now,' the warrior said, looking north across the reed-beds, which were still swollen with rain.

We watched the fire awhile because we knew that Iselle was seeing memories in the flames. Then, without a word, she turned away and we took this to mean she had decided to go with us, though none of us asked her lest the question itself sharpened her pride and purpose against us. For there was something wild about Iselle. A hardness in spite of the incorporeal, waterlogged world which had raised her. A defiance shaped by wind and loneliness. And yet, as we trudged north along hidden ways amongst bristling reeds, the sky as pale as the wood anemones which I had known in another lifetime, I knew that I wanted to be near her.

She led us to a finger of land to the north of the Meare Pool. How she had found the trackways and the low, wave-swept spines through the marsh to take us to the place which Gawain had described was a mystery to the rest of us. 'It has the whiff of magic about it, if you ask me,' Gediens said under his breath as we squeezed water from our cloaks and rubbed warmth into freezing legs. Iselle stood apart, stringing her bow now that we were on firmer ground.

'Instinct, nothing more,' Gawain replied, jumping up and down to get the water out of his scale armour and some heat into his bones. 'How does a hawk know to mantle its kill?' He moved his left shoulder around in its joint, grimacing. It must have been stiff from holding his shield above his head to keep it out of the water. 'In snow, how do wolves know to walk in the tracks of the beast in front?' he asked. 'We are what we are.' He turned his eyes on me. 'No use in trying to pretend otherwise.'

'Easy for you to say,' Father Yvain muttered, 'you who have never tried to sow seed or tan a hide or coppice a wood. The only thing you've ever known is the sword.' The monk swung his knapsack onto his back, where it nestled half-buried in the bear skin. 'But there are other ways.'

Gawain gave a low grunt. 'Other ways.' His lips twisted in his silver beard. 'Like falling to your knees before the Christ god while the land around you burns? Like singing while mothers weep for their starving children? For their husbands slain by the Saxons? And where did that get your brothers, Yvain? What good has it done our people?'

I hated Gawain then, and his words which struck me like a blow to the chest. Because there was truth in them.

Father Yvain said nothing, just set his jaw and fixed his eyes on the path trodden by Iselle. We fell to silence, each alone with our thoughts and fears, and trudged onwards.

'We are close,' Gawain said after a while, leading us now that he recognized where we were. We followed him along a narrow channel which someone had cut through the vegetation and I felt like some creature coming into another creature's lair, for the reeds were so tall here that they leant over to touch above us, forming a tunnel into which the low winter sun cast arrows of golden light. Soon, we came to a ten-foot-high wall of reeds which would have been impenetrable had Gawain and Gediens not drawn their swords to hack a pathway through, now and then stopping to catch their breath. At those times it was unbearably quiet, so oppressive and still. The floor of the bed was an unctuous black mud that would have swallowed us were it not for the broken and flattened reeds which supported our weight. There were no calls of birds. There was no whirring of insects as that which fills the marshes in summer. Just an ominous sense of dread which I knew I was not alone in feeling. It was like a cold hand gripping the back of my neck. It was as if we were passing through a veil from one world to another. And in a sense, we were.

The steading was as poor as any I had seen. There were some swine, two sheep, a goat and some hens pecking in the mud for worms. The outbuildings comprised a small grain store, a smokehouse, an empty stable which was used as a store room, and a run-down byre which would not afford livestock much protection in bad weather.

The house itself was a crude affair of wattle and mud and rotting reed thatch, no better than a hovel. And yet, before Gawain approached the door, he stood a while, his helmet tucked under his arm, regarding the place with such a look on his face as I had never seen there before. It reminded me of how Iselle had looked as she watched the flames consume her home.

Still, I could not imagine why we had laboured, freezing and destitute, through the marsh, seeking out whomever lived in such a place as this. My expression must have said as much, for Father Yvain raised a big hand towards me and shook his head, his own eyes moving from Gawain to the steading in a way that revealed he understood something I did not.

'Wait here,' Gawain commanded. 'Don't follow me.' And with that he walked up to the door, stood a long moment with his hand on the latch, then let himself in and was swallowed by darkness.

Iselle shrugged. 'I've never been here,' she said, in answer to the look I gave her as Gawain disappeared inside the house and we waited on the timber trackway laid between the outbuildings and animal pens. On the eastern side of the steading there was a stand of gnarled and brittle-looking apple trees. On the west, a drainage dyke between fields, which must have taken sweat and toil to dig, though it had won some land from the marsh. And further off, a small wood of sallow, hazel and ash. All of it was bordered by a palisade of reeds whose feathered heads bristled in the breeze, giving it the look of winter wheat in the dying day.

'Such a place could stay hidden even from God,' I told Iselle, watching smoke seep from the thatch to drift eastwards like a faint whisper. Then Gawain reappeared at the threshold and lifted his bearded chin to us.

Gediens and Father Yvain shared a knowing look.

'You ready, lad?' Gediens asked me. *Why me?* I nodded, aware of the sluggish beating of my heart, as though it, too, laboured through the mud of the marsh. I might have relished the thought of a fire to warm my blood, and perhaps some hot food to fill my stomach. But I did not think of either as we made our way along the track towards that dark doorway. All I felt was dread.

'In you come.' Gawain's voice was low, as if he feared waking someone sleeping within. The door clumped shut behind us and my eyes sifted through the darkness beyond the hearth fire's bloom of copper and gold. A small table. A bed against the far wall. A bench beside the hearth. Woven baskets and wooden pails. Spears leaning against the thatch. A brace of ducks hanging from a roof beam, turning slowly in the smoke.

'Closer, lad, so I can get a look at you,' someone said. I took a step towards the hearth. Then another. Still I could not see the man who had spoken, for he stood on the far side of the hearth beyond its light. Beside him, a black hound sat on its haunches, watching us from the shadows. Gawain stood to my right, Gediens, Father Yvain and Iselle behind my left shoulder. 'So, this is him,' the man said. His voice was dry and cracked. Brittle like the apple trees I had seen. 'Galahad,' he said, and it was as though he were speaking aloud for the first time a name which he had kept safe in his mind.

He stepped forward into the fire glow and I saw him. And I knew that those eyes would stay with me all my life. Those blue eyes in which demons danced amongst reflected flame.

'Galahad,' Gawain dipped his head towards the man, 'this is Lord Arthur ap Uther ap Constantine ap Tahalais.'

I heard Iselle behind me gasp and I felt the sting of peat smoke in my own throat as I drew a breath.

Arthur.

Invisible spiders scuttled up my arms. The hairs on the back of my neck prickled in their roots. Could this old man really be the Arthur who had united the kings of Britain beneath his bear banner, with the sword Excalibur gleaming beneath sullen skies? The man who came *so* close to hurling the invaders back into the sea from whence they came? Arthur. The light in the darkness.

No, it could not be. And yet I knelt among the floor rushes and bowed my head and I sensed Iselle do the same.

'Please,' the man said, lifting a hand. 'No!' he said more sharply.

I looked up and saw not a prince or a lord of war. Not even a warrior like Gawain or Gediens. I saw an old man. Hollow-cheeked and gaunt. A man burdened by memories. A man haunted by the past.

'I am not the man I was,' he confessed, seeing the disbelief in my face. He held my eye as I got to my feet, as though needing to be sure that I understood. 'All of that was . . . a long time ago.'

'Not so long ago, uncle,' Gawain countered.

Arthur flapped a hand at Gawain and muttered something under his breath, then he came around the hearth, his black hound padding obediently beside him, and stood before me. He straightened to his full height and only then, with the fire casting his face into shadow, did I catch a glimpse of the man he had once been. Broad-chested and powerful. Handsome and confident. A leader of men. But then a tilt of his head and a change in the light and like the fleeting glimpse of a ghost, the vision was gone.

'My lord,' Father Yvain rumbled from behind me. 'We thought you were dead. All these years. Few dared to hope. But lord . . .' He swallowed down the next words, but they worked their way back up his throat. 'Why do you not fight?'

Arthur looked at the monk. 'Why don't you, Yvain?' he asked with a sad weariness. 'I would not have expected you to turn to the Christians' god.'

Father Yvain did not answer that, and for a heavy moment the only sound was the flap of the hearth flames.

Iselle took a step forward. 'Lord, if the people knew that you live, they would have hope again.'

I cringed inwardly at Iselle's presumption. But Arthur just stared at her.

'How can you deny them hope?' she pressed on, and I turned and looked at her, my eyes willing her to tread carefully, to give Lord Arthur the proper respect. But Iselle would not meet my eye, taking another step so that she was at my shoulder. 'They would fight, lord,' she said. I could smell parsley and mint on her breath, a sharp, clean scent in that musty-smelling hovel. 'They would fight for you.'

Most people would be too awestruck to speak to Lord Arthur, let alone in such a forthright way. But Iselle was not like most people. She had no fear. And now Arthur watched her, as a man might regard a thatch fire from a distance, wondering who had lit the flame and why. I glanced at Gawain, hoping he would break the awkward silence, but he gave an almost imperceptible shake of his head, which I took as him warning me not to interrupt. He wanted to see where this would lead.

Iselle lifted her chin in a gesture that spoke of mistrust or suspicion, as if she had not yet accepted that the man before us was the warlord of the bards' songs, the Arthur whispered of by the wind in the trees and long grass in summer. 'They would fight for *you*,' she added, 'and the kings of the land would have courage again.'

Arthur's eyes hardened at her words. 'Tell me, girl, what you know of courage.'

Father Yvain shook his head at Iselle, but she would not be silenced.

'I know it takes courage just to survive out there,' she said. I thought of the hanged folk in the marshes and the Brothers of the Thorn lying butchered on Ynys Wydryn. Of Iselle's foster mother Alana and of the smoke from half a dozen steadings staining the sky. 'I know that the Arthur of the stories would not hide from the world like this,' Iselle went on, looking into the dark around us. 'I know that the Arthur who slaughtered Saxons would never abandon his people while he had breath and a blade.'

Arthur considered her words, then lifted an eyebrow at Gawain as he leant to stroke his hound between the ears. 'Where did you find this young she-wolf?'

'Galahad found her,' the warrior replied. His lip pulled back from his teeth in a smile. Or perhaps it was a grimace. 'The Christians feared her.'

'I am sure they did.' Arthur lifted his gaze from Iselle and laid it on me as an invitation to speak.

'She saved my life, lord,' I said. 'The Saxons came to Ynys Wydryn.' I saw no need to say more. Arthur stiffened, putting a hand to his chin and pulling his beard between finger and thumb as he turned to glance back into the shadows behind him.

When Arthur turned back to us, Gawain said, 'The monastery is gone, Arthur.'

'They murdered the brothers,' Father Yvain put in, moving into the halo of light cast by a horn lantern which sat on a table beside a jug and two wooden cups.

'May Christ and Saint Joseph keep them,' I said, thinking of the cutting of the Thorn and the eight haws which Father Brice had pulled from the briar and hidden in my knapsack the day he was martyred. Red and cool to the touch, those berries. Hardened drops of blood, one for each of the brothers.

'Hanguis and Endalan are dead.' Gawain's jaw clenched after the words. We looked at one another. It was the first time it had been said aloud and we all knew it was true. Arthur turned his face up to the roof and closed his eyes. Gediens looked at the helmet in his hands, his thumb exploring a dent in the iron. Iselle took her bow string from the scrip on her belt and laid it along the hearth stones to dry, though her eyes never left Arthur. Nor, I noticed, did Father Yvain's. The monk was an ominous presence in that ill-lit place, studying Arthur the way I had seen him trying to read the grain, burrs and knots in a piece of cherry wood or blackthorn. Here before us was the great warlord, whose famous horse warriors had thundered across the land into legend. What was he thinking now? Did the Pendragon blood boil in his veins at this news that the Saxons were rampaging unchecked? Did his heart clamour to raise his bear standard and call spearmen to his side? To be dux bellorum again. The lord of battle.

Arthur's eyes opened. 'Too many have gone,' he murmured under his breath, then pulled up a stool and sat, staring into the flames with the distracted air of an old man lost in memories. 'Too many.'

I looked at Gawain, who was pressing a thumb into the palm of his other hand, kneading away some or other pain. 'How is she, uncle?' he asked. It seemed that Arthur had not heard, but then he looked round into the shadows again and this time I saw something in the gloom.

'She is . . . unchanged,' Arthur said.

Iselle and I caught each other's eye, both of us understanding at the same time. Both of us *seeing* for the first time. My breath caught in my chest. My flesh crawled. There was someone sitting in a chair in the dark. Someone watching us. Father Yvain hissed in shock, instinctively signing the Thorn. He was closer to the seated figure than I, yet no more had he noticed it before now.

I took a step forward.

'She knows you're here,' Arthur told us, his eyes still reflecting flame. 'But only the gods know where she is.'

Yvain picked up the horn lantern and lifted it, his eyes wide as he bathed the woman in its glow. It seemed he was afraid and he glanced at Gawain, who gave the slightest nod, the two old spear-brothers sharing a brief moment of understanding, though the woman herself did not react or even seem aware of the monk. She simply stared ahead, seeing nothing. Or else seeing something which the rest of us could not.

'Does she mind the light?' Father Yvain asked, lowering the lamp a little.

Arthur shook his head and so the monk lifted the lamp again, though he dimmed the light anyway by shielding the lantern with his hand.

The woman was impossibly thin. Her hands lay on her lap, as fleshless as a bird's feet. Her chest was as flat as a boy's beneath a linen dress which had perhaps fitted her once and was the blue of a song thrush's eggs. Her neck was delicate, slender and white as a birch, and her face was gaunt, the pale skin drawn so tightly over the bones beneath that it seemed it might tear open if she made any expression such as a frown or a smile. But there *was* no expression. It was a desolate face and were it not for the faint rise and fall of the woman's chest, so faint beneath that ancient dress that I had to stare a while before I could be sure of it, I would have thought her a corpse. And I would have said Arthur had lost his mind. That here was a madman keeping company with the dead.

And yet she was undead, this silent, spectral woman, and in that way she was a flesh and blood memory which I believed haunted Arthur no less than the demons cavorting in his eyes.

'She's my wife, Galahad,' Arthur said, turning those sad eyes up to me. 'My Guinevere.'

I was unable to speak for the tightening of my throat. I knew who she was. I had known her the moment I saw that long hair, black as a raven's wing, and that face, hollow and starved of joy, yet still somehow beautiful.

I thought back to the day of the great battle, when Tormaigh, my father's stallion, had stumbled weary and blood-slathered from the fray to where I stood on the hill, my eyes filled with unspeakable horrors. I had mounted my noble friend and he had carried me to a clearing in the woods, where I found Guinevere lying among the meadowsweet once so sacred to the druids of Britain. Even then she was already lost, unable to speak. Voiceless and spellbound. Adrift like an autumn leaf on the wind.

'You remember her, Galahad?' Gawain asked.

I nodded. I had tried to wake Guinevere. I had yelled until my voice was a dry rasp. I'd shaken her and pulled at her, desperate to release her from whatever enchantment imprisoned her. Not because I cared for her – I did not know her and had met her only once and briefly – but because I felt alone. Because I was terrified and I missed my mother and I wanted someone to see my tears.

'She has been this way ever since.' Arthur poked an iron into the fire. Sparks crackled and flew.

In the eye of my mind I could still see the faces of the men who had found us there in that glade. Some of Arthur's spearmen fleeing from the final slaughter. They took us to Gawain, who sought out a healer for Guinevere, though the old woman had been unable to cure her. And so, Gawain took Guinevere to the Christian women and me to Ynys Wydryn and the monks of the Thorn. Years in the past. And yet it felt so close again now in that gathering of souls who had been there under that late summer sky, as Britain plunged like a blade into the quenching trough and we watched to see if she would emerge whole or shatter into brittle pieces.

I could hear the great battle again, the screams of men and horses. I could smell the spearmen tearing each other apart with blades and hatred. I could smell Tormaigh too, the sweet hay scent of his steaming breath and the iron stink of the blood matted in his black mane and gleaming coat. I could hear his three-beat gait drumming the earth. Feel the cold bronze scales of my father's armour on my cheek before the battle began, as he held me to him and told me he loved me. Before he walked Tormaigh down the slope and turned to look at me one final time, the last meeting of our eyes.

Arthur sighed a stale breath of old sorrow and weariness. 'My poor Guinevere,' he said. *Not just your Guinevere.* My father had loved this woman too. I had known that the day she came to our door on Samhain eve. I was out gathering valerian root because my father had been plagued with bad dreams, and Guinevere had come. As though the dreams which tormented my father had created her.

I looked at Guinevere now, at those lips which my father had kissed. At those claw-like hands, which he must have held in his own when they were young in the world and happiness seemed as real as the trees and the sky and the wind. And standing in Guinevere's presence, I hated my father because he had given her his soul, and I hated Guinevere for taking it. And I felt like the boy I once was, left alone on a hill.

'Your father took her from me,' Arthur continued. I started and looked at him, struck by the fear that he could somehow hear my thoughts. Iselle's head turned towards me, her eyes wide and bright in the firelight. I saw her hand fall to the bone grip of her knife hilt, seeking the comfort of it, perhaps.

'Your father thought she was his and he took her from me,' Arthur said, and there was an edge of steel in his voice which cut through his weariness. It twisted in my guts.

'None of that was Galahad's doing.' Gawain shook his head. 'Leave the lad out of it.'

Had my mother known about Guinevere? Had it broken her as it broke Arthur? I would've been too young to see it then, but I saw it now in Arthur, his features warped in the flame glow. A mask of bitterness and pain.

'Look at him, nephew,' Arthur commanded, his eyes in me like hooks. 'Don't tell me you can't see *him* in that face. In those eyes.'

'I see him,' Gawain admitted. 'Of course I do. But the lad can't be blamed for any of it.'

'No,' Iselle said, shaking her head at me as if in disbelief. 'You are not his son.' Her voice was tremulous, like cold water with the wind across its face. 'Not Lancelot's son.' She had taken a step away from me, her right hand still clutching the long knife's grip. 'You can't be. You're a monk of the Thorn.'

'Not yet, he's not,' Father Yvain murmured.

All their eyes were on me, heavy as wet wool. Even Guinevere seemed to be watching me.

'Galahad is not his father,' Gawain said, though it did not stop Iselle from drawing an arrow from the bag at her waist and fingering its iron head to ward off bad luck.

I knew what folk thought of my father. What they said about him.

'Perhaps,' Arthur said, his teeth dragging his fair beard over his lip, 'we should wish that he *was* his father. Can you imagine, nephew? You would like that, wouldn't you?'

Gawain did not answer that. Arthur closed his eyes. 'Your father and I were the swords of Britain,' he told me. 'Our enemies trembled at the mention of our names, and where we fought it was as though the gods fought beside us.' He stood like that for a while, remembering. Recalling times and events to himself like the secrets and intimacies of long-lost lovers. And when his eyes opened again there were tears in them. 'I loved your father,' he said. 'Truly, Galahad, I loved him. But he broke my heart.'

The sadness in Arthur's words was almost tangible. The torment in his face terrible. But my own chest was flooding with heat, my muscles tightening in my flesh.

'He chose you over me, lord,' I offered.

Arthur's eyes sharpened. He could see the pain in me just as I could see it in him.

'It's not about choosing,' Father Yvain put in, his gruff voice like a whetstone, grinding into the intimacy of the moment which Arthur and I shared. 'When men fight shoulder to shoulder,' Yvain went on, gripping an imaginary shield, 'when they send their enemies into the afterlife and see their friends taken in blood and agony, they become brothers.' He placed the horn lantern back on the table. 'They can hate each other or love each other, but nothing can change what they are.' He nodded. 'That's the way of it.'

Gediens and Gawain both nodded at that unassailable truth.

I did not know what to say. What did I know of such things? My brothers had been men of prayer. All I knew was that my father, of whose flesh and blood I was created, abandoned me on that hill and rode away to die. And I could not forgive him.

'How can you love her still?' Iselle asked Arthur, looking back to Guinevere with naked disgust. 'After what she did, how can you care for her like this? All these years?'

'Hold your tongue, girl,' Gawain told Iselle. 'It's none of your concern.'

'It is all of our concern,' Iselle said. 'It is the concern of kings and beggars. It is the concern of the gods themselves, for why else did they turn their backs on us?'

'Enough!' Gawain snapped, but Arthur lifted a hand towards him.

'Let her speak her mind.' He nodded at Iselle. 'Nothing can hurt me now.'

Iselle lifted her chin towards Guinevere, who sat shrouded in shadow, returned to the darkness once more. 'She and Lancelot betrayed you, lord,' she said. 'They wounded you more than your enemies ever did in battle. You lost heart. You no longer believed that we could win.' Iselle's hands were clenched by her sides. Her eyes were narrowed, as if she still could not fully believe that the man sitting there by the fire was the same man whose courage and martial prowess was the golden thread and honeyed mead of bard song. Whose victories had brought the kings of Britain together and bought years of peace. The great warlord who, folk whispered, had not died on that savage day of bloodletting ten years ago but still lived and would rise again to lead us out of the darkness.

'And what would you have me do?' Arthur asked her, then shook his head. 'Have I not given enough?'

Iselle unclenched her hands and held them towards him. 'You should be leading us still. You should be High King. You should be Arthur Pendragon.'

With those words hanging in the smoky air, a silence spread among us. We all knew to hold our tongues then, even Iselle. We knew that the next words could only belong to Arthur. He knew it, too, and for a long moment he carried that burden, keeping his thoughts to himself as the fire breathed softly in the hearth.

Then he looked at Iselle and there was such sadness in his eyes that it made my own heart ache. 'I am nothing without her,' he confessed.

I looked at Iselle and she looked at me, and I saw blame in

her eyes. She could not truly hate a woman who was trapped between life and death. Nor could she hate my father, a stranger who had gone to Arawn's realm years ago. But she could hate me, because I was Lancelot's son.

'There may be reason to hope, uncle,' Gawain said.

Arthur looked round, the anguish in his face turning to suspicion. As though he wanted to believe but also did not want to.

'Careful, nephew,' he warned. 'In all the years you have been searching, you have never said as much.'

Gawain acknowledged this with a nod. 'And yet I say it now.'

Arthur picked up the fire iron again and idly poked at the fuel, though he sat a little straighter, his shoulders less rounded than before.

The air in the room had changed. I felt it as a vibration, the way you sometimes *feel* a storm coming before you hear it or see it.

'We've found him, Arthur,' Gawain said. He exhaled as though there were weight in those words and he had been holding them until that moment. 'We've found Merlin.'

6

Shadow and Bronze

OVER THE NEXT DAYS, Arthur seemed changed. It was a gradual change, in any one moment as imperceptible as a marsh marigold's turning towards the sun. But there was no denying it. It was as though some of the years had fallen away from him and, as on the first night, when a play of the firelight had revealed glimpses of the man he used to be, now I saw flashes of Arthur ap Uther in the wan light of the late winter day. I saw it as he worked with a spade on a ridge beyond the orchard, turning the ground and planting a sackful of onions and garlic bulbs which had sprouted new green shoots. I saw it as he climbed up onto the roof with Gawain to pull off some of the old thatch and replace it with new bundles, and as he went into the marsh with Gediens and Iselle and returned later with a duck or some other wading bird for the pot. I even saw it as he listened to Gawain or Father Yvain telling what they knew about the Saxons or the kings of Britain. Or of Camelot, which Arthur himself had made and which yet held out against the invaders, a beacon of hope in the bleakest of days.

There was a difference in the way he carried himself. The wretched apathy which had seemed to cling to him fell away and now there was a restlessness about him. A nervousness.

'This is what he was like the night before he married her,'

Gawain told me one afternoon as we watched Arthur bent over, axe in hand, scraping the slime and rot from the timbers of the walkway, while his dog, who Gawain told me was called Banon, sat patiently nearby. The weather being good, Gawain and I had been out gathering deadfall to burn instead of Arthur's peat turves, and when we returned we found Arthur hard at work. 'He was like this when he and your father dug Camelot's defensive ditches, too,' Gawain added, scratching his beard thoughtfully as I stacked the wood beneath the eaves.

'You've given him a reason to hope,' I said, glancing at the famous lord of war as he worked in the filth. For the flint and steel which had put a spark in Arthur's heart was the news that Merlin had been found. Just as the bards sang their tales of Arthur, so they gilded the dark nights with stories of Merlin, the last of the druids. They recounted the fear which his spells sowed in Saxon bellies, and his vast knowledge of the gods and his ability to speak with them. And of course, the bards told of the sword Excalibur, which Merlin had discovered and given to Lord Arthur so that he might hold it like a firebrand to light the way for the people of these Dark Isles.

The difference was that all folk believed in Arthur son of Uther. Arthur the man. And they hoped beyond hope that he would return to fight for them again. It was not so with Merlin. Folk believed that the druid, one-time adviser to the Pendragon himself, had not been a man of flesh, blood and bone, but rather a mysterious spirit being. A shape-shifter. A legend passed from lip to ear around the hearth, the whisper of the wind among the yews and oaks and ancient standing stones.

I could not recall my father talking of Merlin, though he must have known him. And as for the Brothers of the Thorn, they would not speak the druid's name for fear that doing so was to invoke the old gods and give breath to ideas which they would sooner were buried. But even those who had known Merlin, men such as Gawain and Gediens and Arthur, who had journeyed with the druid and received his counsel, and who could testify to his walking the same ground as mortal men, could not say what had become of him. He had simply vanished like a word on the air.

'No one has seen him in years,' Gawain had explained to me that first night at Arthur's steading, after the reason for our being there had been brought into the light. 'We have been searching, those of us who still hold to our oaths to serve Arthur. Many have died for it. Others who set out never returned.'

'What made you so sure Merlin was alive?' I'd asked, preparing my bed of skins by the hearth. The journey and then the warmth of Arthur's fire had brought a heavy tiredness upon me, but I would say my prayers for the brothers' souls before I gave in to sleep.

Gawain shrugged his broad shoulders. 'If there was a chance he was still breathing, still stirring up trouble somewhere, we had to try. For his sake.' He nodded towards Arthur, who had carried Guinevere to their bed and sat stroking her hair, whispering secret things in a voice no louder than the breath of the flames in the hearth.

I learnt that Arthur had nothing good to say about Merlin. He blamed the druid for Britain's ruin as much as he blamed himself and his own failure. And yet whatever he felt about the man, it seemed Arthur had clung to the hope, as one tries to cling to a dream which fades on waking, that the druid would be able to cure Guinevere. That only Merlin, with his vast knowledge of herb lore and ancient texts and of the gods themselves, could dispel the strange affliction. Arthur believed that Merlin could bring her back.

Gawain told us that Parcefal, another of Arthur's loyal warlords, beside whom he had routed Saxon armies and shared his greatest hopes, and who had, like Gawain, been looking for Merlin across the years, had found him at last, living a hermit's life on Ynys Weith off the south coast of Britain. It was almost unbelievable. And yet Arthur had believed.

'Did he know that I live?' Arthur had asked, his eyes smouldering as the news took hold in him.

'Parcefal's messenger did not say and I did not ask,' Gawain replied, 'but Merlin agreed to go with Parcefal to Tintagel and await me there. We can't risk him being caught out on the roads,' he said, nodding at the door beyond which night had fallen. 'The Saxons would skin him.'

'Not just the Saxons,' Gediens muttered. 'Plenty of Britons would hang the old bastard from the nearest tree and I wouldn't blame them. They think he abandoned us when we needed him most.'

Father Yvain made a gruff sound in his throat. 'Might as well try to guess what a fish is thinking as seek to know the mind of a druid.'

Arthur arched an eyebrow at the monk but said nothing. It was clear by his face that he too thought Merlin had abandoned him. It was loud in the silence.

'He's alive,' Gawain said, bringing us back to what mattered. 'Soon as I have my hands on him, I'll bring him here.' Arthur had nodded and looked over his shoulder into the shadows, where two eyes glowed.

Later that night, Iselle and I had gone out to the smokehouse to fetch an eel and three trout which Arthur had hung some days before. I waited until we were alone in the cramped dark and then asked Iselle what she knew of Merlin. I could scarcely believe I had met Arthur ap Uther, warlord of Britain.

But then to hear that Merlin, the last of the druids, was alive . . . What next? Perhaps Joseph of Arimathea would be seen praying for my lost brothers in the shelter of the Holy Thorn.

'My foster mother met him when she was young,' Iselle said. 'Though she never spoke of him. I think she was afraid of him.' She lifted the eel off the hook, and I found a basket to put it in as Iselle wafted away the sweet, musty alder smoke rising from the ashes of an old fire. 'I don't know why Merlin left,' she said. 'He must have had his reasons. But Gawain will bring him back. Can you imagine it? Merlin and Arthur together again?'

I could not see her face clearly in the murk, but I could sense her excitement. I felt her thoughts thrumming like a bow string in the thick air. 'If Merlin couldn't help Lord Arthur back then,' I said, 'when he needed him most, what makes you think he can help him now?'

'What do you care?' she asked, reaching for a fish and putting it into the basket. 'All you care about is your god and that gnarled old tree which I have seen a dog piss on.'

'I am not a monk of the Thorn,' I said, 'and never will be now.'

'No. You are Lancelot's son. Lancelot the great warrior.' There was scorn in her words, and I wanted to challenge her but instead I gritted my teeth and reached up, ripping the last fish from the hook and thrusting it into the basket.

'I saw the way you looked at Guinevere,' I said. 'You hate her because she loved my father.'

'Don't you hate her?' she asked.

I said nothing. My eyes stung from the smoke.

'They betrayed Arthur and it broke him,' she said.

I had heard others say it, when they thought I could not hear. Or perhaps when they knew that I could. But it was worse hearing it from Iselle. She brushed past me and stood with a hand on the door, ready to open it for me as I was carrying the basket of fish. I did not move. 'So, if you hate her,' I said, 'why do you care if Merlin can heal her?'

She glared at me through the gloom. 'You still don't understand, do you?'

I shrugged. 'I understand that Arthur lives, but he is a broken man. And that Merlin lives and that men died looking for him, for Arthur's sake, even though he may not be able to cure Guinevere.'

She shook her head at my stupidity. 'But what if Merlin *can* bring her back?' she asked. 'What then? Why do you think men gave years of their lives to the search? Why would a warrior like Gawain scour Britain in service to a broken lord?'

I blinked at the smoke, trying to swallow a cough which was in my throat. Trying to think. And then, suddenly, I saw it. I saw what Iselle had seen. What all of them had seen.

'Because if Arthur has Guinevere back, he will return too,' I said. 'He will be Lord Arthur again and wield Excalibur to unite the kings and spearmen of Britain. He'll gather his horse warriors and ride against the Saxons and drive them from the land.' I saw it all. It was laid out before me like a trackway through the tall reeds. And in the gloom, through the smoke rising up to the hooks from which a skinned hare and a brace of rock doves hung, I saw the flash of Iselle's teeth.

Five days after we had arrived at this hidden place, Gawain announced it was time to leave. He and Gediens had been out looking for signs that Cerdic's warriors were still prowling Avalon's willow-edged bogs and twisting marsh trackways. The two warriors would stand silently for long periods, watching the daytime sky for smudges of smoke. We would take turns going out into the night to look for the copper glow which told the sad tale of the murder of some wildfowler, fisherman or basket weaver's family by the followers of Woden and Thunor. At such times, being used to waking during the night to sing the devotions, I would stand by Arthur's pigpen and think of the brothers, of Father Brice and old Padern and Father Dristan, hearing their voices in my head as I quietly hummed the familiar prayers, while night herons and owls glided in the darkness around me like spirits.

But it had been three days since Gediens had spied a party of spearmen in the distance and heard their strange, guttural words carry across the reed-bed, and two days since I had seen fire burning the night sky. Gawain said that the Saxons had moved on. Perhaps gone north to raid in Caer Cynwidion, since King Conyn had taken to his deathbed and left his followers fighting amongst themselves over who should succeed him.

'And if they haven't gone?' Father Yvain asked from where he sat on a tree stump, running a whetstone along the blade of his spear.

A breeze blew from the west and the Hafren Sea, whipping Gawain's silver hair as he watched the pale sun plunging towards the fog-veiled horizon. He shrugged. 'We can't stay here. Parcefal will be expecting us and the longer he waits, the more likely that someone will recognize Merlin, or that the druid will change his mind and vanish again.' He turned and looked towards the orchard where Guinevere sat in her chair, her hands clasped in her lap, her face turned up to the wintry sky. For sometimes, when the weather was kind, Arthur would carry her outside to escape the peat smoke and gloom of the house. He was with her now, leaning against a fallen apple tree with life in it yet, watching a pair of crows mob a marsh harrier, chasing it away from their roosts.

'We leave in the morning,' Gawain said.

I looked back to the trackway and beyond, to the wall of towering reeds from which we had emerged those days ago to find Arthur's steading, and into which Iselle had vanished at dawn in search of feathers to make new fletchings.

'It's all right, she knows,' Gawain said. 'I told her this morning.' I felt a flush of heat in my face and wondered how Gawain had known I was looking for Iselle. 'She's coming with us to Tintagel. There's nothing for her here in Avalon. Nothing here for you, either, lad.'

I knew he was right, but still I did not like his assumption that I would go with him. That his course, upon which he had been set since the day he had left me at the monastery with the Brothers of the Thorn, was now my own.

'Don't look at me like that, Galahad,' the warrior said. 'You may have lived half your life as a priest of the Christ god, but you were never meant to become one of them.' He raised a hand before I could speak. 'I've never been a man who claims to know about gods and fate, providence and charms. I'd leave that to Merlin.' He glanced towards the orchard again. 'Arthur, too. He believed a lot of it when it suited him. But I didn't give you to the care of the Christians so you could spend your life in prayer on some island in the marsh. That's not your fate, Galahad,' he said, scratching the scar that someone long ago had carved from his hairline down to the ridge of bone above his left eye. 'That's not you. I know that much, lad.'

'How?' I asked. 'How do you know?'

He grimaced, pressed a thumb against his broken nose and expelled a wad of snot onto the mud.

'I know because I knew your father,' he grunted.

I did not like this man telling me what I was and what I was not. Nor did I like the awe with which he spoke of my father. Whatever he thought of my father as a man, Gawain clearly admired him as a warrior. More than that, Gawain and Arthur seemed to revere him, speaking of my father as though he had been untouchable on the battlefield. A reaper of lives. A god of war. Could that be the same man who had hidden from the world like an outlaw, so that my childhood was a friendless one? The man who loved another woman more than he loved my mother? The man who chose to fight and die for Arthur rather than to live for me?

'I have to save the Thorn,' I said. 'I have a cutting and berries and must find somewhere safe to plant them.' For I knew that was the task which Father Brice had entrusted to me when he gave me those precious haws. It already seemed so long ago now.

Gawain's frown told me what he thought of that, but I ignored him.

'The Saxons may have found the holy tree and hacked it down,' I said.

'Won't the Christ god send a fog to hide the tree?' Gawain asked. 'Won't he strike the Saxon down who touches the tree with his axe?'

I could not tell by his war-worn face if he was mocking me, but it seemed that he was and the muscles in my arms and legs drew tight like knots, anger flaring in my chest.

'There is no one left on Ynys Wydryn to pray for the Thorn's deliverance,' I said, thinking of poor Father Brice and Father Judoc and the rest, whose corpses would by now have been savaged by wolves and foxes, ravens and crows and countless smaller creatures which flew or crawled or slithered. 'There is no one to protect the Thorn from the enemies of God. I must continue the brothers' work. I will ensure that the tree endures.'

'Plant the cutting here.' Father Yvain pointed the spear he was sharpening in the direction of the orchard. 'Among the apple trees. It's as good a place as any.'

I glared at him. 'This is not safe land, Father.' It troubled me that Yvain did not seem to share my concern. He had never been the most devout of the brothers, far from it, but I thought he would want to honour his fellow monks by doing what he could to protect the Thorn.

'Nowhere is safe,' he replied. 'Not these days.' He spat on the whetstone and ran it along the blade's edge. 'Plant it here and be done with it.'

My blood was running hot. Had they forgotten the slaughter below the tor? I knew that the brothers' sacrifice meant little to Gawain, who was no Christian. But Father Yvain? I expected better of him.

'No,' I said. 'I will find another place. Where there are Christians who will guard the holy tree as the brothers would if they still lived.'

Gawain came at me then. In five paces he was on me, his fist full of my habit as he drove me backward across the mud. 'You damned fool!' he said, his spit hitting my face. 'I lost two good men getting you off Ynys Wydryn! Better men than you, boy.' I struggled against his grip and, hauling myself back, threw up my left hand, knocking his fist away from my throat. He stepped back and so did I.

'Enough!' Father Yvain yelled. He was somehow, suddenly, between us, his broad back before me. His great bulk loomed in the dusk, his spear raised towards Gawain threateningly. 'Leave him be, Gawain.'

Gawain pointed a ringed finger at Yvain. 'You forget yourself, monk,' he spat, and I thought he would draw his sword then.

'No, brother, I do not.' Yvain lifted his spear blade higher still.

A deep rumble came from Gawain's throat. Some instinct

made me look over my shoulder and there was Iselle, standing with her unstrung bow stave strapped across her back. I wondered how long she had been there watching us.

'I've not been a monk so long,' Father Yvain warned.

'Long enough, I'd wager,' Gawain sneered, all but asking Yvain to do something with the spear, whose blade was speckled with rust.

'Peace, Gawain.' Arthur had left the apple trees where Guinevere sat. His face was drawn and pale and the eyes below that furrowed brow, eyes which raked Gawain, Yvain and me, were hard and flat, as though he was angry that we should presume to bring our petty quarrels into his dismal refuge.

Yet Gawain, who either had not heard Arthur or did not want to hear, took a step towards Yvain and threw his arms wide, inviting Yvain to attack him.

Yvain held his ground but did not lower the spear.

'I said peace!' Arthur called, striding towards us, raising a hand to show the palm.

Down came Yvain's spear blade. Gawain lifted a hand towards him, acknowledging that he himself had let the situation slip out of his grasp. Then he lifted his chin towards me. 'He is more like his father than he knows,' he said, his anger dissipating though his jaw was still clenched tight.

Arthur had come to a stop some ten paces away, his booted feet planted in the mud. 'Is that not what you hoped, nephew?' he asked.

Gawain folded his arms over his broad chest and considered this. 'Hanguis and Endalan did not die for nothing,' he told me, then looked at Father Yvain. 'Not for some old tree.'

Father Yvain nodded and planted the butt of his spear in the mud. 'You'll get no argument from me about that.'

Gawain frowned. For a moment it seemed he and Arthur

had more to say to each other, but then Gawain turned and strode off towards the house, muttering about needing a drink. 'We leave at sunrise,' he called over his shoulder.

Iselle held my eye for a heartbeat, then she too went inside.

I turned my attention back to Arthur, who gazed at me with eyes so blue and yet so distant that it seemed they reflected another sky from another time. 'Lancelot was the most stubborn man I ever knew,' he said, pulling his thinning beard through a fist. For the first time I saw the ghost of a smile on his lips. 'Merlin told me once that when your father was a boy, he had a sparhawk. A fearsome, hate-filled bird. A mistrustful, broken-winged fiend of a hawk, but young Lancelot would not give up trying to man her. He'd work day after day, sunrise to sunset, seeking to win the bird's trust, though he knew little about the austringer's art. Merlin said it was a battle between obstinate wills, Lancelot's and the hawk's. The bird was vicious and wild, and no one believed young Lancelot could man her.' Arthur's lips tightened then. He gave a slight shake of his head and turned to look back to where Guinevere sat among the fruit trees, their gnarly shadows distorted by the setting sun so that they looked like dark, grasping hands reaching for her across the ground.

'And what happened, Lord Arthur?' Father Yvain asked. I was glad of that, for I had bitten my tongue to stop myself from asking.

Arthur turned back to me. 'The boy manned the bird,' he said.

'And the bird manned the boy.' Father Yvain smiled.

'In the end that proud hawk would eat from Lancelot's hand,' Arthur said. 'He could cast her at some prey and call her back and she would drop the prize at his feet because she wanted to impress him.'

Yvain nodded, satisfied with the end of Arthur's tale. Then, saying he would carry Guinevere inside, he left Arthur and me standing there, watching the shadows merge and pool, darkness rising like a tide as the sun set.

'Your father never lost that spirit,' Arthur said, looking into the west. 'He did everything he could not to leave you, Galahad. You know that, don't you?'

I felt my face tighten. Felt my throat constrict.

'I did not see the end' – Arthur reached across his chest to press a hand to his shoulder as if to a wound – 'but men have spoken to me of it. They say Lancelot refused to yield. That he would not succumb to death even though it was not possible for a mortal man to deny it. He fought with every sinew. Every breath. For you, Galahad. Because he loved you.'

My chest ached. My breath came in short stabs and I watched a loose mob of jackdaws and rooks winging towards a clump of alders already dark with roosting birds.

'Come, Galahad,' Arthur said, 'I have something for you.'

We stood for a moment, letting our eyes settle into the darkness beyond the glow of the horn lantern which Arthur held. The air smelled of straw and dust, leather and iron and old horse urine, though it was clear that no horse had lived in the stable for years. There were barrels and baskets and some amphorae of the type Greek merchants brought to Britain to trade for our tin. There were bundles of reeds, old spit irons and a rusted cauldron and a saddle and tack, all spattered white with bird droppings.

I followed Arthur deeper inside and saw, leaning against the near wall, a shield like the ones Gawain and his men had, with bleached leather stretched across it and the black bear standing on all fours on the shield boss. Only this shield was even more scarred and battered, the leather torn and begrimed and stained with rust-coloured daubs. This was Arthur's own shield, I supposed. Once a sight to put fear in Saxon bellies. Now, a dust-covered relic. To look at it was to glimpse a glorious time long past, when even the kings of the land had come together under one banner. When the people had hope. When Britain had Arthur.

I was still looking at that shield when Arthur spoke my name softly and pulled a linen sheet from the gloom itself, or so it seemed. He took a step back and lifted the horn lantern before him.

No! I drew a short breath and stepped back, knocking an empty barrel over. I don't know how many times my heart hammered in my chest before I breathed again. I stood there, hands clasped against my mouth, my blood cold. Cold to the very marrow of my bones. Unable to speak or move. Constrained as if by chains or some potent spell.

Because I saw my father back from the dead.

'It's all right, Galahad.' Arthur's voice sounded distant, drowned out by the rushing of the blood in my ears. 'Don't be afraid.'

I blinked. I took a step forward. Then another. My hands moved down to my chest and I felt my heart beating against my breastbone.

It was not my father returned from Annwn, but it *was* his panoply. His war gear, conjured as if from my memories, all hung and mounted on a simple wooden cross stand so that in the dark it had tricked my eyes. So that in that instant when Arthur had removed the sheet, I had seen my father standing there in his war glory. And even now, knowing it for what it was – metal and leather, stitching and wool – I could barely breathe as I gazed at it. My father's long coat of overlapping bronze scales, each little plate shining dully in the dark. The silver-studded sword belt crossed from right shoulder to left hip, and the sword itself, Boar's Tusk, snug in its scabbard, sleeping away the years. A long spear leant against the right end of the cross beam, as though gripped in a hand, and leaning against the bottom of the upright were my father's iron greaves, skilfully wrought to depict the muscles of his legs. On the face of each greave, at knee height, were twin images of a hawk's head, impressed into the bronze by a master smith. It was a depiction of that very same bird which my father had manned as a boy, and looking at those greaves now I felt again the wonder, the thrill that had run through my blood when I would steal a glimpse of them without my father knowing.

'I had them made for your father. A gift to mark our friendship.' Looking down at the greaves, Arthur moved the lantern closer, so that each bird seemed alive as the flame's glow played across the ridges and indentations in the bronze. That fierce eye. That sharp beak. The bristling feathers.

'He told me,' I remembered. I had not wholly believed my father. It had seemed impossible to the child I was then that my father could have been friends with the great Lord Arthur, warlord of Britain.

'Closer.' Arthur beckoned me with a sweep of the lantern, his voice barely more than a whisper. I went closer. I could smell the bronze now and the earthy, slightly sweet scent of the leather to which the scales were laced. I looked at my father's helmet with its hinged cheek irons and its long, white horse-hair plume. I closed my eyes and remembered washing that plume and combing the knots and tangles out until it flowed like water. My father had not said I had done a good job, but I had known that he was pleased. We had both been proud when he put the helmet on and tied the straps beneath his chin. For the last time.

'Why have you kept it here all these years, lord?' I asked, dreading the answer that I knew was coming.

'I kept it for you, Galahad.' He looked back at the armour. He must have cleaned it himself, I realized, for there was no patina on the scales or the helmet.

'Why, lord?' I asked.

Arthur nodded, as if he had expected the question.

'Because it is yours now,' he answered. 'Lancelot was my friend. If he were still here with us . . .' He did not, or could not, finish that thought, but reached out and placed three fingers against the helmet's cheek piece. 'Your father would want you to have it,' he said. 'I knew about you, Galahad. Knew that one day Gawain would return to Ynys Wydryn and bring you to me. And so I kept your father's war gear safe because I thought you would want it. That you would use it.'

My guts had twisted into knots. My chest ached. I was ten years old again, standing on a hillside, watching my father ride away.

'I don't want it,' I said.

Arthur made a hum in his throat and scratched his cheek. However he had imagined this moment, it was not like this.

'I'm sorry, lord, but I don't want it.' I swallowed hard. I needed to escape and so I turned and walked away.

'It's yours, Galahad,' Arthur said as I opened the door and walked into the gathering dark. A darkness which could not dim the sight of my memory, seeing him as he once was. My father, in his scale armour, surrounded by enemies. Engulfed by them.

I had to flee. Though I knew that he never had.

'What would you have me do with it, lad?' Arthur called after me, but I did not stop.

*

I know this creature, and she knows me. She is nervous as we browse the brambles and wild flowers on the fringe of the forest clearing. It is dusk. The scent of new-made hay is on the air, even here among the trees, far from the nearest village and the fields at whose edges poppies flaunt their crimson heads in the summer breeze.

There, twined around a young oak, climbing up and up, a braid of honeysuckle. Sweet and heady on the shafts of golden light which arrow through the clearing. Cream trumpet flowers shivering with the thrill of the embrace.

Too good to leave, and besides, it is not yet night. We move slowly, alert to any hidden danger, twitching at the insects which drone in the heavy air, thick as silt stirred up from a river bed. We move through the dappled grass, the bitter ferns and the sweet-smelling herbs, and I believe I could lead this roe deer right into the clearing and up to the front door of the little dwelling if I chose to. For I have been so long in this other place that I am perhaps more like the creatures whose souls my own soul entwines than what I used to be.

Sometimes, I can see into the world which I left behind. The world in which my body still lingers like an old house going to ruin. Sometimes, I look out from tired eyes and I see him. Arthur. Old now. Grey and broken, but Arthur still. My Arthur. But mostly I roam the wild woods and the grey skies. The wave-lashed shore and the high meadows where the grass grows as tall as a boy. I am trapped, and yet I am free.

What would the druid think if he knew? That my gift, my talent, my curse, is more potent even than his own? That for me the years are a stream? And like a salmon, I can swim with the current but also against it, upstream, back to times and places which are nothing now but someone's fading memory, or a faint echo of feeling among ruins, or a story passed like a drink around a fire.

And here I am now, in the before, spirit-joined with this creature, on the edge of the clearing where he lives.

Lancelot.

I let the roe eat some of the honeysuckle, but then I pull her away and we move on, keeping the wind in her nose, and now I smell him. See him. He is tall and strong. Dark-haired and keen-eyed. He is beautiful. As is his boy, who flies at him now, the clatter of their wooden swords giving the roe a start, though I hold her to this spot amongst the beech and black bryony. A hunter's arrow could not pierce my heart more. I am here, in the past, breathing the same forest air as he. Warmed by the same late evening sun which warms his cheek.

The boy is fast and strong and his father grins to see it. So proud. They move as easily as water, the boy and the man. Like a dance. Twisting and spinning, ducking and thrusting, their practice swords kissing and clacking and whipping the dusk air.

Galahad looks so like his father. It's in his cheekbones and in the way he tilts his head when the two break apart to catch their breath. It's in his hawk's eyes, in that questioning look, as though he is measuring himself against all others, against the world itself, and I remember the boy I knew on the island. That proud boy who swam out in a storm and pulled me from the clutches of some greedy god. The boy who became the man with whom I am entwined now and always. And who waits for me.

But then the door of the little house opens and my hold on the doe almost breaks, for the pain is too much. She is fair-haired and pale-skinned, and she comes to watch them both, and they both turn and smile at her and now I see that Galahad looks as much like her as he does his father. They both love her and she them. It is in their faces and in the air. So thick in the air that I breathe it in, much as I don't want to. The three of them. Three souls hiding from the world.

The boy goes for his father again, but Lancelot parries every thrust and strike until, at last, he seems to misjudge the boy's attack and the boy scores a hit on his chest and my love falls to his knees as

*if mortally wounded, clutching the spot where the boy struck him.
And the boy grins at his mother, who claps her hands like the beating
of a dove's wings.*

*Above me, some startled creature takes flight, yet I hold to the
spot, just as Lancelot tries to hold the grimace of pain in his face but
cannot. The twist of lips, lips which I have known so well, becomes
a smile. He laughs, and in his eyes I see how much he loves the boy.
Loves him to the end of everything.*

*I can look no more. And so I release my grip on the doe, her
bunched muscles bursting into movement, and we fly into the
forest.*

Owl and polecat, fox and badger were out hunting still when I
found myself standing outside Arthur's stable, my cloak pulled
tight against the cold. Dawn had not yet seeped into night's
black hem and the others were deep in sleep when I had eased
the door shut behind me and made my way across the wooden
trackway which Arthur had cleared of slime and moss.

I entered the stable and again I was stopped in my tracks by
the sight of my father's armour. Now, I knew it for what it was:
metal and leather, linen and horsehair, not flesh, blood and
soul, and yet still I half expected it to greet me. Which might
have been why I did something which I would have struggled
to explain even to myself.

'Father,' I said, in a quiet voice. Then a little louder, a little
brighter, as I might have called to him when I returned from
the rabbit snares or the willow traps. 'Father.'

I waited, feeling blood course through my veins. Feeling the
weight of the silence and of my heart, like a stone in my chest.

Perhaps I had just wanted to feel the old familiar greeting in
my mouth again. To remember what it was to be a boy and
have a father. Or perhaps I meant to wound myself, to wallow

in pain by tricking my heart into hoping, beyond reason and sanity, that I might hear my father's voice say *Hello, boy*.

Something rustled in the dark. I lifted the lamp and saw two mice scurry across the reed bundles. Somewhere in the night beyond the old stable, an owl screeched. A long, drawn-out shriek accusing me of stirring up the past and things which were better left alone. I made the sign of the Thorn, went up to the armour and placed my palm on the cold bronze scales. I was closer now than I had been earlier with Arthur, and I saw that many of the little plates were dented. Some of these bent and damaged scales made lines across the coat. Silent echoes from across the years. I closed my eyes and ran my hand over these scars, imagining each sword blow which had made them, each savage blow which my father had felt but which had not put him down.

I moved round to the back of the armour and by the oil lamp's glow I found three small holes, one in the shoulder and two in the small of the back. I explored each one with my fingers, following the course of the spear which had been thrust up beneath the scales to tear through the tough leather beneath. To rip into my father's flesh.

I placed my hands on the same parts of my own body and tried to imagine the pain, but I could not. Then to the helmet, where my father's shade lingered strongest. I touched that white plume which I had seen flying in the wind. I put it to my nose and breathed in its smell. I combed it with my hand, feeling the long, coarse hairs pass between my fingers. And then, heart clenching, hands shaking, I put the helmet on my own head. I caught the faint scent of my father's sweat in the leather liner. After all the years. And in that moment, I was not a man standing in a stable on a winter's night, but a ten-year-old boy pretending to be a warrior. Playing games of war within the protective fortress of a father's love.

'It fits you.'

I ripped the helmet off my head and turned to see Iselle standing just inside the stable.

'What are you doing here?' I asked. How had I not heard her come in? She came nearer, stopping just beyond the glow of the lantern which I had set down on a stool. I saw the glint of bronze scales in her eyes and knew she was awestruck by the war gear, as I had been.

'This is your father's,' she said. Not a question. She just knew.

'Lord Arthur kept it for me.'

She took another step and put a hand on the armour, just as I had done. 'It is magnificent.'

I nodded. It was strange watching her fingers find the battle marks on the bronze. I wanted to tell her that it was not her place to touch the armour in which my father had breathed his last breath. But I said nothing.

'They say your father was the greatest warrior to walk the land since Cú Chulainn,' she said. 'That even the battle god Belatucadrus grew envious of Lancelot and made him fall in love with Guinevere because he wanted to sow the seeds of his downfall.'

'Do you believe that?' I asked.

She cocked her head, studying me as if wondering whether I believed it. 'I am not a child, Galahad. Such stories are for children and men in their ale cups.' She pulled her hand away, as though the scales had burned her. 'But he must have been a fighter without equal. Imagine what he and Lord Arthur could have achieved had Lancelot not betrayed his friend. Had he not broken Arthur's heart.'

'If Lord Arthur despised my father so much, why did he save his war gear and keep it these last ten years?' I asked. 'Look at it.' I lifted the helmet. 'Think of the times he must have come in here to clean and polish the bronze and steel. I expect my father's sword is sharp too.' I looked at Boar's Tusk in its scabbard but left it where it was. 'Why would Arthur do this if he so hated my father?'

Iselle's teeth worried at her bottom lip as she considered her answer. 'He said he kept it for you?'

'But I don't want it,' I said.

'Because you are afraid?'

'My duty is to protect the Holy Thorn,' I said. 'My brothers cannot do it and so I must. I will carry the Thorn to safety. To some secret place.'

I did not want to tell her that I hated my father for leaving me alone in the world. For choosing Arthur and for choosing Guinevere and for not choosing me. For holding tight to his spear and shield and for letting go of me.

'But perhaps you are meant to have it.' She was looking again at the war gear. 'Perhaps that is why I followed you in the marsh. Why I saved your life.'

'You hate the Saxons. That is why you killed those men.'

She did not deny it, and yet I could see that she was thinking other things, trying to untangle knots in her mind.

The owl in the night screeched again but I did not sign the Thorn this time.

'So, what will you do with it?' she asked.

'Nothing. I told you, I don't want it. Arthur can sink it in the mire if it pleases him. An offering to the gods who he believes have abandoned him.'

She touched the scale coat again. To see the awe with which she beheld it, you would have thought the armour had been made by gods. Or worn by one.

'May I?' she asked, nodding at the helmet in my hands.

I wanted to say no. Instead, I held the helmet towards her

and as she took it our fingers touched and a shiver ran through me.

'I asked you what you were doing out here,' I said.

Reverently, slowly, she put the helmet on. It was much too big for her. There was empty space between her high cheekbones and the steel-hinged guards, and she had to tilt it back in order to see properly. And yet it suited her. She looked fierce. She looked beautiful.

'I was awake when you crept out,' she said. 'I thought you were going to pray to your god. I wanted to hear what you would pray for.'

It was not the truth, but I did not challenge it. She removed the helmet and offered it back to me but I shook my head and so she placed it on the pole above the scale coat.

'It will be dawn soon.' I picked up the reed lamp from the stool. Iselle took one last look at my father's scale coat and plumed helmet, his greaves and his sword, and followed me back into the night.

I went back to my blankets by the hearth and I dreamt not of my father riding off to die but of Father Brice. In my dream he had survived the slaughter on Ynys Wydryn and I met him in some dark, cramped, smoky place, which may have been the tunnels beneath the tor or even Lord Arthur's smokehouse. For some reason, the monk could not or would not speak, but I could. I told him over and over that I was sorry I had not stood beside him when the Saxons came. Next time I would, I told him, though Brice seemed more concerned with trying to find our way out of that place, and I cannot say whether we would have escaped, for Father Yvain prodded me awake and I saw it was morning.

Everyone else was awake before me and for a while I just sat there in my blankets, trying to fix Father Brice's face in my mind even as the dream fell away from me. Iselle, I saw, was sitting across from me, the other side of the hearth, her back against the wall, stitching a rabbit skin into the lining of her hood. Arthur, Guinevere and Gediens must have been outside, while Yvain and Gawain were talking in low voices beyond the open door which invited clean dawn air to scour the fug from the room. I shivered to feel the touch of it on my neck.

'You were dreaming.' Iselle looked up from her work.

Father Brice drifted from me like the smoke from the dying fire.

'Did I say anything?' I asked, remembering how, once, Father Dristan had woken me and pulled me through the dark dormitory to Father Meurig's bed because the cook was talking in his sleep. We had stood by Meurig's bed, our shoulders shaking, eyes glistening with tears, and hands clamped over our mouths to keep from laughing aloud as the cook mumbled about some recipe of eels, pignuts, parsnips and milk curdled with wood sorrel.

'You groaned a little. Nothing that made sense,' Iselle assured me.

I pressed my knuckles into a crick in my neck and looked over at Father Yvain and Gawain, wondering what they were discussing. Gawain had a cup in his hand, and I realized how thirsty I was from having breathed in so much smoke during the night. The warrior must have felt my eyes on him for he turned and looked at me, a sourness in his scarred face. Then Father Yvain looked over to me. A heartbeat and his eyes were back on Gawain's, their hushed conversation resumed, and I felt a knot tying itself in my guts.

Perhaps it was the dream of Father Brice, or maybe there was some other instinct whispering to me, for something made me reach for my knapsack. I thrust my hand inside, feeling for the damp linen pouch in which I kept the cutting of the Holy Thorn and the eight precious berries. It was not there. I opened the sack fully and turned the opening towards the daylight so that I could see inside properly.

'It's gone, Galahad,' Iselle said.

For a moment I wondered how she had known what I was looking for. 'Where?' I asked. But even as I spoke, I looked at the hearth and the charred fuel from which, now and then, a small tongue of fire licked, as if tasting the air. My stomach clenched and I couldn't breathe. The little cutting had been green wood, cut from the living tree just days before, so it had not burned well and had retained its shape.

'No.' I was on my feet now, shaking my head at that gnarled, blackened stick which smouldered and smoked in Lord Arthur's hearth. 'No.' I looked round and saw that Father Yvain and Gawain were both watching me.

'What have you done?' I yelled at Gawain, who raised a cautionary hand and opened his mouth to speak.

'I did it,' Iselle admitted, cutting him off. 'I burned it.'

I turned to her, hoping that she was lying. Knowing that she was not.

'The berries too,' she added. 'I took them when you were asleep, and I put them in the fire.'

I felt sick. I looked at the feeble flames and then back at Iselle.

'How could you?' I asked her, forcing the words out between gritted teeth, my muscles quivering in my flesh. 'Who gave you the right?' I was hot with rage which only burned hotter still because I saw no regret in Iselle, no sign that she was sorry for what she had done.

'It's better this way,' she said.

'Better? Are you mad? Who are you to decide what is

better?' I was trembling with anger. I could feel the blood pounding in my head, and I wanted to take Iselle by the shoulders and shake her, but I could not move.

Gawain and Father Yvain came inside, and I knew that they had known. That Gawain was complicit came as no surprise. I did not believe that the warrior cared for anything other than his quest to find Merlin and restore Arthur to his former glory. But had Father Yvain known and done nothing?

'Why, Iselle?' I asked. 'Why did you do it?' My anger was tempered now by a sinking feeling at their betrayal.

'It's done, Galahad,' Father Yvain said. 'Nothing can change it.'

I glared at him. 'Have you forgotten our brothers already, Father?' I asked him.

'I've not forgotten them, lad,' he said, shaking his head. 'But a tree is just a tree.'

Was I still caught inside my dream? If so, I needed to wake up.

'It was an offence to the gods,' Iselle said. 'We are all better off without it.'

'But I swore to the brothers,' I told her, then turned to Yvain. 'I swore to them in my prayers. I would keep the Thorn safe. That was why I could not stay with them at the end. Father Brice knew it and he entrusted the Thorn into my keeping. God helped me carry it to safety.'

'No, Galahad.' Gawain waved a finger at me. 'Not god. Hanguis and Endalan. They're the reason you're alive now.' He pointed at Iselle. 'And Iselle before them,' he added. 'You're alive because we didn't let the Saxons kill you.'

There was a cold truth in his words. And yet I owed it to Father Brice and Father Judoc and all the others to speak for them. I felt that the monks were listening now. That I was being judged and found wanting. Fists clenched, fingernails biting into my palms, I wanted to tell Iselle that I hated her for what she had done. But the truth was I did not hate her.

'Put the Brothers of the Thorn and their god behind you, Galahad,' Gawain said. 'None of it can help you now.' He turned and walked back outside, the new day washing his own scale armour in crimson. 'Get your things, everyone. We're leaving.'

Iselle wound the surplus thread around her bone needle, which she tucked back into the scrip on her belt. Then, without looking at me, she followed Father Yvain outside. I watched her go and I turned back to the hearth. I whispered to Father Bricc that I was sorry. And I watched the Holy Thorn smoulder and burn.

7

The Riven Land

W E LEFT ARTHUR AND Guinevere sitting wrapped in furs among the fruit trees as dawn broke in the east, flooding the marshes with golden light and promising a fine cold day. Iselle led the way, walking an arrow-shot ahead. She was happiest in her own company, it seemed to me, and of us all she had the greatest knowledge and experience of that waterlogged world. Whenever some bird clattered up from the frosty reed-beds at our approach, I realized how clumsy we were compared with her, who had passed those same birds before us and not driven them to seek the safety of the sky. In a glance, Iselle could read the shape of a stunted willow, its extremities combed by the prevailing winds, and know which way we must go. She could taste a drop of water from one ditch and a drop from another and know how far we were from the sea or if the Hafren was surging and we would need to find higher ground. With her bow she could conjure a meal of bittern or duck as easily as think of it, and it soon became clear why she had not merely survived out here amongst the floodplains, fringe streams, rivers, ditches, ponds and lakes, but had thrived.

We went south and, as dusk fell, came across a moss-crept, decomposing hut which we found to be abandoned, though there were snares and traps within which showed that some wildfowler had sheltered there recently. We stayed the night in that draughty place and in the morning we set off again as a thick blanket of cloud gathered above us, prolonging the night and threatening rain which did not fall. The day after that it snowed. The snow did not settle, but swirled on the breeze, hazing the world and making stark, foreboding shapes of the leafless oaks, black alder and ash. And I wondered if Iselle had known it would snow and that was why she had sewn the rabbit pelt into her hood. I did not ask her. We had not spoken since leaving Arthur's steading and the silence stretched between us, heavy as the day.

I smouldered inside my cowl and Iselle glowered from inside her newly lined hood and Father Yvain despaired of us both. 'This thing between the two of you,' the monk nodded towards Iselle, who was out in front as usual, 'it's like ice growing in the water barrel.' He puffed with the effort of climbing a grassy ridge, using his spear as a staff to help him up. 'The longer you leave it, the harder it is to crack.'

I said nothing, and when we got to the top of the ridge the monk stopped and put his hands on his hips, pretending to appreciate the view as snow settled on his bear skin and melted in his big beard. Really, I knew he was trying to catch his breath. 'More like your father than you know,' he said, his gaze ranging along that shoulder of land running south-east beside the Hafren, which snaked inland to the south of Avalon.

'Save your breath, Father,' I said. 'At your age you don't have enough to waste.' Even blowing as he was, he managed to laugh at that. Gawain and Gediens were huffing up the slope behind us, their war gear clinking and clattering as they climbed.

'Have you asked yourself why she did it, lad?' Father Yvain said.

'Because she hates our god,' I replied.

'Maybe,' he said. 'Or maybe it's because she's alone in the world. And she likes you and doesn't want you going off and getting yourself killed for the sake of some old tree. Have you thought of that, Galahad?'

I had not thought of that, but I did now. Iselle had never talked about her real parents, other than to say that they had died in the turmoil of Arthur's wars. And now her foster mother, Alana, was gone too. Her home was nothing but ashes on the wind. The Saxons had taken everything from her, and for all that she had grown up roaming the marsh and the hidden ways alone, like a wolf driven from the pack which must become fierce if it is to survive, could it be that Iselle had grown tired of this solitary life? Perhaps loneliness or curiosity had led her to stalk me through the reed-beds that day I went to the lake village. Or perhaps Iselle hated our Christian god and burned the cutting of the Holy Thorn because she thought me a fool. That was more likely, I told myself as I watched a grey heron beat into the west, its neck outstretched and its legs trailing behind, a grey ghost sweeping through the falling snow. I wondered what it must be like to be up there, looking down on the land. To see everything. Perhaps to know everything.

We trudged on along that high ground. Ahead, we could just make out Camelot upon its hill to the south by the brown tinge its fires gave the snow-laden clouds. Turning my face to spare it the wind's bite, I could not but gaze at that distant hill, imagining Camelot as it once was, when there was still hope in Britain. I could not help but think of my father and Lord Arthur riding their war horses through the great fort's gates, fresh from some victory against the Saxons. Still young. Still friends. The heroes of Britain.

That night we came to the Roman road which Gawain called the Fosse and which he said ran from the Saxon lands of

Lindisware in the north-east to Lindinis in Dumnonia. Wide enough for four horsemen to ride abreast, it was nothing like our own paths and ways, which meandered along animal tracks or watercourses and which so often became quagmires in winter. This Roman road, built on an embankment so that the legions that had once marched along it need not fear ambush, lay for the most part as straight as a spear across the land. And whilst, here and there, weed and grass and bramble pushed through the stony surface, inexorably reclaiming the land, as we longed to do, it was not hard to imagine the road as it had once looked. Awesome, imposing, a thing made of earth and stone, sweat, blood and ambition.

As we prepared a camp in the beech wood nearby, I tried to imagine the many hundreds of men who must have laboured on it. Roman soldiers from Gallia or the Rhinelands, or even from Rome itself, men who lived and toiled and died beneath a foreign sky. I wondered if their souls had found the afterlife. Or did some of those men's ghosts still march along this road, never finding rest, never reaching their destination?

We would have to sleep beneath the cold sky and so were gathering fuel to make a fire that would burn through the night. Some deadfall from the beech trees, but mostly juniper branches, which we knew would give little smoke. As I brought a load back to the camp, I saw Gawain just standing, his arms full of branches, looking back to the road.

'We used to thunder along here,' he said, his thoughts cantering along that road into the past, recalling his years as one of Lord Arthur's famous horse warriors, his cataphracts, who had become the phantoms of Saxon nightmares. 'Arthur would moan that Uther should have kept the roads in good repair, of course, but then he always did admire the Romans.' He grinned at the memory. 'We'd move fast, cover such distances in a day that we could hammer a Saxon war band in Caer Celemion in the morning and cut up another in Cynwidion before sunset.'

'They must have thought there were thousands of us.' Gediens too had stopped to look towards the road, his own head full of the past.

Gawain's smile faded and he shook his head. 'With just another two hundred we could have chased them into the Morimaru and watched them drown.'

'What became of them? Lord Arthur's war horses?' I asked, throwing my branches onto the growing pile beside Father Yvain, who was on his knees setting the fire within a ring made from stones found in the ditch beside the road.

'I heard they vanished. Like Merlin.' Yvain blew into the embers he had nurtured in a pile of birch bark scrapings.

'Folk used to say that Lord Arthur's horses were so saddened by his death that they galloped into the Western Sea, where the goddess Epona turned them into waves,' Iselle said, shaking the berries off a juniper bough.

'Better than the truth, I suppose,' Gawain muttered. 'That they were butchered. Most of them. Those fine, fine horses.' He closed his eyes to better see those horses and when he opened them again, they glistened with tears. He blinked and shook his head to rid himself of the memories. 'Some survived,' he said, turning to Iselle. 'Some ran to the Western Sea, just like in your story. And maybe the sea goddess did turn them into waves.' He shrugged and walked to the fire, dropping his wood with the rest.

'There are others like you?' Iselle asked. 'Alive somewhere?'

A gust sought amongst the trees and Gawain pulled his cloak around his neck to keep its cold fingers off. 'I don't blame a man for wanting to live,' he said. 'If a man is going to stand in the shieldwall or ride into slaughter, he needs to have something to believe in. We've not had anything to believe in for a long time.' He huffed warm air into his hands. 'Maybe that will change.'

The first flames crackled and spat from Yvain's creation and so the monk bent lower still and blew upwards into the fuel, feeding the fire.

'Well, it had better be soon,' Gediens said, holding two sticks side by side to compare their lengths, 'because I'm getting too old to be traipsing across the land and sleeping out in winter.'

'It's a young man's business,' Gawain agreed, easing himself down onto a bench he had made from stumps and deadfall.

Gediens swept one of the sticks through the air with a whipping sound. 'I fear young men these days don't have it in them. Not like we did.' This was for my benefit, I knew, but I ignored it. 'What say you, Galahad?' he asked, and with that he tossed one of the sticks at me and I caught it. He pointed with his own. 'Why don't we see if you have any of your father's talent? Surely the apple did not fall so far from the tree.' He slashed his stick again as if it were a sword. 'First one to land a good hit. Iselle can decide it.' Iselle didn't say that she would or wouldn't, but a smile played at the corners of her lips at my obvious discomfort.

I took three steps and dropped the stick I held onto Yvain's fire, causing him to mutter that it was too soon for pieces that size.

Gediens sighed and lifted his chin to Gawain. 'Are you sure we got the right monk?' he asked.

'Leave the lad alone, Gediens,' Father Yvain rumbled. 'He didn't ask for any of this.'

Gawain was holding his hands towards the new growing flame. 'You think Hanguis and Endalan saw themselves dying on that hill?' he asked Father Yvain. 'You think they asked for that?' The only answer was the crackle of juniper spines catching fire. 'They knew we were there to get Galahad out. They knew what they were dying for.'

'I would not have had them give their lives for mine,' I said, and meant it.

Gawain looked at me and nodded. 'Sometimes we don't get to choose, Galahad,' he said. A gust punched through the woods like a fist, flaring the fire. 'Sometimes we are part of something bigger than what we can see. What I do know is that we have you. And whether you like it or not, you *are* Lancelot's son.' He rubbed his hands together and palmed them towards the fire again. 'We've found Merlin and we'll bring him back. And maybe, if the gods will it, we'll have Arthur again.'

No one spoke for a long while after that, none of us wanting to break the strange spell which Gawain had woven. Each of us perhaps daring to imagine what might be if Arthur rode again. If he unsheathed Excalibur and united the Britons beneath the bear banner, as he had once before, and drove the Saxons back to the coast.

We cooked two bitterns and a tufted duck over the fire, took it in turns to keep watch and slept as well as we could through the cold night. And in the pre-dawn dark we set off again, shivering and stiff, as a robin admonished us from an old oak stump near the road, its percussive *tick tick* unnaturally loud in that otherwise still and murky world.

Sometimes we walked along the Fosse in the footsteps of long-dead legionaries. At other times, particularly if some hill or deviation did not afford us a far view, we kept amongst the trees. For whilst it became less and less likely we would meet any Saxons with every day we journeyed west, it was still possible. We did not want to come across a scouting party out stealing food for Cerdic's army, or a war band probing for signs of resistance from the cowed lords of Britain, like boys poking sticks into a wasps' nest for the bloody-minded mischief of it. Nor did we want to be met by any of Morgana's men or any spearmen who bent the knee to King Cuel of Caer Gloui, for then Lord Gawain would be obliged to travel to their lord or lady's court to pay his respects, which he did not want to do.

'What we are doing must stay between us,' he had warned. 'When we are strong enough, when Arthur is strong enough, we will summon the kings and spearmen of Britain. But we cannot risk a false dawn.'

We all agreed. Besides which, who would believe that Arthur lived? Other than those few loyal warriors who had searched the land for Merlin, no one had seen Arthur these last ten years. He was a memory. A hope to some, perhaps, those who still believed that the old gods of Britain would return with shining swords to save us from our enemies. To most, Arthur was an idea, as intangible as gossamer webs on dewy autumn grass, his name the whispered chant of a raven's beating wings.

'When we're ready, they will come,' Gawain assured us. 'But we are not ready yet.'

He thought our hopes and ambitions as fragile as a new flame on a damp wick and so the fewer eyes that saw us, the fewer tongues that spoke of us, the better.

And yet, we could not weave around ourselves one of the invisibility spells for which Merlin had been famous, and nor could we expect to have the Fosse to ourselves.

We met a man and woman and their three children as they joined the road ahead of us. They had fled their home in Caer Celemion, which was being ravaged by Saxon war bands now that Lord Farasan was in his grave, and were bound for Cornubia. The man was limping, pushing their belongings in a handcart which moaned with every turn of its battered wheels.

Seeing Gawain and Gediens's bear-shields and fine war gear, the man spoke of his family's flight with downcast eyes, his voice tremulous but respectful. His wife, though, spat towards Gawain and Gediens, calling them cowards for going south when they should have been marching north to fight. The man, who by his age and the rusting helmet in his barrow had perhaps earned his limp in the Saxon wars, struck his wife, drawing blood from her lip and perhaps thinking it a small price to pay for saving his family from Gawain's wrath.

But Gawain tilted his spear towards the man, his eyes as sharp as that spear's blade. 'Lay a finger on your wife again and she'll be pushing you and your broken legs along in that barrow,' he told him. The man muttered some apology, his gaze fixed on a weed which had pushed through the road by his feet.

Gawain nodded to the woman. 'Hold on to your anger. Feed it,' he told her. 'There will come a time when it will feed you in return and give you strength.' He gave no further explanation, and we continued on, soon leaving them far behind, the man limping, the barrow creaking, the woman glaring and the children wide-eyed.

We saw other families at a distance. Too afraid of Saxons or thieves, or else too superstitious to use the Roman road, these folk moved among the trees either side of the Fosse. We caught glimpses of wild-looking men and women watching us with dark, sunken eyes. We saw children so thin and starving, their clothes so threadbare and ragged, that they seemed to be made of the same sticks and leprous white bark as the birch trees between which they darted, making games of their tragedy. These were the lost folk of Britain. The dispossessed, drifting south and east like ash from a hundred fires, and whenever I saw them, I prayed to God to guide them to some safe haven. In truth, though, I felt myself drifting further from God the more I saw of Britain. The God I had known on Ynys Wydryn, or at least the God to whom I had prayed daily in that island sanctuary, was said to be merciful and omniscient and all-present. But I saw no sign of Him now, so it seemed to me that if He existed at all, He was confined to that monastery far behind us, the way an oak's shadow is tethered to the tree and can never be parted from it no matter the sun's great journey across the sky.

For there were worse sights even than these desperate, anguished folk. I saw a young man no older than I hung upside down from the bough of a rowan tree. He had been stripped naked, strung up and throat cut, and now turned on that rope above a pool of congealed blood in the leaf litter, arms reaching, his ashen face and staring eyes seeming to ask all the world what he had done to deserve it. Whether these things were done by Saxons, or Britons, we had no way of knowing, though I knew we all preferred to think it was the Saxons than to acknowledge that the land and her people were so riven, that we had fallen so far since the time of Arthur.

A little further on, we were warned by the raucous rasping of crows that we approached another grisly scene. We found a woman face down in the grass. Her clothes were cut or torn, so that her fair skin was as loud as a shout against the dark winter grass. I had to drink from my flask to wash down the bile which had risen in my throat. I saw Iselle muttering a curse at the men who had done this unspeakable thing, while above us the crows eddied in a black, boiling cauldron of noise, incensed by our intrusion.

'We should bury her.' I swallowed hard.

'Cut the boy down too and put them in the ground together,' Father Yvain added, no doubt thinking what we all were: that these two had been lovers. Or brother and sister perhaps.

'We don't have a spade.' Gediens stated the obvious.

'Nor the time.' Gawain looked from the young woman in the grass to Father Yvain with an expression which said that this was what the world beyond Ynys Wydryn had become. The monk shook his head in despair but did not, I noticed, make the sign of the Thorn. 'We keep going,' Gawain said, and so we did.

And there were other sights which soured my stomach and my soul. Other horrors which could not be unseen, and which haunted my sleep. The charred remains of a roundhouse, glistening in the rain yet still smouldering, and inside, a family of five, lying in their beds, their blackened bodies twisted by the flames. A white mare cropping the grass, though her guts had spilled from a savage wound, trailing ten feet behind her like a knotty purple rope and upon which a scrawny dog was feasting, growling with satisfaction. An old man's head mounted on a spear, his white hair wisping in the breeze like bramble-caught wool. A brook dammed with the dead, the water rising against that grim rampart and flooding the banks. We heard wolves howling in the night and sometimes saw them at dusk and dawn, drawn down from the hills and forests by the bounty of flesh. We saw rooks and crows and ravens clouding above settlements whose gates would not normally have been open, and almost every breath that we took was tainted with smoke.

I saw a fox digging an infant from its shallow grave. The fox was so brazen, so emboldened by the prospect of its meal, that it did not run off at our approach but kept pulling until that lost child was brought back into the light. Then, seizing a stubby arm between its teeth as though it were a chicken leg, the fox made off, dragging the little corpse with it.

We saw what Britain had become. And sometimes we wept. And I looked at Gediens and Gawain, at those two old warriors who had fought but failed to hold back the Saxons, just as that dam of corpses would eventually fail to hold the brook, and I wondered where they found the strength to endure, to keep fighting when all was lost. I pitied them for all that they had lost themselves, the years and the friends and the hopes, but I admired them too. More than that, I began to be aware of something besetting my conscience, gnawing at it like a rat's teeth. Not all the time. Often, I was too tired from walking, or too wet, or too cold to think about anything other than the fire at the end of the day and the hot food I would eat. But sometimes, especially when I lay in my furs and skins either in the shelter of the woods or in some abandoned roundhouse, I would feel those rodent-like teeth worrying away, laying bare a shame which I had never admitted to myself. That I had spent the last ten years in prayer and relative safety. That I had been warm and well fed and had hidden away in the monastery on Ynys Wydryn while Britain burned and terror stalked the land.

8

Tintagel

W E CAME TO TINTAGEL under a full moon. The same full moon under which I would have taken my vows as Father Brice gave me the tonsure. I would have looked up to that moon no longer a novice but a full Brother of the Holy Thorn. Father Meurig would have prepared a celebratory feast of swine flesh and hot bread and Father Judoc would have passed around a skin of his best apple wine and no doubt Father Dristan would have danced about like a fool until he spewed and fell into the sleep of the dead, long before even old Father Padern took to his bed. It would have been a celebration and I would have been one of them, my life given to prayer for the preservation of all believers and of the tree which stood on that lonely, wind-scoured hill.

Instead, I was a leaf blown from a felled tree. Carried on a wind which had been blowing long before my birth. There was no monastery now and only one Brother of the Thorn and that was Father Yvain, not me. I was neither monk nor warrior. I was no one. And yet I found myself standing on a gust-harried ridge under a full moon, the sigh of the sea and its crashing against the rocks loud in the night as I stared out towards the great peninsular fortress which was famed throughout these Dark Isles.

That moon's silver spilled across the dark sea to light a trading ship which sat tugging at its anchor, and the breakers which galloped to the shore. It flooded across Tintagel's heights, revealing more than a hundred buildings from whose windows or doors yellow firelight leaked on a murmur of distant voices. And I tried to imagine Parcefal watching the night even now from the shelter of the sea cave at the foot of the cliffs, where his messenger had told Gawain that he and the druid would be waiting.

'Have you ever seen such a place, Galahad?' Iselle asked me. Like me, she was staring across the water, her eyes reflecting the lustre of the silvered sea below.

'Never,' I replied, trying to imagine what it must be like to live on that clifftop. I thought of the hives which the brothers had kept near the apple orchards on Ynys Wydryn and how the bees would cluster, one upon another, thick as a blanket. That was what Tintagel must be like, it seemed to me.

'I would rather sleep here.' Iselle pointed her bow at a patch of tall grass which shivered in the breeze.

'We may have to,' I said, for between us on the mainland and the narrow land bridge leading to the exposed cliff-girt headland was a clutter of buildings, amongst which warriors stood warming themselves around flaming braziers. We had already seen those spearmen turn people away, for it seemed no one was allowed to cross into the fort at night, and several tents huddled in the lee of the ridge near where we stood, canvas thumping in the wind. Gawain and Gediens had been talking with some of those men for a while and now they were walking towards us, their helmets and scale armour burnished by the low moon at our backs.

'We're in.' Gawain picked up his knapsack and threw it over his shoulder, and I looked at Iselle and nodded, trying to reassure her. A crease between her dark eyebrows, she nodded back, picking up her own gear and looking across at the settlement where King Uther's hall still stood. My own blood pounded in my veins at the prospect of being in Tintagel, where lords and kings of Britain had ruled, where High King Uther Pendragon had sat like an eagle on its eyrie. And where my father had spent time as a young man. But I knew that Iselle hated the thought of being there. I had seen her kill men with her bow and rob their corpses and show no fear while doing it. But now she was chewing her lip and running her thumb up and down her bow's grip, digging a thumbnail into the leather binding, because she had lived a more solitary life even than I, and the thought of being among all those people filled her with dread.

We did not ask how Gawain had won over the guards so that we could cross into Tintagel that night, but the way the two spearmen who led us over that crumbling isthmus eyed him told me that they held him in awe. They seemed to know Lord Gawain by name and reputation. Knew that he was a lord of war, a man who had fought at Arthur's side and sent countless enemies shrieking to the afterlife. They respected and perhaps feared him too, for he carried the bear-shield, which showed that he was still waging Arthur's war while most other men, including kings, looked only to their own interests, fought only for their own survival, like rats defending their nests, and had no higher ambitions. They looked at Gawain and saw a man who believed in the idea of Britain, and it scared them, for perhaps they imagined that Gawain would bring war to this south-west corner of the land, this sea-fretted rock, and they might have to sharpen their spears and swords and fight for something greater than themselves.

Once we were on the other side, our escort announced Prince Gawain of Lyonesse and Lord Gediens of Glywyssing to the spearmen above the gatehouse, who leant out over the bulwark to get a better look, the whites of their eyes shining in the moonlight. The next thing we knew, the gates were pulled open and we were inside the fort, traipsing through the same mud which had sullied the great Uther Pendragon's boots. The same ground which had trembled beneath the hooves of Lord Arthur's war horses.

'Met your father for the first time here, Galahad,' Gawain said, as we followed the track which led up to the plateau. I felt the familiar knot draw tight in my guts as it did whenever Gawain brought up my father. 'On the day Uther's balefire lit the world.' He pointed off beyond a clutter of buildings on our right. 'Somewhere over there, I think. Hard to say in the dark. And there's more here now.' As he walked, he lifted his spear high. 'Biggest flames I've ever seen. Loud as a storm.' He shook his head, as if dazzled even by the memory of it. 'They must have seen that fire from Dyfed.' Despite that knot in my stomach, I wanted to hear more about how he had met my father. Still, I would not say as much, and I waited while Gawain sifted through his own mind. 'He was already under Arthur's spell by then. Of course, the mead helped.' A rare grin spread across his lips.

'Mead always helps,' Father Yvain put in. Gediens murmured agreement.

'He must have been your age,' Gawain said and grunted as though this realization meant something. 'You see, Merlin had tricked Lancelot into swearing an oath to serve Arthur.' He looked round at me. 'Did you know that?'

'No,' I said.

'Well, that's Merlin for you.' Gawain shared a knowing look with Father Yvain, who lifted an eyebrow. 'Lancelot swore an oath to protect the next king of Dumnonia.'

'But Arthur was never king,' Iselle put in.

'No, he wasn't,' Gawain admitted. 'But everyone thought he would be. Including Lancelot. In the end it didn't matter anyway because Lancelot and Arthur became as brothers. And once Lancelot had decided on a thing, the gods help the fool who tried to get in his way.' The door of a nearby roundhouse thumped open and a man staggered out, spewing the contents of his stomach into the mud. 'Lancelot saved Arthur's life the very next day, when Constantine betrayed us.'

'I wasn't there, but I heard soon enough,' Father Yvain said. 'Everyone in Dumnonia heard how Constantine made a play for Uther's high seat and murdered Arthur's men in the dawn.'

Gawain cursed. 'As they blinked the sleep from their eyes.' He shook his head as if even now he could not quite believe it had happened. 'I lost friends that morning. Good men. Good horses too.' He was eyeing each building that we passed – the roundhouses and workshops, the stables, granaries, smokehouses, byres, animal pens – and the cobweb of tracks which ran through the settlement, as though he was measuring this Tintagel against the one he had known. 'And Arthur would have died too if not for Lancelot,' he said. 'But Lancelot had sworn to protect him and, as I say, once your father set his mind on something . . .' He did not need to finish.

As we walked on, a knot of children in the shadow of a kilnhouse, who were passing round a wine skin between them, saw us. Or rather, they saw Gawain and Gediens in their scale coats and helmets, their shields slung across their backs. They ran over to us, four boys and three girls, and began dancing around the two warriors like moths around a pair of firebrands.

'Who are you, lords?' the gang's leader asked, a predatory grin on his face. Thickset, fair-haired and no older than thirteen, he trod a fine line between respectfulness and disdain, yet he offered the wine skin to Gawain, who did not break stride and only barely acknowledged the boy. 'Whatever you're looking for, I'm your man,' the boy continued undeterred, keeping pace with us, walking backwards through the mud. 'Wine, ale, women. Boys.' He threw his arms wide. 'I can get you anything. Honoured to help fine lords such as yourselves.'

'The ale house still behind Uther's hall?' Gawain asked.

The boy frowned. 'Uther?' He glanced at one of his companions, a copper-haired boy who shrugged, grinning like a fiend as he capered alongside Gediens. 'You mean Lord Geldrin's hall.'

'He's a Christus man, a priest,' a girl squawked, pointing at me. Her face was covered in sore-looking pustules and her eyes were wide and appalled as she ran them up and down my habit, which, being of undyed wool, was a dingy white but looked bright under that moonlight. I supposed she had not noticed Father Yvain, who was actually a monk, because of his warrior's build, the spear in his hand and the bear skin he wore over his own robes.

The girl spat at me. 'We don't want your kind here.'

'He's no priest,' a tall, whip-thin boy with a mass of dark curls said. 'His head is not shaved.'

'And anyway, the Christians are rich, my father says,' another girl told the one with the weeping pimples.

'Only the Greek ones,' the tall boy said as we walked alongside stables from which now and then came the soft nickers and snorts of contented horses, 'and they're a different sort of Christian.'

'I'm the sort of Christian who can turn you into a toad,' I said, at which most of them laughed and whooped excitedly, though the girl with the pustules looked horrified.

Father Yvain and Iselle seemed amused by the attention I was receiving, but then another girl asked Iselle was she a warrior and had she ever killed a man, and would she consider selling the fine-looking sword on her back because the girl knew a merchant who would buy it off her at a good price. Now it was my turn to grin at her, though as we rounded the stables, the sight of the great hall looming before us stopped us in our tracks. That gaggle of crowing youngsters might as well have dissipated like the smoke which drifted on the night air.

'It's been a long time,' Gawain said. Even he had stopped to look, though whereas Iselle and I stared in awe and wonder, it seemed to me that Gawain was held to the spot by the ghostly bonds of memory.

Gediens put his spear across his shoulders and hooked his arms over the stave. 'A lifetime.'

The hall was huge, by far the largest building I had ever seen, and the moon rising above its eastern eaves illuminated a sloping roof of new golden thatch. By the fitful light thrown from a nearby brazier I could just make out some words painted on a great wooden lintel above the entrance. The red paint was faded, weathered almost away, but the ghost of the words lingered still. *A fronte praecipitium a tergo lupi.*

'First time I laid eyes on this place, I was a beardless spearman,' Gediens mused. 'Nearly pissed my trews when I heard King Uther spitting fury at a groom who had saddled his stallion when he'd wanted his white mare.'

A muffled grunt escaped Gawain's throat. 'Sounds like Uther.'

I could not help but wonder how my father must have felt on that summer day when he had met Uther Pendragon as the king lay on his deathbed.

But there was no king at Tintagel these days.

'You'll have to pay your respects to Lord Geldrin tomorrow,' the thickset, fair-haired boy told Gawain. 'My uncle knows him. I can have him put in a good word for you, lord. Who shall I say has come to Tintagel?'

'We'll be gone tomorrow, so there's no need to trouble Lord Geldrin,' Gawain said. 'But tell me, who is the man to speak with if we're looking to buy horses?'

The boy thought about this, he and his curly-haired friend tossing names back and forth. Eventually they agreed that the man Gawain wanted was a hump-backed trader named Lidas.

'Then we will speak with this Lidas and perhaps do business. After that, we will be gone.' Gawain took a coin from the purse on his belt and gave it to the boy, who nodded, understanding the bargain that had been struck with that small silver disc. He would say nothing to this uncle of his who knew the Lord of Tintagel. Then, because folk needed Lord Geldrin's permission to use the sea steps leading down to the beach after sunset, and we preferring that the Lord of the Heights not know of our presence there, Father Yvain asked the boy where we could find the ale house.

'The other side of the pigs.' The boy pointed beyond the pen, where a group of men and women were arguing or making merry – it was hard to tell. And so Merlin and Parcefal would have to wait until morning.

Yvain thanked the boy and we set off across the slippery timber walkway which led to warmth, hot food, spiced ale and mead, and sore heads.

The noise inside the ale house was the roar of the ocean hurling itself in white fury upon the rocks. It was the seething din in the heart of a great fire. Or the storm wind in the trees. Too much for me, who had lived a hermit's life in the forest and, after that, the quiet existence of a monk of the Thorn on a fog-veiled island in the marshes.

'I can't stay in here,' I told Father Yvain, who just grinned and put a cup of something in my hand. Iselle was already drinking. Though only a quarter of the size of King Uther's old hall, the ale house was choked with folk and hazed with smoke from a central hearth and myriad greasy-flamed oil lamps. I had never seen so many people in one place and the stink of sweat and damp wool, ale breath, foul wind and burning fish oil was enough to bring bile into my throat and tears to my eyes.

'You get used to it,' Gawain told me, smiling at how I sat with my knuckles pressed to my nose.

'The more you drink, the better the stink.' Gediens banged his cup against Father Yvain's. The two of them downed a great wash of ale and slammed their cups onto the table in unison, grinning like a pair of mischievous boys.

To our surprise, there had been no slaves or grooms positioned outside to look after men's blades and war gear while they drank – as was customary to lessen the occasions of blood and ale flowing together when wits drowned and anger surfaced – so the place heaved with armed men, warriors with swords at their hips or on their backs. Men with knives in their belts, their spears leaning against the walls. Some even wore mail shirts; visitors to Tintagel perhaps, who were reluctant to take their eyes off their war gear in a place of strangers. None, though, wore scale armour, which made Gawain and Gediens more conspicuous than they would have liked, though the arrival of two hoary lords of war did persuade revellers to move along the benches and make room for us, which they might not have done otherwise.

'Look at them,' Iselle hissed, lips curling behind her cup as she ran her eyes across those thronging the room. Men bellowed and women cackled, and all were away on a sea of strong drink, slurring their speech, stumbling when they stood, voices fighting against the clamour and by doing so only raising it. 'Do they know what's happening out there?' Iselle asked me. 'The Saxons rape and burn and kill. Britain tears itself apart.' With her cup she gestured at a man and woman across the table who were entwined in each other like the roots of some tree.

'They are free, and the Saxons are far away,' I said, my face flushing as I shifted on the bench, trying to turn my shoulder so that the amorous couple would no longer be in my line of sight.

'Well, they are fools if they think they're safe,' Iselle spat. 'Just as the monks on Ynys Wydryn were fools believing that the Saxons would leave them alone.' She scowled, and I mused, not for the first time, on what a fierce creature she was. Quite unlike any woman I had ever known. Not that I had known many women, other than the nuns who now and again had visited our monastery. Iselle traced a finger over a dark knot in the cup's grain. 'Just as I was a fool to think the marsh and the mists would protect us,' she said.

Gawain, Gediens and Father Yvain were talking amongst themselves, mired in shared memories, but I saw the anger in Iselle, could almost hear it simmering beneath her skin despite the drone of all those voices.

'There was nothing you could have done to save Alana,' I told her.

She shook her head. 'I should have been there, instead of being on Ynys Wydryn. I would have killed those men and Alana would be alive.'

Perhaps that was true. But it was more likely that Iselle would have been dead too, and that, I realized, was an unbearable thought. I felt my face flush hot and so I turned to watch a man who was sharing his food with the greying dog sitting patiently beside him. The old dog was so careful in taking the meat scraps from the man's hand.

'So, I am a coward because I fled Ynys Wydryn and left my brothers to die,' I said, 'and you are a fool because you helped me in the marsh. Because you came to the island when you should have been with your foster mother on the day the Saxons burned your home.'

I looked at her again. She thought about what I had said and did not gainsay any of it. And then I said something which would have had Father Brice tearing at his burial shroud, had he been afforded one.

'Perhaps the gods of this land have not given up and turned their backs on us completely,' I suggested. The words had seemed to come from someone else. Guilt twisted like a blade inside me and I tried not to think of what the brothers would say, as I leant forward so that my next words would not be overheard. 'If Gawain, you and Gediens take Merlin back, and if Arthur rises again, then maybe there *is* a chance for Britain.'

I could see that Iselle was as surprised as I was to hear those words from me. 'You're saying the gods have a hand in all this?' she asked.

I shrugged. 'We cannot say that they don't.'

She thought about that. 'Then you are as much a part of it as I, else you would be dead in the marsh. Or dead on that hillside below the tor.' She drank and dragged the back of her hand across her lips, and I just stared because I had never seen anyone like her.

'I'm beginning to think that you would not have made a good monk of the Christ god.'

The barb in that stung me, but I said nothing. In truth I did not know what I believed. I doubted now that the Christian god, the god of Joseph of Arimathea, cared about the fate of

Britain or the lives of those who prayed in His name. The seed of that doubt had been watered by the blood of my brothers. Nor did I carry in my heart the same embers of hope that glowed in Iselle's heart, that the old gods of Britain would awaken to our need and inspire great armies of spearmen and victories the likes of which the people had not known since Arthur led the fight.

What I believed was that I had abandoned my brothers on Ynys Wydryn, just as my father had abandoned me. And I had failed to carry the Thorn to safety. And maybe Alana would still be alive if Iselle had not helped me to carry the corpse of Eudaf the cobbler back to the monastery.

The ale was strong. I could already feel it warming my insides and blunting my wits. And I was glad of it because I did not want to think any more.

'Take it steady, Galahad,' Father Yvain warned me even as he filled my cup. 'This stuff has a kick like a donkey, and I don't want to be carrying you to your bed.'

Iselle lifted an eyebrow at me. A challenge.

Gediens grinned. 'Galahad's not in some monastery of the White Christ now, Yvain.' He palmed ale from his beard and gestured at the revellers around us. 'He's at Tintagel. Let him enjoy himself.'

Father Yvain grunted, not disagreeing, his attention turning to a woman with long, golden hair and hips as broad as the ship I had seen in Tintagel bay. And I drank long and deeply to show the monk and Iselle too that I did not need looking after.

'Dumnonia needs a king,' Gawain said into his cup.

'Constantine calls himself king,' Gediens said.

Gawain snorted. 'Constantine can call himself the Emperor of Rome as his grandfather did. Doesn't make it true.'

I remembered a day not long after I had come to Ynys

Wydryn, when Father Yvain had returned from one of his trips across the lake with news that Lord Constantine had proclaimed himself king in Dumnonia. I knew that Constantine's father, Ambrosius Aurelius, had been High King of Britain for ten years before he was assassinated and Uther assumed the throne in his brother's place. On his deathbed, Uther had named his own son, Arthur, as heir, and Arthur had fought long and hard, though he had never been king.

'Arthur bought us peace. A peace of sorts, anyway. Your father too,' Yvain had told me, when I had sought him out in his workshop that night to ask him more. 'It was his final act as protector of Britain.' Yvain's brows had gathered. 'Well, you know that better than most, lad.'

I'd nodded, remembering that red day when I had seen things which a boy should never see. The Saxons, being too weak to press on, retreated east to lick their wounds and raise more spears and, in that respite, the noble blood in Lord Constantine's veins had whispered to him of his old ambitions. As the lady's smock rose on that field the next spring, their stems strengthened with the blood of the slain, Constantine rose with them, proclaiming his right to sit on Uther's old high seat here at Tintagel.

These days, King Constantine's high seat was a tree stump in some forest in Caer Lerion, so said Gawain, though he admitted that Constantine yet harried the Saxons with the last of his loyal spearmen.

'We need a king here,' Gawain said now, looking from Father Yvain to me. 'There is no stronger fortress in all Britain. Men and supplies can come by boat and a thousand Saxons could do nothing about it.' He shook his head, drank again and put his cup down on the stained table. 'This is where we should start. When we're ready.'

'What about Camelot?' Father Yvain asked.

Gawain nodded at Gediens, inviting him to answer Yvain's question. 'Too close to King Cerdic's army,' Gediens replied, 'and anyway, we cannot be sure that the Lady Morgana will help us.' He leant forward and lowered his voice. 'Not when she learns about Arthur,' he said. 'The lady is like a spider at the centre of Dumnonia, guarding her web. I don't think she would welcome us.'

'I hear she has never let King Constantine through the gates,' Gawain said, a measure of scorn in the word *king*. 'No, this is where we should raise the banner.' He pressed his finger down onto the table. 'Here. At Tintagel.'

Maybe it was the drink in him talking, but it seemed to me that in that moment Gawain allowed himself to do more than hope. His eyes had sharpened as though fixed on some sight which only he could see. A vision of Arthur's bear banner flapping in the gusts atop that cliff-walled peninsular fortress. Perhaps, rather than the revellers in that stinking, din-filled place, Gawain saw a glimpse of spearmen carrying bear-shields beneath summer skies. Warriors marching to the shrill call of the war horn. Brave sons of Dumnonia and Cornubia, Caer Celemion and Caer Gloui, making a slaughter's dew with Saxon blood. Gawain believed in it. Truly believed, and he sat back on his stool to indulge the vision in peace, as Gediens and Father Yvain argued about whether to stick with the ale or buy a jug of Greek wine.

When I looked around that room, I saw drunks and fat merchants and fugitives who cared only about the skin on their backs and the wine skin in their hands. I saw folk huddled over gaming boards, winning and losing the rings on their fingers and the brooches on their cloaks. I saw couples writhing in the dark corners, needful as beasts. Men and women living for whatever pleasures they could find on this wind-whipped and sea-fretted rock on the south-west edge of the Dark Isles.

A fronte praecipitium a tergo lupi were the words I had read, painted in faded Roman script above the door of Uther's old hall. *A precipice in front, wolves behind.* It seemed to me that those words were no less true now than they were in Uther's day, when my father had walked beneath that sign into the king's hall. Only, back then we had Arthur.

And yet, perhaps Gawain *had* caught a glimpse of the future, I thought later, as the room began to spin around me and Father Yvain bought two trenchers of roast pork and fresh bread, telling me I needed to eat well to soak up the ale in my stomach. Perhaps Arthur would take up his sword and shield and become the Lord of Battles once again.

But there could be no Arthur without Merlin, and so in the morning we would find the druid and take him back.

A precipice in front, wolves behind.

I woke with a sour stomach and a head like the anvil beneath the smith's hammer. Iselle didn't fare much better by the looks of her. She sat scowling in the straw of the stables where Gawain had bought us a place to sleep, her face ashen and her mouth set as tight as a drum skin, as if she were clenching down on all the ale and wine to keep it from rising back up and out. In the corner of the stall, the old mare with whom we had passed the night emptied her bowels, the manure balls followed by a stream of stinking urine.

I sat up, a wave of dizziness flooding me, and through bleary eyes I saw Gediens standing with both arms stretched above his head as he let his scale armour coat fall over him, then shrugged and jumped to help the weight of it settle. I had slept on a bed of fresh straw in just my under-tunic, my cloak laid over me like a blanket, and now I felt awkward in front of Iselle. Not that she seemed in the least interested in my state of undress.

'I thought monks were good drinkers,' Gediens said, a grin on the face that appeared through the neck hole. 'I was mistaken.'

Father Yvain took my habit from the nail on which it hung. 'Galahad is a slow learner.' He threw it at me. I fumbled with the gown, which stank of ale and smoke from the previous night. The smell of it put a lump in my throat but I swallowed it down. 'You wouldn't believe how long it took him to learn how to turn a simple bowl on my lathe,' the monk went on, shaking his head at the memory. 'And even then, it wasn't fit for pissing in.' He chuckled, at which the old mare nickered as though sharing the joke. 'He tried, though. I can't deny that.'

I stood and threw the gown on, as Gediens had done with his armour, and swallowed again. 'Maybe if I'd had a better teacher,' I said, at which the monk dipped his head and raised his hand in acknowledgement of a good counter-stroke.

I drew the belt tight at my waist, the rough wool of the habit chafing my neck and wrists, reminding me of long nights kneeling in prayer with my brothers. Had I truly just spent the night carousing while they lay dead and unburied on Ynys Wydryn? I saw Father Brice's face as he yelled at me to leave, to go or be damned. *Remember us, Galahad*, he had called after me, those words now a dull echo in my head, pulsing with the blood in my ears.

'If you're going to spew, best you do it outside, lad,' Gediens said.

Dizziness welled inside me and I glanced around for a jug of weak beer. Or better still, clean water, my mouth being dry and my tongue feeling like a sliver of old leather. Worse than that, worse even than the dawn sunlight spearing through a stall window into my eyes, were the grins on Gediens and Father Yvain's faces.

Gediens turned to Iselle, who was gathering her hair to braid it behind her head. 'Where are my manners? Good morning, my lady.' He gave an elaborate bow. 'I trust you are feeling better than Galahad this morning?'

The look Iselle gave him was as sharp as claws, but before she could unfasten her lips, Gawain appeared at the door.

'A caravan of slave traders from Caer Gloui has crossed the land bridge,' he told us, taking up his spear and shield. His cheeks and nose were red with the cold that he brought with him into the stable. 'Seems half of Tintagel is swarming to get an eyeful, and the other half is sleeping off last night's ale, which means now is a good time to get down to the cove.'

Iselle and I caught each other's eye, Gawain's words clearing our drink-addled heads like an icy breeze through a smoky hall. We both felt the weight of what we were about to do. For Merlin, the last of the druids, was here at Tintagel, hiding in the sea cave below the cliffs. The man who had advised Uther and Arthur, who communed with the gods of Britain and who heard the whispers of the dead, had been found after ten years of Arthur's loyal men searching for him. And now we would come face to face with him and take him east, to Arthur.

'You found the hunchback Lidas?' Gediens asked Gawain.

Gawain nodded, a steam-like fog rising from his mailed shoulders. 'The price was steep, but the man knows horses. He'll have them saddled and waiting at the gates at noon.'

Gediens nodded. 'Good.'

Gawain looked at Father Yvain, who was testing the edge of his spear blade against his thumbnail. Their eyes met and the monk nodded, his previous good humour gone now. In its place was an air of quiet resolve, a determination to do what must be done, and though he wore a habit like my own, and a bear skin over it rather than the scale armour coats which Gawain and Gediens boasted, Yvain looked no less a warrior than they. In a handful of late winter days, ten years on Ynys Wydryn seemed to have fallen away from him like snow stamped off a boot.

'Are you ready, Galahad?' he asked, his breath clouding in the chill dawn air by the stable's open door.

I nodded. Still I did not see what my part was in any of this, and yet I cannot deny that I felt a thrill of anticipation, a shiver of nerves at the thought of meeting Merlin. So too did Iselle, I knew, though she said nothing of it as she quietly strung her bow, her face showing no strain as she bent the yew stave against her foot. Whispers of Merlin had fluttered across the Dark Isles on the breeze since we were both children, and Iselle was as taut as that bow string at the prospect of rumour made flesh.

We walked out into the dawn and I filled my lungs with fresh sea air only a little sullied by hearth smoke. A gust blew across Tintagel's heights, cutting through my robes and making me shudder as I watched a cormorant skimming beneath a swathe of sullen cloud. Silent and black as a shadow it beat westward, like night itself retreating before the dawn.

'A warning.' Gawain stopped midstride and turned to face us as he slung his shield over his back. 'Merlin was ever a disagreeable shit. I never much liked him, and that was then, when Arthur believed in him.' His lip curled. 'Before he slunk off like a weasel to . . . the gods alone know where. But he should've been there with us that day Mordred betrayed Arthur. Betrayed Britain.' He pulled the shield's carrying strap and shrugged his broad shoulders until it was comfortable. 'He'll be old now. Old and bitter, likely as not. But he's still a druid and in my experience only a fool trusts a druid.' He raised an eyebrow at Father Yvain. 'I'll wager by now Parcefal is wishing he'd sewn the old goat's lips together.'

The monk scratched amongst his coarse beard and grimaced. 'Parcefal never lacked courage,' he said, 'but he was never short of wits either. A druid is a druid.'

Gawain hoomed deep in his throat but did not disagree, and with that he turned around and we set off after him across the muddy ground between the swine pens and byres, the stables, workshops, forges and roundhouses which crowded Tintagel.

There were few people about. Some traders setting up. A brace of children out fetching water, a filthy hound trailing at their heels. A man beneath the eaves of Uther's old hall, bent over and coughing his lungs into the sludge. The wintry sun was breaking over the plateau, throwing long shadows in which the sea wind seemed to gather, rippling the puddles. I shivered again and clutched the wool at my neck to keep out the cold.

And we went to find Merlin.

At first, I thought that we walked through a sea mist, but Gediens told me that it was, in fact, low cloud, rolling across the wind-whipped heights and shredding itself upon the bluffs and crags. Gulls whirred around us in that damp fog, shrieking like tormented wraiths, in and out of our sight from one heart-beat to the next as we made our way to the north-east side of the peninsula. Here, the sound of the surf rose on the gusts which snatched at my robes and whipped my hair, and we came to the ironclad gate through which passed the treasures of the world: olives and oil, walnuts, honey, spices, silks, glass-ware, pottery and wine, all brought here on ships which sailed away from these shores laden with gold and tin.

Father Yvain had to thump his spear against the gatehouse

to wake the guards, while the rest of us shuffled side to side in the damp chill. Iselle was suggesting we go around the gate and scramble down the rocks, when the door clunked open and a guard emerged, bleary-eyed and resentful, squinting into the pale morning as he fastened his cloak with an iron pin brooch.

'You blind? It's low tide,' he called, throwing an arm towards the cliff edge and yawning, his clouding breath smelling of ale and garlic. 'No boat'll be beaching till after noon.' The words were barely out of his mouth when his drink-blurred gaze slipped off Father Yvain and caught on Gawain. His eyes widened and his mouth closed.

'Open the gate,' Gawain demanded.

The guard was not much older than I. Too young, I thought, to recognize Gawain, who had not been to Tintagel in years. But not too young to recognize a lord of battle.

'Of course. Course, lord,' the man mumbled, turning to join another guard who had stumbled out of the little house and was already in place to draw the beam from the gate lock. Then we were through and out onto the worn path which ran alongside the palisade and down towards the stairway carved long ago into the rock.

Out in the bay, the ship which we had seen the previous night lay at anchor still, swaying on the swell, her crew too distant for me to see whether they had the dark complexions of Greeks from the shores of what the Romans called *Mare Nostrum*, 'Our Sea'.

'Watch your footing,' Gawain called over his shoulder, for the steps were slick and treacherous and the wind was beating up at us in salty gusts.

I looked down on the circling gulls and the ebbing tide which had left a dark stain on the sand and shingle, and I saw the cave's gaping mouth at the foot of the cliff. I was struck by the thought that Merlin might take one look at my robes and hate me, if not worse. It was said that with just a few words he could cast maggots into a man's guts. That he could shrivel an enemy's manhood with a muttering and fluttering of fingers. And, like others in Britain who sought the return of the old gods, wasn't it likely that the druid would resent Father Yvain and me as followers of Christ?

I heard Gediens tell Gawain that he would have expected Parcefal to be keeping watch at the mouth of the cave, but we could not see anyone waiting in the shadow as we stepped onto the beach, the gulls crying above us, the rolling breakers breathing and sighing a hundred paces off.

'Something feels wrong,' Iselle told me, drawing an arrow from the bag on her belt, and then we were inside the cave, the wet rock glistening and the sound of the sea distant and muted.

'Parcefal,' Gawain called into the gloom, his voice swimming around the cavernous space. Daylight leaked in through a hole up ahead, some hundred paces from where we stood, showing us that the cave stretched all the way through the headland.

'Up there.' I pointed at a ledge high up beyond the tideline. 'There's something there.'

Gawain nodded. 'Up you go.' And so I hitched up the hem of my habit and climbed, pulling myself onto that shelf of rock with a sense of relief because there was no legendary druid waiting there to curse me or cut my throat.

'Just this,' I said, lifting up the sack which I found leaning against the rock wall, and the top of which I had seen from below. Other than the charred remains of a fire, an iron pot and some knuckles of animal bone – no doubt the remains of a meal – there was nothing else on that ledge to indicate that Merlin and Parcefal were still around, if they had been there at all.

'Nothing,' Gediens called from deeper within the cave. He was working his way back to us, using his spear as a staff to help him across the wet rocks.

I clambered down with the sack to join the others, then drew it open. For a moment I did not know what I was looking at. Shadow in shadow. I leant it towards the cave's mouth and the daylight glossed the blackness within. A whisper of purple. A ghost of green. I put my hand inside.

'Feathers,' I said.

'A druid's cloak,' Father Yvain growled.

Gawain nodded. 'Best leave that be,' he said and so I did, gladly pulling the drawstring to return Merlin's possessions to darkness. 'But don't lose it,' Gawain warned.

'This is blood,' Iselle said, crouching near the cave's entrance.

We gathered around her and we knew she was right. It was not much, just a dark scarlet slick in the sand and shingle, but even in the shadows she had seen it.

'Whatever happened here happened as the sun came up,' Gawain said, 'else the tide would've washed it away.' With that he straightened and walked back outside.

I offered him Merlin's sack, but he curled his lip. 'You hold on to that, Galahad.' He was staring towards the ship anchored out in the bay.

I offered the sack to Gediens, but he raised a hand and shook his head, and I grimaced with the knowledge that I would have to be responsible for the thing. It seemed to me a strange twist of fate that I had lost the cutting of the Holy Thorn and gained a druid's raven-feathered cloak, and whatever else Merlin might keep in that sack.

'What now?' Gediens asked.

Gawain turned away from the sea and strode back up the beach towards the stone stairway.

'We ask questions,' he called over his shoulder.

Two spearmen were tramping down those steps to begin their sentry duty should any boats come in on the next high tide. As they came onto the shingle and we passed them, they frowned at us, no doubt wondering what we were doing down there, but too lazy or uninterested to ask.

'Things have changed here,' Gediens muttered, not for the first time since we had arrived at Tintagel.

'Things have changed everywhere,' Gawain said, his boots scuffing on the wet rock, his bear-shield bouncing against his back.

I followed that bear up the worn stairway, the black-feathered cloak whispering to me from the sack in my hand. And what it whispered of was blood.

9

Lord of the Heights

W E MET WITH THE hunchback Lidas as arranged and stabled the horses where we had slept the previous night. The owner, a short, bald man named Brycham, agreed to let us stay there again, though he seemed surprised that Gawain and Gediens would choose such humble lodgings.

'Lord Geldrin would surely host men such as yourselves in his own hall.' Brycham frowned and scratched at an old sore on his neck. 'No need for you to bed down with the beasts.' His eyes flicked to Iselle, to the Saxon sword on her back, the knives in her belt and the bow in her hand, then back to Gawain. Chances were, he knew who was renting his stables. Word of Lord Arthur's bear-shields being at Tintagel would by now have hopped from lip to ear like fleas from dog to dog, but however much he ached to ask us our business, a stronger instinct told Brycham to mind his own.

'Fresh straw and a roof over our heads are all we need,' Gawain told him. 'Though I shall be grateful if you would feed the horses with the best grain you have,' he said, giving Brycham a coin, which vanished into the man's purse.

'The same barley that makes Lord Geldrin's bread,' the little man replied, dipping his head and raising his hand. 'I'll roll it myself.'

With the horses in good hands, we bought some bread and cheese and salted fish and returned to the ale house, where we hoped to discover something which might help us find Parcefal and his charge.

'We start asking questions and every man and his dog on this rock will know who you are,' Father Yvain warned Gawain, as we stood for a moment eating and watching a dozen slaves being led towards Uther's old hall by a knot of lean, grizzled spearmen. Seven of the slaves were fair-haired Saxons and from the looks of them they had been beaten half to death. Who could say where the other poor creatures were from? Gediens said they had the fierce, proud look of Gaels. Or perhaps they were men of Cambria. Raiders whose arms had driven their boats on to Dumnonian shores, but who would never again cross the Hafren and return to their kin.

Father Yvain tore a hunk of bread from a loaf which he then passed to me. 'Next thing you know,' he said through a mouthful, 'we'll be hauled in front of this Lord Geldrin, who'll be wanting to know why Gawain, son of King Lot of Lyonesse, and the great Arthur ap Uther's right hand, is skulking around his fort unannounced.'

Iselle glared at the Saxons with hate-filled eyes and I knew she wanted nothing more than to sink arrows into their flesh or cut their throats with her long knife. But it seemed this Lord Geldrin would have the first opportunity to view the slaver's stock before those broken, beaten men were driven to the block and sold on the open market. They waited, wretched and miserable, as a steward went inside the hall to announce the traders to his lord.

'We were supposed to be on our way by now,' Gediens said, burying a lump of cheese in a piece of bread and pushing the whole lot into his mouth.

'But we're not,' Gawain said. 'And the chances are every man and his dog on this rock already know we're here.' He looked at Father Yvain. 'Still, we came for Merlin and we're not leaving without him.'

One of the slaves, a scrawny, sallow-skinned man, did or said something which earned him four lashes of his master's hazel switch. He tried in vain to fend off the blows, crying out in pain, and I thought of the whipping I had received at the hands of Father Judoc for going into the marsh without the brothers' permission. After turning away to growl at another man, the slaver spun back to the sickly-looking slave and struck him twice more for good measure.

I shuddered. Was Father Judoc sitting in heaven at Saint Joseph's right hand? Were the Brothers of the Thorn watching me through the veil which hangs between this world and the world beyond? Were they judging my worthiness to have survived, to live and breathe when they did not?

'I want to know whose ship that is in the bay,' Gawain said, 'and whose blood is in the sand.' We nodded, all of us agreed that knowing the answers to those questions was worth the risk of folk learning that Gawain of Lyonesse, once one of Arthur's famed horse lords, had come to Tintagel. And so we sought those answers in the ale house, which to my surprise was just as thronged with beer- and wine-soaked men and women as it had been the previous evening. The clamour filled my head again, a rushing, dizzying noise flooding in where for years there had been only prayer and the devotions and the low murmur of the brothers' voices.

And the stink of that place, of all those people crammed so close that the lice could jump from one to another, of sweat and vomit and piss. Of stale beer and last night's meat dishes and the mouldering thatch above our heads. And of the memory of all that drink which I had poured down my gullet the previous evening. It brought the gorge up my throat and so I picked the least muddied piece from the hay strewn across the floor and held it to my nose, rolling it between finger and thumb to free the scent of a summer long gone.

'No more than two drinks, Galahad,' Gawain warned, though he needn't have, for I could not stomach the thought of drinking anything other than the weakest ale.

'I'll be better on my own,' Iselle said. Gawain nodded, at which Iselle set off, soon disappearing among the crowd. The rest of us split up, Father Yvain and I joining a table of Greek merchants who were awaiting a ship from Ireland to carry them south and home again with the tin they had bought. Being Christians, they were willing to talk to us and, though they had never heard of the Order of the Holy Thorn, they gratefully received Father Yvain's blessings, sharing a jug of wine with us in return.

'The light of Christ is a weak flame in this land,' a man named Anatolios told me in his strange accent as he filled my cup, 'so we are glad to meet fellow believers.' He tapped the rim of his cup against my own, while his friend talked with Yvain. 'Now tell me, young man, about your order. Did Saint Joseph of Arimathea truly bring the cup of Christ to the Dark Isles?' He leant back, a mix of curiosity and doubt in his sun-darkened face, then stamped his foot on the earthen floor. 'Did his holy feet walk upon this very earth?'

I put the cup to my lips, trying not to wince at that first sip of wine, and told Anatolios the stories that I myself had been told by Father Brice when I was a boy alone in the world and in need of tales.

Gediens and Gawain went their separate ways, moving among the crowd, stopping now and then to strike up a conversation, filling a cup here, drinking a cup there, though their faces were so scarred and grim from war, their scale coats and weapons so conspicuous, that men and women seemed to shrink away from them, or even turn their backs and pretend they had not seen them.

A few men, warriors themselves, or at least men who had stood in the shieldwall or carried a spear beneath some lord's wind-stirred banner, dipped a head or dug an elbow into a rib, lips moving behind raised cups as they drew their companions' eyes towards the two figures moving through the hall.

'They can smell the blood on them,' Father Yvain murmured to me as I drained my second cup. He had followed my line of sight towards Gediens, who was fishing for information among a knot of drunken men and women, including Anatolios and his fellow merchants, who had gathered around a girl and her lyre. 'They smell it and fear it and they don't want to get so much as a drop of it on themselves.'

'Gawain says that the war will come to the west, even to Tintagel,' I said, as the first notes of that lyre sang out, almost lost amongst the thrum of voices, tentative and sweet and pure as spring meltwater.

'I think Gawain is right,' Father Yvain nodded. 'The Saxons will come, but until they do, folk here will make the most of being alive.' He lifted the wine jug, his eyebrows too, and I nodded, letting him refill my cup despite Gawain's orders. Then we both drank, and I realized that, if anything, the wine was making me feel better than I had felt before.

'She's a beauty, isn't she?' Yvain was watching the pretty, dark-haired girl whose long fingers danced on the lyre strings, pouring notes into that fug-filled hall like some queen scattering coins among the poor. He had assumed I was watching the dark-haired girl too, but I wasn't. My eyes followed Iselle, catching sight of her now and then amid the human swell. In awe of how easily she seemed to navigate this world, which must have been as strange to her, a young woman of the wind-shivered reed-beds and ancient, secret tracks, as it was to me, who had been raised first in the forest, away from prying eyes, then in a house of prayer on Ynys Wydryn.

Where folk shrank from Gawain and Gediens, wary and watchful, where they scorned or ignored Father Yvain and me, our robes marking us as followers of the new faith, they seemed drawn to Iselle. Their eyes and whispers followed in her wake. I watched men break off from their conversations to put themselves in her path. They offered her drink or invited her to sit beside them and share their meals. They asked about the sword on her back and the long Saxon knife sheathed on her belt, and one or two of them got to see those weapons close up when Iselle drew them, turning the blades this way and that until firelight sang in the ghostly swirls, reminding the blades of their birth.

I saw one man beside her move his hand down and out of sight amongst the press of bodies, a grin on his face as he found what he was searching for. Iselle twisted and there was a flurry of movement, a scuffle in a heartbeat, and then the man dropped, clutching his groin, and only the laughter of those around him reassured us that Iselle had not cut him open, and that the worst he would suffer was pain and embarrassment.

'She's a fierce one,' Father Yvain grinned as we watched Iselle move on through the press of bodies without so much as glancing back at the mess she had made.

'She is too sure of herself,' I said. Really, I was thinking how in awe of her I was. 'She should be more careful.'

Father Yvain looked at me, his eyes and the shape of his

mouth within that thicket of beard telling me that I should have just said what I really thought.

That Iselle was magnificent.

As dusk fell and a gathering wind scattered rain across the plateau in fitful gusts, hissing in torches, whipping the flames to a breathy roar but never quite extinguishing them, we met back at our humble lodgings to share what we had learnt.

'Where's Iselle?' I asked, realizing that she was not among us. I had not seen her since leaving the ale house and now I was worried.

Gediens nodded at the spitting dark. 'I saw her go that way.' He pointed his spear towards the tanner's workshop, beyond which stood a cattle byre and beyond that, the cliff terraces. Between keening gusts, I could hear the sea breaking itself upon the rocks far below.

'Iselle can take care of herself, lad.' Father Yvain cuffed my shoulder before bending to wipe the mud off his shoes with a handful of straw.

'So?' Gawain lifted his chin in a gesture inviting any of us to report what we had discovered.

'Not many would talk to us,' Father Yvain admitted, casting the muddy straw aside and brushing beads of water from his fur with the back of his big hand. His cheeks, where the beard did not hide them, were flushed with drink, his words a little loose off the tongue. 'They've little use for gods here.'

Gawain looked from the monk to me. 'Galahad?' he said. 'Did the Greeks know the ship in the bay?'

I shook my head. 'They've never seen it before. They were more interested in the girl playing the lyre.'

'Aye, well your tales of Saint Joseph and the Holy Thorn even had me falling asleep in my cup,' Father Yvain put in, then shook his head at Gawain. 'The folk here want to drink, eat, gamble and fornicate, and they don't want men of God watching them do it.' He shrugged, swiping his hand across his mouth and looking at the smeared stain of wine. 'Can't say that I blame them.'

Gediens gave a snort from where he stood grooming one of the mares, sweeping a brush along its flank and down to its belly. 'It's a mystery how you lasted ten years in that Christ house, Yvain.'

The monk frowned. 'It's no mystery and you know it.'

I didn't know what he meant by that, but Gawain gave the monk a cold eye and no more was said about it.

'So, no one has seen a man matching Parcefal's description?' Gawain asked.

Gediens shook his head. 'No one has seen a bear-shield at Tintagel for years, before our own,' he said, pulling hairs from the boar-bristled brush and dropping them into the straw litter.

'And no one has seen or heard of men living in the sea cave,' Gawain added, 'though that does not surprise me. Parcefal would have been careful.' His brows knitted. 'What seems to me strangest of all is that no one we have spoken to seems to know whose ship that is out in the bay.' He snatched a grooming cloth from a nail on the stable wall and wiped the rain from his armour lest it tarnish the bronze scales. My father had been just as particular with his own war gear. 'Or if they do, they're not telling us.'

It was not hard to see why men and women who were drinking the short days away had no desire to speak with him, I thought, watching Gawain in the wind-flickered flamelight of the only torch burning thereabouts. He was a big, battle-scarred, broken-nosed warrior from a time before, when there were such lords of the sword in Britain to haunt Saxon dreams.

I wondered what my father would look like now, were he alive. In my mind he was strong and proud and handsome. Flawless. But if he were here now, would he be scarred and worn by war? Weary from campaigning? Haunted by the faces of friends long passed?

Why did you leave me?

'Iselle.' Father Yvain looked up, his eyes sifting the gloaming beyond the stable door.

Iselle came in, throwing back her hood and sweeping the rain from her clothes.

'It's gone,' she said. 'The ship has gone.'

The brush in Gediens's hand went still. He and Gawain shared a knowing look.

'You think it has something to do with Parcefal and Merlin?' Gawain asked Iselle.

'I spoke to a shore guard,' she said. 'He was guarding the land bridge last night and finished his watch at dawn. He was on his way to his bed when he saw a rowboat leaving on the ebb tide, aiming for the ship anchored in the bay. Told me that he thought it strange, seeing as, far as he knew, no one from that ship had yet climbed the cliff steps and announced themselves.' Iselle cupped her hands and huffed warm breath into them. 'I went to see if the ship was still there.' She shrugged. 'It's not.'

For a moment, Gawain considered all this. Then he nodded. 'I want to speak with this shore guard.'

Gediens tossed the grooming brush into a wooden pail. The mare skittered at the sound. 'He might be able to tell us more about whoever was in that rowboat,' he said.

'We'll be back soon,' Gawain told us, and with that he and Gediens picked up their shields and spears again and headed out into the knifing wind and spitting rain. And we three who were left looked at each other.

'Might as well get some rest,' Father Yvain suggested, and went to fetch his spare cloak, which he used as a bed roll. 'It's all right for you young'uns, but I'm still stiff and footsore from all the walking.' He laid the cloak down in the clean straw and winced as he lowered himself onto it.

Now and then the rain gusted in, but for the most part it was comfortable enough. The horses gave off enough heat to keep the chill out, and we'd had worse out there in the woods beside the old Roman road. The wine was warm in my stomach and I did not want to lie down yet in case the world took to spinning around me in a dizzying blur as it had the previous night, and so I fetched the brush from the pail where Gediens had left it and went over to the horses.

The horse I was to ride was a piebald gelding. He was not especially big, under fifteen hands, but he looked well fed and healthy and seemed good tempered, so we knew the boy had advised us well when he told us to seek out the hunchback Lidas. Nor did he need grooming, for his coat shone in the nearly dark, the white like new snow, the black as lustrous as the raven-feathers of Merlin's cloak. But I wanted him to get to know me and so I began to brush him, from his head and its white star shining in the black night above his eyes, down his strong neck to his chest and withers. Long sweeps of the brush, drawing the oils from his skin into the coat to protect him from wind and rain, making him shiver now and then with the pleasure of it.

'My name is Galahad,' I whispered to him, being gentle on his face, only the lightest of touches around his eyes. 'What's your name, I wonder?'

I was not brushing away dust and dirt, but years. I was a boy again, in the stable beside our dwelling in the Dumnonian forest, south-west of Camelot. Grooming Tormaigh, my father's great war stallion and my friend. Brave Tormaigh, who, though old and greying, had lifted his head high and carried my father into battle one last time. And then, somehow, had emerged from that bloody slaughter to carry me to where Guinevere lay, lost inside her own mind.

I had loved Tormaigh and he had loved me, and now I brushed this gelding, whose name I did not know, but in my mind it was Tormaigh that I was grooming. Tormaigh whose scent I breathed in now, the sweet hay perfume of his breath, the comforting dust-and-sweat musk which was strongest where his head met his neck. And, in a way, I was saying good-bye to him now, these years later, because the child I had been had not said the words.

Brave, noble Tormaigh.

'Can I help?'

I looked up. Iselle stood the other side of the gelding's head. She held a rough woollen grooming cloth. I had not seen her approach, but something in her face told me she had been watching me a while.

I blinked to clear my eyes and my mind. 'Best you work on your own horse so you can get to know each other.' Iselle was not used to horses, and I knew she was apprehensive about riding, though she had not said as much.

She said nothing now and I kept working with the brush, sweeping it down the gelding's foreleg to the knee as I had learnt. As my father had taught me.

'He likes you,' Iselle said after a long moment.

'He likes being brushed. Some horses don't. My grandfather had a stallion called Malo. He would bite and kick the stable hands. Even my grandfather's groom.' I felt a smile tug at my lips, the memory of my father's words having caught. 'Malo was a foul-tempered demon. He hated everyone, except my father. And everyone was afraid of him, but my father wasn't, even though he was just a boy. He was the only one who Malo would allow to brush him when he was in one of his moods.'

The mare behind Iselle nickered and snorted.

'I think she wants some attention,' I said.

But Iselle did not move. Her eyes were still fixed on me.

'This is the first time you have talked to me of your father,' she said.

I ran the brush along the gelding's flank to the point of his hip. 'I know what you think of him.' Iselle lifted her chin but held her tongue. 'You blame him for the ruin of Britain. You blame him for loving Guinevere and for breaking Arthur's heart.' The brush went still in my hand. I looked up, seizing Iselle's eyes with my own. 'You believe that if my father and Guinevere had not betrayed him, Arthur would have been unstoppable. That together he and my father would have driven the Saxons back into the sea.'

She thought about this and nodded. 'I used to think that,' she admitted. 'I still think that. But I also think that we cannot decide whom we love. We can control it no more than we can change the flight of an arrow once it has left the string.' She shrugged. 'Your father loved Guinevere. And he loved Arthur. For all his strength, for all his skill with a sword, he could not change that.' She gave a slight shake of her head. 'He could not alter the flight of that arrow.' She placed her hand on the gelding's neck. Near my own hand. Hers on a patch of white coat, mine resting upon a shining swathe of black. A finger's length of gleaming coat was all that separated us.

A tremble ran through the gelding's flesh and I knew that Iselle must have felt it too. Heat flooded through me. I wanted more than anything to place my hand on hers. To feel her fingers and her knuckles beneath my palm.

'I have no doubt your father loved you too, Galahad,' she said.

I flinched. I pulled my hand away and swept the brush along the gelding's flank again.

'You think he did not love you because he left you, to fight at Lord Arthur's side.'

I did not answer. I wanted to tell her that she was wrong. That she knew nothing about me. But that would have been a lie, and so I said nothing as I ran my fingers through the gelding's mane, separating a tangle that was not really there.

'Lancelot was trying to make things right between the three of them,' she said. 'Even were that not so, he had to go to fight beside Arthur. He was a warrior with a warrior's pride.' I was not looking at her now, but I could feel her eyes on me like embers on my skin. 'If you were a warrior, you would understand.'

I had never been kicked by a horse, but just then I felt as if I had. My breath caught in my chest. My limbs seemed gripped by invisible hands and I went still, but for my head, which came up in challenge, my mouth full of words which I had yet to place in order.

But Iselle was no longer looking at me. She was looking towards the stable door and the night beyond. The gelding lifted his head higher, ears twitching, flicking back and forth.

'Someone's coming.' Iselle hurried over to where her bow stave leant against the wall.

'Father, wake up,' I hissed at Yvain, who was asleep in his straw nest. I dropped the brush and moved around the gelding's head to where the monk was snoring in his blankets and furs. I crouched beside him. 'Wake up, Father.' I touched him on his shoulder. He snorted but did not wake and so I shook him. 'Father.'

'Not asleep yet,' he grumbled. 'How could I be, with you

two chattering like two fieldfares on a hawthorn.' He sat up, throwing off his fur and staring at the stable door. 'Gawain's back?'

I did not think it would be Gawain and Gediens. Not so soon. Iselle did not think so either, judging by the Saxon sword which she gripped in one hand, its scabbard in the other; there was no time to string her bow. Seeing her so armed, Father Yvain hurried to his feet. 'You sure you heard something?' he asked her, not taking his eyes from the night beyond the door.

I could hear the rain's hiss and the distant murmur of folk enjoying themselves in the ale house. A laugh. A drunken shout. The faint trilling of a flute now and then, and, far away across the plateau, the incessant barking of a dog.

I looked at Iselle. She did not answer Father Yvain, yet it was clear by the set of her jaw that she believed someone was out there. We had all come to trust her instincts.

Father Yvain took a step towards the door. 'Show yourself!' he called into the darkness, his spear gripped across his broad chest.

The horses were skittish now, one pawing the ground, another curling back its upper lip, baring its teeth. I was aware of the blood rushing through my veins, crashing in my ears like the waves on Tintagel's shore. Iselle and I looked at each other. Perhaps she was mistaken. Perhaps it had been a trick of the wind. Or inquisitive children coming to catch a glimpse of the warriors with the bear-shields, shining helms and scale armour. I was just about to say as much, when Father Yvain growled a curse under his breath.

'Put the spear down, priest.' A short, broad-shouldered man pulled open the low stable door and stepped inside. His sword pointed at Father Yvain. 'On the floor with it, old man, before I take it off you and put the sharp end in your guts.'

Behind him I counted six more warriors, rain dripping from the rims of their grey helmets and the hems of their cloaks and running down the shafts of the spears which they clutched in white hands.

These men came with him, three off his right shoulder, three off his left, all of them with spears levelled and violence in their eyes.

'You're walking mud into my clean straw,' Father Yvain said, tilting his spear's blade down towards the leading man's feet. 'So, I'll ask you once to turn around and leave.'

The short man lifted a hand and his men stopped, set their feet and waited, like obedient hounds ready to kill at their master's word. 'Where are the others?' he asked.

Father Yvain's lip curled in the nest of his beard. 'What others?'

The man almost grinned at that, appreciating Yvain's effrontery. He made a point of glancing at the horses shifting in the shadows and the saddles lined up with our other gear against a partition wall. 'You *are* a priest?' he asked.

Yvain nodded. 'Of sorts,' he said. 'Least, I was.' He shrugged. 'For some years.'

The short man considered this. 'The kind that deals in banes and curses?' he asked, making a slight gesture with his head, at which the three men on his right moved off, closing the gap between themselves and Iselle, who turned to face them squarely.

Father Yvain jerked his spear at them in warning. 'Did you not see the ghost fence which I have made out there?' he asked. 'The one which will shrivel the manhood of any fool who crosses it, unless I have spoken his name to the spirits in the wind?'

The short man tilted his head to one side as he eyed the

monk. By the light of the lamp flame I saw that his face was pockmarked. Perhaps he had reason to fear curses.

'He's lying,' the whip-lean spearman to his left said. 'He's a Christian.' The man spat at Father Yvain. 'You have no magic.'

Father Yvain spun the spear round in his hands, the blade whirring in its circle, whispering in the dark. 'I don't need spells. I have this,' he said, flexing his fingers and gripping the shaft tightly again. Then, with his thick beard he gestured towards Iselle. 'And the girl here kills Saxons for fun. You ever killed a Saxon, boy?' He challenged the thin spearman with his eyes. He was not old, this warrior, but he was no boy, either, and he bristled at the insult.

The leader of these spearmen regarded Iselle, the expression on his pitted face one of grudging respect, then turned his eyes on me. What I saw in his face as he looked me up and down was curiosity, then disgust.

I looked past the short man to the corner of the stable where Gediens and Gawain's spears stood. I would never reach them before one of these men ran me through. My stomach rolled. My saliva tasted sour. I looked at Iselle, who stood defiant in the heavy silence which hung in the stable now that we all knew what must happen. She tossed the scabbard aside and gripped the sword with two hands, her lips pulled back from her teeth like a wolf's, as we waited for the pockmarked man to give the word and send his hounds in for the kill.

I saw his hand come up, then a blur of movement as Father Yvain rushed in, thrusting the butt end of his spear forward to beat the man's sword aside, before swinging the spear blade back across, ripping open his throat in a spray of gore. Yvain stepped back, blocking another man's spear thrust and plunging his own spear into the thin man's belly, twisting and pulling it free before it snarled in guts and flesh.

Iselle parried a spear and swept her Saxon blade up the shaft and I saw a scatter of white fingers fly before another man threw himself at her and they both fell into the straw, Iselle shrieking as the sword fell from her hand, the spearman grunting with the effort of trying to overbear her. Then a blade cut the air so that I felt its passing on my cheek and I ducked as the man scythed the spear back again, the blade flashing above my head. I threw myself up at him, fists flying, knuckles raking across his temple and smashing his teeth into his throat, but as he fell back, I heard Iselle cry out and I turned and the next thing I knew my arms were around the neck of the man who was on her. I hauled his head back and, in that moment, it seemed that everything around me was happening slowly, as if the very air had thickened and our enemies laboured through it like insects caught in honey. I was roaring but I could barely hear it. I could barely hear anything, but I saw into Iselle's wild eyes, our souls touching for an instant. I saw the knife in her hand, that long Saxon blade coming up. Cutting across white flesh.

Then I was in the straw, points of light filling my vision like sparks struck from flint and steel, not yet feeling the pain from the blow which had knocked me down. And beyond the flying sparks, I saw Father Yvain parry a sword thrust and put another man down, his mouth wide in a bellow of fury which sounded far away.

Sword? There had been only one man armed with a sword. I tried to rise, choking on dust raised by booted feet in the litter all around me, knowing that more men had come. We would die. These were our last breaths and I looked for Iselle but saw instead the leather-bound rim of a shield as it came down on my head, knocking me into the straw again.

'Yield, or they die!' someone yelled. 'Drop it and I'll spare them.'

'How do I know?' I heard Father Yvain growl, his breathing like forge bellows. 'How do I know you won't kill them after I'm dead?'

A murmur of voices, then two men took me under my arms and lifted me to my feet. They did the same with Iselle, whose face was blood-spattered and fierce still as she struggled and fought. A man put his spear blade to her throat, just as I felt a blade press against my own, the steel holding the night's cold within it.

A man came into the stable, lifting a lantern and casting light across the faces of the dead men as he stepped over them. He stopped a spear's length from Father Yvain, his men gathering either side of him with spears and shields.

'You'd rather watch them die, and then we'll kill you?' this man asked Father Yvain. 'We can do it that way,' he said, as if it mattered little either way. Broad-shouldered and ruddy-faced, he had seen perhaps fifty winters and had courage enough to stand before Father Yvain with neither helmet, shield, nor a blade in his hand. He was richly dressed, though, and his fur-trimmed cloak of blue wool was fastened with a silver brooch whose long, sharp pin gleamed by the lantern light. 'Well?' he asked, holding a finger up towards the men with the blades at our throats, letting them know that in a moment they would either be killing or not.

Father Yvain looked at me. I shook my head, not wanting him to give up his spear, for I was sure that they would slaughter him the moment he did.

But Yvain gritted his teeth, nodded and threw the spear down, at which moment three warriors rushed in and took hold of him.

'Good.' The man with the fine brooch nodded.

'Who are you?' Father Yvain asked him.

His hair was fair but greying. His beard was short, but his moustaches were long, and he looked to me more like a Saxon than a Briton.

'I am Lord Geldrin,' he said. 'And you, it would seem, are a priest who would have been better suited to war than to prayer.' He looked at one of his men, who was sitting against the wall, pressing his cloak against his face, trying to stem the blood as others kneeling by him demanded in vain to see the wound.

'That was me,' Iselle said, scorn in her voice, pride in her eyes. The man threatening her leant forward, his spear blade lifting her chin so that she could say no more.

'She took my fingers!' another man shrieked, gripping his ruined hand, blood running in rivulets down his arm to his elbow and dripping onto the straw.

Father Yvain grimaced. 'Don't say I didn't warn you about her.'

Lord Geldrin lifted the horn lantern to get a better look at Iselle, whose eyes met his with defiance. 'What is Lord Gawain, Prince of Lyonesse, doing in Tintagel? What is his business here?'

'Ask him yourself,' I said.

The lantern swung, flooding me with light.

'And who are you?' His lips bunched, eyes narrowed. 'Have we met? You dress like a Christian monk, yet you do not have the tonsure.'

'I am Galahad, lord. We have not met before.'

'Galahad,' he repeated, speaking my name as if trying to recall the taste of it in his mouth. His eyes were in me like hooks in my flesh. 'You are familiar to me, Galahad. It is as if I am looking at a ghost.'

I glanced at Father Yvain. He shook his head, and Lord Geldrin noticed the exchange but said nothing, instead drawing his fingers back and forth, inviting me to speak.

'I was a novice at the Monastery of the Holy Thorn on Ynys Wydryn,' I said. 'Until the Saxons came and slaughtered my brothers.' I nodded towards Father Yvain. 'We two survived.'

Lord Geldrin showed neither surprise nor pity to hear what had befallen the Brothers of the Thorn. 'And now you are here, in my island fortress, asking questions of my shore guards and my Greek guests, yet never coming to my hall to pay your respects.' He pulled his long moustaches through his fist to smooth them as he thought. 'How did you come to be travelling with Prince Gawain? Is he a Christian these days?'

I bunched my muscles, testing the hold which the two men had on me. They tightened their grip. 'As I said, lord, ask him yourself.'

Lord Geldrin's brows arched. 'Oh, I will,' he nodded, his eyes lingering on me. Then he turned to his spearmen. 'Bring them outside.'

My vision was still marred, my legs unsteady as Lord Geldrin's men hauled us from the stable into the night, their spears at our backs, pushing us along the timber walkway which was slippery with mud, towards a crowd of folk who had congregated by the main entrance to Uther's hall. Lord Geldrin's hall these days, I reminded myself, wondering what we had done to make an enemy of the Lord of Tintagel.

'Keep your ale hole shut,' Father Yvain gnarred in my ear as those folk saw Lord Geldrin coming, the murmur of their voices rising on the chill night air. The crowd split apart to let their lord through, and there were Gediens and Gawain, their scale coats gleaming dully in the flame-flickered dark, a hedge of spears levelled at them.

Gawain nodded at me, clearly relieved to see that we were all unhurt.

'Lord Gawain, did I not give you my word that I would

bring your friends to you unharmed if you came peaceably?' Lord Geldrin swept his arm towards us. 'Though it was no easy task. I daresay that if the Christ had had a friend like your monk here, the Romans would never have crucified him.' He frowned and gestured at Iselle. 'As for this wild creature, she is the Morrigán made flesh.'

Mention of the Queen of Demons, the shape-shifting battle goddess who could foretell a man's doom, sent a shiver through the crowd. Men and women stared at Iselle, some touching iron or making signs against evil, and she glared back at them, her eyes white in the darkness.

'Is she your daughter, Lord Gawain?' the Lord of the Heights asked.

'No,' Gawain said. 'But I'd be proud if she were.' That pride was in his eyes even so.

Lord Geldrin shared a look with his people, and I knew that here was a man who enjoyed his status and the eyes of the crowd upon him. 'You have cost me dearly,' he told us. 'I will decide how best you can repay me. In the meantime, those scale coats now belong to me. We don't see their like much these days.' He held a hand out behind him and the spearman who had Gawain's sword placed the leather and silver wire-bound grip in his lord's hand. Holding the blade, Lord Geldrin pulled the grip and the pommel to see if they still fitted securely on the tang. Then he took hold of the blade with two hands and flexed it before examining it to check that it had returned to true. Seeming to approve, he made a series of practice cuts which showed that he knew his sword craft, and after a final flourish a satisfied grunt escaped his throat.

'A little heavy towards the point, perhaps, but a fine sword.' He nodded. 'I would expect nothing less from Gawain of Lyonesse, the man who rode beside Arthur. Who fought alongside the great lord of war until the very moment Mordred ap Arthur cut his own father down.' He turned the sword in his hand so that its polished blade reflected flame. 'Was this the sword you wielded that dark day?' he asked Gawain.

Gawain lifted his bearded chin. 'It was.'

'And you, Gediens ap Senelas,' Lord Geldrin turned and pointed the blade at Gediens, 'were you there too?'

'Until the end,' Gediens replied, his back straight, knowing the worth in reputation of being able to say that you had stood beside Arthur on that fateful day.

Lord Geldrin spread his arms wide, a flamboyant gesture made ominous by the gleam of steel in the gloom of night. 'Then why are we spilling blood?' he asked Gawain, 'when we should be sharing wine and food and listening to your tales of the old days and of Arthur?'

Gawain's lips warped amid his beard. 'I am not one for tales. Do we look like bards?' He glanced at Gediens, who gave a sour grin.

They did not look like bards. But they *did* look like the sort of warriors upon whom bards contrived their songs, like women weaving thread on a loom to make patterned cloth. Just like the sword in Lord Geldrin's hand, they were forged in fire and made for war.

Lord Geldrin spun to face the crowd and turned his empty hand palm uppermost. A gesture that asked them what he was supposed to do with such difficult strangers. 'They are too proud, too famous to pay their respects at my hall,' he said with exaggerated deference, 'yet they sleep in a stable with their horses.' He wore a troubled frown.

'*Your* hall?' Gawain shook his head, flamelight from a nearby torch playing on his scarred face. 'It will always be King Uther's hall. Until a king sits in the high seat. Or a man who is worthy of it. A man who makes war against the Saxons. Not a man who sits upon it like a crow atop a dung heap.'

The crowd stirred at that like leaves in a gathering wind. Geldrin's men tensed as if expecting the order to put their spears in our flesh. But Lord Geldrin only smiled to himself as he handed Gawain's sword back to the man who had given it to him.

'It seems we shall have no stories of Arthur this night,' he told his people, before turning back to Gawain. 'But tomorrow I think you will feel differently. At the very least you will tell me what you are doing here. Why you went down to the sea cave this morning and why you are so eager to know about the ship which was moored in my bay.'

He turned his deep-set eyes on Iselle. 'And let us hope that at least one of you has a gift for spinning a tale,' he said, his gaze moving over to me, 'because your lives will depend upon it.' He swept an arm towards us. 'Take them away. Feed them. Wine too. I'll not have it said I'm a poor host.'

'Their armour, lord?' a spearman asked, gesturing at Gediens's scale coat.

Geldren scowled. 'No rush. We are not barbarians, who would so dishonour two lords of Britain by stripping them of their war glory in front of folk who have surely heard of them and know their reputation. Tomorrow, tomorrow.' He waved an arm towards the spitting darkness. With that, we were led away by his spearmen, one of whom waited until we were out of his lord's sight before slamming his spear butt into the back of Father Yvain's head. I heard the crack of it and Yvain stumbled but did not fall.

'That's for Gereint,' the spearman said, spitting at Yvain, who clutched the back of his head but kept walking, eyes on the muddy trackway, mouth clenched on the pain.

My mind showed me again the brief and bloody chaos inside that stable. Father Yvain killing with the skill and instinct of a gifted warrior. My arms around a man's neck as Iselle slashed her knife across his face. The terror and the thrill of it was a faint shiver still in my arms and legs.

Without breaking stride again, Father Yvain straightened to his full height. He took his hand away from his head and I saw it was slick with blood. 'Did your father never teach you how to hit properly?' he growled at the spearman, who muttered some foul insult and raised the spear to strike him a second time.

'You!' Gediens pointed a finger at the spearman. 'Touch my friend again and I swear you'll wish you were washing up on Annwn's shores with this Gereint.'

The spearman spat at Father Yvain again and told Gediens that, lord or no, he was hardly in a position to be making threats. Yet he did not hit Father Yvain again before we were thrown into a kiln-house standing but a spear-cast to the east of Lord Geldrin's hall.

One of the spearmen lit a stinking oil lamp and placed it in the stone oven amongst a litter of potsherds, making sure that the wick took the flame, before they shut the door behind them and took up guard positions around the place.

'Let me see your head, Father,' I said, as the others found stools or slumped down against the circular wall.

'It's nothing,' Father Yvain replied, flapping a blood-red hand at me, but I pushed him down onto a stool so that I could look at the wound.

'The blood has thickened,' I said, relieved, though the gash in his scalp was as long as my thumb.

'Told you, it's nothing.' Father Yvain lifted his chin towards the door. 'That mouthy weasel shit hits like a little girl,' he added loudly enough for the spearmen outside to hear.

My own head hurt in two places, the worst being on my forehead where the shield rim had struck me, and now there was an egg-shaped swelling which throbbed like the surging sea down in the cove.

I sat on the earthen floor, which was dry and cracked from a thousand clay firings in the oven which dominated the space, and for a long while none of us spoke, each lost in the tangle of our own thoughts. Although, looking at Gawain's face, all glower and bridled fury, I knew something was coming. It took as long as a good knife-sharpening for it to work its way up and into his mouth.

'What in Balor's name did you do?' he hissed at Father Yvain.

The monk matched Gawain's glare with his own.

'They came with spears raised. If not for Iselle they would have stuck me in my bed furs.' He put his clean hand to his head wound to check that the bleeding had stopped. 'I killed them before they could kill us.'

'And what if Lord Geldrin wanted only to talk to us?' Gawain asked. 'What if it was simply because we offended him by not paying our respects, and he sought to show us that he is lord here? To embarrass us, nothing more?'

But Father Yvain shook his head. 'They gave no warning and came in the dark. No shields, so not even prepared for a fight. Just spears. Which, if you ask me, speaks of murder, not an invitation to pay respects to their master.'

Gawain grimaced, chewing on his next words.

I said, 'For all we knew, you and Gediens were already dead.'

Gawain's head came around, his eyes seizing mine. 'But we weren't,' he said, then dipped his chin. 'Did you kill any of them?'

'No,' I said.

'Good, that's something at least.'

But the truth was I felt ashamed. Father Yvain had fought so well. Like a champion. Iselle had fought with fierce courage, never asking for quarter. What had I done? Barely more than the horses tethered in the stall.

'I would have done the same as Yvain.' Gediens broke his own silence, not looking up as he worked at a rust spot on his helmet, scraping it with a thumbnail.

Gawain hoomed in the back of his throat. 'And now we will have to pay a blood price,' he said, those words meant for us all. He looked at Father Yvain, who had moved the oil lamp and was setting a fire in the clay oven. 'You should have held back until you knew,' he said. 'You should have waited.'

Father Yvain placed the kindling, leaving a gap at its heart. 'I couldn't wait.' He took a handful of straw to the lamp flame.

'Why not?' Gawain asked.

Father Yvain's head came up. 'You know why.'

Gediens's eyes flicked up at me, then back down to the helmet on his knee. That glance was quicker than a heartbeat, yet Iselle had seen it too, for she looked at me then, an unspoken question in a face still speckled with a man's blood.

'What has it to do with me?' I asked, looking from Gawain to Father Yvain.

Gawain looked at the monk as though inviting him to answer my question, but Father Yvain shook his head.

'What has it to do with me?' I asked again, putting more edge on my voice.

'Tell me this, Galahad,' Gawain said. 'Was Yvain a diligent Brother of the Holy Thorn? Did he take the teachings of your order to heart? Did he serve your god well? At least no less than the other brothers on Ynys Wydryn?'

I wanted to see Father Yvain's face, but he busied himself

with the fire, pushing the ball of burning straw in amongst the kindling.

'Father Yvain was assiduous in his faith,' I replied. 'He worked. Prayed. Sang the devotions as well as any of the brothers.'

Father Yvain snorted at that, then leant into the oven and blew softly upon the new flames, fanning them amongst the sticks.

'Truly?' Gawain asked, lifting an eyebrow at me.

I felt the frown on my face as I searched for the trap in the questions.

'I didn't know half the devotions,' Father Yvain said, placing more sticks into the fire. 'I'd sooner turn bowls and cups than listen to the rest of you droning like bees after a smoking. You know it's true, lad.'

Gediens grinned at that. Iselle too.

My frown deepened. The fire crackled and popped, its coppery red light blooming, vanquishing the dark, yet spawning new shadows.

'I daresay Yvain here volunteered whenever someone was needed to leave Ynys Wydryn,' Gawain suggested, his eyes challenging me to say different. Flames danced in a hundred and more bronze scales that would soon belong to another man.

'Because he knew the marsh better than any of us,' I said, as though it were as simple as that.

'Enough, Gawain.' Father Yvain took a split log from a basket and laid it on the snapping, crackling sticks.

'Because he had vowed to serve the Prior and the monastery,' I said.

Gawain laughed then. Even in that place, with spearmen guarding us and the promise of blood on the morrow. Even though we had failed to find Merlin and Parcefal, Gawain laughed, and the sound of it was like a flame beneath my blood, making it boil.

'Let it be, Gawain,' Father Yvain rumbled under his breath, though we all knew it was too late for that now.

Gawain stared at the monk. 'Brother Yvain ap Drudwas ap Kailin does not serve the Christian god, Galahad, but another master.'

I looked at Yvain, expecting him to deny it. He did not.

'As I serve Arthur, so Yvain serves another lord,' Gawain went on. 'And, like Arthur, this man is but a breath in the wind. A long shadow falling across us from former times.'

Father Yvain sat back on his stool and watched the fire which he had brought to life. He was resigned and knew there could be no putting the stopper back in the bottle now.

'I serve Merlin,' he confessed. 'As Gawain serves Arthur, so I serve Merlin.'

Iselle and I looked at each other.

Yvain shrugged. 'You might as well know.'

'But how?' I asked. My skin prickled. 'How do you serve Merlin?' It seemed, as I stared at Yvain, that his face had changed by the firelight, that he no longer looked like the man I knew.

'I've not seen him,' Yvain admitted, shaking his head. 'Not for ten years. But I had no reason to think he was dead and so my oath held. Still does.'

'What oath?' I asked.

He chewed his lip a moment, then looked at me, his eyes clear with truth. 'To look after you, lad. To make sure you never came to harm. Not that you could get into much trouble on Ynys Wydryn.' He smiled. 'But I swore an oath to Merlin, and an oath is not something you can toss into a marsh once it becomes too heavy to carry.'

'Why?' I asked. I did not understand any of it. 'Why me?'

Yvain's brows arched and he leant forward on the stool. 'You're Lancelot's son,' he said. 'Whether you like it or not.'

I reeled at his words, my thoughts flying this way and that, wild as leaves in a gale. 'Why would you do this for Merlin?' I asked. 'Why would you give him so many years?'

'They were mine to give,' Yvain stated simply.

I thought of the many times, when I was new to the monastery and Prior Drustanus led us in prayer, that the big, bearded monk had been conspicuous by his absence. And I would find him in his workshop among piles of sweet-smelling wood shavings, and he would let me watch him work.

'But you *are* a Christian?' I said.

Yvain nodded. 'As much as a man can be a Christian and yet serve a druid.'

I looked at the others and my stomach hardened. Gediens had found another patch of rust and was working at it with a cloth which he had dipped in the lamp oil. Gawain was using a stick to scrape mud from his boot. Neither man looked surprised by anything Yvain had said.

Iselle, though, could make no more sense of it than I. 'Did Merlin reward you?' she asked Father Yvain.

Gawain lifted his chin towards Yvain. 'Does he look like a rich man?' he asked Iselle.

'I will have all I need because of Merlin,' Yvain replied. 'I will see my wife again. I will hold my son in my arms. I will carry my little girl on my shoulders. My Tangwen.' Tears stood in his eyes.

'I didn't know you had a family,' I said. 'You've never spoken of them.'

It was as if a cloud passed across Yvain's face then. He took a breath. When he let that breath go, it battered the little flame clinging to a reed wick in an oil-filled clam shell. 'They are gone, Galahad,' he said. 'The sweating sickness took them. The summer before Lord Arthur's last battle. I had sought out Merlin, hoping he could do something. He came, but we were too late. Nothing could be done. He took away their pain but not even Merlin could hold them to this world.'

Iselle and I shared a look, neither of us wanting to dig deeper into this wound which I had opened. Both of us wanting to know more.

'Merlin could not save my family.' Father Yvain wiped a tear that had escaped his eye. 'But he could do something for me. Before the end, he put a charm on my wife and my little ones. Henbane, blood and bone.' He waved a hand. 'Other things besides. He marked them, my boy and girl being so small that I feared they would not find their mother in Arawn's realm. And he put the mark on me, too. Merlin swore to me that no matter how many years I lived on after my three loves, when I crossed over I would find them again. That my wife and my son and my sweet Tangwen might even be standing there on the shore, waiting for me.'

Father Yvain wiped the tears from his beard and sat up on his stool, exhaling deeply, then fixed me with his gaze once more. 'In return for doing this for me, Merlin wanted something.' He shrugged. 'I would have given my life there and then, but Merlin needed me to live. He wanted my oath, that I would do whatever he asked of me when he asked it.'

He looked at Gawain. 'I thought I would die on that field, when Mordred betrayed us and Dumnonia's spearmen were cut down like wheat before the scythe. But I lived and, not long after that, Merlin came to collect what I owed.' His eyes swung back to me. 'He said I must join the monks of the Thorn on Ynys Wydryn. That I must look after you, letting nothing harm you. That I should keep you safe, Galahad, at least until Gawain came for you, as Merlin knew he would. One day.' He shook his head. 'I will find my family in the hereafter. And if spearmen come for you in the night, I will kill them.'

'An oath is an oath,' Gediens said in a quiet voice. And even Gawain would not upbraid Yvain more for his actions earlier that night. Nothing could change what had already happened, and there was a sense among us of a collective weariness. As though a painful boil had at last been lanced and all that could be done now was to rest and hope the wound healed.

'We may as well get some sleep.' Gawain stood to pull off his scale armour. 'Tomorrow will bring what tomorrow will bring.'

We made ourselves as comfortable as we could, but I knew I would not sleep. My head was crammed with thoughts and memories. They writhed in my skull like eels in a basket. I understood now why Father Yvain had never seemed as fully immersed in the Order as the other brothers. And why, when we were at Lord Arthur's dwelling, he had seemed to care little for the cutting of the Holy Thorn which I had carried with me from Ynys Wydryn. I tried to understand the sacrifice that Yvain had made. The deal he had struck with Merlin. Ten years for a druid's spell. An oath as binding as chains forged by Gofannon the smith-god, in return for a mark seen only by the dead.

And among those writhing eels were other floundering things for which I had no name. Questions which I could not ask. Not yet, anyway. Such as, had Prior Drustanus and the brothers known Yvain's reasons for joining the Order? And how had Merlin known that Gawain would one day come for me?

No, sleep would not find me as Gawain had. And so I lay on my cloak on that hard mud floor and watched the flickering ghosts of flames cavorting on the whitewashed walls and the dark thatch. I thought of Yvain's wife and children. Three faceless figures standing hand in hand on Annwn's mist-shrouded shore. I thought of Geldrin, Lord of the Heights, who had seemed to know me, and I thought of Iselle and how she had slashed open a man's face, her wild eyes blinking away his blood. And I wondered what tomorrow would bring.

10

Yvain

W E WERE READY WHEN they came for us. Eight of Lord
Geldrin's spearmen, mailed, swathed in pelts and
cloaks against the chill, and resenting having duties before
Tintagel had awoken. Silent but purposeful, they ushered us
along the track in the cold dark before the dawn. We shivered
and clung to our own thoughts, our breath trailing us like
smoke as we tramped towards the old hall, which loomed like
a sleeping giant in the gloom, its own breath palling above the
thatch. But then the spearmen led us off the timber walkway
and onto the mud, which squelched underfoot, and I saw
Gawain and Father Yvain share a look which put a cold blade
of fear in my guts.

'Where are we going?' Gawain asked the lead man of our
escort.

'Where we're told,' the man said over his shoulder, shoving
the butt of his spear at a dog which had been with us since we
left the kiln-house and which seemed determined to sniff the
spearman's trews. The man was the only one I recognized from
the previous night, and I guessed that those who had stood
guard around the kiln-house were now snug in their beds.

Gulls wheeled and shrieked above us in the murk. The moon
still hung above the far horizon, spilling light across the

Western Sea and silvering a shredding billow of cloud which looked to me like a bird of prey with wings outstretched before the stoop.

'There's nothing over here,' I said to Iselle as we trudged up a grassy incline, the breeze cold on my face, making my eyes water. That breeze carried the scent of sea wrack left behind on the sand and shingle at low tide, and the begging cries of guillemots in their rocky roosts.

'Did you think Lord Geldrin would invite us into his hall for warm bread and honey wine?' Iselle asked, as we walked further from the settlement and up a rocky outcrop which we knew led to nothing.

'I hoped that he might,' I replied, my stomach still sour from Lord Geldrin's wine, 'but it looks like we'll know soon enough.' For there on that ledge stood a dark figure against the gradually lightening sky, his cloak billowing in the wind. It was Geldrin, ruler of Tintagel. Lord of the Heights. He had been looking out to sea but now he turned and watched us climb towards him, a spear in his hand, his short-cropped hair standing in tufts.

Beside him stood a young woman swathed in silver fur, her face as pale as the coming dawn, her long black hair flying in the wind like a crow's wing. At this woman's right shoulder stood a huge, mailed warrior whose face was as craggy as the cliffs below, and behind him, four spearmen whose shields, like his, were daubed white with a black raven or crow perched on the iron boss.

'Lord Gawain,' Lord Geldrin called in greeting. 'And Lord Gediens,' he added, dipping his head to both warriors. 'I trust you slept well. The wine was not worth remembering, I'll be the first to admit, but then I didn't think I owed you my best since your friends killed three of my men and maimed two.'

'The wine was good enough,' Gawain rumbled.

We came onto the bare rock and I saw the sea at Lord Geldrin's back, the wave crests breaking white and scudding northwards. I looked east, towards the mainland, and saw the first fringe of light creeping above Dumnonia's dark forests.

'But the meat was tough,' Gawain added, glancing at Gediens, who agreed.

'Think I lost a tooth on it.' Gediens frowned, putting a finger and thumb to his mouth.

'I told you, we're getting too old to eat anything that hasn't been boiled for a day,' Gawain chided him, the two of them talking as easily as if they were in an ale house, denying Lord Geldrin the fear he would have expected to see from men stood at spear-point on a cliff edge in the wind and dark.

Lord Geldrin smiled, and the sea far below could not have been colder. He glanced at the young woman beside him. She nodded but did not speak, her dark eyes passing from one of us to the other, taking hold of every detail from our feet to our heads.

Lord Geldrin turned his face away from the wind so that it would not snatch his words away. 'What are you doing at Tintagel, Lord Gawain?' he asked.

'It is none of your concern,' Gawain said, 'but seeing as you have brought us all up here, it seems to me you are trying to make a point, and so I will tell you, to save us all the trouble. We are here to meet an old friend.'

At this, the dark-haired woman's eyes narrowed and she took a step forward, hands one upon the other below her waist.

'His name?' Lord Geldrin asked.

'Parcefal,' Gawain said.

'Parcefal ap Bliocadran?' Lord Geldrin asked, glancing at the woman, who kept her eyes fastened on Gawain.

Gawain nodded. 'The same.'

A few of the spearmen around us shared surprised looks, for just as men had heard of Gawain of Lyonesse, so they had heard of Parcefal too.

Lord Geldrin's hand tightened on his spear, his knuckles white. 'What would one of Arthur's horse lords be doing here?' he asked, then turned to me. 'It is strange, monk,' he said, 'all these famed warriors who rode with the great Arthur appearing again now like wraiths gathering for Samhain.'

Gawain gave a grim smile. 'It is not our problem that everyone thinks we are long dead.' He shrugged. 'But I have not seen my old friend for a long time and would like to raise a cup with him as we used to.' He threw an arm back towards the roundhouses, workshops, stables and byres. 'We arranged to meet here.'

'Why here?' Lord Geldrin asked.

Gawain shrugged. 'Have you travelled in Dumnonia these last years, lord? The land crawls with Saxons. Famine takes the old and young. Disease stalks the cantrefs and forts. Men murder each other for a coin, or a scrap of iron, or to take another man's wife. And the great kings of Britain?' he said, the words dripping with scorn. 'They won't fight our enemies. They hide behind their walls.' He gestured at the cliff edge. 'Lucky for you, you don't need walls.'

The insult was scarcely veiled, but Lord Geldrin ignored it. 'Where is the great Parcefal now?' he asked.

Gawain pressed a thumb against the side of his broken nose, turned his head and expelled a wad of snot into the wind. 'We have yet to find him.'

'Perhaps he has changed his mind,' Lord Geldrin mused, aiming the words at Gediens. 'Perhaps he does not wish to be reminded of former days, when he was young and men feared him. Would you not rather live out your days in peace?'

'There can be no peace until we take back our land,' Gediens said.

Lord Geldrin nodded, accepting that. 'There is no one else you have come here to find? Just Parcefal, slaughterer of Saxons?'

'Just him,' Gawain said.

The Lord of the Heights lifted his spear and pointed it down into the fortress. 'Why then did you buy eight horses from Lidas? Even if you find your old friend, that's only six of you.'

'Two to carry supplies and arms,' Gawain replied.

'And eight saddles?' Lord Geldrin said.

With his fingers Gawain brushed at some dirt on his tunic sleeve. 'Lidas is a generous man.'

Lord Geldrin smiled. 'No, Lord Gawain, he is not.'

The dark-haired woman raised her hand to Lord Geldrin and lifted her chin towards Gawain. 'Lord Gawain, did you come here to meet the druid Merlin?' she asked.

Lord Geldrin caught Gawain's eye. 'I said nothing of the cloak of black feathers which we found,' he growled too quietly for the woman to hear.

Father Yvain made a show of making the sign of the Holy Thorn, and so I did the same. Gawain and Gediens frowned at one another.

'Merlin has not been seen in Dumnonia, nor anywhere in Britain for many years,' Gawain told the lady. 'He was not a young man when I knew him.' He shrugged. 'Perhaps he had enough magic to keep death at bay. But it is more likely he is in Annwn causing trouble amongst the dead.' He turned his head to look at the warriors with the black birds on their shields. 'Who are you, lady?' he asked.

The lady considered her answer. 'I am Lady Triamour.' She lifted a slender hand to tuck a wisp of dark hair behind her ear. Her voice was thin in the gusts and brittle like new ice.

'Lady Triamour,' Gawain said, dipping his head respectfully. From the way he stared I could tell he thought her beautiful. And she *was* beautiful. Her full brows guarded blue-grey eyes the shape of little spear blades. Her lips were as plump as ash buds in winter, though cracked and sore-looking, ravaged by wind, teeth or nail. A small speck of brown skin sat below her left eye, where a tear might rest, and to me she had a sad, distant look.

Gawain tore his eyes from her and nodded at the warriors. 'Are they crows, or ravens? It is hard to tell.'

'Crows,' rumbled the huge, granite-faced warrior at the lady's right shoulder.

The lady swept an arm towards Tintagel. 'All this used to belong to my great-grandfather,' she said, 'before Uther took it from him.'

Gawain looked surprised, as did Gediens and Father Yvain. 'You are the Lady Morgana's granddaughter?' he asked.

'I am,' Lady Triamour replied, not with pride but rather a sense of weariness.

'Mordred's daughter?' Gawain frowned. She nodded. I looked at Iselle, who lifted an eyebrow. I knew the stories. It was said that before he was High King, Uther desired Lady Igraine, wife of Lord Gorlois of Tintagel, and was prepared to go to war to win her for himself. But Tintagel was as formidable then as now, and so Uther persuaded Merlin to help him take the fortress and the lady by whatever magic the druid possessed. Some said that Merlin wove a spell which made Uther resemble Gorlois, and so complete was the illusion that Gorlois's warriors opened the gates and welcomed Uther in, a wolf into the hen coop. Igraine, thinking her husband returned, took Uther to her bed and soon thereafter was born Arthur.

Other tales said Merlin conjured a sea fog as thick as dragons' breath, within whose concealment Uther's men stormed the land bridge and took the fortress in a welter of blood. Whatever the truth of it, here was Lord Gorlois and the Lady Igraine's great-granddaughter. The granddaughter of Arthur's half-sister, Morgana, Lady of Camelot. And so here, also, was Lord Arthur's granddaughter. I put that thought aside.

'I saw you once,' Gawain said, 'when you were a little girl. You were screaming like a banshee because another child had thrown your straw doll down the well.'

Lady Triamour's eyes narrowed slightly. 'I do not remember that,' she said, and I found it hard to imagine her screaming nowadays. She seemed so calm. Strangely serene.

'You were just a child,' Gawain said with a smile.

In some ways, Lady Triamour looked a child still, with her slender neck and those doleful, unmoored eyes.

'Why has Merlin returned?' she asked.

'Has he?' Gawain glanced at me and at Gediens, as though wondering if either of us had heard anything to support this lady's claim.

'You know he has,' Lady Triamour said.

Gawain sighed. 'I have never been so ambitious as to know the mind of a druid.'

'And yet you rode with Merlin,' Lord Geldrin put in, 'to recover the sword Excalibur from the painted wildlings north of the great wall.'

'I did,' Gawain admitted. 'I was there to keep Arthur alive, not to serve Merlin.'

Lord Geldrin had more to say on this but Lady Triamour spoke first. 'So, you refuse to tell us what you want with Merlin?'

'I told you, I—'

'You're lying,' Lady Triamour interrupted. 'You came here to meet with Merlin for some purpose which must be of consequence. Or why else would the druid have crawled out from whatever rock he has been under these past years?'

'So you say,' Gawain said, sharing a weary look with Gediens, who shrugged and shook his head.

'Lord!' one of Geldrin's spearmen called out, pointing his spear back down towards his master's hall.

A rider was coming through the pre-dawn gloom, trotting his mount up the slope towards us.

'Who is it?' Lord Geldrin asked, but none of his men had an answer for him.

Whoever the horseman was, he shone in the last light of the fading moon, his helmet and the bronze scales of his coat announcing a lord of battles long before we could see his face.

Lord Geldrin's spearmen bristled, some of them turning to face the rider, while Lady Triamour's huge bodyguard stepped up, planting himself between his lady and the newcomer, who reined in some thirty paces from us, his chestnut mare expelling plumes of hot breath from her flaring nostrils.

'Who are you?' Lord Geldrin demanded of the warrior.

'Who do you think I am?' the horseman called back, forgoing the usual etiquette and show of respect that was Geldrin's due as Lord of Tintagel. In his left hand the warrior gripped a thick-shafted spear, while his shield was slung across his back. His shadow-cast face was wreathed in his own breath.

'I think you are Parcefal ap Bliocadran, a lord of Arthur's horse soldiers,' Lord Geldrin said. 'Another name from the past.' He lifted his free hand and fluttered his fingers. 'Another ghost.'

The warrior walked his horse a little closer, stopping just short of where the grassy earth gave way to the rock ledge, his eyes beneath that helmet's rim fastening on me. 'Gods, lad, but you look like your father,' he said.

I felt both Gawain's and Lord Geldrin's eyes on me. 'I believe I look more like my mother,' I said.

The horseman grunted.

'Parcefal,' Gawain greeted the warrior.

'Gawain,' Parcefal called back, before nodding at Gediens and Father Yvain too. 'What's going on here?' he asked.

Gawain lifted his arms. 'It has become like some bard's song that goes on and on. I think the Lady Triamour intends to have us thrown over the edge, brother.' He nodded towards the overhang, far below which the sea broke in ceaseless rhythm.

'This is none of your concern, Lord Parcefal,' Lady Triamour called, her voice finding an edge now which cut through the gusting wind. 'Leave us and you will not be harmed.'

Parcefal's mare tossed her head and whinnied, and her master leant forward to pat her neck, soothing her with words we could not hear.

'I don't think I can, lady.' Parcefal fussed his horse. 'Not now we've come all the way up here.'

Lady Triamour's crow-shields laughed or sneered contemptuously, but Lord Geldrin's men, having to keep us at spear-point, were more wary and looked to their lord for orders. He gestured at them to hold their positions surrounding us, and the men with their spears held towards Gawain and Gediens pushed them forward, drawing the knot of us tighter.

'I have no quarrel with you, Parcefal ap Bliocadran,' Lord Geldrin said. 'That will change if you do not turn around and leave Tintagel now.'

Gulls whirled above us, their yelping *keow keow* cries weaving a blanket of noise.

Parcefal did not turn his horse around.

'I see that he has not changed,' Father Yvain said.

'And you have?' Gediens asked him, alluding to his killing of those men in the stable. Father Yvain accepted the point.

Then Parcefal removed his helmet and his hair was long and white in the moonlight.

'Have you come up here to die, old man?' Lady Triamour's bodyguard called, rolling his huge shoulders. 'I can hear your ancient bones creaking from here.'

Gawain looked at me and shook his head. 'That was unwise,' he murmured. 'Parcefal hates that he is getting old.'

'Lady, let me pull that old fool from his horse and make him apologize to you for his insolence,' the big warrior said over his shoulder, never taking his eyes from Parcefal.

Lady Triamour clutched at the silver fur at her neck, pulling the thing tighter against the chill. 'I need no apology, Balluc. Just kill him,' she ordered, at which Balluc grinned.

'Yes, lady.' He hefted his spear and crow-painted shield and strode down the rock ledge towards Parcefal.

'Make it quick,' Lord Geldrin said as the warrior passed him.

'Where's the fun in that?' Balluc growled in answer, as Parcefal put his helmet back on, turned his mount and walked her in the opposite direction.

'He's leaving?' I asked Gawain.

'No, Galahad, he's not leaving,' Gawain said.

'But he *is* old,' I said, bewildered by Parcefal's lack of concern. He was about to fight for his life, and yet he sat his horse like a man without a care.

Gediens nodded. 'By rights he should be dead by now.'

I watched Lady Triamour's champion walk with the unhurried, even strides of a man off to complete a task he has done a hundred times before, and I shivered as a thin gust from the sea needled through my gown.

'Seems I wasted money on a horse for him,' Gawain said.

Gediens shrugged. 'You weren't to know he has one already.'

When the distance between him and Balluc was no greater than the distance a strong man could throw a spear, Parcefal pulled his mount around.

'Balor be with you, old friend,' I heard Gediens say under his breath as Parcefal walked his mare forward and the horse whinnied her own war cry. And just then I saw that the night was retreating before the dawn. A pale, watery sun had climbed above the summit to wash the rock and heath in cold, grey light, as Parcefal put his heels to the mare's flanks and she came on at the trot.

Balluc planted himself, chin down, one foot behind the other, shield raised, spear couched beneath his right arm, tight against his body.

The mare's head came up as Parcefal brought her to the canter, sitting tall in the saddle, the red plume of his helmet recalling the blood which his spear must have shed in Britain's dark days. Then Parcefal leant forward in the saddle and gave a shout, thrusting his spear at the sky as the mare took up the gallop, her mane flying in the dawn, her hooves drumming the earth.

But Balluc was ready, leaning forward, legs bent, trusting in his shield to take the impact of Parcefal's spear, perhaps hoping to snag the blade in the wood and disarm his enemy. Then, when Parcefal was just ten paces away, Balluc tilted the shield up in order to deflect the blow. But that blow never came. Because Parcefal lifted the spear high, in the same movement turning it end over end and bringing it down again, thrusting backwards as he passed Balluc and driving the blade into the warrior's back between the shoulder blades.

Balluc stumbled forward and roared, then turned to face his foe, who was slowing his mount to bring her around once more.

Not a mortal wound, the blow made contrary to the impetus

of the charge, but it was humiliating for Balluc, who, if nothing else, must have realized that he had underestimated his opponent.

'I've not seen that done for many years,' Gawain said. Even given where we were, standing on a cliff edge soon to be thrown to our deaths, the smile was in his eyes as much as on his lips.

'Not bad for an old man,' Father Yvain admitted, and there was even the shadow of a smile on Lord Geldrin's face, I noticed, as Parcefal charged again, his spear couched under his left arm this time. At the last moment, he turned the spear end over end again, though this time he struck its butt end into Balluc's crow-shield and the big man was thrown backward with the force of the blow, hitting the ground hard.

Lady Triamour's crow-shields cursed and spat. The lady herself said not a word, her cracked lips pressed tightly together, her pale hands clutched before her.

Parcefal wheeled and came again, and again Balluc braced himself for the impact, but this time Parcefal pulled up short, and his mare reared up, squealing into her own fogging breath, her forehooves pawing the air, and Balluc thought his chance had come. He brought his shield down so he might see to make the thrust, and that was when Parcefal threw his spear, his other arm clinging round the mare's neck. The spear took Balluc in his mouth, the blade punching through the back of his skull and lodging there.

A gasp went up from the crow-shields and from Lord Geldrin's spearmen and from us too, as Balluc dropped his shield and stumbled backwards, as the mare's forehooves landed and she tossed her head in a show of equine triumph. Balluc's legs folded and his arse landed on his heels, and he made a strange spectacle sitting like that, a spear sheathed in his head as if cast from the heavens by a god, before the weight of muscle and mail tipped him over onto his back. It was a shocking sight and yet spellbinding too.

'I'm glad I lived to see that,' Father Yvain said.

I looked at Iselle, who looked at me, our eyes wide with wonder.

'Ghosts from another time,' Lord Geldrin said, as Parcefal walked his horse over to Balluc and leant out of the saddle to haul the spear from the dead man's skull. Then he walked the mare back up the slope towards us and I could see the bronze scales rising and falling like waves with his laboured breath.

'See that, lad?' he called and I realized he was talking to me.

I nodded. Of course I had seen it. I had never seen anything like it.

'I'm not as good as I once was,' Parcefal confessed, breathing hard. 'And even then, I was never as good as your father.' He shook his head, his plume sifting in the breeze. 'But then, none of us were.'

Neither Gawain nor Gediens disagreed with that.

'Who was your father?' Lord Geldrin asked me, though I could see in his eyes that he already knew.

'My father was Lancelot,' I said.

Even if he had known it, the sound of that name in the wind still struck him like a blow.

'Lancelot,' he said softly. I could tell he had not spoken my father's name for a long, long time.

Lady Triamour took a step towards me. 'This changes nothing,' she said, though her face said differently.

Lord Geldrin ignored her. 'Your father and I were friends,' he told me. 'When we were your age. Younger, even.' He scratched his neat beard. 'As much as any man could be Lancelot's friend.' The way he was staring, I knew he was looking for my father in me.

'This changes nothing,' Lady Triamour said again. If her voice had been as ice before, now it was cracking like some thin mantle underfoot. 'Kill them, Lord Geldrin.'

Lord Geldrin frowned. 'No, lady. I will not.'

'You will kill them, Lord Geldrin. I speak for Lady Morgana, as you well know, and I command you to kill these men. Her too,' she added, pointing at Iselle.

Lord Geldrin shook his head. 'And I am telling you that I will not,' he said.

'Because you and his father were friends a lifetime ago?' Lady Triamour scoffed, her pale cheeks flushing red. Behind her, the four crow-shields stirred uneasily, looking to each other for leadership. Lord Geldrin's refusal to carry out their lady's command had raised their hackles, but with their champion Balluc lying dead down there in the wet grass, and they so few in number, they did not know what to do. 'Or is it that you fear the dead, Lord Geldrin?' she continued. 'Do you fear meeting Lancelot again in the next life, and what he will do to you if you kill his son?'

Lord Geldrin did not answer these questions. Instead, he gestured at me and Gawain, Gediens and Iselle. 'They will not be harmed,' he told his men, then pointed his spear at Father Yvain. 'But kill the monk.'

'No!' I made two strides before a warrior put the point of his spear against my chest. 'No, lord!' I said, feeling another spear against the small of my back.

'He killed three of my men, Galahad ap Lancelot,' Lord Geldrin said, as two spearmen took hold of Father Yvain by his arms, and another put his spear's point between the monk's shoulders, 'and he will pay with his life.'

'Kill them all,' Lady Triamour commanded.

'Just the monk,' Lord Geldrin told his men.

'Please, lord!' I called.

'Don't do this, Lord Geldrin,' Gawain said.

'It is already done, Lord Gawain.' Lord Geldrin gestured to the cliff edge with his spear.

'Gawain?' Parcefal called, as if asking permission to kick back his heels and charge. Gawain raised a hand at him and shook his head.

'Please, lord,' I said. 'Do not do this.' The blade against my chest was biting now, but still I pushed against it, a tide rising inside me, seething in my veins and threatening to spill over.

'It's all right, Galahad,' Father Yvain said, 'it's all right.'

'You were protecting me!' I said.

'An oath is an oath, Galahad.' He smiled. 'But I'd do it again, oath or no.'

The spearman pulled at him, trying to haul him towards the edge, but he fought against it as if he had sunk roots into the rock beneath his feet.

'Let me hold the boy,' he growled at Lord Geldrin. 'Just once.'

Lord Geldrin nodded, at which the spearmen guarding me, as well as those guarding Father Yvain, stepped back and pointed their spear blades at the lightening sky. And in a heartbeat I threw myself at Father Yvain and he held me so tight that I could not get my breath.

'We'll fight them,' I said.

'No, lad. Not this time.'

'Please.'

'You must let me go. You hear me, lad. You let me go now.'

I held him and he held me, and my tears soaked the fur at his shoulder.

'It's all right, Galahad,' he said, and then his big hand cradled the back of my head and I was a little boy again. 'Now, you remember, lad, you are not him. You are not your father.'

His words were hot in my ear, his beard soft on my cheek. 'You are Galahad. No matter what they want you to be. No matter what you think you should be. You're Galahad. You understand me, boy?'

I tried to nod but he was holding my head so tight. *So tight*. 'Please,' I begged.

'If you see Merlin, you tell him I kept my oath. As best I could. You tell him, lad. Now let me go. They're waiting for me. My little Tangwen and my boy. They've waited long enough.'

And then he broke away from me and I thought I would drown without him to cling to. He nodded and I saw the fear in his eyes.

'Don't you forget. Don't you dare,' he said, as Lord Geldrin's men took hold of him again. 'Don't you dare!' he snarled at me, his fear rising.

I looked back at Iselle. Her tears were falling to the rocks. I looked at Gawain and Gediens, hoping that they would do something. Gawain met my gaze and shook his head and when I turned back to Father Yvain they had him at the edge and his beard bristled in the sea breeze and it glistened with his tears.

Then the spearmen pushed him and he was gone.

I could see Lord Geldrin and Lady Triamour were arguing but I could not hear their words. Above me, the gulls rose and swooped but made no sound. Even the sea had ceased its roar, the waves breaking in silent fury upon the fretted rocks below.

He was gone. He had left me. Though I could still feel his hand on the back of my head, his strong fingers amongst my hair. I could smell him on my own skin, but he was gone.

I turned and saw Parcefal ride up onto the rock. Saw him throw his sword to Gawain and his long knife to Gediens and saw Lord Geldrin's men do nothing to stop it.

Iselle was in front of me and I recognized the shape of my name on her lips, though there was no sound. She took hold of my gown and pulled me towards Gawain, who had taken up a defensive stance beside Gediens and Parcefal, their blades raised towards Lord Geldrin's men and the crow-shields.

Then Iselle struck my face and it was as if she woke me from a dream. The clamour engulfed me, flooding me like freezing water, and I stumbled as Iselle hauled me away from the two groups of spearmen, who were jeering and hurling insults at each other, working themselves up to violence.

'Kill them!' Lady Triamour screamed. Gone was the beautiful young woman with the lost look in her eyes. In her place was a hate-filled creature who craved our deaths. 'Kill them, Lord Geldrin, or I will curse you myself. I will bind your soul to a black kid goat. I will fill your bladder with stones so that you cannot pass water.'

'Enough!' Lord Geldrin roared, cracking the butt of his spear onto the rock and pointing a finger at Lady Triamour. 'Do not threaten me, lady,' he warned her. 'I have kept faith with Lady Morgana, but I am lord here and these are my men to command.' He gestured with his spear towards the sea. 'You have the druid. I did not interfere. But I will not waste another man.' He nodded at us. 'You want them dead, lady, you kill them yourself.'

Lady Triamour hissed at Lord Geldrin and commanded her men to kill us, and so they lowered their spears, raised their shields and walked towards us. Iselle turned and ran down to where Balluc lay and in ten heartbeats she was standing beside Gawain and Gediens, the dead warrior's sword in one hand, his shield in the other.

'Back,' Lord Geldrin told his own spearmen, who shuffled back across the rock, 'this is none of our business.' Then he called my name and threw his own spear to me and I caught it. 'Though I'll not see Lancelot's son murdered without a blade in his hand, even if he is a monk of the Christ.'

I gripped the spear in both hands and it felt familiar. It felt good.

'Get behind me, Galahad,' Gawain said, but I stayed where I was at his shoulder, facing the crow-shields, who were close enough now that I could smell their sweat, leather and dung stink, carried to us on the gusts. My eyes found the eyes of one of them. A tall man, perhaps ten years older than I, and an experienced warrior no doubt, who had risen to serve in the Lady Triamour's personal guard. I wanted to kill him. I craved it, the need rising in my chest, beating like wings.

But the tall warrior went for Gawain, and whatever his experience in battle, it was his last act in this life. He thrust his spear at Gawain, who turned the blade aside with Parcefal's sword, then stepped inside, grabbed a fistful of the cloak at the man's neck and pulled him close, at the same time thrusting the sword into his belly and roaring with the effort and thrill of it. The blade split the leather armour and plunged deeper, into the man's guts, then Gawain pulled the sword out and strode back, giving himself space as the rest of Lady Triamour's men came on past their companion, who dropped his shield and fell to his knees, clutching at his death wound which steamed in the dawn.

'Back, lad,' Gawain growled at me but I held my ground.

'No!' Lady Triamour shouted. 'No more! Back. Back, men of Camelot.' She had changed her mind, and the crow-shields didn't need telling again. They lowered their shields and retreated, gathering close to their lady. She had seen two of her men slaughtered and perhaps she knew that her gods were not with her on that wind-pummelled clifftop.

'Good,' Lord Geldrin said. 'Now I suggest you leave Tintagel, Lord Gawain. My men will return your belongings. You take your horses and you go, and you will not come back here again, do you understand?'

Gawain was breathing hard, his sword dripping crimson into the grass. He nodded. 'I do.'

Lord Geldrin was glaring at me then and there was fire between us.

'You know I had to do it, lad,' he said. 'The dead must be avenged.' He nodded. 'Keep the spear. A gift.'

I said nothing. The spear felt good in my hand. I wondered if my throw was still true, if I could hit Lord Geldrin from where I stood.

'Galahad,' Gawain rumbled. 'We're leaving.'

Still looking at the Lord of the Heights, I nodded. Then I turned and we strode back down the hill towards Tintagel, now and then looking back to make sure Lady Triamour's men weren't coming after us.

'You're looking old, my friend,' Gawain said to Parcefal, who was leaning back against his saddle horns, letting his mare pick her own way down a rocky bluff.

'I *am* old,' Parcefal said, lifting his left arm and wincing at some pain. Below us, Tintagel was waking up to a new day. 'I meant to put that big ox down on the first pass.'

Gawain and Gediens grinned bitterly at that. But I could still hear Lord Geldrin's words on the wind.

The dead must be avenged.

Lord Geldrin's men returned everything they had taken from us, including, to my surprise, the druid's sack, though I was not much comforted to have it again in my possession. Then they escorted us across the land bridge, making sure that the big gates on the landward side were firmly shut and barred behind us. They had not let Gawain sell any of the horses back to Lidas the hunchback, and so we were five riding, with four spare mounts, those horses serving to remind us that we had failed. And that Father Yvain was gone.

I had not gone to the edge of that bluff and looked over, yet still my mind kept showing me his dead body, broken on the rocks. Rolling back and forth in the breakers as the sea worked up the hunger to claim him. He was gone and my heart ached for him.

'He was a good man.' Iselle looked up at the sky as she rode, watching a white egret fly out to sea, graceful and buoyant into the wind, its neck tucked back, legs trailing behind. I fancied it was Yvain's soul escaping his broken body, flying to his wife and children who waited for him on Arawn's shore. Somehow, I knew that Iselle thought the same as she watched that bird.

'As brave as any man I've known,' Gawain said, riding behind me. 'There was nothing we could do.' I could feel his eyes on the back of my head.

I took a breath, trying to swallow the knot in my throat. 'Just as there was nothing we could do for the brothers,' I said, the words as acrid as smoke. 'You remember how we left them to die?'

For a long moment there was just the sound of the horses' hooves clumping softly on the earth, the jangle of tack and the creak of leather.

'There have been many sacrifices, Galahad,' Gawain said. 'There will be many more before this is over.'

'And when will it be over, lord?' I asked.

'When Arthur leads us to victory,' he said. 'When the Saxons are thrown back into the sea.'

'When the gods return to the land,' Iselle added.

'Imagine the Beltane fires,' Gediens said. 'Night will become day.'

'I hope I live to see it,' Parcefal said.

I twisted in my saddle and looked at the big grey mare which Father Yvain should have been riding, and I felt his absence like a great weight, a quern stone sitting in my stomach. A burden of guilt for the years which Father Yvain had given, for the words he had spoken and their binding of him to me. But why had Merlin made him swear such an oath? What did the druid want with me?

'Do you think Father Yvain is with his family now?' I asked Iselle.

She considered this for a time. 'Merlin had the ear of the gods, so they say.' She leant to touch the iron bit in her horse's mouth. 'That is what Arthur believed.'

'But Merlin failed Arthur at the end,' I said. 'Perhaps Merlin had lost his power by the time he made Yvain swear the oath.'

A frown passed like a shadow across Iselle's brow. 'Even if his spell did not work, or if Merlin knew it would not work and meant to deceive Yvain . . .' she spoke the words as if they tasted foul, 'do you think Yvain was the kind of man who would give up searching for his family?'

I did not need to answer that. Yvain would find his wife and his son and his daughter in Arawn's realm. I searched the sky, but the egret was long gone. It had ghosted into the grey somewhere above the Western Sea and so I closed my eyes and watched Father Yvain carrying a laughing little girl upon his shoulders.

We rode east, to Camelot. Gawain had been right to suspect that the ship moored in Tintagel bay had something to do with it all. Parcefal explained that he had gone into the fort to buy supplies, leaving Merlin and his Saxon slave, Oswine, in the sea cave.

'The old bastard was griping day and night about the food,' Parcefal told us, 'like a maggot in my ear, he was. In the end I thought I'd shut him up by fetching some fresh bread and cheese. Some wine, perhaps.' But when Parcefal had gone back down to the sea cave, Merlin and Oswine were gone, only a few drops of blood in the sand to tell of a struggle. 'A maggot in my ear,' Parcefal said again, then cursed under his breath. The old warrior was embarrassed. All those years of searching for Merlin, to finally find him, only to lose him again.

'I don't blame you,' Gawain said. 'Being in Merlin's company is like having a toothache. I rode the length of Britain beside him and it was only because of Arthur that I didn't cut out the druid's tongue when he was asleep.' He grunted and shook his head. 'Mind you, Lancelot hated him even more than I did.'

'Why?' I asked.

'Your father thought Merlin manipulated Guinevere. Because she had the gift,' Gawain said. 'Lancelot thought the druid had his claws in her, and I daresay he did. That devious bastard had his claws in all of us.' He seemed to chew on his next words before deciding to let them out. 'There was a time, when Arthur was at his lowest ebb, when it seemed the gods and men had forsaken him, that he believed that Merlin was behind all of it.' I looked at Gawain and he held my eye. 'That Merlin had *known* Lancelot and Guinevere would fall in love. That he made sure they did. Just like he tricked your father into swearing an oath of loyalty to Arthur.'

Iselle and I glanced at each other. 'Why would Merlin do that?' I asked.

Gawain shrugged. 'Why does a druid do anything?' he said,

using a finger to dig something from his ear. 'Maybe he saw such promise in Guinevere that he wanted the two greatest warriors in Britain protecting her. Or maybe he knew that Lancelot needed to love Guinevere, as a hawk needs flesh, that without that need, your father would never earn the love of the gods. Who can say?'

'I think he knew that Lancelot's guilt would bind him even more tightly to Arthur,' Iselle said. 'So that he would do anything for him.'

Those were heavy words and silence followed in their wake, aside from the soft clump of the horses' hooves on the grass and the creaking of saddles.

I had never met Merlin. To me he had always been nothing more than rumour. A bad taste on the air and barely given breath amongst the brothers of the Thorn. But now I knew he was of flesh and blood and I was already beginning to hate him.

Camelot

WHEN WE CAME TO Camelot four days later, Gediens
told me I looked like a fish pulled from the depths, all
bulging eyes and open mouth. But if that were true, I was not
the only one in awe at the sight. Iselle sat tall in the saddle, her
neck craned as she looked up at that great hill and the wall of
dressed stone and timbers surmounting it. Even Gawain gazed
upon it dewy-eyed, though I knew it was not for how impressive it looked but rather for what Camelot represented, and for
the memories forged there which Gawain carried with him, as
bright and sharp still as the sword in his scabbard.

We came as though summoned by the ringing of the smith's
hammer, as if beckoned by the sweet scent of the hearth and by
the less pleasant stench of humanity and its foulsome dregs.
For there is comfort even in this, Parcefal admitted, when one
has been long on the road.

Rising steeply some five hundred feet above rich farmland,
it was an ancient hill fort. A stronghold of the kings of old, long
before Rome set her hobnailed heel upon our land. And there
was something about the place which made my blood tremble
in my veins as we sat our horses beneath the boughs of an old
oak, to which some brown leaves clung still, having hung on
through every winter gale. It was in the rustle and flutter of

those dead leaves now. Faint voices from the past, whispering of death and war, of the violent dispute or silent disease which had robbed them of their lives. But these whispers were also of love and brief, golden happiness, of bountiful crops and barns full of grain and Beltane fires which licked the skies with flame.

On fine, clear days I had used to look upon this hill from the tor on Ynys Wydryn, knowing that for nearly thirty years it had stood as a symbol of defiance against the Saxons. But only now, with it cramming my eyes, with its memories on the very air and worming into my mind, did I truly understand Camelot. It was the beating heart of Dumnonia. Even without Arthur to man its walls and to lead his famed horse warriors out of its gates, Camelot was the hope of Britain. The last light in these Dark Isles. And perhaps Lady Morgana had taken Merlin because she wanted him at her side in the war against the Saxons, just as her half-brother Arthur had, and Uther before him.

But Gawain and the last of Arthur's loyal men had not searched for the druid all these years to let Lady Morgana wield his power now. There were those who believed, though few would say it aloud, that Morgana had known of Mordred's intended betrayal of Arthur. That she had even planted the seed of it in the young warrior's heart when he was just a boy. For had she not desired Camelot for herself? So men said. And what more terrible revenge could she fashion for the man who had sired their son yet was so repelled by the incestuous act that he tried to have the boy Mordred killed?

'What more vicious revenge than that,' Gawain had remarked one black night by the fire, 'on a man already savaged to the marrow by betrayal?'

'Poor Arthur,' Iselle had said, the flames lighting her face. Dancing in her eyes.

'Aye, poor Arthur,' Parcefal said.

Gawain threw a half-charred stick into the fire. 'And now she has taken Merlin, to use him for her own ends.'

'What if she hasn't?' I asked. 'What if someone else has the druid?'

Gawain shook his head. 'Morgana has him, lad. Why else was that sad-looking granddaughter of hers at Tintagel?'

Parcefal agreed. 'Someone must've seen us and sent word to Camelot.' He folded a blanket and tucked it behind him between his back and a rock, then lay back, watching the fire. 'Have you noticed that we're better at making enemies than we are at making friends?'

Gawain grunted in reply and looked off into the night.

And so we had come to that great hill fort beneath heavy, grey skies, to find the druid.

'It is a sight to rekindle hope.' Parcefal was hunched into both his cloaks, having thrown his spare one over his shoulders. Like the others, he was without his fine war gear; the scale coats, plumed helmets and bear-shields were wrapped and stashed on the spare mounts so as not to draw the eye of any folk coming or going through Camelot's south-west gate. Still, the three men hardly looked like farmers.

'Your father and Arthur dug those ditches together,' Gawain told me, lifting his chin at the ramparts which had been thrown up on the hill's already steep sides. 'Day after day they worked in the mud. It was the only honest labour I ever saw Arthur do, other than making war.' He shook his head. 'This was his dream, Galahad. The two of them were like brothers then. Before it all soured.'

'There's no bond between men that a woman can't sever,' Gediens said.

Iselle lifted an eyebrow at him and he turned his palms up.

'What if we can't find him?' I asked, for only Iselle and I would go into Camelot. The others would be recognized in mere moments were they to ride through those gates. Gawain had been beside Arthur when Arthur killed Mordred, so he could expect no hospitality from the Lady of Camelot. But Iselle and I were unknown and so it was up to us to find where the lady was keeping Merlin, assuming the druid was somewhere inside that citadel.

'He's in there somewhere,' Gawain assured us as we dismounted, Iselle grimacing and pressing a hand to her backside, which clearly ached from riding. 'You'll smell him out.'

The ship on which the druid had been taken would have sailed up the Dumnonian coast as far as the Steart Peninsula, there taking the Parwydydd until the marsh became too shallow, at which point smaller craft would have carried them the rest of the way. Three days at most, Gediens said.

'He's here,' Parcefal grunted. 'I can feel the bastard.'

Gawain held out a hand to Iselle. 'You'll have enough eyes on you, girl, without having a Saxon sword on your back.'

Iselle tensed, her nostrils flaring, and I thought she would refuse, having already tied her bow and her arrow bag to her mare's saddle. Frowning, she handed Gawain her Saxon sword, scabbard and baldric, and he wrapped the belt around the sword, then pointed at the long knife sheathed at Iselle's waist.

'No,' she said. Her hand found the bone hilt.

Gawain pressed his lips into a tight line and nodded. 'Stay out of trouble,' he told us. 'We'll be hereabouts. And be quick about it.' He turned in the saddle and looked back at the muddied track along which we had come. A man and a boy were leading an ox and empty cart towards the hill fort, the wheels creaking and the man now and then goading the beast with a hazel switch. 'Lady Triamour will come,' Gawain twisted back to us, 'and when her grandmother learns that we are alive, she will have spearmen scouring Dumnonia for us and we'll never get the druid back to Arthur.'

'We'll find him,' I said, and meant it. I would do anything to hurt Lady Morgana, for while she had not been the one to throw Father Yvain from the cliff at Tintagel, her pursuit of Merlin was behind it. And so Iselle and I waited until the ox and cart had passed, then followed it up the cobbled roadway towards the gate, above which a banner was draped from the timber-built tower: a huge swath of undyed wool upon which were embroidered three great black birds. Crows, each as tall as a man, their beaks as long as a sword.

Whereas Tintagel had been carved by a god long before the time of kings, Camelot was sculpted by men and was no less impressive for it. It was a fortress built on the bones of our ancestors, the earth turned by muscle and iron, the soil watered with blood and nourished by kinship and common cause. And as we walked along the channel that had long ago been cut through the four great embankments which comprised the ramparts, I could not help but see my father working beneath the summer sun, his skin glistening, his long dark hair tied back as he had used to wear it when cutting timber or turning the ground or teaching me sword and spear. I could almost smell the sweat on his chest and in his beard. I felt his presence here as I had done when I had been alone with his armour at Lord Arthur's steading. And before that, at Ynys Wydryn, when I had dug out the arm bracer from my chest of belongings and held it to my nose, breathing in the still lingering sweet and resinous scent and seeing in my mind my father sitting by the hearth, rubbing beeswax into the leather until it shone.

'What is it, Galahad?' Iselle called back to me. She had walked ahead but now waited near the inner gate, as two guards questioned the man with the cart. 'What's wrong?'

'Nothing,' I said, hurrying to catch up, then turning to look back once more along the rampart. But my father was gone.

We followed the cart through the gates, expecting the guards to ask who we were, but they barely looked at us, and then we were inside the inner rampart. Though we stood on the plateau, some five hundred feet above the old oak tree where we had left the others, the summit was almost windless. I looked this way and that, taking it all in, astonished by the scale of the place and bewitched by the moment of standing where my father must once have stood looking upon the same sights as now greeted my eyes.

'I never thought I'd come here.' Iselle's voice was full of wonder, though hushed too, as if she felt she should not be here. As if someone might tell her to turn around and go back out through the gates, for this was nowhere for someone from the marshes to be. She shook her head. 'I tried to imagine what it was like, but I never thought I'd see it.'

I did not need to answer. We were both overwhelmed, our gaze ranging across the thatched dwellings and workshops leaking smoke into the sky, across the barns and stores, the stables and the smithies and the myriad timber trackways, and all the folk who lived in relative safety within Camelot's walls. Men, women, children, going about their business this grey day.

The noise of the place washed over us like a draught of strong wine: the barking of dogs, the lowing and bleating of cattle in their pens, the cuckoo calls of children playing, the chop of the axe and the squeak and clump of the carts, and the grunts of those driving the oxen, and the neighs and whinnies of horses.

'But here I am.' Iselle threw her arms wide. 'In Camelot. With a half monk for company.'

I took the bait. 'I'm no more a monk than you,' I said, feeling no guilt saying it, just a strange emptiness. Now that Father Yvain was gone, there were no brothers of the Holy Thorn. The order was only as real as a memory, and I alone could carry it with me.

But then, what did that make me?

'It is strange to think of Arthur and Guinevere having been lord and lady here,' Iselle said. 'When you think of them now, hiding in the marsh.' I followed her line of sight towards the great hall which dominated the fortress. Until that moment I had purposely not allowed my eyes to settle on it, as one might leave the meat in the broth till last to better savour it.

It was as big as Uther's old hall at Tintagel, though unlike that hall, whose timbers were warped with age, these beams were as spear-straight as the day Arthur's builder set them in place. The thatch upon the sloping roof was grey but there were no patches of lichen amongst it, and it was not hard to imagine the Lord Arthur and his beautiful wife stepping out beneath a summer sky, their names invoked as folk will call upon the gods for a good harvest, the hopes of Britain on their shoulders.

'Do you think it can be as it once was, Galahad?' Iselle asked me. 'If Merlin can bring Guinevere back into the light. If Arthur takes up Excalibur once more and leads us?' There was so much hope in her proud face. I ached for her.

'Gawain must believe it,' I said. 'And he is not a man given to fanciful ideas, it seems to me.'

Iselle frowned. 'He is a warrior. He knows nothing else. Gawain wants the Arthur of old back because he knows that

Arthur, the lord of battle, is a man whom others will follow. That even the kings of Britain will follow, and so there will be a great army. That is what Gawain wants and he will do anything to see it come to pass.'

'Parcefal and Gediens believe it too,' I said, but she did not answer that, for we both knew that they, like Gawain, were echoes of a time past, all of them searching for the voice that created them.

'Let's try the lady's hall first?' Iselle said.

And so we set off along the timber trackway as a peal of thunder rolled across the western sky and the dogs of Camelot gave up a chorus of howls. Iselle said they sounded like the monks of the Holy Thorn singing their prayers. But she got no rise from me, because I was watching a group of warriors gathered around two bare-chested, mud-slathered men who were grappling, each trying to throw the other down.

We both stopped. 'No,' Iselle said. She had grabbed my arm. I felt her fingers pressing down to the bone. 'It can't be.'

One of the men put the other down and a cheer went up from half of the crowd, as the two wrestlers writhed in the mud, so coated in it that the whites of their eyes shone against the black.

My stomach was clenching, the back of my neck prickling. Because some of the men, eight or nine of them, had long fair hair worn loose or tied into warrior braids, golden beards or beard ropes and ruddy complexions. These were fur-clad and most of them carried hand axes on their belts, and the swords that I could see were longer blades, like the one which Iselle had just given to Gawain.

They were Saxons.

'What are they doing in Camelot?' Iselle hissed, her hand falling from my arm to the hilt of her long knife.

That Saxons could be here, in the heart of Dumnonia, seemed impossible. That they could be here by invitation was unthinkable. And yet, here they were, men wearing at their necks iron or silver amulets of their god Thunor. Men with the grey Morimaru in their eyes and the blood of Britons on their hands. Men cheering for their companion, who had now bound Morgana's man with strong arms and gripping legs, much to the disgust of the Dumnonians, who jeered, accusing the Saxon of cheating.

For a while we watched the bout and though, because of the mud, it became impossible to say which man was which, when the Saxons gave a great cheer and slapped each other's shoulders and sought their winnings from a grey-bearded Dumnonian, neither of us mentioned the bad omen in it. But then, as if to mock our silence, thunder rumbled through the grey sky, closer this time, followed by fat drops of rain which splashed on the timber track and presaged the kind of downpour which has folk running for cover.

And yet, as we wandered amongst the timber-framed buildings, past the smithy and the workshops of the potter, the woodworker, the bronze-caster, the basket-weaver and the barrel-maker, I realized that the rain was helping us. For like everyone else, we threw up our hoods, making it less likely that someone would ask who we were. When I said as much to Iselle, her scathing reply was that the people of Camelot must be growing used to having strangers within their walls.

Behind a barn, we came upon a group of children waging battle against each other with wooden swords and wicker shields. There were four boys and three girls, and the side with four were pretending to be Saxons.

'Look at these fierce warriors,' I called. 'Stay back or they may cut off your head.'

At this the children grinned savagely and resumed their battle with even more vigour now that they had an audience. One of the older boys proclaimed that he was Lord Arthur, and the lad beside him, a small, wild-looking boy whose sword was a blur in his hand, told Iselle that he was Lancelot. And my heart kicked like a horse.

I took a breath, feeling Iselle's eyes on me. The wooden swords clacked and clattered. 'Brave warriors of Dumnonia,' I said, waiting as the two armies separated once more and nursed injuries, checked their weapons for damage or looked at us, one or two of them eyeing my habit with suspicion. 'I have heard that Lady Morgana has found a druid. And that he is here in Camelot. Is it true?'

'It's true!' one of them replied, sweeping his sword left and right.

'His name is Merlin,' the eldest boy added. 'He was a great druid in the old days.' He was still using his Lord Arthur voice.

'Are you a druid?' a younger boy asked me.

'Don't be stupid, Dalam,' one of the others spat. 'There are no druids now but for Merlin. He is the last.'

The younger boy glowered, and another boy explained that I was a Christian, at which I saw the disappointment in the smaller boy's eyes.

'I've seen him. Merlin,' the eldest girl said. She wore a strip of linen around her head and over her right eye. 'My father is one of the guards.' She lifted her chin and her left eye was sharp with pride. 'Lady Morgana gave him a Roman coin once because he fought bravely at the Battle of Giant's Rock.'

I did my best to seem impressed. 'Your father must be a great warrior.'

'Where is Merlin now?' Iselle asked. The girl narrowed her good eye at Iselle.

'I'm not supposed to say,' she said, glancing back at her companions, most of whom were fighting once more, caught up in the ebb and flow of their own great battle.

'We won't tell anyone,' I lied. 'But we would like very much to catch a glimpse of a real druid.'

She considered this and seemed to understand. Then she took three steps towards us, her new and ominous expression seeming out of place on her young face. 'Everyone will have the chance to see Merlin before sunset,' she said.

I looked up at the sky but if there was a sun up there, I could not see it. Then the girl held the point of her wooden sword to pursed lips, deciding what she would and would not say. 'Are you two in love?' she asked, looking from me to Iselle, then back to me. This took us both by surprise. Iselle laughed, which, if anything, fanned the heat in my cheeks.

'We do not even believe in the same gods,' Iselle told her, and then came the rain as we knew it would. It hissed down in veils of grey, blurring the world.

The girl narrowed her eyes at Iselle. 'The north-east gate, before sunset,' she said, then she turned and ran with the others, who scattered and vanished like minnows from a plunging oar blade.

'We may as well find a roof to wait under,' Iselle said, setting off towards the perimeter wall to shelter beneath the concourse, upon which stood Lady Morgana's men, leaning on their spears, heads tucked into their shoulders as they looked out east across the forests of Caer Gwinntguic.

'You don't mind sheltering from the rain with me,' I challenged Iselle, 'even though we pray to different gods?'

She tilted her head to one side and eyed me as I deserved. And then we waited, watching the rain seethe down upon Camelot, wondering why there were Saxons here, and hoping that the girl with the eye patch was not taking us for a pair of fools.

12

Merlin

A T FIRST, WE DID not see him because of the rain. We saw the ox and cart and the man with the hazel switch and the boy walking on the other side of the beast. We saw the folk of Camelot emerging from their dwellings and workshops, from the barns and byres and from Lady Morgana's great hall, all of them wrapped in cloaks and leather capes against the deluge. We saw a party of spearmen crowding around the cart and we knew why the cart had been empty when the man had brought it in through the south-west gate, and we knew that it was not empty now, though we had yet to lay eyes on its cargo.

Then the spearmen dispersed, taking up positions around the cart, and that's when we saw him. I heard Iselle's sharp intake of breath and saw her hand move inside her cloak to touch the iron pommel of the long knife on her belt.

'It's him,' I confirmed. It had to be. Merlin. The man who helped Uther Pendragon seize Tintagel and become High King. The man who served Lord Arthur and helped him find the sword Excalibur, by whose ancient, gleaming blade Arthur united the kings of Britain for the first time in many generations. And the man who was nowhere to be found when Arthur needed him, and who had been barely even a rumour wafting through the cantrefs of Britain these last ten years.

The man struck the ox's muscled flank and it lumbered forward into the dusk, the cart behind it groaning as they set off beside the timber track which ran all the way through Camelot, past the great hall to the south-west gate. I saw the girl who had told us to be at the north-east gate at sunset and I nodded to her in thanks and she smiled.

'The lady means to shame him.' Iselle spat the words. 'Here is a man who speaks with the old gods, the gods of Britain, and she means to display him like a prize slave.'

It seemed to me that most of those who had come out into the hammering rain were as uneasy about this treatment of Merlin as Iselle was. Or perhaps they were just afraid. They kept pace with the cart but from a distance, murmuring in low voices, eyeing the druid from the anonymous shadow of the hoods and cloaks with which they covered their heads.

'The last of the druids,' I muttered, feeling a strange sense of emptiness and dread.

'It is not how I saw him in my mind,' Iselle admitted, as we shuffled along with the rest, catching glimpses of the prisoner between the shifting human tide.

I supposed that Oswine, Merlin's Saxon slave, had been killed already. Or else he was still being held captive somewhere heareabouts.

'He must be very old now,' I said. I felt foolish for not having prepared myself for the sight. What had I expected to see? A druid in all his terrible glory? A priest of the gods who carried the ancient knowledge of Britain with him like a fire in the dark?

Of course, the last days, living in a cave, travelling by sea and by marsh and then being kept as a prisoner, must have taken a toll on the old man. He sat slumped, hands bound with rope, swaying and bouncing with the cart's progress across the bumpy ground, so that I imagined his bones rattling in his skin like a smith's tools in an old sack. He was mud-daubed and wild-eyed, and what hair he still had was grey, long and lank, hanging from his head in matted tangles. And if I had thought Lord Arthur and Guinevere were living skeletons, Merlin was so gaunt, so painfully thin, that it was hard to believe he had eaten in many days. He was an old, gnarled tree root of a man who looked as if he should have been ash on the wind by now, had not some curse held him here past his natural time.

We walked with this strange procession through the shrouding rain, and when the cart reached the great hall, it stopped and the folk around it turned their eyes to the open door, beyond which the leaping flames and copper glow promised warmth and comfort, making me aware of how the rain had now soaked through my cloak and habit to chill my bones.

There was a flurry of movement within the hall and then the Lady of Camelot emerged, blinking reddened, smoke-stung eyes at the rain. She was swathed in black cloaks which had been greased well enough that the water rolled off them in beads, spilling onto the planks beneath, and it was clear to me why her warriors had crows painted on their shields and why a great crow banner hung from Camelot's gatehouse. For Lady Morgana was the living embodiment of the Morrigán. Her hair was long and silver and still thick enough to be tied back in a rope that could bind a man, as once her beauty might have done. Her hands were old, the knuckles swollen, so that even they looked like a crow's feet, and her nose, which once must have looked regal and handsome, was long and beak-like on her age-shrunken face.

Part of me wondered how it was possible that this old crone could wield such power in Camelot and in Britain. And yet she did.

'People of Camelot,' she called in the coarse voice of a rook, as two young warriors took up positions either side of her. 'Look here!' Another man stood off her shoulder and Iselle and I realized at the same time that this was the Saxon warrior who had earlier been wrestling in the mud. He was clean now, though, and wearing a mail tunic, his fair beard braided, a silver brooch fastening an ermine-trimmed cloak. His men stood nearby, similarly adorned for war, their spear blades glinting dully in the day.

'Look upon the ruin of Britain.' Lady Morgana walked over to the cart. The two warriors went with her and, at her signal, one of them grabbed hold of Merlin's hair and hauled his head back so that he had no choice but to look at Lady Morgana. 'Here is the festering wound which poisons the land,' Morgana said.

There was something terribly cruel in Morgana. As cruel as a sharp knife. I could feel it from where I stood, and I feared it, as a murmur ran through the crowd. A young man stepped out and spat at Merlin. The druid neither flinched nor moved to wipe the spittle from his cheek. He just stared at Morgana, who gestured at the warrior to let go of the druid. The warrior stepped back, and Merlin dropped his head and closed his eyes.

'To spit at a druid,' Iselle whispered, appalled.

'Burn him!' a woman yelled.

'Hang him!' a child of no more than eight winters demanded.

Whatever power Merlin had once wielded over folk, whatever awe had kept these people cautious earlier, was gone, dispelled by the sour wind of their lady's words.

'Where was Merlin when Dumnonia needed him?' an old man asked us all, before bending, clawing up a handful of mud and flinging it at the druid.

'Where are the gods now, druid?' a voice from the crowd

screeched. 'We've Saxons within our walls, eating our food and drinking our ale.'

This raised a rumble of agreement as ominous as the earlier thunder, and the warriors flanking Lady Morgana glanced at each other uneasily, though Lady Morgana gave a slight shake of her head, a gesture which told them to let that dissent die away unanswered. I saw that those two men shared so much with each other – the lean face, full lips and contemptuous look in their grey eyes – that it was clear they were brothers, just as something less definable marked them as kin to the lady herself.

'Who are they?' I asked the man beside me. A blacksmith, he wore a leather apron and his eyebrows had been singed away by the heat of the forge, and now the rain was washing the soot from the creases beneath his eyes and beside his nose.

His lip curled in his short, scorched beard. 'That one is Melehan,' he pointed at the man who had yanked Merlin's head back by the hair, 'and the one with the nice new boots is Ambrosius.' The blacksmith spat into the mud. 'Mordred's brood,' he said, and Iselle and I shared a look before turning our attention back to Merlin and Lady Morgana.

'Merlin is a canker,' the lady squawked, 'and we must cut him out if we are to thrive again as once we did.' She turned to the Saxon in the fine war gear, sweeping rain from her clawlike hands, and I feared she would cut Merlin for real. It was all too easy to imagine Morgana taking a blade to the old man's flesh. To imagine a druid's blood puddling in the filth and mud. 'He does not look much now, Prince Cynric, but he was powerful once. Your father will attest to it.'

'I have heard the stories, lady,' the Saxon said with a nod, though he looked less than convinced.

Lady Morgana looked up at the darkening sky. It seemed

that she was waiting for something. Then she told Melehan to see that Merlin was driven to the south-west gate in order that all the people of Camelot should have their chance to see him. Down came the hazel switch and the ox lurched forward, the cart trundling in the animal's wake, and though many of the folk slunk off to their homes to get dry, some walked the rest of the way, and Iselle and I stayed amongst them.

I could see that Iselle was desperate to give Merlin some sign. To let him know that we were there to help him. But I did not have to warn her against it, for the druid had neither the strength nor the will to lift his head. And when the cart had been as far as the gate and turned around again, we lingered amongst the last witnesses of Merlin's humiliation, until the ox was made to stop by a roundhouse behind Lady Morgana's hall. Here, Melehan and his brother Ambrosius took hold of Merlin and hauled him off the cart, Melehan growling at us to go back to our homes because the night would be starless and black and there were no torches to see by because of the rain.

We took shelter beneath the ramparts again, wet through and shivering with cold. 'Gawain will be wondering what has happened to us.' Iselle looked back in the direction of the south-west gate.

'He will have to wait a little longer,' I said, and Iselle turned back to me. 'We do it tonight. Agreed?'

She nodded. There was no moon. There were no stars. The rain fell furious and relentless from the gloom above. And yet I saw the white of Iselle's teeth. Just a glimpse in the darkness. And the wolfish glint in her eyes.

The thatch beneath me was rain-soaked and slick. For a long while I just lay there, my cheek pressed against reeds stinking of moss and smoke and rot, because I feared I would slide down if I tried to move. It may have been the sibilance of the rain but I thought I heard Iselle hiss and so I reached up with a hand and burrowed it into the thatch, taking hold of a hazel spar, by which I pulled myself up. Slowly, so slowly, my habit heavy with water and catching now and then on the thatch, I moved, hoping that the seethe of the rain smothered the sound of my movement from those within and from the spearman who stood guard outside the door on the other side of the roundhouse.

A guard on the ramparts called out. I went still again, my heart thumping hard against the roof beam below the thatch, my flesh trembling with cold and fear. But the call was just a greeting and I breathed again. Surely those spearmen on Camelot's wall were looking out, not in. Surely my grey robes concealed me on this foul and starless night as completely as any spell of Merlin's could. And so I climbed again, finding another twisted hazel stick. Easing myself higher, little by little, because we needed to know if the spearman outside the door was the only one, or if there were more inside.

At last my right foot found purchase and I held that position and held my breath too, my ear to the wet reeds. Listening. Trying not to cough from the smoke seeking through the roof into the dank night. I reached down and pulled Iselle's long Saxon knife from my belt, then slid it into the reed bundle by my head. I pushed it in to half its length, then twisted the blade, trying to force an opening. But although the thatch was old, it was thick and packed tightly and so I used the sharp Saxon blade to saw at the reeds, now and then stopping to pull the cut stalks away.

This was worse than the climbing. I imagined bits falling down inside like chaff. All it would take was a guard inside to look up and see a blade or my hand digging into the thatch and

I would feel a spear rip up into my belly, gouging into my guts as I now gouged into the reeds.

But I could not stop now. I pushed the knife in again, feeling the sudden give as it broke through. I drew the blade out, slid across and put my eye to the hole, blinking against the stinging smoke from the hearth flames below, feeling the rising heat on my skin. And suddenly it was as if I was inside the roundhouse, not lying on its roof in the rain. For I could see Merlin.

He lay on his side on a cloak spread upon the earthen floor, asleep with his knees pulled up to his chest and his head resting on his bound hands. Across the other side of the fire, lying there looking up at me, was a yellow-haired, yellow-bearded man who could only have been Merlin's Saxon slave, Oswine. My blood froze. How long had he been watching me? Was there a man standing where I could not see him, ready to thrust his spear up into me? Oswine made the smallest movement with his head, but it was enough to tell me that there was someone else in there with them.

By now Iselle must reckon I'd been smoked to death, I thought, moving even more slowly than before, because I knew that I could be seen from inside the roundhouse. I used the knife gingerly to lever up some more reeds, then looked in again. I saw the guard, sitting on a stool against the far wall, his spear across his knees, his helmet by his feet, his crow-shield leaning against a roof post. Unlike Merlin, he was not asleep, though he was not far off by the looks.

I looked back at Oswine. He checked that the spearman was not watching him, then turned his hands palms out and nodded to the knife in my hand. I shook my head. I could not risk giving him the blade, for what if the guard saw me drop it and alerted the other outside? Or what if the man inside the roundhouse killed Oswine? Even if Iselle and I escaped, we might never get another chance to break Merlin out.

Again, I shook my head at Oswine and steeled myself to slide back down the roof so that I could tell Iselle about the spearman inside and we could decide what to do. But something in Oswine's face stopped me. In a moment of cold dread, I knew he had decided to test the thread of fate which his gods had spun for him. He sat up and told the guard that he needed the night soil bucket.

The man growled some insult, annoyed at being disturbed, yet he stood to fetch the bucket from beside the door and the moment his back was turned, Oswine's eyes flared and he nodded at me and I did not think, but pushed my hand through the hole in the thatch and dropped Iselle's long knife.

I was moving. With only half the care of before, my blood pounding in my ears. Lowering myself, half sliding, half falling, until I hung over the dripping eaves and dropped to the ground.

'It's happening,' I told Iselle, who was pressed against the wall out of the rain.

She grabbed hold of my shoulders. 'My knife,' she hissed, her eyes searching mine.

'Oswine has it,' I said, and she drew another knife from its sheath as we put our ears to the cold wall, desperate to know what was going on within. A muffled shout. A bucket hitting the ground, and the voice of the outside guard asking his companion if all was well. We edged around the house, keeping to the deeper dark beneath the eaves.

Then the clump of the door being opened.

Oswine was a shadowed fiend with the firelight behind him and the seax in his hand. He came face to face with the outside guard, who met him at the door and levelled his spear at him in an instant. It happened in five heartbeats. Iselle swept in and I did not see the knife but knew she had buried it in the guard's back. As he twisted round to face this unexpected enemy, Oswine was upon him, one arm around his neck, dragging him back into the roundhouse and punching the long knife into his chest again and again.

I looked behind me into the night and saw no one.

'Hurry,' Iselle hissed at Oswine, who cast the body aside and explained to a bleary-eyed Merlin that it was time to go.

One of Merlin's famous concealment spells would have been welcome then, but I feared he would not be able to walk, let alone summon up some powerful charm, and Oswine growled at me to get us away. And so I turned and led them towards the western perimeter wall, which was the closest. We were wraiths in that black night, bent low and our movements more silent than wingbeats across the rain-sodden ground. Seeking the darkest pools of shadow and keeping our eyes low for fear of their whites being seen by some watchful guard up on the ramparts.

Past a sheep pen and through a patch of squelching, boggy ground which might have claimed Merlin had not Oswine picked the old man up and carried him as a father carries his child across a brook or to bed. Then up the earthen bank and to the foot of a ladder, where we waited, needing to catch our breath but not wanting to breathe, for we were looking up at the wooden walkway to make sure there were no guards nearby.

'Now,' I urged, and we climbed, Oswine all but pulling Merlin up, and then we crouched on the rampart and waited for a cry of alarm which did not come. I nodded to Iselle and she and Oswine scrambled up and over the palisade, hanging for a moment before dropping onto the steep bank.

I looked over and Oswine was flapping an arm at me to

lower Merlin down. 'Are you ready, lord?' I asked him. He looked old and afraid and as confused as anyone would who only moments before had been fast asleep by the fire but was now fleeing for their life through the rain-lashed night.

Merlin nodded and, slowly, so painfully slowly, attempted to clamber over the wall, mumbling words which had no shape that I could tell. 'I'm sorry, lord,' I said, and took hold of him, horrified by how little he weighed, and lifted him over, letting his stick-like body slide through my hands until I was gripping just his wrists. He looked up at me, wide-eyed, and let out a little frightened yelp. Then I let him drop to Oswine below and I climbed after.

We slid on our backsides down the steep embankment, and at the next two ditches and ramparts we did the same, but at the final one a sentry saw us and yelled his challenge into the night.

My heart kicked in my chest. Fear flooded my limbs. We dropped from the last palisade onto the plain, just an arrow-shot from the south-west gate and the spearmen in the gatehouse, who took up the alarm, shouting and striking the iron plate which hung there, the hard, flat tone of it filling the night.

We stopped for a moment, breathing hard and peering into the rain-hissing gloom. Iselle held her hand out to Oswine. 'My knife,' she said.

Oswine handed it to her with a nod of thanks and I gave her the sheath. 'They won't open the gate until they know they're not being attacked,' the Saxon said in his thick accent.

'That way.' Iselle pointed the knife into the south.

We moved as fast as Oswine with his burden could manage, but when I next looked back at the hill fort I saw torches flaring on the ramparts in spite of the rain. I had convinced myself that by now they must have found the two dead men and would know that Merlin had gone. And they would wake Lady Morgana and her fury would whip men out of Camelot into the night after us.

'Gawain,' I yelled, not caring if our pursuers heard, so long as we found the others before Lady Morgana's men found us. 'Here, Gawain!' My eyes sifting the dark, searching for the shadow shape of the old oak tree where we had left Gawain, Gediens and Parcefal that noon.

'Galahad,' a voice called out from the blackness. Gediens.

'Here,' I replied. Beside me, Oswine put Merlin down gently, the druid moaning that though he might not be as young as he once was, he was not yet dead enough to need carrying.

'I have them. Here!' Gediens called behind him. And in moments we heard the jangle of horse tack and the snorting of the animals themselves. I saw the dull glow of scale armour and helmets.

'Galahad,' Gawain said, dismounting and coming close enough that we could see each other. Then he saw Merlin and I saw his hand fall to his belt's iron buckle for luck. 'Gods,' he growled.

'That explains all the fuss, then,' Gediens said. Somewhere behind us the iron alarm clanged still, rhythmic and urgent as a heartbeat. There were men and torches too, more than a dozen flames chasing in the dark.

'Gawain ap Lot, Prince of Lyonesse,' Merlin spat, shuffling forward to peer at Gawain from swollen eyes. Bent and crooked as an ancient crabapple tree. 'You look old,' he said.

13

A Warrior Born

W E RODE THROUGH THE night, moving slowly, passing burial mounds and stands of alder and leaning black poplars one hundred feet high: giant sentinels in riverside meadows. Now and then we caught glimpses of flame in the murk, or heard the plaintive bray of horns far away, and sometimes even the cries of our pursuers as they picked up tracks which they thought were ours and called to one another to go this way or that. And so we did not dare stop, though we were careful to let the horses find their own footing, for we trusted their eyes better than our own in the dark.

Gawain led the way, followed by Oswine and Merlin, then Iselle and me and the spare horses. Parcefal and Gediens rode at the rear and I knew that if the Lady Morgana's men caught up with us, these two would turn their mounts and draw their swords rather than see Merlin taken again.

As for the druid, he sat slumped on his small mare, glaring into the north-east as though more fearful of where we were going than where we had been. He was gaunt and grim, bruised and crusted with dried blood. He looked like a corpse dragged from its burial mound, and we rode in the wake of his reek. But he was the last of the druids, the keeper of the knowledge of Britain, and I knew many believed that in him rested our hopes of restoring Arthur to his former self and chasing the shadow from these Dark Isles.

There were spearmen guarding the old Roman bridge across the Cam River. They emerged from rain-glistened tents, armed with shields and spears and resentment, being the ones out here in the cold and damp, far from the comforts of Camelot.

'Why are you travelling at night?' one of them asked, putting on a helmet which was so dented it could have caught the rain. Behind him, ten other warriors stood yawning, shivering and griping. They had seen by now that we were not Saxons and, not anticipating trouble, would rather get back to their dice or ale.

'Because this man is a Christian.' Gawain pointed his thumb at me.

I made the sign of the Thorn at the spearman, who cringed as if he feared I was putting a curse on him.

'So what?' he asked.

Gawain sighed and Gediens shook his head.

'Don't you know anything about Christians?' Gawain said.

The man's answer was to spit into the mud.

'He's a monk,' Gawain said. 'An important one, so they tell me. And his companion, the older one . . .' he thumbed behind him towards Merlin, who was a silent, shrouded figure in the gloom, 'he's sick. He claims that Satan is trying to steal his soul.' Gawain shrugged. 'But Satan cannot find him at night, and so we ride for the church at Caer Gloui, where the Christians keep charms which may hold death at bay and where the abbot will pay us for our service.'

The spearman looked at me. 'You Christus men fear a god who cannot even see in the dark?' he asked.

'Satan is no god,' I said. 'There is only one God.'

'What is this Satan, then?' he asked.

'He is a fallen angel,' I explained, lifting my voice above the burble and gush of the river.

The spearman turned to his men, who shook their heads or spat or touched iron or murmured that Christians were mad and best avoided. Then he looked back at Gawain and I did not need moon or stars to see the disgust twisting his face. 'Are you a Christian, lord?' he asked. He had seen the glint of scale armour and a hint of the sword's grip beneath Gawain's cloak and knew better than to forgo the respect which such accoutrements demanded.

'No,' Gawain leant forward in the saddle and nodded back towards Merlin. 'But I have seen him turn a man's guts to sour water with a word,' he said in a low voice. 'Seen him summon maggots from a man's eyes and so, if I were you, friend, I would not make us tarry here.'

The spearman peered at Merlin through the gloom, but it was clear that he was in no mood to go closer to a sick Christian who could make a man's eyes writhe with maggots. He straightened himself and his spear and waved an arm towards the old Roman bridge.

'Go,' he said.

Gawain nodded and flicked his reins and his mare started forward. We followed. 'Christ be with you,' I said to the spearman and he actually took two steps back and swept his arm towards the bridge again. But their eyes were on Iselle, not Merlin, as we passed. They watched her as men will who have been too long away from their wives, but Iselle kept her eyes on the cobbled path and rode on.

'His fallen angel may not be able to see in the dark, but the Saxons can,' the man with the dented helmet called after us. We were on the bridge now and the hiss of the water running beneath us almost smothered his words. 'They're everywhere, thanks to this damned truce,' he yelled. 'And don't be fooled by it. Those rabid dogs will still kill you for the cloaks on your backs.'

No sooner had we crossed the river than Parcefal urged his big mare forward, the horse tossing her chestnut head as if she too was unsettled by what she had heard.

'Morgana has made peace with King Cerdic?' the old warrior asked.

We had not yet had the chance to tell them of all we had seen.

'There were Saxons in the fort.' I was warming my hands on my gelding's neck where the big veins throbbed beneath his skin. 'Their leader was a man named Cynric.'

'King Cerdic's son,' Oswine put in. 'He will be king of my people one day.' He looked at me, and in the darkness I saw a Saxon. And I wondered how long ago his own people had come to Britain and if they had found good lives or only hardship, blood and death. 'Cynric is Woden-favoured,' he went on. 'Anyone can see that. But for now, he is content to be Morgana's guest, enjoying the view and the lady's wine in his father's stead.'

'And no doubt planning how to take Camelot when this truce fails,' Gediens said.

'He would rather burn it, I think,' Oswine mused.

'Morgana has betrayed Dumnonia,' Iselle spat.

Gawain's face was all scar and frown. 'We will talk it through later,' he growled, picking up the pace, for we knew that soon enough Morgana's men would make sense of who we were and in which direction we travelled. And because voices will drift far at night, we rode in silence across rolling downland and along chalk river valleys. Through low-lying vales and ancient forest. A cavalcade of outcasts. A retinue bound to a dream.

We rode to Arthur.

At noon of the next day, we joined the Roman road north of the River Cary and rode along it as far as we could before leaving it to venture westward into the wetlands. After that, it was slow going as we stuck to the higher ridges and drier tracks because of the horses, even if those paths did not lead directly to Arthur's steading. But we put our trust in Iselle and she guided us with preternatural cunning, so that only three times did we have to turn back and try a different way, and not once did any of the horses become stuck in the sucking mud. Still, it was arduous and tiring and, with no sleep the previous night, we were half dead in the saddle when at last we came to the fenland north of the Meare Pool, and that eerily quiet place beneath the grey sky.

It was dusk again when we emerged from the tall reeds and found Arthur's house as we had left it. This humble refuge in the marsh. This den which seemed beyond the rule of time. But stranger even than the place itself was that we found Lord Arthur sitting on an old willow stump, his black bitch Banon lying beside him, the two of them staring towards the marsh, as if they had known we were coming. And I wondered if Arthur and Merlin were still tied each to the other somehow, joined by some invisible thread which had stretched across the years, and that Arthur had felt the druid's approach the way a spider senses a fly through the strands of his web. I did not see how that could be so, and yet it was preferable to the other explanation, that Arthur had been sitting on that stump all the days since we had left him.

'By the gods,' Arthur said, standing as we walked our mounts into the clearing. Banon stood dutifully at his heel. 'You have him,' Arthur said, his voice tremulous, squinting in the twilight as though he trusted his own eyes no more than the ground beyond that wall of winter reeds. 'Is it real?' he asked, moving stiffly towards us, gripping a fur tightly at his chest though the day was not cold.

'Real enough, Arthur,' Gawain said.

Arthur nodded at me and at Iselle, but then he noticed the spare mounts and the empty saddles. 'Yvain?' he looked at me.

'He is with his family in Annwn, lord,' I said. For I felt sure of it then.

A shadow passed across Arthur's tired face and he nodded. 'So many have gone,' he mumbled to himself, eyeing me with something like suspicion, as if trying to place me, as if he could not quite recall if I was from that old world or this current one.

'We found him, lord,' I said, just for want of something to say. 'We found Merlin.'

This seemed to pull Arthur from the mire of his memories, and he nodded, turning to watch as Oswine helped Merlin dismount, the druid complaining of stiffness and mumbling foul threats which rolled off the Saxon like rain off a waxed skin.

'Guinevere?' Gawain asked of Arthur.

'The same, nephew,' Arthur said, his eyes fixed on the druid, his hands gripping the pelt to his neck, white knots snarled in black fur. His breathing looked deep and laboured, as though he was trying to quell some pain in his stomach, and his jaw was clamped tight, the muscle in his hollow cheek beating like a hawk's heart.

We dismounted and fussed with the reins and saddles, but all of us had one eye on Arthur and Merlin as they stood in the mud, five paces from each other and yet ten years distant.

My presence there felt to me like an offence against some god who had contrived to bring this moment to pass, but I watched anyway, while the world seemed to stand trapped and expectant, like that breathless silence between the lightning flash and the thunder peal.

Merlin swayed and almost stumbled, and Oswine moved in to steady him but the druid hissed and flailed and so the Saxon stepped back. Then Merlin straightened his old back and lifted his chin, his grey beard quivering, and tried to speak. But the words would not come. He chewed at his lip and his blackened swollen eyes widened and filled with tears, before releasing them to roll down his gaunt cheeks.

'Arthur,' he breathed and shook his head. 'Arthur.' His hands gripped each other, the fingers writhing like little serpents, and then he limped across the space between them and Arthur took half a step but no more, his lips a thin line, his eyes all brittle steel.

Merlin wiped tears and old blood from his cheek. 'The gods toy with us still, my old friend,' he said.

We ate well and slept long. And the next day, Arthur asked about all we had seen and heard, though it seemed to me his thoughts were elsewhere. Until we told him that Lady Morgana had forged a truce with the Saxon king, Cerdic. This news seemed to hurt him like an old wound opening.

'Why would she make peace with Cerdic when his war bands are killing and burning in Caer Gwinntguic and Caer Celemion and Cynwidion?' he asked, gently placing his own cloak around Guinevere's shoulders. She sat in her chair by the far wall, watching but not seeing.

'Because no one else will fight and she's not strong enough to fight them alone,' Parcefal suggested.

'My cousin still fights,' Arthur said, meaning Lord Constantine.

Gawain gave a derisive snort. 'Constantine hides in the forests of Caer Lerion.'

'But Camelot is the hope of all Britain,' Iselle said. No one disagreed with that, not even Arthur, and it seemed to me that for all Iselle's fire and thorniness, these old warriors had accepted her into their kinship. More than this, they respected her.

'Camelot has always held,' Gediens said. 'Yet, if there are Saxons in Camelot now . . .' He shook his head, not having the heart to say more.

Arthur sat back against the wall and stared at the cup in his hand. 'Then even the idea of Britain is fading like a dream.'

'There can be no Britain without a man who is strong enough to lead the kings in war,' Gawain asserted. 'There can be no Britain without you, Arthur. You know this.'

But Arthur was lost in that cup and too far away to hear.

We spent the next days hunting and making repairs to Arthur and Guinevere's steading, tending the swine and sheep, spreading the horses' dung to enrich the ground for the growing of fruits and vegetables, ploughing the rich soil in readiness for the spring sowing, cutting reeds and gathering firewood, making plans to unite the kings of Britain, and waiting for Merlin to recover. When we had restored the old byre, at least well enough to keep out the rain and wind, Merlin slept in there with the rest of us, leaving the house to Arthur and Guinevere. But the druid was weak and Oswine said it would be some time before he was ready to attempt what we needed of him. And so we busied ourselves as best we could while the Saxon tended his master.

One day, when Iselle was out in the marsh with her bow, I asked Gawain if he would teach me the use of sword, spear and shield. He had Father Yvain's grey mare pulling a plough, for she was strong and placid and did not seem to mind the collar and traces.

'You sure, Galahad?' he asked, looking straight ahead towards the wood of sallow, hazel and ash beyond the field. Wanting to keep his line. There was not a great deal of arable land, for what there was had been reclaimed from the marsh, but it yielded easily to the coulter, that blade cutting the ground before the ploughshare turned it in glistening banks.

'Yes,' I said. 'I'm sure.'

'Why?' Gawain asked. 'Why now?' He leant into the stilt and clicked his tongue and the mare snorted in reply.

I thought back to that grey day when the Saxons had come to the monastery to kill, and before that, when those Saxon scouts had caught me out in the marsh and I had flailed like an eel in a withy trap. Other memories flashed behind my eyes. Parcefal besting Lady Triamour's champion. Iselle and Oswine killing the men who guarded Merlin, and Father Yvain being thrown from the cliffs at Tintagel. But the vision which clung to me with the sharpest claws, which had, in truth, haunted me since we rode from Tintagel, was of Iselle being thrown backwards and the man upon her, and of the wild terror in her eyes.

'The Order of the Thorn is gone.' I was measuring my stride to keep pace with Gawain and the plough. 'And even if it were not, and if I had taken the tonsure, what use would I be?'

Gawain clicked and encouraged the mare, though she did not need it. 'It is always useful to have a god on your side,' he said.

I leant away from him. 'I don't think you put much store in the gods.'

He almost smiled at that and looked back over his shoulder

to ensure he had not deviated. 'I put store in men, Galahad. In iron and steel. In courage.'

'Then teach me,' I said.

'Did your father teach you?' he asked.

I recalled my childhood. Practising with weapons which were too big and heavy, and which made my arms and shoulders burn with pain.

'Every day,' I said.

Gawain nodded. 'Your father learnt young himself. Learnt from good men. But it was already in him. Maybe it's already in you too.'

And it was. I had always known it. Had felt it in my blood and in my hands, like another man's visceral memories trapped in my own flesh. I had heard the faint echo of it across years, no more than a whisper but nagging like an ache. When I took a bow into the marsh to shoot waterfowl, or a spear into the woods to hunt deer or boar. When I skinned those beasts after, in the sharp scent of them and in the knowing that they were dead at my hands.

'We have time,' Gawain said, 'for Oswine will not have us bothering Merlin until he's better. Or dead.' The ploughshare gouged its furrow, turning earthworms which were pink and naked against the black soil. Behind us, gulls and crows squawked and bickered over the writhing treats. 'We'll teach you what we know. The three of us. And we'll see if you have any of him in you.' He winked. 'Or if you should have taken the tonsure and gone back to Ynys Wydryn to spend your days sitting under a thorny tree.'

We began that same day. Gediens found an old spear in Arthur's stable and, after removing the blade, he cut it in half and wrapped leather around one end of each stick for a grip. Then Gawain and I fought with these and shields too, so that he might humiliate me. Or so it seemed. For I lost count of the times I ended up sitting on my backside or sprawled in the mud. It seemed he could put me down with barely a touch, using my mistakes in footing and balance against me, punishing me every time I overreached or fell for a feint.

On one occasion, he tilted his shield downward at the moment that I struck it, and as my weight carried me forward, he stepped aside and struck me across the back and I went down, face first into the filth.

'You'll never protect her with Christus songs, Galahad,' he growled in my ear, waiting for me to get to my feet.

I rose, spitting dirt, and slammed my shield against his and he grinned. 'Again.' He stepped back and nodded that I should attack him.

I strode forward, looking for a part of him that I could hit, desperate to land a blow that would knock the smile from his face. He saw it in my eyes and so held his shield out wide, inviting me to strike his belly or chest. A trap, of course. But if I was fast enough, I could spring it and still hit him. He was old. I was young. I lowered my weapon, as if catching my breath, then I flew at him and he parried, sweeping my stick aside and twisting at the waist to drive his shield into my right shoulder, putting me down again. I rolled onto my back and looked up at the sky and three crows which were mobbing a hawk, taking it in turns to swoop in and away, driving the predator west, chasing it from their roosts.

'Prayers will not kill your enemies. A prayer is just a fart on the wind.' He gestured with his stick. 'Up you get, lad.'

I got up, hating him. I hammered his shield and revelled in it, and I did not see his stick until it hit me in the belly, driving the air out and leaving me bent double and gasping. 'Anger will get you killed. Skill will keep you alive,' he said.

And so it went. I trained with Gediens and Parcefal too. Gediens was a master with the spear and even though we sheathed the blades in leather, I lost the most blood fighting against him. The stitching on that sheath opened my neck and cheek and the skin on the backs of both hands, so that I learnt quickly to block his attacks with my own shaft, the spears clacking in their own harsh language, our feet moving fast across the ground.

Parcefal taught me how to fight on horseback, sometimes letting me ride his own mare, Lavina, who liked me well enough. She had long been trained for war and together we would jump obstacles, gallop across uneven ground, execute tight circles, sudden turns and stops, I thrusting a spear or slashing a sword at timbers which Parcefal had stuck in the earth, or using the practice sword or sheathed spear against the three warriors, who struck at me from the ground.

I ate mud and tasted humiliation. I limped and grimaced and scowled through the days because of the bruises which bloomed in my flesh like mould in bread. Arthur would watch me work, saying little, but now and then nodding at something which I did well. Or, more often, shaking his head at some failure.

When she was not practising with her bow or with the Saxon sword, or out hunting amongst the reed-beds, Iselle watched, too. Sometimes she laughed when Gawain or Gediens used my own anger or impetuousness against me, and her laughter hurt me more than the bruises and swellings and made me try even harder in the bouts.

On occasion, Merlin left his bed to breathe the air and squint at me from beneath white brows.

'You left him too long with the Christ men, Gawain,' he croaked once.

'Because I was too busy looking for you, druid,' Gawain replied, lifting his chin at me, the sign for me to attack.

They were days of pain and frustration and shame. And they were days of awakening, too. Of memories manifesting in flesh, kindling in a sword-swing or a spear-strike, or in Lavina's whinny as I wheeled her tightly and cut a sliver from a standing pole, and I was on Tormaigh's back again, my father's eyes on us like those of a hawk as we rode down imaginary foes.

At last there were glimmers of spring in the marsh. Mistle thrushes, blue tits and chaffinches poured their liquid songs into the days, marking their territories and seeking mates. Woodpeckers drummed dead timber and herons danced their strange dances, stretching their necks upwards, then lowering them over their backs. Amongst the reeds, toads were emerging from their winter hiding places, lacing the pools with strings of slimy eggs, and in the woods near Arthur's steading foul-smelling dog's mercury, coltsfoot and sweet violets covered the ground like a pelt, shivering in the breezes.

For a while we feared that Merlin would slip away with the winter. Oswine told us how Mordred's sons Melehan and Ambrosius had struck the druid whenever he refused to answer Morgana's questions.

'She wanted his magic for herself,' the Saxon explained, 'but Merlin says he has no magic now. At first, they did not believe him and so they beat him. Not much, for they still feared him. But after a while, when they knew they had not been cursed, when they saw that they were not pissing blood, that their hair was not falling out, that their manhoods had not shrivelled between their legs, they began to believe his power was gone. And so they beat him without fear.'

Oswine had asked me to heat some water so that he could

wash Merlin in the byre, the druid being too weak to clean himself in the brook near the western wood. I carried the cauldron from Arthur's hearth to the old cow shed and, by the daylight flooding in through the open door behind me, I saw Merlin's naked body. Oswine saw the shock in my face but said nothing. Here was the man who had halted Saxon armies with his ghost fences of severed heads. The man who had delivered Tintagel to King Uther and Excalibur to Arthur. The last druid in these Dark Isles. And he looked as helpless and strange as a baby bird that has fallen from the nest. His legs just tendon and bone, his head too big for his scrawny neck, eyes swollen and black, and the white hair on his chest, shoulders and scalp like a hatchling's downy fluff.

I had shivered to see the bruises standing out among the swirls and inscriptions which marked his body, such that he looked to be rotting alive. He was old and weak, and his enemies had beaten him because they wanted whatever power and knowledge still lingered in him.

Yet Merlin did not die. And as life began to return to the land, so Merlin slowly came back to himself. And we who hid within the marsh, in the world and yet not in it, like the ghosts which haunt the margins of sight on Samhain night, dared to hope that Merlin would soon be strong enough to attempt what he had been brought here for.

Then, twenty-three days after we had come back to Arthur, I gave Merlin his raven-feathered cloak. Gawain and Gediens were out checking the animal snares and eel traps. Parcefal and Arthur were in the stable, grooming the horses together and talking of old times and lost friends. Oswine was out in the woods gathering herbs and roots, bracket fungus and berries and whatever else Merlin needed for his healing draughts, leaving Iselle and me with Guinevere and the druid.

I brought the sack containing the feathered cloak to the hearth, where Merlin was sitting warming his bones, clutching a cup of steaming apple wine. Iselle stood beyond the fire's glow, feeding Guinevere a bowl of goose and parsnip broth.

'Your father would have burned it.' Merlin raised an eyebrow when I showed him what was in the sack, lifting a little of the cloak out. The feathers came alive in the flame glow, a lustre of blues, purples and greens, in honour of the birds to which they had once belonged. A murmur of magic. 'Lancelot did not approve of my . . . talents,' Merlin said. 'He did not understand that which could not be gripped in a strong hand or brandished by a trained arm, but which was wielded in here . . .' pressing two fingers against his chest. 'And here,' he added, putting those same fingers against his liver-spotted temple.

He looked over to Guinevere, who by some instinct parted her lips each time Iselle lifted the wooden spoon to them, though sometimes the liquid spilled and Iselle would wipe Guinevere's chin with a cloth. 'That is why he could never truly know her,' Merlin said, 'for her gift was greater than mine.'

'Did my father love her?' I asked. I knew the answer and yet I wanted to hear it from Merlin now, for all that I hoped my mother would not hear it where she was beyond the veil.

'Oh, he loved her.' Merlin took a deep breath. 'He loved her like the sea loves the shore.' He slurped at the spiced wine.

I felt the scowl as a tightening in my face. I said nothing.

Merlin glanced back to Guinevere. 'Your father was a fool because he did not see that his own gift, his talent for war, rose from the same wellspring as her talent,' he said. 'The gods are the fountainhead, Galahad.' He reached a hand down into the sack at his feet, slowly, as though there might be a serpent in there waiting to bite him, and he ran his old fingers across the feathers. 'A dreaming cloak or a sword, it is the same, but your father could not see that. The gods would have worked through him if only he had let them.' He shook his head. 'But Lancelot was ruled by a man's fickle passions. He was not strong enough.' The druid looked into the flames, which danced in his eyes. 'None of us were.'

'Can you bring her back?' I asked.

His own brows furrowed then. 'Perhaps,' he said, but he did not seem confident.

'When will you try?'

His head came up and his eyes seized mine. 'When I'm ready, boy,' he spat. But from what I had seen, the Merlin of flesh and bone was not to be feared, unlike the Merlin of men's tales, and so I held his eyes with my own.

'Did Yvain find his family in Annwn?' I asked.

At that he straightened his back, glaring at me still and, in spite of his frailty, something in his eyes put a shiver in my blood.

'Yvain did not doubt me,' he said. 'Few men would back then.'

'I never asked for it,' I said. Father Yvain was gone but the oath he had sworn to protect me remained like an iron collar around my neck. An encumbrance that grew even heavier when I was around Merlin, for he had forged that collar himself.

'You have not been listening, Galahad.' He sighed. 'Truly, the spark did not fly far from the flint.' He leant towards me, close enough now that I could see the yellow in his eyes and smell the apple wine on his breath. 'Do you think she asked for any of it?' he hissed, and I knew he was talking about Guinevere. 'She married Arthur because I made it so. Because the gods showed me that Arthur and Guinevere would remake Britannia. Your father fought for Arthur because I needed him to. For Lancelot was the greatest fighter since Brân Galed himself. And together he and Arthur were the swords of Britain.'

'And you, Merlin? Did you have a choice?' I asked.

His eyes widened and he gave a snort that became a choking sound, which I realized was laughter. Perhaps he was out of practice. Still, his apparent amusement sickened me.

'I was the only one who could hear the gods of this land. I was the last. Knowing that, do you think they would let me live a hermit's life, curing the occasional leper and talking to the trees and the birds?' He laughed again and Iselle looked over her shoulder, no doubt wondering what could be so amusing.

Merlin lifted a hand towards her by way of apology, and she carried on spooning food into Guinevere's half-open mouth.

'You see,' the druid breathed, bending towards me again, 'the gods toy with us, Galahad.' He looked up at the thatch and the smoke below it seeking amongst the reeds for a way out. 'Even here in this place. You think you are hidden here. You are wrong to think so.'

'Other than Gawain, no one has found Arthur in all the years since the great battle,' I said.

Merlin pointed a gnarly finger. 'No man has found Arthur,' he said, weighting the word 'man'. 'What do you know of her?' He tilted his head towards the back of the room.

'Iselle?' I asked.

He nodded.

'I know that she fears no man,' I said.

He smiled.

Iselle put the spoon and bowl down and left Guinevere in the shadows, saying she would fetch a cup of weak ale for her to drink, and Merlin and I watched her walk out of the gloom and into the day.

When she was gone, the druid nodded at me. 'Go on.'

I frowned at him. I felt disloyal talking about Iselle to this man whom I barely knew. And yet I wanted him to know her. What she had done for our cause. What it meant to her, and all that she had lost.

'I know that she hates the Saxons,' I said. 'That she would do anything to bring the old gods back, for it is said that they left us when they abandoned Lord Arthur.'

His lip curled at that, but he nodded for me to continue.

'I know that she believes in you,' I said. 'And that she hopes that you will bring Guinevere back to Arthur, so that he can be who he once was. So that he will bring the kings of Britain together under one banner and we shall rid the land of the sickness which ails it.' The fire spat an ember at Merlin, landing in the folds of his tunic. He licked his finger and thumb and pinched the life from it.

'You love her,' he said.

I straightened on the stool and looked to the door, relieved not to see Iselle coming through it. 'No.' My eyes slipped from his.

'Yes,' he countered. 'You love her and that is why you spend the days rolling in the mud with a toy sword, making a fool of yourself.' He drained his cup, saw that the jug was empty and scowled around the room, muttering something about Oswine being a lazy Saxon swine. 'Because you have your father's pride and you think that you must protect her, which you cannot do if you don't know one end of a sword from the other.'

'Iselle does not need me to protect her,' I said, not quite denying his accusation. 'She is a warrior. It is in her.'

Merlin grinned and I was surprised to see that he still had most of his teeth. 'Of course she's a warrior, boy,' he said. 'I asked you what you know about her, and you tell me nothing.

I only had to look at her and I know more than you.' He shook his head and sighed. 'I had hoped you would have more clever in you than your father.'

'I know she lived with her foster mother, Alana,' I offered. 'Iselle says Alana met you when she was young.'

He wafted a hand at the hearth smoke. 'Yes, yes, a long time ago. On the island where your father learnt how to slaughter men.' He twirled a finger impatiently. 'How did you meet her? Who found whom, Galahad?'

I cast my mind back to that day I had taken the coracle into the marsh and gone to the lake village in search of a dead man. 'Iselle found me,' I said, at which he lifted an eyebrow, as though that fact meant something to him. 'She saved my life. She killed three Saxons.'

'A warrior born,' he said, and turned his gaze from the flames to Guinevere, who seemed to be watching us from the shadows.

The door opened, the flames leapt and Iselle came in with a jug of ale and two cups. She filled Merlin's cup and then poured a cup for me.

The druid nodded his thanks, his hand in the sack by his feet, fingers caressing the feathered cloak within as he stared at Iselle's face. 'Galahad tells me that he would be a stain on a Saxon blade if not for you, girl.'

Pouring ale into the last cup, Iselle lifted her eyes to me. 'Galahad was a fool to be alone and unarmed in the marsh,' she said, then turned her back on us to carry the drink to Guinevere.

He leant towards me again. 'I think she likes you,' he whispered, then put the cup to his lips and drank. When he had finished, he dragged a stick-thin arm across his lips and grey beard. 'But you *are* a fool, boy. Gawain, too.' He grimaced. 'All of you are fools.' He rolled his eyes up and across the ceiling again. 'And the gods are here in this place.'

I did not know why he said that, nor why he had been asking me what I knew about Iselle, but I did know that he had drunk at least a jug of apple wine and was now holding an ale cup which was already half empty. Instead of leaning across on his stool, he waggled a gnarly finger at me, beckoning me closer. I shifted my stool in the floor rushes and bent, turning my head to put my ear near his mouth.

'*Look* at her,' he hissed. I could see Iselle without having to move, though she had her back to me as she held the rim of the cup between Guinevere's lips and gently tilted it. 'Is it not obvious? Even were she not the warrior you say. Look at her, Galahad,' he whispered, his words little more than the feel of his sour breath on my cheek. 'Your eyes are young and yet you are blind.'

I looked. I tried to see whatever it was Merlin had seen.

'And when you see it, you will say nothing, do you hear?' His face was wolfish in the flicker of flamelight and shadow. 'Nothing! It is not your place.'

I looked. And then my breath snagged in my chest. My skin prickled as though my tunic teemed with lice. My heart thumped its way into my throat, and into the cavity it had left behind flooded a terrible cold: a cold which spread through the marrow in my bones despite the hearth flames that cast the druid's face into shadow, his eyes glittering with pleasure at my sudden understanding.

'Not your place,' he whispered again.

I looked. And I saw that Iselle was not just a young woman who had survived in the marshes, savage as a she-wolf and all but alone in this vicious, dark world. She was not just the proud, copper-haired Saxon-killer who tied my insides in knots whenever we were together and whenever we were apart. I could not say how I had not seen it before, but now it seemed to me that some god must have wreathed a strange fog around her which my eyes could not pierce. But Merlin, this old, broken man, had with whispered words dispelled that fog, so that now I saw it in her regal nose and her wide forehead. In her full lips and in the fire in her eyes. Pendragon fire. For Iselle carried the blood of heroes in her veins. She was a warrior born. And Arthur, the lord of battle, the flame in the darkness, was her father.

14

Old Enemies

W E HEARD THE FIRST deep, hollow calls of bitterns proclaiming the end of winter on the day Lord Constantine came. Rooks were busy rebuilding their weather-ravaged nests, their clamour drifting on the breeze like the sound of distant battle. Blackthorn was bursting into flower, recalling the snow which had fallen when we had set out from Arthur's steading in search of Merlin, and the first furry flower heads were appearing in the goat willow.

Iselle had been the first to see the smoke curling up into the blue sky to the north, beyond the tall trees in whose upper boughs herons were adding sticks to last year's nests. We had feared it was Saxons burning another farmstead or some fisher folk's dwelling, but Arthur assured us it could not be, for no one lived so close as that.

'My cousin has come,' he told Gawain. And so Gawain, Gediens and Parcefal had gone to the place and found Lord Constantine and twenty warriors making camp around the beacon fire which they had lit in accordance with an old arrangement between Arthur and Constantine.

Only Lord Constantine himself came back with Gawain, for Arthur would not have men know where he lived, and I saw that the rumours about the warlord styling himself after a

Roman general were true. He was in his sixties, lean and hardened and scarred by a lifetime of war, and his face reminded me of a statue I had seen on the ramparts of Castle Dore when I was eight summers old and my father took me to see King Cyn-March's great Samhain fire. For Lord Constantine wore no beard or moustaches to hide his grim and austere face. His cloak was the colour of a ripening plum, he wore a breastplate of hammered bronze which had been shaped to mimic a well-muscled torso, and he carried under his arm a Roman helmet which boasted a stiff plume of red horsehair.

He was the nephew of Uther Pendragon and grandson of King Constantine, who had claimed to be Emperor of Rome, and I had never seen a man carry himself with such pride, nor one who looked more at odds with the world, as though he had been born in another time and had spent his life and blood striving to return to it.

Arthur welcomed him and shook his hand, but there was no warmth between them, no friendship that I could see. Just mutual respect between warriors who had faced the same enemies and fought the same wars.

'It's been a long time, cousin,' Arthur said.

'The years pass swiftly, Arthur, and the Saxons still come each spring. I fear we shall never be rid of them.' He spread his arms, turning his palms up. 'But we are still alive in spite of it all.'

For a while the old warriors talked of old battles, as though they could still hear the echo of the steel-song in their ears, and then Arthur introduced me, at which Lord Constantine's jaw tightened, his thumb stroking the ivory eagle's-head hilt of the Roman gladius sheathed at his right hip.

'Galahad ap Lancelot,' he repeated, frowning at my habit, which was crusted with dried mud. 'Your father was the best I ever saw.'

I said nothing, but Arthur filled the awkward silence.

'Galahad is proving himself a skilled swordsman in his own right,' he said, which was being overly generous, but I felt a little taller anyway.

'You are a Christian, Galahad?' Lord Constantine asked me.

'I was, lord,' I replied, for in truth I did not know what I was any more.

Lord Constantine did not know what to make of that. Some said he was a Christian himself, but I had also heard that he maintained a shrine to the Roman god Mithras in some forest cave. He looked at each of us in turn, his hard eyes lingering a moment on the Saxon knife hanging from Iselle's belt.

'I came at the right time, for it seems you are building a new army, Lord Arthur,' he said. He did not even try to hide the note of scorn in his voice. And yet when we went inside to hear his reason for coming, and he saw Merlin sitting by the hearth, hammering a bundle of rosemary with the poll of a hand axe, the warlord's face seemed to drain of blood. His previous disdain gave way to undisguised awe.

'You are a man who holds on to his ambition, Lord Constantine, I'll say that for you.' Merlin brought the axe head down onto the trencher with a thud. He was naked from the waist up, the strange symbols and patterns, long ago pricked into his skin and rubbed with ash or woad, telling their stories by the firelight in a language beyond my understanding. 'Or is it King Constantine these days?' he asked.

Constantine did not answer this, for even if he had proclaimed himself king some years ago, the idea was an absurdity these days, with Lady Morgana still ruling in Camelot and King Cerdic's Saxons running rampant from Rhegin in the south to Lindisware in the north, and in most of the kingdoms between.

'You are an old man and yet still you dream of Uther's high seat,' Merlin said.

The pine smell of Merlin's herbs sharpened the air. Oswine poured a cup of ale and offered it to our guest.

'I dream of killing Saxons, Merlin, and little else,' Lord Constantine replied, nevertheless accepting the drink from a Saxon.

The druid mouthed something under his breath and swept two fingers across the trencher, taking up some of the oil which he had beaten out of the needle-like leaves and rubbing it into the crook of his left elbow to soothe some pain in the joint. 'Then breathe deeply, lord, for the scent of rosemary stirs our memories.' He smiled. 'An old druid trick, it has ever helped us recall the lore. Perhaps it will help you remember how you and Arthur used to slaughter men in the olden days.'

'I fight still,' Lord Constantine said, his pride stung by the insult.

The poll of the axe came down again. Three sharp strikes and Merlin added some of the rosemary to a small iron dish which sat in the hearth.

'Forgive me, lord,' Merlin said, 'but I thought you had been hiding in the forests of Caer Lerion.' He frowned. 'Gawain must have been talking of another king of Dumnonia.'

Gawain lifted an eyebrow at Lord Constantine. Not an apology – he did not like the man enough for that – but an acknowledgement of how Merlin could vex like poison ivy.

'Why have you come, cousin?' Arthur asked, weary of idle talk. Weary of sharing his home with all of us, perhaps, for he had grown more accustomed to birdsong and the drone of insects, and the wind amongst the reed-beds, than to men talking of war and of Britain.

Lord Constantine drank deeply and nodded, and I wondered

how he managed to keep that armour so clean out here in the marsh. It shone like gold, fire reflecting in the smooth curves and bronze muscle which mimicked the physique of a younger man, so that Constantine must have felt the weight of years and of his own long-held ambition whenever he strapped that cuirass on.

'King Cerdic has proposed a parley,' he said. 'He sent messengers to me.'

Parcefal made a scoffing sound. 'Why would he parley now?'

'Because I kill his men, Parcefal.' The jagged vein in Lord Constantine's temple bulged, straining beneath weathered skin.

'You are a thorn in his flesh. A small thorn,' Gawain said. 'And if the rumours are true, you have fewer than two hundred spearmen.'

Lord Constantine lifted his chin. 'I fight,' he said, and turned that Roman face on Arthur. 'I carry the bear banner still, and still it has the power to sow fear in Saxon bellies. But it is your banner, Arthur. Imagine the fear it would sow were you to stand with me beneath it.'

I saw Gawain and Parcefal exchange a look which was almost like thirst. For while neither man liked Constantine, he spoke to their shared hopes and they could not help but drink in his words.

'Perhaps.' Arthur lifted his right hand to his left shoulder, his fingers remembering the old wound. A wound more terrible than any other. A cut to the heart as well as the flesh, because the sword that made it had been thrust by his own son.

If only he knew that his daughter was standing but a few paces away, I thought. Balm for the most grievous wound, surely. I had thought of little else since I had seen the truth with my own eyes. It whirred around in my skull. It nagged at me day and night, and yet I could say nothing. Not yet.

'But why would Cerdic parley now, when you alone bleed him?' Arthur asked his cousin. 'When the other kings hide behind their walls or pay him tribute?'

'And seeing as Lady Morgana will not fight him, either,' Gawain added.

Lord Constantine scratched at an old scar on his cheek. 'What does it matter why?' he asked. 'We need time, Arthur. If you come back, men will join us. I know it.' His eyes met mine and I wondered if he saw my father in me. Was he recalling that Tintagel dawn long ago when he attacked Arthur's men, and my father had run to help Arthur, the two of them forging their friendship in the flames of war? 'Peace will give us the chance to gather our strength,' he said.

Gawain nodded. 'He's right, Arthur. Let Cerdic think his enemies are licking their wounds. But we will send out word across Britain of your return. Scatter seeds of hope across the land. We will gather spearmen.' He looked at the hearth flames dancing for Merlin. 'We will start a fire.'

'It can be done, Arthur,' Lord Constantine said. 'Come with me. Let the Saxons see that you live. That the man who haunts their dreams still lives.'

'Cerdic will be less likely to break the truce if he knows you are back in the fight,' Parcefal said, and with that he put a hand on Arthur's left shoulder. That wounded shoulder. Perhaps chance but perhaps not. 'We have waited so long, old friend.'

I looked at Iselle, who gave a slight nod, her eyes aflame.

But Arthur's brow was furrowed, his own eyes dull, his thoughts not on his bear banner or Excalibur or on fields of summer wheat flattened by Saxon corpses. But on something, or someone, else.

He turned and looked beyond the fire to where Guinevere sat. 'I cannot go,' he said. 'I will not.' He lifted his cup, drank deeply and put it down on the table. 'You have wasted a journey, cousin,' he told Lord Constantine, and with that he walked out the door, leaving us all looking at each other.

Lord Constantine let out a stale breath, and in that moment he looked old and tired, as though the illusion of his bronze armour and greaves, his crested Roman helmet and the eagle-headed sword at his hip had failed. The spell shattered by Arthur's last words.

Merlin poked an iron in amongst the burning logs, releasing a scatter of sparks which crackled noisily in the silence. 'You all see that the Lady Guinevere is lost,' he said, 'but you don't see that Arthur is just as lost.' He grimaced. 'You don't want to see.'

'And what do you see, druid?' Gawain challenged him, lifting his bearded chin towards the fire, his face all granite and scar by its fitful light.

'I see men desperate to taste wine that has long been drunk,' he said, giving those quiet words to the flames.

Gawain glowered.

'Arthur is right,' Lord Constantine said. 'I have wasted a journey and should have stayed in Caer Lerion.'

'There is hope, still,' Gawain told him, then turned back to Merlin. 'You will bring the lady back to him, Merlin,' he commanded, 'or I will give you back to Lady Morgana as her plaything.'

Merlin's lip curled as he turned his gaze on the warrior. 'Only a fool would threaten a druid,' he replied, though the words sounded more like a distant echo than a threat in the here and now.

Gawain ignored him and turned back to Lord Constantine. 'What will you do?'

Lord Constantine shook his head as he considered this. The fuel in the hearth cracked. The druid brooded, sour as old milk. Iselle simmered, hopeful still, and the warriors in that small space, men who had fought all their lives and who would fight until their last breath if only their lord of battles would return to them, seemed burdened by every year on their backs.

'I will meet with King Cerdic.' Lord Constantine pressed his left fist into his cupped right hand. 'I will parley with him and buy us time, if I can.'

Gawain nodded. 'I will come with you,' he said. 'I'll be more use there than here.'

Gediens and Parcefal gnarred in agreement.

'Cerdic will remember us,' Parcefal said, 'and seeing us again will give credence to the rumour that Arthur lives.' He lifted the ale jug but was disappointed to see that it was empty. 'We cannot fight him.' He put the jug back down. 'But maybe we can give him cause to sleep with one eye open.'

'Cerdic will shake like a wet dog at the sight,' Merlin muttered. 'The old men of Dumnonia, come to wave their rusty swords at him.'

Gawain raised an eyebrow. 'Cerdic must be an old man himself,' he said. 'He will know better than to dismiss men who, like him, have lived so long.'

Lord Constantine extended his hand to Gawain. 'I will be glad to have you beside me, Lord Gawain,' he said as Gawain shook his hand. Then the grandson of King Constantine shook hands with Parcefal and Gediens. Old enemies and sword-brothers, men who had fought under Uther's dragon and Arthur's bear, bound once more in a blood pact. Resolved to spend the last of their strength in defence of Dumnonia. Resigned to fan a flame which guttered in the dark, all but gone out.

Gawain rubbed the back of his neck. 'We leave in the morning.'

Constantine nodded. 'I will be waiting with my men.' Then he looked at me. 'Keep up with your training, Galahad. Britain will need every sword.' He turned to Iselle, who looked so much like her father now that I knew it. 'Every bow,' he said to her. I wanted to tell him, tell them all, that she was Arthur's and Guinevere's own daughter. Instead, I clamped my teeth together.

'Dawn, then,' Gawain said.

'We'll be ready,' Lord Constantine said, and with that he left us.

Gawain turned to me and Iselle. 'You'll keep an eye on the druid. He must be ready to attempt the lady's healing when we return.'

'He will be, I swear it,' Iselle said.

I looked at Merlin, who sat rocking on his stool, his eyes closed. And I looked beyond him, beyond the bloom of light cast by the fire, to where Guinevere sat in shadow. So close and yet beyond reach. There but not there. The ruin of Britain.

And our last hope.

The horses were restless in the gloom, disturbed by my presence and by the halo of light and the stink from the fish-oil lamp which I had set down on an upturned barrel. Or perhaps they sensed my unease. My fear.

I placed a gentle hand on the cold bronze, as one might approach an animal so as to gain its trust. More than that, it was as though I sought the armour's forgiveness for rejecting it when Arthur first showed it to me, and my mind had flooded with memories.

When I was ready, I lifted the armour from its stand, the scales rattling softly, stirring from their long sleep. A thousand whispers in the dark. I pushed my arms through the tunic's elbow-length sleeves and held it bunched in front of my chest for a long moment, appreciating its weight. Half expecting a voice to shatter the moment and condemn me for my presumption. But no one spoke, and I lifted my arms above my head and let the long coat fall, leather and bronze and the past, too, pouring over me in a drenching of sound and smell and memory.

My thick woollen habit helped to fill the coat, a foot of grubby hem showing below the last row of bronze scales. I shrugged and bounced up and down to ensure the fit, seeing my father as I did so, then I knelt in the hay and strapped the greaves to my lower legs, holding the position awhile and running my finger over the hawk's head pressed into the bronze at the knee. Tracing the fierce eye, the savage beak and the feathers. Wondering if any man still lived in Britain capable of such exquisite craftsmanship. I would find someone to mend the three holes in the back of the coat, to patch the leather and replace the missing scales. Or . . . maybe I wouldn't. The past would still be the past.

Next, I put on the silver-studded baldric, the leather worn and creased yet still supple, and settled Boar's Tusk against my left hip. That was when the weight of the armour pressed down on me. It seemed too tight now. *Too heavy!* I pulled at the neck. Tried to tug it away from my chest, but my fingers slipped from the scales and I could not grip it. I could not breathe. One of the horses whinnied, sensing my anguish. Another pawed at the ground, and I fought for each breath and thought I must take off my father's armour or die in it as he had.

I was unworthy of it and I knew it. The scale coat and the belt and the sword remembered. They had served the greatest warrior in these Dark Isles and they knew that I was unfit to follow him. I stumbled back against a post and I slid down to the straw, breathing in ragged gasps, clawing at the scales.

'Father.' I choked on the word, my throat too tight. 'I'm sorry, Father.' My voice breaking, scattering into the lamplit dark as I looked up at the helmet still perched on the stand, its long plume a smear of white through my tears.

It must have pained Gawain to see Venta Belgarum in Saxon hands. To see fur-swathed spearmen upon the fort's ramparts. To hear guttural Saxon voices all around us and perhaps even to feel the presence of foreign gods, lingering like the smell of charred timbers and spilt blood. For Gawain, Parcefal and Gediens had fought here alongside Arthur and my father. Many brave warriors, with whom they had shared fire, ale and stories, had died winning this fort back from the Saxon king Aella, who had taken it from King Deroch. It had been a victory, one of many for Arthur, and Parcefal spoke of the fires that had been lit in celebration, their flames whispering to the night sky of glory, courage and loss. And yet what had it achieved?

The Saxon advance into Caer Gwinntguic had been stopped for a year or two, like a wound staunched to stop the flow of blood. But the wound had not healed, the Saxon boats had not stopped coming. Every spring and summer they crossed the Morimaru and spilled their hungry men upon our shores. Every battle waged amongst the meadowsweet and marsh marigold, every skirmish fought in the woods and ancient forests, robbed the rounds and cantrefs of Britain of husbands, fathers, brothers.

We had come to Venta Belgarum in the rain, our shields held upside down above our heads to show that we came in peace, riding through the vast encampment which smothered the land on the fort's western side. For the Saxons had ever spurned buildings of stone and would not live in the Roman halls, temples, bathhouses and villas which still stood within the walls. Father Brice had said that the Saxons were like animals and feared what they did not understand, for surely they could not conceive of how such buildings could be constructed. Father Judoc said that the Saxons believed the Romans to have been a race of giants, while Father Yvain had told me that the reason the Saxons avoided Roman buildings was that they believed them to be crowded with ghosts. But I wondered if the Saxons would not take up lodging in the old villas because they feared that the gods from their homelands across the Morimaru would not know to look for them inside dwellings of stone and brick. And no Saxon fighting in a foreign land cares to be invisible to his gods.

And so we had ridden among several hundred tents, past groups of sullen men sitting or standing around fires which gave more smoke than flame, our hands never far from our weapons, though we knew we would be dead in a matter of heartbeats should any of us spill Saxon blood. A band of twelve Saxons had ridden from the fort to escort us in.

'How does it feel, Galahad?' Gawain had asked me, nodding at the scale coat.

'Heavy,' I said.

He laughed, drawing the eyes of the Saxons around us. 'Give it another thirty years or so and you'll forget you're wearing it.'

'Let us hope that in thirty years Galahad doesn't need to wear it,' Lord Constantine said, back straight, his smooth chin high, ignoring the insults being hurled at him by Saxon warriors who recognized him as the commander who yet defied them, who yet sent their spear-brothers to the afterlife, only to vanish back into the forests to the north.

'He'll need it,' Parcefal assured him, 'for there'll always be someone who wants killing.'

I had known the talk was for my benefit, to steer my thoughts from the thousand Saxon warriors around us and the very real possibility that King Cerdic might order his men to hack us down, ridding himself of a problem. Bright blood in a grey day.

'Well, it suits you better than a monk's robes,' Gawain said, then shook his head at me as he had done several times since leaving Arthur's. 'Even if it *is* like riding with a ghost.'

I knew all too well what he meant, what illusion I had shaped with that bronze scale coat and white-plumed helmet. With the hawk greaves and the fine sword scabbarded on my belt and the white cloak, a gift from Arthur, which fell from my shoulders to spill across the gelding's back. I saw it not only in Gawain's face and in the faces of the other men I rode with now, but in the eyes of some grey-bearded Saxons who watched me pass, leaning on their spears or squatting beside hissing fires, warming their hands and leaving the insults to younger mouths. These men's eyes followed me, and I led them back through the years. Perhaps they heard again the thunder of hooves upon the earth, the screams of kinsmen impaled upon spears. For like Gawain, these old Saxons saw a ghost riding amongst them. They saw Lancelot.

'Will King Cerdic remember my father?' I had asked three mornings ago, when Gawain, Gediens and Parcefal had emerged from Arthur's byre to find me waiting for them in the dawn. I was weary, and Gawain's eyes had seized mine and, in that moment, he knew something of the battle I had fought in the stable while they slept.

He dipped his chin. 'He'll remember,' he said.

'Does a man forget the pain of being kicked in the stones?' Parcefal asked.

I nodded. 'Then let him think that Lancelot ap Ban has come again,' I said, and Gawain had grinned and I grinned too. But then I saw him look past my shoulder and I turned to see Arthur standing with Guinevere cradled in his arms, for he would often bring her out to watch the sunrise. But, his face now. His lips were parted and his eyes stared, and it was not just surprise that I saw there but hate, perhaps even fear, for he glanced down at Guinevere in his arms to see if she was seeing the same apparition.

'Galahad is coming with us, Arthur,' Gawain called out. Trying to break the spell.

Arthur blinked. Closed his mouth. Frowned. Guinevere was looking at me too, but who could say what she was thinking?

'I . . . I thought I should wear it, lord.' The words felt clumsy in my mouth. 'I am no monk.'

Arthur stared a little longer. Then he nodded. 'It belongs to you, Galahad,' he said. Then he carried Guinevere away, past the sheep pen to the willow beyond, whose long slender twigs were studded with downy buds.

'That's as good as having his blessing, lad,' Gawain said, walking to me and gripping my shoulder with a strong hand. 'You already had mine.' He lifted an eyebrow. 'You just brought it all back to him for a moment, that's all,' he muttered beneath his breath.

I nodded, self-conscious in the helmet. Aware of several thousand scales of bronze pulling me down. Reeling, still, from the look on Arthur's face.

'We're glad to have you.' Parcefal rattled the scales on my other shoulder.

Gediens smiled and nodded, drawing my gaze towards the house, where Iselle stood watching from the open doorway. 'Handsome devil, isn't he?' Gediens called to her. He looked like a lord of war in his own armour and plumed helmet, his shield slung across his back.

I mumbled some profanity at Gediens and he chuckled.

'You men are like cockerels flaunting your combs and feathers,' Iselle said through curling lips. 'Next you'll be seeing who can crow the loudest.'

The three sword-brothers grinned at that, and I forced a smile onto my lips, but really I was hoping that they didn't all think me a fool, standing there in the war gear of a great warrior when I had never been in a battle.

And now we stood in an ill-lit hall which had belonged to the kings of Caer Gwinntguic, warrior kings who had been tasked with defending the westernmost reaches of the Saxon shore. Nowadays, this hall resounded with Saxon songs. Tales of Saxon victories and Saxon heroes seeped into these timbers and this thatch, and yet we hoped that rumour of Arthur still drifted from ear to ear like the tendrils of smoke which wreathed among the warriors who had gathered to hear why we had come.

They crowded in on us, pushing us this way and that, their insults and challenges fouling the air with breath and filling the place with a clamorous din.

'Easy, Galahad,' Gawain warned, when I knocked away the hand of a Saxon who seemed determined to wrench one of the bronze scales from my coat.

I felt something wet strike my helmet's right cheek iron and my nose, and I turned, but had no way of knowing which man had spat at me. Then someone yelled for silence and the tumult receded. Warriors came amongst us and, their spears held across their bodies, pushed the crowd back so as to give us space. And then they did the same to open up a channel between us and the raised dais, and only then did we see our host. Or rather, hosts, for to our surprise, and horror too, Lady Morgana sat in the seat beside the old Saxon king. The black cloak which she wore over layered tunics of black wool was fastened with a silver brooch whose pin was long and wicked sharp. The skin around her eyes was dark with soot, her silver hair was braided into a rope and tied off with a leather thong, and at her pale neck she wore a torc of twisted silver which could buy the service of three hundred spearmen for a season's campaigning. Black and silver was Morgana, and her eyes shone with malice.

Melehan and Ambrosius stood beside their grandmother, lean-faced and contemptuous, whilst the fair-bearded Prince Cynric, a warrior in his prime, a king-in-waiting, stood at his father's shoulder.

We removed our helmets and I glanced at Gawain, wondering if he was thinking the same as I, that we would be lucky to ride away from Venta Belgarum.

'I am glad that you accepted my invitation, Lord Constantine.' King Cerdic's voice dispelled the last murmurs in the hall, stilling every tongue. He lifted an ale horn in our direction. 'It is good to meet face to face after all these years.'

'Lord king,' Constantine replied, those two words like poison in his mouth.

Cerdic put the horn to his lips, drank deeply, then knuckled his grey moustaches and gave Constantine a grin which was more raw red gums than teeth. 'And the same to you, Lords Gawain, Parcefal and Gediens.' He swept the drinking horn from right to left. His accent was thick, and he seemed pleased with himself for knowing who was who. 'You have all proved yourselves great warriors in the years since I brought my people to this land. But you, Lord Gawain, son of King Lot of Lyonesse,' he said, leaning forward in the chair, his shoulders still thick with muscle though he was an old man. 'I remember you well. You and Lord Arthur and your big war horses. My people had not fought against such an enemy for five generations.' He took a deep breath and sat back. 'You made many widows in those days. Sent many young warriors to Woden's hall to drink ale with their fathers and grandfathers.' He looked up at the rafters and lifted the drinking horn in honour of the dead.

'I wish we had sent more of your people to feast in the afterlife,' Gawain said, at which those Saxons in the hall who understood our language jeered and called upon their king to butcher us and feed us to his hunting hounds.

But King Cerdic showed no sign of being offended. He just gave his son, the prince, a look which seemed to say, *You see, boy, this is what I have been dealing with all these years*, while Cynric regarded Gawain in such a way that the unspoken challenge was loud enough for all to hear.

'But let us not talk of the past.' King Cerdic batted the air with a hand. 'That is not why you lords of Britain have come.' He turned to look at me then, and I did not see in those eyes the confusion and dread which I had seen in Arthur. What I saw in this Saxon king was curiosity. 'We have not met,' he said.

'No, we have not, lord king.' I could feel Lady Morgana's glare while I held the king's eyes.

'There are whispers in my camp.' He put a thumb and forefinger beside his right ear and lightly rubbed them together. 'There are those who say that you are not of this world. That the sorcerer, Merlin, has summoned your people's greatest warrior from Annwn to fight against me again as he once did.' He smoothed his long moustaches through his fist, and I could see that he hoped the whispers were true. 'They say that you are the great Lancelot, who turned the tide of battle on that day ten summers ago, when the steel storm raged. When your people and mine soaked the earth with slaughter's dew.' He glanced at Lady Morgana, whose claw-like hands gripped the arms of her chair as her eyes gripped me. 'That would be some powerful drýcræft,'

Cerdic said. 'More powerful than anything my own sorcerers are capable of.' His eyes narrowed and he leant forward again. 'Tell me, were you there that day?'

I felt the hairs standing on my arms. Behind us, the fire in the central hearth crackled. Other than that, the only sounds were of men breathing and the scuttle and flap of some bird up in the roof rafters.

'I was there, lord,' I admitted.

The king's eyes widened, and those around us mumbled and hissed and someone growled that they should cut our throats and hang us from the old yew tree by the well outside. Melehan and Ambrosius were each in their grandmother's ears, whilst Prince Cynric's hand fell to the hilt of his sword.

'I was there that day.' I lifted my voice to be heard. 'But I was just a boy.' I felt Gawain watching me. The others too. 'I watched from the hill,' I said, and pressed a hand against my chest, feeling the thump of my heart even through the bronze, leather and wool. 'I helped my father put on this armour which I now wear. Then, I watched him ride to Lord Arthur's side. I watched him cut your men down, as a scythe cuts wheat. I saw him kill Saxons and I saw him kill the traitors who fought for Lord Mordred.'

Lady Morgana did not like that, for Mordred had been her son, but I was glad to see my words warp her mouth. If not for her, Father Yvain would be alive still.

'And I saw him fall,' I said. 'Cut down from behind by men who lacked the courage to face him.' I lifted my chin and swallowed through the tightness in my throat. 'I am Galahad ap Lancelot.'

Lady Morgana fingered the silver brooch pinning her cloak. King Cerdic raised a hand to quiet the hum which rose amongst the assembled warriors and Saxon women.

'Ah, but that is a shame,' the king announced for all to hear. 'I was hoping the whispers were true. That Merlin had found a way to defy death itself.'

'Lord king, have you not invited us here to discuss terms for a truce?' Lord Constantine asked.

The Saxon king's eyes lingered on me a few heartbeats more, then he looked at Constantine. 'There will be time for that tomorrow, after you have eaten and rested. You are our guests,' he swept his arms wide, those arms adorned with warrior rings, 'and tonight we will drink together and talk of past battles.'

'We will not drink with you,' Gawain said. 'Nor talk of the past like old friends.' He glanced at Lady Morgana, which was as good as telling everyone gathered in the hall that he considered her a traitor to her people for welcoming Cerdic's spearmen into Camelot, and for sitting beside the Saxon now as though they were king and queen. 'We will discuss terms and then we will leave,' Gawain said.

Cerdic looked at Lord Constantine, who nodded in agreement with Gawain.

'Again, you disappoint me,' King Cerdic said, his accent shaping our words the way a sea wind will belly a sail. He flicked a hand towards me. 'This man is not Lancelot back from the dead,' he said, then looked at Lady Morgana, 'and now the great warlords of Britain will not stay to raise a cup to our marriage.'

Gawain and Lord Constantine shared a look of disbelief. Parcefal growled a curse and Gediens gripped the helmet under his arm a little tighter, bringing his right hand across to touch the iron against ill luck.

'Lady?' Lord Constantine said.

Morgana brought her hands together, kneading the swollen knuckles with a thumb.

'King Cerdic and I are to marry at Beltane,' she said, which got a chorus of cheers from the Saxons in the hall, though not, I noticed, from her own spearmen. 'We make this alliance for the sake of Britain.'

'There can be no Britain while his people burn and kill and take our people's land for themselves,' Lord Constantine said, his voice containing the anger of hot iron plunged into the quenching trough. Gawain looked too furious to speak.

'The killing will stop,' Lady Morgana said. 'King Cerdic's people may keep the land that they have won. We will rule Britain together as High King and Queen.'

'I can see what he gets out of it,' Parcefal said, 'but what about you, lady? What do you get for betraying us all?'

King Cerdic growled something in his native tongue, but Morgana gestured at the king to let her speak.

'In return for peace, King Cerdic has sworn that the Lords Ambrosius and Melehan will succeed whichever of us leaves the high seat of Camelot empty.' The lady's grandsons grinned. Prince Cynric, I saw, did not. 'This way, we are assured that our own people will rule. That Uther's own great-grandchildren will hold the power in Dumnonia. Two Pendragons to watch over the land.'

'The Saxons will hold the power,' Gediens said, his expression one of incredulity. 'You would give them Britain.'

'I would give us peace,' Morgana said.

Lord Constantine was shaking his head. 'Lady, you cannot trust them.'

King Cerdic pointed a ringed finger at Lord Constantine. 'And you cannot fight us,' he said.

'Now I understand,' Gawain said. 'This is why he asked you here,' he told Constantine. 'To show you . . . this,' he said, gesturing at the king and his would-be queen.

Lord Constantine's face looked as cold as the Roman statues

it resembled. 'Is this true, lord king? You did not ask me here to discuss a truce?'

Cerdic flapped a hand through the smoky air. 'Call it a truce if you want.' His voice sounded like the keel of a ship grinding up shingle. He nodded at Prince Cynric, who stepped forward.

'Come the next full moon, you will ride to Camelot,' the prince told Constantine. 'All of you,' he added, turning his blue eyes on us each in turn. 'You will swear fealty to the new king and queen. You will disband your army—'

'And you will bring me my brother's banner, Lord Constantine,' Lady Morgana interrupted him, 'that I may burn it.' She turned to Gawain. 'I would put an end to these rumours that Arthur lives. As should you, Lord Gawain. For such delusions do not help our people.'

'Arthur does live,' I heard myself say before Gawain could answer, and the eyes of everyone on the dais, everyone in that smoke-wreathed hall, fixed on me. I glanced at Gawain and he nodded, his scarred face saying that I had lit the fire and so we might as well watch it burn. I turned back to Lady Morgana and her new allies. 'Arthur lives and Merlin serves him once again,' I said.

'Lies!' Lady Morgana shrieked.

'No, lady, it is true,' I said.

Gawain held his plumed helmet out wide. 'Did Merlin not tell you that is why he has returned to Britain?' he asked her. 'Maybe if you hadn't beaten him like a dog . . .'

'*You* took him from us?' Melehan challenged, even as his brother Ambrosius pulled his sword from its scabbard and stepped forward.

'Not in my hall!' King Cerdic bawled. 'These men are my guests. You will sheathe your blade, Lord Ambrosius.'

'Do it, brother,' Melehan said.

But Ambrosius hungered to fight Gawain and for several heartbeats he was paralysed with indecision. Ambrosius was a lord of Britain and I could see how he despised taking orders from a Saxon king. And yet, as we had heard, his grandmother's marriage to King Cerdic assured him and his twin brother the high seat of Dumnonia. They would be the High Kings of Britain, if only by Saxon consent.

'Your transgression will not go unanswered, lord,' Ambrosius warned Gawain, pushing his sword back into its scabbard.

'You took the druid from me first, boy,' Parcefal said, 'so be careful before you deal out threats you can't make good on. I'm sure your sister, the Lady Triamour, will remind you what I did to her man.' He glanced at Gediens. 'What was that ox's name?'

'Balluc,' Gediens said with a derisive sneer.

'Aye, Balluc,' Parcefal said. 'Died on his knees as I recall.'

'Balluc was slow,' Ambrosius said. 'I am not.'

King Cerdic raised a hand and Lady Morgana hissed at her grandson to hold his tongue or lose it.

'The next full moon, lords,' the king confirmed. 'You will come to Camelot and bend the knee.' He growled at a slave to bring him more ale. 'If you do not, I will come for you. My warriors will sweep across Caer Celemion and Caer Gwinntguic,' he pointed to the hall's roof, 'like Thunor's chariot rolling across the sky. I will drown your crops in blood, turn the night red with flame and feed the crow and the wolf until one cannot run and the other cannot fly, so glutted will they be with the flesh of your people.' The slave put an ale horn in the king's outstretched hand and Cerdic drank to grease his tongue for the last of his promises. 'Anyone who owns a sword or shield will die. Anyone who breathes the name of Arthur will die, be they man, woman or child.' He lifted the drinking horn. 'In the name of Woden, I swear this, if you do not yield to me.' With that he sat back in his chair.

Prince Cynric raised a hand, stilling the hum which had risen with the king's talk of blood, the way hounds will lift their heads from their baskets when the scent of flesh is on the air. 'No one doubts your courage, lords,' Prince Cynric said. 'You have fought us since I was a boy. You have won many battles. But your time is over.' He frowned. 'You must know this, Lord Constantine. You can no more throw us back than can a man halt the flood tide with a sword and shield.' There was an honesty in the prince's face. A respect for his adversary which compelled him to at least try to see Constantine leave with some of his pride still his own. 'The battle is lost,' he shook his head, 'you can do no more.'

Lord Constantine's jaw clenched. I saw that the knuckles on the hand holding his helmet were bloodless, white as marble. 'My grandfather was Emperor of Rome,' he declared in a voice which had carried above the thunder of shields and the ringing of blades, and which now cut the smoke-thickened air. 'My father and my uncle were High Kings of Britain. Do not presume to tell me what is lost.'

The force of his words landed like a blow. I felt pride bloom hot in my chest and in that moment would have drawn my father's sword had Lord Constantine commanded me. But the effect was short-lived and the Saxons, emboldened by each other and prompted by their king, who hurled his ale horn at Lord Constantine's feet, yelled their insults and threats, baiting us as men will bait captives after a battle.

Yet, we had come to Venta Belgarum in peace and at their king's invitation, and Gawain knew that we must leave the same way, now and in haste, lest Cerdic's bloodlust sluice away his propriety or Lady Morgana convince him that our deaths now would smooth their road to power.

'Come, lord.' Gawain touched Constantine's arm, for the old warrior was eyeballing the king, longing to repay the insult of the ale horn in the rushes at his feet. 'We must go. There's no more to say here.'

Lord Constantine lingered still, as though fixing the faces of his enemies in his mind, then he turned on his hobnailed boots, his purple cloak billowing in the smoke, and we followed him, pushing through the stinking press, my sight crammed with hate-filled faces, my head besieged by the clamour of men vowing to slaughter us.

'Bring me my brother's banner,' Lady Morgana shrieked after us. 'Bring the bear to Camelot and watch it burn.'

We shoved through the crowd and out into the day, relieved to find our horses waiting for us where we had left them in the care of King Cerdic's slaves.

'Don't stop, Galahad,' Gawain warned, as we mounted, my head pounding with noise, the Saxons camped within the fort having noticed us now. 'Not for anything, understand?' I nodded, my hands clutching the reins, my blood thrumming in my legs. For, by our retreat so soon after coming, the spearmen without the hall inferred our humiliation at the hands of their king and bellowed their hatred of us. Some crowded around us with shields and helmets, jeering and barking curses and no doubt foretelling our deaths, but we walked our mounts on towards the gate, staying close to each other: Lord Constantine, then me, then Gediens, Parcefal and Gawain riding at the rear.

Something struck my helmet. A stone from the sound of it. Then a toothless Saxon bent, scooped up a handful of mud and threw it at Lord Constantine. The mud struck his cuirass just above the bronze stomach muscles, at which the Saxons cheered, while Constantine gave the impression that he had not even noticed, his back straight, his face a carving of disdain. Something else must have struck Gediens behind me, for he yelled in anger, but Gawain told us to keep moving.

'Don't even look at them,' he growled, and I tried not to, though my heart was thumping against my breastbone and I could feel sweat running in rivulets down my back.

Then more shouting in our wake and with it the drumming of hooves, and I heard Parcefal invoke Taranis, master of war, thinking that King Cerdic or Lady Morgana must have ordered their men to ride after us and kill us. But when I twisted in my saddle, for I could not help myself, it was Prince Cynric whom I saw cantering through the crowds on a stocky pony, his golden hair flying, a spear-armed warrior at each shoulder.

'What does he want?' Parcefal asked, but Prince Cynric did not stop to speak with us, instead riding past and taking up position ahead, clearing the way and commanding the Saxons to let us pass unmolested. He did this even beyond the gate, all the way to the boundary of the camp, as the noise fell away, the baying insults replaced by the thumping of hooves, the jangle of our gear and the breathy snorts of our horses. Then Prince Cynric eased his pony to a halt and turned to watch us as we passed him.

Lord Constantine dipped his head in thanks, his helmet's stiff red plume bristling in the breeze, and the Saxon prince dipped his head in reply. Then he and his men pulled their ponies around and rode back the way they had come, and we slowed, bringing our mounts closer to each other, riding five abreast.

'That is a man we will have to kill,' Gawain said. As much of an admission of respect as we would hear from him.

'So, there will be no truce,' Lord Constantine said. A woodpecker was drumming in the distant woods to the west. Nearer, by a fallen tree adorned with scarlet elf cups which looked like splashes of blood, two hares were leaping and dancing, as if mad with joy for the end of winter.

'No truce,' Gawain agreed. 'What will you do?'

Lord Constantine considered this, though surely he had known the answer the moment Lady Morgana had revealed her plan to marry the Saxon king in order that Melehan and Ambrosius would rule Dumnonia when she and Cerdic were gone; a treachery which cut as deeply as her son Mordred's had ten years ago.

'I will prepare for war,' Lord Constantine said. 'Raise what spears I can. Send messengers to the other kings. To King Catigern of Powys and King Bivitas, the new ruler of Cynwidion. Perhaps they will be persuaded to join us when they learn what Morgana plans.' He had not shaved that morning and by a shaft of sunlight I saw the beginnings of white bristles above his upper lip and on his chin. He looked old. Tired. As though he had expended his strength and will in portraying a certain vision of himself to his enemies and could keep up the act no longer. 'Let us hope that Merlin has found a way to bring the lady back to Arthur,' he said.

And let us hope that the druid has told Iselle that she is Lord Arthur and Lady Guinevere's daughter, I thought. Or else I would tell her myself. I would have to.

'We don't have long,' Gawain said.

Gediens looked up at the sky. There was no moon to be seen yet, but we knew it would be on the wane when the night revealed it.

For a long moment each of them was lost in his own thoughts. Grim thoughts. For war was coming and we did not have enough time.

'The gods be with you,' Lord Constantine said.

'And with you,' we replied in ragged chorus.

Then the old warrior turned his horse into the north and rode away, and to me he looked like a Roman general riding back into the past from whence he came.

Then we turned our own mounts westward towards the setting sun.

War. Blood to water the summer wheat. Flesh to satiate the carrion feeders of earth and sky.

We rode west. Back to Arthur.

15

The Druid

'THEY HAVE EXCHANGED BARELY a dozen words since you left.' Iselle was sitting on a stool beneath the apple tree, plucking the carcass of a swan which she told me had somehow caught itself in one of her snares. She had already set aside the primary feathers from the bird's wing, which she would split and cut for arrow fletchings. 'I've tried to get them together by the hearth. To make them talk. And listen.' She shook her head, quick, frustrated hands ripping from the flesh feathers which drifted away on the breeze like apple blossom falling in a fruitless year. 'They are both stubborn. Both impossible.'

'But now that Arthur knows what Lady Morgana and King Cerdic intend, he will yield.' I paused. 'He must.'

The previous dusk, when we had arrived back at Lord Arthur's steading and I had seen the flint in Iselle's eyes, I had thought that Merlin must have told her the truth of her birth. But it was soon apparent that she knew nothing of it still, and her anger towards Arthur and Merlin was, rather, due to their bullheadedness.

'Arthur resents Merlin,' Iselle said. 'He says that Merlin abandoned him when he needed him most. Worse than that betrayal, Arthur says, is that Merlin left Britain. Or at least, he vanished from men's sight.'

I looked towards the house. 'But he is here now. Surely Arthur can put aside the past.'

'Arthur believes that Merlin knew about Guinevere,' Iselle said. 'That she was lost. Caught between worlds.' Iselle looked up at me and there was pain, not anger, in her clear eyes. 'And if he knew, why did he not come back?' She was asking on behalf of herself then, not Arthur. She shook her head. 'Arthur cannot forgive him.' She sighed and I knew that we who had ridden into Venta Belgarum to be insulted and threatened by the king of the Saxons had had the easier time of it.

I watched her savaging that swan and after a while she continued, 'Merlin is not the man I thought he was. I have spoken with him. He claims that the gods have abandoned him, that they no longer speak to him, nor can he read the signs they send in the flight of birds or in the entrails.' She shrugged.

'And Guinevere? Did he know?' I asked.

'He says he would have come sooner had he known.'

'Do you believe him, that he has lost his powers?'

Iselle's dark brows came together. 'Why would he say it otherwise?'

'But he will try? To bring the lady back?'

'Yes.' She nodded. 'He'll try.'

I looked at the carcass on her knees. Most of the top coat feathers were out now, but the body was still white with downy fluff and I knew that by the time Iselle had finished, it would look as if there had been a spring snowfall around that apple tree.

'What is it, Galahad?' She was looking up at me as she ripped the feathers out. 'This?' She gestured at her work.

I asked why she wasn't saving the feathers, for on Ynys Wydryn we would use them for pillows or else Father Yvain would take them to sell at the lake village.

'We won't be here long enough to need more soft bedding,' she said, and so those swan feathers lay in the mud. 'I asked Merlin if he thought it was an omen. If we should have left the bird alone or given it back to the water.' She looked down at the carcass, her lips pursed. I could not help but think of Guinevere when I imagined that beautiful bird trapped in Iselle's snare. Iselle shrugged again. 'He said it was not for him to know such things. Not any more. But Gawain said only a fool would waste so much meat. That the gods would not have let the bird trap itself if it was so special.'

'It will be delicious,' I said, and I saw the corners of Iselle's lips tugged upwards just a little. The ghost of a smile.

But the truth was I had not been thinking about the swan or omens, but rather about Iselle being Lord Arthur and Guinevere's daughter and not knowing it. If Merlin would not tell her, then I would, for she deserved to know. I would tell her tomorrow. When I had finished learning my weapons with Gediens, Iselle and I would go into the marsh to hunt birds and I would tell her.

But the next day we did not go hunting, nor did I learn my weapons. Instead, we clung to the roundhouse like elder smoke, Gediens and Parcefal invoking gods in ale beakers or touching iron for luck. Iselle keeping her hands busy by re-fletching a sheaf of arrows which she had found in Arthur's barn but whose flights had been chewed by mice. Gawain wearing his mood like a dark cloak, his thoughts his own but his fears lying upon us all. Oswine mixing herbs, grinding roots, setting dried leaves to smoulder in dishes, warming wine and pouring draughts into cups. Arthur building up the fire before it needed it, stacking peat turves and splitting willow logs for the long night to come; busying himself with any unnecessary task. And I, scrubbing the last journey from my father's armour, greaves and cloak, working the nub ends of old tallow candles into the metal scales and buffing each with a linen cloth until Arthur's overfed fire blazed in the bronze.

Because Merlin was attempting to bring Guinevere back to the world.

Merlin began before sunrise, making the lady drink from a seashell a potion mixed of three substances not procured by human means nor made by the hand of man. These being honey, milk and salt which, combined, created a well-known cure for possession by malevolent spirits, so Merlin muttered as he put the shell to Guinevere's lips, cursing into his beard at every spilled drop. The next draught was worse, being the heart of a crow, beaten up with the bird's blood and drunk still warm. 'She will take this for the next eight days,' Merlin announced, and with the edge of his finger lifted a scarlet drop from beneath Guinevere's mouth and pushed it between her lips, 'providing Oswine and Iselle between them can catch enough crows.' At least I knew now why there had been four of the birds strung up by the legs above the smokehouse door, turning in the breeze, their dead eyes black as curses.

After some mumbled incantations, the druid took a bone needle and, trying to fight the years which shivered in his hands, pierced the shell of a living snail. Then, making Oswine take hold of Guinevere's head and tilt it backward – for Arthur would not do it – he held the snail over the lady, making sure that the fluid which exuded from the creature's shell dripped on her eyes. She blinked. Once. Twice. Then stared as before.

'I would, of course, rub her eyes with the tail of a black cat,' Merlin said, 'but Oswine being a useless Saxon swine could not find me one.' I exchanged raised eyebrows with Gediens, for who would expect to find any cat, black or otherwise, out here in the marsh? And I wondered why Oswine, a Saxon, had remained so loyal to Merlin all these years, when he could surely have slipped away from the druid at any time to rejoin his own people. It seemed to me that Merlin was lucky to have him, though I knew he would never admit as much.

Merlin raised a hand into the hearth smoke. 'Still, we cannot be sure that the lady does not see into this world now and then, just because she cannot tell us as much.'

Kneeling by Banon near the fire, Lord Arthur grunted. 'Do not feel you have to share every part of your scheme,' he said, his mouth slack as though to avoid a bad taste. He was picking burs from Banon's black fur while she sat still and content, her eyelids falling closed now and then. 'Did I tell you each detail of my battle plans?' he asked the druid. 'Which of my cataphracts would form my vanguard? Whether Parcefal, Bedwyr or Cai would circle to attack the enemy's rear? Or when I'd have my men skirmish, when charge and break my opponent's line?'

'You are not the one trapped in here, Arthur.' Merlin dismissed his lord with a flap of his hand. 'Go and pick me some hemlock and willow herb if you don't want to learn something. I am not saying it for you in any case, but rather for me because I have not attempted such an arduous healing for some years, and speaking it aloud helps me to recall the lore.' He gestured to Oswine, who took two handfuls of herbs and threw them into the hearth flames, where they blackened and curled, some bursting to flame and all belching thick smoke, white and yellow like an old man's dirty beard. He had already tied a bunch of mint around the lady's right wrist. 'Go and fetch more wood, Arthur. We will not be finished here until dawn tomorrow.' He picked up a leather flask and poured some dark liquid into a cup and I wondered what he would make Guinevere drink next, but he put that cup to his own lips and drained it in three deep gulps. 'Come here, Galahad,' he beckoned me, 'take the lady in your arms and walk with her three times around the hearth, keeping her face turned towards the smoke. She must breathe it in.'

I felt a fluttering in my stomach and looked at Iselle, who nodded that I should do as Merlin instructed. I had not imagined I would play any part at all in the proceedings, nor did I want to.

Arthur looked up at me, something like suspicion in his grey eyes, and I think he saw my father standing before him. I believed he hated the idea of my participating in Merlin's rites, for though he had escaped from men and from the world, he had never escaped his own memories. Still, he gave a slight nod and so I walked across to where the lady sat, thinking how best to lift her without hurting her, for she was very frail. And when I turned around with Guinevere cradled in my arms, her head resting on my shoulder so that I could smell the iron of the crow's blood on her breath, I saw Arthur walking out of the door, his black shadow, Banon, at his heel.

I walked with Guinevere around the hearth, slowly so as to let the musky, herb-sweetened smoke envelop us, Merlin all the while waving a wooden trencher up and down at the fog to make it chase us. She weighed nothing. My father's scale armour coat was heavier, and yet perhaps she felt my arms trembling under her. For my blood shook with the sin of my trespass; of bearing this woman in my arms, who had been my father's earth, sea and sky. Her warm cheek, once wet with tears of their shared despair, now against *my* neck. Her soft breath on *my* skin, that same breath which had whispered my father's name in the dark.

After the third time around the fire, burdened more by the eyes upon me than by Guinevere, I returned the lady to the chair and retreated back across to the other side of the hearth, hoping the druid would ask no more of me.

'Girl, do you have the skull?' Merlin turned to Iselle, who nodded and fetched a bowl from Arthur's table. From what I could see, that bowl contained a mound of fine, grey-white powder and I shuddered to think that it had been a man's skull before Iselle smashed it into fragments and ground it as one might grind flour to make bread. 'Good,' Merlin nodded, as he took the offered bowl and a cup from Oswine and poured a green-tinged liquid onto the powder. He took up a spoon and began to mix it. 'Nine pieces of a man's skull,' he said, and I wondered where Iselle had found a man's skull, but it did not seem the time to ask, 'mixed with a decoction of wall-rue.' He looked up at Gawain. 'It's a fern,' he explained, at which Gawain shrugged as if to say he didn't care what it was so long as it worked. 'As with the crow's hearts, she will have to drink this every morning until it is all gone.' He raised a finger in warning. 'None must be left, unless we want the dead man to come looking for the pieces of his skull.'

I looked at Iselle, but she was watching Merlin intently. Parcefal muttered something under his breath and said he had to feed the horses.

'I cannot tell you that any of this will work,' Merlin confessed, taking a spoon and waving it in our direction before dipping it into the bowl. 'It has been so long since the lady was first afflicted.' He pushed a spoonful of the skull mixture between Guinevere's lips. 'Such a long, long time she has been lost to us,' he mumbled. 'As I have tried to explain to Arthur, the will of the gods is no more known to me than it is to you.' He gestured at the leather flasks, cups and bowls, the bundles of herbs and tangles of roots and the overturned dishes in which creatures that crawled or slid or scuttled were trapped. 'These cures are for the more common maladies. Blindness.

The falling sickness. That sort of thing.' He grimaced, with his knuckle wiping a drop of the mixture from Guinevere's chin. 'But that which troubles the lady is more grievous and will require intervention by higher powers.'

'Just bring her back, Merlin,' Gawain said.

Merlin's eyes flicked to the door, as if he feared someone walking in at that very moment. Arthur, no doubt. Then he looked up at Gawain. 'In all the years, have you ever considered that perhaps she does not want to come back?' he asked. It was clear from the way Gawain and Gediens looked at each other that they had not considered this. 'Still,' he turned back to the lady, 'I will do what I can, because Arthur is my friend. And because I owe it to him to try.'

'And because if you don't, I'll give you to Morgana and her Saxon king as a wedding gift,' Gawain threatened.

And so Merlin worked throughout the day while we came and went, helpless as men at a birth. Come dusk, when the herons swept eastward above us to their roosts, and the first bats to emerge from their winter hiding places flitted above the reed-beds, Merlin asked me to lift Guinevere from her chair again. This time, I was to put her on the bed in preparation for what he said was the most important part of his rites.

Again, I could hardly believe how little she weighed. I thought of Arthur doing the same thing as I did now, but every night for the last ten years. Carrying her through the nearly dark, laying her amongst the bed furs and climbing in beside her, listening to her breathing and the soft murmur of the hearth flames, and the thought of his loneliness was terrible.

'Thank you, Galahad,' Merlin said.

It was just the three of us then, and I looked over at Guinevere where she lay, and I could not help but wonder what my father would have thought to look at her now, had he still lived.

'When did they . . . when did it happen?' I said, my voice low so that anyone outside would not hear.

'Ah, I wondered when you'd ask,' Merlin said. 'You are slow, like your father was. You might be even slower than he was.' He frowned up at me. 'I haven't decided yet.' He was sitting on a stool, a pile of deadnettle on the table beside him, easing the small flowers from each calyx one by one and putting them to his mouth to suck out the sweet nectar.

'Believe it or not, it was after Arthur had almost burned her alive,' he said. The sound of his old mouth suckling the tiny cuplike flowers was sickening to me. He looked at Guinevere. 'Your father turned the world upside down to save her and, after it all, she slunk off back to Arthur.' He bent an eyebrow. 'The gods told her to do it, I think. What else would explain it?' He picked up another stem of deadnettle and examined it. 'She was trying to set things right in her way.' He plucked another flower and held it up to me. 'Look inside, Galahad,' he said.

I frowned at him but he pushed the flower towards me and so I took it from him.

'Inside,' he said again.

It was dark and I could see nothing much, so I turned the flower towards the firelight and peered inside.

'You see the stamens?' the druid asked.

'Stamens?'

'The threads, boy. Two of them. One black, one golden.'

'I see them,' I said.

Merlin nodded. 'Don't they look to you like two figures sleeping side by side in a bed of white furs?'

I frowned again and looked again and said nothing, putting the flower back down on the table in case the old man wanted to suck out its sweetness.

'They were together one night. Just one.' He looked at Guinevere in her and Arthur's bed, the flame flicker now and then illuminating her pale cheek as she lay so perfectly still. 'But it only takes one night.'

I stared at Guinevere, wanting to hate her. Wanting to feel the pain that my father must have felt knowing that she had returned to Arthur.

'Oh, I doubt your father knew, if that's what's bothering you. Or maybe he did.' The druid shrugged. 'It was all too late by then, anyway.'

It must have been around the same time that my father met my mother, I knew. And though I was born soon after, I had no doubt that my father must have carried Guinevere in his heart still.

Merlin stood, took the ravaged nettle stems and tossed them into the fire, where they smoked and glistened with droplets of water which burst from them like sweat.

'Now I must rest awhile and dream to the gods if I can,' he said. He looked tired, the skin around his eyes tinged blue and so thin it might easily tear. The tremor which I had seen earlier in his hands had spread through his old bones now so that his whole body, and even his face, quivered like heather with a breeze in it. He looked down at Guinevere. 'Keep an eye on her,' he commanded, 'and wake me if she brings anything back up, though the mint should settle her stomach.'

'If she fouls herself?' I asked, for it was not unlikely after all that Merlin had poured into her.

'Then clean her, Galahad,' the druid said with a roll of his eyes, and with that he left us and went to find a quiet place to dream to the gods, or perhaps simply to sleep. And when next we saw him, he was not the same man.

*

Like most of the others, I had fallen asleep by Lord Arthur's hearth, lulled by the soft flicker of flame and the warm bloom of strong mead in my stomach. My bladder being full, though, I woke and saw Lord Arthur sitting on a stool beside the bed, watching Guinevere sleep. He nodded to me and I nodded back, before looking at the others who were lying on furs or leaning against the walls. Gawain and Parcefal were snoring so loudly it was a wonder anyone was still asleep.

Iselle was awake, watching the fire, but feeling my eyes on her she looked up and I mouthed *Merlin?* to her. She shrugged. The screech of an owl and the heaviness of the world beyond the wattle and mud walls told me that we were in the depths of the night, and yet where was the druid? Why was he not neck-deep in his mysterious rites, trying to draw Lady Guinevere from this living death which would not let go its grip on her? I thought to wake Oswine and tell him to fetch the druid from the byre, if that was where he lay sleeping still, for perhaps, being old, Merlin could no longer wake at will, and I feared him ruining the work he had already done this day if he did not proceed as planned.

But then the door clunked open, creaking back on its hinges and waking Gediens, whose hand found the sword in the dry reeds beside him. Silver moonlight washed the darkness, for a heartbeat illuminating waking faces, iron, fur, hearth stones. Then shadow bled in again and with it a great weight pressed upon me so that I could not move, for I thought a god had come down to the marsh and meant to claim Guinevere once and for all, or else challenge us for our meddling in things beyond our understanding.

The god creature stepped over the threshold, black as pitch, shapeless, wanting for arms, and I saw Iselle grab the fire iron beside her to ward off ill luck, and Parcefal half draw a knife, pressing his fingers against the blade. For, like me, they thought that the Morrigán, goddess of strife, had swept down in the form of a great crow, dark as night, sheened purple and green in terrifying beauty. And even Gawain, who was not a man who saw omens in the patterns which cream makes in a pail, or in a flight of rooks, or saw gods in doorways, widened his eyes as he cast off his furs and stood.

It was not the Morrigán who had come, but Merlin, swathed in his cloak of crow and raven feathers; as many feathers, it seemed, as there were scales on my father's coat of bronze. We were all standing now, but I was the nearest to him and it was me he was looking at, though there seemed to be no recognition in his face. I tried to speak. To greet him. To make some show of respect, for here was a druid clothed in his ritual robes, invested with the ancient power of our people. But a heavy foot seemed to be treading down my tongue. No one spoke, and Merlin, the last of the druids, swept past me and went to the small table where were gathered the potions and cups from earlier. Without a word, he picked up two beakers, sniffed them both, put one down and drank from the other. Then he went over to where Guinevere lay, seeming not even to see Lord Arthur, who gave way, almost reluctantly, stepping back into the shadows against the wall.

Merlin lifted his arms and Oswine moved in, taking the feathered cloak from his master, who was naked beneath it, his scrawny body white as chalk but for the shapes and swirls which adorned his skin and seemed imbued with life of their own in the fitful light given and snatched away by the fire. Then he sat on the edge of the bed, staring straight ahead, his eyes wide and bulbous. He showed no sign of seeing any of us or even knowing we were there, as Oswine gestured at Iselle to make up the fire now so that his lord would not get cold.

My mouth was dry, but I did not dare move to fetch a drink. I still needed to empty my bladder, yet I could not leave, so bound was I by Merlin's magic and by the invisible strings which shivered between us all like spider's silk.

Mute, barely breathing, my stomach as hollow as an oak gall, I stood still as Iselle poked the fire, creating space for new fuel, and the fire cracked and spat, and Oswine gently drew the bed skins off Guinevere. And by a brief flare of copper firelight I saw her: the lady lost in a dream. She lay in a blue linen dress which Arthur must have put on her in readiness should Merlin be successful and bring her back to herself and to Arthur. The dress was drawn in at the waist by a delicate gold chain. A fine silver band wrapped around her pale upper arm, though it was much too big, the serpent-head terminals kissing where once they must have challenged each other across a white sea. Her black hair had been combed, her head encircled by a crown of wood anemones and sweet violets and, seeing her thus, my heart ached for Arthur. I did not dare look in his face for fear of seeing the terrible hope there.

Merlin lay down beside the lady, shuffling closer until their bodies touched, then wrapping his hand around hers, one bird's foot grasping another. Talons entangled.

Banon lifted her black head and let out a whine, as if she had heard something which we humans had not. Then Oswine laid the feathered cloak upon the lady and the druid, leaving only their feet and shins exposed.

Wherever you are, lady, he is coming for you. I sent that thought towards her, then I looked at Iselle and found that she was already looking at me.

I run. Like water. Like fire. Clear of the dark woods, the root-nooks and the soft bog. Out under the sky. Into the long grass which whispers to me as I pass through it. Unbound and lordless. Drumming the earth in the ancient rhythm, the song of my kind since long before man sought to bend our spirit. To tame us and taste the wind, flying across the earth at speeds he would otherwise never know.

No men here. In this hidden valley, this secret, sunken place which is guarded by oak wood and steep sides of wind-rippled heather. And I run, not in fear but in joy. Finding peace in movement. The thump of my heart, the passing of my breath, the cadence of my hooves upon the ground and within the ground, honouring the soil which gives us the sweet grass. Echoing the earth thrum of the first herds. When men dreamed us into the white spume of racing waves. When they gave us gods to protect us and used us to collect the souls of the dead. When they first yoked us to gleaming chariots and we carried them into war.

I do not try to impose my own will on this creature. I would be unable to. But I would not want to, either. She is proud and free, this mare, and might run to the world's edge, as a peal of thunder across the firmament. I will cling into her if I can, for I revel in the wind through my soul and in the not trying. And I feel that she knows we are joined. It is as though she wishes to give me this gift of serenity, of letting the world slide off us like smoke. And so I let myself recede, a flame burning out, and give myself to the mare, whose heart's incessant beat is as the ebb and flood of the tides, the turn of the seasons, the death of the old stallion and the birth of the foal.

The world is grey when we come to the pool, which sits low and sullen in the glen like the last water in the cauldron. I lift my head and cry out in triumph and defiance, aware of the slowing of my hooves' song on softer ground. Aware of a savage thirst, my flanks wet with lather, my belly sucking in and swelling out. I walk to the water and turn into the wind, then I drink, cooling the fire in my blood. Then swing my head up, ears swivelling, breathing and blowing and tasting the air. And I feel the mare's fear now, for some part of her remembers being smaller. Weaker. A prey animal forever seeking the protection of the herd, and even now she readies herself to dance away and run again, rather than risk the impossibility of escape.

Then I see her. Emerging from gorse beyond the deer trail, like my own shadow catching me up. A mare the same grey as the sky. Breathing hard. Tossing her head, saying that she has chased me as the moon chases the sun. She whinnies, seeks my permission to come closer, but I jump sideways, away from her and from the pool, and lean back, legs splayed. The mare shrieks again and comes on, inexorable as night, as I swing my head and cry out, my muscles taut, heart thumping, blood in spate.

Still the mare comes on, close enough now that the whites of her eyes gleam like smooth river pebbles and her scent is thick in my mouth. And I know that this mare is possessed by another. I know that he has come. The druid. Somehow, he has found me. After all this time.

Yet, he is too late.

I hold the mare's eyes for another few heartbeats. Then I shriek to the grey sky.

And run.

Afterwards, it was a long time before Merlin would speak. He had thrown off the feathered cloak and sat up, looking straight ahead at the swords and pelts hung from the wall pegs but seeing things that were further away, far beyond our sight. The fire popped and he started, looking at the flames, so that I saw there were tears in his eyes.

'Fetch him a drink,' Gawain growled at Oswine, who had been preparing his master a meal of cheese and smoked eel, having told us that the journeying always brought on a ravenous hunger in the druid.

I did not know if Arthur had seen the tears in the old man's eyes, but he covered the lady with the bed furs again, taking a moment to run his fingers over her forehead into her black hair, as one might wake a lover or a child.

Perhaps we waited out of respect. Or because we thought it was Lord Arthur's right to be the first to ask. Or, maybe we waited because secretly we already knew, yet sought to stretch out the time when all was still possible. But when Merlin had drained his cup, having neither looked any of us in the eye nor uttered a word, we could endure it no longer, and I was grateful when the silence was broken.

'Say something, druid,' Gawain said, at which Arthur flinched as though struck, yet he turned his eyes to Merlin in the same way that I have since seen men look upon a stillborn child or a woman defiled by the enemy; seeing because he must, though knowing the sight will haunt him after.

Merlin had the decency to choose Arthur's eyes out of all those watching him.

'I failed,' he said.

We knew it, of course, for all that I still hoped that he had not. That perhaps the rites were not yet over, or that having been gone so long, the lady might not return at once, as sight does not when eyes first open after a long sleep, but would rouse over the course of the night and the next day.

Arthur held the druid's gaze awhile and it seemed he wanted to ask more, but then he nodded and, telling us he needed to breathe clean air, threw a cloak around his shoulders and went into the night.

Gawain, Gediens and Parcefal looked at one another with tired resignation and it seemed to me that the three of them looked older, as though the small hope which had flickered in their hearts, helping them defy time itself, had been snuffed out and the years flooded in with the dark.

'I'm going to my bed,' Parcefal rumbled.

'And me,' Gediens said.

'I'll see to Arthur,' Gawain said, and drank a great wash of ale before heading out after his lord, uncle and friend.

Iselle put a log on the fire and knelt to blow new life into the coals, her face giving away nothing save that her mind was busy untangling thoughts. I turned my attention back to Merlin, expecting him to give us more. To do something more.

'What is it, boy?' he asked, deliberate with the insult. 'Even Uther knew better than to stare at me like a fool trying to boil water with his eyes.' He pushed himself up and stood unsteadily but Oswine helped him over to the bench by the hearth and sat him down before going to fetch his food.

'What happened?' I asked.

Oswine offered him the plate but Merlin waved it away with a grimace.

'I told you,' he said. 'I failed.' His voice was dry as ancient bones.

I wondered if he was avoiding my eye because he was ashamed, or because there were things which he was keeping to himself and feared saying without a word spoken.

'You did not find her?' I asked.

Iselle looked up from the other side of the hearth, her face washed by new flamelight.

'What does it matter to you?' the druid snapped, a spark of anger in a spent fire. 'It is as I said. As I told Arthur, though I don't think he believed me.' He chewed the next words before he said them. 'The gods have abandoned me. As they have abandoned Britain. The power which I once enjoyed. It's gone.' His eyes turned up to where the smoke gathered, seeping out through the reed thatch. 'They have taken it from me as a mother snatches a toy from a disobedient child.' He held his palms towards the fire and shivered. You'd have thought he had been out in the cold night air. But then, who could say where he had ventured in search of Guinevere beneath that cloak of crow and raven feathers?

He growled at Oswine to bring the plate back, which the Saxon did before filling the druid's cup. Merlin picked up a piece of eel and thrust it into his mouth. 'You would all have been better leaving me to pass my last years alone,' he said as he chewed. 'Instead of dragging me back to the world.' He wafted a hand at me. 'You're like thieves digging up a corpse to steal the coins from his eyes.'

I glanced back at the lady lying in her bed, a ring of flowers in her dark hair. Not a corpse, but not really alive either. 'You could try again,' I said.

He laughed at that. A dry, resentful expulsion which ended in coughing. After, he took his hand from his mouth and grabbed at the air above the hearth. 'And you could try to catch smoke and hold it in your hand, Galahad,' he said, then he looked up at me, his eyes meeting mine for the first time. 'Or try to run back to that hill at Camlan and beg your father not to leave you there and ride to his death.'

I felt that as the pain he had intended, and I wanted to strike him. And why shouldn't I? This man, whom folk called the last of the druids, had done nothing to earn my respect, nor should I fear his power, for I believed he had none. And yet perhaps that was more reason to let him be, and so I swallowed my anger. He was just an old man. Broken and lost. He was nothing more than the soot still hanging in the air from a flame which had been snuffed out.

'It will be morning soon, Galahad,' Iselle said, knowing the heat that was in my blood. I nodded and turned away from Merlin to gather my cloak.

'The gods set us all up, Galahad,' the druid mused, as Iselle and I left him sitting by the flames. 'Like a game of chess,' he called after us, 'they set the pieces up and then they walk away from the game.'

The waning moon was low in the east yet bright enough to throw shadows from the outbuildings and the old crooked apple tree. It silvered the reed-beds and shivered in muddy puddles. It shone in the smoke leaking from Lord Arthur's thatch and it lit the way for a fleet of clouds sailing across the night sky, making me think of the Saxon ships which would soon be crossing the Morimaru now that spring was here.

'It will be full again soon enough.' Iselle was looking up, for we had stopped on the way to the byre, to fill our lungs with clean air before going to our beds.

'It will,' I agreed, not looking at the moon. Looking at her. And though it would indeed wax full soon enough, and we must swear loyalty to the Saxon king and his wife or else witness the final ruin of Britain, in that moment I did not care.

Our hands touched. A shiver ran through me from my head to the muscles in my thighs. Then we were entwined, our mouths pressed softly together, tasting each other. I had never had wine or mead so intoxicating, and Iselle sighed into my mouth and I breathed in her breath, needing her, flesh and soul. Then she broke the kiss, pulling away to look into my eyes, as if to make sure I was the man she thought me to be. As if the taste of me in her mouth had revealed something else.

'Come,' she said, and taking my hand she led me to the stable.

Merlin slept three days and nights after his failed attempt to restore Guinevere. Gawain, Gediens and Parcefal spent much of that time making plans in preparation for King Cerdic's ultimatum and its aftermath. Still they begged Arthur to put on his old scale armour and lead them as he had in former times, but Arthur would not leave Guinevere. For she must want to live, he said, to return to him, or else how could she have endured this affliction for so long?

'The gods test me, still,' he told us. 'They test my resolve and my loyalty. If I remain steadfast, there is hope that they will return her to me. My sins demand a price. I will not abandon her.'

And so Gawain and the others talked of the kings of Britain: which of them could perhaps be persuaded to fight alongside Lord Constantine, given the Lady Morgana's betrayal? Who among them had the most to lose by bending the knee to a Saxon king in Camelot? And who could be called upon to fight in order to prevent the Lords Melehan and Ambrosius becoming joint kings of Dumnonia, having suffered because of Mordred's treachery at the last great battle? Having seen fathers, sons, uncles and brothers killed because of it.

'They must fight,' Gediens said, 'for they must realize that all Britain will be lost if the heartlands of Cynwidion and Caer Celemion are overrun.'

Parcefal shook his head. 'If the Saxon chieftains south of the River Tamesis join Cerdic, as I have heard they will, and bring a thousand spears into Dumnonia, we will never be rid of them. Not without Camelot.'

Gawain agreed. 'So, we must fight this summer.' He scratched his beard. 'Not a raid here and there. Constantine must come out of the forest and plant his banner.'

'Our banner.' Parcefal thumped his chest with a fist. For Constantine flew the same bear which adorned their shields. Lord Arthur's bear.

'We bring them to battle before the wheat ripens,' Gawain said. 'It is the last chance we will have. It is the only way.'

They talked of raising spearmen as though it could be done, throughout three sunny days that woke adders from their dormant state, while goldcrests and greylag geese took to the sky for their breeding grounds further north and east. They talked because the season was turning and at such times hopes will rise with the sap, and it is hard to think of death in the midst of new life. And they talked because they did not want to think about the failure which we had all witnessed. For years they had searched for Merlin, hoping that he could cure Guinevere and that her recovery would return Arthur to them and to Britain. But it was all for nothing, and I think they would have ridden to fight King Cerdic alone rather than face the truth of it.

Iselle spent most of those three days hunting in the marsh, so that I began to think she regretted what had passed between us that night in the stable beneath the cross where my father's armour had hung. I could think of little else. I craved her scent. Her touch. Those parts of her that were secret and hidden but which I now knew. It haunted me like a dream. And so I busied myself with my weapons, throwing the spear until my shoulder muscles burned. Practising my sword cuts against the woven reed target until I could no longer lift Boar's Tusk. Relishing the exquisite pain of swollen muscle and taut flesh. The familiarity of the weapons in my hands had reached me across the years like an echo from my childhood and my father's tutelage, so that his sword hilt and spear shaft felt almost a part of me now.

But then, at dusk on the fourth day, Merlin woke. Gediens and I were fighting with leather-sheathed spears when Oswine came to say that the druid wanted to see us all together. Was he going to try again to heal Guinevere? Or, like the snakes which could be found coiled beneath brambles near the wood, had he woken with new venom to spit at us about the gods and their abandonment of us?

'I have had a dream,' he told us when we gathered around his bed of skins in the byre. He hadn't eaten in four days and he had a wild look in his eyes. 'Or else my mind snagged it in the depths, when I was neither asleep nor awake. As a man hooks a fish on a line which he has left unattended.' He frowned, scratching a hollow cheek, clearly troubled by the not knowing. He lifted a hand to show the palm upon which was inscribed a triskele, the three conjoined spirals the green of old copper. 'Mine to ponder,' he said to himself, then looked up at us again. 'It need not concern you.'

'Believe me when I say that it does not concern us,' Gawain said, stretching a strip of leather between two hands to test its strength. He had taken it upon himself to replace the carrying strap on my father's shield, the current one having perished to the extent it could not be trusted. 'Now, tell us why you called us here or go back to sleep and leave us in peace.'

'Aye,' Parcefal said, 'the horses need feeding and won't thank me for keeping them waiting.'

Merlin looked at me. 'There was a time, Galahad, when men showed me the respect I deserved.' His eyes were aflame, so that for what it was worth, I would have believed that whatever was in his mind, the gods *had* put it there. 'Never get old, lad, that is my advice to you.'

But Arthur, who knew Merlin best, was watching the druid in silence, and it seemed to me that he was expecting something. He knew that fire in Merlin's eyes.

Merlin turned his face to Arthur, nodding before he spoke. 'There may be another way, Arthur,' he said. 'To bring Guinevere back.'

That got everyone's attention. The strap in Gawain's hands went still. Gediens and Parcefal frowned at one another, and I glanced at Iselle but she was transfixed by Merlin, her eyes no less fierce than his own.

'You have heard of the thirteen treasures of the island of Britain?' the druid asked. 'Of Dyrnwyn, or White-Hilt, the Sword of Rhydderch Hael? And the Whetstone of Tudwal Tudglyd, upon which if a brave man sharpened his sword, that sword would kill any man whose blood it drew, yet if a coward sharpened his blade on it, that blade would never draw blood?'

Gawain and Parcefal shared a look which said that even if they had heard some old stories long ago, such things were for children and fools. I shrugged at Iselle and it seemed that she knew nothing much of Tudwal Tudglyd's whetstone either.

Merlin blinked and threw out his arms. 'What about the Horn of Brân Galed?'

Parcefal grinned. 'Whatever drink might be wished for was found in it,' he said, pleased with himself.

Merlin raised an eyebrow at the old warrior. 'I would have wagered the horn itself that of all the treasures, that one you would know.'

Parcefal shrugged. 'No man can remember them all. No man who isn't a druid.'

'Once, I had thought I might seek out the thirteen treasures,' Merlin said. 'Gather them together in one place, Tintagel perhaps, or Camelot. And that being all together, they would draw the eyes of the gods. More than that, their combined power would bring the gods back to Britannia to stand beside our spearmen and cast the Saxons back into the sea from whence they came.' He scratched his iron-grey beard. 'Did you know I have played a game on the Chessboard of Gwenddoleu ap Ceidio?' he asked. 'I won a slave from King Culhwch of Ebrauc, though he ran away and so I cursed his soul,' he added, for Oswine's benefit. The Saxon, who was busy rubbing grease into Merlin's cloak, half smiled. 'But I realized it would be impossible,' Merlin went on, 'to gather them all. Oh, easy enough to recognize the Chariot of Morgan Mwynfawr, if you can find it, mind,' he pointed a finger, 'but not so easy to tell the Crock and Dish of Rhygenydd the Cleric from any other crock and dish.' He grimaced. 'How many whetstones do you suppose you would have to try before you found Tudwal's?' He waved the whole idea away with a hand. 'I would need three lifetimes to do it.' He held up a bony finger to Arthur. 'But, one of the thirteen treasures is not so far away from here.' He put a thumb to his mouth and chewed the nail. 'Well, it is not beyond the walls, anyway, as Excalibur was.'

'My arse still aches from that journey,' Gawain put in, but Arthur was in no mood to reminisce.

'The Cauldron of Annwn is on the Isle of the Dead,' Merlin said.

'Then it might as well be bubbling over Arawn's own hearth fire.' Gediens shot Parcefal a knowing look.

'What about it?' Arthur said.

Merlin nodded. 'The cauldron is one of the most powerful of all the ancient treasures. It can restore life itself.'

Merlin hardly needed to say more. We all looked at each other in the gloom. Surely a cauldron which could revive the dead had the power to cure someone who was not dead, only afflicted?

'Who owns the cauldron? The dead?' Gawain asked, the

flavour of mockery in his tone, but he was already on the hook and Merlin knew it.

'Worse,' Merlin admitted.

Arthur and Gawain shared a look which spoke of old fights and poor odds. And yet here they both were. Alive, still. Friends, still.

'If we get our hands on this cauldron and bring it back here, you'll be able to use it to bring the lady back?' Gawain asked Merlin.

Before Merlin could answer, Arthur spoke. 'I thought you told us your power is gone.' His grey eyes were searching the druid's. 'That the gods have abandoned you.'

Merlin pursed his lips as he considered this. 'And yet perhaps not entirely abandoned,' he suggested, 'for, as I told you, I dreamt of the cauldron, and where do dreams come from if not the gods?' He looked at Gawain. 'I will do what I can.' He raised a hand. 'If I have the cauldron.'

Ever since Oswine had fetched us and I had seen the change in Merlin, I had felt a tightening in my belly. Now, my heart was racing.

'So, we'll go to the Isle of the Dead and find it,' I told Gawain.

'And you think whoever has it will simply give it to us?' Parcefal asked. No doubt his ageing bones were creaking with complaint at the very idea of another long journey, after the years he had already spent looking for Merlin.

'They will give it to us, or else we will take it,' I said, as if there would be no more to it than that.

'It is as though he is here with us again,' Arthur said to me, and I knew he meant my father.

'It is, Arthur,' Gawain agreed, a grin on his face which I had not seen before, but which suited him like a favourite cloak, lost but found again a long time after.

'Well, count me out of it,' Parcefal announced, 'for I'll not go to the Isle of the Dead.'

I grinned at Iselle and she grinned at me, and Parcefal rolled his eyes and growled something foul.

16

The Fisher King

FIRST, WE WOULD GO to Ynys Môn off the north-west coast of Gwynedd. From there it would be less than a day's sail north across the Irish Sea to the Isle of the Dead. But there was another reason for going to Ynys Môn, besides its northern coast being the best place from which to take ship. We would need warriors in order to retrieve the Cauldron of Annwn. Lord Constantine had none to spare, and nor did we have the time to seek volunteers amongst Dumnonia's cantrefs and rounds. But the lord of Ynys Môn, whom men called the Fisher King, was rich in silver, spears and horse, so it was said, and Merlin believed he could be persuaded to help us.

'It will be good to see old Pelles again,' Merlin had said.

'This is no journey for you, old man,' Gawain had replied.

Merlin had let out a bark at that. 'You *do* remember the last quest we went on together, Gawain? And how you and Lancelot and the others were on your knees by that pool, waiting for your turn to be drowned by a pair of painted Picts and a naked priestess?'

Gawain's lip curled in his beard. 'As I said, my arse still aches from the ride. Wish I could forget it.'

'Then you will also recall that I saved your lives,' Merlin said, then turned to me. 'Your father's, too.'

'You were a younger man then,' Gawain grunted. 'And could still catch birds to hide up your sleeves.'

Merlin's grin was sour. 'I am not dead yet. You will need King Pelles and so you will need me.'

'Let him come,' Parcefal said, 'or we may end up dragging the wrong pot all the way back.'

So Merlin had come with us, and in truth from the moment we set off, leaving Arthur and Guinevere beneath the old apple tree, the druid seemed ten years younger. His back straightened so that he was taller now than before. He had waxed his long beard and moustaches, making them into stiff iron-grey blades which accentuated his rawboned face. He had even combed and oiled what little hair yet clung to his head, tying it at the nape of his neck with a thong, into which he had knotted two raven feathers, much to Iselle's delight. He did not wear his old robes, these being threadbare and ragged, but over trews and a tunic which Oswine had washed, he draped a cloak of green wool trimmed with wolf's fur. The cloak was a gift from Arthur, who said that Merlin could not look like a beggar or a wandering priest of the Christ and expect men to respect him or aid his cause. But to me it seemed that the cloak was Arthur's acknow-ledgement of a friendship rekindled by the druid's willingness to take to the road once more in service to him. Whatever the reason, the cloak suited Merlin well and with his ash staff, which Iselle had fashioned and into which Merlin had carved strange symbols whilst whispering secret words, he looked like the druid of our imaginations.

'The Cauldron of Annwn was forged by the druids long before the Romans came to the Dark Isles,' Merlin told us as we rode north, following the Hafren which sprang from the peat bogs high in the Cambrian mountains, sometimes flow-ing so full and fierce that it carried away roundhouses which folk had built too near its banks. 'My forebears kept the cauldron on Ynys Môn, in their stronghold there.'

Iselle had nodded, an ardent look in her eyes, as there always was when Merlin spoke of the old times and of druids and their secret rites. She saw me looking at her, then looked away, a smile touching her lips, and I felt the heat rise in my cheeks. I may have been half listening to the druid, but I had been thinking about that night with Iselle in Arthur's stable and I was sure that Iselle knew it.

'Of course,' Merlin had gone on, 'even those who saw the future in their dreams could not prevent it coming to pass, and the Roman general Suetonius Paulinus came with his legions to extinguish the flame of knowledge in Britain.' At this, the druid's face fell so that you would have thought he had witnessed the slaughter himself, even swung a sword to defend his kind. And yet it had been a catastrophe, the times as dark as those we faced now. The way I had learnt it, the druids had made a desperate last stand before their sacred groves, but in the end the Romans prevailed, as they so often had, and the slaughter had been complete, no druid living to see another sunrise over Ynys Môn.

Not so, according to Merlin.

'Three druids escaped the butchery,' he said now, swaying in the saddle and holding up a leaf so that the setting sun shone through it. 'These carried the cauldron by boat to the Isle, where it remains to this day.' He lifted his hand and the leaf fluttered away and I saw that it was a butterfly, the first I had seen since the previous summer. Iselle watched it until it disappeared from sight. 'Of course, we are not the first to seek Annwn's cauldron,' Merlin said, idly taking up the reins again.

'It's not called the Isle of the Dead for nothing,' Gawain said in his gruff, unpolished way.

Corncrakes rasped amongst the tall grass. A gentle gust

blew into a stand of hazel and alder thickly hung with catkins, sending a billow of yellow smoke into the hogweed and tall grass thronging the brackish margins of the river.

'But perhaps the cauldron wants us to find it,' Iselle said, at which the druid's eyes widened in surprise.

'Perhaps,' he nodded.

And we all hoped Iselle was right as we rode on along the coast of Caer Gloui towards Powys, and warblers plucked flying insects from the air above the river bank, and somewhere amid a far-off thicket a nightingale sang a ballad to the coming dark.

Being accoutred as warlords, Gawain, Parcefal, Gediens and I were not expecting to travel unnoticed. Our armour and helmets gleamed, so that these brighter days with the sun higher in the sky announced us like warriors from fireside tales. We had combed and washed our helmet plumes so they streamed like blood or, in the case of my father's, like snow spilling from a high bough. Even our spear blades must have glinted like stars which linger into the dawn, and one reason we saw so few folk was because they saw us long before we saw them. Several times, though, we saw the backs of men or women running off to hide or to warn their lords of us, and now and then Iselle or I – having the best eyes – alerted the others to children darting from tree to gorse in our wake.

Whenever we came near some round, which we sometimes could not avoid doing, the folk in the fields beyond the enclosure, be they sowing, weeding or ploughing, unbent their backs and stared, and one or two called out to ask who we were, for they could see we were not cut-throats or raiders and so did not fear that we would do them harm. We called back that we were escorting Lord Merlin to Ynys Môn, and I for one enjoyed the bulge of their eyes when they realized who the green-cloaked, grey-bearded man amongst us was. It was the truth after all, and Merlin being a druid and thus respected by all the countries and peoples of Britain, but for Lady Morgana and her Saxon allies, we thought we should be safe enough this far to the west of our enemies.

One night, we were invited into a round to share drink and what news we'd gathered on our travels with a chieftain called Cyledyr, who claimed that Merlin had once cured him of a terrible toothache when he was but a boy. Merlin had the sense to pretend that he remembered the incident and the boy, which had Cyledyr lifting his chin in the company of his friends and retainers and filling our cups again and again until we all fell asleep at the benches and woke to the second cock with aching heads.

On another occasion we were met on the road by spearmen mounted on tough, wild-looking ponies, who said they were King Gwion's men and insisted that we pay our respects to their king and beg his permission to cross his land. They were shaggy-haired, scarred, belligerent men dressed in battered leather armour and animal skins, and it seemed to me that they hoped we would refuse their demands. That they hungered to show us that fine war gear did not prove the warrior's worth, though I'm sure they would have had the scale coats off our backs and onto their own whether by combat or theft given the chance. It was not yet noon when these twelve men accosted us, and we were loath to go with them and lose a day's ride. Parcefal growled that we should kill one or two of them and the rest would scatter like chaff on the breeze, but that is not what I saw in their eyes. Neither did Gawain, and so we went with them to their cantref, whose deep ditch, high bank and palisade, many of the stakes scorched and blackened, confirmed that these were a warlike people and we had done the right thing by accepting their invitation.

King Gwion himself was a bear of a man, who took enormous pleasure in showing us no less than fifty heads which his warriors had taken in recent fights, despite the campaigning season being only just upon us.

'Lord Arthur would see you well paid if you brought spearmen east to fight the Seax,' Gawain told the king over horns of ale, for such men as these, who rode well and took pride in reaping their enemies' heads, would be useful come the summer. But King Gwion only laughed at Gawain's suggestion, like a man trying to prove he cannot be taken for a fool.

'Arthur is long dead, as everyone knows,' he told us, still grinning, 'and the Seax are far away from here. They are not my problem, Gawain of Lyonesse.' He threw up an arm which was thick and gnarled with muscle and scar. 'I have my own enemies to kill and do not need more.' He lifted his ale horn to his warriors, who sat huddled by the hearth though it was not cold, so steeped were they in the habit of it after the long winter. 'Perhaps, when all the ghosts in Powys are headless,' he turned to Merlin, 'and you bring Lord Arthur back from Annwn, druid, I will come and kill the Seax with you.'

There was little point in arguing Arthur's existence, and so Gawain indulged the man, as did we all, lifting our horns and thanking him for his hospitality. And in the morning, King Gwion made a gift to Gawain of a skull, which he claimed he'd taken himself from a famed giant called Berth, who had led a cattle raid against Gwion's people. We all agreed it was almost half the size again of a normal skull, so that this Berth must have been a huge man. Gawain thanked King Gwion for the gift and took the time to dig a sizeable hole to bury it in when we had ridden out of sight of Gwion's warriors, who had followed us for a while on their small, hardy horses.

And that night we saw the glow of Beltane fires in the

darkness and against the black sky, and we knew that in Camelot and by some sacred rites, whether Saxon or those observed by the people of Britain, Lady Morgana had joined herself in marriage to our hated enemy. Yet we barely spoke of it.

We continued north past desolate, wind-flayed hill forts, across meadows thronged with sheep amongst the yellow cankerworts and buttercups, and along river valleys ruled by hare and hawk. Once, Iselle said that she saw the glint of steel up on the crest of a wooded hill behind us, so that we wondered if King Gwion's men yet followed us, perhaps making sure we left their land. But we saw no further signs and when we came to the rugged, cloud-darkened kingdom of Gwynedd, King Cadwallon received us with a feast of mutton, swine, and dark mead which tasted of smoke and heather. Cadwallon, whom men called Longhand, was as Roman as Lord Constantine, and the grim little fort which served as his base was clearly intended to tie his rule with the old Imperial Roman order, to keep alive the idea of stability and martial power, as a child who shouts into a vast gloomy cave takes comfort from the voice which echoes back.

A short, clean-shaven man with knowing eyes beneath a thatch of hair the same copper hue as Iselle's, Cadwallon's cleverness tempered the warlike nature which his people were born with, and Merlin and Gawain trusted him enough to tell him of our quest for the Cauldron of Annwn.

He and his people were Christians, so we did not fear him wanting the cauldron for himself. Besides which, he said we were mad to be going willingly to the Isle of the Dead. He spoke of other parties who had gone in search of the cauldron, not in his time but in his father's and his grandfather's. None of those men had ever returned. Yet, King Cadwallon had enough respect for Merlin, whom he knew from former times, and for Arthur, whose bear he had recognized on our shields, to say that he would pray for our success and for Lady Guinevere's recovery.

'Lord Arthur and I are brothers of the sword,' he told us that evening as we ate, and after Merlin had regaled his hall with stories of the thirteen treasures. 'We both have given our lives to the protection of our people against ravenous devils. He against the Seax, I against the Irish.' He turned his gaze towards his high seat so as to draw our eyes to the red cloak of a Roman officer draped upon it. It had belonged to his grandfather. Too old and too venerated to be worn, yet too obviously Roman to be hung behind a door where no one would see it, or folded in a chest in the dark. 'We have both burned,' he said, 'like torches flaming in the night, holding back the darkness.'

'Arthur will burn brightly again, lord king,' Gawain assured him.

The king nodded, his lips pressed together into a fine line. I doubted he believed Gawain that Arthur would rise again to lead the kings of Britain, but I think he wanted to. For he had helped King Pelles rid Ynys Môn of the Irish, who had been a persistent threat since the legions abandoned their forts overlooking the Irish Sea. Perhaps this was how Cadwallon had earned his nickname, Longhand, for his power which stretched from sea strand to eagles' nest, from mountains to marsh, though I had also heard it was because he could reach a stone from the ground to kill a raven without bending his back. Not that his arms looked specially long to me, but, either way, King Cadwallon was sure of his place in this world, and of the task which his god had given him, and he employed bards to compose songs in order that everyone else would know it too.

We stayed sober that night, because the king himself was a sober man, and because we talked of Arthur and Guinevere and so it would not have felt right to be making ourselves stupid with drink. And in a wet, grey and misty dawn we crossed the shallow water over to Ynys Môn.

Tears stood in Gawain's eyes as King Cadwallon's boat bore us across the slack water. Parcefal and Gediens, too, were mute at the bows, taut with emotion and lost in memory. King Cadwallon had sent an emissary to King Pelles to say that we were coming, and so now waiting on the dunes were a score of spear-armed warriors, golden in bronze scale coats, their large horses up to their knees and hocks in the wind-stirred grass. Helmets glinting dully in the mist, red plumes like drops of blood on the iron-grey day.

'Lord Arthur's Companions,' I said under my breath, and even I, who did not know the men beneath those grey and silver-chased helms, was moved almost to tears by the sight of them. The last of Arthur's famed horse warriors. They could be none other. Men who had forged their own reputation in another time, who had long ago frozen Saxon hearts with terror but then had faded from the world. Seeing them now, I felt I was looking across the water into the past, and it caused my heart to ache.

'There's Cai.' Gawain's eyes narrowed as he peered through the sea fog rolling southward along the channel. It seemed the low clouds were descending to the earth.

'That's him,' Parcefal confirmed with a nod. 'He always sat back in the saddle like that.'

I had heard of Cai ap Cynyr. He had been one of Arthur's commanders as far back as their time fighting in Gaul for King Syagrius. But, two years after Arthur's last battle, when most people in Britain believed Arthur himself was one way or another gone from the world, Lord Cai had led the last of his horse warriors west in search of a new lord to serve. For they numbered too few by then to continue the fight against the Saxons, and rather than see them whittled away in meaningless skirmishes and ill-used by lesser warriors than Arthur, Cai sought to preserve the company, as a man shields a candle flame with his hand as he walks through a darkened room. And in Ynys Môn, far from the maelstrom of chaos which poured into a Britain without Arthur, these cataphracts, as they were known in the twilight of the empire, these knights from another age, had found a worthy king in Pelles.

We came ashore and for a moment we stood on the sand, facing the grim, golden men whose eyes glared from the shadows of their helmets, as their mounts snorted and nickered at our unfamiliar scent, their breath gushing out in plumes on the chill, damp day. Some of those eyes were on me, I noticed, and I knew these men would have known my father, would have fought beside him. One or two may even have fought against him, when he and Lord Arthur became enemies. They knew his panoply as they would know Arthur's, and I was aware of the weight of the scale coat, of the shield on my back and the helmet on my head, in a way I had not been since the first days of training in it.

When he had come ashore, Merlin had fallen to his knees and kissed the ground, then plucked up some coltsfoot, which we used to gather on Ynys Wydryn because it never failed to cure a cough, while a decoction of its leaves would always soothe a cut or burn.

'I am home, brothers,' Merlin muttered, as if to the yellow flowers in his hand, though of course he was honouring his ancestors who had lived here with the sacred groves a thousand years, and would endure here still had ranks of men in scarlet cloaks and hobnailed shoes not brought fire and slaughter to Ynys Môn. Then, the last of the druids picked up his staff and stood, still clutching the yellow stars in his other hand. 'Shall we play these games much longer?' he asked, looking from Gawain to Lord Cai and back to Gawain. Both men's faces looked colder than the water at our backs, which the rowers were churning with their oars as they turned the boat back into the drifting fog above the channel to go and bring our horses across.

Iselle frowned at me, asking if I understood what was going on, at which moment Gawain's face cracked into a broad smile and he strode forward, unable to keep up the pretence longer.

'Brothers!' he greeted the riders, who were all grinning themselves now and dismounting, so that at least I knew that they were of flesh and blood like us, not sombre ghosts from a time past.

Bronze scales rattled, leather creaked and voices boomed as Lord Arthur's former companions greeted one another, embracing and clapping shoulders and gripping forearms. Rolling back the years with the age-old greetings and retorts, and with the casual irreverence of those who know each other, blood and bone, no matter the time which has separated them.

'And this must be Galahad,' Lord Cai said in a voice like a sharp spade in stony ground, squaring his shoulders to me and weighing me with his eyes, from my boots and hawk-faced greaves, to my father's white-plumed helmet. Between the long, greying forks of his moustaches, his jaw tightened, and I feared he did not approve of what he saw.

'If you have but half Lancelot's courage, you will not be found wanting,' he said, and I realized that in that moment he was not seeing me at all, but rather the butchery of the great battle, and that was what had cast a shadow across his face.

'It is an honour to meet you, lord,' I said. He shook the hand which I offered him, and Gawain gripped my shoulder.

'Galahad is as fast as Lancelot was,' he said, 'and it would seem he shares some of his father's . . . talent.'

Cai's eyes widened, their whites bright in his sun-browned face. 'The brothers of the Thorn did not mind Gawain taking you away?' He seemed to be addressing both Gawain and me. 'Having fed and watered you so many years?'

'The brothers are no more,' I answered, the ache of it dulling now, so that I wondered if it would become just the memory of pain rather than pain itself, as it was when I thought of my mother.

'Saxons,' Gawain said. Explanation enough. 'We got Galahad out just in time.' The horse warriors around me murmured and cursed at that. It hurt their pride to think of their old enemies running amok in the east, and perhaps guilt still clung to some of them for having turned their backs and ridden away. The loss of such men as these had surely hastened the end of Arthur's Britain. And yet what can men and horses do to prevent the sun from setting?

'I'm sorry,' Cai said. To me, not Gawain.

'Lord Arthur will come again,' I said, not knowing what else to say.

Cai lifted his grey eyes to Gawain. "That would be a day to light fires all across the land,' he said, 'and for every young man to take up his father's arms and fight.' He nodded at me and then he turned to Iselle, whom Gawain introduced, praising her love of killing Saxons, and her skill, which far exceeded my own, seeing as I had never killed any man, Saxon or otherwise. Cai bowed his head in respect, and his men made a fuss of Iselle, asking to see the Saxon sword, which she drew from its scabbard, handing it to the nearest warrior, a tall, fair-haired man who had lost an eye years ago. He hoomed in admiration and spoke begrudgingly in praise of Saxon sword-smiths and the quality of their steel.

Indulge them, my eyes said to Iselle, and so she did, drawing the long knife from her belt and passing it hilt first to another of Cai's warriors, and I could not help but wonder what these men would say if they knew that this fierce-eyed young woman was the daughter of Lord Arthur and Lady Guinevere.

'Not yet, Galahad.' Merlin was close enough that I could smell the beeswax and tallow which he had run through his beard and moustaches to stiffen them into points. 'Now is not the time.' His words stole my breath. Were my thoughts scattered upon my face for him to read, like the sediment left in the wine cup from which bards make predictions to amuse a crowd? I glanced around, but Iselle was speaking with Cai, who was asking after Guinevere.

'Why not?' I asked Merlin, resenting him for having told me his secret in the first place. 'She deserves to know.' After what she had shared with me that night in Arthur's stable, how could I not share this knowledge with her?

'When it is the right time, then she will know.' His words did not sound to me like those of a man who no longer believes that the gods have a hand in our affairs. 'Besides, Galahad,' he continued, grinning, 'you have other things to concern yourself with, such as making sure to give a good impression to your grandfather.'

He frowned at my face, drumming his fingers on the gnarled head of his ash staff. 'Did I not mention it before?' he asked, clearly taking pleasure in my confusion.

'What are you talking about?' I asked him.

He glanced down at my hand, which was wrapped around Boar's Tusk's grip. 'How quickly your thoughts turn to blood,' he said. 'Just like your father.'

I glowered at him and he sighed. 'King Pelles is your grandfather on your mother's side,' he said, then shrugged. 'Your parents never spoke of the Fisher King?'

My mind waded through memories, back to my childhood. Yes, perhaps there was something swirling there, some recollection of my mother telling me that we would not be seeing my grandfather the king again. Nothing for my mind to grip and bring closer, though. My mother had died shortly after my seventh summer, and it was possible that, after, my father never spoke of my grandfather.

'I don't remember,' I said.

'Some memories are as heavy as the quern stone which grinds the grain for our daily bread,' he said, pointing his staff towards Gediens and another warrior, who were deep in the reliving of some shared experience. The druid lifted an eyebrow. 'Other memories are as dewdrops clinging to a web. A breeze can shake them off.'

'Does King Pelles know me?' I asked, hating that Merlin knew more about my kin and my life than I did.

'He has met you,' he nodded, 'when you were a young boy.' He looked up at a pair of sand martins which streaked above our heads, their undersides flashing white amidst the sea fog. He frowned, perhaps seeing some omen in the birds' flight, or perhaps the frown was because he could read nothing in it and was reminded that the gods had forsaken him. 'Let us hope he remembers you, Galahad,' he said.

The whinnying of our horses from across the water told us that King Cadwallon's men were loading them onto the boat.

'In the name of King Pelles ap Phellehan, scourge of the Irish, beloved of the gods and of his people, welcome to Ynys Môn,' Lord Cai called, catching up with the formal greeting which his games had neglected before. 'I only wish Lord

Arthur were here too,' he went on, stirring murmurs of agreement from his men, 'for then our brotherhood would drink
together this night, the shades of fallen companions sharing
the lamplight with us as if it were Samhain and the wine left
out for them.'

Every man took a moment with that, nodding earnestly,
then smiled again. Our horses were almost at the bank, so we
turned to help bring the boat and its precious cargo safely in,
while Lord Cai's men mounted their fine war horses and took
up the reins.

'He has told you, then, about your grandfather?' Gawain
asked as he and I stood upon the landward side of the gangplanks over which the horses would be led.

'He has,' I said, supposing he must have seen the change in
my face. 'You knew?'

'I did,' he admitted.

'And you didn't think to tell me?'

His brow furrowed beneath his helmet's rim. 'I thought to,'
he said, 'but Merlin persuaded me that your knowing would
change you when you met the king, what with the past being
all stirred up. That it would be better were the king to take you
as he finds you.' He chewed the next words a moment before
saying them. 'King Pelles did not like your father.' He did not
need to explain further. I could easily imagine why the king
my grandfather would dislike my father, knowing, as all Britain did, of my father's love for Guinevere. 'I don't know why
the druid changed his mind about telling you, but,' he grunted,
'I should have told you anyway.'

I knew why Merlin had told me. Seeing that I was thinking
of telling Iselle the truth of her own lineage, he had wanted to
lead my thoughts elsewhere. And it had worked, for I wanted
to ask Gawain about my grandfather and what sort of man he

was, but I did not get a chance, because the horses came clumping onto the planks and we had to guide them ashore.

Then, we mounted and followed the last of Lord Arthur's horse warriors over the grassy dunes and onto a meadow where lady's smock swayed in the sea breeze, which meant there would be adders and so we took care to watch where our horses trod. We rode across the same ground over which the legions had marched, and passed ancient oaks which had, as knee-high saplings, somehow escaped being trodden down by hobnailed shoes or snapped by moving walls of shields as inexorable as the tide. We rode to meet King Pelles, whom men called the Fisher King, and who was my grandfather.

I had never eaten so well as I did in those days before we took ship for the Isle of the Dead. And the feast which my grandfather King Pelles laid on was like something of which the bards sing, when they name each dish with an awe usually reserved for ancient heroes or the constellations in the night sky. We ate goose and duck, spitted boar and fowl, eggs, eels, scallops, oysters and mussels, fresh baked bread and cheese, leeks, parsnips and turnips. We drank wine the colour of a Roman emperor's cloak and which tasted of some faraway country beneath a warmer sun. And ale made with cankerwort, yarrow and the ground ivy which creeps in copses and oak woods. We feasted in a long hall warmed by two round hearths, at a table and benches with all of those men who had once ridden with Arthur but who now served another lord, and it said much about King Pelles that he was able to prepare such a banquet in so little time.

As for the Fisher King himself, he was in his late seventies now, birch-thin and tremulous. He boasted a fine head of hair, white as a swan's wing, and overgrown eyebrows of the same colour which protruded, giving him the look of a learned man who is inquisitive and wise, if not entirely sane. His short beard was white and neat and looked as soft as the fine down from a goose's belly. His watery eyes were the palest violet-blue of harebells, those flowers worn by faithful lovers but which Father Judoc said we must never pick for they are the Devil in disguise, and his cheeks were webbed with red veins as fine as spider silk. He was old and frail, like a man who has lived far beyond his allotted years, and yet he seemed at the same time to have plenty of life left in him.

'My own grandson,' he said, knowing me the moment he laid those startling blue eyes on me. He held a bony hand towards me, tracing the lines of my face without actually touching me. 'So much like your mother, it breaks my old heart,' he said, and he thought nothing of letting the tears slide down his cheeks. 'And what a handsome couple you make,' he added, glancing at Iselle beside me.

We both flushed red and I avoided Gawain's eye as I answered that Iselle and I were merely friends and nothing more. But the king only smiled as one does when indulging a child. He had lived too long, seen too much.

'What was my mother like, lord king?' I asked. He had made me sit next to him and I was glad to be able to ask him about my mother, even though the mention of her awakened something of the old ache, which I hoped would not swell to the chest-clenching pain it had once been.

'Ah, my Helaine.' King Pelles stared ahead but with an inward eye. 'She was so beautiful. A gentle spirit, she was. But no one's fool.' His eyes sharpened again, coming back to me. 'Not even your father's fool.' Then he sighed. 'But she loved him. We can be lords or ladies of a thousand men, but we can never rule our hearts, Galahad,' he said. Gawain and Cai, Parcefal, Gediens and the others were deep in their reminiscing, drowning themselves in wine and the past. Merlin was conversing with the king's bard, a well-fed, ruddy-cheeked man who was all but lapping up Merlin's every word, as a house cat takes milk from a bowl.

'I cannot picture her face any more,' I admitted to the king, though I said it also for Iselle. Wanting her to know me better.

'Then you have only to look in a mirror, Galahad,' King Pelles said, 'and you will see her eyes and her fairness. Her lips, too.'

I did not see how this could be true, how I could look like my mother, when everyone else saw my father in me. But perhaps we sometimes see what the heart wishes us to see. And it was clear to me now that my grandfather missed his daughter, as I missed my mother.

'When I smell wood violets, I think of her,' I said. 'Just a breath of it on the breeze and I am a boy again.'

The king smiled at that, his wide blue eyes turning to Iselle, as if he had known she had something to say. For three heartbeats it seemed that Iselle would refuse the unspoken invitation. Then she said, 'She would have stayed with you if she could.'

I nodded. 'I know,' I said. 'Not like my father. *He* had a choice.'

I regretted the words the moment they were on the air. Their petulance. But there was no judgement in the king's eyes.

'I did not care for Lancelot,' he said, 'and I lost my daughter over it.' He lifted a hand upon whose fingers rings of silver and gold winked with flamelight. 'Yet, some others loved him dearly. Your mother for one. And Guinevere.' He gestured at the grinning, grizzled warriors lining his table. 'The men who fought alongside him. Even Arthur loved him.' He shook his head. 'Arthur loved him after everything.' He picked up his cup, which was made of Roman glass, yellow and cloudy as an old man's eyes, and sipped at the wine. And at his thoughts. 'I am an old fool, Galahad,' he put the cup down again, 'but I know that a man so loved by some and so hated by others must be a man who is true to his heart.' When he smiled, his face fell into the familiar creases and lines, as saddle leather after years of use. 'And besides, he was by all accounts as arrogant as he was skilful. I would wager my kingdom that your father had not even considered the possibility that he might not ride back to you at the end of that dreadful day.'

I pondered that for a long moment, draining my cup while I gave my thoughts time to settle. I did not believe King Pelles about that. As we had stood on that hill overlooking the battle, my father and I had both seen the slaughter being done. We had watched the shieldwalls clash and we had heard the thunder of it. I had smelled death on the air, as had my father's war stallion Tormaigh. Still, my father had held out his hand for his long spear, which I had given him. No man, least of all one with my father's reputation, could have hoped to ride into that bloody maelstrom and ride out again.

King Pelles leant close to me and placed his hand upon mine on the table. I smelled the sourness of his old breath. 'I am heart glad to meet you again, grandson,' he said, squeezing my hand in his.

'And I you, grandfather,' I said.

Then he leant closer still, so that Iselle could not hear him. 'She has the proud look of a queen,' he said, a mischievous glimmer in his eye, his white brows gathered close, like a pair of conspirators.

I returned his smile, watching Iselle, who was watching the room. Pelles's bard was playing the lyre and singing the ballad of King Ban and Queen Elaine in my honour.

'She does, grandfather,' I said.

And she did.

*

The night we feasted in the Fisher King's hall was the night of the full moon. Silver-white light threw shadows over the land. It lit oak and ash and hares fighting in the long grass. It revealed glimpses of owls swooping from high boughs and it brought wolves out of their dens, so that we heard them howling in Gwynedd's high forests. It was a night of shrieks and squeals, of things killing and being killed, so that while none of us spoke of it, we were all in mind of the ultimatum given us by King Cerdic.

And yet, instead of being at Camelot, swearing ourselves to the rule of the Saxon king and his new queen Morgana, we were feasting on Ynys Môn. We were draining cups with men who had turned their backs on the past, and we were preparing to cross the Irish Sea in search of an ancient cauldron that, it was said, would never boil the food of a coward. A cauldron which could bring the dead back to life. Instead of sending his spearmen back to their homes and their farms and bringing Arthur's bear standard to Lady Morgana, who would set it alight and watch it burn and scatter the ashes along with the last hopes of Britain, Lord Constantine was preparing for war.

The king, my grandfather, had shed twenty years in a night, so Merlin said, such was his joy at meeting me, and such the bittersweet draught of familiarity which tugs at the memory of old pain. For in me he saw his daughter, who had been lost to him some years even before the fever took her. It showed in his rheumy eyes which, while they silently enquired of me what sort of man I was, looked inwards too, to other times and places. To the shades of shared moments between a father and his daughter which only now, in the too late, shed their patina and revealed their incalculable value.

He told me stories of my mother when she was a girl, tears in his eyes as he remembered, and Iselle and I listened, not as the young will condescend to the old, but as folk will listen to a bard who can spin a golden tale from old, worn threads. I wanted to know what my mother liked to eat, and how she had once shut herself inside a chest so that the king and queen had not found her for a day and had sent spearmen out across the island in search of her. I wanted to know what was her favourite colour of linen, for I remembered her in blue, and what birds she had favoured. Little things, really, but things which I had been denied, being so young when death stole her from me.

As for Iselle, I think she listened because she felt that knowing my mother was somehow knowing me, and if the old king did not truly remember all of which he spoke, he made a convincing show of it, as around us men and women made merry with a din like the sea thrashing against the shore. The once-famed horse lords of Armorica and Britain feasted on flesh and drank deeply of the past. As though they could share again good wine which had all been drunk years ago. Or ride a full day without suffering the aches in the flesh. As though they could raise Arthur's name to the sky and he would hear it and come galloping on his white mare, Llamrei, his armour glittering under the sun and his red plume streaming in the wind.

Then, when songs had been sung and wine skins emptied, Merlin asked King Pelles if he would help us retrieve the Cauldron of Annwn. Of course, he already knew our reason for being there. King Cadwallon's emissaries had leaked that news as a basket leaks salt, but hearing it from Merlin himself, and so late in the night too, brought a weight upon the old king, as if he had forgotten about it or else hoped that we had. His eyes lost some of their blueness and I saw the thumb of his right hand worrying at a gold ring, turning it round and round a bony finger.

'The isle is death,' he said, stilling every tongue but those of flame which whispered their secrets in the hearth. 'As is the cauldron itself. The craving of it.' He scuttled a hand across the table to touch the iron blade of an eating knife. 'Ever since the day the sacred groves were burned and the streams ran with the blood of the druids, and those who survived the slaughter carried the cauldron across the sea to safety, men have coveted it.' He locked eyes with Merlin then. 'As you well know, my old friend. But none have ever found it.' Just then a candle guttered and went out, and I saw some dark looks around the room for the omen in that. 'None,' he repeated.

It was Merlin who broke the ominous silence. 'We cannot know that, lord king,' he countered, 'that none ever found the cauldron, I mean.' He fluttered a hand towards the rafters. 'Just because a swallow is taken by a kestrel outside your barn in the spring, it does not mean that the swallow did not winter in far-off Africa.' The druid had been drinking steadily but his words just about made sense, for all the frowning faces around me. 'The cauldron is there,' he said. 'I dreamt of it years ago.'

The king's brow furrowed like the sea before the wind. 'There are worse things than kestrels on the isle, Merlin,' he said, stopping short of naming those things.

'So they say,' Merlin admitted with a nod, extending a hand across the table towards Gawain. 'But nothing has managed to kill us yet.'

'Not for want of trying.' Gawain's lips showed his closed teeth as a dog's do. Some of King Pelles's horse warriors thumped their fists against the table's oak planks. Lord Cai nodded at his old friend in a way that told me Gawain had already done his work and convinced Cai to help us, if the king allowed it.

It was my turn now. Despite all the wine, my mouth was suddenly dry. My stomach felt hollow. I cleared my throat and sat straighter. 'We cannot turn back now, grandfather,' I said. 'To beat the Saxons, we need Lord Arthur. But there can be no Arthur without Guinevere.' I looked at Iselle and realized that I did not mind if every man or woman in the hall read what was in my face, so long as the king read it. 'We will go to the Isle of the Dead,' I said. 'We will find the cauldron and take it back to Dumnonia so that Merlin may use its power to cure Lady Guinevere.' I turned back to my grandfather. 'Lord king.' I squared my shoulders and lifted my chin. 'Since leaving Ynys Wydryn I have seen the ruin of the land with my own eyes. I have seen farmsteads burning, their livestock driven east to feed Saxon warriors. I have stumbled upon corpses left to rot in the grass. Seen children wandering the woods, as aimless as smoke.' I felt the skin prickle on the back of my neck. 'Britain itself will become an isle of the dead if we cannot face our enemies and turn them back.'

King Pelles stared at me, pulling his short white beard between finger and thumb. Shaking his head slowly from side to side. 'She is here before my eyes,' he said in a distant-sounding voice. Then he blinked slowly, correcting his thoughts. 'You are both here.' He nodded. 'My daughter and my grandson. Gods, but I was a stubborn fool to let any of it come between us.' He winced at the pain in memories. 'My Helaine.' The name sounded like a man's last breath in this world, and I thought he would shed tears again, but he breathed deeply and held firm. 'What sort of king would I be . . . indeed, what sort of man, were I to turn my back on you, Galahad, my own flesh? My bone and blood?' He looked at Iselle. 'Should I deny you my help because I am old and will not be here to drink to your victory or share in the sorrow of your loss? No,' he shook his head. 'He is a fool who plants no trees because he knows he will never sit in their shade.'

With that he gripped the arms of his chair and pushed himself up onto his feet, shrugging off the courtier who tried to steady him. 'You shall have half my loyal company, Lord

Gawain, and my ship to take you across the sea.' He grabbed at his wine cup and held it aloft, though his arm trembled and some of the red liquid sloshed over the lip onto the table. 'And when you return with the treasure, we shall celebrate with such a feast as will put this night to shame,' he announced, keeping the cup raised towards the roof beams, as fists pounded oak and thunder rolled through the hall.

Then he turned and looked down at me, for I was still sitting, and the thunder died because he had something more to say. 'And I will get to know my grandson better,' he said in a quieter voice. A man's voice, not a king's, and tainted with regret. Even so, men cheered again. Gawain and Cai banged their cups together, spilling ale across the king's board.

King Pelles took Iselle's hand in his and led her off to show her the great tapestry which hung behind his high seat, embroidered with a scene of the ancient hero and king Brân the Blessed being killed by a poisoned Irish spear thrust through his foot during the Great War. Beside the giant Brân, rendered in fine needlework, stood three warriors with swords ready to cut off his head, as the dying hero instructed. But my eye was drawn elsewhere, to Merlin, who was watching me, smirking like a man who has won a wager but knows it would not be wise to boast of it.

17

The Isle of the Dead

W E SAILED NORTH ON a grey sea beneath a grey sky, the westerly breeze spitting rain into my face as I watched the low skerries slide past our port side. Enough wind across the sail to shrug the rain off it and keep us moving at a decent pace, water breaking into white spume across our bows.

'We'll reach the isle well before dusk,' Cai said, stroking the chest and withers of his gelding, a grey Andalusian of sixteen hands. 'So long as Karadas stays wise of drift and tide,' he added, loud enough for the captain on his quarterdeck to hear. Karadas licked a finger and held it up to the thin gusts, calling back that it was not unusual for the wind to squall out of nothing off this northern coast.

'And if that happens,' he said, 'coupled with this westward ebb, it'll be all I can do to prevent her hull being ripped on the skerries and you land men sinking with all your pretty gear.' He gave a gap-toothed grin and Cai grinned back, the two men enjoying the nervous glances which some of the other warriors shared as they comforted their horses, for the animals hated being at sea even more than the men did.

Iselle, who had already given up her breakfast to the fishes, hung over the sheer strake, hiding her pallor from the rest of us, much to Gawain's amusement, while I looked after her horse as well as my own. It was her first time at sea, as it was mine, yet I revelled in the experience, of the sea's breath in my face and hair, the rise and dip of the *Calistra*'s hull up crest and down furrow, and the sense of the unknown, which I found thrilling, perhaps because of my years of confinement at the monastery on Ynys Wydryn, where the days brought few surprises. And though I had heard of men drowning at sea, their ships ripped upon teeth-like rocks so that lives spilled like guts from a wounded beast, I guessed we were safe enough that day. Seamen being more superstitious than most men, if Karadas was joking with Cai, teasing him about sinking into Manannán mac Lir's cold clutches, it must be because there was almost no chance of it happening. Or so I hoped.

What I feared was not the Irish Sea, not on that spring day, nor that terrible sea god, but rather whatever awaited us on the isle. We were fewer than we would have liked. Not that King Pelles hadn't been generous, giving us Lord Cai and nine of his horse warriors, so that we were seventeen in all who would be going ashore. But seventeen did not sound like many given that we were bound for a place from which men did not return. And yet we could not expect the king to lend us more of his warriors for our quest, for all the portents of it being led by the last of the druids, those priests of Britain who had once made this very same journey to save the cauldron. All those long years ago.

Nor could the *Calistra* have taken more men and horses. As it was, the shallow hold, as well as all available deck space, was crammed with men, war gear and skittish horseflesh; a bilious cargo from which fear and unease rose along with the stink of tarred lines, brackish bilge water and wool smeared with tallow, and the beasts' manure, making me stretch my neck to breathe in the clean sea air.

'Arthur used to get seasick something terrible,' Gawain grinned, watching Iselle lean over the side, clutching her copper hair in a knotted fist to keep it from getting spewed on. 'He was green as grass the first time we sailed the Dividing Sea over to Armorica. Said it was the stringy hare he'd eaten the night before, but I ate the same meal and I was bright-eyed and hale.' The big man shook his head. 'Never liked the sea, did Arthur.'

But I liked the sea. Still, it was a strange feeling when I could no longer see Ynys Môn off our stern, but only the grey gloom of sea, sky and cloud, and the occasional sea bird living its life far beyond the troubles and cares of man. A herring gull shrieking as the wind carried it like a leaf on a river. Or, sometimes, a black and white bird with a bill as bright as fire, flying just above the waves, its stocky wings beating impossibly hard. Now and then, I would see these strange birds fall like stones and vanish beneath the surface as though passing between worlds. And it made me think of our journey out here on the Western Sea, beyond which lay Annwn, the world beyond this life. Or so those in Britain believed who had not turned to Christ.

As for myself, I no longer knew what I believed, but as we sailed on that seemingly endless, shifting sea, through veils of rain and sometimes alongside sleek creatures that arrowed beneath the racing furrows or leapt and cavorted as though to see what we were, I felt closer to Merlin's faith than to that of my former brothers, who were now no more in the world than my memories of them.

A tall, striking warrior with a head of black curls called Medyr was the first to call out that he could see low cliffs through the rain and mist. Either the horses understood Medyr, or else they smelled the land, for they began to nicker and stamp and toss their heads so that their manes flew in the wind.

'You'll soon be rid of us,' Cai called to Karadas, who had just been growling curses under his breath at the sight of all the filth which the nervous horses had dropped on his well-scrubbed deck.

'Could be you'll wish I *had* wrecked us and sent you to the crabs,' the captain replied, stepping up to the bow rail to peer into the mizzle haze. 'I wouldn't go traipsing around that island for a year's supply of mead and a raven-haired beauty to drink it with.'

'We have spears and horses, and we have a druid,' said Sadoc, a warrior with a narrow face and bulging eyes. He stroked the flank of his chestnut gelding but watched the land towards which, even on the ebb tide, the *Calistra* was gliding like a crane to its roost.

'I mean no offence to Lord Merlin,' Karadas said, showing Merlin a callused, tar-stained palm, 'but the hateful creatures on that island care nothing for the laws and proprieties that govern normal men. Druid, king, knight or slave. No one should set foot on there and expect to come back to the world of the living.' He lifted a hand again. 'Well, I've said my piece and no man can say otherwise. And I hope by all the gods that you're all on the beach two mornings from now, because I won't be coming looking.'

'Be here,' Cai told him.

'And bring grain for the horses,' Gawain added.

'And ale for us.' Parcefal's request got a nod of agreement from Gediens and several of the others, though how they could be thinking of ale at such a time, I could not imagine.

And then we were all holding reins and tack, speaking soothing words to our horses whilst the *Calistra*'s crew reefed some sail to slow us, and Karadas turned her bows towards a cove which he knew to be sandy enough for him to run her up the beach.

'Whatever we find here, I'd rather that than staying aboard this boat,' Iselle said, still pale, her lips still warped by the sourness of bile.

'I have decided I like sailing,' I smiled. I said it to keep the fear from my face, though surely I was not the only man aboard the *Calistra* who was afraid of what we might find on the island.

Karadas grimaced at the sound of the *Calistra*'s hull grinding up the strand, which we heard even with the horses shrieking and neighing and men cursing as they struggled to steady themselves and their animals against the sudden loss of forward momentum. Six sailors leapt over the side with gangplanks and poles, which they thrust into the sand, leaning them against the *Calistra*'s barnacled hull to steady the ship as best they could while we disembarked the horses.

'Who's got that damned horn?' Karadas called, at which a sailor lifted the horn which hung across his shoulder. For, having beached the vessel on the ebb tide, Karadas and his crew would now have to wait for the flood tide to lift her again, and though the sailors had spears, and some had talked of a recent fight against Irish pirates, the Isle of the Dead was something else.

'If we hear the horn, we'll come as fast as we can,' Cai had assured the captain.

'Aye, you'd better,' Karadas had said, but I knew the *Calistra*'s crew would be watching the dunes and long grass and praying to Manannán to bring the sea up onto the strand.

Men called it the Isle of the Dead, but the place was thronging with life. The horseshoe-shaped bay was noisy with plovers, terns and oystercatchers, and the seals which lay on the offshore skerries, singing their strange lament, so that Gawain said they reminded him of the brothers of the Thorn. The rocky ledges above the shore echoed with the clamour of guillemots, kittiwakes, shags and all types of gull, and I realized I had been a fool to imagine that the island would be as quiet as the grave.

We mounted and formed a column two abreast, taking our time riding up the wet sand to the high tide line, letting our horses find their land legs before we asked more of them. But my own gelding seemed so pleased to be off that ship that he would have gladly galloped if I'd spurred him. His nostrils were soft and round, whereas on the ship they had been tight, thin and drawn. And his lower jaw was so loose that spittle was dribbling from it, which reminded me of Tormaigh, my father's stallion, for he had used to drool when he was content. Perhaps only Iselle was more relieved to be on dry land.

The gelding had not come with a name and so I had called him Seren, for the white star which blazed above his eyes amid the crow-black coat. He had accepted the name so readily that Iselle said I had probably given him the name which he already owned. She was likely right, for you could not look at that mark on his head without thinking of a star.

We rode up among the dune slacks and coarse grass, above which gnats hung in brown clouds, making us cover our mouths and noses. Some of us turned in the saddle and saw Karadas and his men staring after us. The young sailor lifted his horn again, as if to remind us what we must do if we heard its note before the tide was in. I made the sign of the Thorn, from habit perhaps, and I hoped we would see the *Calistra* on the second morning and that the sailors would cheer as they caught sight of an ancient treasure of Britain in our possession.

'Just think what we could do with another hundred like these,' Gediens said. He and Parcefal were riding behind Iselle and me, while Gawain rode at the head of the column with Lord Cai and Merlin.

'It doesn't take much thinking,' Parcefal said. 'We'd drive the Saxons back into the Morimaru and watch them drown.'

But we all knew this would never be any more than a dream. These men, along with their companions who had stayed on Ynys Môn, were the last of Arthur's cataphracts, the feared horse warriors who had fought with him in Gaul and in Britannia. No king in the land was bringing the same quality of horse stock across the Narrow Sea these days. They spent their silver on slaves to dig their ditches and raise their palisades, and on feeding and paying the spearmen who peered over those sharpened stakes into the fretted land.

Who was I to be amongst these few? I felt like an imposter, like a man taking credit for another's deeds, who knows that his transgression will be uncovered sooner or later. And yet even so, I could not help but feel honoured too, being amongst them, these warriors who made a sight to stir the blood and fire the heart. Ring mail or bronze scales burnished so that they held even the dying light of the day. Silver-chased helmets with their cheek irons down and their long plumes washed and combed straight, and the round shields slung across their backs painted with Arthur's bear, because though these men had pledged themselves to King Pelles, they had refused to paint any other sigil on them. Some of the men were as old as Gawain, a couple even as old as Parcefal, but others had been young men of Dumnonia, trained and brought into the company during Arthur's Saxon wars. And all of them were killers. All shared a bond which only death could sever, though such a bond may endure even beyond, so long as the living remember. And all of them had known my father, which I knew made them curious about me.

You are not him. You are not your father. So Father Yvain's words whispered, like the sea breeze on the back of my neck. Words he had spoken just before Lord Geldrin's spearmen threw him over the cliff edge at Tintagel. I was not my father. And yet, I hoped I would have some of his courage when the time came.

'What is it?' Gediens called to Merlin from behind me, breaking the spell of my thoughts. The druid had walked his mount a little way from the column and now sat with his back to us as we passed, watching a distant belt of elder trees that stood on the verge of a steep bank. Oswine sat his horse beside him, patient as a hound who knows that any sound or movement might put up the birds before its master is ready.

'See something?' Gediens called out again. Merlin did not reply, just sat there watching the trees, holding his staff across his saddle in the way other men gripped their spears.

'I'd be surprised if his old eyes can see much past his nose,' Parcefal behind me murmured, not loud enough for Merlin to hear.

'He doesn't need eyes to see.' That from Iselle put a shiver in my flesh.

'Old goat knows something he's not telling us,' Gediens muttered. 'Mark my words.'

And that night, we learnt what that was.

By the light of the waning moon we came down into a wooded glen, through which a stream wound amongst ghostly birch and coppiced ash, shining in the night like a ribbon of black silk. Nestled beside the stream were two buildings, watched over by an ancient wych elm whose far-flung branches, bare of leaves but red with tasselled flowers, must have given shelter and shade to whoever had lived here.

But the place was long abandoned, and before Lord Cai ordered his men to dismount, Gawain sent me in first, to see if it would make a good spot to overnight. And so I walked across the clearing, resisting the urge to draw Boar's Tusk and hold it before me, though I kept my hand on the grip, the blood gushing in my ears as I approached the main roundhouse.

The thatch was all moss and ferns, and some of the roof poles had fallen in, spilling rotten straw into the interior, which smelled damp and had become home to rats or mice. The creatures scurried away from me as I explored the place, my eyes adjusting to the darkness. The wattle walls, once limewashed, were now mouldering and stank, and a table, four stools and three beds stood in the gloom, scattered with droppings and cloaked in spider silk which shivered from the open door, stirring as if waking from a long sleep. But between that roundhouse and the small, weather-beaten barn, we would have shelter for the night and I told Lord Cai, who nodded and shared a look of relief with Gawain. For, even armed as we were, they preferred not to ride deeper into an unknown land in the dark.

'No fires,' Gawain said. The smoke would carry far on that wind. His armour glowed dully by the single rushlight which someone had put in the middle of the hearth, the first tiny warmth those blackened stones had felt since the fires which had blazed there long ago. 'Get your heads down. We ride at dawn.'

The men went about preparing their beds upon the hard floor with the practical efficiency of soldiers long used to each other's company, each eager to get some sleep before it was his turn to guard the horses or stand watch at the edge of the stream or up on the ridge overlooking the valley. We had all brought spare cloaks, skins or furs, and no one really minded not having a fire for warmth, though some of the men grumbled as they chewed cold meat and bread, and it struck me that while they had surely endured hardships in the past, they had grown used to living well in the service of my grandfather the king.

Taking off the helmet and heavy scale coat, I felt a lifting of a burden greater than just the weight of that war gear. It was a shedding of expectation – my own and that of others, too – as I placed the armour carefully with my saddle. But with that unburdening came the fear that the others would see me as I truly was, as a man who had never been part of a brotherhood of warriors nor faced trials of arms nor shared the spilling of blood, as they had.

I could do nothing about that, though, and so I spread my blanket on the earthen floor beside an old loom which stood beyond the hearth. A wide piece of patterned wool cloth lay on the frame still, days in the making but unfinished. Stone weights hung from the warp threads, barely stirring in the breaths of night air questing through the ruined roof, and I wondered how those slender woollen strings had not snapped years ago. I thought of the infant born at the monastery who had lived no longer than the time it took a candle to burn to the nub. I thought of the brothers themselves, bones on the hillside now, and of the corpses I had seen twisting on ropes in the marsh, one of them a child, a boy no older than nine summers. I thought of my mother, too, her shade stirring like the cobwebs in this old place. Close again. Closer than she had been for many years, her presence felt like a tightening in my chest. As though, unable to resist the lure of her father and her son being together for one night, my mother's spirit had wandered to the edge of the veil separating her world and ours and lingered there now in sad and jealous torment.

So many lives cut short, severed by gods or fate or men,

while the weighted threads hanging from the bones of that old loom somehow endured.

I watched an ox-shouldered, scarred-faced man called Cadwy sit down on the edge of a bed to examine something which looked in the gloom like a shoe, and I knew I was not the only one wondering what had happened to the folk who had lived in this place. But none of us wanted to give words to our thoughts, knowing as we did that speaking something aloud can sometimes make it true.

I was also wondering where Iselle was and trying not to feel offended that she had not thrown her blanket down next to mine, when the door creaked open and her face appeared, her hair bright copper under the moonlight, mocking the timid rushlight in the hearth. Her eyes bid me go with her, so I left my gear and stood, taking only Boar's Tusk and wrapping my cloak around me against a night which was damp enough to get into the flesh and stubbornly remain there. I asked where we were going, but Iselle did not answer. I looked past her to the ancient wych elm looming in shadow now as cloud sailed across the moon. A gnarled and twisted tree, its burls like great warts, its boughs contorted like human limbs tortured by fire. And beneath those branches, standing amongst the tree's partly exposed roots, I could make out a knot of five people, one of whom I could see was Oswine because of his fair hair.

'What's going on?' I asked, but Iselle shushed me as we joined the small gathering and Gawain nodded at me in a way which made me think he had sent Iselle to fetch me. Lord Cai acknowledged me with a raised eyebrow, but Gediens and Parcefal did not look up, so intently were they watching the figure who knelt amongst those roots, his hands upon them as if they were mighty snakes and he was commanding them to thrust themselves down into the earth.

The hooded and bowed figure was Merlin. Gone was the green cloak trimmed with wolf fur, which Arthur had given him. His old dark robes covered him again, like a death shroud, without whose long embrace the corpse's bones would fall in a scatter. I had not realized he had brought his old vestments with him. And now the druid was intoning, or rather singing, under his breath. To my surprise his voice was pleasant, younger sounding than Merlin himself and as melodious as water running over a brook's pebble bed. Many of the words were unknown to me, yet I knew it was a sad song, of things lost and of things all but forgotten. It struck me that Merlin was singing to the tree itself and to the tree's memory, for surely the wych elm had sent its great roots into the earth long before the legions came to Britain. It had stood sentinel in this little valley nearly a thousand years and perhaps it had witnessed the coming of the cauldron less than a man's lifetime after Joseph of Arimathea came from a land of sun to these Dark Isles and thrust his staff into the ground at Ynys Wydryn, giving life to the Holy Thorn.

We stood in the dark. We watched and waited, and even Gawain, whose patience for Merlin ran thin as new ice, did not interrupt whatever rites the druid was performing in the moon shadow of that old tree. Iselle, I noticed, was swaying in time with the melody, her eyes closed, so that I believed that she somehow understood what was going on, for she was of the land and the sky, as strong as the wych elm, her roots as deep. And though I was not, like her, bound within the magic of Merlin's song as threads are woven together on a loom to make patterned cloth, I felt the power in it, stronger than the devotions which we had lifted to heaven from our island sanctuary, even with all our voices.

And then, when I was only vaguely aware that I had wandered into the deepest reaches of Merlin's strange liturgy, the song cut off, suddenly, without warning. He pulled his hands off the thick roots as a man does from an iron pot which he had not known was still hot from the fire. And went completely still.

Gawain and I looked around us, thinking Merlin had heard something that we had not. But the night in the valley beyond the farmstead was quiet but for the soft hiss of a breeze amongst the wych elm's flowers and in the gorse and nettles which had risen like a tide against the old animal pens and the ruins of a grain store.

Parcefal and Cai looked at each other, and Gediens lifted his chin to Oswine, seeking his explanation, though no one dared be the first to speak in case they somehow ruined the rites. No one except Gawain.

'What is it, Merlin?' he asked, his scarred face terrifying to look at in the shaft of moonlight spearing between the branches.

Oswine helped Merlin to his feet and the druid turned to us. Inside his hood, his eyes were dark and sharp as flints.

'I am not the last,' he whispered. His voice was not the chime of gentle running water now, but the rasp of a whetstone on a blade. He mumbled something unintelligible, turned his head and spat, perhaps meaning to hit the elm's roots. Perhaps not. We glanced at one another, seeking his meaning, then looked back at Merlin.

'You're not the last what?' Gawain asked him, but Merlin was deep in thought. 'Answer me, druid,' Gawain growled, unwilling to indulge Merlin any longer.

Merlin's eyes widened. I saw their whites in the shadow of his hood. 'There is a druid here,' he said, 'on this island.'

Some of the others touched sword pommels or other iron. I made the sign of the Thorn, annoyed at myself for the habit even as I did so.

'With the cauldron?' Iselle asked. Of us all, she seemed the least astonished by Merlin's revelation. Or else, she had the strongest faith in the old man's ability to divine such a thing from the roots of a tree, or through song, or however he had done it.

Merlin considered her question.

'I don't know,' he told her. But there was something different about Merlin. He stood a little taller, less rounded in the shoulder. He took his staff from Oswine and pushed back his hood, and there was a light in his eyes which I had never seen before, as though a candle flame lit his face from the inside. There was something almost like a smile playing at the corners of his lips, but it was clear to us that he would say no more about this other druid for now. So, Gawain said we should all get some rest and with that he turned and made his way back to the barn, where he had made his own bed.

I had turned to go after him when Merlin flung an arm over my shoulder. It was not raining, but the wool of his black gown smelled damp and foetid. 'I am alive, Galahad,' he said, squeezing the flesh of my upper arm with his claw-like hand. But for Oswine, who hung back several paces behind us, the others walked on, leaving us beneath the elm's branches, which everyone knows is a dangerous place to be. 'For the first time in years, I am alive. I was wrong, Galahad, to think that the gods had abandoned me.' As we walked on, he threw his other arm out towards the sloping ground where yellow cowslips, sheep's sorrel and dove's foot cranesbill shivered in the moonwash. Up on the hill, I saw a glint of steel. Just a wink of light. The spear blade of one of Lord Cai's men who was on first watch.

'Or perhaps we are closer to the gods here, in this place. What do you think, boy?' he asked.

I did not really mind him calling me boy. To a man who had

helped Uther onto Dumnonia's high seat, everyone must seem young. 'I think you should tell Iselle what she has a right to know,' I said, watching her now as she stood waiting by an ancient, moss-draped log pile under the roundhouse eaves. Merlin stopped and turned me around to face him, and I was surprised by his strength.

'You think all that is important now?'

I nodded. 'I think I would want to know if it were me.' And I felt I was betraying Iselle's trust by not telling her, though I did not say that to Merlin.

'Then tell her.' He threw those words away. And yet, the way he was eyeing me implied a challenge to which he was keen to see if I would rise. 'Tell her this night. Why not?' He leant forward and hissed in a quieter voice, 'It's not as though you weren't planning to sneak off in search of some dry ground. When the rest of them are snoring away like hogs.'

His talk of there being another druid on the island had been unnerving, but only now did I believe that Merlin truly did possess a gods-given sight denied to other men.

He shrugged. 'Or, curl up in your furs like a little mouse and dream of your thorn bush,' he said. 'But whichever you choose, Galahad, do not bother me with it.'

He walked off towards the roundhouse and Oswine, following in his master's wake, grinned at me. How I wanted to wipe that grin off his Saxon face, but I just turned and walked back towards the south side of the house and the log pile where Iselle waited.

We met beneath the old wych elm but did not tarry there, sharing the same unease, given earlier events, that it might be a place where the gods linger, and we did not want any eyes on us, not even theirs. Yet we did not think it wise to stray far from the steading and so went just a little way amongst the trees on the glen's western slope. And even then, my heart was galloping in my chest and my ears were straining to catch every sound as we moved further from the roundhouse, keeping to the shadows where the moonlight could not find us.

'Here,' I said, and we stopped by a rowan which was already in full leaf, its smooth bark the bright silvery grey of a polished blade. I recalled Father Brice telling me that it was from the rowan that the cross of Calvary was carved, though I did not think Iselle would be interested to know this, as I bent to press my palm onto the ground. Dry enough beneath that canopy of feather-like leaves, so I took off my white cloak and laid it down, Iselle watching me. Saying nothing.

She had brought her long knife, but not the Saxon sword. I had brought my spear and Boar's Tusk, but no more. If any of the men saw me going outside, I wanted them to think I had gone to empty my bladder, if they thought anything at all before sinking back into sleep.

I laid my spear and sword beside the cloak, then stood to face her. 'I've missed you,' I said.

Her brows lifted. 'We have barely been apart.'

'You know what I mean,' I said.

She smiled. 'I don't think you would have made a good monk.' She glanced down at my white cloak spread across the ground.

I considered this. 'I don't think so, either,' I said.

I took her hands in mine and this time *I* guided *her*, down to the cloak, and she let me do it, a half smile on her lips as though she was curious to watch what I would do from one moment to the next.

Must everyone test me? I thought.

She looked left and right into the moonlit wood then lay back, reaching behind her head and spreading her loose copper hair on the white cloak, so that I thought it looked like the lustrous mane of some magnificent fabled creature.

'I have missed you too.' She took my hand and pulled me gently down, and neither of us spoke for the next thousand heartbeats.

Not until Iselle felt something, or someone, watching us in the night.

At first, I thought I had done something wrong, for she pulled away from me, a hand on my chest, and turned her face away. But I realized she was looking off towards the trees and so I rolled to the side and stood, arranging myself.

'What is it?' I hissed at her, clothing myself, buckling on my sword belt and grabbing my spear from the ground, all the while watching the trees around us, trying to follow Iselle's line of sight.

'There's someone here,' she said.

Fear hardened my stomach. Dried my mouth. I listened, half expecting to hear the mournful note of a horn, which would tell us that Sadoc or Gadran up on the high ground had seen enemies in the night. I wished I was wearing my scale coat and that I had brought my shield. Mostly I cursed myself for being such a fool and bringing Iselle out here away from the safety of the farmstead.

'An animal?' I suggested. 'Badger or fox?'

Iselle had drawn the long knife. She held it before her like a challenge to the shadows.

'I don't think so,' she said.

I looked behind me, gripped by the ice-cold fear that there were unseen enemies amongst the trees around us. Were they spirits? Did that account for my blindness to them? The dead for whom this island was named by those who had heard the terrible stories?

'Come out,' Iselle urged, giving those words to the silver birch and the moon-dappled night, or so it seemed to me. 'Come. We will not hurt you,' she said, and lowered her knife in a show of peace.

I did not lower my spear.

'We will not hurt you,' Iselle said again, in a voice like that which people use when trying to reassure a child that he or she is safe. The moon emerged from a bank of shredding cloud and just then a figure stepped out from behind a young lime tree and I blinked at the sight and looked around again, suspecting some trick. It was a boy. Eleven summers perhaps. No more. Dark-haired and wild-looking, his face pale like the moon. Deep pools for eyes. His trews, tunic and cloak ragged and torn and dirty with muck, leaves and briar.

'Are you alone?' Iselle asked. I had yet to find my tongue.

The boy nodded.

I still did not lower my spear. The moonwash fell across the trees around us now and I looked this way and that, expecting enemies to appear all around.

'Come.' Iselle beckoned the boy with her free hand as she slid the long knife back into its sheath. The boy gave me a wary look but stepped out of the shadows and walked towards us.

'How long have you been spying on us?' I asked.

The boy thought about this. 'Some time,' he said, which was not the answer I wanted to hear. But then he said, 'Since you came ashore.' He frowned, his smooth, white face a mockery of age and woes. 'But I've been watching you for longer than that, too.'

Iselle and I looked at each other, neither of us knowing what to make of that. 'Where are your mother and father?' Iselle asked him. I was still ill at ease with the thought of his having watched us since I had put my cloak on the ground.

The boy's hands balled into fists. 'They were taken.'

'When? By whom?' I asked, but Iselle shook her head at me and took a step towards the boy.

'Come with us,' she said, 'back to the house. It's safe there.'

The boy shook his head. 'It's not safe.' His eyes were wide. 'They are coming.'

Iselle raised a hand to stop me from speaking. 'Who is coming?' she asked the boy, which was exactly what I had been about to ask.

It seemed a shiver ran through his little body then. 'The neamh-mairbh,' he said.

Iselle and I looked at each other again but gave no words to our shared fears, for the neamh-mairbh were the walking dead. Monsters from fireside tales. Hideous creatures who were said to drink the blood of those they killed. The skin crawled on the back of my neck and down my arms, and I lifted my spear again as I looked around, my heart quickening at the sight of a face. Just a pattern in the birch bark. My guts lurching at some breeze-stirred bramble or at the distant crack of a twig which was likely nothing more than some predator venturing amongst the leaf litter.

'What is your name?' Iselle asked the boy.

He did something then which I did not expect. He grinned. 'I'm Taliesin,' he said.

Despite the boy's dire warning about the neamh-mairbh, Iselle managed to summon a smile of her own, all for him. 'Well, Taliesin, we should go.'

The boy's parents had been taken a year ago or more. Not from the farmstead we sheltered in, but another, above the shore on the east side of the island. Taliesin had been alone ever since. A boy left to fend for himself on the Isle of the Dead. And we were the first people he had seen in all that time . . . if we were saying that those who had taken his mother and father were *not* people. Not any more. A thought to make the blood run cold in the flesh.

'Is it possible that you are the one I felt?' Merlin asked the boy. Taliesin did not answer, but Merlin nodded. 'Yes, yes I think so. At first, I thought it was a druid, but it was you. I'm sure of it.' He was watching Taliesin with such a look of curiosity it was a wonder the boy did not melt under the druid's fierce eye like an icicle beneath a candle flame. But the boy was not like a normal boy, whether because of the life he had endured here alone or because of some stranger reason, and he regarded Merlin with a similar inquisitiveness. So much so that, for us who stood around in a darkness barely challenged by the single lamp flame which Lord Cai held, it was like looking at the reflection of a mirror which shows a man his younger self. I doubted, though, that Merlin was ever as beautiful as Taliesin.

'You have the sight?' Merlin asked.

Taliesin tilted his head on one side, weighing his reply. 'I see things sometimes,' he said, and those big eyes swung to the open door, beyond which Cai's men moved in the dark, hissing at one another to be watchful and ready.

'We don't have time for this if there's any truth in what the boy said,' Gawain put in. He put a hand on Taliesin's shoulder and the boy flinched at the touch. 'How many are coming?' Gawain asked. 'Are they thieves and cut-throats? Or warriors? Men with swords and helmets?' He tapped his own crested helmet as if the boy might never have seen such a thing before.

For a moment, Taliesin seemed somehow absent from his body, those dark eyes seeing things beyond the rotting wattle walls. Things that were not easily shaped into words or brought willingly to the lips. Then he shivered and his eyes sharpened on Gawain.

'They're here,' he hissed.

Gawain and Merlin exchanged a glance that was loud with unspoken words, then Gediens appeared at the threshold, his broad shoulders filling the space.

'A horn,' he told Gawain, 'Gadran, up on the western ridge.'

Gawain nodded, shooting Taliesin a suspicious look as he fastened his silver pin brooch, no doubt wondering how the boy had known. Then he strode outside to join Cai, who was forming his men into a defensive position with their backs to the roundhouse's open door.

I put on my helmet and picked up my shield and spear, and Iselle took up her bow, the Saxon sword already sheathed at her hip.

'You'll stay with me, Taliesin,' Merlin told the boy. He gestured at Oswine, who stood in shadow by the old weaving loom, testing the edge of his short axe by shaving a sliver of wood from the loom beam. 'And you needn't be afraid,' Merlin said. 'Whatever is out there, it cannot be as foul or wicked as that Saxon there.'

Oswine grinned, drawing a little iron hammer from inside his tunic where it hung and pressing it to his lips, in this way invoking his god, Thunor.

Outside, Lord Cai and his warriors were arrayed in a crescent formation, facing out, each man separated by a distance of five feet, shield raised, spear levelled, one foot forward, the other planted in the grass. No wall of shields, leather-bound rims kissing, men close enough to feel the rise and fall of their neighbour's shoulders and chest with every fearful breath – not enough men for that – but each would have the space for spear work. Iselle stood in the middle of the open ground behind the crescent, an arrow nocked but her bow held down by her side.

I looked over to the barn, where two men stood guard, protecting the horses which had been taken in there for safety, the night being too dark to fight on horseback.

'Where shall I stand?' I asked Gawain, who was looking up at the crest of the western hill, where rocks glowed in the moonlight. Lord Cai's men had moved almost as one, like a skein of geese pulling together against the sky, so that I did not know where to put myself.

Gawain growled a curse. The rocks up on the ridge vanished, suddenly swathed in darkness, and we looked up at the waning moon to see it swallowed by cloud from the west. Darkness flooded the vale, consuming the farmstead and all of us who stood wide-eyed where once a family had turned soil and tended livestock, but where nettle and bramble now thrived.

'Someone's coming!' one man yelled, pointing his spear off towards the squat black shapes of the coppiced trees at the foot of the eastern slope. Shields were lifted higher. Flesh tensed. Muscles braced.

'It's me,' a voice called from the darkness, and men exhaled, mumbled profanities, touched iron for luck as Sadoc loped into the clearing. His scale armour and war gear jangled, his chest heaving as the crescent of warriors moved apart, absorbing him into the line.

'What did you see?' Cai asked him.

'Nothing,' Sadoc replied, setting himself like the others, his spear blade rising and falling because he was winded from running. 'Heard Gadran's horn. He's still up there?'

No one answered. There was no need. We had all been expecting or hoping to hear Gadran's horn again, or for Gadran himself to return with word of the enemy we should expect.

But the night was eerily quiet. It pressed down upon us and encroached from all sides, an impenetrable darkness hedging us in, heavy with threat like some foul omen which whispers of death. We waited, my blood gushing in my ears, my breath strangely loud in the helmet with the silver-chased cheek pieces down. The muscles in my thighs quivering. I clenched my jaw to stop my teeth clattering together.

What if I cannot fight? What if I am a coward? These men, warriors all, see my father when they look at me. But I am not my father.

I shook my head as if to uproot these fears and scatter them. Then a spear streaked out of the night to clatter against a man's shield and with it came screams.

'Artorius!' Lord Cai bellowed and his men repeated the cry as a mass of beings swarmed out of the dark and the sounds of slaughter filled the world: shrieks and the wooden clatter of shields and the metallic *tonk* of blades on iron bosses. The neamh-mairbh had come. A streak of white in the gloom and one of the fiends went down, clutching at the swan-fletched arrow in its chest.

In front of me, Gawain thrust his spear into flesh, hauled it free, thrust again, then stepped forward and swung his shield across his body to hammer a snarling face with the boss.

'Fight!' he yelled. 'For all the gods, lad! Fight!'

I looked left and right. It was chaos. I saw Lord Cai beset by three of the creatures, desperately fending them off with spear and shield. I saw Parcefal hurl his spear and draw his sword, that blade scything in the dark, taking a head. And I saw Gediens throwing assailants back, swinging his spear to keep them off, like a flaming torch defying the dark. All along the crescent, blades tore night's shroud and helmet plumes danced.

'Fight, Galahad!' Gawain roared, hurling his own spear and stepping back to buy time to pull his sword from its scabbard.

'Damn you!' It was like the deep rolling snarl of a dog, yet I heard it beneath the battle din, and another arrow hissed in the dark and then I saw one of ours fall. It seemed the creatures were all over him, rabid as a pack of wild dogs, too many to fight. He went down and they were trying to haul him away through the grass, but his companions would not give him up, one grabbing hold of a leg while another drove the creatures back with steel and fury.

Gawain cleaved a shield and the fiend behind it fell back, the stump of its severed arm spraying gore.

'Kill them, Galahad!' Gawain cried. Then Cai yelled that Fiacha was down, and in the murk I could make out three of the creatures bent over Fiacha, stripping him of his fine war gear. And I was striding towards them, shield and spear raised, the screams and clashing of arms sounding far away now, like the murmur of the sea beyond grassy dunes. And the darkness encroached, crowding my peripheral vision so that all I saw was the iron blade of my spear and the creatures before me.

The first looked up in time to see its death in my spear blade, mouth open in a silent scream. I hauled the spear from the snagging eye socket, then cast it at the fiend fleeing towards the trees, taking it in the back. The third came at me teeth and blade but fell back with a white-feathered arrow in its mouth, then Boar's Tusk was in my hand and *I* was the fiend in the darkness, stalking for another kill. I found it when two of the savages came shrieking from the shadows, one of them throwing itself against my shield, trying to rip it from my arm. The new strap held, and I twisted to my right, thrusting Boar's Tusk into the fiend's side with a crack of bone. A thin yelp and the creature fell away, but something struck my right shoulder hard enough to throw my head back and flood my neck bones with heat, yet I turned from the waist and scythed the shield rim into a mouth, scattering teeth and gore into the grass.

For a moment I lost sight of the creature, then I saw it on its back amongst the nettles, wide-eyed and trying to scuttle away like some giant insect. Three strides and I was upon it, thrusting down with Boar's Tusk, that shining blade thirsty for blood, and the thing shuddered and went still.

Someone was yelling my name, though it sounded far away, somewhere beyond the flooding pulse of my own blood in my ears. I killed twice more but afterwards could not recall the manner of those killings, and then there was a pale light in the world again and I looked up to see the moon unveiled, slipping free of cloud.

And suddenly the creatures were fleeing back into the trees surrounding the farmstead, vanishing as quickly as a shoal of fish when a hand breaks the surface of the water. One moment they were there, a horde of shrieking madness, the next they were gone, and we were left breathless and fear-soaked. Wild-eyed. Turning this way and that in benumbed confusion. Unsatiated. Blood-crazed. Hating the enemy more for fleeing than for attacking.

Iselle was standing in front of me. I could see her mouthing my name, but I could not hear her. I turned and saw Gediens staring at me, heavy-browed. Just staring. Parcefal was looking at me too, saying something to the man beside him.

I heard the word *hurt* and realized that Gawain was asking me if I had taken a wound. I shook my head, then remembered the blow I had taken on my shoulder and touched the scales there. They were sound and I felt no pain.

'Hold!' Lord Cai commanded, stalking along the line of his men towards me. 'Hold! Let them go!'

He had retrieved my spear and now brought it to me. 'That was a fine throw,' he said, pulling the blade through a fistful of bitter dock to clean it. 'You fought well, Galahad,' he said, holding my eye a moment as he handed me the spear. Then he turned, calling to his men to keep their eyes on the tree line in case the men who had attacked us came again. For they *were* men, I realized as we walked amongst the fallen, butchering any that still breathed.

'Galahad!' Gediens strode up to me. 'Come here, lad.' He pulled me into an embrace, his blood-slick armour pressing against my own, the bronze scales kissing. 'Knew you had it in you,' he said. 'We all knew.' He pulled away and looked into my eyes. 'You fought like Taranis himself.'

'Taranis would never have let his shield drop like that,' Gawain put in.

'This one's alive,' Merlin called out. The druid had emerged from the house, accompanied by Oswine and Taliesin, and was crouching beside a wounded enemy who had managed to crawl a good distance off through the wet, flattened grass. The creature lay gurgling and choking. Oswine rolled the man over onto his back and we saw the blood bubbling at his lips. Like all the others, he was dressed in leather and skins and he gave off a stink of rancid meat and dung, worse than any animal. His hair was long and white, thickened with lime, plastered to his head and tied at the nape of his neck, and his face beneath the slick mask of dark blood was feral, the skin stretched tight across his sharp cheeks and forehead, his lips drawn back from his teeth like a corpse's after a month in the grave. But the strangest thing about him, and the others too, was the green tinge of his skin. Under the fitful glow of the rushlight which Oswine held over Merlin, the man on the ground beside him looked the colour of bread when the mould is in it. The stain seemed worse on his hands and his neck, and this seemed the same with the others, from what I had seen by the weak light of the waning moon.

'See if you can get anything out of him,' Gawain told the druid, so Merlin tried, asking where the others had fled to and why they had attacked us without knowing who we were or our reason for being there. He even asked the whereabouts of the Cauldron of Annwn, promising in return a draught of hook weed and white willow bark to help numb the pain which had made sharp little arrow heads of the dying man's eyes.

But the man showed no understanding and so Merlin spoke other tongues: Irish and Gaulish – of which I knew but a scattering of words – and the ancient language of the northern Picts, yet it did no good. Even if he could understand, the man was too far away now. Like a boat which had sailed out of sight of land and all that can be seen is the horizon and all that can be imagined is the unknown beyond. He spluttered and gasped and clutched the savage wound in his chest, and when it was clear he would be of no use to us, Gawain gave a nod and Oswine cut his throat.

We counted fifteen enemy dead, though some of us had seen the survivors bearing their wounded away, even dragging them off like heavy sacks into the woods, so that we knew we had inflicted terrible losses on whoever these people were. But Fiacha was dead. His mail slick with his blood, his eyes wide, as though still scouring the darkness for enemies. And he was not the only one. Guidan, who had been the oldest warrior in the company and who had ridden with the young Arthur in Armorica as they forged their reputation, had been killed too. A crudely made, bone-handled knife was still lodged under his right arm where there was tough leather but no iron rings.

I looked at these dead men and could not help but feel that I was in part responsible, for I had played my part in convincing King Pelles to let them accompany us to this land. But more than this, it struck me that we were by no means invincible, despite our horses and armour and the skill of these warriors and their vaunted reputation. They could die, as the brothers of the Thorn had died. And we could fail.

When Fiacha and Guidan were laid side by side on the floor of the roundhouse, the men took it in turns to go in and say whatever it was in their hearts to say, while the rest of us stood watching the trees, some even hoping that our enemies would come again, because in fighting there is little thought.

'I'm sorry, Cai,' Gawain said, standing beside his old friend, the two of them watching Taliesin, who was moving through the night from corpse to corpse, spitting on dead faces and murmuring curses which chilled my flesh, so bitter the words from so young a mouth. 'They were our brothers and we will honour them.'

Lord Cai removed his helmet and scratched amongst his dark hair, which was shot with grey at the temples. 'The way we honour them is by finding this damned cauldron and killing as many of those stinking turds as we can before we leave this . . . forsaken island,' he said.

Gawain nodded, and yet doubts must have gnawed at him as he stood with his back to that ill-fated house, his scale armour and helmet glowing dully in the moonlight. It was our first night on the island and the place had already stolen the lives of three amongst us, for we all knew that Gadran up on the western ridge, who had bought us enough time to brace ourselves for the attack, was dead too. He would have been here otherwise.

Iselle came and stood beside me, the two of us watching Taliesin kneel beside a dark shape. I saw a flash of blade and then the boy threw himself down, driving the knife into the body beneath him.

'So, you are a warrior,' Iselle murmured. 'As your father was.'

I said nothing. I hoped that it was still dark enough for her not to see that I trembled as a dog will when the skies are alight with the Beltane fires.

'Maybe . . .' Iselle began, but fell silent again, still untangling her thoughts before laying them out straight. I glanced at her. She looked composed. Her breathing was deep and even. Her jaw was set like that of someone who knows there is a task to be completed which will not be easy but will nevertheless be done.

I did not speak, fearing that the quivering in my flesh would also be in my voice.

After a while, she said, 'Maybe you should accept who you are. What you are.'

And what is that? I thought. One mad fight in the dark hardly makes a warrior. Yes, I had killed. I had killed illtrained, poorly armed enemies who had fought with little regard for their own lives. That hardly made me a slayer of men. And yet. Something *had* awoken in me. I knew it. I felt it writhing in my guts. Crawling in the marrow of my bones, its need warming me like a belly full of steaming broth.

'I'm not my father,' I said.

'Nor do you have to be,' Iselle said. 'But you are not a novice now. There are no walls for you to hide behind. You will find no comfort in the singing of psalms for the Christus. Only in the sword song.'

Her words cut through the heat in my bones like iced water. I looked at her, but she was watching the eastern woods, which were cast in shadow again. Watching the darkness but *seeing* me.

And then we heard Gadran's horn.

18

The Cauldron of Annwn

W E RODE IN THE near dark. Climbing out of that vale as if emerging from some foul dream. Leaving the farmstead with its ghosts and its newly dead, two of whom lay wrapped in cloth amongst the cobwebs on those beds which had not been slept in for so many years. We would collect the bodies of Fiacha and Guidan on our return and take them back to Ynys Môn to be burned on balefires fit for such warriors as they had been. The other corpses we left for the crows and ravens, for the gulls and the wolves, if there were any on that island. For such savage creatures deserved no better.

There had been some disagreement about whether or not we should leave the relative safety of the farmstead while it was night still. At the thin drone of Gadran's horn, we drew close together in the dark, like fingers into a fist, and waited to see what Lord Cai and Gawain would have us do.

'What if it was those who killed Gadran sounding the horn?' a man named Myr asked, glancing towards the trees from where the white-haired fiends had come before. 'What if they mean to draw us out and surround us in the dark?'

It was a fair question and Myr was not alone in thinking we were being drawn into a trap now. And yet all Cai had needed to say was what if it *had* been Gadran? His first signal to warn us, his second, much later, a plea for help. That question from Cai was enough and now we were riding up the escarpment, hoping that Gadran was alive, that he had somehow escaped those wild devils and had signalled us so that we might find him.

But we did not find him and so we rode on, north-eastward, deeper into the island's interior because what else could we do? No one thought it would be wise to make camp. Not that any of us could sleep knowing that Gadran was out there some-where, and with the fight still thrumming in our blood. But then, to our surprise, Taliesin announced that he knew the whereabouts of the neamh-mairbh's lair.

'I followed them,' he told us.

Gawain raised an eyebrow at Merlin, who smiled as if he had been waiting for the boy to come out with it. Iselle nodded at Taliesin, encouraging him to say more, to tell us what he could.

'After they took my mother and father, they came back,' the boy said. 'Looking for me.' I shuddered to think of what the neamh-mairbh would have done to Taliesin had they found him. It seemed impossible that he could have survived on this island with such creatures stalking the night. And yet he was no ordinary child. There was something otherworldly about Taliesin. He was more like a dream of a boy than a child of flesh and blood.

'Find the lair and we'll find the cauldron,' Merlin said. Of us all, he seemed the least afraid. He was old. He was no warrior. And yet he seemed neither tired nor apprehensive about the task at hand. While the rest of us rode twisting our necks to scour the night, seeing in every copse and ditch an ambush, white knuckles gripping rein and spear, expecting at any moment the neamh-mairbh to come shrieking from the shadows, blades flashing beneath the moon, Merlin sat on his horse like a man on his way to a lover. His eyes glimmered like embers in the dark. He seemed unburdened. Seemed to have shed his self-pity and his guilt and his failure as a snake sheds its skin, and now was vital. Younger, even, as if some of Taliesin's tender youth was seeping into him. Or, more likely, the druid was leeching it from the boy riding Fiacha's horse beside him.

I knew the reason for Merlin's reawakening. He had felt Taliesin's presence as a hound smells the hind, and from the moment he had knelt amongst the roots of that ancient elm, he had known that the gods had not abandoned him after all. That he still possessed some of the power which had carried his reputation across Britain on terrifying wings. And I knew I was not alone in thinking that *if* Merlin could become the druid he had once been, then maybe Arthur could become the lord of battle again, and that together they would unite the kings of Britain and reclaim the lost lands.

Once more we heard Gadran's horn. A long, lonely note in the distant dark. And men touched iron and cursed, growled threats to the night and leant to spit onto the ground, because we knew now that it was not Gadran blowing that horn. The neamh-mairbh were leading us on. We had hurt them. They had meant to slaughter us in that vale, but they had failed, and we had killed many of them and now they sought vengeance. They wanted us to find them and so we would.

We rode across rolling hills and rich meadows which, had they been on the mainland, would have been thick with crops: barley and oats, peas, beans and vetches, but were instead a temptation of long grass to our mounts. We crossed a shallow stream and walked our horses up a slope thick with speedwell whose blue blossoms glowed like gems in the moon dark. Iselle and some of Lord Cai's warriors took the trouble to dismount and pick the flowers, which they tucked into the necks of tunics, or stuffed up sleeves, those flowers being said to protect travellers. I could not imagine what good those delicate blossoms would do against the shrieking neamh-mairbh, but I did not begrudge others seeking good luck where they could find it.

The hill led to a shoulder of land bristling with gorse and we followed it, skirting a dark wood until we found ourselves riding north-west now, towards the coast, and it happened almost imperceptibly that the night slipped away, and dawn seeped into the world. We were tired, for we had not slept, but some of our fear dissolved with the dark and it was heartening to know that we had a full day of light ahead.

We came to a stream which Taliesin said he remembered from that night he had followed the neamh-mairbh, and we stopped to drink and perhaps to gather our courage around us again as a man pulls a fur tight before heading out into the cold.

'You don't have to go any further,' Merlin told the boy, who stood on the eastern side of the shallow stream, looking westward and gnawing on a thumbnail.

'Merlin's right.' Lord Cai mounted again and turned his horse. 'I'll leave a man here with you, boy. We'll return here after.'

After what? I thought, but Taliesin shook his head, his dirt-streaked yet beautiful face gripped by a frown. 'I will come, lord.' He glanced at Iselle, who nodded reassuringly, holding the reins of Taliesin's horse so he could remount, though the animal would have stood perfectly still for Taliesin. The boy knew even less of horses than Iselle, and yet he and the gelding already had an understanding of each other that would have seemed strange had the boy been any other child than Taliesin.

'We may not be able to protect you,' Cai warned, no doubt thinking, as was I, how small Taliesin looked sitting on that big gelding which had belonged to Fiacha.

'The boy has survived here alone for a year,' Gawain said, 'yet we have lost three warriors in a night. Seems to me he might be better off without our protection. If he wants to come, let him.'

Cai scratched his beard and frowned, but Merlin nodded. 'Taliesin is a leaf on this wind like the rest of us,' he said. And so we all walked our mounts across that stream and onto a meadow slung with sheets of silken thread which glistened with dew in the morning mist. I could smell the sea now, hear its soft breathing, which grew louder as we passed a stand of stunted hazel and oak which the onshore wind had warped eastward. Cresting a shallow rise of coarse grass, we came to the coast and looked out across the fog-veiled Western Sea. Even through the sea haze we could make out the mountains in the north of Ireland, and I wondered what kind of wild place that was, as I filled my chest with unfettered air, revelling in the feel of the salt-laden gusts through my hair. It was the first time since leaving the farmstead that I could not smell blood.

'There,' Taliesin said, drawing my eyes away from the sea before they had drunk their fill. 'I remember that.' He was pointing north along the coast towards a rugged headland looming some three hundred feet or more above the water which thrashed itself white on the rocks. 'A little further, that's all,' the boy said, so that I became aware of my heart thumping against the cage of my ribs. Soon we would fight again, unless we could somehow persuade the neamh-mairbh to give us the Cauldron of Annwn and let us be on our way. Unlikely, given the island's reputation for swallowing whoever was foolish enough to come here.

And yet I took grim comfort in knowing that I was amongst

a brotherhood of warriors who would stand shoulder to shoulder against any foe. I supposed I had known brotherhood before, on Ynys Wydryn, which seemed a lifetime ago now, but I had never been the equal of Father Brice or Father Dristan and the others. And though I was not the equal of these men either, I had fought beside them and that act bound us in a way. Still, that was but a slim and fragile bond set against the one that held me to Iselle. I knew I would give my life for her. I told myself as much, as the sun, low in the sky now, threw the shadows of men and horses across the gorse-smothered coastal path and we rode towards our fate.

We came to another headland, this spur of land jutting into the dawn-lit sea like a battlement, standing alone and unconquered by the shifting grey mass besieging it, whose legions hurled themselves to white ruin at its foot. White at its crown too, where flocks of seabirds whirled and dived, their disconsolate cries weaving a skein of sound. The landward slope was cloaked in trees hazed green with new leaves.

'What now?' Gawain asked, pulling the stopper from his flask and drinking as the others caught up and reined in alongside us. We had halted on a ridge overlooking a valley speckled with white sea campion and pink thrift. Above us, shreds of cloud drifted eastward in a brilliant blue sky that had been washed clean by the previous day's rain.

'The boy will tell us.' Merlin twisted in his saddle to look at Taliesin, who was riding beside Iselle. Those two had become inseparable since the vale, and it was clear that Taliesin trusted Iselle more than any other of us. More even than Merlin, who was so taken with the boy.

'You want me to put my men's lives in the hands of a boy?' Lord Cai growled.

'It can be no worse than doing a druid's bidding,' Gawain said, pushing the stopper home and retying the flask to his saddle horn.

Merlin lifted his chin in Gawain's direction, his stiff beard pointing at the warrior like a blade. 'And still you searched for me all those years, Gawain,' he said, 'so that I am beginning to think you enjoy my company.'

Gawain did not dignify that with an answer but shared a knowing look with Parcefal, who knew all too well how Merlin's whispers in the ears of kings and warlords had shaped Britain for better and worse.

'You know this place, lad?' Gawain asked Taliesin, who had walked his gelding to the edge of the ridge.

Taliesin nodded and it was enough to make hands grip spear shafts a little tighter.

'See there,' Iselle said, pointing down to the valley floor. 'That dark line in the grass. Like a badger's path.'

Parcefal shook his head in wonder. 'You've good eyes, girl.'

'So, where does it go?' I asked. If that line of flattened grass was a path made by the neamh-mairbh, where did it lead? I had not expected us to come to a hill fort, a great settlement ringed with a palisade and belching smoke into the sky. Nor even a turf-walled settlement like those which were scattered across the kingdoms of Britain as thick as buttercups in a spring pasture. But I had expected a clutter of roundhouses. Maybe two or three such clutters within half a day's ride of each other. But this well-used path seemingly led nowhere.

'Well, lad?' Cai turned eyes as grey as his gelding's coat on Taliesin.

But Taliesin gave his answer to Iselle. 'The night I followed them, they carried fire,' he said, frowning with the memory. 'I was down there. Close. Close enough to smell their stink.' His eyes widened. 'They vanished.' He turned to Merlin. 'Some concealment spell?' he asked.

Merlin pursed his lips. 'Perhaps. Though I don't think the likes of those savages possess the knowledge for such a spell.'

'Well, we are not going to find the cauldron by sitting here,' Parcefal said, and so we tied our helmet straps and closed the cheek irons. We felt for sword grips to make sure they were within easy reach and we threw our cloaks back to keep them out of the way, then we rode down the hill, our horses snorting and nickering now because they could smell something that we could not. Seren was curling his top lip and blowing and I felt his whole body tighten beneath me and so I leant forward, telling him he was a good boy, a brave boy, and that we would look after each other no matter what happened.

'Wherever they are, they know we're here,' Lord Cai warned, 'so don't be surprised if they come out of nowhere, screaming like banshees.'

'And don't kill them all,' Merlin said. 'We need at least one alive.'

Gawain glanced at me. 'You just kill them, lad. We'll worry about the cauldron after.'

I nodded, my palm slick on the smooth spear shaft, my blood quickening in my veins. Then we were on the path which Iselle had seen from the rise, riding two abreast, Cai and Gawain leading, and Gediens and Parcefal at the rear. Spear blades, helmets and scale armour catching the morning sun. Horse tack jangling and hooves scuffing the ground. For Cai was right, the neamh-mairbh knew we were there and so there was more to be gained from appearing undaunted and unafraid, riding into their land more like warlords come to demand taxes or oaths than warriors still reeling from the loss of three of their own. And when we came to a hump of ground which was thick with gorse and ground ivy shivering in the westerly breeze, Merlin raised his staff, bringing us to a halt.

'It was no concealment spell, Taliesin,' he said, a grin stretching his lips beneath the long forks of his beeswax- and tallow-stiffened moustaches. Pleased to confirm that the neamh-mairbh had no magic.

'Where are they, then?' Gawain asked him. We were all looking this way and that, wondering what the druid had seen which we had missed.

'They are in the earth, Gawain.' Merlin struck the ground with his staff. 'Beneath us now.'

'Waiting for us,' Cadwy said, looking down at his feet, his face all beard, scar and grimace.

Iselle and I shared a look of horror. Gawain growled a curse and Lord Cai invoked Balor, god of death.

Because the neamh-mairbh lived in the ground. And we would have to crawl into the earth to find them.

We found the entrance on the east side of the hummock. A gaping mouth lined with broken teeth of rock, many of them scarred with ancient tool marks. Standing before it, I felt warm air on my face, stale as old breath. The greasy, dirty scent of burning fat and something metallic which I tasted on my tongue.

'It is a portal to Annwn's realm,' Sadoc said, spitting at the thought of that.

Gediens clapped him on his shoulder and grinned. 'Then what are we waiting for?' he asked, pointing his spear at the opening. 'We have many old friends there who I would like to drink with again.'

Cai had his men collect green wood to make torches, wrapping the staves in strips cut from his own cloak, which was new, the wool still rich in sheeps' oil. Then he and Gawain looked at each other, knowing it was time to decide who would go into the mouth of that cave and who would stand guard outside.

'Five to stay with the boy and the horses,' Lord Cai said. No one raised a hand. 'There's nothing to say staying out here will be any safer,' he said, knowing that no one wanted to appear afraid of crawling into the darkness. Still, not one man volunteered to wait outside.

'The oldest should wait here,' Gawain said, 'apart from Merlin, who needs to go within because he will know the cauldron, and me because it's my job to keep Merlin alive.'

'Don't think you're leaving me up here,' Parcefal said, knowing that now Guidan was dead, he was the oldest among us but for Merlin.

'Your eyes are not what they were, brother,' Gawain told him. 'You'll be little use to us down there in the dark.' Parcefal muttered something about his eyes being as good as anyone's, yet he accepted Gawain's decision.

'I have hunted in the dark for years,' Iselle said. 'I'm coming.'

All agreed that Iselle had the eyes of a hawk and should go into the cave, but Taliesin grabbed hold of her hand and begged her not to leave him, saying that if she went, he would go too.

'No, boy.' Gawain shook his head. 'You stay here.'

'I'll look after him.' I saw Iselle squeeze Taliesin's hand.

'No,' Gawain said again.

'Merlin?' Iselle turned to the druid, who seemed not to hear her, his face turned away from us, watching a blackcap on a nearby tree stump. The bird's chattering ended in a flourish of flute-like notes to which Merlin listened as though it were a language he alone understood.

'The boy should come,' he said. 'It is what the gods wish.'

Anger passed across Gawain's scarred face like a storm cloud and he swore under his breath, but he was not about to argue with a druid where the will of the gods was concerned.

'Medyr, Tarawg, Nabon, Cadwy, you stay here with Parcefal,' Lord Cai said. 'Sound the horn if you need us. Protect the horses no matter what.'

'Swords and shields,' Gawain ordered, turning the spear in his grip and thrusting it into the ground. 'There'll be no room for spears in there.'

And so we gathered before that gaping mouth which led into the earth, as Merlin invoked the gods with secret whispers and Cai handed a burning brand to Gawain and another to Sadoc.

Ten of us went into that cave. Gawain first, then Gediens, then me. Behind me were Iselle, Taliesin, Merlin and Oswine, and behind them, Cai, Myr and Sadoc.

Just inside the mouth were three tunnels, one leading straight ahead, one branching to the left and another to the right. The one straight ahead was the largest and so Gawain crouched and took that one, his arm stretched before him, the torch hissing in the confined space and throwing fitful shadows across the rock. I was reminded of when we had crawled through the tor, only this tunnel was wider, and I felt less as if I was descending through a burial mound into some pitch-black afterlife. Even so, I was afraid, the hairs standing on my arms and neck, and every instinct screaming at me to turn around and go back.

Looking up, I saw bats snugged in clefts, their little bodies quivering, and I felt my own flesh quivering too, and serpents writhing in my belly, tumbling over each other, knotting and unknotting themselves. Smoke from the burning torches stung my eyes, making them stream. The acrid stench clawed at my throat, and yet I was still aware of another reek too in the airless tunnel. The fetor of dung and blood. And death.

Iselle touched my shoulder and pointed at the rock walls around us, her brows knitted with the unspoken question. For the rock was green in the torchlight. Streaks of green in some places, as though someone had brought seaweed up from the strand and pasted it across the rock. While elsewhere, great swathes of the rock itself were green. I remembered the green-tinged skin of the dead neamh-mairbh back in the vale.

After no more than one hundred feet the tunnel opened into a chamber where we could stand fully and draw together, back to back, shields facing the darkness beyond the blooms of light thrown by the torches. The air was stagnant here, reeking of blood, and Gawain lifted his torch towards an alcove in the far corner, where something white glowed. He hissed at me and the two of us went to see what it was.

Bones. A midden of rib bones, long leg bones, arm bones and leering skulls. Some animal but most of them human. Gawain held the torch closer to this heap, close enough that we both saw the cut marks in one of the leg bones. Some of the other bones bore similar signs of butchery and many of the larger ones had been crushed as if to get to the marrow within.

Bile had risen in my throat. I could taste it. I swallowed several times and saw the disgust in Gawain's fire-washed face and we went back to the others, who had not moved from where they huddled beneath that strange green rock ceiling, peering over shield rims, round eyes reflecting flame. My eyes met Iselle's and I hoped she could not see my fear.

'There,' Merlin whispered, his voice seeming to come not from him but from the darkness around us. He was pointing his staff towards another tunnel, on the opposite side of the chamber from that midden of human bones. Gawain nodded and led the way, and I thought the others must surely be able to hear my heart thumping as fast as the firebrands were burning. Sweat was coursing down my back between my shoulder blades. I felt beads of it bursting from my scalp and trickling out from under my helmet, clinging to my long hair until they dripped onto the worn, scree-covered ground. None of us wanted to go into that tunnel, and yet we knew we had no choice.

We had to stoop as we walked, the green rock walls pressing in on either side, so that there was only a hand's breadth between our shield rims and the walls. I had the sickening feeling that the passage would get narrower and narrower and that I would not be able even to turn around and go back out. My chest had drawn tight and I struggled to find a breath. *I'll suffocate*, I thought.

'Least the bastards can't surround us in here,' one of the men behind me said, which got a hiss from Lord Cai, who had told us to move as quietly as possible.

Then there was a grunt and a scuffling sound, and I looked over my shoulder to see a flurry of flame and movement.

'Sadoc!' a man yelled, his voice reverberating off the solid rock. 'Sadoc!'

'What is it?' Gawain shouted, caring nothing for the noise now.

Those behind me were cast into darkness. Sadoc's fire was out and the light from Gawain's torch did not reach those beyond Iselle and Taliesin.

'He's gone!' Lord Cai said.

'What do you mean, gone?' Gawain asked. There was fear in his voice, and it turned my bowels to liquid to hear it.

'Gone. They took him.' The warrior who had called out, Myr, was facing back the way we had come but turned to speak over his shoulder. I could hear the dismay in his voice. 'He was right behind me, close enough for his torch to singe my neck hairs.'

Lord Cai trotted back down the tunnel and was swallowed in the darkness. 'Sadoc! Answer me, man!' he called. But there was no reply.

'You saw nothing?' Gawain asked Myr.

'Nothing,' Myr said.

Then Lord Cai reappeared in the light-bloom from Gawain's brand. He looked at Gawain and shook his head. Gawain growled a curse and Lord Cai took up the rear behind Myr.

'We keep going,' Merlin said.

So we did, and the tunnel opened into another chamber. Bigger than the first, perhaps the size of four roundhouses together. Gawain moved his torch this way and that, the fire breathing louder with each swing of his arm, the flames chasing the dark away for only a heartbeat before the blackness flooded in again. But by the flying tail of that flame we caught glimpses of things which told us that this was the neamh-mairbh's lair. Animal skins on the ground. Crudely made wooden stools. Iron pots, beakers and trenchers. Furs and old saddle cloths and, standing against a wall, old battered shields, slung with cobwebs, their devices long faded. There were more bones and several spears, and a barrel by the wall which was half full of rain water, which seeped through somewhere above so that we could hear it dripping in the dark. And as we ventured further in, Gawain's torch showed us something else too. Something which stilled the fire in his hand and the breath in our throats. He held the torch steady, the flame seething, guttering now as it ate through the last of the cloth binding. Enough light, though, that we all could see the stone-ringed fire pit and what sat within it. As if waiting for us.

*

The Cauldron of Annwn did not look much like a treasure. Sitting on four piles of flat stones, so that a fire could be kindled beneath, it was black, encrusted with soot and filth and whatever food had been cooked in it and had spilled over. And with a sudden heart-stopping horror, I knew what that food was. It was in the air, metallic and sickly. A raw odour cut with the lingering scent of a fear not entirely our own. But it was Cai who confirmed it, some foreknowledge compelling him to hasten to the cauldron and peer inside while the rest of us approached, half watching the darkness beyond the withering bloom of Gawain's dying torch.

'Gadran,' he said, his voice gruff, the word hanging in the dark.

'We have it.' Merlin was crouching, spitting on his fingers and trying to rub off some of the grime to reveal the metalwork beneath. Already he had uncovered a patch of silver. A serpent, coming alive under Merlin's touch, seeming by the flickering flame to move again after a slumber of lifetimes. 'We have it, Gawain,' Merlin said again. And we did. We had within our grasp one of the ancient treasures of Britain. The very cauldron which had been saved from the slaughter amongst the sacred groves of Ynys Môn. A prize which was said to have the power to restore life to the dead. And yet, in that moment it paled against the truth of what had become of Gadran, whom we had believed dead but for whom we had yet carried hope.

'I will return to this island and kill them all,' Cai said.

Gadran had been disembowelled and dismembered. His pale limbs thrown in on top of his torso and lastly his head, his beard and hair having been burned off to leave a mess of charred tufts and blistered skin. His eyes were closed. A small mercy, though it was impossible not to imagine the horror in them *if* he had still been living when the neamh-mairbh brought him into that place. The revulsion I had felt previously, that sickening disgust which had brought bile to my mouth, ebbed now. Or perhaps it was drowned by something else. A welling anger which rose hot in my chest and in my limbs, and ran like scalding water through my veins, consuming me. Here before me was death and horror. And yet I wanted to kill. More than wanted to. I needed to.

'Let's get it out of here,' Gawain said.

'Should empty it first,' Gediens said.

Cai nodded at Myr to help him, and the two of them took hold of the cauldron's rim to tip it.

That was when they came.

I did not see where they came from, only that a moment before, the darkness around us had been empty, but now it was glutted with bodies.

'Shields!' Cai bellowed.

'Around the cauldron,' Gawain yelled, and we moved fast, surrounding that treasure of Britain, our shields close together facing the shadow all around. 'Stay tight,' Gawain said, and then they struck. A shrieking fiend hit my shield, but I had braced myself to take the impact and I thrust Boar's Tusk around the shield into flesh. The neamh-mairbh grunted and fell away, but another one had two hands on my shield's rim, trying to pull it from me. I let him haul the shield away from my body, then punched Boar's Tusk forward, taking him in the neck, and twisting the blade as I hauled it back, covering my body with the shield again. Iselle beside me, the Saxon sword in her right hand, the long knife in her left, hacked into a white thigh, then slashed a face. Her enemy dropped, clutching its ruin and screaming.

'Kill them, Galahad,' Merlin rasped behind me, gripping his staff across his body, guarding the cauldron and Taliesin both, while Oswine fought in the circle with the rest of us.

A rock struck my helmet with a metallic clang. Another hit the helmet's right cheek guard and would have otherwise broken my jaw. Instead, it fed my rage. I rammed Boar's Tusk into a man's side and felt the rush of hot blood on my hand and the scrape of the blade against ribs as I pulled it free. I lopped off a hand, which fell at my foot, and I scythed into the neck of a neamh-mairbh who had knocked Iselle down and had raised his spear to thrust it at her. Standing above Iselle so that she could get to her feet, I saw Myr take a spear in his throat and go down. On the other side of the cauldron, Gediens was on his knees, grasping at his neck while Cai shielded him, holding the neamh-mairbh at bay, his sword flashing in the fitful, dying flamelight.

'Galahad!' Merlin called, and I turned and saw him swinging his staff, fending off a wild, white-haired creature who had broken through the ring. But I could not leave Iselle, who was on her feet again now, crouching, blades raised as the chaos swirled around her.

Then Oswine was there and he buried his axe in the man's back, but even as he did so, two more of the devils were on him, stabbing him over and over. He fell to his knees and Merlin screeched and his staff struck a head, and all was movement and flame and shadow and screams and the ringing and scraping of blades.

And then Gawain's torch guttered and died. He hurled the brand and there was a last flicker of flame and a trail of smoke, and then nothing but utter darkness. The neamh-mairbh fell back into the shadows, hissing. Like us they were lost for a moment, blind in the murk between light and dark. I lifted my shield, heaving for breath, knowing that in another few heartbeats they would come again.

And then Taliesin started to sing.

*

I had never heard a voice like it. Clear as water in a mountain stream. Sweet as the flowers of the woodbine, which children suck for their nectar, yet strong enough to bind us in the dark, as honeysuckle stems will twine into the branches of trees. It swirled around that chamber, seeming to come from everywhere at once: a single voice, yet many. Like a chorus of echoes from the past, trapped but seeking to escape. He sang of the forest and the ocean, of a horned god and a ram-horned snake, and a silver torc which shone as brightly as the moon.

I did not know the song, but I would not have been surprised had that melody risen to crow and raven long before Rome's eagles came to Britain. And there was magic in it. I stood sweat-drenched and breathing hard, peering into the gloom over my shield's rim, just able to discern the neamh-mairbh by their lime-plastered hair and the soft glow of their eyes. For some reason they waited. Perhaps they feared our blades. Perhaps they knew there were enough dead in that chamber to feast upon for many days. But I believed it was Taliesin who held them at bay, his song having awoken in them some shared memory, recalling some story within which their people had once walked, lived, worshipped, mourned. The warp and weft of a cloth which once clothed them.

It was a spell, perhaps as powerful as any that a druid ever wove, and I felt it holding Iselle beside me, too. She was still as death, and I knew that some part of her was lost in the song.

'We leave now,' Gawain rasped.

'Not without the cauldron,' Merlin hissed.

I sheathed Boar's Tusk, slung my shield across my back and helped Cai and Gawain to tip the cauldron, spilling Gadran across ashes and hearth stones. 'I'll carry it,' I said, squatting to wrap my arms around the cauldron's belly. Gods, it was heavy! But I was strong and the neamh-mairbh would have to cut me down to stop me carrying that treasure of Britain out into the light.

'We move and we keep going and we get this thing out of here,' Gawain said, his teeth showing in the soft green glow of the cave's walls. Taliesin was singing still, his voice entangling the neamh-mairbh and rooting them in place, and it struck me that this was how the boy had survived alone on the island. That perhaps these folk who dwelt in the dark feared him. Or revered him. This young boy in whose pure voice a deeper, ancient power moved. As though his song was the first song, given by a god to men. That they might name the trees and the moon, the sun and the stars, and pass the knowledge of these wonders to their children.

And yet even such a spell as this was as delicate as a spider's silken threads strung amongst heather, and it seemed impossible that the boy could hold the neamh-mairbh much longer. Now that they knew we had come to steal the cauldron, they would surely attack with renewed and desperate savagery.

'Ready,' Gawain said. It was not a question. He would lead, with Merlin and Taliesin behind him, then me. Iselle took up position on my right, blades raised to the darkness. Gediens was on my left, paying no heed to the bloody wound in his neck, and Cai would defend our rear.

Gawain hefted his shield. 'Now,' he said, and we were moving. And the spell was broken.

Gawain's sword flashed and something died, and I heard fighting behind me, too, but I kept moving. We hurried back along the narrow tunnel, one line again, the rock walls either side tearing open my knuckles and the backs of my hands because the passage was only just wider than the cauldron itself.

In front of me, Gawain stopped. 'Which way?' he yelled,

while Cai yelled at us to keep going and my arms trembled with the precious burden. I saw Taliesin's eyes, wide and luminous amid the gloom.

'Your left,' Iselle called. That was good enough for Gawain, who set off down another tunnel, and I felt my back would break, so stooped was I beneath that rock ceiling, my cheek pressed against the cold metal of that cauldron which had cooked the flesh of men. But Cai was keeping our enemies at bay no less than Taliesin had, and we came into the smaller chamber with the bone midden, then into another tunnel, and now I could feel a breath of air, cool against the raw skin of my hands.

'Nearly there,' Gawain said. 'If they follow us out, we'll slaughter them.' And we would, because Parcefal and the others were out there beneath the clear sky and when they saw us emerge bloody and fewer than we had been, they would mount their horses and cut the neamh-mairbh down like barley before the scythe.

'Faster, Galahad!' Iselle demanded, and at last I could straighten again and my lower back burned with pain and the muscles in my arms were taut and trembling, but I ran, and I would not drop the cauldron.

'Cai is down!' Gediens roared, his voice filling the tunnel.

'Don't stop!' Gawain yelled.

'Go!' Gediens roared, and I could not breathe but I kept going because there was no room for Iselle and Gediens to pass me and if I was not fast enough, they would die.

Stumbling, half falling, but keeping my feet under me. My shield hammering against my back. Shoulders and arms striking the rock over and over. My blood gushing in my ears, drowning out my curses which were thick on the air because I could not see where I was going but must follow Gawain by the sound of his boots scuffing the ground and his breath and the jangle of his war gear and his helmet's cheek irons. Then a shaft of light and an incline up which I drove with the last of my strength, roaring with the agony of it and blinded by the day.

Out of the creatures' lair, and I let go the cauldron, which struck the ground with a hollow clang, rolling and coming to a stop in the tall grass beside the path. I unslung my shield and drew Boar's Tusk and turned in time to see Gediens and Cai emerge from the cave's mouth, walking backwards, shields raised, both men sheeted in blood.

'Galahad!' Iselle cried. I spun back round and saw Parcefal wheeling his horse, his spear raised to the sky. Medyr, Tarawg, Nabon and Cadwy were all mounted, forming a line facing north, spears gripped in their right hands, shields on their backs, their helmet plumes dancing. Facing them, a spear-throw away amongst the grass and the yellow cowslips, were a score of neamh-mairbh brandishing spears and knives, and some gripping bows to whose strings they were nocking arrows. Even from that distance I saw the green tinge of their skin, and in their ragged clothes and with their white hair they looked like corpses who had clawed their way out of their burial mounds. As if summoned from some story told around the fire to draw an audience and, after, haunt their dreams.

At the centre of this band, standing forward from the rest, was a huge man holding a huge axe. There was a torc of twisted copper, thick as a rope, at his neck, and more copper bands on his wrists, and of course it was copper ore which was in the walls of the caves.

He wore a bear's fur over his animal skins and looked like a man who had won that pelt wrestling against the bear itself. His long white hair was plastered back over his wide head, his nose was broad and broken, his eyes were deep set and I saw him look at the Cauldron of Annwn lying where I had dropped it. Saw his lips pull back from his teeth as he said something to the men behind him.

'We should have blocked the entrance,' Lord Cai said. He was bent over, breathing hard. 'Two of us could have held them.'

'Too late now,' Gawain said, because the neamh-mairbh whom we had fought were spilling out of the cave's mouth, as though the sickened earth vomited poison. They came blinking into the day, startled by the brightness, hands shielding their eyes, many of them wounded and bleeding.

'Shall we mount?' Gediens asked, gesturing with his bloodied sword at our horses. They stood twitching and tossing their heads nervously, not liking being hobbled. Seeing the other neamh-mairbh coming, Parcefal must have done it to stop them being driven off.

'No time for that,' Gawain said. We were all but surrounded now, though the cave-dwellers were keeping their distance, perhaps because they knew that we were dangerous and that many of them would die, or else they were waiting for the big, axe-bearing warrior to command them.

'We must protect the cauldron.' Merlin was fierce-eyed, his face blood-spattered and his beard and moustaches frayed. But despite the odds, he was alive, thanks to Oswine who was still in that underground chamber. It was his tomb now.

'Stand with me!' Iselle called. She had hurried to retrieve her bow and bag of arrows from her horse and now stood beside the cauldron, the Saxon sword thrust into the ground beside her for when she ran out of arrows or if the neamh-mairbh were too close. She was ready to make a last stand and my heart swelled in my chest to see her defiance. Beside her, Taliesin stood gripping Iselle's long knife in two hands, meeting his old enemy with those big eyes of his.

Gediens and Lord Cai took positions beside Iselle and in front of the cauldron and I joined them, catching Iselle's eye for the briefest moment, trying to say in that one fleeting look what could not be spoken aloud if we were to cling to the illusion of hope. But Gawain did not stand with us. He was striding towards the other neamh-mairbh warriors, his back straight and his chin high and a spear in his right hand. He walked past Parcefal and the other mounted men, ignoring his old friend, who growled down at him from his mare, asking what in Balor's name he was doing.

'You!' Gawain roared, left arm outstretched as he walked towards the ragged-looking war band, pointing at their bear-like leader. 'You!' Gawain yelled, still walking. He was closer to the neamh-mairbh than he was to Parcefal and the others, so I knew that if the cave-dwellers attacked, Gawain would be dead before the fastest horse and rider could reach him.

Then Gawain pulled his arm back and cast the spear and it flew like I had not seen a spear fly since I was a boy watching my father train. It rose into the sky, the shaft spinning, then fell, gathering speed, and would have impaled the axe man through his chest had he not twisted his upper body at the last, so that the blade buried itself in the ground, the shaft standing there like an insult, as straight as Gawain's finger pointing at the huge warrior. 'You and me!' Gawain said, still striding towards him, but drawing his sword now, giving the leader of the neamh-mairbh no time to consider what he should do, but enough time to know that this was a challenge which he could no more ignore than refuse.

'You rancid turd of a she-giant!' Gawain yelled. 'Fight me, you coward! Fight me, or the horse warriors of Lord Arthur, son of Uther Pendragon and Prince of Battles, will slay your people and scour you from the land.'

Arthur's warriors, he called them, not King Pelles's warriors. Yet I saw no disagreement in Lord Cai or in any of the four men mounted beside Parcefal.

Up came the axe. The big man bellowed something in his own tongue and strode out to meet Gawain. He did not break stride but swung the axe with two hands and Gawain danced out of the way like a man half his age. Then the two warriors circled, weighing each other with their eyes, the neamh-mairbh a head taller than Gawain and broader in the chest and shoulders.

'He was always a fool,' Merlin said, but there was admiration in his eyes, because he knew that Gawain had seized what might be our only chance. That by killing the leader of the neamh-mairbh in single combat, he might buy us our lives, as champions in the past stood between armies and spilled their own blood to decide the day and prevent a slaughter.

The huge man lowed like a bull and swung his axe again and this time Gawain lifted his shield and the axe struck it with a crack as Gawain pulled the shield back to absorb the blow. He scythed his sword at the giant's neck, but the man was fast for his size and threw himself back out of the blade's reach and swung the axe around his head. It smashed Gawain's shield, sending splinters of limewood flying.

The watching neamh-mairbh hooted and shrieked and Gawain walked backwards, using his sword to hack away the ruined wood from what remained of his shield. Arthur's bear still stood on the iron boss, but its top half was gone and a long sliver of wood, sharp as a needle, ran with the grain across almost the whole width of the shield.

'He's lucky the green-skinned devil didn't take half his arm too.' Cai dragged an arm across his sweat-sheened brow as, exulting in his own strength and in the ruin of his enemy's painted shield, the monstrous warrior lifted his chin and howled at the sky, then came on, swinging the axe as though cutting a swathe through a mass of ghostly warriors only he could see.

Gawain's red horsehair plume danced as he twisted and ducked, leapt and retreated, sometimes avoiding that flashing axe head by a finger's length, sometimes by a foot, but always staying close enough to entice the man on. To keep him swinging that heavy weapon. Working the fiend into a slathering frenzy of bloodlust. Making him crave the sensation of cleaving not just limewood but flesh and bone.

'Take him now,' Gediens murmured under his breath. The neamh-mairbh around us were as transfixed by the fight as they had been by Taliesin's singing and had taken up a low chant of *'Bredbeddle! Bredbeddle! Bredbeddle!'*, which I guessed was the giant's name.

And now Bredbeddle's axe rasped off Gawain's shield boss and his next swing bit into the top of Gawain's shoulder, sending bronze scales flashing in the day and eliciting a cry of pain from Gawain and shouts of triumph from the neamh-mairbh. *'Bredbeddle! Bredbeddle! Bredbeddle!'* they chanted, louder now, like a drum beat announcing Gawain's doom, for they thought it was all but finished. They expected to see their champion standing over Gawain's corpse. They were already imagining a feast the likes of which their kind had not known for many years.

'Now,' I said in a low voice which Gawain could never have heard, yet it was as though he had, for the axe head flew and Gawain threw himself back, the blade whispering past his throat stone. But as he planted his rear foot, he suddenly thrust himself forward and now he was inside that long axe's reach where its wicked blade could not harm him. He threw his head forward, ramming his helmet into Bredbeddle's face, and I heard the splinter of bone across the distance.

Then as the bigger man stepped back, Gawain swung his half shield across and into Bredbeddle's neck with enough muscle to send him staggering away. But he only made three careening strides before Gawain, who had turned and dropped to one knee, brought his sword across to slice into the hamstrings of Bredbeddle's right leg. The giant went down onto his knees, bellowing in fury and pain, and clutching at his neck, and the long sliver of wood which had skewered it. Gawain was up and he gave a flourish with his sword before stepping in and, in one sweeping cut, taking Bredbeddle's head off his shoulders.

The head fell into the grass and the lifeless body slumped beside it.

We braced, watching the neamh-mairbh. Expecting them to attack. But they did not. They just stood there, looking over towards where Bredbeddle lay. Then, giving us a wide berth, the ones who had followed us from under ground walked over to join the others, who were already moving to recover their champion's body and head.

'There was a time Gawain could have slaughtered that ox in the flap of a raven's wings,' Merlin said. 'Truly he's getting old.'

But Merlin had it wrong. Gawain had known what he was doing. Had he gutted the man in the first exchanges, the neamh-mairbh would have been furious and eager to exact revenge on us. And so Gawain had given them a spectacle. He had let them witness their champion's courage and strength. He gave them hope and then ripped that hope away from them, leaving them hollow, sagging like an empty wine skin, the fight gone out of them. Maybe he had even let the axe glance his shoulder. Or perhaps he *had* been too slow in that moment. Merlin was right in that Gawain was older than he had been in Arthur's day. But I knew he could still have killed Bredbeddle without breaking a sweat. And I knew he had just bought us our lives.

19

Spirit Walkers

W<small>E SAILED BENEATH A</small> sky of iron and rust. Behind us, the Isle of the Dead was slowly consumed by mist and weighed upon by shrouds of sullen cloud which slid inexorably southward, coerced by that same wind which leant into the *Calistra*'s woollen sail. As before, we stood amongst the horses, only this time we needed them more than they needed us. We leant against them, almost clung to them, needing their strength for we were bone-weary. But also, perhaps, coveting their equine indifference. Hoping it might seep into us and numb us, as ale will numb a wound of the heart, so much did we ache for the loss of our brothers. We had not been able to retrieve Gadran's dismembered body. Oswine too, who had served Merlin so many years, would never again be touched by sunlight. And Sadoc, who had vanished in the dark, and Myr, whom I had seen fall, remained in the dark still. But we had taken some small satisfaction in recovering Fiacha and Guidan from the old steading where we had left them, and so those two at least would return to Ynys Môn and from there be borne to Annwn on the smoke of a hero's pyre.

We had come to the beach rather than linger inland, and found the *Calistra* anchored offshore in the dusk, waiting for the morning tide to carry her up onto the sand and shingle.

Karadas simply raised a hand in greeting, but even across the distance we could see the wide eyes of his crewmen as they stared at the cauldron which we had brought, slung from a pair of spears fixed to the saddle horns of Oswine's and Sadoc's horses. They could also see that we numbered fewer than when we had left them, and they knew better than to celebrate our success in the absence of the lost. That night none of us really slept, but kept our eyes on the dunes and rocks, fearful that the eaters of the dead would come, so that in the morning we were tired beyond words when we finally embarked and set sail accompanied by the cries of gulls and the thrashing of the sea upon the strand.

I stood with Seren, beyond weary, my head against his, my body leeching the warmth from his flesh, my hand resting gently behind his eye where I could feel the thump of his heart and know that we both still lived. It was strange but we did not feel that we had won. Karadas barked his orders at the crew and they went about their business of ropes and sail, steering oar and tiller, and the *Calistra*'s bows churned the sea as we hastened towards Ynys Môn, as though the ship herself sought to put ten thousand grey furrows between her stern and the receding land. But we who had ventured into that land, and under it, were in some way there still. In the valley of the deserted farmstead, peering into the night after lost souls. Or fear-soaked in the cramped blackness of the caves, where hungry things lurked like monsters in the shadows of a dream.

We who had survived looked at the cauldron as one would look upon a curse, if a curse could be seen. I did not blame Merlin. I had seen the anguish in Lord Arthur's eyes, sharp still after all the years. I had seen the Lady Guinevere, had with my own eyes, long ago, beheld the dissolution of her body and mind. And so I knew why Merlin sought the cauldron.

But Cai and Medyr, Tarawg, Nabon and Cadwy blamed him. They did not say as much, but they did not need to. They stood among the horses, legs braced against the *Calistra*'s pitch and roll, silent as stones raised in honour of the dead. Stunned from the loss of their spear-brothers. Now and then I caught one of them looking over at the cauldron by the mast with suspicion or disgust, perhaps thinking the price they had paid for it far exceeded its worth.

'Did you know I found him hiding in an ash?' Merlin said. I lifted my head from Seren's neck and looked at him across the gelding's back. 'Not an easy tree to climb, the ash,' he said. I knew he was talking about Oswine. 'But he had just seen his father run through by Uther's champion and so I suppose he had good reason to climb it.' He smiled at the memory. 'And he was a boy, not yet thirteen summers, and boys can do extraordinary things if they don't stop to think about them.'

'You saved his life?' I asked.

Merlin frowned. 'Uther's men were blood-crazed. Killing anything that breathed.' His brow darkened. 'And doing worse things too.' He placed a hand on Seren's withers, as though he needed to know what comfort I drew from the gelding. 'I told Uther's brutes that whichever of them touched the Saxon boy would piss blood for a year.' He looked up to the grey sky, where a gull sliced in and out of the northerly, its raucous mews offered like a lament for the dead. 'Men feared me in those days,' he said. 'Now, they do not even fear the gods. They fear only for their own small lives. Will the barley grow tall? Will they survive childbirth or plague or famine? Will they stay warm in winter?'

'Will the Saxons come?' I added.

He nodded. 'That too. Always that.'

I clasped my hands together but did not make the sign of the Thorn, instead pressing my left thumb into my right palm, kneading the flesh, which was tender from how fiercely I had gripped Boar's Tusk in the caves.

'Men still respect you.' I kept my head low and nodded towards Gawain and Cai, who were talking in the bows. Beside them, Gediens sat against the side of the ship as Iselle, with Taliesin beside her, close as a shadow, examined the cut which the warrior had taken in his neck. We watched her lift the bloodstained linen binding away and pour Karadas's wine over the wound, much to the captain's distress. 'Look what they have done because you said they must.'

Cai too was hurt, I knew, from a spear thrust which had not penetrated his armour but had badly bruised his shoulder, and from a blow to the head from which he was still seeing double, so Gawain said.

Merlin scowled. 'And they hate me for it.'

I looked at the Cauldron of Annwn, that treasure of Britain, still tarnished with age and filth and soot, and still smelling of Gadran's blood even after Cai and Gawain had rolled seawater around inside, before Merlin had rasped at them to stop insulting the god. 'But, if it restores Lady Guinevere.' Those six words so heavy with hope that they fell from my mouth like ballast into the sea, and no more followed them.

Merlin scratched his bearded cheek, for a long moment ensnared by his own thoughts. Then he leant over Seren's neck and I knew to turn my ear towards his cracked lips. 'The truth is, Galahad, I think we must prepare for the worst,' he said in a voice that could have been a creaking of one of the *Calistra*'s tarred ropes. 'Even if I *can* reach her, I fear she will not survive the journey back.'

I pulled away from those sour words and from the sourness of his breath and fixed my eyes upon his. 'You don't believe it can be done?' I asked.

Merlin scowled and hissed at me to keep my voice down, though only Seren had heard me above the sea's murmur across the ship's bows and the groans of the timbers and ropes, and the whinnying of the other horses.

The druid leant towards me again. 'I am only saying that we must look to other outcomes.'

My legs weakened. I looked to where Guidan and Fiacha lay in their shrouds beside the cauldron, anger flaring in my chest, hot as fire. How could Merlin tell me this now, after all we had been through to retrieve that so-called treasure of Britain? I looked around me at the men who had risked their lives and lost brothers because we – not just Merlin, as I had played my part up to the hilt – had asked for their help. And I looked at Iselle, her hair flying in the wind like flame, for she was Britain and she burned with the hopes of a people. And I felt sick to my stomach, almost feverish with shame because I could not unhear what Merlin had told me. And knowing it when others did not made me as deceitful as the druid.

'Why did six men give their lives for it?' I asked him. 'Why are we here?' I gestured at the indistinct blur of grey sea and grey sky. 'Instead of standing with Lord Constantine against our enemies?'

'Don't play the fool, boy, you know why,' Merlin said.

And I did. 'For Arthur,' I said.

I let out a shivering breath and glanced at Gawain, whose call upon the blood bonds of brotherhood was the real reason why Cai and the other horse warriors, the last of their kind, had joined us. I knew that if he learnt the truth of Merlin's doubts, he would likely throw the old man overboard.

'For Arthur,' Merlin whispered to himself. 'It has always been for Arthur.'

Seren snorted and lifted his head in irritation at my neglect, for I had ceased stroking his neck and flank. His tail was pressed tightly against his buttocks. His ears were flicking forward and rearward at every strange sound, every creak and snap of the sail, and it seemed to me that, like the rest of us, he wanted to be somewhere that foully used and begrimed cauldron was not. 'Soon, my friend. We're almost there,' I said, putting my cheek against his muzzle and breathing in the sweet scent of his honest breath. 'There's my brave boy.'

'What would you do for her?' Merlin asked.

I frowned at him. He rolled his eyes. 'You know who I mean.'

My eyes found her. 'Anything,' I said.

His eyebrows lifted. 'Even journey to the Isle of the Dead to recover a relic because she clings to the hope that Arthur will ride again?'

I nodded.

'And so would I do anything for Arthur.' He paused. 'Try anything.' He shook his head, his long grey beard and moustaches fraying in the sea wind. He looked old and gaunt, like a tired hound whose coat seems to have shrunk upon its flesh so that the bones can be seen. His eyes, though, were not the eyes of an old man, not rheumy nor clouded, nor their whites tinged red like those of an old hound. Merlin's eyes were embers amongst the ashes, pulsing with secret life, waiting for the breath that would ignite them. 'I failed him before,' he said, throwing out his arms to hold round Seren's neck as the *Calistra* bucked over a wave. Some of the horses shrieked in fear. 'I gave Arthur Lancelot. And I gave the gods Guinevere. And so Arthur had the sword of Britain – I mean your father, not that trinket which he waved around the land to impress the kings. *And* he had the gods.' Both hands resting on Seren's back, he was stroking his right palm with two fingers of his left hand, tracing the triskele of conjoined spirals that had long ago been etched into the skin and still showed green as a vein. He shook his head. 'I thought it would be enough. I should have seen what would happen. I should have known that love can destroy like fire.'

What had happened was that my father had loved another man's wife and that love had poisoned everything. I did not see how any of that was Merlin's fault, but if he claimed a part of it, it was not for me to argue. Had not the druids always stirred the brew?

'I failed Arthur and I failed Britain. And so, Galahad, I must try to fix what is broken.' He looked beyond the *Calistra*'s bows, where, through a darkening veil of rain, the cliffs of Ynys Môn rose from the sea-fretted rocks. Did he mean Britain, or Guinevere, or Arthur? Perhaps he meant all three.

'You *will* cure Guinevere,' I said, as though saying it could make it so, 'and Arthur will lead us again.'

Merlin said nothing to that but pulled his beard through a knotty fist as he turned his gaze upon the Cauldron of Annwn.

I did not know what the druid saw when he looked at that begrimed metal bowl which his forebears had carried across the sea, fleeing the flames which the Romans had loosed upon their sacred groves. But when I looked at that cauldron, what I saw was death.

We watched a boy and girl disappear over the brow of a hill, running to deliver the news of our return, and later, when the guards in the palisade gatehouse saw us emerge from the tree line with the Cauldron of Annwn swinging gently between two riderless horses, they sounded the horn. I expected we would be greeted with cheers and acclamations, with children running alongside us and with sorry looks from those who knew all too well what it had cost to bring the treasure of Britain back to Ynys Môn. But there was no cheering, not even when we passed through the gateway and walked our mounts into the courtyard as the setting sun broke through cloud to spill a strange red light across the fort.

One of Lord Cai's warriors stood waiting for him, while those others of his red-plumed horse warriors who had stayed behind fell in beside us, or rather, beside the cauldron, bear-shields and spears in their hands as they greeted friends, acknowledged empty saddles and asked what had happened on the Isle of the Dead. And at first, I thought their surrounding of the cauldron was some act of respect, done to honour us and those of us who had not returned.

But then I saw the crow-shields.

My chest tightened and I looked at Gawain in time to see him lean from his saddle and spit, because he had noticed the shields, too.

'What in the name of the horned god are they doing here?' Parcefal said, lifting his spear from where it had rested across his saddle horns.

'They came the day you left,' one of Cai's men, walking beside us, said. 'The Lords Melehan and Ambrosius. Their father was Mordred,' he added, touching the iron of his shield boss at his own mention of Arthur's son who had betrayed him.

'We know who they are,' Gawain said. 'Why are they here?'

I had the sudden and terrible fear that Morgana and the Saxon King Cerdic had not waited to make good their threat. That their combined army had already fought and defeated Lord Constantine, and that now they had come to demand oaths of loyalty from the kings of Dyfed, Powys and Gwynedd. But it was Iselle who plucked that fear away, sowing a new dread in its place.

'They followed us,' she said. She had drawn the Saxon long knife from its sheath, its blade catching the setting sun.

'She's right,' Gediens said, and I recalled Iselle having seen a warrior's mail or a helmet amongst the trees above a river valley to the south of Gwynedd. We had thought they must be King Gwion's men, shadowing us to ensure that we were what we purported to be, but now it seemed likely that Melehan and Ambrosius had followed us. I wondered if they had trailed us from Venta Belgarum all those days ago but then lost us in the marsh, only to pick up our trail when we left Arthur. Or had one of our hosts from any of the forts and rounds along the way sent word of us to Camelot and Morgana, selling us to our enemies even as they shared their food and ale with us?

'We stay with the cauldron,' Gawain said loudly enough for us all to hear. 'We don't let anyone else come within twenty feet of it, understand?' Men who were hungry and thirsty and bone-weary mumbled their assent, sitting taller in their saddles now, gripping spear shafts, eyes sifting the crowds for signs of trouble. For now, though, the crow-shields just stood in their knots, some thirty men in all that I could see, watching us. And watching the cauldron.

Then a commotion drew our eyes to the hall, as King Pelles the Fisher King, my grandfather, stepped from the dark, flame-flickered interior into the dusk. He walked leaning on a staff, clinging to the thing with two hands because he was old and lame, and though he must have heard the news already, his old eyes beneath their bushy brows were round as Roman coins as he regarded the cauldron.

'There will be no trouble,' he called out, taking a tremulous hand from the staff and hoisting it towards the crow-shields. 'No trouble here!' he called. His hair, so white, white as a dove's neck, ruffled in a breeze which carried the sour scent of the white wood sorrel which grew on the earthen bank in the shade of the palisade. 'Our guests are here in peace,' he shouted in his dry, thin voice, and this for our benefit. And now I heard Merlin behind me rasp a curse, because Melehan and Ambrosius came in the king's wake, walking slowly so as not to cause offence by overtaking the lame king. But then the brothers let King Pelles go on without them, having the sense to halt ten paces from where we sat our horses. For my weariness had flown from me like starlings startled from their roost, and I wanted to heel Seren into a canter and sink my spear into those traitors. Those sons of a traitor.

'Lord Gawain,' Melehan said. 'My lords,' he added, nodding in greeting at Parcefal and Gediens; a feigned respect as ill-fitting as the smile on his brother's face. 'It is good to see—'

'What are you doing here?' Gawain interrupted him, having no use for false courtesy. But far from taking insult, Melehan nodded, as though the cold faces which he looked up at were only to be expected.

'We came to offer King Pelles an alliance with Queen Morgana and King Cerdic.' He threw his hands wide and half turned to his host the king. 'For Gwynedd is not so far away from Camelot.'

'Nowhere is far enough away from traitors and Saxons,' Gawain muttered, as some of the men around me cursed and spat to hear this confirmation that Lady Morgana had married the Saxon king, as she had told us she would when the Beltane fires licked the night sky. Nor could I believe that Mordred's sons could be truly happy about it either, to see their grandmother wedded to the man whose war bands had, since the days of Arthur, stalked across Britain like predators scavenging for flesh. But the marriage ensured Melehan and Ambrosius the rule of Dumnonia, perhaps even as Pendragons of Britain, their twin high seats set upon the raised dais of Arthur's old hall at Camelot, casting long shadows over these Dark and yet still darkening Isles. Gods but I hated them. My gelding sensed it in me and whinnied and pawed at the muddy ground.

'Sadly, King Pelles has declined our queen's offer of an accord,' Ambrosius said, making sure to let no ill will show in his face. The men and women who had gathered at news of our return stood around uneasily, their eyes jumping from us to the groups of crow-shields, fearing a fight and yet drawn towards the cauldron. Meanwhile, the wives and families of the men who had not returned had eyes only for the horses they knew and the empty saddles upon their backs. Heedless of the potential violence, indifferent to the treasure of Britain for which their men had died, they clung to each other, little islands of grief in a sea of conflicting currents.

'If you've had your answer, why are you still here?' Gawain asked, looking from brother to brother.

'They are my guests, Lord Gawain.' King Pelles turned a hard eye towards Gawain. 'I have their word that there will be no bloodshed, as I will have yours.'

Gawain looked at me. Not at Cai or Gediens or Parcefal, but me. I think he could feel the hatred on me, as a hand feels the heat of a flame even from a distance, and I knew that if I said that we should fight the crow-shields, Gawain would unleash a savage fury upon them.

'No, Galahad.' Merlin was behind me and must have seen the way Gawain was looking at me. 'There has been enough death. Now is not the time,' the druid said, despite the cruelties which he had suffered at the twins' hands. 'We have the cauldron. It is our only concern.'

I twisted in the saddle to look at Iselle, who sat mounted beside Taliesin, holding his hand with her free hand while she gripped the long knife in the other. The boy looked more frightened of the crowds who had gathered around us than he had of the ncamh-mairbh and their dreadful caves. It must have been a long time since he had seen so many people together.

I straightened and shook my head at Gawain, who blinked in a gesture of understanding, while King Pelles sent servants forward to lift the two shrouded corpses from the horses over which they had been slumped and carried with such indignity home.

'The king and queen have taken your failure to go to Camelot and swear fealty as a declaration of war.' Melehan's voice rose so that all might hear. 'And yet here you are, not standing with Lord Constantine, whose pitiful army will be routed before midsummer.'

'Which has us thinking,' his twin brother said, taking up the thread as easily as if it were a game between them, 'that perhaps you don't intend to fight a war which you know you cannot win, but have come all this way in search of a wedding gift worthy of Queen Morgana and King Cerdic.'

With that he pointed at the cauldron, a smile lifting the moustaches on his narrow face. 'It does not look much to me, but I'm sure Merlin can tell us why it was worth men's lives.' He gestured at the bodies of Fiacha and Guidan being carried past King Pelles towards his hall.

'I am still waiting for your word that there will be no bloodshed here, Lord Gawain,' the king said, leaning on his staff. With considerable effort he lifted that stick and pointed it at Lord Cai before sweeping it towards some of the other red-plumed warriors who sat their horses around the ancient treasure of the druids. 'These men may be your brothers in arms, but they serve me. They are sworn to *me*.' This last was spoken to Gawain but meant for those men themselves.

'On my honour, lord king,' Gawain dipped his head, his helmet catching the dying light of the day, 'I want nothing but ale and a bed.'

The king accepted that and told Lord Cai to bring the Cauldron of Annwn into his hall, where we would be welcome to sleep, while the Lords Melehan and Ambrosius and their spearmen would spend the night outside the fort in the grazing meadow beyond the south wall.

'I would offer you the floor of my hall again, but my men have suffered much,' he explained to Melehan and Ambrosius. The king – my grandfather, I reminded myself – was old and lame, but he was no fool. He knew that we must guard the cauldron. Not that it went well with Morgana's grandsons. Melehan's mouth worked, as though swallowing something foul, while Ambrosius crossed his arms over his chest, a thumb pressed to his lips as if to keep in words which wanted to be spoken.

'We understand, lord king,' Melehan said.

'We will leave for Camelot at dawn, King Pelles,' Ambrosius said. 'If you change your mind about the queen's offer, we would be honoured to speak with you again in the morning.'

'If you live as long as I have, young Melehan, you will learn that changing one's mind takes too much precious time and strength,' King Pelles said, and with that he winked at young Taliesin, though he must have wondered who the boy was. 'Besides which,' he said, twisting around the staff to look back at Melehan, 'it takes a better memory than I possess. If one changes one's mind like the wind, how can you be sure what your current position is?'

Melehan mumbled some reply to this but the king was not listening now, as he limped to where I sat astride Seren and stroked the gelding's muzzle as though the two of them were old friends.

'I am glad to see you unharmed, Galahad.' He searched my face with his pale blue gaze. 'But you are tired, I see. And you have suffered.' He frowned, his white brows drawing together. 'And you have changed, too,' he continued, studying my face.

'We are all tired, lord king,' I said. 'Grandfather,' I added, forcing a smile which I knew had not reached my eyes.

But the old man's smile was warm and sad, and he nodded as if in thanks for that small thing. 'Come, then, my boy, and take your rest.' He gestured with his staff towards the hall, whose thatch of wheat straw, usually grey, was made new again by the setting sun. On the crest of that roof, upwind of the smoke seeping out through the thatch, sat a hawk, watching us with its fierce yellow eye. Grey-brown plumage. Bars across its chest. A female. I spun a picture in my mind. My father as a boy, with such a bird as this on his arm. The two of them passing the days together. Yet both alone in their way.

'Comfort awaits you all,' the king announced, breaking the spell that had bound me for a moment. Around us, the others were dismounting, stretching aching muscles, chasing the numbness from legs and backsides, as stewards and grooms came to lead their horses to stable. 'Tomorrow you will tell us how you retrieved the cauldron,' the king said. 'We will give the names of the fallen to the gods,' he added, loud enough for the grieving to hear, 'and we will raise our cups to honour them.'

I threw my leg over Seren's back and slid to the ground, my armour, cloak and helmet pulling me down as if through deep water, down and down to the depths. I had never been so tired and could have fallen asleep on my feet had my legs the strength to hold me upright.

A boy took Seren's reins and I started, for a heartbeat wanting to snatch the reins back, to not be separated from the gelding. But I knew that he and the other horses would be fed and brushed and guarded well and so I told Seren I would see him soon enough and then I walked towards the hall, following Gawain, Parcefal and Lord Cai, who went in after Merlin and the cauldron.

'So, boy, who are you?' I heard the Fisher King say.

'Taliesin, lord king,' the boy replied.

'I am pleased to meet you, Taliesin,' my grandfather said, and Taliesin must have been sure enough to let go of Iselle's hand, because she was beside me now. I could smell her sweat on the air, sweet and earthy, and I breathed of it deeply as we walked together towards the king's hall, the crow-shields among the crowd watching us as we went.

Beech and birch, alder and oak. The deep woods falling from the hillside down into a valley, a flowing current of tremulous, wind-stirred leaves which I follow, my wings supple, my heart beating in my breast, the wind coursing through my feathers. Then down to the pocket of air which hugs the land and in which the sparhawk can be what she was born to be. Elusive like a ghost. Here, and then gone. A killer.

Skimming dog-rose and bramble, mossy tree stump and bracken, fast and low now like a scythe. Then up to the outstretched arm and the leather glove which is rich with the boy's scent and the scent of blood.

This boy, this loyal Lancelot, is the only one she trusts. He has fed her and protected her, and his fierce eye is a comfort. She hates all others. But she tolerates the boy. And now, in this wet, grey dawn, she would kill for him.

Half hidden behind a stunted trunk, we wait, making no sound. I feel the hawk's body drawn tight like a knot, her sinews clenched in readiness, and I feel, even through the leather glove, the boy is just as tense, just as eager.

There, the rock dove. The boy has seen it too; I feel the spate of the blood in his arm, though he has not made any movement. Then, we ghost off the glove, quick and low against the ground, and up, and I feel the dove's terror as the talons pierce her flesh. Feel her life flee like a breath, and then we bank round and drop the torn and bloody body at the boy's feet.

I could unbraid my soul from the hawk's and fly. But I like being close to the boy and so I stay awhile and watch him. I feed from his hand and let him stroke my wing and neck, and when he leaves me tethered to the perch, I watch for his return, wanting to punish him for going.

Then the door opens, and thin light floods the darkness, hurting my eye, but I know by the scent that it is not him, but another boy. And I feel the hate on this one. I tell myself to go, to sever my bond with this creature and find another soul to cling to.

Go now!

But I stay. I watch this boy come close and I feel the hawk's fear. It wells up in her racing heart and spreads to her outstretched wings, and she shrieks, warning this stranger to stay away, threatening him, yet he comes closer still, and we bate, wings attacking the empty air, and this gives the boy pause, for he must see the fury in our eye. But his hatred is stronger than his fear, and he snatches up a fire iron from beside the hearth.

Go! Leave this creature!

He lifts his arm and I know I should be away, should send my spirit soaring, but I don't, and the fire iron comes down, striking my wing, and the pain is like nothing I've ever known.

Fly!

The hawk shrieks and tries to bate, and the boy takes a hold of the leash and winds it around our broken right wing, once, twice, and we fight, stabbing at him, drawing blood on his arm, then he backhands us off the perch and the leash pulls taut and now we are spinning around and around, and screaming in pain and rage and fear.

I had never been more tired, yet sleep would not come. I lay looking up at the bird-dung-spattered roof beams and the drifting spider silk and the underthatch upon which flamelight played as fitful as my mind. Some of the men had fallen into sleep the very moment their heads fell upon the furs or the cloaks which they had rolled up to use as pillows. Their snores made a ragged, discordant chorus, at times coalescing, then breaking apart again, like surf in the suck and plunge of shoreline rocks. Others talked in low voices, a soft and ceaseless drone, and a few, who like me could find no sleep, sat drinking their way to numbness. And in the middle of us all, silent and yet alive in the firelight, pulsing like a fevered heart, sat the Cauldron of Annwn. An ancient and empty vessel, and yet not empty at all but brimming with ghosts, boiling with the whispers of the dead who would not let me sleep.

I rolled over and saw the whites of Iselle's eyes. On her far side, Taliesin was sound asleep, his face so serene, so beautiful, it seemed impossible that he had seen such terrible things in his short life.

'There is no other way,' Iselle whispered.

I nodded. We held each other with our eyes a long time, and then, silently, we rose and made our way to where Gawain sat in the shadows beyond the hearth light's reach. We crouched by him, and he looked from Iselle to me and put a finger to his lips before glancing over to where Lord Cai lay amongst his bed skins, perhaps sleeping, perhaps not. Looking back to me, Gawain nodded that I should speak, and in that moment, I knew that I did not really need to say anything.

'You know what must be done,' I said in a voice barely louder than a whisper.

'I do,' he said.

'You gave your word ...' I said, meaning his pledge, demanded by King Pelles, that he would spill no blood.

'I don't value my honour as once I did,' he said, too tired even to lie to himself. 'But we can't ask Cai.'

That was a blow, yet I understood it. Cai had already given much and lost much, and Gawain would not now ask his friend to disobey his sworn lord or, worse, to bring shame upon him by desecrating the hospitality which the king had extended to his guests from Camelot.

'And you?' Gawain asked me. 'You are his blood.'

I recalled how the king had looked at me out in the yard. He had seen something in me which had not been there when first we met. I knew he had seen it because I had felt it in me. Like a welling up of dark water, or like a dream whose malevolence clings to you long after the dream itself is forgotten.

'What choice do we have?' I asked. I did not know my grandfather beyond the one night we had spent talking of my mother. And yet it was because we both shared her that I dreaded the disappointment which I would see in the old man's pale eyes after it was done. When he would no longer see his daughter in me. Only my father.

But I had seen the way the Princes Melehan and Ambrosius looked at us when we rode in through the gates with the cauldron. There was every chance that they would attack us this very night, that they were already gathering out there in the dark with steel and fire. But they need not go to that trouble, nor go to war with King Pelles. All they need do was leave at dawn as promised and wait for us in the forests or hills of Gwynedd or

Powys. They knew that we meant to take the cauldron south, back to Dumnonia, or Cornubia perhaps, though they cannot have known what we wanted with it. They would try to keep Merlin alive, but they would slaughter the rest of us and carry the treasure back to Morgana, who had always put store by the gods and would use the cauldron's power for her own ends.

All this was as certain as the dawn, and so we must kill in the night.

Iselle hushed us, looking back round towards the fire. There were eyes glowing softly in the dimness. Eyes reflecting the flames which flapped in the hearth, lazy as a pennant in a gentle breeze. Parcefal and Gediens were watching us. So was Cadwy, his scarred face leering and savage-looking in the half-light. And Merlin, who just moments before had looked to be asleep, was now sitting cross-legged beside the cauldron, one hand upon it, fingers tracing the figures and shapes which had been hammered into the metal so very long ago yet which could barely be discerned now beneath the sooty crust. But his eyes were on us. Perhaps, like us, these others could find no sleep and had watched us cross the firelight to Gawain, curious to know what we were talking about.

Then another figure crouched down in the shadow beside us, pulling his long moustaches through a fist of knuckles gnarled as old tree roots.

'So,' Lord Cai said, his eyes flicking from Gawain to Iselle to me. 'How do we do it?'

We were ghosts. Spirit walkers stalking through a night haunted by bat and fox, badger and polecat and, now and then, the blood-stilling shriek of an owl in the woods to the west of the Fisher King's hall. A night haunted by us, too, for we had made ourselves a part of it, rubbing dirt onto the backs of our hands and besmirching our faces and necks. Throwing dark cloaks around ourselves to prevent starlight and the last cold light of the waning moon from catching in the bronze scales or iron rings of our armour, or on sword hilts. We wore no helmets, having stashed them in sacks tied to our saddles, and those with horses whose coats were white, or partly white, had laid dark animal skins upon them, or smeared the white patches with mud.

I recalled that night when I had stolen out of the monastery of Ynys Wydryn and taken a coracle into the marsh, afraid of the thrys, those creatures who dwelt among the sedges and in the secret fears of men. And I thought that we seven who had left by the north gate and rode now, round-shouldered, heads slung low, silent as the dead, were more like the thrys than men.

We rode north across ancient earthworks or burial mounds which humped the ground like the arched backs of sleeping dragons, using the fort behind us to shield us from the sight of those camped outside the main southern gate. Then we turned and rode eastward onto grazing meadow, following an old track which wound up towards a rocky ridge upon which a copse stood dark and forbidding against the night sky, like the palisade of some other fortress.

I rode at the rear of our little column, now and then twisting in the saddle to peer into the night, my ears alert for any sound not of our own making. And we made hardly a sound, just the occasional scuff of hooves or a horse's snorting breath, or the soft clink of one chewing its bit, for they were nervous too, of our blackened faces and of being out in the dark and because they could sense our unease.

In front of me rode Merlin and in front of him the Cauldron of Annwn swung gently beneath the two spears which were lashed to the saddle horns of Gediens and Parcefal's horses. Iselle led us, a cloaked and cowled figure, her strung bow lying across the saddle horns in front of her, just as my own spear lay in front of me, its blade looking forge-black because I had smeared it with molten tallow and thrust it in the hearth ashes.

No one spoke as we walked our mounts up towards that copse, but perhaps I was not alone in beginning to think that we had escaped unnoticed, that we had succeeded beyond what we had thought possible in merging with the night itself, in making ourselves as invisible as the dead who pass through the veil on Samhain.

I was thinking this even as Seren's ears swivelled and twitched and I felt him quiver beneath me, for he had heard them before any of us. But then I saw them. We all did. Men on the higher ground to the south-east, lit by the moon, hurrying up towards the same ridge line. Iron helmets and round shields. Spear blades pointing at the sky. Men of Dumnonia. Men who should have been fighting alongside Lord Constantine or guarding Camelot's earthen defences against King Cerdic's Saxons. But these Britons served the sons of Mordred and so they were our enemies.

'We keep going,' Gawain growled.

The crow-shields were on foot, but even so we could not hope to outrun them, not with the cauldron suspended between Parcefal and Gediens, and their horses joined by two seven-foot lengths of ash. So, we rode on as if we had not seen them loping like wolves through the tall grass, and I felt the battle thrill awaken in my flesh. Felt the quickening of my heart and my blood flooding in spate to the muscles in my thighs and through my arms to the hands gripping rein and spear.

'Keep going,' Gawain said again.

Melehan and Ambrosius had known that we must try to

escape that night or else be slaughtered in the Gwynedd hills far from the Fisher King's protection, and so their men had stood watch in the dark, waiting for us to fly the roost. And when they had seen us, they must have thought us fools for supposing we could make ourselves as invisible as the pine marten and slip away with our lives and the ancient treasure of Britain. I imagined the grins on the brothers' faces as they hurried up the drover's path beyond the spine of land to our right, eager to gain the high ground and put cold dread in our hearts when they revealed themselves to us. As they did now, striding up onto the crest of the ridge to the right of the trees, so that they showed against the skyline.

Iselle lifted a hand and pulled back on the reins and we all did the same, halting at once, as if we had seen the crow-shields for the first time. One of the horses whinnied and Gawain's mare shied, jumping sideways so that he fought to wheel her back around, though I suspected he had feigned the whole thing.

'We want the cauldron,' Melehan or Ambrosius – it was impossible to know which – called down.

'And we want the druid,' the other brother yelled.

They knew we had come too far to turn around and ride back to the safety of the fort, but they must also have known we would never give them the cauldron. Nor Merlin either.

'Come and take them,' Gawain shouted, and he dismounted, which was his way of showing that we did not intend to run. It was his invitation to Mordred's sons to walk down the hill and slaughter us, to finish the bloody work which their father had begun that day ten years ago when he had turned on Arthur and betrayed Britain. When so many brave warriors had fallen beneath Saxon and Dumnonian blades, and my father, too, had fallen.

Parcefal and Gediens, who could not have fought on horseback anyway with the cauldron slung between them, dismounted then, and so Iselle and I climbed down, she taking the bow from her saddle while I took my helmet from the sack tied to the saddle horn and ran my fingers through the white horsehair plume before putting it on.

'Stay close,' I told Iselle, throwing off my cloak and unslinging the shield from my back.

She gave me a wicked grin. 'Don't get in the way of my arrows,' she said, taking a white-fletched shaft from her bag and nocking it to the bow string.

'Shields.' Gawain pushed his helmet down and closed the cheek pieces. Gediens and Parcefal stepped up beside him, their own helmets glowing dully against their dirt-smeared faces, and I put myself on the right of the line, half expecting Gawain to tell me to get in the middle, for being on the right is the most dangerous place to stand because you have no neighbour's shield to protect your right side. But neither Gawain nor any of the others said anything and I took that as a sign of respect and my heart thumped, wild and urgent, and my ears were full of my own pulsing blood.

'Here they come,' Gediens said as the brothers brought their spearmen down the southward-facing slope of the ridge.

For now, Iselle stood in front of us all, an arrow on the bow string and two more stuck in the ground by her right foot. I hoped she would not take any chances but get behind us before our enemies were close enough to throw their spears.

Merlin stood to our rear with Taliesin, the horses and the cauldron. I could hear him murmuring some incantation and I wondered if the crow-shields felt any doubt at all, any creeping fear as they strode down the slope towards us, knowing that we had a druid with us, for all that we made the most pitiful shieldwall they had likely ever faced.

Iselle loosed and I saw the white fletchings streak towards our enemies and heard the thunk as the shaft embedded in a shield. I looked over my shoulder, back down towards the distant fort, which was shrouded in darkness, though a pall of hearth-fire smoke showed as a lighter brown against the charcoal sky.

'Is that all of them?' Parcefal was leaning forward as if that would help his old eyes see the crow-shields better.

'It's enough,' Gediens said, as another arrow flew from Iselle's bow, disappearing somewhere out there among the warriors whose shield bosses and helmets now and then caught some little moonlight and vanished again in the dark. There were at least forty men trudging down the slope towards us, which meant that Melehan and Ambrosius had probably brought their whole force up from their camp outside the southern wall of King Pelles's fort. Which was what we had hoped they would do.

'Iselle!' I called, because our enemies were close enough now that I could see the soft white glow of their faces and the sheen of belt buckles, knife hilts and those domed shield bosses of polished iron.

As Iselle pulled another arrow from her bag, a spear buried itself in the earth just three feet in front of her. Yet she did not flinch but nocked the arrow, drew and loosed, and I did not see that arrow fly but I heard the man it struck scream in the night and saw him fall, clutching his face.

'Iselle!' I called again and another spear appeared in the ground beside her as if it had suddenly sprouted from the soil. She drew once more and this next arrow tonked off a man's helmet and then she turned and strode back to our position, fitting another swan-feathered shaft to her bow as she walked.

'Don't you die, Galahad,' Gawain growled at me from the other end of the shieldwall. Our enemies were so close now that even in the dark I could see the crows which they had painted on their shields in honour of Lady Morgana. And I hated them for it.

'Protect the horses and the cauldron,' Parcefal said.

I lifted my shield and levelled my spear. I could smell the approaching spearmen now. Wool grease and sweat. Leather and dung and the onions they had eaten.

And they came for us just as we had hoped that they would.

A horn blared in the night somewhere to our left beyond the sloping ground to the west. A horn whose braying note had filled Lord Arthur's enemies with gut-twisting terror so many times over the years, and now sounded again with breath from the same lungs as then. And following in the wake of that fateful note, the thunder of hooves rumbling through the earth, as over the rise came horsemen with levelled spears and helmet plumes flying and yelling to their gods and for Arthur.

The crow-shields had not formed a wall of limewood and steel. They had not needed to, thinking they would flood over us, as cold shadow surges across the land when the sun falls to the horizon. But now they turned to see the wave of steel-tipped death rolling towards them across the hillside, and some of them bunched together and threw up their shields, while others, driven by some desperate and vain instinct, turned away and fled. And perhaps if cloud had veiled the moon at that moment, some of them might have found sanctuary in darkness. But as it was, the silvery light fell like a blade across that land.

Lord Cai rode at the tip of the wedge formation and so was the first to strike, though in half a heartbeat the others hit too and a terrible noise rent the night; the splintering of shields and bone, the clang and clash of steel and the screams of the dying and the shrieking of horses and the shattering of men.

Cai and the others broke through the ruin they had wrought, spurring their mounts on across the slope, for they were just fifteen strong and Cai knew that if they got snarled up in a melee with so many spearmen, the enemy's numbers would tell and men and horses would die. But neither would horses charge a well-built shieldwall, and so Cai yelled for his men to wheel their horses and form the wedge again, which they did with the fluid ease of long practice.

'Shieldwall! Shieldwall!' Ambrosius was yelling, and though the crow-shields were scattered across the slope like autumn leaves before the wind, many of them had found their wits amongst the wreckage of the night and were hurrying to either Ambrosius or Melehan, who was a spear-throw away on the left, roaring commands and beating his spear against his shield.

But Cai and his cataphracts were cantering again, plumes dancing, shields bouncing on their backs, their war horses' iron-shod hooves drumming their three-beat gait upon the ground.

'By the gods, I've missed that sight,' Parcefal bellowed, as Cai and his men spurred into a gallop and that wedge punched through Ambrosius's loose wall, and spears plunged down and the horses in their leather armour broke men where they stood. This time Cai didn't lead them on but wheeled his grey Andalusian and drew his sword and his men did the same, pressing among the living, the dead and the dying, hacking down with their swords like men chopping down briars around some long-abandoned shrine.

Over on the left, Melehan had gathered a score of spearmen now who were as yet untouched by Cai's second charge. By the grey light I could see them arraying themselves shoulder to shoulder, left legs forward, feet planted, shields overlapping, and I knew they would be hard to beat.

'To Cai!' I yelled, and then I was running, my breath loud inside my helmet, my legs working hard, though the weight of my scale coat and leather tunic, my shield and greaves felt as nothing. All I felt was the hunger to kill. Perhaps some part of me knew that if Melehan brought his wall of warriors into the melee against Cai, the cataphracts would eventually be speared in their saddles or pulled from their mounts and butchered on the ground. But in that moment the battle lust was in me and so I ran towards the killing, towards the carnage of steel and flesh, and only when I was amongst it, like a stone around which a river flows, did I realize that Gawain and Gediens, Parcefal and Iselle had run with me.

I killed men. My spear was a living thing in my hands, its blade ripping and piercing, and when I left it in an enemy's guts, I drew Boar's Tusk and reaped lives with that blade as my father had done before me. I was fast and strong, and I had some skill, but I was also savage, and I saw that savagery reflected in the terrified eyes of those I killed.

'For Arthur!' Parcefal bellowed, lopping off an arm which fell with the shield still attached.

'Arthur!' Gediens echoed, plunging his spear through the neck of a man who was trying to spear one of Cai's riders from behind. The whinnies of horses and the screams of men blended in a terrible cacophony and I scythed men down until my sword hand was slippery with blood and my face was slick with sweat and blood, and then there was no one left to kill.

'Form up! Form up!' Lord Cai was yelling, pulling his grey gelding round in tight circles, his bloodied sword raised to the waning moon like an offering.

'Enough, Cai!' Gawain roared. He was bent double, heaving breath into his lungs, but he was watching the crow-shields who stood in their wall some eighty paces away.

All around me were dead men and none of them our own.

'Hold!' Cai and his men fought to control their horses, the animals' blood running hot in their great muscles, their flesh quivering with the terror and thrill of the fight.

Parcefal and Gediens were gathering up spears and handing them to the riders so that they would not have to dismount to arm themselves again should Cai give the order to attack Melehan's shieldwall. Iselle was retrieving her arrows. I watched her pull one from a dead man's throat and bend to wipe the point on the grass.

'Are you hurt?' I asked her.

'No,' she said. 'You?'

I shook my head and Iselle thrust the arrow back into the bag on her belt, then nodded to draw my attention to something behind me.

Gripping his sword in two hands, Gawain raised it above his head and for a moment the polished blade hung there like a judgement which will bind the fates of men, then it came down onto the dark shape in the grass by his feet. He wrestled with the blade to free it and brought it up above his head again, and this time he roared with effort as he hacked down. He bent, snatched something up with his left hand, straightened and set off across the slope towards our enemies.

'Galahad, with me,' he commanded, and so I fell in at his right shoulder, breathing hard, blinking sweat from my eyes, my own blood still in spate and my hand sticky on Boar's Tusk's leather and silver-bound hilt, which was slathered with other men's blood.

'Melehan!' Gawain called. 'Melehan ap Mordred ap Arthur!'

Mordred's son pushed his way out of the shieldwall and set himself in front of his men, who stood firm though they must have been inwardly reeling to have seen half their number butchered in the time it takes a man to bridle and saddle his horse. They were men of Britain and they would never have thought they would have to face Arthur's famous horse warriors.

'Look, traitor,' Gawain's voice carried in the still night air, 'son of a traitor.' With that he lifted his left arm and held up the severed head by its dark hair. The gory neck dripped rhythmically into the grass.

From the tightness of the prince's face, Melehan already knew that his brother was dead. That all of his men save those at his back lay where they had fallen and would never rise again. But seeing now his brother's dead face, its moon-washed pallor, the sightless eyes and the grimace, where just moments before there had been vigorous life, Melehan coughed and spluttered and spewed steaming puke onto the sheep's sorrel.

Gawain pointed his gore-slick sword at me. 'This here is Galahad,' he said.

'I know who he is,' Melehan spat, dragging a hand across his mouth.

Gawain nodded. 'Then you'll remember his father. Lancelot ap Ban. Reaper of lives. Slayer of Saxons and killer of men. The greatest warrior since Taranis, lord of war, walked the land.' Melehan did not answer this but spat a glistening string of foulness into the grass. 'Galahad here just killed your brother,' Gawain said, 'butchered him like a man putting down a rabid dog.'

Melehan's eyes turned on me, the hatred in them sharp and raw, and I glared back at him, then glanced at the head which Gawain was still holding up, because I could not remember fighting Ambrosius and thought that another look at his dead face might recall it to my mind.

'We have a new lord of war, Melehan ap Mordred.' Gawain

lifted the point of his sword towards me again. 'Go and tell Lady Morgana and that Saxon swine Cerdic that. We have Galahad ap Lancelot.' With that he hurled Ambrosius's head at Melehan, who all but jumped out of the way and watched horrified as his brother's head rolled across the ground, coming to rest by the foot of one of the spearmen behind him.

'Go, traitors,' Gawain commanded those men of Camelot.

They looked at each other and they looked to their lord, who for the moment just stood there, his eyes still in me like hooks. But even Melehan knew that to stay was to die. He could not have known that we had attacked him without the Fisher King's blessing, and so he must have believed that even if by some miracle he could beat us there on that corpse-strewn slope, the king would send spearmen after him and they would die before the dawn.

'Go now,' Gawain said.

The big warrior behind Melehan's right shoulder pointed his spear across the hillside. 'What about our dead?' he asked.

'They are traitors to Dumnonia and will be left for the crows and the dogs,' Gawain answered. 'But you may take that.' He pointed his sword at the head which lay amongst the sorrel, staring up at the night sky.

Melehan did not turn to look at it but gestured for one of his men to pick up the head, which someone did, wrapping it in the cloak which he had taken off his own back, tying it closed with a belt.

'You cannot win,' Melehan told Gawain, then lifted his chin. 'You are ghosts!' he bellowed so that Lord Cai and all of the others could hear. 'You are ghosts from the past. Soon enough you will join the dead and I will be High King. I will be High King!'

I felt Gawain beside me tense and for a heartbeat we both

thought that Melehan was going to fight, that his men would beat their swords against their shields and the butchery would begin again. But then Melehan pointed his spear into the east and walked away and his men followed him, half watching us as they went, as though they did not trust the gift of life which Gawain had given them. As though they expected Lord Cai's warriors to spur their mounts and charge, their spear points thirsting for blood.

But Lord Cai and his men just sat their mounts, their spears laid across their saddles before them, and watched those men go.

'We'll have to fight them again,' Parcefal said, coming to stand beside me. Iselle and Gediens were with him.

'We will,' Gawain said.

'Only, there'll be more of them than there are hairs on a bear's arse,' Parcefal said.

'There will,' Gawain agreed.

'But we will have Arthur,' Iselle said.

No one answered that, and I thought of what Merlin had told me, that he feared that even with the cauldron he would not be able to bring Lady Guinevere's mind back to her body. And without Guinevere there would be no Arthur.

'I'll send men to make sure they leave Gwynedd,' Lord Cai said.

'They'll leave,' Gawain said. 'Let the men rest. They've a long journey ahead of them.'

I saw no surprise in Cai's face. He rolled his shoulders and looked off into the night after the retreating column of spearmen.

'You're coming back?' Gediens asked him, looking from Cai to Gawain, as if expecting one of them to explain himself. Gawain stood watching Cai, his arms folded across his chest like a man guarding himself against the possibility that he's wrong. Beside him, Parcefal stood open-mouthed, also watching Cai, who twisted in the saddle, looking at the mounted men around him. Some of them nodded, their faces grim, granite-hard in the darker shadow of their helmets. Then at last Cai, lord of Arthur's horse warriors, looked down at Gawain.

'We're coming back,' he said. 'If there is a chance that Arthur will ride again, we have to.'

Gawain nodded. No smile on his scarred face. Just acceptance, an acknowledgement as if of something preordained. As inevitable as death.

20

Guinevere

W E MUST HAVE MADE a sight which would live long after
our deaths on the lyre strings of bards. A vision to linger in the mind like a dream which clings to the soul long years
after the night which spawned it. Men in bronze scale armour
and plumed, silver-chased helmets, each of which held the
flames of the summer sun, and their spear points tied with red
silken ribbons which caught the wind and played like tendrils
of blood in water. Men on war horses whose coats gleamed
upon their muscles and who wore, as proudly as the men on
their backs, their own armour: breastplates and shaffrons of
boiled leather rubbed with beeswax so that they looked like
polished oak. We rode south through Gwynedd and Powys
and Caer Gloui, and the ragged-looking folk in the fields, the
gaunt men scything the long grass while the women and straw-
limbed children followed in their wake, turning the hay so that
it dried evenly, and those shearing their sheep, taking the
fleeces early while they could, would stop their labours and
stare as we passed.

Some would ask who we were, and we would say we were
Lord Arthur's men come to reclaim Britain. Others would
watch us from a distance, not daring to approach, as if they
feared we were not men of flesh and blood but the spirits of men

returned to the land, come through the veil which separates this world from the world beyond, as if seeking vengeance for the betrayals of the past.

And in a way that is what we were.

Lord Cai sent riders to the lords of Britain, to King Catigern and King Bivitas and Lord Cyndaf of Caer Celemion, telling them to forge spear blades and swords, to make arrows and shields, and to gather their spearmen and prepare for war. For Arthur would come again, they said, and so he who does not make ready to fight beneath the banner of the bear is a traitor to the land of his ancestors and an enemy of the gods of Britain.

We also sent a man east to Caer Lerion to find Lord Constantine and tell him to march his men south into Dumnonia, for it was in Dumnonia that Arthur's heart had beat loudest and where the echoes of his past glories could still be heard, faint as the notes of distant war horns on the wind. And so it was in Dumnonia that we would make our stand.

King Pelles had been sad to see me go, but I think I was not the same man leaving his hall as the one who had come, and that when my grandfather bid me farewell, the tears gathering in his old eyes as we stood in the shadowed courtyard, the sun not yet risen above the eastern palisade, he saw more of my father in me than my mother.

He had taken both my hands in his and nodded towards Iselle who was nearby, saddling her mare, her breath and the mare's pluming in the pre-dawn chill. 'She is the land and the hearth and the dream,' the king told me. 'Whatever else happens, Galahad, do not forget that.'

For a heartbeat I thought he knew that Iselle was Arthur and Guinevere's daughter, and I held my breath beneath his scrutiny, wondering how he knew it. Had Merlin told him? Or maybe the old man did not know the truth of who Iselle really was, but simply knew that I loved her – for I did love her – and his meaning was that it is for those we love that we must hope and dream and fight.

Whatever my grandfather knew, or did not know, I told him that I would remember his words and heed them. Then we had ridden out, each of us in turn dipping his ribbon-bound spear point to the king as we passed, Cai and his men giving thanks and honour and love to the man they had served for ten years and who had released them from his service now.

'You were always Lord Arthur's men,' Pelles had said, when Cai formally requested the king's permission to ride with us back to Dumnonia and war. 'I shall not see you again in this life.'

It was a sad parting, for King Pelles had been kind and generous to them and they had served him loyally, but it was true that they belonged to Arthur and he to them, and so we had ridden out through the gates with heavy hearts and to the sounds of weeping from King Pelles's people, who stood in the dawn and watched us until we were gone from their sight.

And these men, who had been gone from the world so long, now let the tears stream into their own beards as they saw for themselves the ruin of Britain. For the further east we rode, the more degradation and suffering we saw. Rounds left charred and smoking from some raid, men, women, children lying where they had been slain. We were forewarned of the dead by the crows and ravens thick upon them like black cloaks rippling in the breeze. The birds covetous of their feasts so that only when we came within a spear's length would they take wing, croaking with indignation. Or else it was the dogs that warned us of corpses among the ruins and ash, the beasts snarling at each other over their spoils of flesh, snarling at us too, though we kept our distance, for no one wanted to see such horrors if they could help it.

We saw men who had been mutilated and hung from low branches as warning to others of the fate which awaited those who dared fight. We saw women and children wandering the fields or drovers' paths, sometimes in small groups but often alone, perhaps the sole survivors of their household, walking as if lost or half asleep. We saw the smouldering remains of pyres and the piles of newly turned earth under which folk had buried their dead, and we saw gates shut against us and palisades lined with frightened faces, though we called out that we were Lord Arthur's men returned from Ynys Môn to fight against Lady Morgana and her Saxon king.

'You have been gone a long time, brother,' Gawain rumbled to Cai as we rode past a group of fugitives on the road, a dozen old men, women and children pushing handcarts or hefting their belongings in sacks on their backs. They had fled from their village on the northern border of Caer Celemion and sought protection now in the walled town of Caer Baddan, which the Romans called Aquae Sulis. And they watched us with expressions of fear, wonder and disbelief; though, seeing our bear-shields, one greybeard, who must have been old when Uther still reigned, told us he would take up his own shield and spear again if Arthur returned.

Lord Cai and his men saw much but said little, though it was clear that they were shocked to learn that Saxon war bands were pushing so far along the Tamesis valley. Some of them even dismounted to share their cheese and bread and ale with these dispossessed folk and it seemed to me that Arthur's horse warriors blamed themselves for not having been here to fight on in the years after the great battle. And yet how could men hope to prevent the shadows lengthening as summer gives way to autumn? Or the leaves falling from the trees?

When we came to the south of Caer Gloui we stayed by the coast, keeping as far from Camelot as was possible, for we knew that Melehan would have sent word of us and the cauldron to Lady Morgana and she would have spearmen out looking for us.

With provisions running low, we bought food where we could, and we hunted and foraged too and found that Taliesin was almost as knowledgeable as Merlin when it came to which plants, herbs and berries could be safely added to our broths. The boy even had us pulling up clumps of hellebore from shady spots beneath trees. These he dried over our camp fires before cutting up the flowers and giving some to each of us to distribute about our person. For this was a charm which would make us invisible to our enemies, Taliesin said, and when some of the men had looked to Merlin, seeking confirmation of this, Merlin grinned and asked them why in the name of the gods would they doubt the word of a boy who had survived alone for a year on an island of man-eating cave dwellers.

Fourteen days after leaving Ynys Môn we were back amongst heath, fen and marsh, where the harrier, the bittern and the great white egret ruled and the air was thick with insects and the reed-beds teemed with resonant life. We left Lord Cai and his men in oak woodland to the north-west of Ynys Wydryn, whose tor we could see wreathed in morning mist as night fled into the west, and Gediens, Parcefal, Gawain, Iselle, Taliesin, Merlin and I went on together. We took only two of the horses, which we needed to carry the cauldron, and left the others with Cai, for it was better not to risk taking them deeper into the marsh. And we pushed on past stands of elders and coppiced boles of sycamore and hazel which had not been tended for years and so now stood in groves forty feet high, the tall, straight poles shivering as we moved among them and Taliesin peering up at them with innocent wonder. Then, with the heat of the day waning and dusk not far away, we came sweat-drenched and tired to the high wall of dense reeds which surrounded Lord Arthur's steading like a golden palisade. And I realized that I was shivering like those coppiced boles, because we were returning to Arthur and Guinevere and we had the Treasure of Annwn and we carried the hopes of so many.

It was as if we had never been away. The little steading was unchanged, Guinevere still sat in her chair in the half-dark of the roundhouse, and Arthur seemed a desolate soul still, a man haunted by demons. A man trapped between the past and a future that never was. And yet, though he regarded the Cauldron of Annwn with suspicion verging on contempt, I saw some small flicker of fire in his blue eyes when Gawain told him that Cai and the last of his horse warrior companions had returned and were waiting nearby.

'The Fisher King let them go?' Arthur asked, his brow furrowed as he watched the sun, as round and orange-red as an egg yolk, slipping behind the reed wall to the west.

'Pelles is an old man,' Gawain said. 'He has no need of Cai now, but I don't think he would have stopped them leaving anyway. They would rather fight and die for you than die in their beds on Ynys Môn.'

Arthur said nothing to that, though I saw tears in his eyes as he watched the slow, ghostly flight of a nightjar as it trawled for moths above the reed-beds.

'I will try tomorrow, Arthur,' Merlin said. Then he, Iselle and Taliesin set about cleaning the cauldron, first by softening the sooty crust with hot water, then by rubbing at the dirt with cloths dipped in tallow.

'I daresay the king was happy to meet his grandson after all these years.' Arthur turned to me, trying to smile but failing.

'I think I reminded him of my father,' I replied, regretting the words because of course I had reminded Arthur of my father too, and that must have been to him like a knife in the old wound.

He nodded. 'Lancelot is in you, Galahad, just as Uther is in me and Constantine was in Uther.' He lifted an eyebrow and brought it down heavily. 'And I was in Mordred,' he added. There was a gruffness in his voice which could not hide the tone of regret. He turned away from me, back to the west, but the sun had slipped out of sight now and the air turned chill. 'Nothing we can do about that. They are in us. In our blood and marrow. In our heads, too,' he added, tapping two fingers against his temple, 'but we are not them. Our triumphs are our own to make. Our mistakes also. We may love, hope, hate, kill . . . regret.' He sighed. 'We don't need our fathers for any of that.'

He turned to me once more, and his face looked so gaunt now: dark pools beneath his eyes and in the hollows of his cheeks, as though the shadow that fell in the absence of the sun had sought out Arthur and clung to him and claimed him for its own. 'I loved your father,' he said. 'And I hated him.' He bit his lip and made a guttural sound deep in his throat. 'No, not hate. But I envied him. And there was a time when I wanted him dead. And yet, when I needed him one last time, he came.' He was not seeing me now but the past. Or one day in the past. The same day which I had lived a thousand times since, imagining a different ending. 'Lancelot changed the tide of that fight. He rode down to us and when my men saw him, when we all saw him, we felt hope again. I cannot believe but that the gods rode with him that day, for he fought like a god. But he died like a man. He died as my friend. As my brother.'

I tried to swallow. I clenched my teeth together and I believed this man, that he had loved my father. And perhaps for the first time I understood why my father had ridden down that hill and into that red carnage. Why he had ridden away from me.

'You are not him,' Arthur said. 'But in some ways, Galahad, you might hope to be like him.'

I thought about that, looking back towards the sun which was no longer there, before I answered. 'I will be honoured to fight for you as he did, lord.'

Arthur's lips pressed into a tight smile. 'I am not the one you will be fighting for,' he replied.

I would have asked him what he meant by that, but Taliesin called to us, excited to show us what he and Iselle and Merlin had uncovered.

The Cauldron of Annwn had been black and begrimed, so that Merlin had even been forced to use his eating knife to dig away the thick crust which had grown upon it over years of sacrilegious misuse and desecration. But underneath that layer of soot and grease the cauldron told another story, a tale of Britain and her gods and her heroes.

'It's silver,' Iselle told us, though we could see that for our-selves, even though only half of the surface had been uncovered. The cauldron had been made by fitting many silver plates together, the plates soldered in place with molten tin and strengthened with a hoop of iron around the rim. And those silver plates seemed alive now in the dusk as the light seeped from the world, each one decorated with figures: animal, human and divine, all of which stood proud of the metal, as if emerging from the silver itself, such was the skill of that master craftsman who had long ago hammered the plates from the inside to create the figures in relief on the outer surface.

I recognized the horse goddess Rhiannon riding the fleetest of steeds, and I saw creatures for whom I had no names, but which were horned and clawed and savage-looking. There were warriors holding swords aloft and sacred bulls and some god or hero riding in a chariot whose wheels resembled fiery suns. Each plate bore a different scene, stories perhaps known only to Merlin, tales which were told round hearth fires long before the Romans came to these island shores with their legions and their eagles.

'Here is Gofannon,' Merlin pointed at the figure who held a forge hammer in one hand and a sword in the other, 'and here, see, is the moon goddess Arianrhod.' He placed two fingers on the figure and on the past, touching the world which his druidic forebears had known.

Taliesin sat on the other side of the cauldron, rubbing at the silver with a cloth, his face under that thatch of dark hair clenched in concentration, his top teeth half buried in his bottom lip.

I peered inside the cauldron, trying not to think of what we had found there when we had come across it in the caves of the Isle of the Dead. The inner surface was badly tarnished, but on the bottom plate I could make out the central scene of three figures holding a fourth above a cauldron. I remembered what Merlin had told us about Annwn's Cauldron, that it could restore life itself. Is that what those figures were attempting? Were they placing the other into the cauldron to bring him back from the dead?

'It is beautiful,' I said.

'More beautiful than I ever imagined,' Merlin admitted. He looked up at the darkening sky. It seemed to me that he was looking for some sign from the gods, that they knew we had recovered this ancient treasure and were perhaps even grateful for its return.

Taliesin took his cloth away from the plate which he had been cleaning and turned his big eyes to Iselle. 'Eirianwen,' he said, saying the name with wonder, though quietly, as if careful not to invoke the goddess. 'She could change herself into a wolf.'

Merlin looked up at the boy. 'Eirianwen has been all but forgotten here.' He lifted a hand and fluttered skeletal fingers. 'She drifted away with the smoke from the sacred groves.' He tilted his head on one side as he regarded Taliesin. 'How is it that you know of her, child?' he asked.

Taliesin shrugged. 'She comes to me when I sing,' he said, the evenness of his voice belying the strangeness of the confession. Words which put a shiver in my flesh and made the hairs on my arms stand up. He ran a forefinger over the two finely wrought figures which he had uncovered: the goddess and the wolf. Arthur looked at Merlin. I looked at Iselle.

'Lord,' Taliesin said, lifting his gaze to Arthur, his unblemished skin so pale, but for the spread of brown speckles across his nose and cheeks, that you would have thought he had been the one living in a cave, beyond the sun's reach. 'I hope the lady will come back to you.' It was said with such pure feeling that it stole my breath.

Arthur couldn't summon the words to reply. He stared into the boy's large eyes, and it seemed to me that he was trying to remember what it was like to be so young, with all the years stretching before like a wide and dewy meadow to be galloped across. That he was trying to feel some of Taliesin's hope. His faith in unseen things. In gods and timeworn tales and in dreams only half remembered.

'Thank you, Taliesin,' he said at last. 'Thank you.' Then he turned and walked back to the house, leaving us with the Cauldron of Annwn and the tales of which it whispered, and I knew he would carry Guinevere to their bed and lie beside her in the night.

'I will begin at dawn, Arthur,' Merlin called after his old friend, who did not reply but nodded and then was gone.

I looked up and saw Gediens and Parcefal hefting a joint of meat and a brace of waterfowl which we had smoked and hung before setting off for Ynys Môn and the Isle of the Dead. They would take the food to Lord Cai and the others and I supposed that they would stay the night with them and perhaps the next day too, rather than linger here, helpless and tormented by fear and hope while Merlin performed his rites and endeavoured to restore Guinevere for the sake of the lady herself, and for Arthur, and for Britain.

I was woken by pallid dawn light spearing through cracks in the byre's roof. I found Iselle outside by the old willow stump, loosing arrows into a target of woven reeds. Nearby, Taliesin was on his knees playing with Banon, wrestling the black dog, placing Banon's forepaws upon his own shoulders as though the dog was some savage black beast which could not be withstood, and Banon growling to make good the fable. He looked like any other boy, giving himself utterly to the moment, so that it was strange to think of the power which he bore within himself. The talent by which he had bound those hateful and ill-favoured creatures in the darkness.

The dawn was damp and cold, and a mist was rising above the reed-beds. Now and then a bittern called from its hidden place in the marsh, a forlorn sound which spoke of loneliness and yearning.

'They've begun.' Iselle grunted as she sent another arrow, which thumped into the interlaced ring of marsh violets which she had made and pinned at the centre of the target.

I looked towards the house and immediately smelled the herb-tainted smoke leaking from Arthur's thatch. I went over to the target, pulled out the three shafts which were inside the ring of flowers and took them back to Iselle, keeping one in my right hand.

'Arthur is with them,' she said. 'Gawain is checking the traps.'

I nodded. She handed me the bow and I nocked the arrow to the string. There was old blood on the shaft near the iron head and some red staining on the white fletchings.

'Do you think she will be . . . normal,' Iselle asked me. 'When she comes back?'

I took a step forward as though lining myself up with the target. In truth I didn't want her to see my face. I pulled the string and pushed the bow and held the draw.

'How could she be as she was before, after so many years like this?' I asked, feeling the taut string and my fingertips on my chin. I wanted to tell her what Merlin had told me, about his doubts that he would be able to cure Guinevere even with the cauldron. But what purpose would that serve now, when the rites were under way and we would know soon enough if he had succeeded or failed?

'I was thinking how happy Arthur will be,' Iselle said, 'when she comes back to him. He will be *so* happy.'

I loosed and the arrow seemed to shiver in the air and struck the target with a thump. Outside the ring of marsh violets. I glanced at Iselle and lifted an eyebrow that asked her to say nothing about my poor shot.

'It's hard to imagine Arthur smiling,' she said. 'But he must have smiled when he and Guinevere were young, before he had to fight all the time. And before all the other things,' she added. There was no need to mention my father. We both knew what she had meant by *other things*. 'But it is hard to imagine a smile on that face now.'

'It is,' I said. 'But I hope he is smiling before the end of the day.' I truly did hope that even though the doubt sown by Merlin's words to me on the voyage back from the Isle of the Dead stayed with me.

I held out my hand. Iselle gave me another arrow. She frowned. 'What if Merlin brings Guinevere back and Arthur is so happy and the lady is happy, and he does not want to go to war again? Who wants to fight if they are busy being in love?'

I had fitted the arrow to the string, but I did not draw the bow. Instead, I turned to Iselle. 'Isn't love sometimes the reason why we fight? To protect it?' I looked over to where Taliesin was playing with Banon, the two engaged in a tug of war with a stick, the dog's long teeth revealed in a rolling snarl. 'To protect those we love?'

Iselle thought about this and I looked back at the target, exhaled slowly and loosed. The arrow streaked spear-straight and struck the woven reeds in the centre of the marsh violets.

'Lucky,' Iselle said.

I smiled. Then the roundhouse door clunked open and Arthur stood there, white smoke billowing around him, his face drawn and fearful and terrifying in the dawn. He caught my eye and, without a word, he walked off towards the marsh.

'Galahad, come,' Merlin called from inside the house. I looked at Iselle. She nodded that I should go, so I did, my stomach rolling over itself as I crossed the mist-damp ground, dreading what I would find inside.

At first, all I saw was smoke. It was thick and acrid, hanging in palls and slowly rising to the roof, and I saw that much of it was coming from the Cauldron of Annwn, which sat on stones above the hearth, too heavy to hang from the iron tripod like a normal cooking pot.

'Shut the door, you fool,' Merlin said. He was standing by the bed where Guinevere lay covered by a bear's fur. I coughed and blinked and turned to suck in one last breath of clean dawn air before pulling the door shut behind me. 'Here, come here,' the druid said. 'Hold this.'

I went to him and he handed me a wooden cup. Turning it in my hand, I saw that it was just like the one which Father Yvain had been turning on his lathe that day the infant boy had died on Ynys Wydryn.

'Do precisely what I say.' Merlin took Guinevere's arm out from under the fur and laid it on top.

'And Arthur?' I said, thinking that he should be here doing this, not I.

Merlin reached to the table at the head of the bed and took up his knife, which was already unsheathed, its blade honed and polished and wicked-looking. 'I sent him out looking for bugleherb,' he said. 'Which men sometimes call thunder and lightning.'

'Will it help?' I asked, feeling a creeping chill in my flesh despite the hearth flames which now and then licked up the sides of the Cauldron of Annwn, tormenting the figures who seemed to writhe in light and shadow upon its silver surface.

'Bugleherb can be useful,' Merlin said, distractedly. 'Good for cuts and bruises, for stomach ulcers. For healing.' He lifted Guinevere's arm, which was as thin as a birch sapling, then placed the tip of the knife blade on her pale forearm where, by the fitful light of a rush flame, the green veins showed just beneath the skin. 'I needed Arthur out of the way. Try working with him glaring at you.' One of his white brows lifted as he gestured for me to hold the cup beneath the lady's arm. 'Besides, he wouldn't like this part,' he said, pressing the point in to pierce the skin, then drawing the knife along Guinevere's arm, slicing into the flesh.

I winced to see it, though there was no sharpening of her eyes in pain. No flinch of her arm at the blade's bite. She just lay there, staring up at the thatch, her face drawn but peaceful-looking. Her hair shining like the gloss upon a raven's wing.

There was more blood than I expected. It was bright and hot, running in rivulets across that pale skin and dripping from it, tapping an urgent rhythm into the cup, which I held with two hands so as to ensure I did not waste a single drop. When it was full, I held the cup while Merlin bound the wound, and tried to avoid looking into Guinevere's face. Yet I could not stop myself. What would my father think if he could see her lying there like this, trapped in this living death?

'Here,' Merlin said, taking the cup from me and walking it over to the cauldron. There he stood a while, muttering under his breath, invoking gods and the ancient knowledge of his order. Then he poured Guinevere's blood into the cauldron and it hissed, steam rising, and I peered into the silver bowl to see the blood bubbling and blistering amongst the blackened herbs which lay across the bottom.

The smoke was making me dizzy and I stepped back, and Merlin took up his druid's staff and used it to stir the contents. Round and round, murmuring and counting and now and then thumping the staff down to further crush the leaves. He made me fetch water from the rain barrel and he added this bit by bit to the mixture, and when at last he was satisfied, he told me to put out the hearth fire, which I did with water, making the fuel hiss and the smoke become so thick that I could barely breathe.

'*Now* I need Arthur.' Merlin looked towards the door. 'If he doesn't come soon, Iselle will have to help me.'

I didn't ask why I could not help. In truth I was relieved, so I said I would go and fetch Arthur. But he returned moments later, as though he had known that he was needed. He looked surprised to see me inside the house, sharing that flame-gleamed and shadow-played room which was thick with smoke but thicker with ritual and conjuring. He looked almost angry, but Merlin pointed at the plants in his hand and muttered that Arthur had done well, and in that moment, Arthur seemed to forget that I was there, his eyes drawing back to Guinevere. His mind snagging once more on the thorn of hope.

'Out with you now, Galahad,' Merlin said, and so I left them to the druid, though I paused at the threshold and turned to take one last look, seeing Merlin pull the bear skin off the lady, who was naked beneath it. I saw Arthur looking down at her, holding the purple flowers he had gathered which Merlin did not need, then I turned away and stepped out, pulling the door closed behind me, drawing clean air into my lungs, my head spinning from the smoke and my guts squirming like a bag of eels.

The voice startled rooks from the nearby copse and punched into my chest like a cold hand reaching for my heart. Banon's black head came up from her forepaws and she whined towards the roundhouse. One of the horses in the stable whinnied and stamped. Gawain, Iselle and I looked at each other with wide, questioning eyes.

The voice had been Arthur's, and we turned our ears to the house, expecting to hear something more, some coherent words or explanation. For what we had heard was equivocal, a shout of pain as much as of exquisite pleasure and release, like a cry from the bed of lovers, and it hung unanswered in the dusk.

'Has it worked?' Taliesin asked Iselle. We had made a fire outside and sat watching the day seep from the world and dragonflies whirring through the warm air. The boy reached out to Iselle. She took his hand but could not answer him.

Banon pushed herself up and walked towards the house, cocking her head to listen to that which we could not hear. Then Arthur's voice again. Muffled. Something about the gods.

The door clunked open and he staggered from it and dropped to his knees, his face white as bone and his eyes spilling tears across the hollows of his cheeks.

'Arthur?' Gawain said, standing. We all stood. It did not feel right to remain seated while Arthur knelt on the dried mud. 'Arthur?' Gawain said again, his tone wary. Almost afraid.

Arthur held his fists clenched before him and his eyes were closed and his nostrils were wide because he was breathing deeply of the clean air like a man who fears what he has seen, or fears that he has seen what he knows is not there.

Gawain was four paces from his lord and friend when Arthur opened his eyes and looked up at him.

'Well?' Gawain said. We had followed him but stood behind now. He was our shield against the worst.

'She is here,' Arthur whispered, looking into Gawain's eyes, his own eyes welling with tears and all the sorrows of his life.

Iselle and I looked at each other, hardly daring to believe what we had heard. Thinking that Arthur must have made some mistake born of his long torment.

Gawain looked round at me and gestured that we should go in and see for ourselves. I looked at Arthur, who made no move, nor gave any word to forbid it, and so we went inside.

Herb-scented smoke still hung in the air but in thinner veils now, lingering below the thatch and in the dark corners and drifting towards the open door. The cauldron lay above a pile of grey ashes which now and then pulsed with copper heat, though gave no flame. Merlin was at the table, pouring wine into a cup. He looked a broken man, bent and tremulous, the last withered leaf on a dying tree.

'Cover her,' Gawain rumbled under his breath.

Guinevere lay on her bed as before, naked, though her skin was as dark as the shadows, which were deeper now that twilight lay across the marsh. Only the whites of her eyes showed, stark against the filth, and seeing Merlin's hands the same colour, I realized that he had taken the contents of the cauldron, those herbs and the water, the blood and the tallow, and smeared it over Guinevere's skin. He had even daubed it over her hair and the soles of her feet, and I shuddered to think of the ritual to which Guinevere and Arthur had been subjected.

Iselle laid the bear fur over Guinevere as Merlin took her head in his hand, lifting it so that he could hold the cup to her lips. She seemed to breathe a little of the liquid in, watching Iselle, then watching me, her eyes sharp in a way that I had never seen them. She was seeing us. There was no doubt in my mind.

The door creaked and Arthur came in and we moved apart to let him through.

'You did it,' Gawain said to Merlin, his voice as gruff as ever but his face almost young again with wonder.

Merlin stood frowning, pressing a thumb into the triskele inscribed on his palm, as Arthur sat on the stool by the bed and took Guinevere's salve-stained hand in both of his own.

'My love.' Arthur exhaled the words. He had fled from her and from the magic which had brought her back. But he was Arthur, warlord of Britain, and he had gathered his courage now. 'My love. My Guinevere.'

Arthur's eyes were in Guinevere and Guinevere's eyes were in

Arthur and there was no distance between them now. No years. No bitterness.

'My Arthur,' she said, or tried to say, her lips making the shape though her voice was thinner than the smoke tendrils snaking towards the door.

'You have been gone for so long,' Arthur said. 'So long.' His tears dripped onto the bed.

Guinevere clenched her teeth together and I saw the joints of her jaw pressing against the thin skin stretched across her face. She tried to speak but no words came and so Merlin brought the wine back to her lips and she drank, though some of the red liquid spilled down her chin and Arthur gently wiped it away with a finger.

'Get this filth off her,' he said to Merlin.

Guinevere closed her eyes. Gathered herself. Opened her eyes in which the tears shivered. 'I cannot stay, my love,' she said.

It had seemed to take all her effort just to speak, but the words themselves, though merely breath on the air, were savage and she knew it. For she looked at Arthur as though wishing she could take them back but knowing she could not.

Arthur shook his head. He looked up at Merlin, as if he suspected the druid of having played some malicious trick on him. But Merlin did not flinch from Arthur's terrible stare, and seeing no guile in the old man's face, Arthur looked back to Guinevere.

'I've waited through the years,' Arthur said, and Guinevere's hand looked small in his. So small. 'The gods have brought you back to me.'

Her eyes fell shut and she exhaled a long time, as if that breath had been trapped inside her all the years. 'I cannot stay, my love,' she said.

'Why not?' Arthur asked, his voice frayed with anguish. His face a mask of torment such as I had never seen nor would ever see again. It was as if Arthur's soul was draining away before my eyes, like a man with a spear wound in his belly bleeding and bleeding until he is gone. 'You will grow strong,' he said. 'We will have our time at last.'

Guinevere's eyes closed and it seemed she slipped away again, and Gawain put a hand on Arthur's shoulder, his own face, so scarred and broken by violence and hardship, now the face of a boy who is afraid of the dark.

I felt I should not be there. This was not for my ears. Not for my eyes. And yet I could not walk away, because something told me, some voice whose vibration I could feel in my gut, that my father needed me to stay. To hear and to watch and to know.

Arthur snatched a breath. And another. And with a look, Iselle sought Merlin's permission to clean Lady Guinevere's face with a linen cloth and bowl of water which she'd warmed in the hearth ash.

Arthur looked up at her. 'Thank you, Iselle,' he whispered, as with the tenderest hand she wiped the dark paste from Guinevere's face, revealing the white skin streak by streak. When it was done, Iselle took the bowl and the dirty cloth away and Arthur put a hand on Guinevere's shoulder and gently shook her awake.

'Arthur,' she murmured, seeing him as if for the first time.

Arthur managed a tired smile.

'Let me go,' Guinevere said, and Arthur's smile died on his lips.

'No.' He shook his head, as if his will alone was enough. 'No, I can't,' he croaked, his voice crumbling like ancient mortar threatening to bring down everything that ever was.

Iselle and Taliesin were holding each other, and I envied the boy and yet I knew that Iselle's touch would break me.

Arthur lifted Guinevere's hand to his lips and kissed it. 'Why won't you stay with me?' he asked. Her eyes slid from Arthur onto me. I gasped, a sudden coldness flooding my bones. Yet I could not look away from those eyes, and Arthur looked up at me and I saw hatred in him, deep as an ocean. Dark and churning currents. Swallowing him.

He looked back to Guinevere. 'Because of *him*?' he asked.

I knew he meant my father.

Guinevere's eyes were mires of sadness and they held Arthur as a mother might hold her child. 'He waits for me,' she said, simply. Tears tumbled down her face, but her gaze clung to Arthur. 'And I must go.' She paused. 'Please, my love, let me go.'

Arthur closed his eyes. Tears fell into his beard. His chin fell to his chest and Guinevere watched him, their hands still clasped, their fingers entwined. Then Arthur took three shallow breaths and leant forward and kissed her forehead, pressing his lips there for a long time. Then he stood and turned and walked out of the house.

We stood for a long while in Arthur's wake. Afraid. Not knowing what to do. Having no words to hurl into the rising black water like offerings to appease some hateful god. It was Iselle who eventually broke the silence, asking Taliesin to heat more water so that she could continue to clean Guinevere.

Merlin sat against the wall, brushed away the floor rushes to reveal a patch of hard earthen floor and took some bones from a pouch, which he spread before him. They looked like knuckles in the half-light. Gawain went to the table and poured himself a cup of wine, which he threw down his throat before refilling the cup. He was not the only one who sought escape from that place. From that night.

I turned to the open door and the moonlight spilling through onto the rushes. 'Leave him, Galahad,' Gawain called out, his voice weary. 'He won't want anyone.'

But perhaps Gawain was wrong. Perhaps Arthur would want Iselle. If he only knew. And so I left the others and, once outside, looked towards the grain store, smokehouse, stable and byre. I let my eyes sift the steading, then I looked in the direction of the marsh and that's when I saw him, no more than a shadow moving towards the tall reeds. Where was he going?

I followed him into the marsh and the moon-washed reed-beds, keeping my distance, careful not to fall from the narrow wooden track. Now and then, some creature, some frog or vole, plopped into the water. Moths and bats flitted above me, while all around me the reeds clattered and hissed. From somewhere to my right came the pig-like squeal of the secretive water rail skulking among the stems, and I kept going, needing to follow Arthur and yet not knowing why.

An owl shrieked and I turned my eyes towards the distant woods, which I could not see for the tall reeds, and when I looked back along the shadowed track, I could not see Arthur either. Had he known I was following him? Who was I to intrude on his grief, a grief so terrible and deeper than the water around me from which the stink of rotting vegetation rose like steam from a foul broth? But Arthur still had Iselle. He still had his daughter. Surely, he would see that. And if he could not, then I would make him.

And so I hurried along that ancient causeway, deeper into the marsh, where the reeds thinned and the moon sat in dark pools. Here the track was more substantial, made of large oak planks laid on top of dumps of brushwood and transverse timbers, so that I could move more quickly without fear of falling into the dark water.

And yet I began to wonder if I had been mistaken about seeing Arthur. Had it been a trick of the night, or something more sinister? I stopped, looking back the way I had come. Something brushed my hair. A moth, I hoped. A vixen shrieked from the heathland margins to the north, between the nearby woodland and the reeds, and I drew my knife against the night.

What if Lord Arthur was still back at the steading, and what I had seen was a thrys or some apparition from beyond the veil trying to lure me ever deeper into the marsh?

A bird clattered up from the reeds and I turned to the sound, watching it clapping up and up towards the moon. Then I saw a dark hump on the wooden track and my heart kicked against my breastbone. There he was. He was crouching, or on his knees perhaps, leaning out over the water. Reaching for something.

I took two steps and stopped. Arthur lifted his head and looked around. I stood still, the tall reeds brushing my right shoulder, and he did not appear to see me, for he turned back and lowered himself off the causeway and into the coracle that sat tied to the pilings.

I wanted to call out to him. But I wanted to hide, too, and in that moment the sense of being an interloper, of meddling in things which I should leave alone, overwhelmed me and so I held my tongue and remained still. There was something else too. Some other sensation which I could not name but which lay upon me thick and heavy, so that I might not have been able to move even had I wanted to. As though some higher power, some god even, had cast his unseen net upon me and held me fast.

I saw the dark shape of Arthur and, as he turned to push himself away from the causeway, his face washed pale in the moonlight. And it seemed that he saw me then. That he looked right at me. His eyes seeing into my eyes across the night as if across a dozen years, our lives no longer sharing the same night, our lungs not the same air. He was gone even before he was gone, yet I heard the *splosh* of the paddle in the water. Saw Arthur, the great warlord who was to have led us to victory, lean forward in the small craft and sweep it through the moon which shivered on the surface.

I watched until the darkness swallowed him.

I feel the animal's fear. It is in her like a sickness and she pants in urgent rhythm, only ceasing and holding a silence now and then to listen. Then the panting again. She knows that her master has gone. She feels his absence and she fears it, the loneliness, as her wolf ancestors feared exclusion from the pack.

His scent lingers in the night air still, but faintly, and ebbing all the while. Fading. And so, beneath the moon, we pad over to the gnarled old tree where his scent lingers strongest, having seeped into the trunk, having laced the long grass like some ethereal, consoling dew. And we lie down there, as though to rest beside him a while, as though to share the warmth which his flesh has sent into the soil at that place, like roots going down.

Part of me, the part which can still disentangle my own awareness from Banon's, wants to stay here, on this spot, for the dog's sake. For she has been as loyal to Arthur as any man or woman ever was, and more loyal than some. More loyal than I. And it is a comfort to sense her absolute love. A faithfulness which cannot be sullied. An allegiance beyond corruption. And yet we cannot stay. I cannot stay.

The door clumps open and the young woman steps out, smoke hazing behind her like a veil caught by the wind. Banon gives a whine, perhaps in protest at my coercion, but she cannot withstand me, and we rise, wearily, and leave the apple tree and the ghost of

Arthur, padding towards her across the familiar ground, silent and as black as shadow.

Tears glisten on her cheeks as she looks up at the stars and the moon. Banon nuzzles against her leg and she crouches and runs a gentle hand between the dog's ears and speaks in soft words which we feel no less than her kind hand. Then we walk away, towards the byre, and look back, but her upturned face is washed in moonlight again, and so we give a plaintive whine. We walk a little further, turn back, whine again. The woman calls softly to Banon, and the dog replies with a sharp bark, then we are moving again, and I can feel that she is following. Iselle.

My own Iselle.

The byre door is ajar, and we slink into its dark interior and into the ancient scent of animals and old straw, dung and dust and the acrid stink of sheep from the grease on tools. Banon yips again, but she did not need to, for the young woman slips into the darkness and stands for a moment, letting it envelop her, letting her eyes grow accustomed, and sifting the shadow with them.

I don't have long. My hold on this animal is slipping away. If she were wild, I would already have lost her. But she is far from wild. And she is afraid and already misses Arthur, and perhaps she draws some comfort from my presence now and so lets me abide awhile. We walk into deeper darkness, and though Banon does not know why we do it, she does not fight me, and then she sits, tall on her haunches, her nose full of the scent of the rusty iron sickle leaning against the timber wall, and of the chain strung from a nearby beam, and of the coarse woollen cloth bundle which lies across an old scarred, mossy tree round once used as a chopping block.

The voice beckons me, but I hold Banon still, and she whines in protest now, not wanting to stay in the dark byre but wanting to go outside and wait for her master. And yet, the whining draws the young woman. She moves through a shaft of moonlight lancing through a split in the timber wall and stands beside us, scrubbing Banon's nape and withers and speaking soft words. Banon touches her nose to the cloth bundle and licks it for the animal fat on it. But I am fading as fast as Arthur's scent on the night air, losing my grip on the animal. I cannot stay. But I must.

Just a little longer.

The hand pulls us back towards the door and the night beyond, but I hold Banon to the spot and she barks once, and I feel my soul untwining from hers now, and her own nature flooding in. She stands. Turns. Trots back towards the night air. But the young woman picks up the cloth bundle, weighing it in her hands, and she takes it into the shaft of moonlight and unwinds the wool.

Going now. To him.

I rise into the dark.

I am coming.

Below me, the young woman lifts her discovery in the moon-wash. Iron and steel. Ivory gleaming like cream. Polished wood. A blade to cut through the darkness like a firebrand.

I'm coming. My love.

Guinevere died in the night. Perhaps even at the same moment that Arthur drifted away into the lonely dark.

'She is free now,' Iselle told me when at last I returned to the steading. I had stayed a long time at the water's edge, looking west into the night after Arthur. Dawn was breaking across the marsh in bands of pale gold, the air already alive with insects and brimming with bird song. Just like any other day. 'I held her hand as she went,' Iselle said, looking off towards the old apple tree against whose trunk Gawain sat clutching a wine skin, watching a hawk soar in circles high above the deep reed-beds, sweeping their expanse. 'Merlin gave her a draught. For the pain.' Iselle's eyes found mine in such a way as to question this draught of Merlin's without saying as much. What did it matter anyway?

So, Guinevere was gone too. I felt no jolt of surprise or fear, just the settling of weight upon my soul, like the peat turves stacked one upon the other under the eaves of Arthur's house.

'It's over, then.' My own words sounded far away, as empty as the wide sky above us.

Iselle untied a leather thong from around her wrist, pushed her copper hair back with both hands and tied it at the nape of her neck. There were dark shadows beneath her eyes and a tiredness in them that sleep could not cure. Yet still her savage beauty defied the callous dawn.

'Where's Taliesin?' I asked. I could see Banon over by the tall reeds, her black tail swaying as she whined softly to the west, pining after her master, but the boy was not with her.

'He is with Merlin,' Iselle said, looking in the direction of the wood of sallow, hazel and ash.

I was surprised at that, for Taliesin had not strayed from Iselle's side since we had found him, or rather since he had found us, on the Isle of the Dead. But then, who could blame a young boy for wanting to be away from this place and its ghosts? Especially a boy already burdened by ghosts known only to him, from which he could never be free, unless Merlin knew of some way.

I looked back at Iselle and her eyes were in me like a hawk's talons in some prey's flesh.

'Did you know?' There was a flush of blood in her cheeks but no suspicion in her face. She was beyond that. 'I want the truth, Galahad.'

An unseen hand clutched at my throat. My chest tightened. I wanted to turn my face away, to slip the leash of her stare, but instead I looked into those green eyes which were so like those others which had closed in the night and would never open again.

'Yes,' I whispered. 'I knew.'

I imagined the scene in the previous night, of Guinevere telling Iselle that she was her mother. I could picture Iselle's face. The confusion and then the understanding. The sadness and then the anger.

'Damn you!' she said.

She closed her eyes, breathed deeply and exhaled, as someone trying to endure physical pain. When she opened her eyes, they were almost sharp enough to pierce my skin. 'When did you know?' she asked.

I held her gaze. 'Merlin told me. When we came back here after Camelot.'

She hated that, hated that I had known for so long. Her teeth fretted at her bottom lip as she fought her anger. 'Damn you, Galahad,' she said again. 'Why did you keep it from me?'

I considered the question. I had been afraid to tell her. That was one reason I had kept Merlin's secret. But that was not the only reason. 'I did not think it would help you to know.'

'Merlin made you swear to say nothing?' she asked, as if hoping it were true. As though that would at least be something.

I shook my head. 'No. It was my decision.' I paused. 'There were many times I thought to tell you, but I chose not to.'

Again, she let a silence grow between us, spreading like a bloodstain in linen. Banon looked around to us, crying, asking us where Arthur was.

'You decided it was not my right to know who my parents were,' Iselle said.

'It was a burden which I would have spared you,' I said. 'I

know about such burdens.' I reached out to take her hand, but she pulled it away, pointing a finger at me.

'You had no right,' she spat. 'No right to keep that from me.'

'I know,' I said. 'I'm sorry.'

She pressed her palms to her face, then pushed her hands up through her hair, dragging the tresses back, pulling on them, her hands shaking.

'And I'm sorry that your father left you on that hill, Galahad. I'm sorry that he never came back for you.' She threw an arm wide and gritted her teeth. 'But perhaps my father would have stayed if he had known.'

'Maybe he did know,' I said. 'But Arthur could never have been a father to you. He was a warlord. That was his reason for breathing. That and Guinevere.' I should have held my tongue. I was a fool. And yet it was true. Arthur and my father were the same in that way. Both impelled by greater ambitions than the raising of children. Both spurred by crueller demons than those which taunt normal men. Both in thrall to the same woman, too, and perhaps to the exclusion of all other love.

'He might have stayed.' There were tears in her eyes.

'No, Iselle.' I gestured at the animal pens, at the sorry-looking sheep and swine and the clutter of near derelict buildings which comprised the farmstead. 'Look at this place.' She did not need to look. 'Arthur son of Uther has been gone for years,' I said. Iselle's eyes hardened then and I knew that I had wounded her and I hated myself for it. I wanted to tell her I was wrong to keep it from her. That I wished I had told her when Merlin had shown me the truth. I wanted to say that perhaps Arthur *would* have stayed if Iselle had asked him to, even though I knew he would not have. But I said none of this.

Iselle strode over to the house and snatched up her arrow bag and her bow and her long Saxon sword, which leant in its scabbard against the wattle wall. Then she turned towards the rising sun and headed for the trees.

And I watched her go.

21

Iselle

'WHAT DO YOU MEAN she's gone?' Merlin said. 'Gone after Arthur?' Taliesin stood at his shoulder, a dead hare in one hand, a bunch of red campion in the other. Behind them, the horses stood head to tail in the shade of the byre, swishing their tails, shivering off clouds of flies and cropping the long grass.

I shook my head. 'No, she went east. Towards the woods.'

Merlin swung his ash staff at me, so that I had to step back or else be hit. 'And you let her go?' he accused, glaring. Taliesin was looking towards the tree line, his young face clenched with worry.

'She was angry,' I said.

The druid lifted the staff and pointed it at me as though about to cast some curse or spell. 'Of course she was angry, Galahad,' he said. 'You have known all this time that she was Lord Arthur and Lady Guinevere's daughter and yet you kept it from her.'

I frowned at him. 'As did you.'

'But she does not love me, you fool.' He planted the staff on the ground and placed both hands upon its knotty head.

Merlin's horse lifted its head, flared its nostrils and gave a loud snort followed by a nicker. I followed its line of sight and saw riders coming through the orchard of gnarled old apple trees, their armour, helmets and bosses gleaming and their spear blades winking in the late afternoon sun.

'We fetched them,' Merlin said, lifting his staff in welcome to the Lords Parcefal, Gediens and Cai, and the rest of the horse warriors who rode at their shoulders.

'Do they know?' I asked. 'That it's over?'

'I told them that Lady Guinevere was free at last.' Merlin shrugged. 'So perhaps they know that Arthur will not ride again.'

Gediens and I greeted each other silently across the distance and when they had walked their horses into the steading they dismounted, looping reins over the top rails of the animal pens and some of them looking around as if in wonder that this was where their lord, the great warrior of Britain, had lived these past ten tears.

I did not want to face Gediens and the others, to be the one to tell them. But Gawain was still slumped against the apple tree, drunk out of his mind, and some of the men were already looking at me and so I walked to meet them, a painful lump in my throat and a sour taste in my mouth.

'Where is he, Galahad?' Parcefal called, while I was still three spear lengths from where they had stopped and stood now as though unwilling to cross some invisible threshold. A threshold of knowing.

'He's gone.' I gestured behind me. 'Into the marsh. Last night.'

Parcefal and Cai shared a look which seemed to confirm their fears, while a low rumble rose amongst the men around them. Gediens, though, watched me quietly, waiting for more.

'I don't think he will return,' I said.

'You can't know that.' Lord Cai pointed a finger at me, as though warning me against speaking thus.

'Maybe when the fighting starts,' Cadwy said. 'Maybe then he'll come.'

Medyr, who had removed his helmet to run a hand through his black curls, agreed with this. 'When we need him most, he *will* come.' He looked at me. 'As Lancelot did.'

I did not gainsay either of them, but held my tongue, knowing that I was witnessing the death throes of hope.

'It's over,' someone growled. I turned to see Gawain lumbering towards us, a wine jug in his hand. He lifted it to his mouth and emptied the contents down his throat, some of the liquid spilling through his greying beard onto the grass. 'Over,' he snarled, and hurled the jug against the roundhouse and it shattered into pieces. 'Arthur is not coming back. It has all been for nothing.' He stood on unsteady legs, swaying like a lonely ash in the wind.

'Stop your wallowing, Gawain,' Merlin snapped, coming to join us, planting his staff with every other step, his grey beard braided and stiff as rope. 'It does not become a Prince of Lyonesse.'

For a heartbeat Gawain gawked at the druid, then he lumbered forward, snarling his hands into Merlin's cloak and tunic and lifting the old man off the ground.

'You are the reason she's dead, druid!' Gawain spat, as Gediens and I rushed to intervene, each of us taking hold of one of Gawain's arms and pulling to bring Merlin safely back down, Gawain bawling at us to get off him.

'Leave him, Gawain,' I said, as Merlin pulled free and staggered back out of the big man's reach.

'He brought her back, knowing she would die,' Gawain accused the druid. All eyes turned on Merlin then. 'You found her before, didn't you? When you put on the feathered cloak? You found her, druid,' Gawain spat, his words slurring one into another. He hurled an arm towards the sky. 'You found her out there somewhere, and she told you she wasn't coming back.'

Merlin may have been old and frail, but he had courage enough to square his shoulders to Gawain, and there was a hawk-like fury in his face that put ice in my belly and had some of the men touching iron to ward off whatever malicious spell they expected the druid to cast.

'I found her,' Merlin admitted, 'and I tried to bring her back to Arthur. But Guinevere's heart belonged to Lancelot. It always did.' His voice was steady, something in it compelling every ear to attend his truth. He stepped forward, back into Gawain's reach, and pointed a gnarled finger at the warrior. 'You knew that. You've always known.'

Gawain turned his head and spat into the grass. 'What does it matter now?' He shrugged. 'It's finished. We cannot fight without Arthur. No one will come.' Then he turned to me and his scarred face was almost unrecognizable. 'Your father has cost us everything,' he snarled. 'Even in death, he has ruined us.'

Rage took hold in me, sudden and hot. I flew at him. I hit him so hard that he staggered several steps and fell onto his arse amongst the grass and the yellow and white bone flowers which seemed to stare like a thousand eyes.

'Peace, Galahad,' Gediens hissed, taking hold of me, for I had taken three steps towards Gawain, my blood boiling. 'Peace now.'

'There he is.' Gawain stared up at me, a grimace of a smile warping his mouth. 'There's the man who would have ridden with us to drive the bastard Saxons back into the sea. He's a damned killer, just like his father.'

Breaking free of Gediens, I hauled Boar's Tusk from its scabbard and held its point against Gawain's throat, and Gawain lifted his chin, offering me the kill, and in that moment, I wanted to thrust the blade forward, as Gediens and Parcefal yelled at me to lower my sword and back away.

'It's lost,' Gawain said. 'It's all lost.'

My vision cleared and I saw Boar's Tusk at Gawain's neck. Saw Taliesin staring at me with round eyes. For a moment I thought I heard his voice, the intoxicating enchantment of his singing, swirling in my head like a warm breeze amongst summer leaves. But it could not be, I knew. The boy's lips were fastened.

I pulled the blade away.

'Galahad, find Iselle,' Merlin said, his voice coming to me like wind seeking through a cave. 'Do you hear me? Go now and bring her back.'

I was half aware of Parcefal and Cai lifting Gawain to his feet. And of Tarawg, Nabon, Medyr and some of the others saying that they wished to see Lady Guinevere in spite of everything, for they had once loved her and served her and they would pay their respects before we burned the lady on a pyre and gave her ashes to the western wind.

'Go, Galahad,' Merlin snapped, his teeth bared, his hair fraying in the breeze. 'Find her.'

I felt I was drowning, flailing for something to hold on to, thoughts whirling in my head, and each breath too thin and weak to sustain me. But I had wits enough to know that I must escape that place. And I had blood enough in my veins to know that I wanted Iselle. That I needed her. And so, I turned my back on them all, fetched a spear from the byre and set off towards the trees, above which the rooks eddied in a black cloud, crying for the death of our dream.

I did not find Iselle. She found me. I heard the whip crack of the arrow hitting the willow trunk beside me and was relieved to see that the fletchings quivering at the end of the shaft were white.

'What do you want?' she called. The arrow told me to look for her amongst a clump of alder to my right, though I could not see her. I was reminded of the day we met, when she had killed the Saxons who would otherwise have killed me.

'Merlin wants you to come back,' I said. Like the coward I was.

'Why?' she asked, still not revealing herself.

In truth I did not know why Merlin had sent me to fetch her. Maybe to stop me killing Gawain or Gawain killing me.

'Gediens and Lord Cai and the others have come,' I said.

Somewhere nearby, a sedge warbler was chattering, rejoicing for the bounty of mayflies, moths and lacewings that were on the air, thick in the gloaming.

'It is over.' There was such sadness in her voice. 'They will not fight now. Not without Arthur.' She stepped out from behind an alder, her bow down by her side. My heart kicked in my chest. 'The war is lost before it ever began,' she said.

'Lord Constantine will fight on,' I said.

'He can't win. You know that.'

I nodded. 'Come back with me. It will be dark.'

'Why didn't you tell me?' she asked.

I took a breath. 'They would have brought you only pain. They were not what they once were.'

Even across the distance I saw her brows draw down. 'You never believed that they could be together again? That Arthur would lead us in battle?'

'I wanted to believe it,' I said honestly. I looked into the west, where the sun was a fiery shield sinking to the horizon. Swallows and swifts skimmed the reed heads, taking insects on the wing.

'It will be dark,' I repeated.

She said nothing. Her silence said everything.

'I should have told you,' I said. 'I'm sorry.'

Whatever Iselle was thinking, she kept it to herself, but I saw in her face that she was asking questions of others now, not of me, and so I took my chance and walked towards her.

'I'm sorry,' I said again, and I put my arms around her and she gathered into herself, taut as a drawn bow, but I held on and she softened and I kissed her copper hair and breathed her in as though they were my last breaths.

'Do you think he knew?' Her voice was so quiet that it almost did not invite a reply.

'How could he not?' I whispered. 'You are his blood. But Arthur was never meant to be a father. He loved war and he loved your mother. I think he feared everything else.'

She looked down at her bow and ran her thumb over the horn knock, which had worn smooth. 'He tried to burn her,' she said.

'I know.'

'Would he have done it? If Lancelot had not come?'

I thought about that, but before I could answer, Iselle said: 'Perhaps he was just trying to trap your father.'

'We cannot know,' I said.

I could not see her face, but I felt her body tense against mine.

'Why would she go back to him after that?'

I had wondered the same thing myself, though only now did I see a possibility that made any sense. 'She blamed herself,' I said. 'For coming between the two men who together were the hope of Britain. She was trying to make things right.'

Iselle said nothing to that, but I knew that she did not believe it. I felt it in her.

I held her, waiting for her next question, knowing what it would be. She would ask why Guinevere, why her mother, gave her up. I waited for that question. Fearing it. Fearing that I would be able to give her no answer, nor had I the courage to plead on Guinevere's behalf, for Iselle deserved better than that. But the question did not come.

I held her. I sowed more kisses amongst her hair, and, should the sun fall beyond the horizon, flooding the world with darkness, I would have happily wandered the marshes with Iselle for ever, the two of us haunting the reed-beds and meadows, restless spirits unburdened of memory and fear and even hope.

Iselle pulled away and looked me in the eye. 'How did she have such a hold over them?' she asked, and in that moment, as my soul trembled and the light leached from the world, I knew how.

I knew how.

I reached out and thumbed a tear from her cheek.

'I will never leave you,' I said.

When we returned, it was night. The moon hung white and fat, making spear blades of the reed heads and silvering the smoke rising from the fire which Lord Cai's horse warriors had made near Arthur's old apple tree. That tree where I had so often seen Arthur sitting beside Guinevere, watching the sunset.

Merlin had told everyone to gather there, much to Gawain's annoyance by the looks, for he had got hold of another skin of wine – from one of Cai's men presumably – and having resumed his position against that gnarled tree trunk was busy sluicing his insides.

Seeing me by the fire glow, he lifted the wine skin, offering it to me, and I took it and drank, knowing that I should have been the one to make the peace and wincing when he turned his face away and the firelight revealed a bruise across his jaw, the reddish-purple of knapweed flowers.

I handed the skin back. 'What's he up to?' Gawain slurred, lifting his chin towards Merlin, who stood further off beneath the moonlight, looking up at the night sky and the stars clustered there as if they whispered in quiet yet eternal voices which he alone could hear.

I shrugged, but thought that he must have something important to say, because he was wearing his black robes and carrying his ash staff, and he had braided his beard into an oiled rope and darkened his eyes with ash.

'We should have left him in his hole on Ynys Weith,' Gawain rumbled, gesturing towards Merlin with the wine skin. 'Better if you hadn't found him, Parcefal.'

Parcefal was walking from the house to the fire, cradling a load of split logs. 'We had to try, old friend,' he said. He dropped the fuel onto the ground near the fire and looked at Gawain, the scar that started below his right eye and ran down his cheek, through his lips and down his chin, giving him a terrible aspect by the firelight. And yet that awful scar spoke less of pain and suffering than did the sad smile which he gave his friend then, the two warriors beset by the past and all that had been hoped for and lost.

I looked at Merlin. The druid had failed to give Guinevere back to Arthur, and we had failed to give Arthur back to Britain, and yet he looked more austere and enigmatic than ever. It seemed that he took strength from the night around us, that something sustained him even after the loss of Arthur and Guinevere, while the rest of us withered like fruit on a poisoned tree.

Then I looked for Iselle and saw her by the smokehouse,

talking with Taliesin, who held something in two hands, something wrapped in cloth. Whatever the boy was telling her, it looked as though Iselle did not want to hear it, nor did she want whatever he was trying to give her. She shook her head and turned her face away, her expression cold under the white moon. But Taliesin took her hand and pulled her towards the fire and for a moment I thought Iselle would break away from him. But she did not, and they came to sit upon the animal skins which Cai's men had laid on the ground. I asked her with a look what had happened, but she shook her head and then Merlin strode into the bloom of golden firelight.

'Friends! Men of Dumnonia! Warriors of the Cauldron!' he said, lifting his voice above the murmur of men and the crack and pop of the fire. A score of faces turned towards him and a hush fell upon the clearing, so that the marsh around us, the wall of reeds and the dark shadowed trees seemed suddenly to close in on us, reminding us that we were few and the darkness was great. I shivered. 'You have fought across Britain and even across the Dividing Sea in the dark forests of Gaul. You have bled for this land and for Arthur. But the fight is not over. The enemies of Britain, who have stalked the land since Arthur's last great battle, have gathered once more. They mean to drive us from our land and our gods. We have been betrayed by the Lady of Camelot, who has taken the Saxon king to her bed. Desperate to hold on to some measure of power in Dumnonia, Queen Morgana has joined with King Cerdic, who has sworn to cede the high seat, Uther Pendragon's high seat, to Morgana's grandsons. Thanks to Taranis, master of war, and to Galahad's sword, one of those foul-hearted sons of Mordred is dead.'

Men's eyes fell upon me then. Some nodded in respect and acknowledgement of that shared night of blood, and it warmed me.

'But the other lives,' Merlin said. 'Melehan ap Mordred ap Arthur will rule in Dumnonia.'

Some of the men cursed into the flames. Gediens shook his head for shame, while Gawain lifted his wine skin as though in honour of the future king of Dumnonia.

'He'll be a puppet king, nothing more,' Lord Cai said, tossing a stick into the fire. 'The Saxons will rule. Melehan will not have the spears to wield true power.'

'They'll never let him sit in Uther's high seat,' Medyr said, helping Cadwy to run a spit through four waterfowl which would be set above the fire later when the flames had died. 'Melehan will have his throat cut before he's ever proclaimed king.'

'Perhaps,' Merlin nodded. 'Either way, by then it will be too late, and Britain will be lost.'

'Britain is already lost,' Parcefal growled, stirring mutterings of agreement from those around the fire.

'Perhaps,' Merlin said again.

'So, what do you want from us, druid?' This from Gawain, who sat apart from the others still. A shadowed shape beneath the twisting trunk of a moon-silvered apple tree.

'I want you to fight, Gawain, son of King Lot of Lyonesse,' Merlin said. 'That is what you do, is it not?' He swept his ash staff across the assembly and the men's faces which were lit by flame or moonlight. 'I want you all to fight. One last time.'

'It's over, Merlin.' Tarawg shook his head. 'We cannot fight without Arthur. The other kings will not fight without Arthur.'

'So, you will abandon Lord Constantine, who has fought on against our enemies while you feasted with the Fisher King? You will let him fight alone with the last of his brave spearmen?' Merlin asked us. No one answered this, though I saw the disquiet in Gawain's drunken face and knew it hurt him to forsake Constantine. 'Then perhaps Constantine was right all those years ago when he believed he should have been proclaimed king as Uther lay dying. For he has never given up, nor ever will. Not until he is cut down by a Saxon blade.'

'Which will be before this summer ends,' Nabon put in, lifting a bulging wine skin to his lips. Some of the men fell to talking among themselves, discussing the inevitable fate of those who still held out against the Saxons and their new allies. But Merlin took a step towards the fire and lifted his staff, commanding men's attention again.

'There was once a dream of Britain.' His voice was clear and strong, and yet as soft as cream in the pail. 'A dream of Camelot,' he said. 'Arthur believed in that dream and I believed in Arthur. We all believed in Arthur. He was the best of us. He was the light in the darkness.' There were murmurs, and cups were raised, and some men gave Arthur's name to the night around them. 'You think it is over, but it is not,' Merlin said. 'There is still a flame and that flame can become a fire which will wake the gods.' With that, Merlin opened his hand towards the fire and there was a sudden flare of flame, a leaping copper tongue that licked into the dark and made us gasp and throw ourselves back in fear and surprise.

I saw Medyr and Nabon and some of the others touch belt buckles or knife hilts, seeking protection from Merlin's magic.

'I was like you,' Merlin told us. 'I thought the dream had flown away.' He lifted a hand and fluttered his fingers. 'I believed that the gods had turned their backs on us. That only the faintest whiff of their power remained in Britain, like the smell in the air after a rain storm.' He looked at the stars and shook his head. 'I could not hear them. I could not dream to them, and so I thought my own abilities had drained from my body, like the blood that spilled from so many brave warriors on that field at Camlan.' He pointed at Parcefal and Cai, at Gediens and Cadwy, Tarawg and Nabon. 'You were there,' he said. Almost an accusation. 'You all bled.'

'We were there, druid. Where were you?' a warrior named Culhwch asked, eyeballing Merlin from the other side of the fire.

'My body was not there, Culhwch ap Cynan, but there is more to a man . . . and a woman . . . than flesh and bone.' He grimaced. 'I fought for Arthur in my own way, just as you fought in yours. But after, I was spent. We stopped the Saxons but the slaughter was great and I feared we had given too much and gained too little. The gods took away my second sight. That was their punishment, for I had made mistakes.' He glanced at me then and I knew he was thinking of my father and Guinevere. 'But the gods are still here,' Merlin said, holding out his arms as if to invite the stars and the moon, the flame and the darkness to turn themselves into Taranis or Balor, Epona or the horse goddess Rhiannon. 'I felt it on the Isle of the Dead and in the boy Taliesin.' Men looked at Taliesin then, some no doubt recalling the tale of how he had sung in the caves of the neamh-mairbh and how his voice had benumbed those foul creatures, binding them in the dark. 'I felt the gods in the Cauldron of Annwn and I feel them here. Now. In this place.' He lifted his eyes and looked around him and, in that moment, it was as if we were not there. Just Merlin and the gods wheeling in the night like moths around a candle. 'They want us to fight for the old dream. They want us to fight for Britain.'

'We needed Arthur,' Gawain called. 'But Arthur's gone.'

Merlin smiled and looked about him. 'And yet we are all here,' he said.

'Hardly an army,' Parcefal said, raising a smattering of quiet laughter.

'It only takes one leaf from the hemlock plant to kill a man, Parcefal,' Merlin countered. 'We are no army, but we are the beginnings of an army. We are the flint and steel from which a hundred fires will be lit. A thousand fires.'

Some of the warriors shook their heads. Some told Merlin that he was too late. That he should have been here ten years ago and maybe then there would have been a chance. To regroup after Camlan and throw the Saxons back into the sea.

'I am here now,' Merlin said. 'And I have more power than I ever did, because I have the greatest of the ancient treasures of Britain. I have the Cauldron of Annwn.' Merlin looked at me as he said that, and I saw the glint of triumph in his eyes and I felt snakes writhing in my guts because in that moment I realized that we had not ventured to the Isle of the Dead to fetch the cauldron for Guinevere and Arthur, but for Merlin. He had known that even if he could bring Guinevere back to her body, she would not stay. That she *could* not. But we had given Merlin the cauldron, that treasure once belonging to the druids of old, and that treasure was what Merlin coveted. It was in that silver bowl that Merlin had found the gods whom he had thought gone for ever.

His gaze lingered on me, because he knew that I knew, and he was enjoying the moment. 'And we have Galahad ap Lancelot,' Merlin said, staring still, pointing his staff at me. 'A warrior who has it in him to be even greater than his father. For though Lancelot was without equal in battle, he was blind to the needs of Britain. He saw only the lady. Galahad here has his father's great heart.' He clenched a bony hand and thumped it against his own chest. 'But he sees more than Lancelot ever did.' He pressed a gnarled finger against his temple. 'He has more brains. He knows what we are trying to build here. He knows what Britain can be, if we only stand together now.

Here, in this place.' I felt men's eyes on me, heavier than any armour, yet I stood square and tall because in my heart I wanted them to believe what Merlin was saying. I wanted to believe it myself. 'Galahad will be the one to reach out and take what the gods have shown me in my dreams,' he said, then he paused to let his words sink in, looking up towards the star-domed vault of heaven, and but for the flapping of flames, the night was silent, as if it too hung on the druid's words.

Then he lowered his face and swung his eyes to Iselle, and I looked at her and she at me and we both knew what was coming. Her jaw was set, her cheekbones sharp beneath the fair skin, her lips pressed into a tight line.

'Our enemies already know that Galahad killed Ambrosius ap Mordred,' Merlin went on. 'They fear him, and they are right to fear him.' He threw a hand towards the tall reeds through which I had followed Arthur the previous night. 'But what about Arthur? you cry. How can we fight without the Pendragon's son to lead us?' He turned to face Iselle fully now, and he paused again, letting the silence flood in, while he simply stared at her, as if he had never really looked at her before, never really seen her until this night beneath these stars.

'Stand up, Iselle.' His voice was even and rich, and in the dark one might have thought it was the voice of a younger man. Iselle looked at me, as if for help. I had never seen her look so afraid as she did in that moment, but all I did was nod that she should do as the druid asked. 'Come, Iselle,' Merlin said, 'let us see you now.' This time Iselle stood, and she balled her fists and lifted her chin rather than show her discomfort. She had no inkling that she looked like a queen.

Merlin dipped his head. 'This young woman standing before us now, standing *with* us now, is Lady Guinevere's daughter by Arthur.' A murmuring rose around us, a low rumble as of hooves drumming soft earth. 'This is Arthur's daughter,' Merlin said, and at this the rumbling grew louder and men swore and growled and some were climbing to their feet, or touching iron to ward off ill luck, or invoking the gods, all of them glaring at Iselle as if she had suddenly appeared, like some spirit on Samhain come among them. 'She is a warrior, as you know,' Merlin said. 'Uther's blood flows in her veins. Guinevere's too, and Guinevere had a power that even I could never possess.'

Culhwch took three steps towards Iselle and lifted his cup, looming in the flame shadow and frowning. 'You're Arthur's daughter?'

Iselle nodded.

'I can see it now,' another said.

'Balor's eyes,' Parcefal growled.

'You kept this from me, Merlin?' Gawain said. On his feet now. Unsteady. Pointing a finger at Merlin.

'Gawain, you look at a meadow and you see a meadow. You do not see the cloth dye in the shepherd's knot or the healing power of coltsfoot, or in the four-leafed clover the name of whoever is practising witchcraft against you.' He shrugged. 'You are a warrior.'

Gawain turned to me. 'Did you know?'

'I knew,' I said. 'After Camelot.'

Gawain spat a curse and kicked a smoking stick which had fallen out of the fire, sending up sparks like a swarm of fireflies. But Iselle said his name and he swung his drunken eyes to her. 'I only learnt it last night,' she told him. 'Guinevere . . . my mother . . . told me.'

'And now you all know,' Merlin said, lifting his staff with two hands and sweeping it through the fire glow. He looked at the faces around the flames, letting the revelation seep into the men like the fire which ate into the logs, making them crack and pop. 'Iselle will lead us,' the druid said.

Cadwy muttered something under his breath and several of the others frowned or shook their heads.

I stood. 'Iselle is a warrior,' I said. 'The day I met her she killed three Saxons before they could kill me.' I looked at Iselle and she shook her head at me, her eyes telling me to say no more. 'She did not know that she is Lord Arthur's daughter and yet she shared more than Arthur's blood. She shared his dream of Britain.'

'You would have her lead us in battle?' Cadwy asked. 'I mean no offence, girl, but—'

'There is no man here who has more courage.' I heard the challenge in my voice, but no one denied it. They all knew Iselle and they had seen her fight.

'No one will believe she is Arthur's daughter,' a bald, big-bearded warrior named Hardolf said, turning the spit upon which the waterfowl glistened and dripped juices which hissed in the flame.

'Do you believe it, Hardolf?' I asked him, throwing an arm towards Iselle, inviting the man to look at her again.

The meat sizzled and Hardolf frowned. 'Yes,' he said, 'there's no mistaking it now.'

I nodded. 'So will everyone see it.' For, suddenly, I saw it myself. Iselle was our hope. She would be what the sword Excalibur had been those years ago: the talisman to draw the kings and the warriors of Britain into the fight. Merlin was watching me, and he knew what I had seen in my mind. The stag antler banner of Powys and the bristling boar of Caer Gloui, the spearmen of Dumnonia and Cornubia, of Caer Celemion and Cynwidion, lining up in their shieldwalls beneath the summer sun, and all of them brimming with the belief that we *could* win because we had Iselle ferch Arthur ap Uther. Merlin grinned because he knew I saw all that. And perhaps he had known I would.

But Iselle could not yet see the same things in her mind and she shook her head. 'I do not want it,' she said to herself. I saw her lips make the words. She lifted her eyes to Merlin and me. 'I do not want it,' she said. 'I am not a leader like Arthur was.'

'But you can be,' Merlin said. 'It is the will of the gods. I see it now.' He put a hand to his eye. 'It is what we have been waiting for.' He swept his staff back towards the house and the treasure which sat above the cold hearth ash. 'We have the Cauldron of Annwn,' and again the staff swung towards the men around the fire, 'and the last of Arthur's famed horse warriors, and the son of Lancelot,' he said, accusing me with that gnarled rod of ash. 'It is no accident. The gods have stirred us into this broth, girl, and even if you did not want this, it is not your choice to make. Not now.'

He thrust the heel of the staff upon the ground in a way that made me think of the stories of Joseph of Arimathea planting his own staff into the ground of Ynys Wydryn, where it had sunk roots and burst into bud, becoming the Holy Thorn. But there in that lonely steading in the marsh it was not a tree that Merlin was planting, but hope.

Beyond the fire, Gawain growled something and pulled his sword from its scabbard. He threw out an arm, pushing past Tarawg and Cadwy, and strode towards Iselle, and for a terrible moment I thought he had lost his mind in the wine. But then, when he was a spear length from Iselle and I had half drawn Boar's Tusk and taken three strides, Gawain stopped and gripped the sword by hilt and by blade.

'Lady, if you will lead, I will follow,' he said, and fell onto his knees, lifting the sword above his head, his eyes fixed on Iselle's face. 'My sword is yours,' he said.

And so I kept walking and when I got to Gawain I knelt beside him.

'Get up,' Iselle hissed.

'My sword and my life are yours, lady,' I said, lifting my sword to her as Gawain had.

I saw the turmoil in her, her fists knotting and unknotting, her brows drawn together and her teeth dragging at her bottom lip.

'Get up, Galahad. Both of you,' she hissed again, but we did not get up, and Gawain and I glanced at each other, both of us thinking that we must look the biggest fools in Britain, kneeling there in the grass before a woman who did not want to lead us, pledging our lives as if we two led armies of spearmen who would fight when and where we commanded.

But then I felt them at my back like a shadow sweeping to engulf me. Felt their footfalls in the ground beneath my knees. Heard the soft hiss of swords being drawn up the throats of leather scabbards. They gathered around us and they went down onto their knees and they raised their swords in the firelight.

'We are your men, lady,' Parcefal said. I looked at the old warrior and saw a glistening of tears running to his grey beard.

'We are your men, lady,' others said in a ragged chorus. A gruff, wine- and smoke-dried chorus which was more beautiful than any of the sacred chants that had risen to the thatch in the monastery on Ynys Wydryn.

'We will fight for you, lady,' Lord Cai said.

'Our swords are yours,' Cadwy said.

And it was then that Taliesin came up and offered Iselle the cloth-wrapped object which earlier I had seen her refuse.

Again she shook her head and so Taliesin pulled the leather thongs away and drew a sword from the cloth and there was an intake of breath from the men around me because they recognized that long, straight blade, the gleaming ivory grip which was shaped to fit into the hand, and the guard and spherical pommel of dark wood. I had heard it called Caliburn and Caledfwlch, but these men, and all of Britain, knew it as Excalibur.

As surprised as anyone to see the sword, Merlin spoke some secret words to the gods and hissed at Iselle to take it, which at last she did, holding Excalibur down by her side. Then Merlin beckoned Taliesin to him and gave the boy his staff to hold. The druid stepped up and from somewhere amongst his robes brought out a garland which had been woven from the red campion that I had seen in Taliesin's hand earlier that day. *Blodau neidr*, snake flower, was the name some folk gave it, for the seeds were said to cure snake bites. But I had also heard folk say that if you picked red campion, someone you loved would die, and I thought of Guinevere and I wondered when in the previous night Taliesin had pulled those flowers from the hedgerow or woodland floor.

Merlin reached out and placed the garland on Iselle's head, crowning her as the Romans had crowned their champions.

'The gods are here among us,' Merlin said and, still kneeling, we looked around us at the flame-thrown shadows and the moon-paled night, expecting to see Epona riding her great mare, and Cernunnos the horned one, the Morrigán, Queen of Demons, and dread Balor, his single baleful eye shining in the dark. To see Taranis the thunderer, lord of battle, lifting his spear to Iselle as we had lifted our swords, eager to march with us into battle as he had done many lifetimes ago when the tribes of Britain had gathered against the might of Rome.

We were few. We were the last. And the darkness was all around.

But Merlin and Iselle had lit a flame of hope in our hearts. And we were going to war.

'You need a banner, lady,' Gawain said. He was sitting on a stool, sweating under the sun as he polished his war gear. His face was grey, and his eyes were swollen with wine and lack of sleep, and Parcefal had joked that if he worked any more lustre into that helmet, Gawain would have the shock of seeing his own face in it. 'A queen should have a war banner.'

'I'm not a queen,' Iselle said.

'You need a banner,' Gawain insisted, and I nodded at Iselle that Gawain was right.

'The bear,' Gediens said, as if surprised that there was any question about it. He was pulling a comb through his helmet's long red plume, while Parcefal and I were saddling our horses. 'She's Arthur's daughter. The bear is hers,' he said.

Gawain shook his head. 'Constantine flies the bear and has done for years,' he said. 'It should be something else. Something that our enemies have not seen.'

'Uther's dragon,' Parcefal suggested. 'Let the Saxons know that they've woken the beast.'

'Morgana would hate that,' Gawain agreed through a half-smile, turning his scale coat this way and that, catching the sunlight in the bronze plates to ensure that each and every one was free of any patina.

'Aye, she'll think Uther has returned to haunt her,' Gediens said, for Uther had killed Morgana's father Lord Gorlois and taken her mother Igraine for himself, along with their clifftop fortress of Tintagel.

'No,' Iselle said. 'I want my own banner.'

Merlin was securing a sack of provisions onto the back of one of the spare horses, but I knew he had been listening carefully and now he smiled.

And I knew what Iselle wanted.

'A wolf,' I said.

She nodded.

Gawain, Gediens and Parcefal grinned at one another.

'A wolf,' Iselle confirmed, for she had lived like a lone she-wolf, wild and free, but now she had gathered a pack of her own. It was perfect.

'What do you think, Taliesin?' Iselle asked and we all looked at Talicsin, who was over by the rain barrel, filling our flasks and empty wine skins with fresh water. The boy tilted his head back and howled at the blue sky, at which a dozen waterfowl clattered up from the reeds, and the rooks in the far-off tree tops squawked in alarm, and we laughed like old friends gathered at a Beltane feast.

And we *had* feasted the previous night. Having killed the last of the swine and the hens, we ate our fill and Lord Cai lifted his cup towards the marsh and thanked his old lord and friend for this final gift. Then, as the shadows crept, seeming to rise from the marsh around us, and the reeds whispered to the coming dusk, Gawain and I fetched Guinevere's linen-shrouded body from the house and laid her upon a pyre of dry reeds and deadfall. She weighed less than my scale coat, helmet and greaves, this woman whom my father had loved nearly all his life. Whose soul had entwined with his like the bindweed which Iselle and Taliesin had pulled from the hedgerow beyond the apple orchard and laid upon the lady, blanketing her in white blossoms.

Merlin thrust the burning brand in amongst the dry fuel and the fire took with frightening haste, as if the flames had been waiting for Guinevere too long. They surged through the pyre, searching and ravenous, and I watched as the white flowers wilted and browned in the heat, and Merlin spoke to the gods in the gloaming.

The fire's ardent breath and the crackle of the dry fuel drowned the piping of teal and the purring trill of the nightjar, and then we saw the first flames reach her and some of the men lowered their eyes rather than watch. I watched, though. The flare of red gold as the linen caught, then the blackening of it and a glimpse of pale skin before I too looked away.

Guinevere was free. She and my father were together again in some other place, and perhaps that was how it was meant to be, but I wondered about my mother, who must have been waiting for my father since she passed through the veil those years ago. Had my father found her when he fell in battle that summer's day? Or had he found the shade of some leafy tree and waited for Guinevere there, as Arthur had waited for Guinevere beneath that old twisted apple tree? Had my father abandoned my mother in death, just as he had abandoned me in life?

We watched the black smoke rise like the night itself, pluming up and up as if reaching for the stars which were revealing themselves in the fading sky. Men who knew each other like brothers let their tears fall into their beards as they stood heavy with memories of days when they were young and strong, and everything was possible. They were proud men. Warriors. And they cried for all that was lost. And as they watched that smoke eddy and surge like the last breath of a god freed of some curse of immortality, I knew that they were saying goodbye to Arthur too.

In the morning, we had gone over our plan, such as it was, and said our farewells, pledging ourselves once more to our purpose and to this last fight that would breathe life into the fading dream of Britain or else see it fade for ever.

Cai led his fourteen shining warriors east to round up what spearmen they could, and to be seen in their war glory, their helmets and scale armour glimmering beneath the summer sun, their long red plumes foretelling of the blood they would spill. Time would tell if the kings of Britain would heed the summons which Cai's riders had carried across the land on our departure from Ynys Môn. Meantime, we wanted word to spread that Arthur's famed horse warriors had returned to Dumnonia. We wanted the lords and spearmen of Britain to know that the great warriors of the past were gathering, and the time had come to fight. And so, Cai would fan the flames of rumour, but he would also learn as much as he could about our enemy's strength before riding west to join us on Ynys Wydryn, where we would make our stand.

'That's it, then,' Gawain said, when we had driven the two sheep and the goat out of their pens and Taliesin had done his best, telling the animals that they must find their own food from now on and to stay away from the reed-beds. None of us doubted that the boy was able to make the creatures understand him, even if we did not know how it could be.

As we walked our horses away from that sad little place in the marsh, Arthur's black bitch Banon walking beside us, I thought of the laughter which we had given to the sky when Taliesin howled like a wolf. The first real laughter of delight that place had heard in many years, perhaps ever. The last, too.

'Do you think he'll ever come back?' Gediens wondered out loud, turning in the saddle to look upon Arthur and Guinevere's steading one final time.

'Perhaps, if it looks as though all is lost,' Parcefal said, gazing eastward towards the rising sun, whose molten copper light showed all the old scars and scratches on his scale armour, and the lines in his face, and the grey stubble on his weather-worn cheeks. 'Perhaps then he'll come.'

We rode with that thought tugging at our hopes. Iselle, Gawain, Merlin, Taliesin, Parcefal, Gediens and me. We seven rode south to meet with Lord Constantine and to go to war.

22

Swords of Britain

'Lord Cyndaf has gone,' Gediens said, removing his helmet and pushing a hand through his short hair, which looked more fair than grey in the bronze light of the brazier. King Cuel had been relaying the positions of the Saxons and Morgana's own spearmen but had broken off mid-stream because everyone could see that Gediens had news on his lips.

'Gone?' Gawain lowered the cup from which he had been about to drink. 'Gone where?'

Gediens shrugged, heavy-browed, looking down at the table upon which Gawain and King Cuel had drawn Ynys Wydryn in charcoal. Several smooth pebbles represented our own forces, while three empty cups stood for the enemy. 'Seems he waited for dark, then led his men east.'

'Damn him.' Lord Constantine thumped the tent pole beside him. Gawain spat a curse and King Bivitas of Cynwidion growled that he was not surprised, as the men of Caer Celemion were cowards and always had been.

'We have to hope the Saxons didn't see him go,' King Catigern of Powys said, eyebrow raised as he dug between his teeth with a slender splinter. There were twelve of us in that tent, crowded around the table or by the fire or lurking in the shadows. The kings and lords of Britain who had answered the call.

'Cerdic will know,' Merlin said, watching the flames in the brazier leap and cavort. 'The man is a Saxon, not a fool.'

King Catigern grimaced and spat away the morsel which he had rooted out.

'Better Cyndaf, or anyone, leaves now than deserts their position tomorrow,' Gawain said. 'Or worse still, goes over to Morgana.'

'I shall curse nine times any man who does,' Merlin hissed under his breath, a warning for every lord and king to share amongst his men.

We all knew that Gawain was remembering Camlan and how Lord Mordred had betrayed Arthur during the battle, turning the tide in the Saxons' favour. Such was the hatred which had festered in Mordred all the years since Arthur had tried to have him killed so that Arthur might bury his own shame, of having begot the boy with his half-sister Morgana. Such was the secret poison which turned Mordred against his own people and which Arthur had drawn forth, along with Mordred's blood, on that death-gorged field.

'We're better off without that snake among us,' King Bivitas muttered, having nothing good to say of his southern neighbour.

'Lord Cyndaf is no coward,' King Catigern rumbled in a voice like boulders tumbling down a hillside. As king of Powys, Catigern was one of the most powerful rulers in Britain and certainly the most powerful man in that tent. He had brought four hundred spearmen south to fight under Iselle's wolf banner and, as Merlin said, when Catigern spoke even the gods turned an ear towards him. 'A king who deceives his men, those brave spearmen who have pledged to fight for him . . .' He walked over to the brazier and tossed the sliver of wood into the flames. 'That man dishonours his high seat.'

I saw some dark looks and furrowed brows. We needed the spearmen of Powys, and now we feared that King Catigern was having doubts.

'Speak plain, King Catigern,' came a voice from the shadows at the far end of the enormous tent. Lord Geldrin stepped into the fire glow, pulling his long moustaches through a fist. Everyone in that tent knew the reason why Lord Cyndaf had taken his men of Caer Celemion and slipped away in the dark, but Lord Geldrin wanted to hear King Catigern say it.

The king glanced at Iselle, who stepped away from Gawain as if to show that she neither sought nor needed his protection, for perhaps she, most of all, knew what was coming, as Catigern turned his gaze onto Gawain. 'You promised us Arthur,' he said.

There it was, unsheathed and sharp in the night.

'Arthur is gone,' Gawain replied. 'Nothing can change that. But we have Arthur's daughter. Uther's granddaughter.'

King Catigern was a big man. Barrel-chested and broad but running to fat. Even when he did not speak, he was loud. 'We had Arthur's son ten years ago and that did us little good.' There were some murmurs at the memory. 'Now we have his daughter and you think that is enough?'

I had heard of other men stealing into the woods or the marshes, as a fox will skulk away from the hen coop before dawn. They had come for Arthur and victory, but now they believed in neither.

Colour flooded Iselle's pale cheeks. She lifted her cup towards the king. 'And yet, you are here, lord king.'

Catigern made a sound deep in his throat. 'I am here, lady, because if we do not stop the Saxons now, you will all be bending the knee to them come winter.' He looked at King Bivitas of Cynwidion and King Cuel of Caer Gloui and some of the others whose lands were nearer the Saxon frontier than his own. 'And I will be paying them tribute within three years.' He turned back to face Iselle. 'I am here because I believe we have to fight, lady.'

Iselle nodded and held the king's eye a moment, the two of them sharing an unspoken moment of mutual respect. Then she turned to Lord Geldrin, who was pouring himself a cup of wine. 'And you, Lord Geldrin, why have you come? Surely the Saxons cannot trouble you in your clifftop fortress?'

In truth, we all wanted to know why Geldrin had come. The Lord of the Heights was no friend of ours after what had happened at Tintagel. He had ordered Father Yvain's death. His men had taken my old friend to the cliff's edge and cast him down onto the sea-worn rocks below, and though he defied Lady Triamour by refusing to kill the rest of us, I had hated him and burned to avenge Father Yvain.

But then, to our surprise, Lord Geldrin had arrived on Ynys Wydryn with eighty warriors and swore to fight in the name of Lady Iselle ferch Arthur ap Uther, and I had no choice but to swallow my hatred of the man.

'I have little to fear from Saxons,' Lord Geldrin agreed, dipping his head towards Iselle. 'Or from Lady Morgana, though she pays well for my wine and olive oil and I will be a poorer man when she is no longer the Lady of Camelot.' In three steps he was beside me. 'But this man's father and I were friends,' he said, reaching out to take hold of my shoulder, his eyes gripping my eyes. 'Your father had a sparhawk, Galahad. A savage little creature, all beak and claw and hatred.'

I nodded. 'A boy called Melwas broke its wing. My father told me.' Someone behind me rumbled that Melwas had been Mordred's man.

'The bird died soon after,' Lord Geldrin said, a shadow

falling across his face which even the flamelight could not dispel. 'I could have stopped it, stopped Melwas, but I didn't, and I've never forgotten it.' He looked at King Cuel and King Bivitas and shrugged. 'Strange how a little thing like that can haunt you through the years,' he said, then he turned to Iselle. 'And I knew your mother, lady. She was kind to me.' He nodded, an echo of the oath he had sworn to her the previous day, then he turned to King Catigern. 'I fight for Galahad and Lady Iselle,' he said. 'And when it's over, I will return to my eyrie and you can all fight amongst yourselves over the scraps.'

I could not like the man, but I admired him. In a tent full of kings and lords, he had unveiled a simple truth, that no matter a man's power and riches, he cannot escape the debts he owes to his own honour.

'We are all here to fight,' King Cuel said, eager to bring us back to important matters. 'But the loss of Lord Cyndaf and his two hundred spears hurts us.' He scratched amongst his red bird's-nest beard, which I doubted had ever known a comb. 'We will be thinner still come dawn, I suspect,' he said, by which he meant we would lose more spearmen to the dark. He opened his big hands towards Gawain and Iselle. 'Even against twice our number, when we thought Arthur would lead us there was hope. But now?' His red brows drew together.

'You think we should seek terms, King Cuel?' Merlin asked him. 'You think Morgana and her Saxon king will let you lead your men back to Caer Gloui and forget that you raised the boar banner here against her?'

'She will know by now that Arthur did not come,' King Cuel said.

'She will,' Merlin admitted, 'and she will see that we are all here even so,' and he threw his arms wide. 'Don't you see?' His robes were black, but his eyes held flames within them like two bronze scales from my father's armour. 'We are here.' And those three words were given like beats on a drum. 'And this is just the beginning. And though it may be that we cannot win this fight, we will cut our enemies deeply. We will bleed them and the other kings and lords of Britain, the men of Gwinntguic and Caer Lerion, of Elmet and Rheged, those who did not come to stand with us, will smell Saxon blood on the air. They will gather like wolves around a wounded deer and they will strike.' He pounded a fist into the triskele on his other palm. 'But I believe we *will* win.' He turned to Gawain. 'Why am I alive still, an old man like me, if not for the will of the gods? They have given me another chance, you see? I failed them before. I failed all of you.' He pointed at me then and it seemed that the candles guttered as heads turned. 'Here we have Lancelot's son. A man who does not share his father's weakness.' He swung his finger to point at Iselle. 'And here we have Uther Pendragon's blood, held in the flesh of a warrior unburdened by her father's failure.' He raked the assembled lords and kings with his flaming eyes. 'This is our chance to finish what Uther began.'

'And how many young men have to die tomorrow for you to make amends with the gods, druid?' This from Menadoc, King of Cornubia, who had taken the high seat after the death of his brother, Cyn-March, in the way that Uther had seized power in Dumnonia following the assassination of his brother Ambrosius Aurelius. Menadoc was old now, as old as Merlin perhaps, and Cornubia being a sub-kingdom of Dumnonia, he knew how his people would suffer at Morgana's hands if we lost. He had not spoken until now, and his words were heavy, as though he had weighed all that had been said and found that the scales did not balance.

'The gods have always demanded sacrifice, King Menadoc. You know this,' Merlin said.

Menadoc knew it, and yet he begrudged it. He had seen too many of his spearmen die in other people's wars. 'You were wrong about Arthur. Yes, he held back the tide for a while, but he was not the Pendragon you prophesied.' He threw an arm in Cuel's direction. 'He was not even a king,' he said. 'What if you're wrong about this girl?' He frowned at Iselle, then shook his head at Merlin. 'Our world has changed. Our gods are changing. The time of the druids is long passed.'

'Don't be an old fool, Menadoc.' Merlin turned on the man, but Iselle stepped forward, stilling Merlin's tongue with a raised hand.

'I killed my first Saxon when I was thirteen,' she told King Menadoc, who lifted his chin, inviting her to say what she would. 'He was alone,' Iselle said. 'Lost in the marsh when a mist rose and separated him from the others in his hunting party. He was a big man. As big as Gawain. But he was afraid.' She lifted a hand to her pale throat. 'He kept touching the silver hammer of his god. He was asking his gods for help when I let him see me through the reeds.' She let that sink in, lingering awhile in the memory of it.

'I don't think he wanted to harm me,' she continued. 'I think he was relieved to see someone out there, to know he was not alone after all.' She shrugged. 'Maybe he thought I would help him. I remember his face. It was a good face. A strong face. I smiled at him to show that I was not afraid, and he spoke in a soft voice as he came closer, his hands away from his blades, because he did not want to frighten me away. And when he was close, so close that I could smell his stink, I drew my knife and I buried it in his eye.' Her lips warped with the telling. 'I watched as he fell into the black water, clutching at that knife, and all I thought was that I was a fool for not killing him with an arrow, because he thrashed and went down where I could not reach him and I never saw that knife again.'

Iselle had never told me that story, and hearing it now made my blood run cold. I was not the only one by the looks on the faces around me. That a young girl could do such a thing. Could be so savage.

'I was killing Saxons long before I knew whose granddaughter I was. Whose daughter,' Iselle said. 'And tomorrow, when we face our enemies, you will not see me hiding at the rear, no matter what plans Merlin has for Britain and for me.'

My fists clenched at my sides. My chest tightened and I tried to catch Iselle's eye, to urge her to say no more, for I did not want her risking her life to prove anything to these men. But she avoided my eye. She knew what she was doing.

'Tomorrow, I will fight,' Iselle told us all. 'Not because Arthur was my father, but because I must fight. We must all fight. Here in this place. Or else we will lose everything. Our people will be driven out or killed or enslaved. Our gods will abandon us, never to return, for we will have proved ourselves unworthy of them. And so I will fight.' She took a deep breath and lifted her chin. 'But will you and your brave men fight with me, King Menadoc?' she asked.

The old king gave a grimace to reveal the last of his teeth. 'Aye, we'll fight, lady,' he grunted. 'The men of Cornubia will not be found wanting.'

'And we'll fight, lady.' This time it was King Cuel who spoke. 'And we'll send the Saxon dog and his traitor bitch back to Camelot with their tails between their legs.' With that he lifted his cup towards Iselle, and all around me kings and lords raised their cups in the fire-licked dark and swore death to our enemies, and so loud was the clamour that those warriors outside in the camp around us, men awaiting the dawn and the carnage it would bring, must have thought that some battle god had stridden into that tent and promised us the victory.

Gawain nodded at me and I nodded back. Then I looked at Merlin. He stood pulling his beard rope through his fist, watching Iselle, the ghost of a smile on his lips and his eyes full of flame.

Our enemies swept towards us like the shadows of fast-moving cloud darkening the summer meadow. They came in three great bodies of men, five hundred warriors in each advancing mass, walls of shields whose bosses glinted in the sun, great hedges of spears whose blades promised pain and death, the ruin of men and the torment of mothers and wives.

To the left, a huge war band of Saxons, their banner a moss-green ship's prow beast on a dun-coloured cloth. Some in ring mail but most in leather and skins and even furs despite the warmth of the new day. Here and there, steel helmets. Most in leather skull caps. All with spear and shield and a hunger for good, rich land to farm and upon which to raise more Saxons.

In the centre were Morgana's Dumnonians; spearmen of Camelot and those of the lady's allies whom she had gathered in beneath her banner of three crows like sheaves of wheat. Gawain had muttered that he could hear the dead, our fathers and their fathers and all those who had fallen to Saxon blades, moaning in heartfelt pain in the afterlife to see Britons standing with Saxons. Marching against the men who had fought for Uther and Arthur and Lord Constantine.

On the right, and the largest of all the contingents, came King Cerdic's Saxons, their shield rims kissing, their rampart of limewood, iron and leather as tight as the strakes of their ships' hulls. These were men who had fought for what they had taken from us. What they had won from us. Many were young men, sons and even grandsons of those first men who had crossed the Morimaru from their homelands. Men who had answered the old king's battle cry because they hungered for land and riches and renown of their own and hoped to find it in Dumnonia and Caer Celemion and Cynwidion.

No nightmare could have conjured such a sight, and warriors around me invoked their gods or emptied their bladders or vomited amongst the meadowsweet or murmured last words to lovers, as if those words being given to the air would somehow find their beloved's ears. Some men near me tried to raise an old battle song from their fathers' and grandfathers' time, but the song withered and died after a few lines and no one had the heart to take it up again.

The smell of human dung was thick in the air and my own guts were sour and my mouth was dry, and I felt *so* heavy, all but paralysed by the memory of when last I had seen such a war host. When I had been a boy and had watched my father ride towards that hate-filled, fear-soaked maelstrom and had never seen him again.

'We will beat them today and take back what they have stolen from us!' Lord Constantine yelled. He and his two hundred spearmen were arrayed in our centre beneath Lord Arthur's bear banner, which was stretched between two long boar spears and rippled in the breeze blowing across its surface, making the black bear shiver in its red field. 'We will drive the Saxons from Dumnonia. We will remake Britain as it once was.'

'Does he mean as it was before the Romans, or after?' Iselle grinned beside me, for Constantine wore his helmet with the stiff red crest, and his breast- and backplates of hammered bronze, and his purple cloak. His men were similarly accoutred, each wearing a long cloak of purple or red, so that they looked like the legionaries who once marched along the roads of Britain.

'Are you ready?' I asked her.

She nodded, sweeping her copper hair back from her face, then putting on her iron helmet with its moulded eyebrows and the snake's head which came halfway down the nose guard. The helmet was a gift from King Menadoc of Cornubia, who had had it made for the son he never had, and with its liner stuffed with horsehair it fitted Iselle perfectly.

'How do I look?' she asked me.

Bronze armour like mine would have been too heavy for her and so she wore a long coat of leather scales which had been a gift from Lord Constantine, taken as a prize in some long-ago battle. But Iselle and I had cut nine of the small bronze scales off my own coat – which I had never mended and so still bore the scars from my father's last fight – and Gawain, Gediens, Parcefal and Lord Cai had each given nine scales from their own coats, and all of these we stitched here and there into the leather of Iselle's coat, so that they caught the sunlight, winking with fire as she moved.

'Well, how do I look?' she said again, for the sight of her had robbed me of words. This was what she had craved, I realized. To be a part of something bigger than herself. To add her voice to the song which carried on the breeze, calling the old gods back to Britain. To chase the shadows from the land or, in failing, give her blood to the soil.

'Like a queen,' I managed. 'You look like a queen.' And she did.

She clenched her jaw and nodded that she was ready, so I called to the spearmen to say we were coming through and those men parted for us. I hefted the wolf banner which the women among King Cuel's camp followers had made, along with the two spears, and together we walked through that channel to calls of 'Lady Iselle! Lady Iselle!' And 'Iselle ferch

Arthur!' 'The Lady of Dumnonia!' And, from some mouths in savage glee, 'Saxon slayer!', for it seemed the kings and lords who had been at that war meeting the previous night had recounted Iselle's story to their warriors, so that her reputation had spewed from that tent like smoke from unseasoned wood, spreading far and wide. And though Iselle was untested in war and unknown to all but a few of those who had brought their blades and their courage to Ynys Wydryn, when they looked at her now, they saw a warrior goddess sprung up from the rich earth like summer wheat. A hero to lead them against the invaders, a new Boudica, who had united the Britons and led them to many victories against the formidable legions of mighty Rome.

'Saxon slayer! Saxon slayer!' men roared in unison, in voices as rough as steel on a whetstone, a chorus that stood the hairs on the nape of my neck and on my arms. We stopped beside Arthur's bear banner and Lord Constantine himself came forward and thrust his spear into the dew-damp earth that he might help me plant both shafts of Iselle's banner deep enough that they would stand even with the wind playing across the wool.

When it was done, Iselle and I took a moment to admire the leaping wolf, black as shadow upon its field of green cloth, then we both turned to look at our enemies, who had halted in their shieldwalls two arrow-shots away and now stood at rest, their spear blades pointing at the sky.

'There are so many of them.' There was almost wonder in Iselle's voice.

'That's a good thing,' I said. 'The more there are, the more we can kill.'

A grunt escaped Lord Constantine's throat. 'I hope you're not as reckless as your father was. This battle will not be over quickly, so you want to make sure you're still alive at the end of it.' He fixed his old eyes, eyes which had seen so many battles and so much butchery, on the Saxons and their Dumnonian allies. 'We'll bleed them, Galahad. Drop by drop, we'll bleed them until they've got nothing left.'

His armour, with its moulded stomach and chest muscles, gleamed beneath the dawn sun and, though he was old, I suspected that the body beneath that breastplate was still hard and muscled. He was an echo of Rome, was Constantine, a lasting vestige of discipline and implacable will and, like the Roman statues and palaces, the walls and the amphitheatres which still stood in these Dark Isles, I could imagine Lord Constantine outlasting us all. 'Don't throw your life away, lad,' he said. 'Make those whoresons come and take it.'

I nodded, took a breath, held it, released it. It was Constantine who had chosen the ground where we would make our stand, and even Gawain, who could not like the man, had agreed that it was the best place to plant our banners. And also the worst. For Ynys Wydryn was more or less an island, only connected to the mainland by a narrow strip of land to the east, and it was on that strip, which was cut across by a ditch built long ago, that we stood blocking the way. And that was why our enemies in their three bodies of spearmen had stopped. There was only solid ground enough for one of those bodies of men to attack at any one time, so that most of Cerdic's Saxons and Lady Morgana's Dumnonians would have to wait their turn before they could fight. This negated their superior numbers to a great extent, though of course they could disengage and replace tired men with fresh ones in ways that we could not.

But it was also a desperate place to hoist our banners of the Wolf and the Bear, King Catigern's stag antlers and the shining sun of Cornubia and the bristling boar of Caer Gloui, because if King Cerdic and Lady Morgana chose to, they could keep us on the island as a stopper holds wine in a flask, and we twelve hundred would live on fish and fowl and grow old on this island, in the shadow of the tor which stood at our backs two miles away, as it had once seemed my fate to do. For this island had been my home. And now, perhaps I would die here, my blood seeping into the rich soil as had the blood of the brothers who had raised me in the shadow of the Holy Thorn. I hoped that I would possess the same courage as they.

'Look.' Iselle pointed with the spear.

The crow-shields parted, and two figures emerged, one a warrior with a silver torc glinting at his neck, the other a black-haired woman in a black gown, so that she looked like a crow as they made their way towards us. I recognized both. Then a third man stepped out from King Cerdic's shieldwall and joined the other two. Not Cerdic's son, Prince Cynric, but a man I had never seen before.

'How good is your throw?' Lord Constantine asked me, nodding at the spear in my hand.

I hefted the spear, testing its weight, but Iselle shook her head.

'No, Galahad. Let us hear what they have to say.'

'They want to get a better look at what they're facing,' Lord Constantine said. 'We shouldn't let them.'

But Iselle was already walking down the embankment. Constantine looked at me, eyebrows raised, a half-smile on his lips, and together we followed Iselle down and across the ditch and up onto level ground again, from where Lord Melehan, Lady Triamour and the Saxon, whoever he was, would be unable to see much more than the first four ranks of our spearmen.

We went no further, letting brother and sister and their Saxon ally walk all the way, carrying the burden of our gaze, until they stopped six paces away. There, they nodded in greeting and we nodded back but did not speak, making it clear that we had nothing we wanted to say to them.

Lady Triamour broke the silence.

'Is it true, lady?' she asked Iselle. 'You are Arthur's daughter?'

'I am, lady,' Iselle said.

Lady Triamour gave a sad smile. I had never seen a sadder face than hers, nor, perhaps, a more beautiful one. 'Then you know we are related by blood,' she said, which of course they were, Lady Triamour being Mordred's daughter and Melehan being his son. 'Your father was my grandfather,' the lady said. She looked at Iselle as though curious to know what her aunt made of that. But Iselle did not give her the satisfaction of appearing to make anything of it.

'Where have you been all these years?' Lady Triamour asked.

'I've been living as best I can, away from all this,' Iselle replied. 'And killing Saxons when I could.' Her words paid the big, mail-clad, fair-haired Saxon no heed. As if he was not there. 'And you?' she asked Lady Triamour.

Lady Triamour did not answer. I glanced at Lord Melehan and knew that his eyes had never left me. For I had killed his brother and he wanted to fight me, wanted more than anything to kill me. I believed he would have given up the high seat promised by King Cerdic and his grandmother, in exchange for my head on his spear.

'You could join us, lady,' Lady Triamour said to Iselle. 'Rather than die here with them.' A pale hand gestured at Lord Constantine and me.

'And you could join me,' Iselle replied, 'and together we could beat Cerdic and destroy the Saxons' power in Britain for a generation.' Once again, Iselle did not even acknowledge the

Saxon, but I looked at him to see if he understood. Of course he did. That was why King Cerdic had sent him with Melehan and Lady Triamour. I had seen a faint amusement in his eyes when Iselle had suggested that Lady Triamour should join us.

'My grandmother wants the same thing you do,' Lady Triamour said. 'Peace in Britain.'

'Morgana would give Britain to this man's king.' Constantine now spoke, lifting his smooth-shaven chin towards the Saxon. 'But it is not Morgana's to give.'

'When my brother is king, he will protect Dumnonia,' Lady Triamour said.

'Your brother is a coward and a traitor and will never be king,' I said. Melehan *was* a traitor but he was no coward, and I had hoped to provoke him to draw his sword, but he let the insult slide off him, promising me death only with his eyes.

'I think the time for talking has passed,' Lord Constantine said, but Melehan raised a hand as if to beg his forbearance a moment longer and gestured to the ivory-hilted sword at Iselle's left hip. 'Is that Excalibur?' he asked.

'It is,' Iselle said.

Melehan hungered to kill me, but he also coveted Excalibur and I knew that he was imagining that sword at his own side. 'Arthur could not win.' When he spoke his grandfather's name, it was as if it tasted rotten in his mouth. 'What makes you think you can?'

Iselle smiled. In spite of the battle to come and the overwhelming numbers facing us, in spite of all the death and the pain and the anguish which would soon glut the day, Iselle smiled. And I saw how Melehan hated it and the Saxon was confused by it, and Lady Triamour feared it. 'We have Merlin,' Iselle said. 'And Merlin has the Cauldron of Annwn. And we have the gods.' She spoke as if these were simple truths, and yet her words had my blood trembling in my veins. I was in awe of her.

'Your gods are weak,' the Saxon spat. His first words. 'As weak as a woman.'

Iselle looked at the man for the first time, and he grinned because he thought he had managed to offend her.

'And we have Galahad,' she said, looking into the Saxon's blue eyes.

She caught me off guard with that, given how she had been talking of a treasure of Britain, a druid, and of the gods themselves, but an instinct, unforeseen and unbidden, told me I ought to do something.

And so I killed the Saxon.

It happened so fast. Lady Triamour stared at the dead man and Melehan half pulled his sword from its scabbard, but Lord Constantine levelled his spear.

'I wouldn't,' Constantine said, loudly because our men on the ridge behind us were cheering, and Melehan let his polished iron blade wink once beneath the morning sun before thrusting it home into its dark bed.

'You have no honour,' he rasped at me, his eyes round and so full of hate I thought they might burst.

'I let him draw his sword.' I pointed my own blood-slick blade at the dead Saxon, who lay soaking the green grass and the rich Dumnonian earth with his own blood, like so many of his people before him. And I *had* let him draw his sword. More than that, I had told him to draw it. He was experienced enough to know that I was serious and had pulled his sword and come at me with a scything attack, fast and deadly, but I was faster and twisted aside, his sword's tip hissing down my scale coat before I spun back, punching Boar's Tusk into his throat and driving it on until the gleaming hilt was in his beard. When I had hauled

Boar's Tusk free, blood sprayed more than five feet, hitting Iselle across the cheek and somehow spattering Lady Triamour too across her pale face and leaf-bud lips.

Lady Triamour wiped at the blood now, smearing it across that speck of brown below her left eye, but Iselle left the blood where it was. Holly berries strewn across snow.

Our spearmen cheering and my flesh trembling, I took the Saxon's head from his shoulders. 'Take this back to the old hound who shares your grandmother's bed,' I said, thrusting it at Melehan, who must have been sick of being given men's heads, yet he took it.

Lady Triamour looked up at the wolf banner and the bear banner and the grim-faced men who lined the summit of the embankment and thumped their spear shafts against their shields. Some of them were yelling at me to kill Melehan too, others were asking Lord Constantine's permission to come down and do it themselves.

'You will all die here.' Lady Triamour's words rose above the din, her beautiful, sad face seeming to show regret.

'We expect no quarter, for we shall give none,' Lord Constantine said.

Melehan stood there, holding the Saxon's head by his long, pale yellow hair, the ruined neck dripping into the grass, the dead eyes staring as if in disbelief.

'I will find you in the battle, Galahad,' he snarled.

'I hope so,' I said.

Then he looked at Iselle and jerked his chin in Constantine's direction. 'You will wish these old men had not pulled you out of the marshes,' he said. 'Arthur is not here to save you now.'

Iselle remained silent, having said everything that she wished to, and so the last word was left to the man who had been flying the bear banner all these years.

'You are a fool if you think Arthur is not here now,' Lord Constantine said, looking around him at the shivering grass and the distant reed-beds and the hawthorn tangles down by the brook on our right.

Melehan and Lady Triamour shared a look which had some meaning known only to brother and sister, then they turned and walked back towards our enemies. Our own men up on the low ridge took to hurling insults at them both, calling Melehan the son of a worm and a traitor and far worse yet, while others assured Lady Triamour that they would find her after the fighting, and these threats made my skin crawl, for they were far worse than anything they promised Melehan.

We watched them walk away, each of us lost within our own thoughts and aware of the weight of what had just happened. For there could be no peace now, only battle and pain and death.

'I don't think you would have made a good monk of the Holy Thorn, lad,' Lord Constantine said, his eyes shadowed beneath his helmet's rim and furrowed brows.

'I don't think so either,' I admitted, remembering that Iselle had said the same thing before we had made love on the Isle of the Dead. I glanced at her now. Her jaw was clenched, the muscle in her cheek bouncing beneath the blood-speckled skin.

Then Constantine, son of Ambrosius, nephew of Uther Pendragon and warlord of Britain, turned and walked down into the ditch and up onto the bank, and we followed him.

And no sooner were we standing beneath our war banners again, than did the mournful tones of Saxon war horns carry on the dawn air, and the mass of spearmen with their crow-shields lurched forward onto the green meadow.

*

'Back! Get the lady back!' Lord Constantine yelled, his face a grimacing, gore-spattered mask. 'Get her out of here, Galahad!' he screamed. I hacked into a neck, then thrust Boar's Tusk into a mailed shoulder, breaking through the iron rings into the leather, flesh and bone beneath. I had long ago lost my spear but I still gripped my shield and now I drove my left shoulder into it, heaving against the weight of bodies pressing in on me, trying to stay on my feet, to not be sucked under where men writhed and screamed and suffocated and died.

'Iselle!' I caught sight of her amongst the rolling human tide, this swell of desperate terror, and though she was only two paces away, she was unreachable. Then I saw a young warrior holding his spear in a two-handed grip above the press, its blade pointing at her.

I called to her but the clamour filled the world: a clashing of blades and the thump of shields, the terrible shrieks of pain and the gasping of men fighting for every breath. I had never heard anything so loud, not even the crashing of the sea in some raging storm.

My strength was useless against the thronging mass and so I brought Boar's Tusk up and sawed through the shield straps, letting the shield fall away. Then, by touch alone, I found Boar's Tusk's scabbard and pushed the blade home, for there was no room for sword work now.

Our shieldwall had held until a vast swathe of cloud, as grey as charcoal, swept across the noonday sun, at which time the crow-shields established a footing on our embankment and carved deeper and deeper into our position. To my right and left, our shieldwall yet held, but in the centre it was broken, and chaos was lord of the field. And so I pulled my long knife and punched it into necks and chests, into bellies and groins, and with my other hand I pulled and clawed at the flailing bodies of those I was butchering, hauling them out of my way, forcing them down into the carnage below, treading on them to get to Iselle.

Blades scraped on my armour, hands grasped like tangles of gorse at my greaves and my legs, but I would not be stopped and I killed and maimed and then I came face to face with the young spearman, who could not get his weapon down in time to stop me ramming my knife into the hollow beneath his raised right arm. He screamed into my face as I twisted the knife free and hacked into him, taking his lower jaw in a spray of hot blood.

'Galahad!' Iselle was wild-eyed and daubed in crimson. She looked lost. Confused. As though she had woken from deep sleep amid this stinking, convulsing carnage and could not imagine how she had got there.

'Back!' I told her, putting myself in front of her and drawing Boar's Tusk, and together we moved backwards as Lord Constantine led his best men in a desperate counter-attack against the crow-shields.

'For Lady Iselle!' our warriors cried. 'For the lady!' and they surged forward, driving the crow-shields back up onto the ridge. 'For the lady!' They drove on, sending the enemy tumbling down into the ditch onto those who were trying to clamber up, so that the trench became a seething mass of struggling men.

Then a great crack tore the sky, drowning the uproar of mortal strife, so violent that I felt it in my chest, felt it in the ground and rising up through my legs. A deep rumble followed, rolling on and on through the decisive moments of men's lives, sounding like some god driving his chariot across the roof of the world. Then a giant serpent's hiss as rain lashed down, fogging the day, sluicing blood from helmets and shields and faces. In an eye-blink the grass became treacherous and men were losing their footing and going down. Those who were not in the front ranks or caught up in the melee at our centre turned their faces to the grey sky and opened their mouths to catch what water they could, and when I looked over my shoulder I saw Merlin standing up on the crest of the rise, his arms and his staff raised to the rain-heavy sky as though he had called that downpour upon us, his beard rope jutting from his chin, the black dye with which he had darkened his eyes running down his gaunt cheeks.

Another peal of thunder ripped through the western sky, the rain arrowed down, bouncing from helmets and drenching the war banners so that they sagged heavily between their spear poles, and Constantine's men on the bank hurled spears down at the men struggling in the ditch, who roared and shrieked and writhed in a welter of despair.

And then Lady Morgana's war horns called her spearmen back.

Some fifty or more of our men chased them across the bank but most of us let the crow-shields go, content to yell insults after them and relieved to see their backs instead of their faces. I looked over to our right, where King Bivitas of Cynwidion stood with his spearmen. Still solid. Still defiant. I caught the king's eye and he nodded. Beyond the men of Cynwidion stood the warriors of Caer Gloui under King Cuel. I could not see them, but I saw the bristling boar banner standing firm in the seething rain. And behind them, in reserve, some fifty or so brave men of Caer Celemion who had not abandoned us and tramped home with Lord Cyndaf.

All around me men were bent double, sucking air into their lungs. Some tasted the rain on their tongues and took off their helmets to catch it, for there was so much coming down.

'Are you hurt?' I asked Iselle, looking for any wounds, any

damage to her leather scale coat. My eyes were full of sweat and my vision was blurred by the rain, and I was terrified that she might have taken a blade but did not know it yet, as can happen.

'No,' she said. She gripped Excalibur in her right hand. The blade was red with gore. Her eyes sharpened and she came back to herself. 'No,' she said again, as if confirming it to herself. 'You?'

I shook my head and took her arm, wanting to lead her to the rear, to where King Menadoc of Cornubia and Lord Geldrin waited with their men as a reserve, but she pulled away and removed her helmet so that the men around us could see that she was alive and unharmed.

'Get her away from here, Galahad,' Lord Constantine bellowed, striding over to us, pushing men out of his path.

'No, Galahad,' Iselle said. 'I won't go.'

'You must,' I urged her, but then Constantine was upon us.

'You need to get to the back, lady,' he said, blood-slathered and furious, still in the grip of the battle lust. Glaring at her. 'If you die, it's over.'

'I'm staying here,' Iselle told him.

Lord Constantine's head snapped back as though he had been struck. 'You'll do what I tell you, *lady*.' He ground the words out.

Not even a heartbeat and Boar's Tusk was at his throat.

'Careful, lord,' I rasped. For I too was thrumming with the savage thrill of battle and I blamed myself for having been carried away from Iselle in the thick of the fight, and any man who threatened her now, Saxon or Briton, would pay with his life.

'Lower your blade, Galahad,' Morvan, Lord Constantine's second in command, ordered, his own sword close enough to my face that I could see the rain washing the blood off it.

'Galahad.' Iselle's voice, wanting me to do as Morvan said.

I did not lower Boar's Tusk, nor did I take my eyes from Constantine's, ignoring Morvan as though he was of no more consequence than the rain dripping from my helmet's rim. I knew that there were other warriors around us, gripping spears and swords and waiting for their lord's command. Beyond them, and all around, the cries and moans of the broken and dying.

Constantine made a gesture which told Morvan to lower his sword, which the man did, glowering at me.

'Then you had better keep her alive, boy,' Constantine snarled at me.

'I will,' I said, and removed my blade from his throat.

'Here they come!' someone yelled, and we all turned to look east again, our small enmities falling away in the face of King Cerdic's Saxons moving forward in a shieldwall forty men across and five ranks deep. The retreating crow-shields were streaming past both flanks, some getting stuck in the treacherous, marshy ground because there was no way through the oncoming Saxon rampart.

'Cerdic made Morgana send her men first,' Constantine said, 'to prove their loyalty.'

'And to soften us up,' Morvan said.

Our men were gathering spears and discarded weapons. Some were down in the ditch, looting the enemy dead, pulling off helmets, arm rings and finger rings, stripping armour from bodies which had moments before been living men, drinking from flasks for which the dead had no use, cutting amulets from the cords around men's necks and searching for coins and anything else of worth. But there had been no time to gather up our own dead and they lay where they had fallen, dozens of them in their scarlet cloaks, once the flower of Britannia, given now as some appalling sacrifice which we knew would appease neither men nor gods.

'This will be harder,' Constantine announced, sweeping his shield- and bone-blunted sword towards the coming mass of foes, 'for this Saxon king knows that we are all that stands between him and the high seat of Britain.' His voice carried as if on wings, far over the clamour. 'On this day, in this place, will the fates of Dumnonia and Caer Celemion, Cynwidion and Caer Gwinntguic and even mighty Powys be decided,' he yelled, nodding over to his left at King Catigern, who stood at the forefront of his men. 'We must not fail!'

I nodded at Iselle, who dipped her head in grim resoluteness, both of us admitting in unspoken accord that Lord Constantine was a leader and we were lucky to have him.

'You will not find the warriors of Powys wanting, Lord Constantine,' King Catigern boomed, spitting the rain which ran down his thick moustaches and beard. 'Send the Saxon dogs to die on our spears.'

'Powys! Powys! Powys!' they chanted, clattering their spear staves against their shields in a woeful echo of the thunder, for though the men beneath that stag antler banner had repelled some half-hearted assaults from Morgana's crow-shields, they had yet to face the onslaught that we in the centre had faced, and they craved to prove themselves our equals or betters.

I picked up a scarred but sound shield from the ground nearby, prised a spear from the hand of a dead crow-shield and took my place in the middle of the mound once more. Beside Iselle.

'Can we win?' she asked me. She was looking straight ahead, a shield in her left hand, Excalibur in her right, her helmet's cheek irons down so that her face was mostly obscured, though her eyes were visible and as fierce as a hawk's.

'If we kill enough of them,' I said.

The Saxons had taken up their chant of 'Woden! Woden! Woden!' The stench of open bowels and the startling iron stink of blood tainted the air, too strong even for the rain to wash it away, and yet I could still smell the Saxons. Their soaking, rancid furs and their swine-reeking sweat and their ale breath which fogged around their faces as they came on, invoking their god, who once had resided far away across the sea but who now, it was whispered, dwelt in these Dark Isles too.

'Make way!' a familiar voice called, 'make way, damn you!' A channel opened behind us and Merlin came through, leading a white stallion. 'Don't let them kill me, Galahad, there's a good boy,' he cried, as he led the stallion by its bridle down into the trench and up the other side onto the plain.

'Where did he find that?' Iselle asked, for it was a beautiful horse, a stallion which Lord Arthur himself would have coveted back in his prime when he was the lord of horses.

'What are you doing, Merlin?' I called down to him, but the druid ignored me. He stood there with that noble beast, which could have torn itself free at any time, or even killed Merlin if it had wanted.

'Do you think they have all seen him?' Merlin yelled back at me, holding the bridle still and facing the Saxon shieldwall.

'Seen him?' I shouted. 'King Cerdic will be riding him if you don't get back up here!'

Merlin nodded and raised a placating hand. He took a knife from his belt and put his face to the stallion's muzzle, seeming to whisper or sing to him, and the beautiful creature lowered its head, accepting the old man's embrace. Merlin's arm moved quickly and the blade cut, and still the horse stood there, uncomplaining as Merlin's hands and gown and even his face were sheeted in blood that steamed in the rain.

'Merlin!' Iselle shouted, for the Saxons were no more than an arrow's flight away now. Soon the strongest of them would be trying to claim the glory of killing a druid with a spear throw; a deed for their scops to sing of. And yet Merlin clung to the stallion's head still, cradling it, whispering soothing words like a man who is thanking his horse after a good ride.

'Merlin, they're close!' Iselle cried, and with those words still fogging on the air, the stallion's forelegs buckled, and it fell to its knees and it was now no longer a white horse but half red. And Merlin stood and pointed his bloody knife at the Saxons, who came to a halt, their shield rims kissing and their chant of *Woden* draining away like the stallion's lifeblood.

'A waste of a fine horse,' grunted a man beside me. And perhaps he was right. But perhaps he was not, for I knew what Merlin was doing, or at least I knew why he was doing it.

That magnificent stallion, as handsome in his way as my father's stallion Tormaigh had been, slumped onto his side with a soft snort, raised his head one final time, then laid it back down on the grass, his belly rising and falling with his last immense breaths.

'The bastards have stopped,' another red-cloaked spearman said. He wasn't watching the horse but rather the Saxons. 'Why have they stopped?'

'Because Merlin has cursed King Cerdic,' I said.

'By cutting a horse's throat?' the first man asked.

'Cerdic claims to be descended from the Saxon chieftain Hengist,' I said, 'who was himself descended from their god Woden. Hengist and his brother Horsa were the first Saxons to win land in Britain. Hengist became king in Ceint.' I also knew that Hengist meant stallion, but I did not say it. I had learnt all this from Father Brice many years ago, for it had been expected of me in my novitiate that I should know how the ruin of Britain had begun.

Now, I watched the Saxon shieldwall waiting there, afraid of Merlin's magic, afraid that the last druid in Britain had cursed their king by cutting that noble stallion's throat, and I wondered if Father Brice and the other brothers' bones still lay unburied amid the ruins of the monastery. If I lived through the day, I would bury the brothers as they deserved. I swore it to myself and to any gods who cared to listen. But first I would avenge them. The blood in my veins, hot and in spate, demanded it. There was no fear in me then. I hungered for the fray. Here, on Ynys Wydryn, on this island in the marsh, I would stand as the brothers had done.

Lord Constantine ordered a score of men to gather up any last spears or weapons from the ground and butcher those crow-shields who lay groaning in the ditch. Others took the opportunity to drink or exchange their battered shields for better ones, to ask Taranis for strength and skill at arms or to beseech Arawn for swift passage to the afterlife should they fall in the coming battle.

'How long will the druid's curse hold them?' Morvan asked, but no one could answer that. Not even Merlin, who, leaving the stallion to pump the last of its blood into the grass, ambled back across the ditch and up the embankment with all the urgency of a man out gathering fungus and herbs.

But I hoped his magic *would* fade, or that the wizards whom King Cerdic had sent out ahead of his shieldwall to counter Merlin's magic would break the chains which bound them. I wanted the Saxons to find their courage again, to defy the druid's curse and come for us, because then I would kill them. I would slaughter them as my father had done. I was Galahad ap Lancelot, and I was a killer of men.

*

It took the three Saxon wizards the time it takes a candle to burn halfway down to counter Merlin's curse with the horse. Enough time for our men to get their wind again and steel themselves for the next fight, but not so long that doubts and fears could gnaw too deeply at their souls.

'Stay close,' I told Iselle.

'Not too close,' she said, one eyebrow raised.

I nodded. I knew I was wild in the maelstrom of battle. 'No, not too close.'

Some of our men at the rear had bows, and when the Saxons were less than fifty paces away, these archers sent their arrows streaking over our heads like swallows to roost. We cheered for every arrow that struck a Saxon face, shoulder or leg, and even when one tonked off a helmet, though most missed or buried themselves in the ground or in shields.

Their shieldwall hit ours with a clattering thump and a ragged chorus of grunts and then the shoving began. This was when you were close enough to your enemy to smell the sour cheese, garlic or onions he had eaten and the ale he had drunk, and you could smell his fear, too. I leant into my shield and thrust Boar's Tusk through any gap I could find, while Iselle rammed her spear over my shield rim into men's faces, screaming at them, her eyes flaring.

The man throwing his weight upon my shield went down and Iselle ran her spear into his belly to make sure he was dead, but another man took his place and when we killed him too, another came on, and so it went, until we were gasping for air but could find none.

Like the Black Crow traitors before them, the Saxons concentrated their attack on our centre, for they knew that was where Iselle stood, beneath her wolf banner, and they believed that if they killed her, we would break. I knew that Constantine had been right, that it was madness for her to be in the thick of the fight. But I also knew that her being there inspired our warriors to incredible efforts. Seeing her fighting at the fore, as she had promised, stabbing and killing and shrieking like some goddess of war, shamed them or emboldened them to push harder, to hack and hew with renewed strength, to not give ground but to take it from the enemy. Iselle carried the blood of the Pendragon in her veins. She was the beating heart of Dumnonia, of Britannia, and we fought for her.

But the enemy were too many and we were too few.

'Hold! Hold!' Lord Constantine bellowed in a voice which had carried across battlefields for more than twice my lifetime. 'Hold, damn you!' he roared, 'hold!' but we could not hold.

Risking a look over my shoulder, I saw King Menadoc's sunshields running in groups of a dozen to plug the holes that the Saxons had carved in our shieldwall. They came shouting: 'Cornubia! Cornubia!', proud of the land of their birth as they lent their shoulders and shields and blades to counter the Saxons and tried to drive them back. But as I heard that call more and more, I knew that our line had been breached in too many places and that our rampart of flesh, wood and steel was disintegrating like a mound of sand on a beach before the relentless surging of the waves.

'Back!' I roared. 'Do not break!'

I looked along that line, my view obscured by thrusting blades and snarling, bearded faces and the rain which still hammered down from the slate-grey sky, but I saw Lord Constantine and he saw me. He bared his teeth and nodded, then gave the same order. 'Back!' he yelled. 'Slowly! Keep those shields up! Back! King Catigern!' he screamed. 'Damn you, pull your men back!'

I saw the big king of Powys spit a curse and order his men to withdraw in line with ours, lunging and shoving as we ceded the ridge. We gave ground, retreating en masse, still facing the enemy, our shields still pressed against theirs, back down the mound onto the flat. I saw thirty or so of Menadoc's sun-shields hurrying to our right to meet a body of Saxons whose intention was to outflank us and attack our rear, and there was a crash of shields and a roar when those two groups met.

Then the man beside me tripped on a tussock or his own feet and went down, and I buried Boar's Tusk in the earth and reached out to him, yelling at him to take my hand, but the weight of the enemy on our shieldwall was too much, their advance as inexorable as night, and just as our fingers touched I was driven back and only just managed to snatch up my precious sword before it was too late. I caught one more glimpse of the man, of his pleading eyes and the terror in his face, but then he was gone. He had been younger than me.

'What can you see?' I asked Iselle, for I was crouched behind my shield, and whilst spearing over my head she had a better view.

'Saxons,' she said, which was not the answer I'd hoped for.

Back we went, leaving our dead and dying behind. Two hundred paces from the ridge now. We could not stop the Saxons, but they had not broken our wall. Not yet.

We did not do much killing then. Our only ambition was to survive long enough to see the Saxons haunted by their nightmares made flesh, and so we gave up that narrow strip of ground between the reed-beds, though I knew that we must make a stand soon or else we would come onto the island proper and once there, Lady Morgana and King Cerdic would throw every man at us and we would be overwhelmed and surrounded and it would be over.

'There!' Iselle gasped, blinking away sweat and rain and

looking beyond the enemy shieldwall. The Saxon leaning into his shield against me was tiring. I felt it through the limewood, though the men at his back were shoving him on. I lifted my head above my shield's rim to see that we were three hundred paces from the embankment now and only a hundred paces from the wider ground at our backs. 'There! On the ridge,' Iselle said.

'I see them,' I snarled, manoeuvring my shield boss above the Saxon's so that I could press his shield down. His strength was gone. Down went his shield and I saw the surprise in his eyes as Boar's Tusk smashed through his teeth and out through the back of his skull.

King Cerdic and Lady Morgana were up on the ridge. They stood surrounded by their household warriors, Cerdic in ring mail, his hair, beard and long moustaches as silver as his helmet, Lady Morgana swathed and cowled in black like her granddaughter Lady Triamour. An old bear and two carrion crows looking over a field of corpses.

Come on, I willed them. *Here we are.*

Back we went, step by step, getting nearer to the sloping ground which led up to the tor, nearer to the open ground, upon which our enemies would roll over and around us in a wave of steel and death.

Come on. Come and kill us.

The battle din was not what it had been before. Men were tired. Their arms weakening. Blades bit into shields less, rasped off helmets less. Mouths were too dry to yell insults. Rain flayed us, seething in ground churning to mud. We slipped and stumbled in the sludge, and the muscles in my thighs, shoulders and arms screamed with hot pain. The sound of my own rasping breath was loud in my helmet, the pulse of my blood a rhythmic thump in my ears, and it all seemed somehow far away. The battle. The struggle. This savage contest. It was distant and I was a boy again watching from the hilltop at Camlan. Watching my father riding to his old friend, the two of them flickering like flames in the night.

And the next time I looked up I thought Lady Morgana and her Saxon king had retreated back over the ridge, but then I saw Cerdic striding forwards with his score of mailed, fair-bearded warriors, as if he was eager to join the fray now that victory looked certain. The old warrior, who had fought Uther and Arthur and Lord Constantine and now us, wanted to be close enough to see the end with his own eyes. He hungered to see the defeat in our faces, to feel the last hope go out of us. To see the last light of resistance extinguished.

So, what must the old Saxon have thought when he heard the long, ominous note of Lord Cai's war horn carry across Ynys Wydryn like the judgement of a god?

They came in the shape of a spear, and in a way they *were* a spear, cast by Taranis, one of the old gods of Britain. Or a bolt of lightning, perhaps, for Taranis is the god of thunder and this was a day when the sky itself seemed to be at war.

Lord Cai led them. He was the point. On his left shoulder rode Parcefal and Cadwy, and on his right rode Gawain and Gediens, and storming behind came the rest of them, a dozen shining warriors, galloping across the summer flowers, red plumes flying from silver-chased helms, spears couched beneath their arms, their mounts armoured in leather: boiled shaffrons covering their faces, breastplates to protect their mighty hearts.

The last of Arthur's horse lords. Men from another time, riding to one final battle.

And though they were not even a score, the earth itself

thundered beneath the pounding of the horses' iron shoes, and we cheered for them even in the tumult of that desperate fight.

'Hold here!' Lord Constantine yelled.

'Hold!' I shouted, and behind me someone blew a horn so that we all knew that this was where we must stand. We must give no more ground to the enemy but stand and hold them and kill them here.

A shudder ran through the Saxon shieldwall. I felt a lessening of the great weight bearing down upon us as men risked a backward glance, struck by the worst of all fears to afflict those fighting in a shieldwall: that you find enemies at your back.

Iselle felt it too. 'Kill them!' she screamed, parrying a spear that was aimed at her face and thrusting her own spear into a Saxon's throat. 'Kill them!'

Sometimes doubt will kill a man, and Lord Cai and Gawain had sown doubt in the enemy, so we drove into them, hacking and cutting, and on the left, the men of Powys were not merely holding the ground but were taking it back, their warrior king living up to all the bards' songs which celebrated the courage and martial skill of his people.

Iselle had killed the man in front of me and for a brief moment I caught sight of Gawain and Parcefal driving their spears down into King Cerdic's warriors, who, rather than fleeing, bravely stood their ground, surrounding their king. I saw Gawain hurl his spear and draw his sword. Saw him spur his horse into the thick of the fray, hacking down to his left and right, driving the mare on. I saw Gediens lop off a man's head and I saw Parcefal cast his spear, which struck the man beside the king. And I saw a huge Saxon swinging a long axe at Gediens's mare, cutting away both forelegs at the knee, toppling horse and rider. *Gediens, no!*

A spear blade struck my helmet but glanced off. Another

punched into my shoulder but did not break through my scale armour. I hammered Boar's Tusk down onto a leather skull cap and felt the keen edge bite.

'Gawain needs us,' Iselle rasped, and I saw fear in her eyes and so tried to peer over the shield. But now I could see nothing of the distant fight, a long arrow-flight away, between the horse warriors and the Saxon king. What I could see were those other Saxons, the ones who had stood under the banner of the ship's prow beast and had yet to fight. They were running to help King Cerdic. A great roaring horde of men with shields, axes, spears or swords, charging through the veiling rain. And I knew that Cai and Gawain, Parcefal and the others, in their desperation to kill King Cerdic and rip the hearts out of our enemies, had not disengaged and formed to charge again, but had stayed in the melee, hacking and hewing and spurring their mounts through Cerdic's best men to get to the king.

'If we don't help them, they'll die,' Iselle said.

'If we try, we'll die,' I snarled.

But Iselle was right. The Saxons would swarm around each of the horsemen like hounds on a stag, wounding the horses over and over, bleeding them. They would thrust their spears up at the riders and the horse lords of Britain would fall one by one until they were no more.

I looked to my left. The spearmen of Powys were ahead of the rest of us now, though they were no longer making ground. To my right, King Bivitas had fallen. I had heard the desperate cries of his warriors and felt the news of it spread amongst us like an ill wind. And yet his men fought on, as did the warriors of Caer Gloui led by King Cuel, though their shieldwall was only three men deep in places now. But the fifty men of Caer Celemion, led by a grizzled-looking man named Gralon, still held their position at the rear.

'Somebody bring me Gralon,' I yelled.

Moments later, Gralon had muscled his way to me through the ranks. His spearmen stood at his back, tall and grim-faced and war-ready.

'Are your men ready to fight?' I asked him. For a heartbeat he looked at me askance, as though not sure I had enough years on my back or blood under my fingernails for him to take orders from me. But then he grinned, which was all the answer I needed. For Gralon was eager to emerge from the shadow which his lord, Cyndaf, had cast upon the men of Caer Celemion, and so I told him what we would do.

When he brought his men into position, Gralon was like a war dog wrenching at the leash. His beard was spittle-flecked and his eyes were bulging in his head and I saw him thumping his plain iron helmet with the heel of his hand, working himself into a rage while his men formed a column four abreast behind him, gripping their shields two-handed before them.

'Now, Gralon!' I called. 'For Caer Celemion!' I turned to Iselle, who had come up beside me and put half of her shield behind mine. 'Take a deep breath and hold it,' I said, then Gralon's men behind us struck, driving the air from my lungs like a gush from a smith's bellows. The pressure against my back was immense and I saw Iselle's face gripped in a rictus of pain which even the cheek irons of her helmet could not hide. But we were moving. Forward. And if we'd lifted our feet we would have been carried like flotsam on the tide, but as it was we tried to stamp down, some vain attempt at control, as Gralon and his column of spearmen drove on, crushing us, driving the breath and the life from our bodies but driving the Saxons back too.

I tried to tell Iselle to hold on, to breathe, but I could not make the words. I was seeing black motes floating through my vision like ash, and I thought I had killed us both and even then, I could not tell Iselle that I was sorry. Her eyes were heavy-lidded. Closing. I felt her body going limp against mine and I cursed the gods, if only in thought, but then the enemy gave way, crumbling before us like rotten wood before the driven nail, and in three heartbeats we broke out from their rear rank into the empty, grey, rain-washed day.

Stumbling, I sucked in air and rain, and my vision sharpened again as my senses returned in a flood tide of noise and stench and the warm hardness of the sword hilt in my hand and the weight of the scale armour on my body. Iselle had fallen to her knees but she was up again now, though bent over, gasping for breath, and she nodded to let me know that she was unhurt, then followed the direction of my gaze. And there, an arrow-shot away, were the horse lords of Britain, fighting for their lives.

A roar behind me. The warriors of Caer Celemion pouring out from the channel which they had forced through the Saxons.

'Keep going!' Gralon roared at them, at those who were hacking at the backs of Saxons at the rear. 'Keep going, you bastards! On, Galahad!'

I pointed Boar's Tusk across the field. 'To the horses! To Lord Cai!' I called, and then Iselle and I were running across the torn and muddy ground, over flattened flowers and past corpses which stared with dead, lidless fish eyes at the world of which they were no longer a part.

I was young. Not yet a lord of war as my father had been. But I could run, even in my war gear, even with lungs still screaming from having been starved of air, and I killed the first Saxon before he had fully turned to face this unexpected threat. Iselle was close behind and she hammered Excalibur against a

Saxon shield, but then two big Caer Celemion men jumped protectively in front of her and hacked the Saxon down.

It was madness. Lord Cai's men were wheeling their mounts, their long horsehair plumes dancing as they struck down with their swords, cleaving heads and lopping arms off at the shoulders, and even the horses themselves were fighting, biting men's faces and swinging their armoured heads down to break noses, cheeks and necks. And now Gralon and his men were on these Saxons whose fine mail and helmets could not intimidate the men of Caer Celemion. Having been held in reserve, Gralon's warriors fought now with the savagery of hounds kept too long from the meat.

Through the swirling maelstrom I saw Gawain, twisting in the saddle, hacking down at men on either side, crimson spraying, shrieks ripping the air. I saw Parcefal on his big mare, Lavina, lean out of the saddle to drive his sword down into a Saxon's back. Saw the sword's tip burst from the man's chest before Parcefal hauled it free and the body fell forward to be trampled beneath hooves. Lord Cai was on Parcefal's other side, and together those three were driving their mounts towards King Cerdic, who gripped a long axe now and stood his ground with the last of his bodyguard, three Saxons who were tall and wide and grey as cliff faces in their iron ring mail.

'Crow-shields.' Iselle pointed Excalibur towards the ridge where we had planted our banners that dawn.

'Too many,' I said. They were swarming over the embankment, too many to count, and I caught sight of Melehan at the fore, leading Lady Morgana's men to save the Saxon king.

Gawain had seen them too. He bellowed a challenge at Cerdic and dug his heels into his mare's flanks and scythed his sword against a shield.

But there was no time. The crow-shields were almost upon us.

'We can hold them,' Gralon grunted, in between gasps for breath. His greying beard was speckled red. 'Get the lady away.'

I looked back to where the shieldwalls were battling. We had broken through, but we had not broken the Saxons, and now, rather than two shieldwalls, the lines were less distinct and at several places huge melees raged.

'Gawain!' I called. He looked up at the crow-shields and I saw the desperate, hopeless fury in his face, because he knew we had failed. King Cerdic would live and we would lose.

'Galahad, get the lady away.' There was no fear in Gralon's face. His men stood around us, bloody and breathing hard and wide-eyed, waiting for Gralon's orders. I nodded and he nodded back, then he growled at his men of Caer Celemion to make a shieldwall two men deep facing the oncoming tide of crow-shields.

Seventeen of Cai's men still had their mounts. Gediens was dead. I saw him lying there in the mud, eyes looking up at the sky, rain bouncing off his pale face.

'Take my horse, Galahad,' Medyr said, limping towards me, leading his stallion by the reins. His helmet was gone and there was blood in his black curls, washing down his face with the rain. His right arm was slashed below the short sleeve of his scale shirt. 'I can't ride.'

'No, Medyr,' I said. 'No.'

'Do what he says, Galahad.' I looked up as Gawain's horse made its way to us, plumes of hot breath pouring from its nostrils beneath the leather shaffron. 'Get Iselle to safety.' Iselle was staring at King Cerdic, who had his back to us as he beckoned the crow-shields on with the long axe, hungering to avenge his slaughtered hearth men. 'We have to get you away now, lady,' Gawain said, the words hurting him.

Iselle did not seem to hear him. She was still watching King Cerdic, hating him across the distance. Knowing how close we had come and knowing it all meant nothing now. Then she swung her gaze to Gawain and then to me. 'I won't run while others stay and fight,' she said, and my stomach clenched with pride but with fear too.

'The tor,' I told the others. 'We'll make our stand there.' There was a clash of shields as Lady Morgana's men struck Gralon's small force.

Parcefal wheeled his horse around, peeling away from the rest of Lord Cai's riders, who were milling nearby, encouraging their mounts with words and familiar touch as they awaited their commander's order. 'We can punch our way through. There.' He was pointing beyond us towards the far right of the Saxon lines. He shrugged at Gawain. 'Can't stay here,' he said. And he was right, because the crow-shields were already swarming around Gralon's pitiful shieldwall and would be upon us soon.

I picked up a heavy Saxon spear and mounted Medyr's horse, and Iselle climbed up behind me, while Lord Cai pulled Medyr up behind him because he refused to leave any of his men behind.

'I'll lead,' Parcefal said, and no one argued with him as we started to move, the rest of the horse warriors forming into an arrowhead shape as easily as geese in flight, most with spears they had recovered now couched under their arms in readiness for the charge.

The wind was gathering now, sweeping the shrouds of rain east and into our faces, so that we had to squint against it. Some of the Saxons in the rear ranks were turning or casting nervous glances over their shoulders because they knew Lord Arthur's famed horse warriors were behind them, though they could not have imagined we would try to charge into such a dense mass of shield-bearing men, not least because they knew that to reach safety we would have to pass through our own lines too.

'Gawain once told me that the horses won't charge a proper shieldwall,' Iselle said. Her left arm was around my waist, her hand a fist around my belt buckle, while in her right she gripped Excalibur. Somehow, she had wedged herself between me and the two rear saddle horns, so that we both sat high, and Medyr's stallion whinnied and complained but I leant forward and stroked his muscled neck where it was not covered by his shaffron and told him we were friends and that all would be well, but that we needed him to be brave and to run and not to stop until I told him to. In my legs I felt the tremble in his flesh and the great strength in him, and I knew he had Tormaigh's spirit and would not let us down.

We trotted at first, towards the centre of the Saxon line because we did not want those men on the far right to know our intentions and form a rampart of shields facing us. Besides which, seeing us coming towards them, the Saxons in the centre turned to face us, which relieved some of the pressure on Lord Constantine's men facing them.

Hooves drummed the earth and my pulse drummed in my ears, and even through her leather armour and my bronze scales, I felt Iselle's heart thumping against my back as we left the carnage behind us, moving towards the greater butchery ahead. Then, without warning, Parcefal cut across the field at a diagonal, and we followed, Cadwy on our left, Gawain on our right, the horses' two-beat-gait becoming the three beats of the canter.

Helmet plumes jumped and shattered. The horses' breath trailed in tendrils through the cold rain. We had come almost to the northern edge of the land bridge, almost to the reed-beds into which the rain hissed like some malevolent serpent, when Parcefal straightened his course and kicked back his heels and we all did the same, and then we were flying.

Realization spread across the Saxon line like a ripple through a pool, and some were turning, bringing their shields up, a few even making ready to hurl their spears at us in the hope of emptying a saddle or two before we closed.

'Artorius!' a rider behind me yelled.

'Artorius!' another echoed, then, 'Iselle!'

And others took up that battle cry. 'Iselle! Iselle!'

We flew. Still we did not know if our horses would carry the charge, but we had to ride as though we had no doubts at all.

'Iselle!' I called. Not a war cry but a declaration, to gods and to men. That should I die, it would be for her. And then Parcefal's mare struck the line with a clatter and shriek and Lavina did not slow and we poured into the breach. The noise was like the ending of the world. Screams of horses and men. Shields and spears and bones splintering. Iron and steel rasping and clanging and singing in long, clean notes which rose to the grey sky. Grunts and roars and breath punched out of bodies, and iron hooves sending thunder rumbling through the ground.

I put the Saxon spear blade through a man's neck and pulled it free as we rode on. Iselle swept Excalibur and took a head clean off. I saw a Saxon thrust a spear up at Cadwy but the impact drove the butt of the spear straight back into the Saxon's chest and Cadwy galloped on.

Most tried to escape, throwing themselves into their companions, screaming at their countrymen to move so that they might live, doing anything to not be in our path. At least the men of Powys had some warning and they moved left or right, forcing a channel as best they could, while the horse lords of Britain manoeuvred into a column two abreast, so that we passed through our own ranks as neatly as an arrow through tall grass.

I pulled the reins to the right and we rode to where Lord Geldrin seemed about to commit his reserve to help the men of Cynwidion, who were being overrun now that they had no king to lead them.

'Nice ride, Galahad ap Lancelot?' Lord Geldrin asked me.

I pointed my bloody spear to the west and the hill I knew so well. 'Get your men up the tor,' I said. 'We're falling back.'

His brows gathered. Rain dripped from the ends of his long moustaches. 'We can hold them here,' he said, gesturing with his own spear to the chaos in front of him. He wanted to fight.

I shook my head. 'No!' I could feel the impatience of the horse beneath me, his need to run. His anxiousness because I was holding him still. Or trying to. 'The crow-shields and the rest of the Saxons are coming.' I did not want to think of Gralon and his brave men of Caer Celemion. By now they would all be dead. 'Get to the summit and make a shieldwall. We'll plant our banners there.'

Lord Geldrin turned his gaze onto Iselle behind me. 'What say you, lady?'

'They call you Lord of the Heights, don't they?' she answered, and I imagined her teeth white against a mask of blood. 'We make our stand on the tor.'

Geldrin smiled at that, gave a shallow bow and turned to bark the order at his men, who hefted their shields, turned west and set off at a run.

I looked back at Lord Cai and the others. Not all of them had made it through, but I caught Gawain's eye and he gestured to the tor as he mouthed the word, *Go*.

And so I rode to where Iselle's banner had been planted, so far from where it had begun the day. Not planted, really, the two spear butts thrust into the ground in haste and not deeply enough, so that the whole assemblage leaned like a storm-beaten tree and might fall to the next gust. I pulled one shaft free, walked Medyr's stallion forward and snatched the other spear from the soil, trying not to think of the chaos and struggle at my back, whose clamour flooded over me, growing louder with every passing moment.

There was no sign of Merlin, I noted, and I wondered if, smelling our defeat on the air, he had vanished again, deserting Iselle as he had deserted Arthur at the last. I said nothing to Iselle about it, but I knew she would be aware of his absence.

'Are you sure about this?' I said over my shoulder, laying the long spears and Iselle's sodden, heavy wolf banner in front of me across the saddle and the stallion's strong neck.

'Do you really need to ask?' she replied.

'Once we're up there, we'll be trapped,' I said. 'We might never come down.'

'I know.'

Those two words were like the shutting and locking of a door, and there could be no going back. And for the first time in my life, I envied my father. Before that day when he chose to leave me, knowing we would never see each other again in this life, he had lived according to his own will, his own nature. He had loved and that love had been a deep wound which had never healed. It had tortured him until the moment of his death, and yet he had been able to love. But if Iselle and I planted the wolf banner at the tor's summit now, we would give up love, its anguish and its joys. There could be no future, for we would not live, and so I would never have what my father had. Not even that.

The stallion whinnied and tossed its head, and I let these thoughts untether themselves from me and be carried off in the gusts. Iselle had given her answer and whatever our fate, neither of us could turn from it now. So I pressed my right knee against the stallion's flank and whipped the reins and we rode towards that rain-veiled hill which had loomed above me for so much of my life, while Gawain and Lord Cai rode behind our shieldwall, yelling to the kings and lords of Britain that they must give up the ground they had fought long and hard for and retreat to the tor, where we would make our final stand. Where we would bleed our enemy until that hill's terraced slopes ran with blood and the corpse halls of the Saxons' gods were so glutted with souls that the dead could not feast with their ancestors.

We rode up from the south, along the whale-backed ridge, the rain gusting against the left cheek irons of our helmets with enough vehemence to make us turn our faces away, while Lord Geldrin's men had taken the direct approach and were climbing the steeper eastern side, their shields slung on their backs as they pulled themselves up with the help of the long grass. So few of them that they were almost lost on that hillside.

The stallion was blowing hard, for we were a far heavier burden than he was used to, and I told him I was sorry I did not know his name. Then I asked Iselle what she could see to the east, over the brow of the ridge. I had an idea myself, but I hoped I was wrong, that the rain in my eyes and the greyness of the day were making me see things not as they truly were.

'Well?' I said.

'Just ride,' she said. And so we rode.

23

A Flame in the Dark

'So, THIS IS IT, Galahad,' Merlin said, looking out over the struggle, as our men scrambled up the hill, breathless and sodden, fugitives of the slaughter, taking their places in the shieldwall which stood upon the crest like a bloodied crown. 'This is the fire in which we shall recast Britain.'

'You shouldn't have brought the boy up here.' I nodded at Taliesin, who stood beside the druid, pale and wide-eyed, his hair flattened against his head. Looking lost in the midst of that desperate chaos.

When we had gained the summit, where the old Roman ruins stood, Iselle and I had both been surprised to find the druid and the boy there, as if they had been waiting patiently for us. As if they had known we would come. We'd been even more surprised to see the Cauldron of Annwn sitting there, shining dully in the rain which was sploshing inside it.

'In my experience, boys do not like being left behind.' Merlin turned an eye on me. Did he know how often I had lain in bed in the monastery dormitory, waiting for sleep to come, trying to fashion a dream in which I shared my father's saddle and we rode together, my arms around his waist as Tormaigh carried us down to Arthur?

'But never mind all that,' he said, sweeping a hand through

the rain as he walked towards us. 'Here, both of you,' he snapped, handing Taliesin his staff. 'Quick now!'

We had dismounted, and I looked at Iselle and she looked at me, then together we strode across the wind-rippled grass to meet the druid.

'I know!' Merlin said, sweeping towards us, a skeletal dark wraith in the storm, and before I could stop him, he threw up his claw-like hands and took hold of my cloak where it fastened at my shoulder. 'I know, Galahad!' he said, 'why Guinevere went back to Arthur.' His eyes were wild as he blinked the rain from them. 'Why she spent one more night with him.'

He turned those wild eyes onto Iselle. 'You must have wondered,' he told her, 'why your mother would go back to Arthur after he had bound her to a stake and lit the fuel upon which her pretty feet stood?'

Iselle glared back at him. 'Because her mind was gone even then,' she spat, but did not mean it.

Merlin shook his head, water flicking from his lank beard and moustaches. 'No, child,' he said. *Child.* Even as Iselle stood there in blood-smeared scale armour, and as her wolf banner flapped in the rainy gusts, and as men fought and died with her name on their lips. 'It was because she saw this day,' he said. 'Her talents were ever greater than my own. The gods showed Guinevere this day.' He threw his arms wide to encompass that hill and the tumult boiling around it. 'Don't you see?' Iselle glanced at me. I gave a slight shake of my head, and Merlin sighed with dramatic effect. 'She saw her child,' he said. 'Arthur's child. She saw you, Iselle, and she knew what she must do. Just as you know what we must do.'

'I know how to kill Saxons, druid,' she said through a grimace.

Merlin turned his rain-glistened face up to the grey sky. 'I see it all now.' He laughed and there was joy in it, and several weary spearmen turned at the sound, no doubt thinking that they had enemies in front and the mad behind.

'I thought it was lost. All lost. But it never was.' The druid shook his head. 'I am an old fool.'

Taliesin came up and lifted an old sack which he held towards Merlin. 'Will we do it now?' he asked.

'Not yet, boy,' Merlin said, reaching out to scrub Taliesin's head with a bony hand and taking back the staff. 'But soon, I think.' He looked back to Iselle. 'Well, then, let them see you, Iselle, daughter of Arthur, granddaughter of Uther Pendragon.' He gestured towards the summit's edge. 'Let them all see you, including the gods.'

Iselle held Merlin's eye for a long moment, then she nodded and turned and went to take her place in the shieldwall, and men cheered her in rasping voices that sounded like a chorus of rooks.

'How do you know?' I asked Merlin.

He half turned and gestured. 'The cauldron told me,' he said. 'I saw it all in the cauldron.'

He was grinning and I found it unnerving given the circumstances. Given that even now spearmen were climbing the hill to fight us. So, I thought to bring the old man's head down from the clouds by asking how he had got the cauldron up the tor. But he told me it was a spell which had persuaded a flock of gulls to grip the cauldron's rim with their strong feet and carry the treasure up to the top of the hill. There were no birds on the wing that I could see. More likely Merlin had paid or threatened some of the camp followers to lug the thing up the tor and had since sent them away, knowing what must now follow.

And what must follow was slaughter.

As Iselle and I had ridden up the tor, we saw the ruin of the men of Powys. Being fierce and proud, they had been loath to withdraw, their warrior king fighting in the heart of the struggle, his spearmen gathered around him. But as the other kings and lords of Britain obeyed the command to retreat to the tor, walking backwards, shields and weapons raised to defend themselves against the oncoming enemy, the men of Powys had become isolated, the Saxons and Lady Morgana's men flowing around them, as a stream will find the easiest route around a boulder. We had watched King Catigern being cut off. It had sickened me and now the survivors – in separate knots of five to ten men – were coming up the slope, fleeing the massacre of their countrymen. I could not see King Catigern amongst them.

Only Lord Constantine and his red cloaks had prevented a rout. They were the finest warriors in Britain, having fought shoulder to shoulder against the Saxons for so many years, and they did not break now, but stood halfway up the steep eastern slope around Arthur's bear banner, their shield rims kissing, their stiff helmet crests bristling in the wind. They bought us time and we used that time to build a shieldwall around the summit.

'This is where we make our stand!' Gawain roared, pulling men into that wall, slapping the backs of warriors he knew and sharing knowing looks with some of the older men. His bronze armour, like my own, was sheeted in blood and would stay that way now the rain had stopped. 'This is where we will beat them. Up here where the gods can see us.' He had never put much store in the gods, but he knew what men wanted to hear, and his words gusted in the wind which bellied Iselle's wolf banner, the cloth straining between the long spears which I had sunk deep into the soft earth.

Having hobbled their horses by the old ruined tower, Lord Cai and the rest of his men came to stand with Iselle and me at the eastern edge of the summit, from where we could watch our foes gathering for the final push. They grouped into a dozen or more shieldwalls, many of them six men deep, Morgana's own men and her allies on the left of Lord Constantine and his red cloaks, the Saxons facing him and spread across the rest of the terraced slope.

'Constantine needs to get up here before the Saxon swines get around the back of him,' Lord Cai said, palming sweat from his eyes.

'His men are exhausted.' Iselle shook her head as if in wonder, putting a hand to her neck and the dark bloody grime smeared there. I was relieved when I saw no wound in the pale skin revealed. 'They need to rest.'

'They'll be resting for ever if they don't move now.' Parcefal worked a whetstone along the blade of his spear. His face was gaunt-looking, his eyes sunken and the skin beneath them puffy and swollen. He was old and tired and yet I would not have wished to fight him.

'Come with us, Galahad,' Merlin suddenly ordered, levering men aside with his staff so that he and Taliesin could pass through the shieldwall. He had put on his feathered cloak, so that he shone purple and green as the wind played across the feathers, and men stepped aside, making room for him to pass, none of them wanting those black feathers to touch them, for they feared that cloak and its magic. 'I want to show you something which would have your monks of the Thorn pissing in their cassocks,' the druid called back to me, 'and in return you'll make sure no harm comes to me or the boy.'

I looked at Iselle. 'Go,' she said, and so I followed Merlin and Taliesin down onto the next terrace below the summit, as men told Merlin to turn the Saxons' gut ropes into snakes or boil the brains in their skulls or fill their mouths with maggots, or whatever other horrible affliction they could think of.

'You will have to wait and see,' Merlin called to them over his shoulder, a mischievous grin on his pursed lips. I noticed that Taliesin held a crow tightly in his small hands, though where he had got it, who could say? Then Merlin lifted his staff above his head and held it there, his arm quivering, until enough of those down below had seen him and word spread among the different shieldwalls.

'Men of Britain!' he called out, his voice the creak of a thick rope under strain. He turned his head slowly, raking his eyes across the spear-armed ranks of our enemies. 'You damn your own souls. You serve an enemy of the gods!' He half turned his face to me and frowned. 'Can they hear me, Galahad?' His feathers were ruffling, and I wondered if he had plucked some of those feathers and breathed life into them to make the crow in Taliesin's hands.

I shrugged. 'It's windy,' I replied.

'Give it here, boy,' he said, and Taliesin stepped up and handed the crow to Merlin, taking the staff in return as Merlin lifted the crow to his face and whispered to it, his beard rope jerking up and down. The bird croaked and twitched its head this way and that, the black bead of its eye blinking as Merlin lifted it up for all to see. 'Morgana has betrayed us all!' he shouted. 'And for that I curse her. She will die before Samhain and all who fight for her here today will suffer. But those who fight *beside* us now against the invaders will be spared. Here is my curse!' With that, he opened his hands and the crow flapped its wings and took flight, croaking as it rose into the grey, flapping into the east above our enemies. And such was Merlin's reputation, even then, that hundreds of pairs of eyes followed

547

that bird. In that moment the battle and the butchery were overshadowed by a bird; everyone on the tor watching the crow and wondering if Merlin really had the power to lay down such a curse.

And then the bird fell. It plummeted towards the ground, spinning, its wings dead and useless, its little body limp, and I did not see where it landed but I heard the gasps and murmurs and saw the men touching iron to ward off the evil of Merlin's curse. I shuddered inside my scale coat.

Had Lady Morgana seen it? I hoped so. I wanted her blood to run cold, as mine did. I wanted her to see how her spearmen, those warriors with the crows painted on their shields, looked at one another now, all of them pulled and plucked by the fear which Merlin had sown in their souls. Some of those men were arguing amongst themselves now, some even turning their shields and spears towards the Saxons across the slope, who could no more than they understand how Merlin had killed a flying bird with thought or words.

'Come, Taliesin,' the old druid said, and together we clambered back up to the plateau and I thought I caught a glimpse of something small and white between the druid's finger and thumb before he dropped it in the grass. Just a sliver of bone, perhaps. A needle sharp and slender enough to stitch a wound or a feathered cloak. Or to pierce a bird's heart. Or perhaps my eyes had deceived me because some part of me needed an explanation.

What Lord Constantine had needed was an opportunity, and Merlin had given him one. As the fear and uncertainty swept over Morgana's men, he led his red cloaks up the tor and we on the summit cheered as those brave men joined us. We cheered those men and we cheered for Merlin and we taunted the enemy because many of them were now cursed along with their lady.

And we were still cheering and taunting when the Saxons came to kill us.

I stood with the horse lords of Britain, with Arthur's Companions, those proud men who had ridden with him and fought for him in Britain and in Gaul. Men who had been tempered by war, so that even now, as old as some of them were, they stood firm and fought with the ceaseless rhythm of the turning of years. A brotherhood of blood. They had known my father, for he had been one of them, and now they would know me.

'Hold!' Lord Cai bellowed, thrusting his spear at the lower edge of a Saxon shield, tipping the top edge forward and giving me a glimpse of beard and teeth. I did not miss, and the Saxon died with blood bubbling and frothing at the gash in his throat. Then the clash of shields as their wall struck ours, they pushing upwards, their blades snaking at our shins and legs, our strokes raining down upon their shields and helmets, for we held the high ground and would not, could not, cede it.

'Hold!' Iselle shrieked, big-eyed, blood-spattered, ramming her spear down into bear fur and leather and flesh.

A blade scraped off my right greave where the hawk's head sat over my knee. Another, or perhaps the same, cut through my trews and sliced into the flesh of my left thigh and the pain seared like fire.

'Push them back!' Gawain roared, hammering a shield with his sword, his features twisted with hate, spittle flying from his mouth. 'Give no ground!'

But there were too many of them. Cadwy took a spear in his belly, the blade ripping him open so that his gut rope sprang out and he fell to his knees, clutching at himself and groaning. Nabon tried to grab his comrade under his arms and pull him back, but a Saxon spear skewered him through his calf, and he bent to grab the offending spear, roaring in fury and pain. I lost sight of him for a moment, but when I saw Nabon again, his eyes were staring and his mouth was still open. His scream was silent, though perhaps it echoed in the other world.

I saw Lord Constantine's sword rising and falling. I saw Gawain fighting like some hero from the old tales, hammering Saxons into the ground and challenging their best warriors to fight him. I looked over to the northern edge of the plateau and saw King Cuel and his men of Caer Gloui fighting hard beneath their boar banner, and with them was old King Menadoc and his sun-shields of Cornubia, striving to hurl back the shadow that sought to overcome us.

Further down the slope, two of the Dumnonian shieldwalls – some three hundred men – were facing off against the Saxons who fought beneath the green ship's prow beast, so that it seemed Merlin's curse and that crow falling from the sky had turned half of the crow-shields against Lady Morgana, though whether they would fight was yet to be seen. And even if they did, it would likely be too late, for King Cerdic's warriors and those men yet loyal to Morgana still numbered more than a thousand and we could not hold them.

A huge Saxon got both hands on my shield and ripped it off my arm and then he was on me and I was falling backwards. Even as I fell, the big warrior landing on me, driving the air from my lungs, I saw Saxons driving our men back. Heard their animal grunts as they broke our shieldwall, then the cheer as others flooded in through the breach.

Iselle!

I got my left hand under the Saxon, whose hands were around my neck, and I pulled my knife from its sheath and punched it into his side, felt the blade scrape against his ribs and smelled his breath as he made a guttural sound like some beast. Then he went rigid and his eyes swelled, and I felt the tip of the spear which Parcefal had thrust into his back and almost into my chest.

'On your feet,' Parcefal growled, before spinning to face another Saxon while I heaved the dying man off me and turned to see Culhwch shielding Iselle with his own body, three Saxons running him through with spears. We were breaking. But I was up, Boar's Tusk in my hand, for I would be no less than *he* had been. And then that odd sensation again, as though all the swirling chaos on that hill had receded like the tide and I was caught in a waking dream. A dream over which I had full mastery, so that I was creating it.

I cut and moved, spun and ducked and thrust. Boar's Tusk flashed in my right hand, the long knife in my left, and my enemies were slow. Clumsy. And I slaughtered them where they stood.

I saw Culhwch go down. Saw a Saxon slam his shield boss into Iselle's face and saw her stagger back as I killed the man and caught Iselle before her legs gave way.

'I've got you,' I told her. She grimaced and spat out the blood which was spilling across her lips from a cut above her right eye. Somehow, though, she kept her feet and still gripped Excalibur, holding it before her as I searched for a way out.

I saw Tarawg, sheeted in blood, swinging an axe, screaming in defiance as they cut him down. I saw brave Medyr, his black curls flinging blood as he held two Saxons at bay, though a third was coming at his back.

I looked this way and that, seeking a way out but there was none. I looked into the south-east and saw smoke, black as pitch, rising from Camelot, but there was no time to think more of that, and I parried a spear thrust. Then another. Holding Iselle against my body, consumed with wrath for any man or blade which sought to hurt her.

Medyr was gone but Gawain was beside me now and Parcefal was still fighting nearby. But the enemy were everywhere. They had broken through all around the summit and were trying to get to Merlin, who stood by the Cauldron of Annwn, Taliesin at his side, the two of them performing some sort of rite as the slaughter whirled and eddied around them.

I turned a sword thrust aside and put a man down and Gawain hacked a head from its shoulders.

'I won't leave you,' I growled at Iselle.

A sword bit into my left shoulder, sending bronze scales flying like sparks from a fire and causing me to drop the knife, though I held on to Iselle and she put Excalibur's point into an open mouth and twisted the blade.

There were too many of them.

But we would not yield. We would never yield. My left arm around Iselle, we stumbled but we did not fall, and in my desperation to see a way out, I hauled my helmet off my head and let it drop, the white horsehair plume trailing to the ground. And then a score of men cut their way through to us and I saw that Lord Geldrin led them. He threw himself at the enemy and his men formed a shieldwall around us, around Iselle, and then King Menadoc and his sun-shields were there too, throwing the Saxons back with savage, desperate strength.

And somewhere to the east, horns sounded.

I could not breathe. Blood was in my eyes and in my mouth. I thought my heart would burst from its hammering. But I stayed on my feet and Iselle did too, and we watched the Saxons on our side of the tor being pushed back off the plateau.

'Why?' I rasped, my mouth too dry to say more. We saw others of the enemy overlap their shields and we thought they would march to sweep us off the tor, but instead, they walked backwards, blades held high towards us. They retreated, and then we realized that the horn blasts were calling them back, though we could not imagine why King Cerdic would recall his men when they were on the cusp of winning.

'What's happening?' Gawain's great chest was rising and falling, his sword dripping gobbets into the grass. 'Why are they retreating?' But no one could say, and nor was the fighting over. But the Saxons *were* falling back from the summit, being drawn like an ebbing tide, back to their king.

'See there!' a man called, pointing his broken sword down the tor's eastern slope. I thought he was pointing at the crow-shields, who looked to have driven the other Saxon force off. One of the shieldwalls stood jeering at the Saxons and hammering spear staves and sword pommels against their shields in thunderous rhythm. The other wall of crow-shields stood facing the woman whom they had served that morning but did not serve now, not since they had seen the last druid in Britain make a crow fall from the sky through the power of his own will and maybe that of the gods too.

But then I saw what the warrior with the broken sword wanted us to see. There was a third Saxon war band. Another three hundred warriors gathering in the gloaming at the foot of the tor, their spears pointing at the darkening sky.

Men around me groaned. Some cursed the gods. A few fell to their knees, exhaustion flooding into the places within them where there had remained some small vestige of hope.

'Is there no end to them?' Parcefal spat, taking off his helmet, too exhausted even to sweep the lank, grey hair from his eyes.

'It's Prince Cynric,' Iselle said, and she was right. I recognized the man: his fair beard and long golden hair and his hauberk of polished mail which shone like silver.

'Maybe they'll be tired out by the time they get up here,' one of King Menadoc's sun-shields said, stirring a smattering of bitter laughter, as men *will* laugh who know there is nothing left to do but die. For they supposed that King Cerdic had withdrawn his attack so that his son, the newly arrived prince, could share the glory. That together, they would come and sweep us from the tor and into oblivion. That together, they would snuff out the flame of Britain once and for all.

'I was beginning to think he would never come.' Merlin's voice was like the squawk of a rook, loud in my ear, for I had not seen him come to stand beside me.

I turned to stare at the druid. 'You knew he would come?'

Here and there, knots of men still fought, not knowing or daring to stop, but for the most part it was as though the battle and the day itself held its breath.

'We hoped,' Gawain answered on behalf of them both. 'Though the bastard waited until half of us were dead.'

'He's ambitious, not stupid,' Merlin said, squinting down the hill with his old eyes.

Gawain shook his head, spat into the grass and stalked off to tell Lord Cai and Lord Constantine what apparently only he and Merlin knew.

'Prince Cynric won't attack?' I asked Merlin.

'No, I don't believe he will,' Merlin said. 'Well, not us, anyway.' And then I understood.

'You've been dealing with him?' I felt a flush of anger at him for having kept it from me.

The druid batted that suggestion away with a hand. 'We sent a messenger or two.'

I spat a curse at myself for not having seen it, but then Father Yvain's voice carried to me from the past. *Might as well try to guess what a fish is thinking as seek to know the mind of a druid.*

Then my attention was pulled to halfway down the tor, where Prince Melehan was screaming at his men, trying to get them formed into a shieldwall facing not us, but Prince Cynric at the foot of the hill. For Melehan understood what was happening. He knew that the Saxon prince intended to kill him, because Cynric had never accepted the deal which his father had struck with Lady Morgana; that in exchange for peace now, the sons of Mordred would sit on Dumnonia's high seat after Cerdic and Morgana were dead. Why should Melehan be given what it was Prince Cynric's right to take, if he could? And so Cynric would try to kill Melehan now and it would be up to his father the king whether he chose to fight his own son, or else waited to see how things turned out. Perhaps he would even join the prince now and together they would wipe out Morgana's power in Britain.

Either way, there would be more blood on that grey day, I thought grimly.

I looked back into the south-east and the hill fort there, that old bastion of defiance and hope whose earthen ramparts my father and Arthur had dug with their own hands, but which now stood beneath a pall of smoke that was spreading across the eastern sky like a stain. Gawain and Iselle and some of the others were looking towards Camelot too.

'The gods are cruel,' Parcefal muttered.

No one else spoke of it. It was too heavy a thing.

Cynric had come, as Merlin and Gawain had hoped he would, but first he had burned Camelot. What choice now then for Lady Morgana, but to fight or run? To survive if she could, one way or the other.

'Cynric won't attack us?' I asked Merlin again, for it still seemed impossible that we might live after all.

'If he does, I shall turn his guts into three rats, and they will eat him alive from the inside. We have a truce.'

'A truce?' Iselle repeated, wincing as she touched two fingers to the gash above her eye to see if it was still bleeding. Even then, after everything and having come so close to death, she seemed to despise the idea of peace with the Saxons. 'For how long?' she asked, wiping the fresh blood on her trews.

'Who can say, lady?' Merlin replied, 'but the gods are with us and that is what matters now.' He nodded to Iselle and to me and winked at Taliesin. Then, telling the boy to stay close, he set off across the hilltop, declaring to all in a thin voice which was whipped this way and that by the wind, that *he* had summoned the gods with the help of the Cauldron of Annwn. That the gods had answered him and had fought beside us and carried his curse to our enemies, so that they would die, and we would live.

So that Britain would endure.

For a while we watched the fighting. I saw Melehan leading his best men in a desperate bid to kill Prince Cynric. A great wedge of crow-shields carving their way towards the Saxon. The man was no coward, but then he had every reason to crave Cynric's death. I did not see what happened, for I knew we should not linger on that hill while we had the chance to slip away. We would have to come back for the dead, but it would be night soon and we must go while we could.

I found Gawain and together we made our plan. I was reintroducing myself to Medyr's stallion, asking the horse if he would carry me again now, and in return I would see his brave master burned on a hero's pyre, when Morvan, Lord Constantine's second in command, came over to say that his lord wanted to speak with me. Constantine had made sure it was he who had taken the surrender of those three hundred crow-shields who had abandoned Lady Morgana, and he was taking each man's oath there and then, on that hillside, in full view of anyone who cared to notice.

'Lord,' I said, at which he turned from the rows of kneeling warriors, gesturing that Morvan should continue the proceedings. 'We should go before the issue is decided.' I nodded down towards the clashing shieldwalls below. For now, at least, it seemed King Cerdic was letting his son fight his own battles.

'The Saxons won't fight us again today,' Lord Constantine stated, and gestured at his new recruits, those many spearmen who had come over to us. 'They know the victory would cost them too dear.' He gave a tired smile. 'It seems the druid proved his worth at last.'

I nodded, suddenly so weary. 'I must go, lord.'

'Go where?' he asked.

I did not answer that.

'Come with me, Galahad,' he said. 'I saw you fight today. You arc gifted. As good as your father was, perhaps. But I think you have something which even the great Lancelot did not possess.' I did not ask what that was, but it did not stop him telling me. 'You have it in you to be a leader of men,' he said. 'I saw it. They fought for you, lad.'

'They fought for Iselle,' I replied.

He took a step towards me. 'She is Arthur's daughter. Of that there's no doubt. And that helped us here today. Because Arthur's name was still . . .' He turned an eye up to the bear banner which rippled beneath the darkening sky. '. . . still in the air,' he said with a flutter of bloodstained fingers. 'Men wanted to see Iselle for themselves. I daresay a good many of them half believed . . . hoped, at least, that Arthur himself would come after all.' He lifted an eyebrow. 'But you and I both know that Arthur is not coming. He will never ride again, and so we need a new warrior to give the people hope. We need a king, Galahad.'

'I thought you were a king,' I said.

He ignored that. 'I am old. And I'm tired. I've been fighting all my life, but I can't fight for ever.' He straightened as if in defiance of his own words. 'Come with me and learn from me.' Again, he extended a hand towards the kneeling men who had been spared the slaughter now taking place at the foot of the tor. 'We have the beginnings of an army. In time more will come, because we made a stand here today and even with so few we were not beaten.'

I turned and my eyes found Iselle. She was helping Lord Cai get a wounded man up into the saddle.

'But they will not follow her,' Constantine said.

'Because she is a woman?' I asked. 'She is as much a warrior as any man on this hill.'

'We need more than a warrior,' he said. 'We need a king.'

I stared at him, aware of the blood simmering in my veins. Hot and needful.

'Come with me to Caer Lerion,' he said. 'There are men there who will join us. After today.' He came forward and took hold of my forearm, its muscles screaming from wielding Boar's Tusk all day. 'We will start there and together we *will* remake Britain.'

I remembered my father telling me about that morning on Tintagel's heights, when Uther was dead and Lord Constantine, furious at not being named Uther's heir, had slaughtered Lord Arthur's men and hamstrung their horses. My father said he only had to think of that day to hear the screams of the horses again. He and Arthur and Gawain and Merlin had narrowly escaped with their lives.

I pulled my arm away and glanced up at the dusky sky. 'Will you kill her now?' I asked him, 'or in the dawn?'

His dark eyes sharpened. The muscle in his cheek twitched

beneath an old scar and grey stubble, but he said nothing. And so, I turned and walked away from him. Back to Iselle.

We rode into Camelot unchallenged. Iselle and I, Gawain, Parcefal, Merlin, Taliesin, Lord Cai and the last of the horse lords of Britain. Twenty-three of us in all. More followed on foot, including Lord Geldrin and his men, King Menadoc and his sun-shields, and some others who wanted to rest before setting off for their homes. Meanwhile, the surviving men of Cynwidion, those of Powys and King Cuel of Caer Gloui were already on their way back to their respective kingdoms, intent on using the cover of darkness to put as much distance between themselves and our enemies as possible.

But we had come to Camelot and now we walked amongst the charred and smoking timbers, the scorched and blackened thatch and the small fires which still burned here and there. And the bodies. Dozens of them, grey with death and ashes. And red too.

Only a skeleton garrison had been left behind, for what had Morgana to fear from Saxons? But they had run or been slaughtered.

'Prince Cynric will be a formidable enemy,' Gawain said.

But not today.

Some of the survivors wandered through Camelot like the walking dead themselves. Seeming lost and confused, as if they hardly recognized the place. Others sat by the ruins of their homes or beside their dead, while a few were still putting out fires which had not taken properly because of the earlier rain.

None opposed us. All stared at us, for we came on war horses, wearing armour and helmets that were damaged and dented and sheened with blood. Our faces were grimy and drawn and pale, and our eyes were swollen with horrors.

Lady Morgana's hall, which had once been Arthur's hall, still stood. The Saxons had tried to fire it but the timbers had not caught and the thatch had not taken the flame, and so it stood there and Iselle and I stared at it awhile, she because her father and mother had lived there, I because I could almost feel the pain my father must have felt when he looked upon the place, knowing that Guinevere lay under that roof. In Arthur's bed.

Parcefal growled that Prince Cynric would not be the opponent Gawain feared, if he was not even clever enough to leave a garrison of his own men in Camelot. But I knew Cynric would have needed every spear in case his father the king opposed him. And as for Camelot, I supposed he despised the place, just as the Saxons had always despised the stone villas and palaces which the Romans left behind. Camelot had been the heart of Arthur's defiance and so he had burned it. Or tried to.

'I want the gates reinforced and the walls manned!' Lord Cai announced, sweeping his blunted sword across the fort, and weary men hefted shields and spears and tramped up onto the ramparts, even kings and lords. And we knew it would be a long night.

I turned away from Arthur's hall and, limping because of the sword cut I had taken in my thigh, fetched the wolf banner from where I had left it by Medyr's stallion, whose name I still did not know. I carried the banner to a patch of ground which had been churned to mud, where the ashes stuck but for those which were being swirled about by the wind. And there I drove in one spear and then the other, stretching out the banner until the wolf could be seen clearly and for what it was.

When I turned back to Iselle, Taliesin was beside her. Iselle put her arm around the boy's shoulder and we all watched the wolf banner, hoping it would stay upright in the soft ground. Behind it, in the west, the light was fading, leaching from the world. It would be dark soon, and in the darkness, we are prey to our fears.

I looked over at what had once been Arthur's stables. When we had come through the gates it had been burning still and had collapsed in on itself, throwing up a shower of sparks. Now, some spearmen were trying to stamp out the flames which still licked amongst the ruins, but Merlin shooed them away with his staff.

'Here, Galahad,' he called. 'Build this up. We need a fire, and this is a good place for one, don't you think? Good as any.'

I dragged some of the fallen timbers back into a pile and soon the flames were leaping high, chasing away the shadows.

Author's Note

PLEASE BE AWARE, this note contains spoilers!

Camelot is, perhaps, more of a companion novel to *Lancelot* than a sequel in the usual sense. This was ever likely to be the case. When I wrote *Lancelot*, I had no intention of following it up. *Lancelot* was to be a big, fat, standalone volume. A reimagining of one of the great figures of British myth and legend. It was never in my mind during the writing that I should leave the story open-ended, or that the characters might go on to live again on the page. However, in the event, both my agent and my editor persuaded me that I wasn't yet finished with this world and these characters, whom I had come to know so intimately. After all, *Lancelot* had sold well, and some reviews expressed disappointment that there wouldn't be more, and, well, hadn't I spent too long and put in too much effort creating that vision of Arthur's and Lancelot's Britain just to walk away now?

And I remembered the boy who was left alone on that hill in the last pages of *Lancelot*. I could see him in my mind's eye, standing there, waiting for his father, who would never come. My own brother had been particularly upset with me for that ending. How could Lancelot have just left his son there? he asked, the disapproving frown on his face intimating that I had ruined what, up to that point, had been a good book.

But Lancelot *had* to ride to Arthur's side, I explained. For their old friendship. For honour. For Britain. For Guinevere! And who knows, maybe the great warrior thought he would ride back up that hill to the boy? And even if not, even if he *had* chosen those other things over his own son, didn't that just show that, for all his talent, for all his brilliance, Lancelot was, in the end, a flawed man? Like his father before him.

And yet. That boy alone on the hill. He was standing there still, and would be for ever . . . unless I gave him his own story. Didn't I owe him that? Certainly enough people thought that I did.

I wanted to call the book *Galahad*. It seemed right after *Lancelot*. But I accepted that Galahad simply wasn't such a familiar name, whereas Camelot looms large in the public imagination. More than a fortress of timber and stone upon an ancient hill, it is a dream. The evocation of hope, unity and defiance against the darkening world. A fading dream now, though, after the climactic struggle of *Lancelot*'s final pages.

But I knew that this would not be *Lancelot* part II. *Camelot* would be a different story. It had to be. And Galahad would be a very different character to his father, and not just because, in writing another first-person story, it was important to distinguish the narrator's voice to avoid it feeling like a continuation of the previous book.

No, here was a different kind of man. In the traditional tales, Galahad embodies purity and virtue. He is a sinless virgin all his life. Obviously, I wasn't going to go that way! Having replaced Perceval as the Grail hero, Galahad was raised in a nunnery, yet he was the greatest warrior in the world, a man whose arrival was prophesied from the days of Joseph of Arimathea. As such, he was preordained to be the only one to attain the Grail. Hard to make that work, I thought, in a sub-Roman Britain that had, since the story told in *Lancelot*, become a brutish hellhole of cut-throat anarchy, slaughter, filth and darkness, where famine and pestilence rule and the uneasy truce between the Saxons and the Britons is breaking. Sticking a pure-hearted golden boy into that mess seemed incongruous to me, even cruel. Moreover, protagonists in drama require motivation. Where's the conflict, where's the challenge, if you're a pre-selected winner? Where's the suspense?

I did know that Galahad wasn't going to have Lancelot's uncompromising confidence and his obvious talents. In some ways, Galahad is the antithesis of his father. He is unsure of himself and his place in the world. He fears the unknown and does not possess Lancelot's hawk-like focus. Galahad is a young man burdened by his father's legacy and, frankly, haunted by his father's abandonment of him. He tries for as long as he can to reject everything his father was, refusing the call of the martial life and the whispers of his own blood. And yet, how far from the tree can the apple fall?

The principal characters would be very different from the previous book, then, but I went about the writing in a similar way, taking up threads of the well-known stories and weaving them into something new. Of course, even having made a basic chapter outline, I watched the story take on a life of its own, as I suspect is usually what happens to authors and their best-laid plans, and I think that's only healthy. After all, what would be the point in recycling an existing version of the Arthurian myth? Indeed, the fascinating, and frankly mind-boggling thing about the stories of Arthur created between the sixth century and today is the sheer variation in the characters, places, themes, objects and events. Writers have been changing and adding to the canon (no doubt deviating from their own carefully laid plans) for . . . well, forever.

Lancelot himself was most likely an invention of Chrétien de Troyes in the late twelfth century (there are scholars who have different ideas about this), though his character is much developed in the later Old French prose-romance Vulgate cycle. Either way, Chrétien, or someone else, decided that what the tale was lacking was a brave and brilliant knight, a sidekick for the story's hero. A man whose love for his best friend's wife would ultimately lead to tragedy.

Or take Gawain, one of Arthur's most famous knights. Early French romance considered him the epitome of the chivalrous warrior. But in the Vulgate and post-Vulgate cycles Gawain is a thug who murders other knights during the Grail quest. And then there's Morgan le Fay (Morgana in *Lancelot* and this book), who is so very inconsistent throughout the Arthurian saga. In some versions she's evil, in others compassionate and generous. In some, beautiful, in others ugly. Sometimes a real woman, other times an enchantress, and even, on occasion, a metaphorical figure.

My point is that the Arthurian stories are always changing, evolving, and that's good. That's as it should be. Nothing, after all, stays the same, and it's only to be expected that writers will reflect their own times and their own experiences in their tales, and seek to create something different from what's gone before. You will, if you were looking carefully, have found my versions of some familiar themes. There's Gawain and the Green Knight in here. There's the raid to the otherworld in search of the Cauldron, too. And, of course, it is in the poem *The Spoils of Annwn* that Taliesin first appears, hence his inclusion in my own story. The inspiration for my cauldron, by the way, was the magnificent Gundestrup cauldron, which held me utterly spellbound when I saw it with my own eyes at the British Museum's Celts exhibition in 2016.

As for Arthur having a daughter . . . Well, why not? If my Galahad wasn't going to be the sinless virgin in this brutal, divided land, then the famous and charismatic warlord Arthur, son of Uther Pendragon, was ever likely to sire several offspring, both in and out of wedlock. And if we're allowing that any of this might really have happened, is it not possible, even likely, that, being a woman, she was written out of the texts? But, of course, anything is possible, because it's all stories. And, so with *Camelot*, as with *Lancelot*, I've reimagined the myth and the man in a way that made sense to me, from my perspective, informed by my own experiences, my own heart, my own soul.

It is, of course, the quest for the Holy Grail with which Galahad is inextricably linked. So where is my grail, you may wonder? Is it the Cauldron of Annwn, whose discovery sets in motion Merlin's schemes and leads to his ultimate realization about the destiny of Britain, as laid out before him by the gods? Or is the Grail in this story not an object at all, but a person, namely Iselle, who brings purpose to Galahad's life through his love for her? Or, perhaps the Grail here is purposefully absent, its shadow glimpsed only in metaphor, in Galahad's journey of self-discovery, as he seeks to unburden himself of the past, find direction and meaning in the present, and hope in the future. Is his ultimate attainment of the non-featuring Grail, in essence, his acceptance, at last, that he is, for better or worse, his father's son, but that he is also his own man and free to take his own path?

I'll leave that for you to decide.

Giles Kristian
21 January 2020

Dramatis Personae

Galahad – The narrator of the story. Son of Lancelot
Iselle – A young woman of the Avalon marshes
The man in the marsh
Merlin – Druid and former adviser to Uther Pendragon and Lord Arthur
Oswine – Merlin's Saxon slave
Guinevere – Wife of Arthur. Lover of Lancelot
Taliesin – A boy
Lady Morgana – Ruler of Camelot. Arthur's half-sister
Lady Triamour – Daughter of Mordred, sister of Melehan and Ambrosius
Melehan – Son of Mordred, brother of Ambrosius and Lady Triamour
Ambrosius – Son of Mordred, brother of Melehan and Lady Triamour
King Cerdic – A Saxon king
Prince Cynric – Son of King Cerdic

Father Yvain – A monk of the Holy Thorn
Father Brice – A monk of the Holy Thorn
Father Judoc – A monk of the Holy Thorn

Lord Constantine – A warlord of Dumnonia. Nephew of King Uther and son of Ambrosius
Lord Geldrin – Ruler of Tintagel

Gawain – One of Arthur's warriors
Gediens – One of Arthur's warriors
Hanguis – One of Arthur's warriors
Endalan – One of Arthur's warriors
Lord Cai – One of Arthur's warriors
Parcefal – One of Arthur's warriors

King Pelles – King of Ynys Môn, called 'the Fisher King'

King Bivitas – King of Cynwidion
King Catigern – King of Powys
King Cuel – King of Caer Gloui
King Menadoc – King of Cornubia

Acknowledgements

There are many levels to finishing the writing of a novel before one has no choice but to let it go, to send it out into the world like a message in a bottle, hoping it will find its way to someone, somewhere. These endings are, in a way, false dawns, because, of course, the final incarnation is the only one which really matters. Nevertheless, each 'finishing' marks the end of a challenge and is, in my opinion, worth celebrating. The rush of emotion when you type 'End' on the first draft can be quite something. But as someone, somewhere once said, the first draft is really just the author telling the story to him- or herself. After this, you need to get some perspective, which is hard when you're so close to the story. What seems obvious to you turns out to be invisible to the reader. Those subtle touches of character, theme and symbolism are, well, too subtle. You know your protagonists so intimately that you forget that they haven't also been living in the reader's head for the last year or more.

This is when eyes other than your own become invaluable, and where the editor, that too often unsung hero, must call upon all his skills to help you shape the manuscript. They must use their experience of the craft, of the business, of the market and the intended audience (and of the author!), as well as oversee the whole publishing process, in order to give the book the best chance of connecting with readers.

When music artists release records, the producer is always

credited. It seems to me that editors should appear in the credits on books. And so, the first person whom it is my great pleasure to acknowledge here is my long-suffering editor, Simon Taylor, whose sage advice, as ever, helped me whip this tale into shape.

I also want to acknowledge some of the other brilliant people whose talents and skills have helped create this story and this book, in whatever format you have consumed it.

My thanks to the eagle-eyed Elizabeth Dobson, whose meticulous and astute copy-edit has saved me countless blushes. Any mistakes that remain are entirely my own. Thanks also to Nancy Webber and Anna Hervé for their proof-reading prowess. I'm indebted to you! Thanks also to the production editor, Vivien Thompson, for coordinating all this work on the script and collating the many corrections and tweaks to the final pages. To Dredheza Maloku, for ensuring the words and metadata earn their keep. To Phil Lord, for the book's interior design, and to Liane Payne, who created the splendid map, thank you very much indeed. I'm grateful also to Phil Evans in production for organizing the typesetting, the page proofs, getting the book off to print and no doubt more besides. As ever, I think Stephen Mulcahey has done an inspired job with the cover, and I must thank Anthony Maddock for his artwork and his labours on the book proof.

To Philip 'the voice' Stephens, I'm thrilled and honoured to have you narrating the audiobooks, and thank you, Alice Twomey, for making the audiobook happen. My heartfelt thanks to Lilly Cox for marketing this book and to Hayley Barnes for striving to get it noticed. I appreciate your efforts enormously.

Thanks to Anthony Hewson for reading *Camelot* in its first draft form, which must have been like trying on a hessian sack,

Acknowledgements

and thanks, as always, to my astonishing wife, Sally, and my ever-patient agent, Bill Hamilton, for putting up with me.

Lastly, I feel I must mention the book which has been a constant feature on my desk (partly because it's too heavy to move) throughout the writing of *Lancelot* and *Camelot*. *The Arthurian Name Dictionary* by Christopher W. Bruce (Taylor & Francis, 1999) presents a comprehensive dictionary of characters, places, objects and themes found in the legends of King Arthur and the Knights of the Round Table. It's a mighty tome and a staggeringly prodigious piece of work by Christopher W. Bruce, for which I'm very grateful.

If this were one of those Arthurian tales with a great round table in it, you would all be seated around it with the wine flowing and the bards singing. As it's not quite one of those tales, I hope you'll be happy with a muddy stool in the Avalon marshlands, as the sun sinks below the reedbeds and the darkness closes in.

For his next novel, Giles Kristian is taking an exciting leap forward in time, to the present day, with a thrilling tale of endurance and survival set in the snowbound mountains of Arctic Norway . . .

FAR WANDERER

Here are the opening pages of this pulse-racing novel in progress . . .

The woods are lovely, dark and deep,
But I have promises to keep,
And miles to go before I sleep,
And miles to go before I sleep.

Excerpt from
'Stopping by Woods on a Snowy Evening'
by Robert Frost

They whisper to him of a man. Lost in the forest. Up to his knees in snow. For it is their charge, to fly out with the dawn and return at nightfall, bringing him word of all that passes in the world. The man is far from the path and floundering, says Hugin.

What has that to do with me? he says. I have my own troubles.

The man cannot endure, says Hugin the ever-vigilant. The snow is deepening. Soon he will be gone.

Again, I say, what has this man to do with me? There are many like him. Let him drown in the snow. I have my own cares.

Munin the sharp-eyed flaps black wings, which are like shadows thrown upon the face of the world.

There are other tracks near this man, Munin whispers. He is not alone.

They wait. They know he is curious. Would he have given his eye were he not?

Where is my staff? he says, unbending himself from his watch-tower throne.

CHAPTER ONE

Erik lifted his eyes to the rear-view mirror. Sofia was holding a finger against the window, tracing the staccato movement of a snowflake as it melted and journeyed across the glass, leaving something of itself in its wake until it was gone.

Even as he looked back to the road, he knew that Sofia had sensed his glance, and so he looked to the mirror again and this time their eyes met. Just for a second, then she turned her face back to the window, her gaze fixed on an old red timber farm and outbuildings that passed in a snowy blur.

It had been a game once, with Sofia's sister. He would glance at Emilie but she would look away immediately. Was Sofia remembering now, too, as she watched the snow-laden pines and the dirt-blackened drifts whir by? He knew that she was.

The sat nav said they would arrive in sixteen minutes. They would fill the boot with supplies, then head up to the cabin. Elise was determined that they would sit down and eat together before bed. Comfy clothes. Candles. He would get a fire going. Some music. A cosy family dinner. The first night in the mountains. The start of something new.

The drive from Tromsø had been easy enough. Two and a half hours, including a toilet and snack stop, and the thirty-minute Ullsfjord ferry crossing from Breivikeidet to Svensby. On that near-silent crossing, he'd lost himself gazing at the summits and upper slopes of the snow-cloaked mountains cast in dawn's pink blush. The sky the infinite blue of azurite copper ore, the water before the ferry's bow still black, fathomless and indifferent, a dark mirror between worlds.

It had been snowing on and off for three days, the ploughs shaping canyons of cleared snow along the roads while people slept. He had lain awake listening to them, welcoming their interruption of the deathlike stillness of the night. Now the only snow on the roads was that which the wind whipped across the black asphalt in ghostly swirls before the headlights.

The whole idea of coming out to the Lyngen Alps was to escape the last ten months. Not to forget – who could forget? – but to feel something else. To breathe again. And they needed it. So Elise had told him over and over, and no doubt she was right. She usually was.

Her employer, Friends of the Earth Norway, couldn't have been more understanding. They had welcomed Elise back to work, had orchestrated this posting to ease her back into the job. And hadn't Erik himself suggested they rent a cottage away from everything and everyone? Fresh air. Ski trips. The Northern Lights.

More than once he had seen Elise's eyes flick up to the mirror. Seen her looking at the empty back seat across from Sofia.

'There must be something going on today,' Elise said, breaking into his thoughts. They were coming into town already.

'Never thought it would be so busy,' he said, leaning forward over the steering wheel, searching for somewhere to park.

'The demonstration.' Elise was peering at a throng of people a hundred metres ahead, gathered before a makeshift stage in the small town square. 'Karine told me about it, but I forgot it was today.'

'Who's Karine?' he asked, anticipating the eye roll that followed.

'Karine Helgeland,' Elise said. 'She did say I should come to the protest if we arrived in time.'

He knew that Elise had been chatting online with this local Sami campaigner, being kept up to date about the mining company which had bought land and an old copper mine around here somewhere.

'You have some days off before you start work, though, right?' he said when they were parked up. His tone had sounded more confrontational than he'd intended.

Elise turned to him, frowning. 'I told you, we'll have the week's holiday before I start.'

He glanced up at the rear-view. Sofia was staring out of the window. He needed to get out. The car was full of tension. Most of it his own.

'I can do some research in the evenings,' Elise said. 'Maybe speak to a few people. But we'll have the days.'

He said nothing, then twisted around to give Sofia a smile which felt like a stranger on his face. 'Let's get some supplies. Some chocolate?'

Sofia's smile was her answer, as she plucked her woollen hat from amongst the clutter of bags and Amdahl family belongings and pulled it on to her head.

'Stay close,' he called to Sofia behind him as he forced a way through the crowd, his arms wrapped around the bag full of groceries.

'I see her, Pappa,' Sofia said, pointing.

'Keep up, Sofia,' he said, pushing his way towards the stage. A group of men and women stood holding up signs saying things like: SAY NO TO MURMANSK NICKEL and WHAT HAPPENS IN THE ARCTIC DOESN'T STAY IN THE ARCTIC. One sign in particular caught Erik's eye. It bore a photo of a Sami herder and a reindeer below the words: WHERE WILL WE GO NOW?

The protestors, some in the bright blues and reds of traditional Sami dress, gathered thickest around one of their number who stood at a microphone, addressing the crowd. Her words were clear even through the screech and squeal of the low-rent P.A. Murmansk Nickel would reopen the old copper mine, she said, and destroy more of the ancient reindeer grazing land. This corporation's greed was yet 'another assault on the fragile Arctic environment'.

Elise would be into the thick of it. This wasn't the biggest of battles which she and Friends of the Earth were fighting on behalf of the natural world and its myriad species. But better that Elise was here than five hundred miles away lobbying against the transportation of used nuclear fuel from the Gulf of Finland to Siberia, like her last job. Better that they were together.

'There, Pappa!' Sofia pointed again as she squeezed between a knot of phone zombie teenagers, and caught up with him.

'I see her, Lillemor,' he said.

'Pappa!' Sofia said, trying to look crosser than she was at his use of her pet name. He suspected she still quite liked it now and then.

Elise stood to the side of the stage, looking up at a larger woman who was making her way down the wobbly steps towards her, smiling and waving at Elise as though they were old friends.

Erik headed forward again, then suddenly stopped dead, up on his toes. A man had stepped hard and fast into his path, face to face, so that some of the shopping spilled out on to the filthy snow between booted feet in the crowd.

He shook off the man's gaze, cradled the bag in one arm and bent to pick up a pack of minced beef.

'Watch where you're going,' the man said, looking down at him.

Fuck. Really? Erik thought. He put the bag down on the slush and ice and stood to face the man. Fought to subdue the adrenaline rushing through him.

'You walked into me,' he said, his tone calm and matter-of-fact.

'Pappa,' Sofia said.

'You couldn't see over your shopping bag,' the man said. Russian, at a guess. He was shorter than Erik but broad across the shoulders, his neck thick with muscle.

Erik held his eye and straightened. He knew he was being challenged.

'Pappa,' Sofia said again. More urgently this time. Fear in her voice.

Erik shook his head and stooped again. 'Help me, Lillemor,' he said, and Sofia bent and gathered up two tins and put them in the bag.

'Let me,' came a voice. Another man from the crowd dropped into a squat beside them, picking up a can of beer which had broken free of the pack. He swept the dirty water off the can with the back of his hand. 'I prefer Ringnes,' he continued. The same accent as the other man. 'An Oslo beer but owned by the Danes. Like Norway used to be.' He handed Erik the can. Erik placed it back in the bag with the other items, and the two of them stood together.

Erik nodded in thanks.

The man smiled. As he stood, Erik noticed a scar that ran through his lips on to his chin. He was tall. Six-two, six-three. Face lean as a wolf's. 'I apologize for my friend,' he said, gesturing at the bull-necked man. 'He is . . . clumsy. Has no manners.'

Erik glanced at the man, who dipped his head in some sort of acknowledgement-cum-apology which he didn't mean. Then Erik nodded to the tall man again, wrapped his left arm around the shopping bag and held out his other hand to Sofia, who took it tightly.

The audio speakers on the stage squealed. 'We must protect what is ours,' the Sami protestor said. 'Doing nothing would be a betrayal of our ancestors, our children and our children's children.'

'Let's find Mamma,' he said, squeezing Sofia's hand, and together they continued through the crowd until they reached his wife, who stood with the other woman.

'Erik, this is Karine,' Elise said, smiling at her friend.

'Pleased to meet you, Karine,' he said, letting go of Sofia's hand to shake Karine's, then wrapping his right arm around the shopping.

'And this must be Sofia.' Karine stepped back to examine Sofia, who said a shy hello. 'I have heard all about you,' the older woman said, nodding with approval.

'Karine has been helping me prepare for the investigation into Murmansk Nickel,' Elise told Erik. She glanced at Karine. 'I don't know what I would've done without her.'

He suspected Karine had been helping Elise with other things too. There was usually wine or G&T involved in these late-evening Skype calls. And a week or so ago, when he had gone into the study to take Elise her usual cup of green tea, he could tell she had been crying. He hadn't said anything. If Elise could open up to Karine Helgeland about Emilie, well, that was good, wasn't it?

'Quite a turnout,' Erik said to Karine, nodding at the press of people around them.

'We are doing what we can,' she said. She looked in her late fifties, and though an outdoor life had weathered her face, giving her a stern look, her eyes had a youthful mischief about them.

'Isn't Mrs Helgeland's kofte beautiful, Sofia?' Elise said, gesturing at Karine's traditional felt dress with its ribbons of contrasting colours, its pewter embroidery and her red wool bonnet.

Sofia nodded.

Karine smiled at her. 'I usually only wear it on Sami National Day—'

'The sixth of February,' Sofia interrupted.

Karine gave Elise an impressed glance, then turned her bright eyes back to Sofia. 'But today is a day to be proud of our heritage and to speak up for the land, which cannot speak for itself,' she said. Then, to lighten the tone, she took off her hat and leant towards Sofia. 'Although, to be honest with you, this can get very itchy.' She scrubbed her short, brown hair with thick fingers, then she straightened and put a hand on Elise's shoulder. 'We are so grateful to have Elise here,' she said, raising her voice above the loudspeaker a few feet away on the stage. 'Together we must make sure that the land is protected.' She and Elise shared a look of solidarity and determination.

'But you've just arrived after a long journey,' Karine said. 'You'll want to be settling in up there,' she added, looking up at the snow-covered mountains to the west of the town. 'Why don't you come for dinner on Saturday night?' She turned her head, fixing her dark eyes on Erik. 'If you don't already have plans.'

Before he could answer, Karine turned away to greet a handsome man with silver hair rattling the platform's metal stairs as he descended towards them. A warm smile spread across his sun-browned and wind-beaten face.

'This is my husband, Lars,' Karine said. 'Lars, this is Elise Amdahl and her husband Erik.'

Lars nodded to Elise and shook Erik's hand firmly.

'And who is this?' Lars asked, stepping back and holding his arms out towards Sofia. 'A young adventurer coming all the way up here to see how we mountain-trolls live?'

Sofia glanced at her mamma for reassurance. 'I'm Sofia,' she said, looking back to Lars Helgeland.

He dipped his head. 'You must be what, fifteen? Sixteen?'

'Almost thirteen,' she told Lars.

'Ah, so! I'm glad to meet you, Sofia.'

Karine and Elise shared a smile. 'The Amdahls are coming for dinner on Saturday,' Karine told Lars, who raised his eyebrows, as surprised as Erik at how fast that had happened.

'We look forward to it,' Elise said, smiling. 'Message me with the time and if there's anything we can bring. We'll see you Saturday.'

Erik had already turned away, but he lifted a hand in farewell. Then, through a gap in the crowd, he caught sight of the tall, scarred man who had helped him pick up the shopping. Their eyes met and the man nodded cordially, then Erik turned to Sofia.

'Come on, Lillemor,' he said.

Sofia loved the drive up to the cabin, especially when they left the roads which the ploughs had cleared and had to fit the snow chains. He let her attach the levers and clips. It added a half-hour to the journey but it was worth it to see her face when she got back in the car, huffing into cupped hands, cheeks red from the cold.

Sweeping her hat off and rubbing her own hands together in the warm air from the AC vent, Elise smiled at him in a way which he realized he had missed. They continued along the twisting, climbing track up into the mountains, towards Jiekkevárri, at nearly two thousand metres the highest peak in Troms county. Past half-hidden shacks and winter cabins built forty years ago, between fields dense with snow and tall spruce bent and burdened with it, as though cursed by some spell and frozen in time. The Mitsubishi's gasoline engine purring now, generating power for the electric motors. The chains rattling on the wheels, biting into the deep snow. They came like pilgrims from the new world seeking to make their sacrifice to the old.

Now and then they passed other vehicles on the road; the 4x4s of other cabin owners, most with a Thule ski-box on the roof like their own, or the occasional yellow plough with flashing lights, creating their own blizzards as they hurled snow into drifts either side of the road. Three thousand kroner a year would see one of these drivers keep the track to your cabin ploughed.

'We owe someone,' Erik said when they took a left off the road and saw that the track to their cabin had been cleared. On the roof, though, the snow was piled four feet deep. It overhung the gables, defying gravity, as if suspended in time by the same magic which made ice sculptures of the water which should have been gushing down rock faces, and which held the trees unnaturally still beneath their thick white burdens.

The same spell which held him, too.

It was two-fifteen and already growing dark when Elise turned the key in the door and pushed it open. The smell of the pinewood interior took Erik back to a hundred vacations boy and man, by fjord and mountain. Lamps were switched on, candles were lit, and he set a fire in the Jøtul wood-burning stove in the lounge, while Elise made filter coffee and Sofia introduced herself to her bedroom. He had cleaned the soot from the stove glass before making the fire, and now he watched the flames, their tentative questing, then their growing hunger as they fed on the kindling and licked the seasoned birch, whose leprous white bark caught like paper. Soon after, the fire was softly roaring, tongues of flame caressing the glass, and the iron stove started to ping and tick as the metal expanded with the heat. It was a ritual, this waking up the cabin. Saying to the place, *we will get to know each other, but for now just know that you are ours and we are yours*.

He felt a calm which had evaded him these past ten months. A settling in his stomach and in his heart. But no sooner had he acknowledged this welcome change, than the memory of the scream came back to him. The twisting in his gut as he watched. The lurch forward, far, far too late. He shook his head hard to dislodge the vision, swallowed back the bile that had risen to burn his throat, shoved himself out of the chair and headed outside to fetch more logs for the fire.

In the morning, after four cups of coffee to offset another night's broken, haunted sleep, he dug out two snow shovels from the shed. He and Elise set to work clearing a path from the car to the cabin door, where the plough hadn't been. Sofia helped out for a while, emptying last night's ashes from the stove, refilling the log basket from the pile under the eaves, and bringing the skis and snowshoes from the car's roof box to the porch. She arranged them neatly, a set between each of the pegs. After that, she disappeared inside, as he carried a ladder from the shed along the path which Elise was still busy clearing with the scoop. He'd decided to clear at least half the snow off the roof before lunch.

'Please don't fall,' Elise shouted to him as he reached the top of the ladder and prepared to haul himself on to the roof.

Her needless warning struck him like a blow to the chest. For a moment he held tight to the ladder, not wanting to look down at Elise. Knowing that she would be inwardly cringing at her own words. Emilie had fallen. Twenty feet. A survivable fall, but as they say, falling doesn't kill you. It's hitting the ground.

He pulled himself up on to the roof, then took two tentative steps to retrieve the shovel which he'd already thrown up there. He could hear the thrust and cut of Elise's scoop as she resumed her own work, and he was just trying to guess where the roof ended and the overhang began, when he caught movement from the corner of his eye and looked up. Dressed in all her Helly Hansen gear and snowshoes, as if ready to join one of Amundsen's Polar expeditions, Sofia was setting off up the slope towards the pine woods behind the cabin.

'Where are you going?' Erik called down to her.

Sofia stopped dead. She stood with her back to him for a moment, as if she had known she would be challenged. Then she turned around. 'I'm just exploring,' she shouted, lifting a gloved hand in which Erik knew would be the pocketknife she had so desperately wanted for Christmas. A Victorinox *Huntsman* multi-tool with fifteen functions, it had been the only thing she had asked for, but Erik's toes crunched up in his shoes every time he saw her opening and closing the sharp gadgets and blades.

'No, Sofia, I want you to stay here,' he said, gesturing with the shovel.

'But Pappa, I just want to look around,' she called back.

'And I'm telling you I want you to stay here where we can see you,' he shouted.

'Because you don't want me to die too,' she said. Her words were quiet, but sound travels far across snow, and he heard it. Elise had too. They looked at each other, making an unspoken agreement not to react.

'What if she promises not to go far?' Elise said, looking at the sky and then at her watch. He guessed it was midday. 'It will be light for another two hours,' Elise said. 'It's a shame if she can't make the most of it.'

'No,' he said, more forcefully than he'd intended.

Elise gave a slight shake of her head, then turned, dropped her shovel on to the snow beside the path that she had cleared and set off towards the porch.

'Where are you going?' he asked.

'Somebody has to make lunch,' she said, as she disappeared from view.

His daughter followed, head to the ground, fists clenched. A moment later, he felt the vibration of the door slamming shut below his feet.

'Shit,' he said. It was only the first day and already Sofia was sulking with him and Elise was pissed off. So much for the cosy family trip to the mountains. 'Shit,' he said again, thrusting his shovel into the snow and hurling a wedge of it over the side of the roof. *And I'm hiding up here on the damn roof,* he thought, *like that's going to help anything.*

Down came the shovel. Off flew the snow. He lost himself in the task. The truth was he enjoyed the repetitive drudgery of it, the heat that bloomed in his arms and lower back. The rhythm of his breath and the pulsing of blood in his ears. Peace in movement.

It was in stillness that his mind beat madly, like a bird trapped in a room, hurling itself against the window glass.

CHAPTER TWO

He is having the dream again. He knows he is dreaming and still he cannot steer its course. He never can. The figure is more shadow than man. More dark presence than human form. More of a sensation, like that heaviness in your gut when you have lashed out to hurt the feelings of someone you love. Or that clenching tightness in your chest when something is broken which you know cannot be fixed.

He feels all this even in the dream. Knowing he is in the dream. But this time it's different, and despite the dread, he moves closer.

What are you? he asks.

He sees in that dark form the outline of a face. An eye. And Sofia is here too. *Here I am!* he shouts to her but she cannot hear him. The terror is on him now. In him. Its claws sinking into the soft meat of his heart. *Sofia!*

She is moving towards the figure. *No. Stay away! Sofia, stay with me!*

He hears his daughter scream.

'Erik!' He woke with a start, Elise's voice bringing him back. The fuzzy blue display of the alarm clock sharpened as he swung himself out of bed, heart racing, knowing that the scream had been real. Three twenty-two a.m.

'She's having a nightmare,' Elise said, already on the landing.

Erik stumbled after her and through the doorway. Elise pushed open her daughter's bedroom door.

'Shh, darling. It's just a dream,' she soothed, as she sat on the bed beside Sofia and took the girl's hands in her own. 'Just a dream.'

Erik exhaled sharply, still trying to blink away his own dream, which clung to his mind and body, heavy as wet clothing.

'Pappa,' Sofia said, perhaps awake, perhaps still dreaming.

Erik sat on Sofia's other side, gently running a hand through her sweat- and sleep-tangled hair, pushing it back from her face. 'It's okay, Lillemor, Pappa's here.'

'I'll bring her some water,' Elise said, leaving Erik with Sofia.

'It's okay. You go back to sleep now. I'm here.' He leant and kissed her on the forehead, holding his lips there a moment. 'Mamma and Pappa love you so much.'

She smiled and squidged her head back into her pillow as he stood.

'Love you,' she said, her words slurred, as if she was already drifting off.

The next morning, he got up early and set to work clearing the rest of the roof. When it was done, he found Elise at the dining table, laptop open, coffee beside her, those two vertical furrows between her eyebrows and nose as subtle as a *do not disturb* hanger on a hotel room door.

She didn't need to look up to know what he was thinking. 'I just need an hour or two,' she said, frowning at the laptop screen as her fingers danced across the keyboard. How she could type and speak different words at the same time was a mystery to him.

He couldn't help himself. 'I thought you weren't starting for a week?' he said.

Her right hand left the keys, index finger pointing up. 'You were on the roof.'

'You were still in bed,' he said.

She took a weary breath and looked up at him now, the creases of her concentration frown melting away. 'It's my first job back with them. I want to be prepared.' She gestured at her laptop. 'And it's important.'

So he and Sofia drove into town to the Vinmonopolet to buy wine. Once back in the car, he turned, taking a moment to look at her.

'I can't believe you're going to be a teenager,' he said.

She raised her eyebrows, no doubt recalling the times they had called her a sulky teenager long before the eve of her thirteenth birthday.

'I mean it.' He shook his head. 'Where has the time gone?'

'Pappa,' she said, staring ahead through the windscreen. 'You promised to take me on the Long Ski when I was thirteen. Remember? A proper trip. Sleeping in snow shelters and everything.'

He kept his eyes on the road. A knot tying in his stomach.

'You promised, Pappa,' Sofia pushed.

'I know,' he said. 'But that was a couple of years ago.' *Before Emilie died*, he left unsaid, though it was loud enough in the silence.

'I'm thirteen tomorrow. I'm old enough.'

'I don't think we can do it this time,' he said.

'But you promised,' she protested. 'Emilie asked you, the Easter before last, and you told her to wait until I was thirteen and then the three of us would go together.'

'I know what I said.' His words were sharper than he'd

intended. Just the mention of her name. 'But so much has happened since then. It's different now.'

He glanced at her and she shook her head and turned her face to look out of the side window.

He remembered that day in crisp detail. Emilie had borrowed her grandfather's well-thumbed maps, still pen-marked from his own trips, and plotted a five-day, four-night ski tour through woods and across frozen lakes. She had been so excited. But Sofia had been too young to go. And so Erik had told Emilie that they would wait until Sofia was thirteen and they could go together. He had known how disappointed Emilie was. And yet she had explained the route plan to Sofia, who had listened wide-eyed and announced to the whole family that she would remind Erik of his promise the day she turned thirteen. He'd known she wouldn't forget.

But it wasn't Easter now, with its fourteen hours of daylight, when the crisp sunlight offered warmth for the climb and gently melted the snow's surface, creating perfect grain snow conditions for the descent. It was only just February, and the days were short and cold.

'Let's give it another year, Lillemor,' he said. 'Just one more year and then we'll go on the Long Ski. A real adventure, I promise.'

Silence. Another promise he wasn't sure he could keep.

'Thank God for the directions you emailed me,' Elise told Karine as they'd stood in the Helgelands' front porch, stamping snow off their boots and hanging up coats and hats. Turning on the happy family show like throwing the light switch at a winter fair.

'We're expecting more snow,' Lars said, leaning out to look up at the grey cloud blanketing the sky. 'In a few days you won't be able to get up here in that.' He was pointing at the Mitsubishi. 'Snowmobiles are the only way when we get a heavy fall.'

Karin and Lars were perfect hosts, generous and welcoming, and Lars clearly enjoyed a beer, which gave him enough in common with Erik to see the evening off to a better start than he had expected.

Elise asked it ever worried them, being so remote, but Lars just chuckled.

'We love to live out here,' he said, gesturing towards the window. The curtains were open and the snow beyond the glass glowed gently in the black night. 'We are not city people, as you can tell.' He looked over at Karine, who was in the kitchen showing Elise her recipe for *fiskebollar*. 'If we wanted visitors all the time, we would live in Tromsø,' Lars said, a mischievous smile on his face.

Lars must have been in his early sixties, Erik guessed, but he was still broad-shouldered and solid, his hands tanned from so many summers of outside work, even now after the long winter.

'Ah, there are cabins being built all the time,' Lars said. 'Beautiful things of cedar wood. Even the roofs are cedar. Inside, everything cladded in oak. Huge windows with views of the mountains, the sea. Built to follow the contours of the landscape and laid out . . . just so,' he said, then waved a broad hand. He rubbed the bristles on his cheek. 'Well, you know all this; Karine tells me you are a carpenter? You must be a busy man with all the houses that are springing up these days.'

'Actually, I'm taking some time out,' Erik replied, feeling Elise's eyes on him from the kitchen doorway. *Time out.* When was the last time he fitted a staircase, window frame or skirting board? Or looked at a set of blueprints? Ten months ago he had hung a digital *Sorry . . . Temporarily Closed* sign on his website, and there it hung still. Amdahl Carpentry closed until further notice.

Once dinner was underway, the conversation inevitably turned towards Murmansk Nickel, and how the locals felt about the Russian-owned company buying the mineral rights to the old Koppangen copper mine west of town. Lars, Karine and Elise shared their fears about waste being dumped in the fjord. About how the Sami Council was ignored, and that the government was willing to destroy the indigenous land in the north of Norway.

On and on it went, and he listened. Barely. Swirling the wine round his glass as Karine retrieved a letter from her cork board beside the fridge.

'This came yesterday,' Karine said, handing it to Elise.

He saw Novotroitsk Nickel's logo on the letterhead, two blue Ns interlinked to look like a pair of mountain peaks. 'At first they said it was just an exploration project,' Karine said. 'To see if the old mine had industrial potential. This was about a year ago.' She gestured at the letter in Elise's hands. 'That outlines their intention to explore the abandoned tunnels further and dig three new test pits, pending the results of a feasibility study.' She pushed her plate away as though talk of the mine's reopening had soured the food.

Truth was he was bored of the conversation. Angry too, because he knew that this was what Elise cared about. What obsessed her. And he had been wrong to think they could find each other again here in the mountains. Plus, the wine had gone to his head in all its euphoric *fuck it* brilliance, and so he told them that the world needed copper. That it was how electricity worked.

'We're all for electric cars, right?' he said. 'If we're going to electrify the world to save it, then maybe we have to be prepared to lose some of the old ways.'

'Are you joking?' Karine Helgeland asked him, her aspect hardening, suddenly expressing all the cheer of a granite rock face.

'It's just the wine talking,' Elise said, a smile on her lips but anger in her eyes.

Karine suggested they talk about something else, and Lars stood, telling Sofia he had something to show her.

Elise left the table too, carrying dishes to the kitchen. And so he sat alone, watching Lars showing Sofia the contents of a beautifully carved wooden box which sat on the windowsill. Beyond it, the night loomed, filling the world with black nothingness. Sofia seemed genuinely interested in the old photos of the Helgelands' ancestors. In the other treasures too: a comb made of reindeer antler which Sofia said looked just like the ones she had seen in The Viking Ship Museum in Oslo. A horn needle case engraved with little reindeer. A leather purse with tin thread embroidery which had belonged to Karine's great-grandmother. And most exciting, judging from Sofia's wide eyes, a huge knife which Lars took down from the fireplace above the stove.

'We call this a *stuorraniibi*,' Lars told her. He smiled at her frown. 'It just means big knife.' He shrugged for comic effect, before drawing the blade from the reindeer leather sheath and making a chopping motion with it. It was nearly ten inches long. 'Long and wide enough to cut firewood or small trees to make shelter poles. Strong enough to split reindeer bones.' He turned it around to hold it by the spine of the blade. 'Feel the handle.' He offered it to Sofia. She touched the wood. 'Birch,' he said, 'for a better grip in cold and snow.'

'I have a Swiss Army knife,' Sofia said, and no sooner had she said the words than the knife was in her hand and she was easing the little blades and tools out one by one, and now Lars was shaking his head as if he had never seen something so wonderful, much to Sofia's delight.

Sofia looked more engaged, more curious than she had about anything he'd done with her for a long while. What exactly *had* he done with her in the last year? They had had gone hiking a few times, picking late summer berries along the trail. He'd taken her to the Alfheim Stadium to watch Tromsø IL lose to Rosenborg in the fourth round of the Norwegian Cup. Oh, and there was the funeral of her sister. That had been a long family day together.

He got up, grabbed hold of the three empty wine bottles and carried them to the kitchen counter.

'Will you have coffee?' Karine asked them, fetching mugs down from the cupboard.

Elise glanced at him and he knew the answer. At least they could still communicate without words.

'No, thank you,' Elise replied, 'our little girl turns thirteen tomorrow. We have a big birthday breakfast to get up for.' She smiled.

Erik looked over at Sofia. She stood at the window, looking west into the night as Lars told her about Karine's brother, Hánas, who was a reindeer herder.

'Right now, while we are cosy and warm,' Lars said, 'Hánas is somewhere up there on the plateau with his herd.' He pointed at the night and the dark shape of the mountain.

'Sometimes, we see a light in the dark and we know it is Hánas in his tent,' Karine said, coming over to join her husband and Sofia at the window.

'It must be beautiful up there,' Sofia said.

'But so cold,' Elise said, miming a shiver as she put a hand on Sofia's shoulder.

But Sofia was still looking up at the mountain. Elise and Karine shared a smile, acknowledging the girl's preoccupation.

'So, have a very happy birthday tomorrow, Sofia,' Karine said, 'and make sure your mor and far spoil you all day, starting with a special breakfast.' She looked out of the window and nodded to the dark, distant peaks. 'Did you know, on my thirteenth birthday, my father took me up there and taught me how to lasso a fully grown reindeer? He was a big bull. I can still see him in my mind. His antlers were like this,' she threw her hands up. 'One and a half metres.'

'Ha!' Lars exclaimed, wafting her words away with a hand.

'Were you there, husband?' she asked, lifting her chin in challenge, so that Erik could see the stubborn young girl she once was. 'Whose story is this, anyway?'

Again, Lars batted the air with a big hand.

'So, after many attempts I lassoed the bull, over his great big antlers, and my father had to help me hold the rope, like this,' she said, miming the action, 'or that bull would have carried me off and I would probably still be hanging on now. But then we had to get home before dark because we didn't want to meet a *stallo* up there.'

Sofia screwed up her face. 'What's a *stallo*?'

'Sofia is too old now for stories of *stallos* and trolls,' Lars said. He was standing by an antique cocktail cabinet, pouring himself a brandy in the soft light from the cabinet's interior.

'I was just telling Sofia what I did on my thirteenth birthday,' Karine said. 'You have to have adventures when you are young.'

Erik was watching Sofia as she turned to look at him. He knew what she wanted to tell the Helgelands; that he had promised to take her on the Long Ski when she turned thirteen. Her silence knotted him up inside.

After declining Lars's offer of brandy, he and Elise thanked their hosts for a lovely evening, said their goodbyes and crowded into the porch with Sofia to put on their coats, boots and hats.

'Sofia,' Lars said, coming out after them. 'I have something for you.' They turned and waited as he tramped through the snow after them, their warm breath pluming around their faces. 'Here, Sofia, for your birthday,' Lars said.

Sofia held out her hands and took the *stuorraniibi* he offered her, looking at her mother and father for reassurance.

'Of course, you must only use it with your parents' permission,' Lars said, nodding at Elise, then Erik. 'But I thought . . . well . . . you have your modern pocket knife which can do everything you can possibly think of, but you should also have something from the past, to remember those who came before us.'

Sofia stared at the gift in her hands, open-mouthed. Not knowing what to say.

Erik looked at Elise. Surely *she* knew what to say. Like, *what the hell's wrong with you, Lars, giving a bloody great Sami knife to a thirteen-year-old girl? Who does that?*

'You lucky girl,' Elise said, putting her arm around Sofia's shoulder. Subtly trying to squeeze a *thank you* out of her.

'Thank you, Mr Helgeland,' Sofia managed, tearing her eyes away from the knife to look Lars in the face.

'Take care of a good knife and it will take care of you,' Lars said. Then he raised his hand. 'So, see you all again.' He turned and walked back to the house. 'And happy birthday, Sofia,' he called, his breath fogging in the glow of his porch light.

LANCELOT
Warrior. Friend. Lover. Legend.

The legions of Rome are a fading memory. Enemies stalk the fringes of Britain. And Uther Pendragon is dying. Into this uncertain world a boy is cast. A refugee from fire, murder and betrayal, he is an outsider – his only companions a hateful hawk and memories of those he's lost.

Under the watchful eyes of Merlin and the Lady Nimue, he begins his journey to manhood. He meets another outcast: Guinevere – wild, proud and beautiful. And he is dazzled by Arthur – a warrior who carries the hopes of a people like a torch in the dark.

But these are times of blood when even love and friendship seem doomed. The old gods are vanishing. Treachery and jealousy rule men's hearts and the fate of Britain rests on a sword's edge. This young renegade is now a lord of war. He is a man loved and hated, admired and feared. He is a man forsaken but not forgotten.

He is Lancelot.

'A masterpiece'
CONN IGGULDEN

'Kristian's finest novel to date. Glorious. Tragic. Lyrical. Totally gripping'
BEN KANE

'A gorgeous, rich retelling'
THE TIMES